# SHADOWS OF EMPIRE

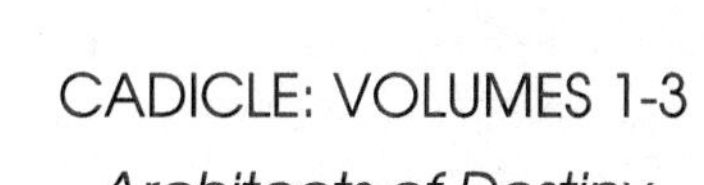

CADICLE: VOLUMES 1-3

*Architects of Destiny*

*Veil of Reality*

*Bonds of Resolve*

**A K DUBOFF**

SHADOWS OF EMPIRE

Published by Dawnrunner Press


ISBN: 1954344325
ISBN-13: 978-1954344327

0 9 8 7 6 5 4 3 2

Produced in the United States of America

# CONTENTS

# PROLOGUE

A GENETIC EVALUATION couldn't lie. The code was definitely corrupted.

The scientist frowned at the results. "It was a complete failure."

"We need to try again," the Priest said from the shadows.

"This damage can't be undone. The abilities are all but lost."

"Then start over," the Priest insisted. "There's still the Archive."

The scientist sighed. "Even if it's possible, it would take generations—hundreds of years."

"Then we must begin immediately. Our enemy won't be forgiving."

"That's what the Bakzen are to us now? An enemy?"

The Priest took a slow breath. "They'll overpower us if we don't find a way to match their strength."

"Well, the Archive is our best hope, but that will only get us one genetic line, if we're lucky. Will a handful of people be enough?" the scientist asked.

"If it's the right person, we only need one."

VOLUME 1

# ARCHITECTS OF DESTINY

# PART 1: NEW BEGINNINGS

# CHAPTER 1

*I* MUST LEAVE *tonight. I can't stay here any longer—* Cris Sietinen ducked to avoid the electronic rapier swinging toward his head.

"Stay focused." His tutor jumped to the side as he stabbed at Cris' torso.

Cris parried the blow, a challenging glint in his cobalt eyes. "You haven't hit me yet."

"You haven't struck me, either." His tutor circled him, steel-blue eyes locked on Cris. "Get inside your opponent's head, just as Marina taught you. Movements can deceive, but what's in the mind can't be faked. Trust your intuition."

Clearing his thoughts, Cris prepared for a telepathic assessment. "It's not intuition, Sedric. Science has told us that much."

Sedric Almar sighed. "Telepathy, clairvoyance, call it what you will. You are one of the few with the gift. Use it." He took a swing toward Cris' right leg. Though decades past his prime, he still possessed the same youthful vigor as the day he joined the Royal Guard. Now a trusted captain, he remained a formidable opponent in any close-quarters combat, gray hair or not.

With his mind cleared, Cris reached out to read the thoughts grazing the surface of Sedric's consciousness—catching a glimpse of his next move. Before his instructor could complete his swing, Cris deflected the attack. "If it's such a 'gift', then why does everyone treat it like a curse?"

"Don't be so dramatic." Sedric jabbed toward the main sensor on the chest of Cris' training jumpsuit.

As he dodged the attack, Cris brought his own blade to Sedric's collar in one fluid motion. The sensor lights illuminated red. A kill hit.

Sedric held out his hands in defeat and nodded his approval. "Next time I won't go easy on you."

Cris took a step back to rest. "I can't rely solely on telepathy to win. There must be a reason the Priesthood condemns the use of such abilities." His covert lessons from Marina were defiant enough, flirting with the boundaries of legality.

Sedric reset his jumpsuit using the controls on the sleeve, and the sensors returned to blue. "It's not our place to speculate about matters regarding the Priesthood. Not even yours, my lord."

"But you have to wonder," Cris pondered. "On Tararia and most of the colonies, there's nothing but anti-telekinesis propaganda. Yet, an entire division of the TSS is dedicated to honing the abilities of those rare Gifted individuals, and the Priesthood does nothing."

"The Tararian Selective Service is unique in many ways," Sedric replied, dismissing the dispute with a shake of his head. He gripped his sword and took an offensive stance. "Now, we have a lesson to finish."

Cris was resolute, determined to finally get an answer to the questions his teacher was always so eager to dodge. "You spent a year with the TSS, didn't you? You must have seen so much—"

A single crease deepened between Sedric's dark eyebrows. "My lord, with all respect, your father doesn't appreciate discussion of the TSS."

Cris' restraint slipped. "Of course he doesn't. He wants me to ignore my abilities, just like he did. Why should I listen to someone who wants me to live a lie?"

"I'm sorry, I—" Sedric brought his slender sword to a resting position with the illuminated tip on the ground.

Cris fought to maintain composure; the years of battling the strained relationship with his father had taken their toll. "You don't understand what it's like… to have all the privileges of being born into this family, and yet it doesn't mean anything." He shook his head, letting out a pained scoff. "He'll never be happy with who I am, not after the son he lost years ago. Me? I'm just the replacement heir to the Sietinen Dynasty—a tool to perpetuate our familial empire." *A disappointing shadow of the brother I never knew.*

"You mustn't think that way, my lord," Sedric said with a gentleness that belied his hardened exterior.

*Stars! Just a few more hours…* Cris swallowed, his throat tight. *Then I can get away from Tararia and stop being compared to the impossibly perfect memory of Tristen.* "Shite, it's no wonder he and Mother avoid me. I guess by now I should be used to seeing my instructors more than my own parents." Cris met Sedric's gaze for a moment before looking down.

Sedric put an encouraging hand on Cris' toned shoulder. "You're true to yourself, and that's the best thing you can be."

Cris undid the collar of his dark gray training jumpsuit, extinguishing the subtle blue sensor lights. "I've had enough for today."

He stepped from the black rubberized tiles in the training arena onto the white marble found throughout the estate, stowing his sword on the rack of training weapons. As he removed his jumpsuit, he stared out the window at the clear sky above the manicured grounds. He couldn't wait to be out among the stars.

To Cris' disappointment, when he glanced at the time displayed on the viewscreen integrated into the wall, he saw that it was only halfway through the scheduled lesson time. He sighed.

Sedric rested both hands atop the hilt of his sword. "Why the sudden interest in the TSS?"

Cris returned to the arena, wearing only the gray t-shirt and black workout pants that had been beneath his training attire. "It's a significant institution, but all I ever hear are rumors. You were actually there. What was it really like?"

"Very different than anything here on Tararia," his instructor replied after a moment.

"How so?"

Sedric scowled. "You're trying to get me in trouble."

"This is just between us, I promise."

The old soldier eyed him, still on edge. "First off, nothing of anyone's life outside the TSS mattered. You could come from one of the High Dynasties or from the streets—everyone was treated the same." He paused, but Cris' pleading eyes drove him on. He smoothed his light gray uniform as if reliving a morning muster. "Though I was just in the Militia division, I had a few chances to meet the Agents. They have a commanding presence unlike anyone else I've met. I was always awed by their abilities—such power. It was something timeless."

*Unrestricted telekinesis... What can they do?* Cris was captivated. "So, why did you leave?"

A grimace flitted across Sedric's face, barely perceptible. "Many only attend for the first year. It just wasn't the life for me."

Cris examined his instructor. "If many leave after the first year, it must be easy to join. How do—"

Sedric let out a gruff laugh. "Oh, I see! I never should have said anything. Now you're getting fanciful ideas."

A disarming smile brought out Cris' natural good looks. He ran a hand through his chestnut-brown hair. "Please, Sedric? I'm only trying to broaden my knowledge of the outside world."

His teacher scrutinized him. "There's an open application process for Militia, but most Agent slots are by invitation. However, it is best if you permanently remove such thoughts from your mind."

Cris composed his face, but the mischievous smile never fully left his eyes. "I was just curious."

The old guard was not convinced. "You have a duty, my lord. Whether you like it or not, you are the Sietinen heir and will one day be in charge of SiNavTech and the Third Region of Tararia. That is an extraordinary responsibility. I only hope that you will embrace that power."

"Oh, I will—eventually." *Just as I will embrace the power that I have within.* "But I'm only sixteen. That's still a long ways off."

Sedric was about to respond when the door opened.

Cris turned to see who had entered. His gaze rested on Marina Alexri, one of his father's Court Advisors; the intrusion did nothing to improve his mood. Marina was in her mid-twenties and pretty, but she had a frigid demeanor that could silence a room. Her position as his sole telepathy instructor was the one redeeming element of their relationship.

He instinctively bolstered his ever-present mental guards, careful to bury his plans for that night. *Stars! What does she want?*

"Working hard with combat techniques, I see," Marina said, gliding forward. Her dark blonde hair was pulled up into a complex bun with braids and twists, and she wore a rich emerald dress befitting her Lower Dynasty upbringing, tailored to her slender figure. Her green eyes surveyed the room, missing no detail.

Sedric came to attention. "We were exploring the finer points of verbal battle, madam."

"Naturally." Marina smiled curtly. "Come, Cristoph. There is a matter your father must discuss with you."

"It's 'Cris'," he corrected, despite failing with his hundreds of previous attempts.

"As you wish, my lord." The Court Advisor withdrew from the room.

When Marina was out of sight, Cris let out a slow breath and turned to Sedric. "I'm sorry for arguing. You're a wonderful teacher. I don't mean to be difficult." His throat constricted. *You're the only one I'll miss… You always believed in me.*

Sedric beamed. "Think nothing of it, my lord."

Marina returned to the doorway. "Come along. Your father is waiting." She disappeared again.

Cris smiled one last time at Sedric before he followed Marina, trying to ease the knot in his chest.

"I'm surprised my father sent you to fetch me. Now you're running errands for him?" Cris asked the Court Advisor as he approached. Since coming into the employ of the Sietinen Dynasty three years before, Marina was almost always posted in one of the administrative offices throughout the estate to oversee dynastic operations. Cris' twice-weekly telepathy lessons over the last year were one of the few exceptions.

Marina's brow twitched. "Actually, in light of a recent development, he wished me to terminate your telepathy instruction. I thought that best said in person."

The news should have been a huge disappointment, but instead it only confirmed Cris' decision to leave. Those lessons had been one of the few things he was reluctant to give up; if that was being taken away, there was nothing worthwhile left for him on Tararia. "I see."

"Such training was an unnecessary distraction," Marina

continued. "It's time to focus on what matters."

Except, what mattered to Cris was of no concern to the rest of his family. He shook his head and looked down.

The Court Advisor pursed her lips. "What are you hiding?"

Cris quickly suppressed the thoughts of his upcoming departure. "Do you really want to know?"

Marina rolled her eyes and set off down the corridor. "We're already late."

Cris stood his ground. "On second thought, I'm not in the mood for another lecture. I think I'll pass on the father-son chat."

Marina spun around on her heel to glare at Cris. "How can you be so flippant? You know he's busy tending to all of the political and economic issues *you've* never bothered to understand—"

Cris crossed his arms. *Oh, don't I? Try quizzing me sometime and we'll see who knows what.*

"—while overseeing the transportation industry for known civilization. You should be more appreciative of the time you get with him." She flourished her arms with exasperation. "Honestly, Cristoph, you become more insolent every time I see you."

*That's what happens when you're treated like an outcast in your own family for your entire life.* He shrugged. "Sorry. I guess I just have insurmountable faults in my personality."

Marina's eyes narrowed.

Cris glared back. "Since I'll apparently be berated anywhere I go, let's get the worst of it with my father out of the way."

The Court Advisor let out a huff and resumed striding down the hallway.

*No snide response? I'll count that as a win.* Cris followed her at a safe distance.

He wished their relationship was different, but all of his attempts to find common ground had inevitably led to assertions that he needed to become a model politician while Cris insisted that there was more to life. The tension had been mounting for years, and the past several months had brought Cris near his breaking point. He needed to get away. He didn't know for how long, but enough time for him to learn who he could be outside the context of his highborn family.

As he trailed Marina through the spacious corridors of the

Sietinen mansion's southern wing, he glimpsed the landscaped grounds of the estate through towering windows overlooking the city of Sieten below and the great Lake Tiadon in the distance. Sieten, the capital city of the Third Region, was nestled in the breathtaking foothills of the Bethral Mountains. Its temperate climate was pleasant in the peaks of summer and winter even without weather modification, making it envied by Dynasties throughout the five other Regions of Tararia.

Though it was the only home Cris had ever known, he wanted to see what else the galaxy had to offer and experience how other people lived. He couldn't imagine being an effective leader without understanding what life was really like throughout the Taran Empire. *I'll come back here eventually. I just need to find myself while I still have the chance.*

Marina and Cris arrived at the palatial outer administrative office for the Head of the Sietinen Dynasty. The attendants and advisors throughout the room looked to be working furiously at various computer consoles and desktop holodisplays, though Cris had doubts about how much was actually being accomplished.

Cris spotted his father. He, like all Sietinens before, had the distinctive chestnut hair and striking cobalt eyes that defined the bloodline; carefully arranged marriages ensured the continuation of the traits. Cris knew his mother's Talsari heritage was nearly as pure, but the prestige of Sietinen was paramount.

Marina led Cris toward the elder Sietinen, who was absorbed in conversation with two advisors. To Cris' displeasure, Marina halted just beyond earshot of the discussion, leaving Cris to stand idly while the exchange concluded.

*How typical—after all the rush to get here, I still have to wait.* He glanced over at Marina. She returned his gaze with a decidedly hostile smile.

After a few minutes, the advisors were dismissed and Reinen Sietinen-Monsari turned to look Cris over silently. Gray touched his temples, bringing a sense of distinguished age to his handsome features. He wore a deep blue suit embellished with silver accents, the finest available. "Marina informed you of the change to your instruction, I presume."

"Hello to you, too, father," Cris replied. "Yes, she told me."

Reinen nodded. "Let's go into my office."

Cris followed his father into a smaller room off to the right. Reinen sat down on a sleek brown couch near the center of the room and gestured for Cris to sit in one of the upholstered chairs across from him. Behind them, a desk was framed by an arched window that stretched nearly the width of the room, looking directly over Lake Tiadon. The sun was beginning its descent, shadows emphasizing the features of the lush landscape.

"Why the sudden end to my lessons with Marina?" Cris asked as he sat down.

Reinen's eyes narrowed the slightest measure. "You've already learned enough to guard yourself. There's nothing further to explore."

"Would a little object levitation really hurt anyone?"

His father leaned forward, stern. "The laws apply to you, too. We're supposed to lead by example."

"Right, by supporting the policies that make it illegal to learn about oneself."

Reinen grunted. "Maybe you should take the matter up with the Priesthood."

Cris was about to brush off the statement, but there was a seriousness in his father's tone. "What do you mean?"

"I received a communiqué this afternoon. The Priesthood has requested a meeting with you."

Cris froze. "Why?" His pulse spiked, knowing how rare it was for any individual to be singled out by the powerful organization. Marina's instruction had always stayed within the governing restrictions around telepathy, but if they suspected Cris had crossed the line into telekinesis, there was no telling what the meeting might entail.

"The representative only stated that they want to interview you as soon as possible." Reinen shook his head. "Whatever it's regarding, it's not the kind of attention we need."

*Stars! How do I get out of this?* Cris gulped.

The Priesthood of the Cadicle oversaw all Taran affairs, governing even the High Dynasties and their respective corporations that were the pillars for interplanetary society. As the critical regulatory body for the Taran worlds, the organization controlled everything from laws, to the flow of information, and the application of new technological advances. Given its roots as a formerly theological institution, the Priesthood had been unquestionably viewed as Taran society's moral compass and ultimate authority for generations.

"Did you set an appointment?" Cris asked, holding his breath that it wouldn't impact his departure plans.

"No. They wanted the interview to take place on their island, but I refused. The representative said he'd get back to me with alternate arrangements."

Cris relaxed. *Good. I'll be gone by morning.* He felt his father's eyes on him and looked up.

"You're getting older, Cris. People are beginning to take more of an interest in you."

He bit back an exasperated sigh, familiar with where the conversation would lead. "You mean dynastic heads are trying to marry me off to their daughters. I'm still way too young to have any interest in those discussions."

"One day soon you'll have to."

"But not yet."

"Cris, I— I just worry about you."

*Why does he pretend? At least Mother just ignores me.* He crossed his arms. "Is that so? You've never expressed much interest in me before."

Reinen seemed taken aback, his brow furrowed. "What makes you say that?"

Cris shook his head. "It doesn't matter."

"No, if something is bothering you, I want to know about it."

He met his father's gaze. "When you say you worry about me, what do you mean? My political future? My future as the leader of this dynasty and as an executive of SiNavTech?"

"Well, of course. You seem disinterested."

"What about my feelings as your son?"

"I always assumed you were content."

*"Content"... What about feeling loved?* He almost said it aloud, but the words caught in his throat. The damage was already done. "Well, I'm not," he muttered instead. "I can't say I ever really was."

Reinen was silent for a long time. "I'm sorry."

Cris shrugged. "It is what it is. I know I'm not the one you wanted to be your successor."

Reinen looked down, his face contorted in an attempt to hide his anguish.

"If there's nothing else, I'll return to my studies." Cris stood up.

There was the slightest shake of his father's head. "No. That's all."

Without another word, Cris left the office.

Though not what Cris had envisioned for his departure, the conversation had been a fitting sendoff. He didn't doubt that his father meant well, deep down. There was just too much residual pain for Reinen to have been a real parent to him; he had already raised a child to adulthood and poured his heart into that relationship. When that legacy had been stripped away with Tristen's death, Cris had been born out of obligation, not desire. It was no wonder their interactions resembled a business transaction.

Cris hurried away from the administrative center, trying to clear his mind in preparation for the critical tasks ahead. Now, more than ever, he needed to focus.

Upon reaching his residential suite, he passed straight through the lounge area and stepped onto the generous balcony. A calm breeze ruffled his hair, cooled by the lake below.

He breathed in the pure air. *I'll miss this.*

For a moment, he felt a twinge of regret. But, he knew staying on Tararia wasn't what was best for him or his family.

Cris returned to his bedroom and activated the touch-surface workstation on his desk. He began what had become a routine exercise of hacking into the secure central system for the Sietinen estate. Though not particularly easy, part of Cris' grooming had involved study of the complex system, so he knew shortcuts through the security blocks.

Once inside the system, he created an alias under the guise of a high-ranking guard and catalogued it in the central computer. Using the alias, he checked out a transport vessel at a secluded port on the southern side of the Sietinen compound. It would be waiting for him at midnight on the twenty-five-hour Tararian clock. He also set up a standard maintenance reboot of the central security system to correspond with his departure. If he timed it right, he could slip out undetected and be well on his way before anyone knew he was gone.

All of his preparations over the last six months came down to tonight. For two years, he'd dreamed of starting a new life. Now, it was about to happen.

With the final pieces of his departure plan in place, Cris admired one last sunset out his bedroom window. By daybreak, he'd be in space.

# CHAPTER 2

IT WAS 24:45. The world outside Cris' window was dark. Only the glow from Tararia's two moons, Aeris and Denae, illuminated the sky.

Dressed in plain street clothes, Cris gathered his provisions. Only a select few knew the electronic frequencies needed to illuminate the normally invisible identifying Dynastic Mark on his arm or read his imbedded ID chip, so all he needed to do was blend in. If he looked the part, he could become anyone he wanted.

Cris was accustomed to slipping out to walk the gardens in the middle of the night, but never had the stakes been so high. *They'll put me on complete lockdown if I'm caught leaving. No second chance.*

He crept from his suite into the corridor. As a precaution, he reset the door's electronic lock so there would be no record of what time he left. He peered into the dimmed hallway. Clear. He ventured toward the nearest exit.

The security system reboot was still five minutes away, set for 24:50 and scheduled to take twenty minutes. To avoid triggering alarms in the meantime, he used the less monitored servant passageways. He encountered no one, to his relief, and was soon outside.

Cris broke into a light jog along the main path that ran the length of the mansion. He made it no more than ten meters when he caught sight of a surveillance light.

*Hide!* He dove off the path into some bushes. The branches scraped at his bare face and hands, but he found a hollow within the foliage.

He quickly retrieved a scrambler from the front pocket of his travel bag and activated the device; it should be enough to throw off the guard's sensors. He checked the time on his watch: 24:52. It was within the reboot window for the central system. He would be fine as long as he stayed out of sight.

Cris nearly held his breath as the guard approached. He could make out the armored form through the leaves, made more imposing under the moonlight. The guard was walking slowly, inspecting a handheld. He stopped in front of Cris.

*Stars!* Cris' heart raced. He stayed motionless, barely breathing.

The guard tapped the screen on his handheld a few times, then muttered something under his breath. After another minute, he continued strolling down the path in the direction Cris had come from.

Cris breathed a sigh of relief. When the guard was well past, he carefully extracted himself from the bushes and looked around to make sure no other guards were nearby. No one else was in sight. He smoothed his hair and brushed off a couple of leaves that had affixed to his jacket.

Cris returned to the path and resumed jogging toward the ship port. Excitement welled up in his chest, but he kept it at bay. *I'm not free yet.*

He reached the port at 24:57. Half a dozen shuttles occupied a paved area amid the foliage of the grounds. Each craft was approximately six meters long, with streamlined aerodynamics specifically designed for breaking through the planet's atmosphere.

Cris was about to enter the port when he spotted a figure in the small shelter used by port attendants during the day. He froze. There wasn't supposed to be anyone there overnight. His entire plan rested on using an automated kiosk to check out the shuttle under his guard alias. Needing to interact with a person changed everything.

He bit his lower lip, thinking. *I can't turn back now.*

Seeing no other option, he strode confidently into the port

and headed straight for the kiosk. He kept his face oriented away from the shelter.

The kiosk was dangerously close to the building, and it didn't take long for the attendant to rouse.

"What may I do for you?" the attendant asked.

Cris kept his head turned to the side so the attendant couldn't see his face. *I have every reason to be here. I'm in control.* "Official business," he said, faking a deeper voice. "You can verify my credentials on your own screen."

The attendant crossed his arms. "I'd like to see some ID."

*Don't panic.* Cris continued walking toward the kiosk with feigned assurance. "And I'd like to report you to your supervisor for impeding an official investigation. I don't think you want that on your performance record so close to review time."

"Your ID, sir," the attendant requested again.

Cris reached the kiosk. "I'll get it, hold on." Before the attendant could protest, Cris brought up his shuttle reservation in a few quick taps. He entered the access key for his guard alias. "There, satisfied?"

The attendant glanced at the authorization on the screen inside the shelter. "It checks out." He seemed unsure.

"So, do I need to have that chat with your supervisor?" Cris turned toward his assigned shuttle.

"No, sir," the attendant said. "Have a good night."

Cris let out a slow breath as he set off toward his shuttle. *We really need better security.*

The assigned shuttle was at the end of the row. Cris went to the far side of his craft and entered his specified passcode to open the main door. Once inside, he stowed his pack in a cargo area behind the eight passenger seats in the main cabin.

Cris moved to the cockpit to initiate the startup sequence. The touchscreen controls and holographic interfaces cast a cool glow in the cockpit. As the system ran its automated check, Cris strapped into the pilot's chair. He suppressed another wave of excitement.

When the shuttle was ready, Cris deftly lifted the vessel off the ground and launched it into space. Flight lessons had always been his favorite. He savored the exhilaration as the antimatter pion drive smoothly propelled the craft, feeling the power through the low vibrations in the controls. The muted rumble intensified as he pointed the vessel upward, locking in his destination. As he gained elevation, he became just one of many ships scattered throughout the night sky.

The acceleration of the vessel slowed as the sky turned from deep blue to black. Cris felt the artificial gravity automatically activate when the shuttle achieved orbit, settling his stomach.

*I'm actually leaving Tararia.* He relaxed just enough to smile. *But I still have a long way to go.*

Cris passed through one of the gates in the planetary shield and followed the course to the primary space station orbiting the planet. He sent a preset message requesting docking clearance. An affirmative response came immediately, and control of the shuttle was handed over to remote operators at the station.

Once the remote pilot took over, Cris allowed himself time to admire Tararia from above. *It's so beautiful from space—so peaceful.*

Sieten was a mere speck of light on the western edge of the massive Third Region in the northern hemisphere, with the smaller Fourth, Fifth and Sixth Regions below it to the south. Across the sea to the west, he could see the edge of the crescent-shaped Second Region and the First Region to its south. In the sea between the Third and First regions was an island Cris knew to be the seat of the Priesthood. From space it seemed very small for someplace so important.

His shuttle was drawn into docking position and clamps locked onto the hull. Apprehension replaced his excitement as the small vessel shuddered under the docking clamps. It was the first time Cris had ever been off-world on his own, and preparing for such an adventure was never part of his lessons.

He set his jaw, determined to not let nerves get the better of him. *I need to find a ship.*

Cris gathered his pack and made his way down the gangway into the space station. He was struck by the metallic quality of the filtered air, a harsh contrast to the fresh breeze off the lake. The foreign feeling of the station was heightened by an intense energy permeating the structure, felt both in the air and through the metal deck plates underfoot. The sub-audible hum of motors and electricity felt oppressive at first, but he centered himself and soon let the vibrations wash over him.

He moved from the gangway into the main corridor of the concourse, where smooth metal walls arched overhead toward the center of a massive ring. Gangways stretched out to ships along the perimeter, and several broad concourses branched out to other rings with even more ships. Cris admired the sweeping metal forms through viewports overhead and along the sides of the passageway. Even more wondrous was the blackness of space beyond, with dazzling stars holding untold possibilities.

The space station was more populated than Cris had anticipated for the late hour, but he had to remind himself that space travel didn't follow the same schedule as his home time zone. People moved about their business in the corridor, paying no attention to Cris as he eased into the flow of the foot traffic. Everyone was moving quickly, and where there were no openings in the crowd, someone would shove their way through. Cris found himself jostled as he tried to navigate the steady stream of travelers.

Just as he was starting to get comfortable, he was pushed from behind. His bag came loose from his shoulder and almost fell to the floor. He took a few rapid steps to regain his balance, eventually catching himself on the wall of the corridor. He looked around.

A large man with cropped, thinning hair and a dingy jacket was cutting his way through the mass. Others stepped to the side to make way without missing a step. It was orchestrated chaos, and everyone but Cris knew the rhythm.

Cris pressed his back against the wall, trying to get his bearings again. A couple of people glanced over at him, but he may as well have been a decorative plant based on their reactions.

He took a deep breath. *Don't fight the crowd.*

With an assertive stride, Cris reentered the stream of travelers. He had two more near-collisions but managed to avoid any further incidents. Following overhead signs, he made his way to the nearest directory where he could access the status of all ships at the port.

The directory was located in a bay off the central corridor. It was surrounded by an even denser throng of travelers. Cris spotted what looked to be a queue and took his place in the group. After several minutes, he noticed that people kept cutting in to take an open station when one became available.

His face flushed with frustration. *They have no sense of order.*

Another person pushed ahead to grab a terminal at the directory, knocking Cris to the side. Cris tightened his grip on the bag over his shoulder. *I guess I need to act like them.*

A moment later, when a woman tried to push past Cris, he firmly held his place. The woman relaxed and waited behind him.

Cris took the next available terminal. He pulled up the transport directory, first looking over the outbound passenger transports. There were over a dozen cruisers to choose from, ranging from economical to luxurious. However, those would certainly be the first place anyone would look for him. Cris closed out of the list. That left the cargo freighters, and he found there were at least six times as many of those. Far too many choices. He filtered out all of the ships with large-volume, hazardous, or unregistered cargo. After discounting any with scheduled departures in more than one hour, only two potentials remained.

*I should check them out in person before making a final selection.* He made a mental note of the docking coordinates for the two ships and cleared his search on the terminal, moving aside as someone lunged forward to use it.

Cris returned to the central corridor and made his way toward the docking location of the first ship. As he approached, he immediately felt uneasy, an instinct which Sedric and Marina always encouraged him to heed. Some members of the ship's crew were standing near the entrance to the gangway. They watched him pass, a touch of malice in their gaze. He moved on.

The second ship looked far more promising. Only a single man was near the entrance gangway, working on a tablet. He looked to be about sixty-years-old, and was somewhat grizzled. Attached to his belt was a red and white badge with his credentials, marking him as the ship's captain. Cris stood back and watched as another man exited the ship and engaged in conversation. *What are they talking about?*

Carefully, Cris reached out telepathically toward the two men. Though his abilities were not yet well developed, he was able to gather a few impressions. The captain seemed good natured, and he was on friendly terms with the other man. Cris dove deeper and saw some flashes of the ship's flight deck. The other man was plotting a course. He was joking with the captain. There was a sense of homesickness.

Cris pulled back. He tried to make sense of what he had seen and felt. *The ship's Navigator, maybe?*

The two men continued to talk for three more minutes and then parted ways. The other man carried a duffle bag as he walked away.

*Did he just resign? This might be my lucky day.* Cris walked up to the captain of the cargo freighter, trying to be unassuming. It proved harder than expected. "Excuse me, sir?"

The captain pivoted around to look at Cris. When he saw who had spoken, he rolled his eyes. "Fok, this is all I need. What do you want, kid?"

Cris was shocked by the tone, after the deference he had been given his whole life. *Remember, you're not that person anymore.* "I was hoping to buy myself a ride aboard your ship."

"We're not a passenger vessel." His annoyance was apparent.

"I can pay—"

"We're not a passenger vessel," the captain repeated.

*Fine, then I'll put my education to use.* "What about openings on your crew?"

The captain didn't respond at first. His eyes narrowed. "Not unless you know long-range navigation."

"I do."

The captain smirked. "Right."

Cris looked the captain in the eye. "Let me prove it."

The captain scratched his stubble. He sighed. "All right, I'll give you a chance. What's your name?"

Cris was about to respond, but stopped himself, knowing he couldn't let anyone know his true lineage. "Cris Sights."

"I'm Thom Caleri, and this is the *Exler*," the captain said, gesturing to his ship. "Let's go to the flight deck and I'll see if you're full of yourself."

Cris smiled with trained charm and followed Thom onto the ship.

The *Exler* was a small freighter compared to many. Built exclusively for space travel, it was long and boxy with a forked backend for the jump drive and a protrusion at the top for the flight deck and living quarters. It was to this upper deck that the gangway led; as with standard freighters, cargo would be offloaded to smaller transport shuttles using a bay in the belly of the ship.

Inside, the *Exler* matched its captain. There were scuff marks along the walls and some deck plates were missing the occasional screw, but the bones were solid. The flight deck was at the end of a short hallway leading from the gangway entrance. It was a cramped room with only two seats. An expansive viewport spanned the far wall, giving a partial view of the space station and surrounding ships. Most of the controls looked to be physical buttons and switches. However, there was a horizontal touchscreen at the center of the room between the seats, supported by a console marked with the same SiNavTech logo found on all navigation systems.

"Have at it," Thom said, pointing to the touchscreen.

Cris glanced at the branding on the navigation console beneath the screen and noticed it was an older model from around the time he was born. The interface would be slightly different, but the underlying firmware would be identical to the modern systems he had studied during his education about the family business.

Cris tapped the touchscreen and it illuminated. A holographic spatial map hovered just above the screen's surface. "Where to?"

"Gallos System," Thom instructed.

*Not exactly a tourist destination, but I'll take anywhere other than here.* "Okay."

Cris went through the time-consuming navigation programming sequence with expert precision, identifying an optimized route for the subspace jump that would take them on a direct course to the destination. He ran four different scenarios and after half an hour settled on a beacon sequence that would allow access to several space stations during the required jump drive cooldown stops along the way. He tested the course with a dummy lock to the first beacon, and it verified his route.

"This is my recommendation. Transit time will be eleven days, including the cooldown times for the jump drive."

Thom had watched him closely at every step. A navigation system was a sensitive piece of equipment for a stranger to access, but there was no other way to vet a new Navigator. "That looks right to me. Except add a few days to the time estimate to account for longer stops so we can sleep."

"I'm happy to change the stopovers if you'd prefer—"

"No, the locations are fine. You did everything correctly." Thom crossed his arms. "I'm just surprised someone your age has experience with course plotting. You can't be much older than what, sixteen?"

"Is that a problem?"

The captain looked pensive. "I suppose not. That's legal age for crew work."

"Does that mean I have the job?"

The captain smiled amiably. "Shite, why not? Some company would be better than none. You can be my Navigation Officer for the trip to Gallos—for starters—in exchange for room and board. If it works out, we can negotiate a salary for the next run."

*It's more than a little ironic I'd end up working as a Navigator after being groomed as an heir to SiNavTech.* "That's a reasonable offer. I accept."

Thom nodded. "Good." He looked Cris over again. "I have three rules. First, no stealing from me or other members of the crew. Second, no picking fights. And lastly, I won't ask you prying questions if you don't ask them of me."

That last one worked to his advantage. "Agreed."

The captain turned the palm of his right hand upward in greeting, the Taran custom for new acquaintances who had not yet earned the trust of physical contact. "Welcome to the *Exler*."

# CHAPTER 3

AMAZED BY HIS good fortune, Cris accompanied Thom from the flight deck into the belly of the *Exler*. The captain introduced him to the two other crew members, Dom and Neal—both thick, muscled men in their thirties who were responsible for the cargo hold—and gave him a tour of the ship. There was little to see beyond the cargo area, workout room, kitchen, and shared washroom. Though it was simply appointed and lacked many of the comforts Cris had grown up with on Tararia, the *Exler* was clean enough and mechanically well-maintained from what he could tell.

The last stop in the tour was Cris' new quarters. It was a tiny room with only a bunk, toilet, sink and storage locker. Cris smiled politely when he saw the space, and Thom left him to get settled in. When he was alone, Cris set down his bag and looked around the modest accommodations. *I need to reset my expectations.*

He sat down on the bunk to test it. The mattress was firmer than he would prefer, but it was sufficient. *I wanted to see what life was really like outside the Sietinen estate. It doesn't get more authentic than this.* He took a deep breath. *My entire life is changing.*

He gave himself a few minutes to settle in and then made his way up to the flight deck. Thom was waiting for him.

"Ready to head out?" Cris asked.

"Yes. All stocked and ready to get underway," Thom

confirmed.

Cris brought up the saved beacon sequence he had plotted during his interview and set it as the active course in the navigation computer. He locked in the first segment of the trip, a series of five beacons. “All set.”

Thom smiled. “Let’s go.” He strapped into his chair and triggered buttons and switches at the front of the flight deck.

A holographic control interface illuminated over the front panels. Using a combination of the holographic display and buttons beneath, Thom undocked the *Exler* and used thrusters to direct the ship away from the space station.

Anticipation swelled in Cris’ chest. *I’m leaving for real.*

When the space station orbiting Tararia was a distant speck, Thom activated the jump drive.

A hum filled the air as the drive charged. The entire ship began to vibrate, rattling every rivet. It felt like the ship was going to fall apart, but Cris tried to hide his worry. As the vibration crescendoed, a shifting blue-green aura formed around the ship. It grew steadily brighter and more solid, drawing the ship inward. For a moment, time elongated. The ship slipped into subspace.

Cris let out a slow breath as the rattling subsided. The view through the front viewport was nothing but shifting blue-green light.

“It’s beautiful, isn’t it?” Thom said.

“It really is.” Cris had taken previous trips via subspace, but the mode of travel was still a novel experience. Even more rarely had he been able to look outside while in transit. *I could get used to this.*

The first sequence of beacons would take several hours to traverse. Cris and Thom settled in for the journey, keeping a casual eye on the navigation beacon locks to make sure they stayed on course. It was uncomfortably quiet.

As much as Cris wanted to be social, he knew his background was very different from Thom’s. He had little way of knowing what might give him away as High Dynasty. *What’s a safe topic?*

Silence was the safest option, but Cris’ lack of sleep from his midnight escape began to catch up with him. He’d need some conversation or he wouldn’t make it through the rest of the jump.

"So, Thom," Cris said, breaking the silence, "what's the craziest cargo you've ever had to transport? If it's not something confidential."

Thom smiled. "A herd of horses."

"Horses, really?"

The captain nodded. "I imagine you haven't been out to the far colonies. Some worlds that have taken a more agrarian approach to life. They prefer horses to hoverscooters."

"Go figure."

Thom chuckled. "It was messy business. Sweet animals, but I'll take a depleted power cell over a pile of manure any day."

Cris laughed. "I'm with you."

"That was a long time ago." Thom leaned back in his chair. "I now make it a point to steer away from any cargo that isn't inanimate and doesn't fit neatly into a crate."

"Smart move."

"I've been doing lots of textiles transportation for Baellas recently."

Clothing and home furnishings weren't the most grand of the High Dynastic ventures, but important nonetheless. "Is that what we have on board now?"

"Yes, but I'm ready to switch things up after completing this delivery."

"What do you have in mind?" Cris asked.

"I heard about some new food distribution contracts with Makaris Corp in the Outer Colonies. It'd be steady work for several months at a time. I don't particularly love it out there, but can't argue with the pay."

Cris nodded. "That does sound like good, steady work."

Food and water filters were a necessity everywhere. It had made Makaris one of the most powerful dynasties, though the reliance on SiNavTech's navigation network and VComm's communication infrastructure kept those two at the top.

"I've learned that it all comes down to the specific contract terms. It doesn't really matter what the cargo is when it's all packaged up. In the end, all of the Big Six are pretty much the same to work for."

Cris' brow furrowed in spite of himself.

Thom must have noticed his confusion. "The six High

Dynasties," he clarified.

"Oh, thanks," Cris said as casually as he could. "Hadn't heard that before."

"I had already pegged you for being from the Central Worlds, but that confirms it."

"Tararia itself, actually." Cris regretted the statement the moment he spoke.

The captain nodded. "I'm not surprised. Well, out here, you'll hear a lot of different opinions about the Big Six. Generally speaking, the farther out you go, the less favorable they will become."

"Interesting." *I'll have to watch what I say.*

"Don't get me wrong," Thom continued. "Tarans in aggregate recognize the importance of the core services the Big Six provide, but most worlds try to have their own identity. The descendants of the older colonies even look and sound different—an entirely divergent race from a native Tararian like yourself. To them, the High Dynasties and the Priesthood feel like very distant and often inconvenient overlords."

*But without the services provided by the High Dynasties' companies, everything would fall apart.* At least, that's what Cris had been taught. "I could see that."

"Since the outermost colonies try to make it on their own as much as possible, they sometimes get neglected by the central oligarchy. It's one of the reasons I was looking to pick up those Makaris contracts."

"That's good of you." Cris' instruction had made it sound like there was equal access and opportunity for every colony world, but maybe that wasn't the case. It was all the more reason to see it firsthand.

"Well, first we have to offload this Baellas shipment. Need to take it one contract at a time."

Cris smiled. "Of course."

Thom sat up straight. "Hey, do you know how to play Fastara?"

*What in the stars is Fastara?* Cris shook his head. "I can't say I do."

"Hold on." Thom searched through a cabinet near his seat and produced a deck of plastic playing cards. He removed them from their clear box and fanned them out. There were a series of symbols in different colors on the cards. “I’ll teach you. There’s no better way to pass the time out here.”

“Sounds great.”

Thom deactivated the holographic course projection from the navigation console and moved the most vital information to a head-up display over the front viewport. The touchscreen top of the console became a perfect tabletop for laying out the game.

“The objective is to win,” Thom said with a toothy grin.

The captain went over a series of rules that Cris tried his best to follow. There were a lot of contingencies based on the specific cards in play. After a few confusing explanation attempts, Thom dealt out the first game and walked Cris through an open-hand demonstration. Even with the coaching, Thom won by a ridiculous margin. They played three more rounds in the same manner before switching over to private hands. Cris was still terrible at the game, but he started to understand the mechanics. While reading Thom’s mind would have been an easy solution, it would defeat the purpose of the game—and, that kind of invasion was no way to begin a friendship.

The hours sped by with the rounds of Fastara. Cris was startled when the navigation system flashed, indicating their approach to the exit beacon in the sequence. They cleared the game and moved the display back to the center console.

With a shudder, the ship dropped back into normal space. The swirling blue-green dissipated and they were once again surrounded by blackness and stars.

Cris looked at the map. It was officially the farthest he had ever been from home. “Jump complete.” *They’ll have a hard time finding me now.*

“Now we take a break,” Thom said as he got up from his chair. “The jump drive only needs four hours to cool down, but we’ll stay here for eight so we can get some sleep. After this, we’ll do two jumps in a day.”

“That works for me.” Cris got up from his seat, feeling stiff after remaining stationary for so long. “Hey… Thank you for the job.”

“Everyone deserves the chance to start a new life,” Thom said. “Get some rest.”

Cris went to his room and got into bed. The ship's engines produced the perfect background hum to lull him to sleep. *I'm free.*

—

An alarm sounded, echoing through the tiny metal room. Cris' eyes shot open. A red light strobed above his door. *Stars! What's going on?*

He rolled off his bed, clutching his ears to muffle the alarm. *Are we under attack?*

The metal deck plates felt like ice under his bare feet. Wearing only pajama pants and a t-shirt, he stumbled toward the door. Something didn't feel right.

Cris' stomach turned over. He tried to take a step and couldn't get traction. Slowly, he lifted off the ground.

*The artificial gravity is shut off! Shite!* He continued to drift upward as he struggled. An acidic burn filled the back of his throat, a combination of nerves and the weightlessness. *I'm going to be sick.*

He grasped at the walls and managed to propel himself toward the toilet in the corner. No sooner had he raised the lid than his stomach emptied. He coughed and spat for a moment, only to be horrified to see the vomit rising upward without gravity to hold it down. He slammed the lid down to trap the contents in the toilet bowl.

Still feeling queasy, he gripped the wall and shimmied himself back toward the door. He hit the release to slide it open.

Red lights flashed in the hallway, casting eerie shadows across the riveted planes.

Cris' heart raced. *Where is everyone? Are we going to die?*

His heart pounded in his ears. The taste of sick still in his mouth made him want to hurl again. He tried to suppress the feeling as he gripped the bulkhead outside his door to move toward the flight deck.

"Thom!"

No reply.

Cris inched along the wall, afraid to let go. He couldn't hear anything over the deafening alarm and the pounding in his ears.

"Thom, where are you?"

Cris made it to the gym and opened the door. Empty.

He knocked on the doors to Dom and Neal's rooms, but there was no reply.

He kept pushing forward. As he approached the kitchen, the door slid open.

Inside, the three other members of the crew were floating comfortably in midair. Thom was grinning and Dom and Neal were laughing hysterically.

Cris stared at them in shock. "What…?"

Thom laughed at Cris' bewildered expression. "You didn't think you could come on board without a little hazing, did you?"

Cris felt his face flush. "So, there isn't an emergency."

"Not at all." Thom hit a button on the wall and the alarm silenced, though the red flashing light remained. "However, I am pleased to report that all emergency systems are functioning perfectly."

*Bomax.* Cris steadied himself against the doorframe, his ears still ringing from the alarm. "Well played."

"So sullen! It was all in good fun," Thom said.

*Right.* "Now can you restore the gravity? I feel like I'm going to puke again."

Dom and Neal burst into another round of laughter.

Thom looked slightly apologetic. "Again? You planet-lovers never fare so well at first. Cleaning supplies are in the cabinet over here, if you need anything."

*No more servants to pick up after me.* "Thanks. I think most of it was… contained."

"Well, let's get you back on your feet." The captain glided toward the door.

Cris eased out of the way so Thom could get by, and then followed him through the hall toward the darkened flight deck.

Thom pulled himself into the pilot's seat. Even in the challenging light of the red strobe, he easily manipulated the buttons and switches on the control panel. "This is why we have physical buttons rather than exclusively touchscreen interfaces," he said. "You can run on backup batteries for days this way. Holographics are a massive power drain. And difficult to control in zero-G."

"Ah, I was wondering." *I can't believe they messed with me like that.*

The red light was replaced by the normal soft yellow ambiance. Simultaneously, Cris felt himself drawn toward the floor, and he repositioned accordingly. He breathed a deep sigh of relief as his bare feet made contact with the ground once more.

His stomach settled. "That's better." *I hope I'm cut out for life in space.*

Thom beamed. "Congratulations. You've been officially inducted."

*Yay.* "I'm going back to bed." He heard Thom chuckling in the flight deck all the way back to his room.

# CHAPTER 4

OVER THE NEXT several days, Cris embraced his place in the *Exler*'s crew and set aside thoughts of his old life. By sheer will, he fell into the ways of space and vowed to leave behind his former existence. He spent long hours in the flight deck with Thom, hanging on every word of the captain's stories. As Thom promised, Cris was never asked intrusive questions and he never pressed Thom.

His daily activities were nothing like his schooling on Tararia, and Cris relished the change. By ship's day, he kept Thom company in the flight deck while they traversed the vast network connecting the star systems. It was the first real contact Cris had ever had with the impressive SiNavTech infrastructure, and he couldn't help but feel pride for what his family had built over the generations.

As the days stretched on, Cris incrementally improved his skills with Fastara. He could only win one in twenty games against Thom—if the captain got a particularly bad draw—but it was progress. Ultimately, the win rate didn't matter; life was good if the biggest decision he had to make was regarding which card to play.

The jumps toward Gallos grew monotonous. By the end, Cris was ready to see more than the four rooms where he'd spent the majority of his time for the last two weeks. Though some of their stopovers were near space stations, Thom insisted it wasn't worth the docking fees to berth. They were confined to the *Exler* until they reached their destination.

The final jumps went by quickly, knowing they were nearing the end. When they dropped out of subspace after the last jump, Cris' heart leaped with excitement as he glimpsed the distant outline of a sprawling space station. *Gallos. Finally.*

He had learned from Thom that the Gallos System was a commercial hub for the surrounding colonies. Its central space station dwarfed even the massive port at Tararia. There were rambling offshoots in every direction, seemingly constructed to meet ad hoc demands for expansion over the years. The result was a daunting labyrinth of corridors and gangways where Cris imagined a person could get lost and never be seen again.

"We have a docking reservation where our client is meeting us," Thom stated. "I'll go to the Makaris field office later today to talk about a distribution contract."

"What should I do?" Cris asked.

Thom rubbed his chin. "Are you interested in staying on with me?"

*He's been good to me, even if it's been a little boring at times. I can't imagine a much better setup for now.* Cris nodded. "If you'll have me."

"I can offer you continued room and board, plus five percent of my profits."

It was probably a terrible deal, but he didn't need the money. "That works."

Thom seemed surprised. "Okay, well good. You've been great company. It'll be nice having you around."

"Do you want me to come with you to the Makaris meeting?"

"No, best leave that to me. Take some time to wander around and enjoy yourself. We'll head out in a couple of days."

They finished docking with the station and Cris was soon left to fend for himself. He took some time to shower in the shared washroom and change into clean clothes before venturing from the *Exler*.

The space station was a completely different environment than the port at Tararia. It was immediately apparent that the pace was slower, with individuals and small groups strolling as they talked business or caught up on personal lives. Cris found it easy to walk off the *Exler* and wander down the corridor without coming close to anyone else.

At first, he couldn't resist sneaking a few telepathic probes on the passersby. Most minds were preoccupied with business dealings or the other mundane aspects of life. He was tempted to look deeper and stretch the skills he kept in check around his friends, but he held back. It wasn't polite to pry, friend or not.

Furthermore, while telepathy was a practical skill, what he really desired was to learn telekinesis. Thus far, all of his attempts at object levitation had been non-starters. He knew he needed instruction, and a spaceport in the Outer Colonies might be his best bet to find a teacher to get him started. As much as he'd like to join the TSS and get official training, reaching out to them would give away his position to Tararian authorities—granting him a one-way ticket on a transport back home. Keeping a low profile was his safest option, even if it meant taking longer to reach his goals.

As he made his way down the hallway, foot traffic slowly picked up. After a short while, he found himself at an intersection with what appeared to be a central mall. Shops lined the broad corridor, with merchants barking their wares.

There were significantly more people in the shopping district compared to the docking area near the *Exler*. People with every variety of skin tone and feature, dressed in all manner of clothing styles, were going about their business. The hum of conversation filled the space, making it feel lively without being frantic.

*Now this is what I had imagined.* Cris looked around in wonder. *There's so much to explore!*

The colorful storefronts with illuminated signs and attention-grabbing holographic gimmicks stretched on for as far as he could see in both directions, broken up only by other side corridors to the various docking wings. He made note of the shops near the *Exler*'s docking location so he could find his way back, then arbitrarily set off down the mall to his right.

As he strolled, there was a slow change in his surroundings—so subtle that he didn't notice at first. The vibrant colors and flashy ads gave way to metal signs with static typography. The wording on most of these signs was vague, such as 'Sundries from far and wide' or 'Trade, Barter and Pawn'. The people also changed. Though still covering the spectrum of physical traits, their clothing was more worn and they appeared to be constantly assessing the value of everything they surveyed.

Cris was so taken in by the freedom to wander on his own that he didn't realize he was growing increasingly anxious under the scrutinizing gaze of the shopkeepers and their patrons. When he finally became aware of his surroundings, he realized he stood out from the few people left roaming the corridor. *Maybe it's time to get out of sight for a while and do some shopping.*

One of the shops off to Cris' left caught his eye. The printed sign boasted discount ships and parts. *How discounted? Maybe I could buy my own ship one day and have real autonomy.* He decided to investigate.

The entrance to the shop was an open doorway two meters wide. Inside, on both walls of the shop, tiered shelving rose to the three-meter-high ceiling. Other shelves were positioned perpendicular to the wall, forming a maze of forgotten artifacts. Random ship parts were nearly overflowing from the shelves, and some larger items rested on the floor. The disorganization and compact layout were unappealing, but Cris was too intrigued by the dream of eventually having his own ship to care.

The perpendicular offshoots from the shelves prevented a direct view deeper into the store. With no proprietor in sight, Cris headed toward the back. He weaved through the shelves until he came to an open area.

A young woman was lounging on a metal counter, her long legs crossed with one of her booted feet bobbing in the air. She looked to be a few years older than Cris, and had dark hair with fuchsia highlights that was pulled up into a sloppy ponytail. Long bangs fell over her maple eyes. When Cris approached, she looked up.

She appraised him and smiled. "Well, hello there." She slid off the counter.

"Hi," Cris replied. "Do you work here?"

"I do." She looked Cris over again. "What can I do for you?" She shifted her weight to one hip and stood akimbo. Though she was fairly tall and thin, her revealing clothing emphasized every curve.

Cris tried to keep his eyes on her face. "I saw on your sign that you have ships for sale."

She nodded. "That's right. In the market for anything in particular?"

"Just browsing for now. How much for a basic craft with a jump drive?"

"Well, let's take a look at our inventory." The woman sauntered around to the back side of the counter and grabbed a tablet from underneath. She placed the tablet on the counter and activated a holographic projection of the inventory list, which included images of the craft and some basic features. She drummed her fingers on the counter. "Need room for passengers? Traveling with anyone?"

"Not really. Just me." Cris looked around the equipment in the shop. Some of it was worn, but much of it appeared to be almost brand new.

"Okay, let's see..." After flicking through the list of ships, the woman selected one and brought up a more detailed display on the projector. "This would be your best bet. For something entry-level."

The ship was only ten meters long and had the aerodynamic look of a craft designed for atmospheric entry. While it would be functional, Cris doubted he could stay sane in such a small space for any prolonged period of time. "How much?"

"76,000 credits."

Though not outrageous, there was no way he could spend that much without drawing suspicion. "Not bad, but it's a little more than I was hoping to spend."

The woman shrugged. "Well, you're paying for the scrubbed ID, of course."

"Of course." *Stars! These are ships for smuggling.* He realized with dismay that the new equipment around him was likely scrap from stolen vessels.

"How would you pay?" the woman asked. "We might be able to work out a deal."

The discomfort that had been pestering the back of Cris' mind since he entered the shop washed over him full-force—a wave of ill intent that now seemed impossible to have missed before. "Really, I—"

He was cut off by the woman turning to yell deeper into the store. "Merl! We have a customer."

The sound of creaking metal drew Cris' attention to his side. A man with arms nearly the size of Cris' torso emerged from a hidden doorway, blocking the exit path.

Simultaneously, another man emerged from a back room behind the counter. He was two heads taller than Cris, all muscle, and had geometric tattoos on the side of his face and going up his bare arms. With his eyes fixed on Cris, he approached the counter. He put an arm around his slight companion. "Oh, Danni, you got us a good one."

"He's pretty, isn't he?" Danni said. "Traveling alone. And he comes with a nice bank account."

*Shite! This is bad.* Warnings flashed in Cris' mind, sending a chill down his spine. *I don't think they just smuggle ship parts…*

"How much do you think we could get for him?" Danni asked.

"Looks like good breeding," the tattooed man—presumably Merl—replied as he evaluated Cris. "Probably at least 50,000 credits to the right buyer."

The man from the side room took a step toward Cris.

*Run!* Cris bolted, ducking past the towering man who had come to block him in. He felt the breeze from the man's arms trying to grab him, but managed to make it through.

After tearing around the maze of shelves, he ran full speed as soon as he was in the open corridor. He didn't slow until he was again surrounded by lively merchants and bright ads.

Cris stepped off to the side of the hall. He leaned forward, hands resting on his thighs—shaking and his breath ragged. He found an open stretch of wall to lean against.

*I should have seen that coming.* Reading everyone's minds might not be polite, but perhaps some way necessary to protect himself.

He took a couple minutes to calm his breathing and racing heart. Despite his excitement from earlier, when he looked out at the crowd again, he felt like everyone in the port was staring at him suspiciously.

The *Exler* seemed like the only safe place. He took a direct route back, thankful he had paid attention to the docking location.

When he made it to the ship, he was about to go into his room when he saw that Thom was in the flight deck. He continued down the hall and poked his head in. "Hi, Thom."

The captain looked up with surprise. "Back already? I figured you'd be partying all night."

Cris collapsed into his Navigator's chair. "It was a lot to take in at once. I think I'll just turn in early."

Thom raised an eyebrow. "Everything okay?"

"Yeah, just… acclimating." *Probably best if he doesn't know how inexperienced I really am. There's no way I'm traveling alone any time soon.*

Thom nodded. "Yes, it's quite different out here than around Tararia."

*I'll say…* Cris sighed inwardly.

"And even more so in the Outer Colonies where we're headed."

Cris perked up. "You got the Makaris contract?"

Thom smiled. "I did—and a good one. Fifteen months, with scheduled stops on a service route. We'll have supply pickups every two weeks at stations, so you'll have plenty of time to get used to everything."

"Perfect." *All this will start feeling normal eventually, right?*

"I got us a little something to celebrate." Thom pulled out two small glasses and a bottle of a dark brown liquid from the cabinet by his chair. "I know you're not quite of age, but one drink won't hurt you." He filled the glasses and passed one to Cris.

*Stars! It would be rude to turn him down.* Cris took the glass. *Besides, I think I could use a drink.*

Thom downed the contents of his glass in one gulp.

Cris took a cautious whiff of the liquid. It seemed more like a cleaning supply than anything fit for a person to consume.

*Here it goes.* He took the full glass into his mouth and swallowed. It burned all the way down and left his stomach feeling warm. He coughed a couple of times, feeling the burn up in his sinuses. "Wow, that's…"

"That's real liquor. Not like those 'liqueurs' and sparkling shite everyone drinks back in the Central Worlds."

*Everyone drinks those because they actually taste good.* "I appreciate the introduction to the real stuff." *And now I know what to avoid as much as possible.*

"It'll knock you on your ass if you're not careful." Thom poured himself another glass and offered Cris some more.

Cris hastily declined. "I'm sure it can." Without warning, he started to feel a little light-headed and tingly. *This stuff acts fast.* "I think it's bedtime for me."

Thom seemed disappointed. "All right. Sleep well."

Cris rose. "Thanks for the drink." *And thank you for taking me in.*

— — —

The news was not what TSS High Commander Jason Banks had hoped to hear. "What do you mean he's 'gone'?"

Agent Jarek's image on the viewscreen, almost indistinguishable from real life, looked uncomfortable. "His parents didn't want to talk to us. We were able to glean that he slipped out in the middle of the night a couple of weeks ago."

*Shite! We should have been keeping a closer watch.* Banks didn't let his frustration show. "We need to find him. As soon as possible."

Jarek frowned. "He could be anywhere, sir. We checked all the registries for passenger ships, but there was nothing. If he's on a cargo freighter, there are hundreds of possibilities, multiplied exponentially by transfers at another port. I think we need to wait it out until we get some kind of lead."

*This is a disaster.* Banks rubbed his eyes under his tinted glasses. "Fine. Make some contacts out there to keep watch for us. We'll wait it out." *Let's hope we find him before the Priesthood does. I don't want to risk a repeat of last time.*

# PART 2: AWAKENING

# CHAPTER 5

"GAME." CRIS LAID down his victorious hand of Fastara.

Thom threw down his cards in disgust. "That's five in a row. I've created a monster."

"Oh, come on now. Be a good sport."

"Constant loss kind of takes the fun out of it."

*Right, like it was awesome for me when we first started playing.* "You had a good run. This was bound to happen eventually. After all, I've had a year of daily practice." Cris grinned. He knew he had just been lucky with his last several draws—he and Thom were equal in their playing ability, despite the recent winning streak. *I can't resist getting in a few jabs while I can.*

They were nearing the end of another delivery cycle on their Makaris contract. After only ten months with Thom, Cris could hardly believe he'd ever had any other life. Since his initial mishaps, he had become comfortable with the customs of nomadic space life. With dozens of stopovers in space stations, he had learned how to identify the good areas from the bad, and he was proficient at using covert telepathic probes when needed.

To his relief, the food distribution work offered far more variety than the initial, dull trip to Gallos. They traveled for no more than two days at a time without making a stop to offload, which helped the time pass.

Privately, Cris had kept up with his studies and physical training in the *Exler*'s small gym, not wanting his skills to atrophy; however, it was because he enjoyed it, rather than feeling like it was something he had to do. He kept steady watch for news about his parents back in Sieten, but heard little. There was never an announcement about his disappearance—that would have been a disastrous political move—but he figured there must be private detectives looking for him. The prospect was disconcerting, but he tried to feel confident in his ability to remain undetectable. He was the Navigator for a cargo freighter, and as far as anyone else was concerned, he was born to fulfill such a duty.

The navigation system beeped. They had reached the last beacon in the sequence.

Thom jumped at the chance to clear the cards from their play surface. "Thank the stars! I need some time away from the onslaught."

Cris shook his head and laughed. *He'll get over it.*

He checked the lock on the exit beacon; it was solid. "Aldria, here we come."

The *Exler* dropped out of subspace. Ahead of them, in the distance, was one of the smaller stations in the sector. They had previously been there four times on their delivery rounds. Unlike many other stations, Aldria was predominantly a stopover for merchants, rather than serving as a residence for any sizable population.

They went through the docking protocol with the remote attendant.

As soon as the clamps were in place, Thom rose from his seat. "I'll handle the offloading. Go get some of that fried thing you like so much."

"Best fried leeca in the Outer Colonies!"

"So you've told me every time since we first came here." Thom shooed Cris away with his hand. "Now go, before I change my mind."

Cris eagerly complied. There were few things he missed from his home, but fried leeca was one. It was common street food on Tararia, but the Sietinen family chef had made it for him one time and he was instantly hooked. He had stumbled across a vendor in the Aldria Station on their first stopover and was thrilled to discover that the rendition thoroughly lived up to his memory.

The vendor was on the opposite side of the station. Cris took his time taking in the sights, happy to stretch his legs in a manner other than on a treadmill. They stopped at stations frequently enough, but rarely was he afforded free time to idly gaze at wares.

Even after a year of travel, he was still amazed by the quantity and breadth of products available in ports. There was a gadget to fulfill every purpose—both real needs, and those invented strictly for the sake of sales. It was difficult to imagine all of the inventory selling, yet the system perpetuated itself.

Cris was struck by the scale of it. *How many millions of people pass by just out of sight in space every day?* Thinking in those terms put his own miniscule existence in perspective. Except, despite his current anonymity, he was important. Every one of those countless people would recognize his birth name. It was humbling.

Cris took a wrong turn at first, but eventually found the fried leeca vendor's red cart. A rich scent of frying dough wafted down the hall. The cart was a freestanding box a couple meters square and just tall enough to stand inside, with a half-open wall to the front. Its crimson color made Cris think of his favorite flower patch in the Sietinen estate's gardens. He beamed at the proprietor as he approached.

She was a sturdy woman of middle years, named Roselyn based on the credentials displayed in front of her cart. There was a warmth to her that reminded Cris of the nanny who had cared for him until he was six. She tilted her head and gave Cris a slight smile in return. There was a hint of recognition in her burnt umber eyes. "You're back."

"I could never pass up the opportunity to get a taste of home."

"It's been almost two months, hasn't it?" Roselyn asked as she rotated the contents of the basket in her fryer within the cart.

Cris nodded. "Yes, sadly. Our rounds only bring us here every nine weeks."

Roselyn frowned. "What a shame. I've missed that adorable smile of yours." She winked at him.

*Stars! Is she flirting with me?* He smiled politely and took half a step back. "I'll take two orders, please."

"Absolutely. I'll have a fresh batch ready in a couple minutes." She flipped the contents of the basket again.

"I've been looking forward to it all week."

Roselyn inclined her head. "You flatter me. Are you here for long?"

"Just for a few hours to pick up our cargo, then on to Elarine," Cris replied with a dour expression. It was his least favorite of all the ports.

"Elarine…" The vendor's brow furrowed. "I've heard of it, but never been."

"Don't bother. There's nothing to see. It's small and unremarkable in every way."

Roselyn grinned. "Looking forward to your visit, then?"

"Can't wait."

"Well, I hope this makes it easier for you." Roselyn removed the basket from the fryer and placed six fried patties onto a plastic plate. The golden dough of the leeca was still sizzling. She set the plate on a ledge atop the front opening to her cart. "Four credits."

Cris pulled the physical currency chips out of his pocket and gave her five credits. Electronic transfers were far more common, but he feared the faked credentials on his alias bank account wouldn't hold up to thorough scrutiny. As a precaution, he had adopted the practice of using chips instead.

He blew on a piece of leeca to cool it and took a bite—warm and savory with just the right touch of sweetness. It brought him back to his early life, before preparing for his future responsibilities became the sole focus. *I did have this as a kid. I guess it wasn't all bad.*

"It's excellent," he said while still chewing.

"Enjoy," Roselyn said. "Have fun in Elarine."

"Heh, thanks." He waved goodbye and began wandering back toward the *Exler*.

Cris finished up the leeca while casually strolling through the port, reflecting on some of the good times from his childhood on Tararia. He wandered by some shops and looked at completely impractical, unnecessary items. As he browsed, he even noticed oversized pulse guns that couldn't possibly be legal and some openly displayed narcotics. *It really is different out here.*

With romanticized thoughts of Tararia still floating through his mind, Cris was on his final approach to the *Exler* when he happened to overhear the Sietinen name mentioned in a conversation. It had been so long since he'd heard the name directly—rather than a generic mention of the Big Six—that it caught him off-guard. He stopped and looked around to identify who was talking. After a moment, he spotted two merchants drinking at a walk-up bar. Curious, Cris walked over so he could hear the details.

"You're right, the entire government system is corrupt," the first merchant was saying. "Regardless of what Sietinen and Vaenetri say, the Priesthood runs the show." He took a sip of a green liquid from his glass. "But it doesn't matter who's in charge. Nothing happening out here matters to any of them."

Cris had heard numerous similar conversations over the last year. Each one was a series of unflattering generalizations about the High Dynasties and how no individual could possibly ever care. He was sick of hearing it. *We're not all like that. I'm different. The Priesthood is the real menace, not the Dynasties.* He was about to walk away.

"Real conflict is headed our way, but they do nothing," the other merchant said. "I've been to the outermost territories recently. It's brutal, and it's only getting worse."

Cris hung back. *That's new...*

"They're certainly not going to tell us what's going on out there," the first merchant agreed. "Meanwhile, countless people are starving and being taxed to death."

"No shite. All of those purists think alike. It's about maintaining power and getting richer, not helping people."

"Thank the stars for the TSS! I hear at least they have the decency to tell their first-year trainees about some of what's going on in the rest of the galaxy. Give people a chance to get out of whatever hole they were born into."

"It's hardly enough. We're all foked."

The first merchant gulped the rest of his glass. The second did likewise.

*What kind of conflict are they talking about?* Cris knew it wasn't his place to intrude, but he was feeling inspired after his recent reflections on Tararia. He stepped up to the merchants. "The High Dynasties do care about their people. You shouldn't be so dismissive."

The merchants stared at him, taken by surprise. Both burst into uproarious laughter.

"How naïve!" the first merchant exclaimed. "Generation after generation it's always the same shite. They ignore us out here, and that's never going to change."

"There is always hope for change," Cris countered.

The merchant scoffed. "Hope, maybe, but that doesn't mean it will ever happen. The Dynasties and Priesthood control everything, and we're nothing to them. You or I can't do anything about that." He turned back to his companion with an indifferent smile, shaking his head.

*Perhaps there isn't anything he can do, but I am in a unique position.* "Then someone already high up has to bring about change," Cris said with renewed vigor. "Someone who doesn't share their predecessors' ideals."

The merchants shook their heads, laughed again as they turned to face Cris.

"You're still here?" the second merchant jeered as his drink was refreshed by the bartender.

The first merchant sighed. "The problem *is* the people with influence! Everyone has been born into their position, and no one would give that up."

*I would. There have to be others.* "The Dynasties are only as powerful as the people let them be."

"If that's the case," said the second merchant, "then the Dynasties are doing a foking good job of keeping the populace placated through lies."

Some passersby took notice of the debate and stopped to listen.

"I'm sure people are told what they need to know," Cris said.

The merchant's expression became completely serious. "What about a war? Is it right to keep the war a secret?"

*What war?* Cris hesitated. "Someone thinks so." *Have they kept secrets even from me?*

The merchant shrugged and waved his hand, brushing Cris off. He tried to crack a smile. "Then what does it matter? Whether it's the Priesthood or someone new, it'd still come down to one group deciding what others should know."

*Could there really be a conflict going on that I don't know about?* He'd never heard mention of a war. There were plenty of political secrets kept from the general population, so if there *was* something going on, there had to be a reason. "Knowledge and power come with a price," he said. "Perhaps it is necessary for a few to bear the burden."

A murmur of agreement passed through the small crowd watching the discussion.

*What does he know about the war?* Cris was about to reach out to the merchant's mind to see what he could glean, but a jeer pulled his attention back to the present.

"What do *you* know? You're no one!" The merchant's eyes narrowed as he focused on Cris.

Cris looked around the crowd. "Everyone can do something." *I might not love politics, but maybe I can do what no one else has been willing to do.*

The merchant shook his head. "The Dynasties and the Priesthood have been this way for as far back as anyone can remember. There's no point in talking about change. Anyone who does would likely end up the same way as the Dainetris Dynasty—ruined and all but forgotten. When it comes to matters of Tararia, civilians have no influence."

Cris examined the expectant faces in the crowd. "Then the remaining Dynasties have to listen. With their help, the Priesthood could be brought down."

The merchant recoiled, eyes darting. "Watch what you say—the Priesthood hears everything."

*No wonder they have so much control. People shy away at its very mention.* "I don't fear the Priesthood."

The merchant froze, his gaze fixed on Cris.

Cris looked at the ground. *Stars! What am I doing?* He glanced up, noticing all the people around him looking on with a mixture of wonder and apprehension. *I have to end this.*

"I'll be on my way now." He turned away from the merchant. "Excuse me." He pushed his way past the onlookers before the merchant could protest. As he retreated, he thought he saw Thom standing in the crowd.

Cris rushed back to the *Exler. Is the Priesthood really concealing a war?* He went straight to his quarters and sat down on his bunk, his mind spinning. *Who is the enemy? Over what? Why would everyone on Tararia keep it from me? Do they even know…?*

He'd heard about the occasional civil spat, surely, but not a war. He tried to rationalize the claim, but got nowhere. After several minutes, he caught himself. *It doesn't matter. I'm trying to forget that life.*

With a deep sigh, Cris forced himself off his bunk. He figured he may as well distract himself by preparing the next route for their upcoming deliveries.

An hour of sporadic work passed in the flight deck. Though some questions still churned in the background, Cris soon felt much more settled. However, he became anxious again when Thom entered, looking concerned.

"What is it, Thom?" Cris asked.

The captain shifted uncomfortably on his feet. "I— I was just surprised to hear you say those things at the bar earlier."

Cris dropped his gaze to the floor, regretting his encounter with the merchants. "I'm sorry for my behavior, Thom—"

The captain shook his head. "You were just speaking your mind." He took a deep breath. "But, you can't threaten the Taran authorities like that. People can complain and wish things were different, but what you said about bringing down the Priesthood—that's just foolish."

"I understand."

"Good." Thom looked around the small room, not meeting Cris' gaze. "Now, can we just move on?"

Cris nodded, but Thom still looked distraught when he left the room.

Cris' heart began to race. Something about Thom's demeanor had changed. *Stars, of course! Only someone from a Dynasty would dare speak out against the Priesthood in public... and Thom knows it. Shite.*

For two days, he and Thom avoided eye contact, but they eventually returned to their normal routine. Still, the debate with the merchant had moved Cris, and his subliminal thoughts turned to Tararia. He had the power to make a difference—in a way few others could. However, he couldn't bring himself to go back. Yet. He wanted no part of the current political system. But, with the right alliances, perhaps things could change one day. *For now, there is no place for me there. I still have so much to see.*

# CHAPTER 6

CRIS STROLLED THROUGH the Elarine spaceport, thankful to be on leave from the delivery routine. *Even a stopover at Elarine is better than being cooped up on the* Exler.

The selection of wares in the shops was limited and bland compared to those in the larger ports, but it passed the time. He wandered from shop to shop, keeping to himself. There were few travelers in the corridors, and most of the shopkeepers seemed disinterested until someone wanted to make a purchase.

As Cris came out of one of the establishments, he was startled to see two men watching him from across the hall. They were dressed entirely in black, with tinted glasses and sleek overcoats that hung to their knees—a stark contrast to the colorful merchants. He tensed. Something about them felt unusual.

He headed down the corridor deeper into the port, wanting to distance himself. Out of the corner of his eye, he noticed that the men were heading in his direction.

*Who could they be?* He thought for a moment. *Stars! Are they my parent's detectives? Bomax, I probably gave myself away in that argument during our last stopover at Aldria.*

Pulse racing, Cris abruptly turned around to hurry back toward the *Exler*. To his dismay, the men followed.

*I can't let them take me back!* Cris broke into a run.

He came to the central mall of the port and darted through the crowd, careful to avoid colliding with any of the travelers. When he came to an intersection, he nimbly stepped off to the side and sprinted around a bend in the hall in an attempt to evade the two men. He took a few more turns, but he soon found himself in a dead-end passage.

*Shite! Where can I go?* Cris halted. He was about to wheel around, but in the stillness noticed the pounding of footsteps right behind him.

Before he could turn, Cris was thrown to the ground, tackled from behind. With his arms pinned to his sides in a horrific embrace, he fell forward. Lurching to the side, his shoulder took the hit to avoid smacking his head on the metal deck plates.

He rolled to his stomach, weighed down. Someone was on his back.

His hands found the floor, and he pushed up, throwing all of his weight sideways to flip his assailant to the ground and crush him against the deck plates. The attacker's grip loosened.

Cris jabbed with his elbows and broke free. He scrambled across the hallway.

He expected to see one of the two men dressed in black. Instead, he saw a man of average height, robed in brown with his face hidden in the shadow of his hood. Cris recognized the golden symbol hanging from a chain around the man's neck, marking him as an associate of the Priesthood of the Cadicle.

*The Priesthood.* Cris suddenly remembered the conversation with his father the afternoon before he left Tararia. *I never did find out why they wanted to meet with me.*

As the Priest recovered on the floor, the two black-clad men emerged from around a bend in the hall. There was a hint of shock on their otherwise stoic faces.

Cris was about to address the men when the Priest leaped to his feet. He pulled out a pulse gun from underneath his robe. "Give me all your valuables."

Trembling and sore, Cris grabbed ten credit chips from his pocket and threw them on the ground. "I have nothing else." It was the truth.

His heart pounded in his ears. *Why would a member of the Priesthood be mugging people at a spaceport?*

"Hand over everything you have or die," the Priest threatened.

Cris looked more closely at the figure and caught a brief glimpse of piercing red-brown eyes under the hood. The eyes contained such intense sadness that Cris felt a twinge of sorrow, despite his peril. But, the gaze was also one of complete fear. The gun hummed as it began to charge.

Cris looked back toward the two other men, but they remained at the end of the hall. He was on his own.

The Priest murmured something that Cris couldn't quite make out. He pointed the gun toward Cris' chest.

"No!" Cris held up his hands. He felt dizzy, a buzzing in his head. *I don't want to die.*

Undeterred, the robed figure fired.

It should have only taken an infinitesimal moment for the shot to reach him, but the beam halted just beyond the muzzle of the gun. There was no perceivable motion. Cris looked around, seeing the Priest holding the gun and the two people in black observing from a distance. The moment continued.

*I can get away.*

Cris dove to the side, but didn't fully feel the movement. He was in midair, falling, but he didn't feel connected to himself. Nothing stirred around him. He blinked.

Cris hit the ground hard. There was a flash as the pulse beam struck the empty wall.

The Priest spun to face him, mystified.

Cris could barely breathe. He felt charged, as if filled with electricity. He looked around with wonder—he was in a different place than he had been a moment sooner.

*What's going on…?* He shoved his confusion aside as he saw the Priest raising his weapon once more. *This isn't a mugging—it's an assassination!*

"Stop!" he pleaded.

As the Priest was about to fire again, Cris held up his hand in what he thought to be a futile act of protection. However, the motion threw the Priest backward against the wall—slamming him into the metal plating with enough force to dent the sheeting. He slid into a crumpled heap on the floor.

Cris scrambled to his feet. *Did I just do that? How…?*

He turned to the men in black who were still standing motionless at the end of the hall. "Who are you?" he stammered.

Without responding, one of the men walked over nudged the Priest with his foot. Cris got a sickening feeling in the pit of his stomach that the Priest was dead, but then saw that he had responded to the nudge. The other man returned to his companion.

The brown-robed Priest rose unsteadily and looked around, dazed from the impact with the wall. When he caught sight of Cris, he backed away, terror evident in his trembling movement. After a moment, he noticed the two men in black clothing and froze, apparently recognizing them. His eyes darted between Cris and the men. He said something to Cris, but it was so quiet that he didn't catch the words; it sounded different than the galactic common New Taran, but somehow familiar. With one more glance at the two black-clad men, the Priest passed them and fled down the hall. He didn't look back.

The man who had nudged the Priest bent down to pick up the pulse gun from the floor. He placed it inside his coat and turned toward Cris.

"Who are you?" Cris repeated, still shaking. He took an unsteady breath. *Why didn't they help me?*

He looked the two men over and tried to assess their minds, but found only an impassible void. They appeared to be wary of Cris, but that was understandable after what he had just done.

*Stars! What do I do? I can't outrun them.* He took another breath. "Why were you following me?"

"Are you Cristoph Sietinen-Talsari?" the man finally asked.

"That depends. Are you here to kill me, too?"

The two men exchanged looks. "No, we're not here to harm you," the second man said.

"Did my parents send you to find me?"

"Have you ever done that before?" the first man asked, ignoring his question.

Cris was about to make an indignant remark, but stopped himself. "No." He looked down. "I don't even know what 'that' was."

"No, your parents didn't send us," the other man said after a slight pause, coming to join his colleague. "If you come with us, we can explain everything."

Cris shook his head, finding it increasingly difficult to remain calm. "After what just happened, I'm not in the mood for vague answers. And I'm not going anywhere with people who stood by and did nothing while someone attacked me! Who are you and why are you here?"

The first man nodded to the second. They each pressed their jacket lapel, which activated a projection of their credentials.

Cris examined the holographic images hovering in front of him. His eyes widened. *The TSS!*

"I'm sorry, we're not allowed to intervene in matters regarding the Priesthood. We're with the Tararian Selective Service," the first man said. "I'm Agent Jarek and this is Agent Dodes." He gestured to his partner and then deactivated his ID.

*The Priesthood is so powerful that not even the TSS will stand up to them.* Cris crossed his arms. "What do you want?"

"The TSS is here on our own accord," Jarek continued. "We were deployed to your family's estate on Tararia to speak with you, only to find that you were missing. Your parents probably have their own people looking for you, but it looks like we found you first. Just in time, it seems—especially considering what you just pulled off without any proper training in telekinesis."

Cris swallowed hard. “And what was ‘it’? I have no idea how...” *What if I can’t control it? I could hurt someone—Thom, myself... And why does the Priesthood want me dead? Everything was going great. I fit in, I was normal...*

“We’re not the best people to answer that,” Jarek said.

“Then what do you want from me? You still haven’t told me why you’re here.”

Agent Jarek studied Cris. “We’re here regarding your future.”

Cris tensed. “My future?”

“The TSS has been following you with great interest for the past few years,” Dodes said. He looked over to Jarek, who nodded. “We would like to extend an invitation for you to train with us.”

*There was a time when that would have been a dream come true, but now...* Cris’ stomach turned over. The attack. His vow to change things on Tararia. There was so much to consider. “I’m not sure what to say.”

“I know this comes as a surprise,” Jarek responded. “But, the TSS feels you have great potential, which is only evidenced by the abilities you’ve demonstrated today. I’m sure that our superiors can deal with any reservations you may have. If you’ll accompany us to Headquarters, our High Commander can answer your questions.” He glanced at the spot where the Priest had been. “And, we can offer you security.”

Cris looked down. He might not be so lucky if the Priesthood came after him again. *I still have no idea why they would try to kill me...* He didn’t want to give up his newfound freedom, but that had never been his true objective. More than anything, he wanted to learn about the full range of his Gifted abilities. Training with the TSS might be the only way for him to truly protect himself.

“What would I have to do?” he asked the Agents.

“Just gather your things and come with us. We have a ship waiting on the other side of the port,” Jarek said.

Cris nodded. "The *Exler*'s back this way." *I have absolutely no idea what I'm getting myself into.*

Upon reaching the ship, he left the Agents at the foot of the gangway and went in to gather his belongings. He only had a handful more possessions than when he had left Tararia, but it didn't feel right to leave it all behind. He sighed. It was time to tell Thom he was leaving.

Cris found the captain in the flight deck, reviewing the ship's inventory. "Thom?"

He looked up. "What is it?"

"Something's come up." Cris swallowed, a sudden heaviness in his chest. "I've just been offered a training opportunity with the TSS."

Thom searched Cris' face. "Are you accepting?"

He nodded. "This is something I have to do."

The captain sighed and stood up. "When?"

"Right now. I'm sorry."

Thom nodded, processing the loss of his travel companion. "I understand." He took Cris' hand, shook it. "I always suspected you were destined for greater things. I hope you find what you're looking for."

Cris looked down. *He might not know my real name, but he always saw me for who I am.* "Thank you for everything. I couldn't have asked for more."

The captain smiled and patted Cris on the shoulder. "Best of luck, Cris."

"Thank you, Thom. You too." Cris turned to go.

"Oh, and here." Thom grabbed his Fastara deck. "Take these."

Cris smiled. "I'll teach everyone who'll listen."

Before he could change his mind, Cris exited the flight deck and hurried down the gangway to meet the waiting Agents. With only his single bag slung over his shoulder, Cris felt bare and alone.

Jarek and Dodes led the way to their TSS transport ship. The Agents were unlike anyone he had met before. They moved with a sort of elegance, as though they were one with their surroundings. Even their tailored black uniforms, which were casual compared to attire of the Tararian Guard, projected a sense of regality, making Cris feel like he would be underdressed even while wearing his finest suit. There was also an energy about them that he couldn't quite identify—a magnetism that made him have difficulty looking away.

Over the last year, Cris had become used to blending in and downplaying the authority that had been ingrained in him through years of tutoring. Now, even in the most refined state he could muster, he still felt insignificant compared to the Agents. *How long before the TSS changes me, too?*

As they passed through the spaceport, passersby looked on with wonder and gave the party a wide berth. On the rare occasions Cris had been permitted to visit Sieten, he had received similar looks from the city's residents. There was a sense of awe, but in the same way someone would admire a majestic animal that could readily kill its handlers.

*What will that make me, as both an Agent and dynastic leader?*

Cris' thoughts were interrupted by a glimpse of the TSS ship in the distance down the spaceport's corridor. He had previously seen TSS vessels while visiting a Sietinen shipyard—one of the ancillary businesses to SiNavTech. The TSS vessel stood out from the other craft in the port by its iridescent hull and smooth lines. The materials for the hull were far too expensive for everyday civilian use, but the superior impact absorption was an asset for combat applications and for minimizing the structural stress of subspace travel. At eighty meters long, this particular craft was much smaller than those he had previously seen, though it made sense that the Agents wouldn't take a warship on a recruitment mission.

"How long will it take to get to Headquarters?" Cris asked as they approached the ship.

"About four hours," Jarek replied.

"I didn't realize it was located so close to the Outer Colonies," Cris commented.

"It's not," Jarek replied. "Headquarters is located in Earth's moon."

"Earth?" Cris asked, incredulous. "That seems like a strange place for TSS Headquarters."

"What makes you say that?" Dodes asked.

"Earth isn't part of the Taran government, for one."

"Which makes it a perfect location for training those with telekinetic abilities, doesn't it?" Jarek pointed out.

"I guess it does." *Far from the control of the Priesthood who's outlawed those skills.*

Like most children, Cris had learned the story of Earth as a cautionary tale. Over millennia, Taran descendants seeking to escape the perceived oppression of Tararian rule had fled to Earth and mingled with the native population born from ancient panspermia. Each group of Taran colonists had brought with them elements of the unique cultures from their home worlds, but they shared the common vision of a new start—leaving behind the advanced technologies that connected them to the rest of Tarans in an attempt to disappear. As the 'lost colony' of Earth gave rise and fall to its own great civilizations, Tarans had watched their divergent brethren from a distance—but apparently from far closer than most of Earth's population would have ever imagined.

"Headquarters is within a subspace containment shell inside the moon. Our space dock is fixed just above the surface on the dark side, so we keep to ourselves," Jarek continued.

Cris' brow furrowed. "Subspace containment shell?"

Jarek smiled. "A sustained subspace pocket surrounded by a really big wall. Basically, breaking into Headquarters would be extremely difficult."

"I'll take your word for it," Cris replied. *I guess if their ships are any indication, the rest of their tech is pretty advanced, too.*

"It all might seem strange to you now, but we like being a little hidden," Jarek said as he led the way up the gangway to the ship.

"Wait, you said it would only take four hours to get there. Isn't Earth in a sector that's two or three weeks' travel from here?"

Dodes smirked. "With a civilian jump drive, maybe."

"What does the TSS use?"

"We have long-range subspace transit," Jarek explained. "It works the same basic way as commercial vessels—locking onto SiNavTech beacons. But, rather than the short jumps used by cargo freighters and civilian transports, our ships can lock onto beacons at much farther intervals to expedite the jump. Since our drives don't require cool-down, travel time is reduced by a factor of thirty."

The revelation caught Cris by surprise. "I'd heard theories about long-duration drives, but I didn't know the technology was ever developed."

Jarek nodded. "There are many ways the TSS is outside the mainstream. Travel technology is one of the big ones."

They reached the top of the gangway. Inside, the TSS ship was simply appointed but comfortable. Gray carpet covered the floor of the hall, and metal wall panels were inset with tan accents. Jarek headed down the hall to the right.

"I'm surprised I was never told about the extent of SiNavTech's work with the TSS," Cris said.

"I'm sure you would have been eventually," Jarek said. "But it is kept pretty need-to-know."

*What else haven't I been told? Like the war?* "I guess so."

The hall ended at a lounge room. In the center of the space, there were four plush chairs upholstered in a matte black fabric, which circled a low table with chrome legs and a glass top. An expansive viewport filled the outer wall, and one of the side walls had a broad viewscreen.

"I hope this will be acceptable for the next few hours," Jarek said.

*It sure beats the flight deck on the* Exler. Cris smiled. "It'll be fine, thank you."

"Make yourself comfortable." Jarek gestured toward the chairs.

Cris settled into the seat with the best sightlines to the viewport, and Dodes took a seat across from him.

Jarek remained by the door. "Excuse me, I'll get us underway." He inclined his head to Cris and left the cabin.

Dodes pulled a handheld out from his pocket and began looking at something on the device.

Cris took the opportunity to clear his head, closing his eyes. *I never thought I would be joining the TSS. Especially not like this.* He'd always thought growing his abilities would be useful and fun, but now he was scared to see what he might be able to do. *I never wanted to hurt anyone.*

After a few minutes, Cris felt the low rumble of the jump drive through the floor. Unlike the *Exler*, the vibration seemed muted and controlled. He opened his eyes. The stars out the viewport slowly became masked by blue-green light as the ship slipped into subspace.

"It's nice to just be a passenger for a change," Cris said.

"I'll bet," Dodes replied, looking up from his handheld. "Relax while you can. The TSS isn't exactly known for easing people in gently."

"What should I expect?"

"I honestly don't know. You're a unique case. The High Commander wants to meet you, and he'll figure out where to place you."

Cris crossed his arms, pulling inward. "Is it because of what I did earlier?"

Dodes hesitated. "Yes, but not just that. You have a lot more potential than most."

He looked down. "I didn't know I could do those things."

"Soon enough you'll be able to do a lot more."

Cris leaned back in his chair and stared out the viewport at the swirling blue-green sea of light. *I hope this is the right choice.*

"Did you really have another option?" Dodes asked in response to Cris' thought.

Cris realized he had let his mental guard lapse and raised it again. "No, not anymore."

"We'll take care of you, don't worry," the Agent said.

*At least I'll finally be around other people like me.* Cris stared back out the viewport. *Maybe I'll finally fit in.*

— — —

"Sir, we have him. It sounds like he wants to join."

*Thank the stars, finally!* Banks leaped up from his desk and walked toward the main viewscreen to speak with Jarek. The tension began to ease in his chest. "Good. Did you have any trouble?"

"Yes, actually. Much more than expected," Jarek said.

"Did he resist?"

Jarek's brow furrowed. "No, he came quite easily."

"Then how so?"

"He was attacked."

*No, don't tell me...* "Attacked? By whom?"

"An assassin from the Priesthood. They must have been acting on the same information about his whereabouts that we were."

*Bomax! What were they thinking?* Banks was careful to hide his indignation. "How did he escape?"

Jarek looked away. "Sir, he 'stopped time'."

"What?" Banks tensed.

"I don't know, sir. He seemed distraught. I asked him afterward, and he said he'd never done it before."

"It's unheard of, pulling off that maneuver without extensive coaching."

Jarek looked shaken. "I know, sir. I barely knew what I was seeing. I've only witnessed it once before. But that's not all."

Banks took a slow breath. "There's more?"

"Then he threw the assassin against the wall telekinetically. I was struck by the power of it—absolutely astounding. There was a great measure of control, even though he claimed to not know what he was doing."

"This development complicates matters considerably." *I can't possibly put him in with other new Trainees. Not with that level of ability.* "But he's safe?"

"Yes, sir. Shaken, but unharmed."

Banks nodded. "We'll decide what to do after I meet with him." After all of their careful planning, they back to making up a strategy on the fly.

"Yes, sir." Jarek inclined his head.

"Dismissed."

# CHAPTER 7

THE TSS SHIP dropped out of subspace, revealing a partial view of Earth in the distance. Its large continents reminded him in some ways of Tararia. The planet was soon obscured by the moon that stood out as a white orb against the surrounding darkness, barren compared to most of the moons he had encountered in his travels.

The TSS ship taxied toward a sprawling space dock fixed with a gravity anchor fifteen kilometers out from the hemisphere of the moon facing away from Earth. There were craft of all sizes, from shuttles only four meters in length to massive warships. Cris exhaled slowly with wonder. *I haven't seen a fleet like that outside of a shipyard.*

"It's something, isn't it?" Dodes commented. "And to think most people on Earth have no idea all this is up here. It takes a lot to keep it that way."

Cris couldn't take his eyes off the viewport. "It's impressive, for sure."

The door opened, and Jarek looked in. "Time to get going."

"Come on," Dodes said, gesturing toward the door.

Cris tore himself away and grabbed his bag off the floor. A wave of nerves suddenly struck him. Joining the TSS meant a new future for him. A path he never thought was possible. *I need to do this. It's the only way I'll ever learn to use my abilities.*

He swallowed and took a deep breath. Resolute, he followed Dodes into the hall.

Jarek led the way to the gangway off of the ship. The transparent walls afforded an impressive view of the moon's cratered surface and the surrounding ships in the port. The lights along the port's structure reflected off of the iridescent hulls of the ships, making the more distant vessels look like gems against the dark starscape beyond.

At the bottom of the gangway, Jarek turned to Cris. "Best wishes. I know the TSS will be quite a change for you, but I hope you'll find a sense of community here."

"Thank you. I hope so, too." Cris shifted the pack on his shoulder.

Jarek and Dodes took Cris down one of the wings of the spaceport. The port was unadorned, with plain grated metal floors and matte metal structural beams. Curved glass panels swept toward the ceiling.

They approached a row of small shuttles. Waiting for them was a woman dressed in dark gray. She appeared to be in her early-thirties, with dark eyes and hair pulled back into a tight bun.

"This is where we leave you," Jarek said. "Trisa is one of our Militia officers. She'll take you to the High Commander."

"Okay. Well, I'll see you around," Cris said.

"Yes, I'm sure," Jarek replied.

"Take care," added Dodes.

Trisa held out her arm toward one of the waiting shuttles. "This way, please."

The oblong shuttle was only four meters long with viewports uniformly wrapping around the perimeter, making it difficult to distinguish between the front and back of the craft. A hatch on the side connected directly to the spaceport's corridor. The interior was one open room with dark gray padded seats along the walls, each with a four-point harness. Cris took a seat in the middle, and noticed a control panel inlaid in the wall next to the door.

Trisa sat down next to the control panel. She didn't secure herself in a harness, so Cris left his off, as well. Without a word, Trisa made a few inputs on the panel. The shuttle door closed with a hiss and the craft pulled away from the port. It glided toward the surface of the moon, accelerating.

Cris swiveled around to stare out the viewport at the cratered, dusty surface. *Is there really a whole facility inside there?*

It looked desolate and barren, but an illuminated ship port stood out at the base of one of the craters. The port was a simple structure consisting of three corridors with docking slots for transport shuttles to either side along each of the wings. Approximately half of the slots were occupied by a craft.

The shuttle slowed as it approached an open docking slot between several other shuttles. It set down with a barely perceptible bump. The door automatically sealed with a portal in the wall of the corridor, and the door slid open after a moment.

Cris gulped. *I guess I'm committed now.*

Trisa led Cris across the port through a security checkpoint at the end of the corridor. Beyond the security gate, the port opened up into a central dome at the intersection of the three branches. On the far side, there was a bank of what looked to be elevator doors arranged in a half-circle.

Trisa stopped in front of the doors. After a minute, one of the doors opened, revealing an elevator car with an upholstered seat around the perimeter and room for a dozen people.

Cris took a seat along the back wall, and Trisa sat near the door. As soon as the door closed, there was an initial feeling of acceleration. Trisa glanced over at Cris on occasion, but made no effort to converse. Minutes of silence passed. The only indication of movement was a pulsing white light to either side of the door.

Suddenly, there was a loud thud outside.

Cris' pulse spiked, startled after the quiet. "What was that?"

"Entering the containment lock for the subspace shell around Headquarters," Trisa stated. She folded her arms and leaned back.

*She said that like it's a normal thing.* Cris leaned back and tried to relax.

Eventually, the elevator slowed and came to a rest. Cris' heart-rate quickened as the doors opened, revealing a circular lobby surrounded by elevator doors. The floor was dark gray marble with decorative black inlay. Trisa headed straight across the lobby, entering a surprisingly decorated hallway.

*This is way fancier than I pictured.* Cris looked around in wonder at the carpeted floor and wood paneling, with show weapons and holopaintings lining the walls.

They went past several offices before the hall ended in a set of double wooden doors.

"Here is the office of the TSS High Commander," Trisa said. "This is his jurisdiction and you're his subordinate."

"Understood."

"All right. Go in," she said.

Cris nodded. Trisa swung one of the doors inward, and she directed Cris into the High Commander's office.

Cris' first impression of the room was that it was too ornate, like the hallway, to serve much practical purpose. He had been brought up with the utmost luxuries, but he had always been under the impression that the TSS would have no use for elaborate furnishings.

He did have to admit there was good taste behind the selection of the leather couch and carved wooden desk, but it all seemed superfluous until he examined the items more closely. The couch was facing an extensive viewscreen integrated into the side wall. The desk was decorative, but its touch-surface top also served as a workstation. The display cases likely held the High Commander's personal combat implements, rather than purely show weapons, as Cris had initially thought. Once he looked at it that way, Cris realized the TSS simply had style.

The High Commander stood on the far side of the room across from the door, seemingly staring out at the snow-capped mountains depicted in a holopainting on the wall. The moment the door closed, he turned to look at Cris. He wasn't presently wearing the tinted glasses typically worn by Agents, so Cris could clearly see the peculiar eyes associated with advanced telekinetic abilities. The eyes were the High Commander's natural gray color, but they seemed to be slightly bioluminescent—glowing with a captivating inner light.

He stepped forward and stopped in front of Cris. "I'm High Commander Jason Banks," he said with a voice of obvious authority. "You're Cristoph Sietinen, I presume."

Cris nodded. "Yes, sir, I am. I go by 'Cris' most of the time, though." He looked the High Commander over. He had dark hair and appeared to only be around thirty-years-old, though that seemed improbable given his rank. *He carries himself as if he were much older. He must be at least a decade older than he appears.*

"Well, Cris, you're a difficult person to find." Banks looked at him levelly.

Resisting the urge to squirm under the High Commander's scrutinizing gaze, Cris ventured a smile. "Then I accomplished my aim. Until you found me."

"You were careless. It almost got you killed."

"In retrospect, I would have done things differently, that's for sure."

Banks sighed. "That's all you have to say for yourself?"

Cris faltered. "I'm sorry."

"Don't say things you don't mean. It's unbecoming."

*Stars! Maybe aligning with the TSS was a mistake.* "Then what do you want? *You* brought *me* here. I was perfectly happy on the *Exler*, minding my own business—"

"Hardly!" Banks' glared at Cris, stern. "Do you realize what would happen if the general population heard the Sietinen heir was threatening the Priesthood?"

*He knows about that?* Cris' face flushed. "How can you defend the Priesthood? They hate people like us! I thought the TSS, of all organizations, would see things my way."

Banks laughed. "Your way? You have so much to learn."

Cris was taken aback. "Maybe I should just go."

"Go ahead. It wouldn't surprise me."

*What's his problem?* Cris glanced toward the door but stood his ground. "You went to an awful lot of trouble to find me, only to let me walk away."

"I'd rather you walk away now than when you have a ship full of people counting on you," the High Commander replied.

Cris crossed his arms. "I wouldn't abandon my crew."

"You ran away from Tararia," Banks shot back. "Why should I expect you to be any more loyal to the TSS?"

"It's not like that. I just want to learn about my abilities."

Banks looked skeptical. "And once you've mastered them? Given your track record, I would expect you to walk away whenever something new and interesting catches your eye."

"That's not why I left."

"Well, I have no idea what will make you stay here." The High Commander shrugged. "Jarek and Dodes brought you in because that was their last standing order, but after the way you've behaved, I don't know if I want you to be part of the TSS."

*Stars! Is he serious?* An unbidden wave of fear struck Cris. "You'd turn me loose, knowing the Priesthood will kill me the first chance they get?"

Banks' eyes narrowed. "I'm simply not convinced you're cut out to be an Agent. The TSS isn't a good fit for people who like to take the easy route."

Cris stared back at the High Commander with disbelief. "You think it was easy for me to leave Tararia? I didn't *want* to go. I just knew if I didn't, I'd be stifled for life."

"The TSS won't exactly give you freedom, either," Banks stated. "We can teach you how to use your abilities, but it's a lifetime commitment of service in return. I don't think you're ready for that."

"I was born into a lifetime of service. That responsibility isn't new to me."

Banks tilted his head. "But you ran away."

"I didn't!" Cris insisted. *I left, but I'll return when it matters.*

Banks stepped toward Cris. "Take some personal responsibility! You'll make a piss-poor leader if you always blame others for everything that doesn't go 'your way'. Do you want to keep running, or do you want to man up and do something that really matters?"

It took all of Cris' will to keep from cowering as the High Commander approached. "All I've ever wanted is to find a real home where I can be true to myself."

The High Commander softened. "We can give you that, Cris. But I need to know that you're fully invested. You have so much potential—we can unlock abilities that you never dreamed possible. But I can't let you gain all that power and then go rogue."

Cris straightened. "I only left so that I could become the kind of leader Tararia deserves."

"You've gone about it pretty poorly," Banks said.

Cris looked him in the eye. "Then show me another way."

"So, you *do* want to be here?" Banks asked.

"Yes. Please, just give me a chance."

Banks let out a slow breath. "Even if I do let you join, I don't know where we'd place you."

Cris looked down. "Find a place. I *need* to be here. And not just because it's away from the Priesthood—this is the only place where I can learn to become my full self."

Banks was silent, pensive. He cocked his head slightly as he looked Cris over from head to foot. "You demonstrated you already know how to handle yourself, as far as hand-to-hand combat is concerned. What about telepathy?"

*Does that mean I'm in?* Cris' heart lifted. "I received some basic lessons from a Court Advisor, but I haven't practiced much since I left the family estate. With things as they are on Tararia, I was never able to practice anything too advanced."

Banks nodded. "That's what makes things so tricky. You already know more than any other incoming Trainee. Yet, even if we enrolled you directly as an Initiate, you don't have the requisite experience in free-fall spatial awareness training."

Cris hung his head, growing increasingly more concerned about his prospects with the TSS. "No, I don't." *What would I do if he turns me away? Would I even be safe at the Sietinen estate?*

"One of the few options available," Banks continued, "would be to put you into an apprenticeship with an Agent for a few months to catch you up to a second or third year Initiate class. Would you be comfortable with that arrangement?"

"I'm used to tutors, so that would be fine. Whatever you think is best." *Just please let me stay.*

Banks evaluated Cris, seeming to weigh something that was unseen. "Very well."

Cris perked up. "Does that mean I can join?"

The High Commander nodded. "Yes. I just wanted to make sure you were here for the right reasons."

"I like to think I am."

Banks smiled. "I can see that. Now, I don't suppose you have a preference for an area of specialization?"

Cris shook his head. "No. I'm sorry, but I'm not familiar with the different classes of Agents. One of the few TSS-trained people I know is my former combat instructor, but he was Militia."

"I see," the High Commander said. "Well, since you certainly won't be in Militia, I suppose you could be placed along the Command track with an Agent in Primus, our top division. With your background, you're a natural fit for a leadership role, so a support position in the Sacon or Trion Agent class doesn't make sense. Though we select only a small number of trainees with the highest potential for Primus—especially the Command track—I'm not too concerned about you meeting the requirements of the designation. If you apply yourself, I'm sure you could graduate as one of the best in your cohort. You have too much potential to fail completely."

"Sir, what is this 'potential' that keeps being brought up? Does it have something to do with what I did at the spaceport?"

Banks paused for a moment. "Everyone has an innate level of telepathic and telekinetic ability, which varies greatly among individuals. Those abilities manifest in different ways. From what I heard, you created a spatial disruption at the spaceport. We often call it 'stopping time', but it's actually telekinetic dislocation—you hovered on the edge of subspace, where the perception of time passage is different. Very few can do it."

"Why me?"

"Luck of the genetic draw," the High Commander replied with a slight smile. "It is a sign of potential in other areas, too. You can go far."

"Lucky me, then," Cris said. "I'll try my best to live up to your expectations."

Banks nodded. "Just apply yourself."

*I'll do what it takes to succeed, but what does the TSS want in return?* Cris searched for the right way to ask. "There is another question, sir."

"Yes?"

"A few weeks ago, I had an encounter with a merchant. He spoke of a war in the outer realms. He said that the TSS told their trainees the truth about what's going on at the end of their first year."

Banks swallowed, barely perceptible. "You can't believe everything you hear at spaceports."

"But, *is* there a war?" Cris pressed.

The High Commander took a deep breath. "There is mounting tension with a race called the Bakzen. We suspect it will escalate to full-out war within our lifetime. Since the TSS is a lifetime commitment, we need individuals who will be steadfast to the cause when the time comes. So, we give our trainees the chance to leave after their first year if they are not willing to participate in a war, should they ever be called upon." He looked Cris in his eyes. "Does that change your decision to train with the TSS?"

Cris looked inward. *I have to stay, regardless of what may be going on elsewhere in the galaxy. The TSS can give me what I need.* "No, sir. I would gladly fight with the TSS."

Banks nodded. "That's good to hear." He paused. "You know, I'm sure your parents would like to know that you're safe and that they can halt their detectives. Since you're seventeen now, once you sign the training contract, we can grant you immunity so they can't bring you home against your will."

*Thank the stars! My parents would never consent to this.* Cris inclined his head. "Yes, I'll let them know. Thank you."

"I can draw up the contract now before you contact them," Banks offered. He took a step toward his desk.

"That would be great. One more thing, though…"

Banks stopped. "Hmm?"

"I would like to keep my true identity confidential. As you know, sir, the Sietinen family name comes with a reputation." *The last thing I want is to go back to that way of life.* He couldn't pass up the chance to truly begin anew, and in a far better way than on the *Exler*. He could become a worthy leader—prepared to face the changes on Tararia in the future.

"As you wish," Banks agreed. "The contract must be with your legal name, but you may go publicly by something else if you like. Others do the same thing. Do you already have a name in mind?"

Cris smiled. "I went by 'Cris Sights' on the cargo freighter." *This is it! I actually got away for good.*

High Commander Banks nodded. "Well, Cris Sights, welcome to the Tararian Selective Service."

— — —

Banks sat down on the couch in the middle of his office, unsure how to proceed. Cris Sights, as he was to be known, was perhaps the most remarkable student the TSS had ever seen. He was confident and insightful, but also quick to anger—though that would mellow with time and the discipline of training. Banks sensed the power in him that Jarek had witnessed; was cautious of it. Cris was not someone to deceive, but that was precisely what had to be done.

The High Commander sat for a long while, pondering the situation. *The Priesthood tried to kill him. Why? We can't afford to start all over again. They can't be foolish enough to think we could hold on that much longer… But why did they want him eliminated?*

"CACI," Banks intoned, directing his attention to the Central Artificial Computer Intelligence interface for the TSS Mainframe via the viewscreen on the wall, "contact the Priesthood. Let them know I want to talk to them immediately about Cristoph Sietinen."

As expected, it did not take long for the call to be accepted. The life-like image of a figure robed in black appeared on the screen, piercing red-brown eyes shone out through the shadow cast by the hood.

Banks stood to address the High Priest. "Thank you for granting me audience," he said in Old Taran, the standard language of the Priesthood.

"I was told you wanted to discuss Cristoph Sietinen."

"Yes," Banks replied. "We agreed that this was a TSS matter. Sending an assassin—"

The Priest gave a slight nod. "If we had been able to properly evaluate him a year before, as we wanted, it would not have come to that."

"What is the problem with him, exactly? I thought he had all the qualities we hoped for."

"He is too independent. Powerful, yes, but he will not easily be bent to our wills. Escaping from Tararia was proof enough, but he's also publicly spoken out against the Priesthood."

*That's what makes him so perfect. We need someone with initiative.* Banks kept his expression impassive. "It's the child he will one day father that matters. In the meantime, the TSS can mold him. He is eager to learn."

"For the sake of the entire Taran race, I hope you are right."

"Your dissatisfaction with his brother set us back twenty years, as it was. You waited far too long to decide what to do with him." *If only he had come to the TSS when we first extended an offer.*

"We are aware. But he refused to embrace his abilities. We had no other choice."

*And so he met his end in a 'tragic accident'.* Banks had learned long ago that the Priesthood would go to any means necessary to accomplish its objectives. Tristen Sietinen had failed to fulfill his role in the plan—not that the young man could be blamed for turning away from his abilities. "The anti-telekinesis sentiment you promote is dangerous. I've warned you—"

"You know the reasons why it's necessary."

"It's crippled us."

"Perhaps in a few more years we can reconsider." The Priest's level gaze was one of finality.

Banks looked down and took a deep breath to calm himself. "All concerns about Cris aside, we need to move forward with him. He's in our custody now, and I'd appreciate you consulting me first if you have any reservations in the future."

The Priest reluctantly inclined his head. "What does he know of our intentions?"

"Very little. I'm sure he'll figure out that we're keeping something from him, but there's no cause for concern. As for the Bakzen, he will learn the standard story."

"Good. You have your mandate." The Priest ended the transmission.

# CHAPTER 8

CRIS QUICKLY LEARNED that life with the TSS was far more exhausting than he could have ever imagined.

Immediately upon leaving the High Commander's office, he was ushered back into the central elevator and taken further into the Headquarters facility. Without warning, he was run through a barrage of tests. Hours passed as he took written exams, was placed in all manner of scanners, and was hooked up to more machines than he could count.

Tired and cranky, he was beginning to regret his decision to join the TSS when suddenly it was over. An attendant handed him a set of light blue clothes and he was left alone in a small room to change.

Cris donned the pants, t-shirt, and jacket, then collapsed on the single bench in the room. *What was I thinking coming here?*

He closed his eyes and was on the verge of dozing off when the door opened. A man in all black with tinted glasses stood in the doorway. He was tall and had dark features, and he carried himself with assurance. An Agent. Cris blinked wearily.

The Agent cracked a smile. "Looks like they wore you out." He removed his tinted glasses, revealing luminescent warm brown eyes.

Cris let out a non-committal groan.

"I'm Agent Poltar. I've been assigned to train you over the next few months."

Cris tried to rally, but couldn't quite muster the energy. "Pleasure to meet you, sir. I'm excited to get started."

The Agent smiled. "I'll be nice and let you rest up before we dive into things. Let me show you to your quarters."

Poltar led Cris to the second level of the Headquarters structure, making small-talk along the way. Cris learned that Poltar was from the eastern part of the First Region on Tararia and had been with the TSS since he was sixteen-years-old. Cris shared a little of his time on the *Exler*.

When they exited the elevator, Poltar said, "We were unsure where to house you since you're in between ranks right now. At first, we were going to put you in Agent's quarters temporarily, but then we thought it best that you be around fellow trainees. In the end, we decided to place you in Junior Agent housing for the time being."

They walked down a long hallway with carpeting and paneling similar to the top level by the High Commander's office, though not as ornate. Small fern-like plants with delicate oval leaves were placed every few meters, contained in glass cylinders with down-lights. Holopaintings of nebulae lined the walls.

Poltar stopped at a door halfway down the hall, marked as JAP-227. "Fortunately, we had an opening with some of our top Junior Agent trainees. They'll take good care of you." Poltar pressed the buzzer by the door.

A young man with light-brown hair and hazel eyes slid open the door; he looked to be a few years older than Cris. He wore dark blue clothes, which Cris had gathered were for Junior Agents. "Good evening, Agent Poltar."

"Hi, Scott. This is Cris Sights. He's the new recruit who'll be staying with you for a while."

"Right!" Scott extended his hand to Cris for a handshake. "Scott Wincowski, nice to meet you."

Cris grasped his hand awkwardly, not used to the colloquial greeting. "You too, thanks for having me."

“Sure thing.” Scott stood aside to give Cris room to come in. “I can take it from here tonight, Agent Poltar.”

“Thank you. Cris, I’ll be by at 08:00 to begin your training tomorrow. Rest up.”

“Will do. Good night. And thank you, sir.”

Poltar nodded and left in the direction of the elevators.

“Come in,” Scott said, gesturing inside.

Cris took his lead.

The door opened into the common room of the quarters. Like the hallway, the living room presented like a well-appointed home. Padded carpet covered the floor, a plush sectional couch faced a large viewscreen on the wall, and holoart depicting exotic mountain ranges and beaches lined the copper-colored walls. A table surrounded by four chairs stood at the back of the room.

“You’re quite lucky, you know,” Scott said as Cris entered. “I had to sleep on a tiny bunk in a room with four other guys for the first year I was here.”

“I would have been happy with anything, just to be here.” Cris took in the room. It was spacious and inviting after his sterile cabin on the *Exler*.

“Regardless, they must see something special in you.”

“I’ll try my hardest not to let anyone down.”

“Well, anyway,” Scott moved backward past the couch, “let me show you your bedroom.” Cris noticed two doorways on each side of the common room. Scott approached the doorway in the back right. “We’re still down a roommate, even with you here,” Scott went on. “They like to pair Junior Agents in multiple cohorts so there are mentorship opportunities. We just had the two oldest roommates graduate.”

“I take it most Junior Agents don’t get brand new Trainees for roommates,” Cris ventured.

Scott studied Cris, serious. “No, never.”

Cris dropped his eyes to the floor, feeling out of place.

“As I said, they must see something in you.” Scott slid the door to the bedchamber open. It took Cris a moment to realize that he hadn't physically touched the door. "This will be your room."

Careful not to gape at Scott's open use of telekinesis, Cris peeked inside. The room was compact but not cramped. It was simply furnished, containing a large bed, corner desk and dresser. The bag containing his personal articles from the *Exler* was sitting on the bed. "Excellent."

*This is a resort compared to where I've been for the last year.* The bed beckoned to him.

"The bathroom is through there." Scott gestured to a wider doorway at the back of the common room. "They set up a locker in there for you."

"Where do you eat?" Now that he was standing still, Cris felt hunger mounting.

"They didn't feed you?" Scott seemed a little irritated, but not at Cris directly.

Cris shook his head. "I've been on the move constantly since I got here. I don't even know how long it's been."

Scott looked Cris over again. "You'll never live it down if I take you to the mess hall like this, looking wiped out and lost. Not a great first impression. Do you think a couple protein bars would hold you over until the morning?"

Cris shrugged. "I'll take whatever I can get."

"Let's see…" Scott rummaged through a cabinet by the table and chairs at the back of the common room. He produced two bars in shiny metallic wrappers. "These should take the edge off, at least."

"Thanks." Cris took the bars from Scott. "I have no idea how anything works around here." *And I thought that the* Exler *was different than Tararia! This is something else entirely.*

"Sure." Scott rubbed the back of his neck. "Well, my room's the one right across the way if you need anything else."

"Thank you. See you in the morning." Cris entered his room and closed the door.

The lights faded on automatically as he entered and a screen on the wall behind the desk illuminated as soon as the door was closed, displaying the TSS logo. Cris ripped open one of the protein bars and devoured it. He kicked off his shoes and was about to sit down on the bed when he noticed that the desktop was a large touchscreen, similar to his desk back home. There were also a handheld and a tablet sitting on the desktop to charge. Still chewing, he placed his palm on the desktop.

"Welcome, Cris Sights," said a friendly female voice. "Would you like to configure your preferences?" The TSS logo on the screen changed to read: 'Welcome'. The sleek black desktop surface illuminated, and various colored menus and windows appeared. Cris was especially taken by the icon for the TSS Mainframe.

Cris sighed, noting the late hour on the computer clock. "Not right now," he replied, though a large part of him wanted to explore. "Can you set an alarm for the morning?"

"Yes. Please state the desired time for the alarm."

Cris did some quick mental math. "07:15."

"Alarm set."

Cris grabbed the handheld from the desk. Thin and the size of his palm, it appeared to be solid, but he tugged the edges and the device slid open, revealing a screen on one side with an opaque backside for privacy. He swiped along the display, activating a holographic projection of the contents on the screen, which he could manipulate in the air. He closed the device, and browsed the settings for the external notifications that illuminated in the otherwise smooth black outer casing. It was just like the handheld he'd used back home.

*VComm has a presence even within the TSS. I guess I shouldn't be surprised, given they use SiNavTech beacons for navigation.* He set the handheld back on the desk.

A yawn overpowered Cris. He shoved his travel bag onto the ground. After stripping down to his underwear, he climbed in bed, feeling his muscles relax as he eased into the soft mattress. "Lights off," he ordered, already drifting to sleep.

—

Soft beeping intruded on Cris' dream, getting louder. He opened his eyes.

The screen on the wall displayed the time, 07:15. Cris rubbed his eyes and stretched.

He dressed and wandered into the living room. Scott and another young man were stretched out on the sectional couch, apparently reading on their tablets. They glanced up when Cris emerged.

"Good morning," Scott said. "How'd you sleep?"

"Really well."

"Cris, this is Jon Lambren. His room is the one next to mine."

Jon gave a little wave but barely lifted his eyes from whatever he was reading. His dark hair was cut short and he had a seriousness about him.

"Hi," Cris greeted as though he hadn't noticed Jon's disinterest.

Scott's attention returned to his own tablet. Cris let them be and headed into the bathroom. He was pleased to see that the facilities were smartly designed to easily accommodate four people. He found all the necessities in a locker with his name on it, including a change of clothes. After the nonstop events of the previous day, he was happy to take a leisurely pace getting ready.

Cris emerged from the bathroom feeling ready to tackle whatever Agent Poltar could throw at him. Since he still had some time before Poltar was scheduled to arrive, Cris decided to take the opportunity to do some of the electronic sleuthing he had been too tired to attempt the night before.

CACI—which he learned was the interactive interface for the TSS Mainframe—walked him through the configuration of his personal notifications, gesture calibration and setup of his telecommunication accounts. As he walked through the setup, he munched on the second protein bar Scott had given him the night before, pleasantly surprised by how filling it was. He was just finishing when a window popped up with a video feed, showing Poltar standing at the front door.

"Meet me out here, Cris," Poltar said, looking straight into the camera.

The exploration of the TSS network would have to wait.

Cris grabbed a light blue jacket to match the rest of his uniform and hurried out. Scott and Jon were already gone.

"Good morning, sir. I can't wait to get started." Cris closed the door to his quarters.

"We'll see how long you can hold onto that enthusiasm."

Poltar took Cris down the long central elevator to the bottom level of the Headquarters structure once again. This time, Cris noticed that the elevator passed through another containment lock like the one coming from the moon's surface.

Cris was wary. The last time he was down there, it had meant seemingly endless testing. *Is this a place of torture?*

Poltar led Cris down a hall that bore no resemblance to the elegant comfort of the upper levels. Though the floor was still carpeted, it was a plain industrial gray, and the walls were unadorned metal that looked to have had little treatment after fabrication. Cris followed Poltar through the halls in silence, trying to decide if he'd rather know what he was in for or remain sheltered by ignorance for as long as possible. They passed no one in the corridor.

Poltar stopped in front of a nondescript door identical to a dozen others they had already passed. The doors were placed far apart, each one was smooth metal, recessed in the wall, with glowing red or blue lights illuminating the perimeter. A control panel was positioned next to each. Poltar made some inputs on the panel by the selected door, and the light turned from blue to red.

"Let's see what you can do." Poltar grinned at Cris.

Cris swallowed.

The door opened, revealing a plain room. The threshold between the hallway and the adjoining wall of the room was nearly a meter. What appeared to be a door was centered on the back wall, a square too high off the ground to step through. The surface of the room was completely smooth, aside from handholds recessed around the door on the far side. Poltar stepped inside.

Cris hesitated. "What is this?"

"Have you ever been in zero-G before?"

His stomach tightened with the memory of his first night on the *Exler*. "Once."

"Then what are you waiting for?"

Cris entered the room. "Sorry, sir."

Poltar activated an interior control panel, and the outer door closed. He placed his tinted glasses into a sealed pocket inside his jacket, then moved to the back wall and grabbed a handhold.

Cris followed his lead.

"Take slow, steady breaths," Poltar said. "It can be unsettling at first."

The energy in the air around Cris changed. His stomach dropped, and then began rising into his mouth. He felt like he was being stretched and compressed at the same time. Ever so gradually, he felt himself rising off the ground. He tried to keep his feet rooted on the floor, but the struggle made him queasy so he relaxed. He floated upward until he was parallel with the door. Concentrating on his breathing, he centered his mind and tried to settle the nausea in his stomach.

"Are you doing all right?" Poltar asked, looking Cris over.

He nodded. "A little unsteady, but I think I'm okay." *I'd die of embarrassment if I threw up in front of an Agent.*

"Good." Poltar looked pleased.

The square door in the center of the back wall opened automatically. Cris peered into the next room with wonder. The entire room was black, illuminated only by pinpricks of light that looked like stars across all the surfaces. There was no sense of up or down, and Cris had difficulty judging the size of the space.

"This is one of our spatial awareness training chambers," Poltar explained. "We'll also work on your telekinetic skills, once we've covered some of the basics. This setting is ideal for honing your sense of what's around you and learning how to manipulate your environment."

Cris took an unsteady breath. "Tell me what to do."

Poltar pushed himself into the chamber. It was eerie to watch him glide without his overcoat fluttering. He moved deftly, a master of his surroundings. He stretched out a hand and stopped himself in the middle of open space.

Cris stared at him in wonder. *How did he do that?*

"Come here," Poltar commanded.

Cris let go of the handhold and pushed off the door frame with his feet. As soon as he was out of contact with the wall, he realized he had pushed far too hard. His aim was true in the direction of Poltar. Too true. He panicked, seeing he was on a collision course with his teacher.

Poltar calmly lifted his hand, palm outward toward Cris. Cris felt the air congeal around him, a buzz of energy filling his ears. He slowed and came to rest a meter in front of the Agent.

"How did you…?" Cris took a deep breath, feeling exposed floating in the middle of the dark room.

"In time, I'll teach you," Poltar replied. "The universe is filled with energy. Those of us who are Gifted and able to sense the electromagnetism around us can learn to manipulate those fields. This allows us to perform incredible feats, such as levitating objects or focusing energy into a concentrated sphere you can hold in the palm of your hand. Even thought is energy at its most basic level, which is where telepathy comes in. We know these skills have a transdimensional component, though it's unclear what in our biology grants the abilities to some and not others.

"The greater your connection to the unseen energy that surrounds you, the more control you will gain. There is a limit, of course, to how much energy a person can physically handle. We have objects that can help us focus more, and we can work in teams. But alone, each person has a finite limit. This limit is a principal factor when determining an Agent's Course Rank.

"As part of the graduation exam, each Junior Agent is placed in a room with a single sphere made of ateron, a rare element that behaves like a quantum particle, simultaneously existing in this spacetime and a higher dimension. The Junior Agent is instructed to focus all the energy they can handle into the sphere, and we measure the input to determine the person's capacity. By the time most Junior Agents graduate, their abilities will be as fully developed as they will ever be in life. Though it can fluctuate for some, it's very uncommon.

"My responsibility is to teach you to focus the energy around you and control the maximum amount you can physically handle. Safely. Pushing too far or too fast can destroy a person. We'll begin small and work up from there."

Cris grinned. "Let's get started."

Poltar glided a couple meters away from Cris. "Close your eyes."

*What's he going to do to me?* Cris hesitated for a moment but complied.

"Can you tell where I am?" Poltar asked.

"I just saw you. You're right in front of me."

"Oh, am I?" The voice came from Cris' left.

Cris opened his eyes. Poltar had indeed moved to be three meters off to his left. "That's a nice trick."

"Not a trick at all," the Agent countered. "If you were paying attention, you would have noticed that I moved."

Cris sighed. "How, exactly, would I be able to tell?"

"Every living thing has an electromagnetic signature. As someone sensitive to such things, you should be able to pick up on the presence of someone even without your eyes."

*That's not very helpful instruction.* Cris crossed his arms. "I don't feel much of anything while floating here."

"The zero-G will make it easier for you to pick up on what's important, if you apply yourself. Come on, give it a shot."

With a sigh, Cris unfolded his arms and closed his eyes again. He tried to clear his mind and focus on the energy around him.

After a few moments, he did start to feel a certain presence coming from the last place he had seen Poltar. *It's like the intuition Sedric always told me to use in combat.*

He honed in on Poltar, judging his exact location. "Okay, I think I know what you mean." *Was I really using these abilities all along without knowing it?*

"I'm going to move around now," Poltar said. "Stay oriented in my direction."

"I'll try." Cris focused on Poltar's position.

Initially, he didn't detect any movement, but slowly the energy seemed to shift. Cris started by turning only his head to track the movement, and then rotated his whole body. He moved back and forth several times, and then spun around entirely when he thought he sensed something behind him. The movements continued, becoming increasingly more erratic. It was difficult for Cris to follow at times, but whenever he started to feel lost, the presence seemed to come to a resting place. It was a fun game at first, but Cris started to feel bored with the tedious exercise as it stretched on.

"You may open your eyes," Poltar said eventually.

"How did I do?"

"You seem to be tracking well," the Agent replied. "I'd like to see how accurate you are at judging distance."

Cris tried to keep his boredom hidden. "All right."

"For reference, I'm currently three meters away," Poltar said.

*This just keeps getting more thrilling.* Cris closed his eyes and made note of how Poltar's presence felt at that distance. "Got it."

"Whenever I stop, call out how far away I am."

Cris sensed movement, and then Poltar stopped.

Cris thought for a moment. "Five meters." It was a guess, but he thought it was a reasonable attempt. There was movement again. Cris turned to his right as he tracked. "Seven meters." After the next movement, Poltar seemed closer. "Two meters."

Like the previous iteration, the exercise went on for far longer than Cris found engaging. *Why won't he tell me if I'm guessing right? I can't improve if I don't know what I'm doing wrong.*

"All right. Let's try something else," Poltar said, breaking the silence.

*Finally.* Cris opened his eyes.

Poltar moved toward the entrance door. He touched the wall, revealing a compartment. Inside, there were several chrome spheres. Poltar took four spheres from the compartment and closed it again. "These are probes. They will emit a minute electromagnetic pulse. I want you to identify the active probe."

*That sounds like more of the same.* "Okay," Cris acknowledged, a little disappointed. *I'm sure he has a reason for doing this, even if it doesn't make sense to me now.*

Poltar used telekinesis to distribute the probes around Cris at varying distances. "Point to the probe when it's active," he instructed.

Cris tried to locate the probes, but he couldn't detect anything other than Poltar himself. "I have no idea."

"It's subtle. Just give it your best guess."

Cris sighed inwardly. "Fine." He kept his eyes closed and started pointing in different directions—wherever gut instinct told him. He didn't consciously detect any signal from the probes, but following his initial reaction seemed reasonable.

Poltar gave no indication of how accurate he was, just made generic statements of encouragement every so often. Though Cris felt like he was randomly guessing, he continued.

"Okay, open your eyes," Poltar said, breaking the silence. "That's enough for a solid baseline."

"Did I get any right?" Cris asked.

Poltar pulled out his handheld. "It's more important to judge your improvement than where you are now."

"Yeah, but—"

Poltar returned the handheld to his pocket. "It's been almost three hours. Want to break for lunch?"

*He's smart to distract me from my question with food.* "That would be great." Cris' stomach felt like it was about to eat itself, having only had two protein bars in the last day. "I really am curious how I'm doing, though."

Poltar yielded. "You're a little more advanced than I anticipated. But there's a lot for me to teach you."

*I hope we're almost done with the testing and can get to the fun parts.* Cris smiled. "I look forward to learning."

Poltar pulled Cris telekinetically toward the entrance door. He opened the hatch and they passed through the lock to reacclimate to gravity. Once outside, Poltar led the way to the central elevator that would take them up to the main levels.

After some prodding, Cris got Poltar to explain the setup of the Headquarters structure during the elevator ride. The facility's eleven Levels were self-contained rings connected by a central shaft, and each served a distinct function. There were multiple floors on each Level, which could be accessed by stairways, but the central elevator was the only way to get between the separate rings. The top Level was for Command and Medical. Agents were on the next three Levels, with Level 2 for the Primus Agents, Level 3 for Sacon Agents, and Level 4 for Trion Agents. Each of those Levels had Trainee quarters for the new students that were not yet assigned an official Agent class or area of specialization. There was also ample classroom space where the trainees in all ranks would convene.

Levels 5 through 9 were housing and training space for the Militia division. Level 10 contained primarily research labs and Engineering. The bottom ring of Headquarters, Level 11—where he had thus far spent most of his time—was suspended away from the rest of the facility. Since it was specifically for practicing telekinetic skills, Level 11 was outside of the subspace containment shell. Telekinesis could only be used sparingly in the rest of Headquarters, due to the natural dampening properties of subspace; it kept the trainees from getting out of hand.

Poltar took Cris back to Level 2, for the Primus class. There was a mess hall on every Level, Cris learned, except for the training area. Though Agents and trainees of any class were permitted into the other classes' mess halls, it was convention to use the facilities on the same Level as one's quarters unless invited to another—and such an invitation was always necessary for Militia members. The TSS culture dictated that at mealtime, Agents and trainees could come together in one place without the distinction of rank.

When Cris walked into the mess hall, he was pleased to see Agents, Junior Agents, Initiates and Trainees sharing tables, though the clothing colors indicated that people still tended to stay within their own group more than not.

The Primus mess hall was large enough to accommodate four hundred people at the same time. Long tables with seats for ten people on each side filled the center of the room, and smaller tables dotted the perimeter. There were even some booths behind a short wall at the back of the room, for those seeking a more private conversation. The entire space was decorated with warm wood tones accented by gray and black fabrics, and potted plants stood out amongst the tables and the matte black floor. Along the right wall, people moved through a buffet line before selecting an open seat.

"Help yourself." Poltar gestured Cris toward the buffet.

Cris took a heaping tray of steaming meats, vegetables and bread with a few more cookies than would be considered appropriate. Poltar raised a skeptical eyebrow, but said nothing.

After surveying the room, Poltar led the way to one of the smaller tables along the left wall. Cris felt like everyone watched him pass by, not sure if it was because he was an unfamiliar face or that he was in the company of an Agent.

Cris dove into his meal, ravenous now that food was in front of him. Poltar had taken only a light lunch for himself and ate in silence across from Cris. While eating, Cris took in the people around him and tried to identify a pattern to the social framework. The more he observed, the more he realized that the co-mingling he thought he'd noticed when he first walked in was actually just a commander seated with their trainee group. Cris was the only individual below the rank of Junior Agent seated alone with an Agent.

"Why am I getting such unusual treatment?" Cris asked once he was most of the way through the plate of food.

Poltar tilted his head, questioning.

"I'm the only one here with a one-on-one mentor. I might be more advanced than some, but why not just throw me in with other new Trainees?"

"You have a lot of potential, Cris. Probably more than anyone else in this room. And now that you've begun to tap it, you need to be taught control before it overwhelms you."

Cris shook his head. "All of this has happened so fast. And all this talk of 'potential'. I hardly feel like I know myself anymore."

"I heard about what happened at the spaceport. That kind of power is extraordinary. Most wouldn't be able to do those things without years of training. Without a foundation. Jumping right in at that level… well, the holes need to be filled in quickly. You could never get that in a normal training group."

"I just don't see how I'll ever fit in." He looked down. *Yet again, I'm set apart. Is that just how it's destined to be for me?*

Poltar smiled. "Don't worry about that. I'll help you get control of your abilities, and then everyone will want to work with you. Who wouldn't want to have the best on their team?"

Cris shrugged. "I'm sure there's someone."

"Then they're shortsighted and ignorant. Anyone worth your time will respect you," Poltar said, looking Cris in his eyes. "There is greatness in you. It's apparent to anyone who knows what to look for. They already see it in you." He surveyed the trainees and Agents throughout the room.

Cris looked around the room again. No uncertainty remained about whether he was being observed. People were engaged in their own conversations, but they kept glancing over at Cris. Darting glances, trying not to be caught. "What if I'm not what everyone thinks I am?"

"That kind of humility will get you far." Poltar eyed Cris' empty plate. "Ready to get back to it?"

*There's no use fighting it. It's not my fault if they're wrong—I didn't ask for any of this.* "Yes, sir."

# CHAPTER 9

CRIS FELT LIKE the walls were closing in on him. There was too much energy buzzing around him to concentrate.

A red cube hung in midair at eye level, spinning slowly. Poltar raised his hand and rotated his wrist, and the cube responded likewise. He lowered his hand, and the cube returned softly to the metal floor.

"Is it always so intense?" Cris asked.

Poltar shook his head. "This room is an amplifier. It's designed to assist trainees like you. Even moderate exertion from a full Agent can seem like much more than it is."

There were four cubes on the ground in front of them, in ascending size. The smallest cube, green, was the size of Cris' fist. A yellow cube was twice that size, and the red Poltar had used for demonstration was about the size of his head. A blue cube, nearly a meter on each side, dwarfed the others.

"Clear your mind. Focus on the green cube. Command it." Poltar stepped to the back wall behind Cris, out of his view so he was not a distraction.

Cris stared at the cube. He squinted, willing it to obey his command. With clenched fists, he thought about it hovering in the air. Nothing happened. He sighed.

"You're trying too hard," Poltar said from behind him.

"I have no idea what I'm doing." *I threw a person across the hall without thinking about it, and now I can't do anything when I try.*

"Treat it as an extension of yourself," Poltar said. "Like a limb. When you're first learning to walk or write, you need to concentrate on what you're doing. Eventually, it will come without thinking."

Cris frowned. "I tr—"

"No, *really* clear your mind. Open yourself to knowing the cube. Feel it."

Letting go of his frustration, Cris breathed slowly and evenly—just as Sedric had taught him for combat. He envisioned a void, with the green cube as the only object in existence. He explored the cube, noting the way the light hit each of its planes. He evaluated its weight, the way it would feel to be held.

*Rise.*

The air began to buzz, vibrating. In Cris' mind, he saw a faint glow around the green cube, white light that seemed to shimmer. Ever so slowly, the cube began to lift off of the ground.

*Rise!*

The cube rose to a meter off the ground, a faint, glowing white column supporting it from the floor.

Cris looked back to Poltar, excited. "I'm—" The cube crashed to the floor. "Or, I did."

Poltar grinned. "Not bad at all." He leaned back against the metal wall. "Maintaining the levitation while talking is another lesson."

Cris smiled. "I've never seen anything like it. It was glowing."

Poltar nodded. "That was the energy field. Everyone seems to visualize it a little differently. I see yellow electric sparks, myself. Putting an image to it is common, helps with control."

"It just appeared."

"The mind is an amazing thing," Poltar said with a smile. "Now that you have a way to visualize the field, it should be easier to control."

"Huh." Cris stared at the cube, now seeming so plain and dull. *I don't know if I can ever look at things the same way again.*

"Why don't you try a larger one?" Poltar suggested.

"Okay."

Cris focused on the yellow cube next. He cleared his thoughts again and made the yellow cube the center of the void in his mind. After several seconds, a white glow emerged, billowing into a column beneath the cube as it rose.

The buzz of energy filled him, fueled him. He thirsted for more. Feeding the energy into the cube, he brought it up two meters off of the ground before slowly lowering it.

*I did it!* He felt warm from the exertion, but invigorated.

"Good, and the next," Poltar instructed.

Cris concentrated. The red cube became surrounded by a white glow, but it didn't rise at first. Cris focused on it more intently, picturing it levitating in his mind, seeing the column pushing it upward.

*Rise!*

The cube inched upward, gaining speed as it rose. It overshot the height Cris had intended, nearly hitting the ceiling, and then descended quickly to the floor with a thud.

"Almost," Cris said sheepishly.

"Try the last one." Poltar nodded toward the largest blue cube. It was a significant jump in mass compared to the progression of the others.

Cris evaluated it dubiously. "Okay…"

He focused on the blue cube, envisioning the white glow around it. The cube began to shudder as it was infused with energy.

*Rise!*

The cube quaked on the ground, rattling against the metal floor. Cris focused even more intently, seeing the energy flow into the cube. It glowed brighter, almost enough. He pressed harder. A corner of the cube rose off the ground, lifting—

"Stop! Don't strain yourself." Poltar put his hand on Cris' shoulder, and Cris felt the energy dissipate.

Cris nodded and let out a breath. *That felt incredible! The power…* He grinned at Poltar. "I was so close."

Poltar nodded, suddenly serious. "Go back to the yellow one."

After the difficulty of the blue cube, the mid-sized yellow object rose easily from the ground. He brought it to eye-level, and began slowly rotating it clockwise. The cube spun at a fixed height, steady. It was an island in the void of Cris' mind, surrounded by glowing energy. He felt like he could maintain the hold forever.

"Good, that's enough for today," Poltar stated, breaking the moment.

The cube faltered but didn't fall. Cris regained his serenity and lowered the cube slowly to the ground. The glow faded when the cube was at rest.

Cris rubbed his temples.

"Nicely done." Poltar clapped Cris on the shoulder. "How do you feel?"

"My head hurts. I feel wired." The buzz that had been in the air still hummed in his head. He wasn't sure if he was feeling it or hearing it.

"You should get in some physical exercise, too," Poltar added. "It's easy to get over-charged from telekinesis, until you know exactly how far to extend yourself. Exercise is a good release."

Cris nodded. Aside from any post-telekinesis benefits, there was no need to explain the importance of exercise while in artificial gravity. He had neglected his exercise routine for three weeks in the middle of his stint on the *Exler*, and the rapid atrophy he had experienced was enough for him to never lapse again.

Poltar took Cris into a large open room with a track around the perimeter and weight equipment in the center. Only a few pieces of equipment were presently in use and several people were jogging around the track at various speeds. "You can use this track for now. A lot of trainees run laps in the residential halls, but we'll wait on that until you know your way around."

"All right." Cris' mind was still reeling, shocked by what he'd been able to do through telekinesis. The buzz had yet to subside.

"I'll leave you to it," Poltar said. "Run some laps and help yourself to the weights, if you feel up to it. We'll put together a formal physical training routine tomorrow. I'll meet you at the same time in the morning at your quarters."

"Yes, sir. Thank you." *I need to clear my head. Running laps is just what I need right now.*

"Great work today, Cris." Poltar hurried off.

Cris sighed. The entire day felt like a blur.

He jogged laps around the track, taking a leisurely pace for most of it but occasionally surging forward into a sprint. He noticed a few of the other runners were with a partner, but some were by themselves. *Finally, somewhere I don't stand out.*

The buzz in his head lessened with each lap, eventually fading entirely. He thought about using some of the weight equipment but decided against it. Though the oppressive hum was gone, his mind was still racing, and he thought it best to just take some time to unwind back in his room.

Cris made his way back to the central elevator and rode it up to Level 2. Upon reaching the Primus level, he realized that all of the corridors branching from the central lobby looked the same.

*Some more prominent signage would be nice.* He examined his options and ultimately picked the hallway that seemed the most familiar.

Fortunately, his memory served him well and he traversed the remaining route to his quarters without making any wrong turns. When he reached his quarters, he placed his hand on the panel next to the entryway and the door slid open automatically for him.

"How was your first day?" Scott asked as Cris entered. He and Jon were lounging on the couch.

"Exhausting."

"Yeah, that tends to happen." Scott smiled. "So, what did you go over today?"

Cris collapsed on the couch across from the Junior Agents. "First, he took me down to one of the spatial awareness chambers, I think they're called. He circled me while I had my eyes closed, and then had me sense some probes."

Scott and Jon looked at each other. "What did the probes look like?" Jon asked tentatively.

"Chrome, about the size of my fist."

The two Junior Agents shook their head and let out long breaths. "What then?" Scott questioned.

"We went into an empty room with some colored cubes on the floor. He had me try to lift them telekinetically," Cris went on, cautious.

"Could you?" Scott was expectant.

Cris swallowed. "I could only make the heaviest blue block shudder, but I didn't have too much trouble with the others. I held the yellow block for a few minutes."

Scott's jaw dropped open. Jon exclaimed, "That's impossible!"

Cris was taken aback. *Am I really that different?*

He tried to sink into the couch, but he still felt completely vulnerable. "Is that bad? Poltar won't give me any specific feedback. He just keeps giving me different things to try."

Scott laughed. "Bad? It's incredible."

"Most are lucky if they can hold an object in suspension for a few seconds prior to being raised to Junior Agent," Jon added.

Cris' mouth went dry. "I didn't know."

"I can see why they took an interest in you," Scott said after a time.

Jon kept shaking his head.

Scott cleared his throat. "Hey, would you like to go to dinner with us?" Jon shot Scott a disapproving glare, but it was gone in an instant.

Cris had noticed the look but shrugged it off. "That would be great." *Was Poltar right? Will my power draw others to me?*

Cris felt much more confident walking into the mess hall with two Junior Agents rather than an Agent. His own light blue was not nearly as stark a contrast as it had been against the Agent's black.

Scott led them to one of the larger communal tables and introduced Cris to some of the other Junior Agents, both men and women. The other Junior Agents were friendly and welcoming, though he did get some strange looks when Scott explained Cris' unconventional training situation. It soon seemed to be forgotten, and Cris became the center of attention, telling of his travels on the *Exler*.

By the end of the evening, he was among old friends. He went to bed that night feeling content. *Maybe I do belong here.*

—

The next morning, as he waited for Poltar to retrieve him for the day's studies, Cris finally took the opportunity to attend to some overdue business. After giving himself a little pep-talk, he sent a short note to his father's personal email letting him know that he was with the TSS and would not be coming home anytime soon. *He'll love that.*

Cris then turned his attention to the Mainframe. There was a seemingly endless wealth of information, even more than what he'd had access to on Tararia. It would take a lifetime to explore everything. He looked over entries about the TSS' spacecraft and navigation systems, but one specific item still stood out in his mind.

*The Bakzen.* The main entry was frustratingly sparse and no more than he knew already—a rising enemy, living in the outskirts of explored space. "CACI, is there any more information on the Bakzen?"

"Restricted access. Additional clearance required," CACI replied.

*Bomax. Looks like I won't be finding out any more for now.*

He resumed his perusal of the other files until a video feed from the front door popped up. Poltar had arrived.

Cris went out to meet his instructor. "What are we doing today, sir?" he asked as he stepped into the hallway.

Poltar smiled. "First, we eat. Then, we get to work. I have it on good authority that you slacked on your workout last night, so we'll need to make up for it. I also need to see how you handle yourself in combat."

"I had a great teacher." *Sedric's lessons saved my life.*

"There's always more to learn."

"Will we be practicing any more telekinesis?"

Poltar nodded. "Absolutely."

— — —

"He's been a very quick study, sir," Poltar said. "I know you want to keep his true identity hidden, but people will take notice of him all the same."

Banks paced across his office, weighing his options. "Many already are."

"We should just advance him," Poltar urged.

"It goes completely against protocol." *Then again, so does everything about this.*

"I'm aware of that, sir. I just think anything less would be an unnecessary delay. You instructed me to move him through as quickly as possible, and, in my professional opinion, he'll be ready in four months."

Banks stopped his pacing in front of his desk. He slumped down on the edge, torn. "Moving him straight to Junior Agent will be an administrative nightmare. But, it's my duty to take your recommendation under advisement. We'll need to conduct a formal evaluation."

Poltar nodded. "Of course, sir."

"Thank you for the update. You're doing great work."

"Thank you, sir." Poltar bowed his head.

"Dismissed."

Poltar bowed again, a little deeper, and left.

Banks rubbed his eyes. *Advanced to Junior Agent after four months?* Unheard of and unorthodox, perhaps, but there was no more time to waste.

# PART 3: FULFILLMENT

# CHAPTER 10

"COME ON, JUST one more lap."

Cris eyed Scott with open skepticism. His lungs and legs burned.

"It's good for you!" Scott grinned.

Cris had always thought he was in good shape, but Scott had proved to be a demanding training partner. Even after more than three years of training together as Junior Agents, Cris couldn't figure out where all the energy came from. "*One* more."

"That's the spirit!" Scott took off down the hallway.

Cris willed his legs to move again and followed, centering his mind to block out the aching and burning he felt everywhere.

Scott set the pace at a fast jog, following the corridor that looped around the perimeter of the Primus residential wings on Level 2 in the Headquarters structure. The loop was approximately five kilometers, which seemed even longer by the end of an already exhausting workout.

Despite the cool temperature, Cris was hot and slick with sweat. His t-shirt was off, tucked into the back of his pants, to let the air cool his bare chest and back. Scott ran shirtless a few paces ahead of him, showing no intent of slowing down. Cris urged himself onward.

They neared the halfway point in the lap. *Almost there*. Cris' legs and lungs ached for relief.

A group of fellow Junior Agents were sprawled out on the floor of the hallway up ahead, resting their backs against the walls. Such impromptu study groups were a common sight on their afternoon jogs. Cris picked his way carefully through the first sets of legs sticking out into his path, weaving around other bystanders blocking his way. He was so focused on avoiding the obstacles that he didn't realize Scott had stopped.

"Hold up, Cris." Scott returned his attention to a pretty blonde with short hair and bright blue eyes who was sitting on the floor with some other Junior Agents.

Scott crouched down to talk with her more closely. She laughed.

Cris sighed. *Here we go again.* He untucked his shirt from his pants, using it to wipe the sweat from his face.

Scott looked over at Cris and then back at the blonde. She nodded vigorously.

*Oh no.* Cris looked around for a quick escape, but it was too late.

"Cris, come here." Scott waved him over.

Cris reluctantly complied, trying to control his panting breath and racing heart.

"So, Cris," Scott said as he approached, "this is Marsie Katz. We were thinking it would be fun to go on a double date tomorrow."

The last setup had been a complete disaster. "That would be something…" he began while trying to think up a credible excuse to get out of it.

"Great!" Scott grinned at Marsie.

"I'm looking forward to it," someone said from below Cris in a gentle female voice.

Cris startled backward. Her back had been to him, but she now twisted around to look at him. Her long, dark-brown hair was pulled up into a ponytail, leaving the ends in a loose wave about her shoulders. Bright hazel-green eyes that had begun to glow with bioluminescence drew him in.

She was by far the most beautiful woman he'd ever seen, but there was something else… He felt instantly connected to her.

His breath caught as they locked eyes, and he felt like his heart had stopped beating. Her lips parted in a sweet, genuine smile, and he felt suddenly at ease with her while still being overcome with anxious anticipation.

"Hi," Cris finally stammered, thankful that his cheeks were already flushed from the run.

"Hi," she replied, taking him in. Cris couldn't quite read her expression, but it seemed favorable. "I'm Kate."

"Nice to meet you," Cris managed to get out, still lost in her eyes.

"Well, this will be great fun tomorrow!" Scott jumped to his feet. "Later, ladies." He jogged a couple of steps. "Come on, Cris, time to get back to it."

"Bye," Cris said, pulling himself from Kate. He took a few steps and glanced over his shoulder, seeing that she was still watching him go.

*Wow.* Cris didn't feel any of the burn for the rest of their run.

—

Cris relaxed on the couch, thankful for the magical healing properties of a hot shower. Scott emerged from the bathroom, toweling his hair.

"I have to admit," Scott began, "that it really wasn't fair of me to drag you into a double date like that."

Cris' heart skipped a beat, thinking about Kate again. "It's fine, I know how you are."

"No, not like that." Scott screwed up his face, searching for the right words. "Here's the thing…"

"What?"

"Uh…" Scott took a deep breath. "She's… High Dynasty."

Cris' mouth dropped open involuntarily. "Wait, *what*?"

"Man, I'm sorry. Like I said… Look, Marsie is her roommate and they're good friends. Some people are kind of wary about hanging with Kate because of who she is, and Marsie wanted to give her a chance to get out, so we thought a double date would be good. And you and I are friends, so—"

Cris felt sick. "Which Dynasty, Scott?" *Fok, who is she?*

"Vaenetri. She's Katrine Vaenetri."

Cris let out a shaky breath. *Thank the stars, not a relative! But Vaenetri, of all the families. After Tristen and her sister…* "That's… unexpected."

Scott sat down on the couch, wringing his towel. "I know, I know. I'll make it up to you. I'm just asking for one night."

"It's fine." *Kate Vaenetri…*

"Fine? Fine! Great." Scott leaped to his feet. "Yes, it's going to be just fine."

Cris raised a quizzical eyebrow. "Are you okay?"

"Yes! Of course." Scott bit his lip. He sat back down. "How are you so calm about all of this? A *Lady* from a *High Dynasty* and you're 'fine'? I'm kind of freaking out here. How do you even talk to someone like that?"

Cris laughed inwardly. "High Dynasty or not, they're still just people. They're not all that different."

"Hah! Right." Scott rose to his feet, tossing his towel over his shoulder. "I knew I was bringing along the right guy." Scott went into his room, muttering something under his breath.

Cris sighed, and it turned into a chuckle. Even coming all the way to the TSS couldn't get him out of a dinner with an eligible High Dynasty bachelorette.

—

The day went by far too slowly. Cris had spent the whole night and following day thinking about Kate, despite himself. She didn't exude the elitist air that he'd come to expect from anyone born into the High Dynasties, and he was anxious to see if that perception held true once he got to know her.

After finishing up his classes for the day, he was finally free to return to his quarters and prepare for his double date. *Excited for date night? What's happened to me?*

Cris went about showering and dressing in his quarters, the only home he'd known since coming to the TSS. After TSS command had decided to promote Cris directly to Junior Agent, he'd stayed in the same quarters he was first assigned with Scott and Jon. Jon had recently graduated, and like many new Agents had been sent on assignment to Jotun in the outer realms. They had never been assigned a fourth roommate, so it was temporarily just Scott and Cris. Scott had learned to take full advantage of the arrangement, often kicking Cris out for several hours so he could engage in more private activities with his female companions.

Once dressed in the same dark blue t-shirt and pants that now comprised his entire wardrobe, Cris went out into the common area. Scott emerged from his room at the same time.

"Ready?" Scott asked.

"As I'll ever be."

Cris and Scott made their way to the Primus mess hall. As they approached, Cris saw that Marsie and Kate were waiting for them outside the main door. Both women wore the standard dark blue tank tops that normally served as undershirts for the women's uniform, with a scoop neckline tapering into thin straps that crisscrossed their backs. Their pants were more form-fitting than the men's uniform, slim down to their knees and flared slightly around the cuff covering their boots. Marsie had added some curl to her short blonde hair, and Kate now wore hers in a loose braid.

*I've never seen someone so naturally stunning*, Cris thought to himself as he admired Kate. She smiled in greeting when she saw him, and he felt his heart flutter. *Gah! Stay cool.*

Marsie gave Scott a hug when he walked up to her, and they exchanged a playful glance.

"Shall we eat?" Scott said, gesturing toward the large doorway into the mess hall.

They loaded their trays and selected a booth along the back wall. Scott slid in next to Marsie, leaving Cris the spot next to Kate. *You can do this!* He sat down next to her, trying to judge an appropriate distance apart.

When they started eating, Cris noticed that Kate still followed the proper etiquette instilled in all members of the High Dynasties, so he was especially diligent in maintaining the more casual mannerisms he'd picked up aboard the *Exler* and from those around him at the TSS. As best he could, he tried to walk the line between politeness and commonplace. *Something as simple as how I hold my fork could give me away to a trained eye. If she's interested in me, I want it to be because of who I am as a person, not for my pedigree.*

They engaged in idle small talk as they ate. Some big tests later that week. Wish lists for their internship assignments that would be announced any day. Cris was careful to keep his mind guarded against any potential telepathic probe.

"Cris, here," Scott ventured after a time, "spent a year on a freighter touring the galaxy before joining the TSS. I think he's seen more than any of us."

"How fun!" Marsie exclaimed.

"What was your favorite part about it?" Kate asked.

"How I got a different perspective on life. Saw how others lived," Cris reflected.

"I've appreciated that about the TSS," Kate said. "There are so many people from different backgrounds here. My life back home was so sheltered by comparison."

"It's hard to get the big picture from one vantage, no matter what it may be." He'd had arguably the best education available, but what he'd learned since leaving Tararia has been far more valuable.

"Cris, where are you from originally?" Marsie inquired.

*Here we go...* Cris had his back-story down, but it was something else entirely to recite it in front of another noble. He glanced at Kate, before proceeding. "I'm from Tararia, the Third Region. Sieten." Kate looked over in interest, but Cris didn't detect any recognition or suspicion. *She doesn't expect to see me as highborn, so she doesn't.*

"I've never been there, but I hear it's beautiful," Marsie replied. "I would have tried to get into the University there if I hadn't been recruited by the TSS."

"Yes, it's quite lovely." *I wish I still had the view from my bedroom window.*

"Do you miss it?" Kate asked.

Cris looked. *That's such a loaded question.* "Sometimes, but it wasn't the life I wanted."

Kate nodded. "I know exactly what you mean." She looked down at her own plate, seeing past it.

*She does?* Cris saw a new somberness in her softly glowing eyes. *Is she like me?*

"Sorry, I didn't know it was such a touchy subject!" Marsie said with a little laugh.

"Oh, don't mind them," Scott said, putting his arm around Marsie. "Homesickness can get everyone down sometimes."

Cris forced a smile. "There's way too much going on here to miss home much."

"Too true!" Scott said, squeezing Marsie. "Gorgeous women, cutting-edge tech, and free food. What else do you really need?"

Everyone rolled their eyes in exasperation, but they knew there was truth in his statement. They were in the midst of one of the good times in life, and they had enough perspective to recognize it.

The Junior Agents finished their meal between more light conversation and laughter, enjoying each other's company. As the evening went on, Scott and Marsie inched closer together and talked quietly to each other so that Cris and Kate couldn't overhear. Eventually, when there was a lull in the conversation, Marsie leaned in and whispered in Scott's ear.

"We should probably get going," Scott announced.

"This has been a lot of fun," Marsie added. "It was great to meet you, Cris."

"You too," he replied.

"Well, you two have fun the rest of tonight," Scott said as they got up. "Try to stay out of trouble." He winked at Cris.

Cris sighed and shook his head when they were beyond earshot. "That guy…"

Kate smiled. "Marsie is no better. They were made for each other."

*What do I do now that I'm alone with her?* They sat in silence for a few moments.

"You're under no obligation to spend the rest of the evening with me," Cris blurted out.

Kate shook her head. "Nonsense. I'm enjoying your company." She scoped out the buffet from afar. "I could really use some dessert."

"I'm game."

They procured some chocolate mousse and returned to the booth, sitting across from each other.

"So, Kate, I'm sure you get this all the time, but I have to ask. How did you come to join the TSS? As far as I know, it's rare for anyone from a High Dynasty to come train here, especially beyond the first year." Cris took a bite of the mousse; not quite as good as the Sietinen private chef's, but still delicious.

Kate sighed. "I'm… a bit of an anomaly. I have an older brother, who's heir, and two older sisters. Most High Dynasties only have one or two successors. As a fourth child, I'm of little consequence."

"Are you close with your siblings?"

She shrugged. "Not really. They were adults by the time I was born. I'm twenty years younger than my closest sister."

Cris just about choked on his mousse, but was able to hide it. *Twenty years younger…* That meant there were no children in between Kate and Krista, his brother Tristen's betrothed. It was too big of a coincidence for Kate to be Cris' age. *Even after what happened, they still wanted to unite the two Dynasties.*

He swallowed. “I know what it’s like growing up alone.”

“At any rate,” Kate went on, “when my abilities started to emerge, it was decided that I could come train here. There wasn’t any reason for me to stay on Tararia.”

*I was gone, and they knew it.* The situation became all too clear. She was the very person his parents would have wanted him to meet had he stayed on Tararia. He’d always imagined such an arranged pairing would be horrible, but now he found himself eager to get to know her.

“I hope you feel like you made the right choice to leave,” Cris said. He didn’t have any regrets, but for the first time in years it struck him that his decision to leave Tararia had changed the lives of people outside his immediate family.

“Yes, I do. How about you? What brought you here?”

Cris picked his words carefully. “I didn’t get along with my parents. I think my father actively disliked me. My mother, on the other hand, barely acknowledged my existence. They especially disapproved of me embracing my abilities. So, as soon as I could, I left home. I met Thom, the captain of the *Exler*, on my first day out on my own, and he took me in. I got really lucky.”

“I heard the TSS actually tracked you down to recruit you. And that you trained privately with an Agent when you first got here.”

Cris opened his mouth to reply, but didn’t know what to say. He shrugged it off. “We’re all in the same place now.”

Kate looked at him thoughtfully with eyes that contained wisdom beyond her years. “I’ve never met anyone quite like you,” she said. “You act so casual, but you have a certain… poise.”

“I’m me. It’s just the way I am.”

Kate smiled. “I like it.”

They both looked down at their empty bowls.

“What now?” Cris asked. It was still a little early to go back to his quarters, if he knew Scott’s habits.

“Let’s go up to the spaceport,” Kate suggested, excitement in her eyes. “It’s been too long since I’ve seen the stars.”

"Okay," Cris agreed, ready to follow her lead anywhere she wanted.

Kate took Cris' hand and led him to the central elevator that would take them on the long ride to the surface of the moon outside of Headquarters. They didn't have the clearance to take a transport vessel up to the dock with the TSS fleet, but they could go as far as the terminal on the surface.

The surface port was all but deserted, and they went over to one of the expansive windows that curved in a half-dome overhead, providing an unobstructed view of the starscape beyond.

"I love coming here," Kate said, staring out. They leaned against the railing in front of the window. "It all looks so different from space. You can't get a view like this on Tararia."

"No, you certainly can't," Cris replied. He could never tire of gazing out into the impressive blackness of space with its amazing spectrum of stars.

Kate inched closer to Cris. After a moment, he took the hint and put his arm around her. She relaxed against him. Nothing else mattered with her next to him like that. He was completely at peace. He had no idea how long they stood together, but he savored every moment.

A wave of tiredness washed over Cris. He checked the time on his handheld: 24:13. *How is that even possible?* It was past curfew, though that was rarely enforced for Junior Agents. "We should get back." He reluctantly unfurled himself from Kate.

Kate checked her own handheld. "I had no idea it was so late!"

"It's probably safe for me to go back to my quarters now."

Kate stifled a yawn. "Yes, I imagine so."

They took the central elevator down to the Primus level and walked back to Kate's quarters, her arm linked around Cris'. *I could walk like this forever.*

"I had a great time tonight," Kate said when they were outside her door. "I hope we can see more of each other."

"Me too."

She looked up expectantly at Cris, but he hesitated, not sure what to do.

"Well, good night." Cris smiled and turned to go, his heart pounding in his ears.

"Aren't you going to kiss me goodnight?"

He turned back to look at her. She gazed into his eyes, searching. "I didn't want to presume. You are a Lady, after all," he said.

"Consider the invitation extended." She took a step forward.

Cris swallowed. Coaching about girls hadn't been a part of any of his training. *I have no idea what I'm doing.* He let instinct take over, cupping Kate's face in his hand and drawing her to him.

Their lips met, sending a tingle through Cris' entire body. Kate placed her arms around his neck and pulled him closer. Despite his inexperience, Cris felt at once comfortable with her, following her every cue. She wanted more, but he pulled back slowly from the kiss. "Good night." He kissed her again lightly, lingering just long enough.

# CHAPTER 11

"HOW WAS YOUR date?" Scott asked as soon as Cris emerged from his room in the morning.

Cris grinned, in spite of himself. "It was good."

Scott laughed. "Someone is smitten!"

"Well, I wouldn't go that far," Cris said, trying to sound casual. *She's the most incredible person I've ever met. I didn't know someone like her could exist.*

"Uh huh." Scott didn't seem convinced. "When are you seeing her next?"

"We didn't make any plans yet." *Stars, I hope it's soon.*

"Marsie sent me a message last night saying that Kate was gushing about you."

*Really?* "I'm glad she had a good time."

"By the look on your face, the feeling was mutual."

Cris shrugged it off. *Stay cool. It was only one date. But stars! It was great.*

"Anyway, I'm glad it worked out." Scott pulled out his handheld and checked it. "Hey, I have to check in with the lab. I'll see you later."

"Have a good one." Cris rubbed his eyes. It had been a wonderful night, but they had been up far too late to now be awake at this hour. He suppressed a yawn.

Cris took a quick shower before heading over to the mess hall for breakfast. He got his tray of food and was about to sit down at an empty table when he spotted Kate eating alone. She was reading something projected from her handheld.

*Do I go over to her?* As he was trying to decide what to do, she looked up from the text and smiled at him. She waved him over. *Okay, that answers it.*

"Good morning," she greeted as he approached. She collapsed her handheld and put it away in her pants pocket.

"Hey." Cris took a seat across from her, instantly energized in her presence. *How could I miss her so much after just a few hours?*

"You don't have to sit here if—"

"No, I'm glad you called me over. I didn't want to interrupt you."

Kate poked at her food with her fork. "I was afraid you might take it as me being too clingy or something."

Cris chuckled. "Not at all." He took a bite of potato scramble from his plate. "It's good to see you again."

Kate blushed slightly. "You too." She took a couple bites of her own meal. "I had a great time last night."

"Me too."

They resumed eating in silence.

Cris kept his gaze downcast. The quiet was awkward. *Maybe it was a bad idea to come over here. I remember Scott mentioning something about a waiting period between dates…*

"I'd like to get to know you," Kate said suddenly.

Startled, Cris looked up and their eyes locked. The awkwardness melted away.

"It felt right, last night," Kate continued. "I know Scott and Marsie are just fooling around, but there seemed to be a real connection with us."

*And I still feel it now.* Cris couldn't look away. "I agree. I'd very much like to get to know you, too."

Kate smiled. "Good." She tore her gaze away and looked down for a moment. She cleared her throat. "Now, you said you were from Seiten, right?"

Cris' breath caught. *Stars! Exactly how well do I want her to know me right away?* "Yeah, from right outside the city." *Do I come clean?*

"And you said you grew up alone. Only child?"

"Yes. Well, sort of. I had a brother who died in an accident before I was born." *If she makes the connection between Tristen and her sister...*

Kate's brow furrowed with sympathy. "That must have been difficult for your family."

Cris breathed an inward sigh of relief. *She doesn't suspect me. Or at least doesn't want to admit it.*

He nodded. "It was tough growing up in a shadow. Aside from my parents disapproving of my abilities, that's the other key reason I chose to leave Tararia." *I want to tell her everything, but I need to know that she cares about me, not who I am.*

"I can relate." Kate withdrew in thought for a moment. "Anyway, what interests you? What do you enjoy studying?"

"I love flying. Any chance I have to get in a fighter is welcome. On the more academic side, recently I've been diving into the deepest layers of subspace mechanics."

"Scott mentioned you had a knack for navigation."

*I couldn't escape the family business entirely.* He tried to dodge the question. "Yes, admittedly, much of the subspace studying has navigation applications. I did work as a Navigator before joining the TSS, so it's a familiar subject. But, it's something I'm good at, more than something I enjoy."

"I know what you mean. That's like me with telecommunications systems, because of my family. I can construct a holographic projector from parts, but I'd much rather help plan a battle strategy." She grinned.

*Of course. She was educated in the operations of VComm, just as I was groomed to take over SiNavTech.* "I second your sentiment about battle strategy. Agent Reisar's class was incredible."

Kate's eyes lit up. "It was! When you took it, did he give you that lecture on using phantom subspace jumps?"

"Yes! That was awesome. I mean, I'd hope to never find myself in that situation, but—" Cris was interrupted by a loud chirp from his handheld. "Sorry." He reached into his pocket to silence the device.

A moment later, Kate's handheld made the same chirp. She groaned and pulled it out from her pocket to look at the message. She frowned. "I've been summoned."

Cris examined his own handheld. The message read: >>Proceed to Junior Agent Lounge JAP-271C.<< He showed Kate.

"Same for me," she confirmed.

*Are we in trouble?* Cris took one final bite of breakfast. "I guess we should go."

They bussed their table and walked together to the lounge. A handful of other Junior Agents were already there, including Scott.

"Any idea why we're here?" Cris asked.

"No," Scott replied.

"Internships?" Kate speculated.

Scott shrugged. "Maybe."

After five more minutes, a dozen Primus Junior Agents were gathered in the middle of the room, including Marsie and some other common acquaintances from various classes. Everyone chatted amongst themselves, throwing out increasingly far-fetched theories about the meeting.

The door slid open again and everyone immediately fell silent when a figure dressed in black entered. Cris recognized the man as Lead Agent Nilaen. He was one of the oldest Agents Cris had encountered, with almost fully gray hair. However, he still held himself with the same regality as his younger counterparts. Cris had never interacted with him directly, but he knew his reputation for fair issue resolution and attention to detail.

Nilaen beamed at the crowd. "I'm sure you've all had time to theorize why you have been gathered here." The Junior Agents nodded. "Well, I'm pleased to tell you that the day has finally arrived. Your internship assignments await you."

The Junior Agents looked at each other with anxious anticipation.

Kate shot Cris a smug look. "I knew it." She clasped her hands. "Please, be somewhere warm."

Nilaen checked his handheld. "The details of the assignments have been transferred to your accounts. Good luck." He departed as the Junior Agents scattered to review the assignments with their friends.

"Let's see what we got," Cris said to Kate. They pulled up the files on their handhelds. Cris scanned through the information. It seemed like a straightforward assignment on a pleasant planet, but the subject matter was pretty low on his wish list. *Great. I have to deal with diplomats.* He looked to Kate. "What did you get?"

"Valdos III," Kate replied with disdain. "This looks awful! Just completely… boring."

"How so?"

She continued flipping through the file, looking increasingly distraught the more she read. "Well, their flag is solid beige. I think that says everything."

Cris gave her a sympathetic smile. "I'm sure it will be fine."

Kate sighed loudly. "Easy for you to say, since you won't be stuck there for the next year. Where did you end up?"

*She won't like this.* "Marilon II. Fairly temperate climate and mountainous landscape—pretty picturesque, actually. But, it would seem the Districts don't know how to play nice with each other and they need a mediator." *I'll be stuck in the role of politician after all.*

"Let me see." Kate grabbed his handheld and brought up a holographic projection of the planet's landscape. Towering trees stood out among dramatic rocky cliffs. A modern metropolis was nestled in the foothills with a clear blue river bisecting the city. "You have to be kidding!" She shoved the handheld back at him.

"To be fair, I'll probably spend all of my time in conference rooms," Cris pointed out.

"At least you'll have something to look at out the window." Kate pulled up a holographic display of her own location on her handheld.

Cris wanted to laugh, but held back. The capital city of Valdos III was flat, featureless, and bland. The inhabitants all appeared to wear loose-fitting clothes in an awful shade of gray-tan, giving the entire civilization a completely monotone appearance. "It's… quaint? And it looks like you did get your wish for somewhere warm."

Kate's eyes narrowed into a malicious glare. "Don't even try."

"Hey, I didn't make the assignments!" Cris held up his hands in self-defense.

"Someone doesn't look happy," Scott said from behind Cris.

*Perfect timing!* Cris turned to his friend. "Not every planet has high tourist appeal. How did you fair?"

"Meh, fine," Scott replied. "I'll be managing supply distribution on one of the recently settled colony worlds in the Outer Colonies. You?"

"Diplomatic relations on Marilon II," Cris told him, trying to block out Kate's seething glare.

"How is this fair?" Kate exclaimed, taking ahold of Cris' handheld again and directing it toward Scott.

Scott looked it over. "Hmm, that's not a typical internship assignment. Lucky you."

"I'm sure I'll be miserable in my own way." *If only they knew how much I loathed these sorts of political dealings.*

"Fair enough," Scott said. "Be nice, Kate. At least you'll get to practice advanced telekinesis on Valdos III—I've heard it's one of the only planets where it's integral to their culture."

Kate placed her handheld back in her pocket and crossed her arms. "Lovely." She sighed. "What about Marsie?"

Scott shook his head. "I don't know. She muttered something about 'may as well be going to a convent' before storming off."

*Every assignment is deliberate, designed to address our greatest weaknesses. I guess we're finding out what parts of ourselves we need to improve.* Cris shrugged. "Well, we have a couple months to get used to everything before we ship out."

"Very true," Scott agreed. "I need to start this reading."

"Yes, I should do the same," Kate said. "I'm sure there's *some* redeeming quality about this place. I may as well know what it is."

"That's the spirit," Cris said. "Catch up later?"

"Sure. I'll message you." She smiled at him, all of the discontent from earlier forgotten.

Cris smiled back and nodded.

When they were several meters from the lounge, Scott shook his head. "You two are already sickening together. I'm regretting setting you up."

"You're just envious."

Scott rolled his eyes. "When you're playing with your grandkids, remember I was the one who made it all possible."

Cris gave him a playful shove.

Scott grinned and leaped ahead of Cris. "And name your firstborn after me!" He took off in a sprint down the hallway.

When Cris eventually arrived at his quarters, Scott had already retreated into his room. Cris settled onto his own bed so he could begin the arduous review of the mission details for his internship. He was about to start reading when he noticed an unread email notification.

His stomach knotted when he saw the message details. *Ugh, not again.*

It was from his father. The subject was simply: 'Checking in'.

Cris groaned and deleted the message. He had received dozens of similar emails and video recordings over the last three years. All of them said the same thing, even though the packaging varied: 'Your training with the TSS is pointless. You have no future there. Come home to where you belong.'

*Except, I don't belong on Tararia. And now I have Kate here. They can't argue about a High Dynasty match.* He flipped to the internship brief. *This is the last step. Soon I'll be an Agent. Kate and me, together as Agents. We'd be unstoppable.* He couldn't picture a brighter future.

# CHAPTER 12

AFTER REVIEWING THE details for his internship, Cris was convinced Banks was playing a cruel joke on him. Mediating political negotiations would be Cris' version of a nightmare.

To make matters worse, the more time he spent with Kate in the ensuing weeks, the more the reality of their impending time away sunk in. They would be apart for at least five months, maybe a year. *Already I can't imagine being away from her. Why couldn't we have met after we got back?*

Knowing their time was limited, they saw each other almost every day at meals. Occasionally over the next few weeks, there were opportunities to spend an evening together, but most of that time was spent studying. Still, Cris was happy to get any time he could with Kate, even if it was just sitting in the same room.

One such evening, Cris and Kate were working on their tablets in the common room of Cris' quarters. Scott was away for a few hours completing a project in an engineering lab down on Level 10.

Kate looked up from her reading. "Do you ever stop to think about just how rare we are?"

"What do you mean?" Cris asked from the adjacent couch.

"There are forty-two trainees going on internships this year," Kate said. "According to this article, there used to be hundreds in each cohort."

"What changed?"

"The article doesn't go into it." Kate set down her tablet on the coffee table. "I can't read any more today."

"I second that." Cris stretched and set down his own tablet. It was late and his eyes were glazing over.

Kate came over to Cris' couch and cuddled up next to him. "It makes you wonder, though."

"What do you think happened?"

Kate thought for a moment. "I bet people with abilities are too scared to come forward. The TSS comes across some by chance and will recruit them, but thousands—maybe hundreds of thousands—are probably hiding their abilities. Without any training, all of that talent just gets suppressed and ignored until it may as well not exist at all."

*Like my father. And Tristen, in his attempt to be the perfect son.* "That very easily could have happened to us."

Kate nodded, pensive. "I was pretty lucky to be a fourth child, I suppose. Otherwise, I would have been pulled into the responsibilities of the Dynasty rather than being allowed to train with the TSS."

"Your siblings weren't so fortunate."

Kate frowned. "If my sisters and brother are Gifted, they certainly never let on."

*She doesn't know...* Cris swallowed. "Abilities come in Generations, Kate. If you have them, then they do, too."

"Are you sure? It seems strange that they never would have said anything."

Cris carefully composed his response. *Kate could very well be the ally I've always hoped to find. But I can't reveal my full hand yet.* "The Priesthood's influence is strongest on Tararia, especially with the High Dynasties who are supposed to be leaders and set example for others. How bad would it look for dynastic members to publicly display the abilities the Priesthood tries to denounce?"

Kate looked sick. "Stars! No wonder they let me come here... I always thought they were letting me do what I wanted, but maybe they just wanted me out of the way."

"I'm sure that wasn't the only reason." *I know exactly how she feels... Realizing your family wishes you would blend in, just like them.*

"Now I don't know what to believe." She looked away.

Cris rubbed her shoulder. "I'm sorry, I didn't mean to upset you."

She shook her head. "No, it's not you. I just hate the idea of being lied to."

Cris bit his lip and swallowed. *I haven't been completely honest with her, either.*

"I just never thought about it before," Kate continued. "Sometimes I feel like I was living under a rock. You must have heard all sorts of things in your travels—the kind of things they'd never talk about on Tararia or here within the TSS."

"I did come across some really disgruntled people. Everything might seem fair and balanced in the inner worlds, but it's completely different in the border territories. Out there, people would rather the central government not exist."

Kate's jaw dropped. "No Priesthood or High Dynasties?"

"I know, it surprised me, too."

Her brow furrowed. "What do they have against them?"

"I think it's more that they feel they don't have a voice. The services provided by the High Dynasties are supposed to be for the good of the people—providing the necessities for life and prosperity. But in reality, the Dynasties' companies are complete monopolies and the average person has no say in the type of service they receive or how much it costs."

Kate nodded. "Which is why the Priesthood provides oversight."

"But what does the Priesthood really know? Their decision-makers live a luxurious life on Tararia just like any member of the High Dynasties. Even if they have advisors on other worlds, decisions will always be skewed in favor of the majority leaders."

"And you think there's a better way?" Kate asked.

Cris shrugged. "I don't know, maybe. It just doesn't seem right the way it is."

Kate tilted her head back to look up at him. "What would you propose?"

"I'm probably not the best person to ask…" *This could be my chance to find out if she really does think like me or is content with the way things are on Tararia.*

"No, I'm curious," Kate insisted. "What do you have in mind?"

He decided to make a bold assertion to see how she'd react. "Make the Dynasties' corporations public. Their operations would be dictated by the vote of the populace."

Kate stared at Cris, stunned. "Whoa. That's…"

Cris made a dismissive motion with his hand in an attempt to downplay the radical proposition. "I know. Like I said, I'm probably not the best person to ask."

"The Priesthood would never go along with that," Kate said after a pause.

"Of course not."

"Wait." She caught Cris' gaze. *"Are you suggesting to remove the Priesthood from power?"* she asked telepathically.

Cris looked down and closed his mind to her. *This is a dangerous conversation. The Priesthood already tried to kill me once.* "Never mind."

Kate reached up to turn Cris' face toward her. "Do you think it would be possible?"

Cris let out a slow breath. "I've thought about it. Under the right circumstances, it could be done."

"How?"

*I didn't mean to go this deep now, but she does seem intrigued.* He decided to reveal a little more. "It would require a majority vote from the High Dynasties."

"I guess." Kate let out a little laugh. "Like they'd ever agree."

"If you could convince your family, that would be one vote. It would just take three more." That would only leave two more to convince, once Cris was in charge of Sietinen.

"Right. I can just say 'pretty please' and they'll relinquish control."

"Forget it. I'm clueless when it comes to politics. Maybe I'll learn something on my internship." He leaned down to kiss Kate.

She kissed him back but was still distracted. "It would take years to get the alliances in place for that kind of overthrow."

*Do I let this continue?* Cris hesitated. "Probably a generation or two."

Kate nodded. "Even if the Dynasties went along with it, what about the financial infrastructure and biomedical? The Priesthood plays an important role as a neutral third-party."

"The function would need to be replaced under the new system. I'm far from having all the solutions at this point. I just know I see a problem with the way things are presently."

"It is tough to support the Priesthood when they don't want people like us to exist," Kate murmured.

"My sentiment exactly."

Kate looked distant, then her face softened and she laughed. "What are we doing? We're going to be TSS Agents. This isn't our problem to worry about."

Cris forced a laugh. "You're absolutely right. I tried to warn you about me!" He grinned, both as a cover and out of genuine happiness for discovering he had more in common with Kate than he'd ever dreamed possible. *We could really do it. We could lead a revolution together.*

"I never thought of myself as the type to hang out with the bad crowd."

Cris pulled her in for a kiss, wrapping his arms around her. "I'm a rebel, what can I say?"

She ran her fingers through his hair. "You're going to cause so much trouble on Marilon…"

"I bet you'll be just as bad by the time you come home, after all that time in one of the only places that doesn't share the anti-telekinesis sentiment of the Central Worlds."

Kate made a playful frown. "Between your influence and that, I'm doomed."

"Try not to think of it as 'doomed'—more, 'enlightened'."

"Uh huh..." She repositioned on his lap. "And I take it you're going to help me continue preparing for this internship?"

"Naturally. I still have a few more weeks to get you talking crazy like me."

"With so little time, is talking really the way you want to spend it?" She kissed Cris' neck.

A warm tingle ran through him. "I'm open to other suggestions." *The revolution can wait.*

— — —

Banks was reviewing some weekly reports from his commanding Agents when his desk lit up with an incoming message notification. He looked at the caller. *The Priesthood always has impeccable timing.*

He composed his face and accepted the call as he rose from his desk.

"Hello," Banks greeted in Old Taran while he stepped toward the viewscreen. "To what do I owe the honor of your call?"

The Priest did not look like he was in the mood for pleasantries. "How are matters progressing?"

"Everything is on track."

The Priest glowered. "So you keep saying, but we have yet to see any results."

"These things take time. We can't push too hard without drawing suspicion. You'll have what you want in a few short years, I assure you."

"Years?"

*Your decisions are what got us in this position.* Banks was steadfast. "We'd be done by now if you hadn't abandoned the last attempt. This is the new timeline."

The Priest bowed his head. "Very well. I will inform the others."

"Be patient. I have everything under control. Just let me do my part."

"We await your next update."

# CHAPTER 13

KATE WAS SNUGGLED up against Cris in the crook of his arm, a position he'd come to know well and cherish over their two months together. They fit perfectly, in a way he'd never imagined possible.

*What will I do without her?* The departure for their internships was only a little over a week away; a countdown he'd rather forget.

Kate reoriented in Cris' arms, bringing her face close to his. "You know," she began, kissing him between words, "we have the place to ourselves tonight."

Cris kissed her back, his mind racing. *Stars! Is she suggesting…?*

He had been careful to hold back, knowing they'd soon need to part ways for their internships. But, bit by bit, the physicality of their relationship was progressing despite his efforts. His resistance was twofold. First, there was the Tararian custom for highborn to maintain chastity until engagement—a custom that didn't seem to be a high priority for Kate as a fourth child. While he wasn't overly concerned with tradition, the truth about his identity was another matter. *How can I even consider being with her in that way when she doesn't even know who I really am?*

"You can stay the night, if you want." She moved her hands over his chest, working their way downward.

"Kate, I'd really love to stay, but I have a report I should work on."

"That can wait." She continued to run her hands over his body, knowing just where to touch. "Before we go away, I want to be with you." Her eyes searched his, looking for affirmation. "I lo—"

*No mistaking that!* Cris throbbed with desire, but he resisted—barely. *I can't...*

"I really have to go. I'll see you soon." He extracted himself from her and gave her a quick kiss before rushing out the door.

"Cris, wait!"

*Keep it together.* As soon as he was in the hallway, he located an alcove and ducked out of sight. He leaned against the wall, fighting the competing impulses within. *Why now? I know I need to tell her who I am first, but this isn't the right time. I just wanted to go on the internship and deal with all this when we get back. Shite, I should have anticipated this.*

He steadied himself and made his way quickly to his quarters.

Cris closed the door and sunk to the floor, his back against the wall in the common room.

*Stars! Maybe I do need to tell her before we go. But how? I'm in so deep now, this could ruin everything.* His pulse raced.

Scott walked out of his bedroom. "Hey. Wait, what's wrong?"

Cris tried to talk but couldn't force anything out. He hid his face in his hands.

Scott walked over. "Cris, what is it?"

Cris shook his head. "I haven't been honest with you. With anyone."

"What do you mean?"

Cris rose slowly, still leaning against the wall for support. "Truths have a way of getting lost sometimes. Buried. And once you start down that path, it's hard to turn away."

"I don't like it when you start getting all philosophical on me. What's going on?" Scott looked concerned. He leaned against the couch across from Cris.

"It's Kate. Things have gotten serious between us. She's wanting to take it that next level."

"That's great!"

Cris shook his head. "It would be, but…" He searched for the words. "She thinks I'm someone I'm not. I don't know if she'll accept me for who I really am, and that terrifies me. I can't lose her." *I love her. Stars, I love her so much. More than I ever thought I could. Why didn't I just tell her the truth from the beginning?*

Scott looked confused. "Why, what did you tell her?"

Cris shook his head. "It's what I *didn't* say. I never lied. Not to her, or you, or anyone. You need to know that."

"Okay. What's the issue?"

*Do I tell him? Gah, I have to tell someone or I'm going to explode.* Cris swallowed. "Scott, I don't want this to change anything. You're one of the first real friends I've ever had. That means so much to me."

"You too, man. Nothing could come between us."

Cris nodded. "Well, you know how I said I was from Sieten? That's true. But what I didn't mention was where I lived… at the Sietinen estate."

Scott's face drained. "What are you saying?"

"I'm the heir to the Third Region. I'm Cristoph Sietinen."

Scott worked his mouth. Shaking his head.

"Scott…"

His friend held up his hand. "I just need a minute." He paced on the far side of the room. "Heir to Sietinen, really?"

Cris nodded. "I swear it."

"Well shite." Scott paused. "Wait, so I unwittingly played matchmaker for the High Dynasties?"

Cris nearly collapsed into nervous laughter. He regained some semblance of composure. "It would seem so."

"Bomax."

Both men were distant, chewing unconsciously on their lower lips. They didn't know whether to laugh or run away from each other. Cris felt relief at releasing one of his most guarded secrets, but he felt for his friend. Scott just looked lost.

Eventually, Scott tousled his hair and sat down on the couch. He was coming to terms. "You have to tell Kate."

Cris sat down on the couch across from him. "I know."

"She's crazy about you. You know that, right?"

Cris nodded. *I can only hope it's enough to see past my deception. I need to think of what to say…* "I'll tell her tomorrow."

# CHAPTER 14

THE PIT IN Cris' stomach was even deeper than the night before. His only solace was that Scott had been surprisingly casual about everything that morning, so perhaps there was hope.

After completing his work for the day, Cris went to Kate's quarters, knowing what he had to say but hating that reality. He hit the buzzer, ready to accept the fate he was dealt.

Kate practically leaped into Cris' arms the moment the door was open. "You left so suddenly last night!" She gave him a passionate kiss. "Must have been a busy day. I didn't see you at breakfast or lunch. "

*I needed to wait until we could talk alone.* Cris held her close. "I'm sorry. I hate being apart from you." *And soon we'll have to say goodbye for who knows how long.*

Kate led him inside with her arm still around him. She directed him onto the couch and climbed onto his lap, straddling him. "I really don't want to be apart from you any longer. In any way." She slid her hands down his stomach, stopping tantalizingly close to his groin, her eyes filled with desire.

It took everything to keep Cris from giving in to her advances, but he held back. "Kate, there's something we need to talk about."

She leaned forward and whispered in his ear. "Talking can wait."

Cris took her hands and slid her onto the couch next to him. "Not this." Kate tried to protest, but he was persistent. "We've been spending a lot of time together recently. I feel like we've really gotten to know each other, and you're such a beautiful person, inside and out. You mean so much to me."

Kate smiled. "You mean a lot to me, too. I think you're amazing."

Cris forced a smile through his nerves. "But the thing is, you're from a High Dynasty."

Kate shook her head. "That doesn't matter, I told you. None of that matters here."

"Isn't there a part of you that holds onto that old life?"

"No, this is my life now."

Cris took a deep breath. "What I'm trying to say is, would you really spend your life with me, even marry me, knowing I'd be nothing more than a TSS Agent?"

Kate searched his eyes. "Are you proposing?"

Cris blushed and let go of her hands. "No. I mean, not formally. More hypothetically."

Kate was silent, but her elation was apparent by the upturn at the corners of her mouth and fire in her eyes. "If you're asking if I think such an arrangement would be 'beneath me', no. I never had aspirations of marrying within the Dynasties. There was a single eligible suitor for someone of my birthright, but he would never so much as meet me."

"He was an idiot." *I was that idiot.*

"Regardless, none of that ever mattered to me. All I want is to be happy. To have someone who's as crazy about me as I am about him. I can say with absolute certainty that you make me happier than anyone ever has. You're all I think about."

Cris smiled, reveling in the connection between them that he couldn't put into words. "You too."

Kate gave him a coy grin. "So, yes, in this hypothetical of yours, I would happily marry you."

Cris leaned forward and kissed her. He couldn't help himself. *You still need to tell her.* He pulled himself away. "That means more to me than you know."

"Why are you so nervous?" She took his hands in hers.

"I wasn't completely upfront with you about who I am. I've phrased things in a way to give you a certain impression about me. I feel awful about it, Kate. I shouldn't have, but I just needed to know you care about *me*, not who I am by reputation." He looked into her eyes, trying to make everything okay.

"All right…"

"Kate, my real name is Cristoph Sietinen. And I'm very much in love with you."

"You're…?" She pulled back.

Without hesitation, Cris pushed up the sleeve on his left forearm and turned the inside of his wrist upward for her to examine his Mark to confirm his identity. Instinctually, she pulled out her handheld and tuned the light to the closely guarded frequency that everyone born into a High Dynasty had memorized practically since birth. She ran the light over his wrist, and the Sietinen crest and Cris' full birth name glowed light purple on the surface of his skin.

"It's true…" Kate ran her fingers over the Mark, tracing the form of the serpent in his family's emblem; she touched the falcon invisibly imprinted on her own wrist. She caught herself. "This changes everything."

"Kate—"

"No, don't you realize what this means for me? That's a bomaxed big truth to hide!"

*Uh oh.* "I know it was wrong of me. When I found out who you were, I panicked. I've been 'Cris Sights' for so long now, it's my default."

Kate stood up and stepped away. "I need time to process this. Alone."

Cris rose, but gave her space. "I'm sorry I wasn't upfront with you. I just needed to be sure."

"About what?"

"That you were interested in me as a person, not my title."

Kate stared at him with disbelief. "You think I'm really that shallow? After everything we've discussed?"

"No. I..." *Shite! How do I salvage this?* He took a breath. "I didn't have very good experiences with other highborn in the past."

"After our first date you should have had more faith in me." She crossed her arms. "And especially after a few weeks."

"I did."

"Why wait this long, then?"

"There just never seemed like the right time to tell you."

Kate looked like she wanted to cry. "Oh, really? Not when I was pouring my heart out to you about my own crappy childhood on Tararia? Or talking about my poor sister whose betrothed—your *brother*—died? Or when we speculated about a new Taran revolution?"

"Well... yes." *Fok, this is bad.*

Kate laughed to herself, resentment building in her gaze. "Let's not overlook the fact that my suitor on Tararia was *you.* You cast me aside without ever giving me a chance."

"I maintain that I was an idiot."

"It seems you still are."

Cris winced. "I meant everything I said. I do love you, and I want to spend my life with you."

She looked down. "You should go."

Cris' heart dropped. "Can't we talk this through?"

Kate shook her head, staring past the floor. "Yes, but not right now."

*I don't want to leave things like this, not so close to leaving for our internships.* "Kate, please." Cris took a step forward and held out his arms for a hug, but she raised her hand to stop him.

"That was really selfish of you to not tell me sooner. I have plans for my own life, too. I'd started to think about what that could be like with you."

"We can have everything we talked about and more," he said. "We can be the kind of leaders Tararia deserves."

"The kind who keep secrets from the people they care about the most?"

"No—"

She looked down again. "Give me some time to think. Then we'll talk."

Reluctantly, Cris nodded. "I'm sorry." He let himself out, his stomach in writhing knots. *How do I fix this?*

He hurried back to his quarters, avoiding the gaze of other Junior Agents in the hall. If he couldn't be with Kate, then he wanted to be alone. To his disappointment, he found Scott sprawled on his favorite couch in the common room of their quarters.

"Hey," Scott greeted when he entered. "I thought you'd be at Kate's for the night."

The knots in Cris' stomach pulled tighter. "Things didn't go well."

Scott sat up. "You told her?"

"And now I think she hates me."

"Oh shite."

Cris eased himself onto the adjacent couch. "Yeah."

"What happened?"

"I told her I loved her and wanted to spend my life with her—"

"Whoa, you didn't tell me that part before!"

Cris ignored the interjection. "When it was clear she felt the same way, I told her who I was. She's furious I misled her."

Scott let out a slow breath. "That was a lot of revelations all at once."

"I really foked up." Cris rubbed his eyes with the heels of his hands.

Scott shrugged. "I suppose that depends on how you look at it. Maybe she never even would have talked to you, if she'd known who you were upfront."

"You're not helping." Cris glared at his friend.

"My point is," Scott continued, "you might have missed out on seeing what you could have together. But now you both know.

The connection is obvious, even to an outside observer like me. Don't give up."

"I'm not. I just wish things were different." *Stars! Why did I ever let it go this long without telling her the truth?*

"She'll come around." Scott gave him a supportive smile.

"Yeah." *I can't talk about this anymore or I'm going to drive myself crazy.* Cris headed to his bedroom. "I'll see you tomorrow."

"Hang in there."

Cris felt like banging his head against his bedroom wall, but tried to bury the feeling. At first, he laid down on his bed, but it was soon apparent that he was far too wound up to sleep. With a frustrated groan, he forced himself up to grab his tablet off of the desk.

There was a notification that he had several unread messages in his inbox. His first instinct was to ignore them and try to distract himself with a mindless game. *But what if Kate wrote me?* Gritting his teeth, he opened the inbox.

Most of the messages were an email chain between some of his classmates regarding a group assignment. He scanned through the other senders. *Nothing from Kate.* He sighed. Then, he noticed one message in the list unlike the others. It was addressed from his father, with the subject: 'I want to talk to you'.

*As if this day could get any worse.* It had been a while since he'd received anything from his parents. With a groan, he decided to open the message. The body read: >>You can't ignore me forever. Next time I call, please answer.<<

*He's the last person I want to talk to right now.* Cris was about to close the message when he noticed that it was tagged with an automatic 'read' receipt back to the sender. *Great, now he'll know I'm at my computer.*

Sure enough, an incoming call from Tararia popped up on the viewscreen above his desktop. Cris wanted to decline, but he knew if his father was serious about reaching him, he would keep trying until he got through. *If I just hear him out, then maybe he'll leave me alone.*

Cris settled into his desk chair and initiated the video call. "Hello, Father."

The image of Reinen appeared on the screen. His hair was a little more touched with gray than Cris remembered. "Hi, Cris. I didn't actually expect you to answer."

Any other day and he probably wouldn't have. "You seemed pretty insistent."

"Well, I'm glad you did." Reinen looked him over. "I try to forget how long it's been, but seeing you now… You've grown up."

Cris crossed his arms. "Well, it has been almost five years."

"Did you get him?" came Cris' mother's voice from out of the camera's view. Alana came to stand next to her husband. "Cris! We've been so worried about you." She was a regal woman, touched by the years, but carrying them with grace.

*A full-on family reunion.* "Hello, Mother." He was surprised she has any interest in seeing him.

"You look well." Reinen ventured a smile.

"I'm well enough." *Everything was great until yesterday.* He suppressed the ache in his chest as his thoughts started to drift back to Kate.

"Is everything okay?" Alana asked.

Reinen searched his son's face. "Are you happy?"

*They see your pain. Don't let them bait you.* He forced a smile. "Happier than I ever was there."

Alana paused. "We miss you, Cris."

"Look, I've had a pretty shitey day. What do you want?" Cris snapped.

Alana looked aghast and turned away.

Reinen recoiled. "We just wanted to wish you a happy birthday."

*Birthday?* Cris glanced at the calendar on his computer. *Stars! It is. With everything going on, I completely forgot my own birthday.* He looked down, having just assumed they had an ulterior motive.

"You're our only child to make it to twenty-one," Reinen added faintly.

*Now I feel like a jerk.* "I… Thanks."

"We'd have a party for you, but…" Alana said, still looking down.

*I'm not there.* "I know." Cris took a deep breath. *I abandoned them and didn't look back.* Despite his own feelings of discontent, he knew it wasn't a fair thing to have done to his parents. "I'm sorry I left with no explanation. I was only thinking of myself."

Reinen was caught off-guard. "It's nice to hear you acknowledge that," he said eventually.

"It wasn't until recently that I had the proper perspective."

Reinen sighed. "All these years I've tried to understand."

"It wasn't any one reason." Cris ran a hand through his hair. *I can't possibly explain to him what it felt like to be an outcast in my own family.*

"Alana, dear, will you give us a moment?" Reinen gently placed his hands on his wife's shoulders and directed her away.

"It was good to see you, Cris. Please stay in touch," Alana said as she turned to go.

Cris doubted it was a genuine request. "Goodbye, Mother."

Reinen gathered himself as soon as Alana had departed. "I still wish you would come home."

"Please, don't start—" *Can't we just talk without it turning into a lecture?*

"What kind of life can you possibly have there?" Reinen's eyes narrowed.

Cris had to fight to keep from immediately going on the defensive. *He does have a right to be angry with me. I ran away from my responsibilities.* "The TSS has given me something I couldn't get anywhere else. I finally have friends here with the same abilities. I feel like I belong here."

Reinen began to pace across the room and the camera followed his movement. "That was fine for a while, but at some point you need to assume your proper place in society. You're a dynastic heir! You need to start acting like one."

Cris glared at the image of his father. *The sentimental act was all a façade after all.* "There's more to me than my social standing."

"Regardless, you need to look at your marriage prospects. I can't imagine you have a great selection within the TSS."

Cris smirked. "You'd be surprised."

Reinen stared down his son. "I won't let this bloodline be destroyed by you trying to marry a commoner."

*He hasn't changed at all!* "Thank you for reminding me why I left Tararia in the first place."

"You're meant for more than this, Cris," Reinen implored.

*I am. Just not in the way you think.* "Don't bother calling me again." Cris ended the transmission with a disgusted groan.

He returned to his bed and stared up at the ceiling. *I won't be like him. The TSS is my home now, with or without Kate. But I hope it's 'with'…*

# CHAPTER 15

STILL NOTHING FROM Kate. After three days of obsessively checking his email and receiving no message, Cris was beginning to despair. *Is she going to avoid me forever?*

The conversation with his father had left Cris feeling bitter, and it made him miss Kate's companionship even more. He had tried to keep himself busy with class work, but he was cracking. After finishing up his remaining assignments for the day, Cris headed into the common room of his quarters to find Scott.

To his relief, Scott appeared to be done with his own assignments and was playing a game on his tablet while sprawled on the couch.

"Hey," Cris greeted.

"You want something," Scott replied.

There was no sense denying it. "Has Marsie said anything about Kate? I'm losing my mind."

Scott set down his tablet. "I told you, you need to be patient."

Cris groaned. "But has she said anything?"

"Just that Kate was really upset. I haven't talked to her since the day after your little blowout."

*That's not helpful.* Cris collapsed on the couch and crossed his arms. "I don't know what to do."

Scott let out an exaggerated sigh. "You're going to drive *me* crazy if you keep this up! Try to track her down in one of the lounges or mess hall if you're so intent on talking to her."

*Yes! A seemingly random encounter.* "That's a great idea."

Scott shook his head with exasperation. "Try not to get into deeper trouble."

Cris grabbed his tablet out of his room. *I can look like I'm just going to study in the lounge.* It was a feeble plan, but he was desperate.

Intent on the mission at hand, Cris set out to comb the common Junior Agent recreation areas.

The first three locations were a bust. Cris was on his way to the mess hall when he spotted Kate at the end of the corridor.

His heart leaped. "Kate!"

She turned away to walk in the other direction, but Cris jogged over to her. "I still need more time," Kate said as he approached. She kept her gaze downcast.

*I can't wait any longer. We leave in three days.* "I miss you."

Kate sighed and looked up at Cris. "I miss you, too." She groaned, seemingly frustrated with herself.

Cris wouldn't let her look away. "Can we talk? Please?"

After a moment, Kate yielded. "Fine."

*Progress!* "Come on." Cris headed down the hall toward a row of study rooms. He led Kate into an empty one.

"You really hurt me, you know," Kate said as soon as the door was closed.

Cris set his tablet down on the table. "I'm so sorry. I didn't mean to."

Kate took a deep breath. "I know you didn't." She crossed her arms. "This isn't easy for me."

"It wasn't right of me to keep my identity from you."

Kate shook her head. "It's not just that. I'd already mentally left behind my life on Tararia and committed to the TSS. I didn't think I'd ever look back."

"I have no intention of leaving the TSS, either."

"But, like it or not, you're still an heir. You'll have two lives—one here, and one out there. If I'm with you, that means I'll still have a responsibility to Tararia, too. I could never have the clean break that I'd envisioned. Especially not if you were serious about that plan of yours."

*I hadn't thought about that part of it.* He nodded. "I was serious. We could have two votes between our families, when the time comes. But, you're right. It was a lot of me to ask of you."

"No wonder you had thought through all the steps. I should have known then that you were highborn." She sighed. "I guess these last few days have surfaced a lot of bad memories from my childhood on Tararia, back when I felt like I didn't have any direction. I'd wanted so badly to leave all that behind, but then thinking of being with you at the center of all that… it's a complete shift."

"I'm so sorry, Kate." Cris brushed her cheek with his finger.

She shrugged him off. "You should have been upfront with me."

"I know. You were absolutely right about what you said. I was thinking only of myself." He took her hands; she didn't resist. "When I ran away from Tararia, I didn't know that also meant running away from you. At the time, I felt like I had to get away, at any cost. My parents… Tristen's accident devastated them. I knew they had me out of necessity, not want. All my life, they looked right through me, or when they did see me, I saw them wishing I was someone else."

Kate nodded. "I would have run away, too, if they hadn't willingly let me go. I'm surprised your parents allowed you to stay here."

"Hah! My father writes me at least once a month begging me to come home."

"Oh."

"Everything about Tararia was toxic. I know I've brought up some pretty revolutionary ideas at times, but I honestly believe there's an opportunity for real change. Being here at the TSS is a chance to buy time and leverage." Cris caught her gaze. "I promise you, I may have left out my birth name and title, but the rest has been all me."

Kate searched his face. "You really meant it, about wanting to be with me?"

"Absolutely. I want nothing more than to have you as a life partner."

Kate squeezed his hands. "I feel the same way."

Without hesitation, Cris pulled her in for a kiss. She relaxed into him, releasing the anxious tension of the last few days. After a few moments, Cris pulled away just enough to look Kate in her eyes. "I promise to never mislead you again. I love you."

"I love you, too. We can do so much together."

Cris' heart skipped a beat with the words. *To think I could have lost her… I'll never make that mistake again.*

Kate grinned. "But you should work on your proposal technique, because your first one kind of sucked."

"Don't worry, the real one will be much better."

—

A great weight had been lifted. Kate had accepted him, even if things hadn't gone quite like Cris imagined. *Then again, I didn't think anything through.*

Still, Cris knew better than to believe all challenges were behind him. His relationship with Kate would be difficult within the TSS. It was one thing to casually date, but marriages among Agents were extremely rare. Furthermore, they would no doubt face long periods of separation—first with their impending internships, and after graduation, any random assignment could keep them away from each other for unthinkable spans. Then there was the matter of their parents. *One step at a time.*

The most immediate need was having the High Commander officially sanction the relationship; without that, many other factors would be moot. Cris grabbed his tablet off his desk and sat down on the bed to draft an email to Banks, requesting a meeting. Given the unusual subject matter, he kept the message brief and somewhat vague. In the back of his mind, Cris knew he would leave the TSS before giving up Kate, but hopefully it wouldn't come to such an ultimatum. Nonetheless, he felt a twinge of dread as he sent the message.

Cris set the tablet down next to him on the bed and sprawled out. He yawned and settled into the pillows. A nap was very appealing, having stayed up well past curfew to talk with Kate after reconciling. It was a necessary conversation, and it had left him feeling even closer to her.

As soon as Cris closed his eyes, he heard an email notification chirp. *Response from Banks already?* His heart skipped.

Propped up on his elbows, Cris read the new message. It was indeed from the High Commander, and it stated that he was free to meet at the start of the hour.

*That's in ten minutes!* Cris jumped up from the bed. *So much for preparing a thoughtful speech.*

He rushed out of his quarters and took the elevator up to Level 1. He arrived at the High Commander's office a couple minutes early and found the door open.

Banks was examining his desktop inside, and he looked up when Cris approached the door. He gestured Cris in. "You may close the door, if you like."

Cris entered and took Banks' offer. "Thank you for agreeing to meet with me on such short notice, sir."

Banks smiled. "You caught me on a good day. Have a seat."

"Thank you, sir." Cris sat down across from Banks in one of the two guest chairs facing the desk—cozy leather seats with padded arms that gave a homey feel to the room.

"What can I do for you?" Banks asked, examining Cris through his steepled fingers.

Cris swallowed. "This is admittedly kind of awkward. I'm not sure what to ask, exactly."

Banks cocked his head. "You had some reason for meeting with me."

"Well... I'm not sure if you're aware or not, but Kate Vaenetri and I have been seeing each other for a few months now. And, we've decided we'd like to get married."

Banks' eyes widened behind his tinted glasses and he sat up straighter in his chair as he folded his hands on the desktop. "That's some big news."

"It's all happened rather quickly." *I had no idea my entire life would change like this, but already it's hard to believe it was ever any other way.*

"Congratulations are in order," Banks said with a smile.

"Thank you, sir, but it's not quite official yet. I still need to get her a ring, and somehow convince our parents to go along with it." *That's going to be a fun conversation.*

The High Commander looked intrigued. "A starstone ring, I imagine."

Cris nodded. *That's one tradition I won't break.* A privilege only for the High Dynasties, such stones were rare to the point of being incomprehensibly expensive. "Yes, I'll need to go in person."

"I guess I'll finally get to see one up close. I hear they're breathtaking."

"They are. She's definitely earned it, putting up with me."

Banks smiled. "Well, I'll grant you the leave whenever you need it. I know wedding planning is stressful enough without having to worry about getting time away from work."

"Thank you, sir. That's still a ways off, but I wanted to talk to you as soon as possible, since I know this sort of thing is unusual within the TSS."

Banks steepled his fingers again. "It is, yes. Then again, we don't get many High Dynasty trainees."

Cris shifted in his chair and looked down. "I don't mean to place you in a tough spot."

"No, not at all," Banks assured him. "The lack of long-term relationships among Agents is self-imposed more than any TSS policy."

*It can't be easy. Are we crazy to try?* "I'm glad it's not a direct violation of anything."

Banks shook his head. "Far from it. Many Agents do settle down, eventually—often with a local after an extended planetary assignment. Those people don't pass through Headquarters very often, though. You'll definitely be an anomaly around here."

"Is there any way to guarantee long-term assignments together?"

"Of course, Cris. I wouldn't send you off to opposite sides of the galaxy."

"Thank you, sir."

Banks leaned forward against the desk. "In all honesty, you'll likely stay right here."

Cris came to attention. "Oh?"

"You're on pace to have the highest Course Rank on record." Banks gave him the hint of an approving smile. "That'll put you far up in the Command hierarchy."

Cris sat in shock for a moment. "Sir, I'm not sure what to say."

"You can be very proud of yourself."

"Thank you, sir." *I wasn't expecting a leadership role immediately after graduation.*

Banks paused. "I'll do what I can to make sure you and Kate can have a happy family life here."

"I wasn't really thinking that far ahead."

"I have to. I know you're a dynastic heir, and that comes with a responsibility to your bloodline."

"I suppose it does." *Stars! That always seemed so far away, and now it's just around the corner.*

"Besides, it's probably for the best that you be here, at Headquarters, when that time comes."

"Why's that, sir?" He didn't want to raise a child on Tararia after his experience, but TSS Headquarters wasn't exactly an ideal setting, either.

"I can only imagine a child of yours will be… extraordinary," Banks stated, seeming to choose his words carefully.

"What do you mean?"

Banks hesitated. "Your father was the first in recent generations to have abilities, correct?"

*Though he pretended he didn't.* "Yes, I believe so."

"That makes you 9th Generation. As far as I know, Kate is, as well. So, your child would be 10th Generation on both sides, which is typically the peak of ability. And since you're two of the strongest Gifted I've ever seen, I can only imagine what the combination would produce."

Cris swallowed. "I hadn't thought about it."

"I didn't mean to worry you with idle speculation."

"No, sir. Just caught me off guard a little."

Banks waved off the comment. "Well anyway, consider your request approved. Sorry to have jumped ahead."

"Thank you, sir." *I'll try to be a better father than mine was to me when the time comes. No matter what, I can offer love and support. Unconditionally.*

"As for the wedding," Banks continued, "would it be possible for you to wait until after graduation? With the internship departures in just a couple days..."

"I agree. It would be best to wait."

Banks nodded. "Okay, good. We can work out any administrative details later on. Thank you for coming to me with this."

"Of course, sir."

Banks caught his gaze. "Please, let me know if you ever need anything."

*Something tells me he isn't that friendly with all the trainees.* "Thank you, I will."

"Take care, Cris."

He nodded his thanks and showed himself out. *I guess that went well?* He had no doubt that the coming years would be difficult at times, but at least he could take comfort in knowing he'd have a partner to share it with—and, apparently, an advocate.

Cris smiled to himself. *I can have a life here. A family. This is what I always wanted, even when I didn't know it yet.*

— — —

Banks could hardly contain himself until Cris left the room. *I can't believe the plan is finally coming together!*

Banks called his contact at the Priesthood on the viewscreen.

The Priest answered after several seconds. "Yes?"

"I have excellent news," Banks said with a smile. "Cristoph Sietinen just approached me with plans to wed Katrine Vaenetri."

The Priest's grin was visible beneath the hood of his robe. "We were beginning to worry."

"It was inevitable that they'd arrive at this decision eventually," Banks replied.

"True. Our interventions made sure of it."

"Cris has agreed to wait until after graduation for their wedding. That will allow us to ensure their position as contracted Agents and keep them here at Headquarters."

"Very foresightful."

"I do have one concern," Banks continued. "We've had to move Kate through the training program quickly, to keep her in the same cohort as Cris. I've arranged for her to keep training while on her internship—hopefully, it's enough to catch her up. But, she still might not score an accurate Course Rank."

"Accurate scoring is not a high priority in this matter."

"My concern is that she'll score below her potential and not justify her Primus Command rank." It was the only way to ensure them assignments together without drawing suspicion.

"Then make sure she does. It's imperative they are secure in their relationship and feel comfortable enough to bear the Cadicle—your Primus Elite—as soon as possible."

*The result of our generations of planning and manipulation.* "What do we do until then?" It would still be decades before their future child would be grown and ready to come into the war.

"Our forces can't hold out against the Bakzen in the Rift for much longer. We need more Agent recruits if we're to last until then."

The Priest thought for a moment. "Perhaps now it is time to once again embrace such abilities—change the public consciousness to revere the TSS and the duty it serves. Maybe the denouncement of telekinetic powers has outlived its usefulness."

*People have finally forgotten that those abilities were once core to our race, and how they came to be lost.* "Thank you, that has been my hope for many years. Such a change would be to our benefit in winning the war."

"Consider it done." The Priest looked at Banks levelly. "But the true nature of the war must remain our best kept secret."

Banks looked at the floor, uncomfortable under the Priest's intense gaze. *So few others know the truth I must guard, but it is a necessary burden.* "I faithfully serve Tararia and the Priesthood."

VOLUME 2

# VEIL OF REALITY

# CHAPTER 1

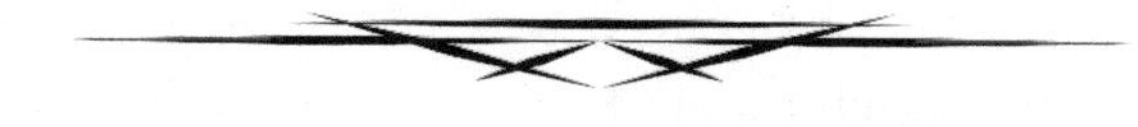

CRIS SIGHTS RELAXED as the docking clamps locked onto his transport ship in the TSS Headquarters spaceport. Being away on extended field assignments never got any easier. *Home at last.*

He stood up from the plush chair in the passenger cabin of the transport vessel and stretched. It had been another long week of diplomatic relations on behalf of the TSS. Following the success of his internship on Marilon II, Cris had become High Commander Banks' first choice for any matters requiring a political liaison. Much to Cris' irritation, the assignments had continued even after he advanced to Lead Agent. *I should have known that there was no escape from politics. Even after two decades with the TSS, I'm still babysitting dynastic delegates.*

A young Militia officer named Dylaen popped his head into the passenger cabin. He had accompanied Cris on other diplomatic missions and had been immensely helpful with the administrative aspects of their most recent assignment on Bashari Prime. "All set, sir?"

"Yes, we made it back just in time. I think most of my sanity is intact." Cris grabbed his travel bag from next to his chair and walked toward the door.

"Didn't go how you'd hoped?" Dylaen asked.

"Not every outcome is as favorable as we may like." Cris shrugged. "My report has been submitted. We'll see what Banks thinks." At least there was that benefit to his field assignments;

once the report was filed, his work was complete. Few other responsibilities as Lead Agent had such a clear distinction.

Dylaen accompanied Cris toward the gangway off the transport ship. "Any plans with the family now that we're back?"

*I wish.* Cris almost laughed. "That's a rarity these days. Kate and I are able to grab Wil for dinner once a week, if we're lucky."

Though expected, it was still difficult to see his son drifting away. Wil was already a Junior Agent, despite only being fourteen years old, and no one else in that position would have their parents around demanding attention.

In recent years, Cris frequently found himself questioning the decision to raise Wil at TSS Headquarters. There had been no examples to follow—being the only High Dynasty heir to ever become a TSS Agent. Having a child to carry on the Sietinen Dynasty legacy was a given, but there were no systems in place within the TSS to accommodate that parental responsibility. Cris had fought to make it work—desperate to provide an alternative for his son that would offer a vantage other than that of Cris' own privileged youth. The chance to raise Wil within the TSS, surrounded by others with telekinetic abilities and from all walks of life, seemed compelling at the time. Yet, it meant Wil had always been the sole child among teenagers and adults. Never did Cris anticipate the full effects of such an arrangement.

He descended the gangway from the transport ship, with Dylaen in tow, and headed toward the docked shuttles that would take them from the space station down to the port on the surface of Earth's moon.

"I'm not surprised Wil is so busy," Dylaen commented as they approached the waiting shuttles. "People always want to talk to him about all sorts of stuff—subspace navigation theory, engineering spec reviews, or even for tips on high-speed maneuvering in combat fighters. I have no idea how he's picked up so much."

*Everyone is so eager to exploit Wil's intellect, they forget he's still a kid.* Cris entered an empty shuttle and took a seat. "I've told him he needs to establish boundaries or he's never going to have any time for himself."

"Don't worry. I'm sure he'll find a balance eventually,"

Dylaen said, initiating the auto-pilot to take them down to the surface. "You must be proud of him. Making Junior Agent so quickly is really impressive."

"Very proud, but I worry sometimes. I want him to be happy." Cris knew all too well what it was like to have demanding responsibilities at a young age and how much of a burden it could be. He'd hoped to offer a carefree youth for his son, but it hadn't worked out that way.

"I'm sure he'd come to you if there were any issues."

He nodded. "I hope so."

"He'll graduate in what—a couple more years?" Dylaen asked.

"Yes, most likely."

Wil had been an exceedingly quick learner as a child. However, his exceptional aptitude had become most apparent when he began his formal training with the TSS at the unprecedented age of twelve. Seeing how Wil's performance contrasted that of his older peers, it was evident that he would complete the training program in record time. As he'd continued to grow stronger, it'd also become clear that his future rank would be well above that of any existing Agent—warranting a 'Primus Elite' designation. Though no one wanted to acknowledge it outright, there was a strong possibility that Wil would even break the elusive Course Rank of 10. There was no telling what he might be able to do with that kind of power.

Dylaen shook his head. "Crazy. He'll be an Agent the same age as most incoming Trainees."

"You're telling me. I'll probably get kicked out as Lead Agent." At the time of his own graduation, Cris' Course Rank of 9.7 was unmatched—an accomplishment that gave him automatic seniority above much older and more experienced Primus Agents. Out of respect, he waited to assume the Lead Agent title until his predecessor, Nilaen, had retired, but it had made for some awkward moments with the other Agents. *I never imagined my own son could be my superior, especially not at sixteen.*

"Oh, come on. You're far too much of an institution around here to be unseated so easily."

Cris cracked a smile. "Thanks for the vote of confidence."

"Anytime, sir."

When the shuttle docked at the surface port, Cris and Dylaen parted ways. Cris checked the time on his handheld and realized it was almost midnight. *Everyone else is probably smart enough to be in bed by now.*

He took the central elevator down to the main Headquarters structure, grateful to have the car to himself. After enduring near-constant conversation over the past few days, he appreciated the silence.

TSS Headquarters had been his residence for almost twenty-one years, and he couldn't imagine living anywhere else. He felt instantly at ease as the elevator descended through the containment lock that kept the main Headquarters structure suspended inside a permanent subspace bubble. The natural effect of subspace dampening his telekinetic abilities helped quiet his mind.

When he reached Level 2, Cris made the trek through the dimmed hallway of the Primus Agents' residential wing. Sconces illuminating potted plants decorated the walls between doors, interspersed with holopaintings of nebulae.

At last, he reached the long-awaited haven of the quarters he shared with his wife. He entered quietly, aware of the late hour. All the overhead lights were off, but there were faint nightlights along the baseboard casting an orange glow throughout the room.

On the right side of the living room, the sliding door to the main bedroom was cracked open. Kate was in bed, asleep.

Seeing her, Cris still felt a swell of love and excitement, even after seventeen years of marriage. Throughout the challenges they had faced as TSS Agents, their love and bond had been a constant that sustained them. And it had given them the enduring strength to form a united rebellion against the Priesthood's anti-telekinesis sentiment throughout the Taran colonies. No member of a High Dynasty had ever openly embraced their abilities, and the public display of Cris' TSS Agent's uniform at their wedding had made a bold statement—even though the images had been scrubbed from most of the major publications. Cris had expected his parents to outright denounce him and any involvement with the TSS, but they had been surprisingly agreeable from the moment he announced their engagement. However, he was willing to bet they would have done anything to finally unite the Sietinen and Vaenetri Dynasties.

Cris placed his handheld on the nightstand and took off his outer layer of clothes. As he lay down on the soft mattress, he felt content for the first time in days. *There's nothing better than your own bed after a long trip.*

Kate stirred as he adjusted the covers. "Welcome back," she murmured, still half-asleep. "I missed you."

"I missed you, too." Cris gave her a kiss and then settled into his pillow. It was good to be home.

— — —

The dimmed hallway stretched before Wil Sights. No one else was present in the corridors of the Primus residential wing so late, nearly 01:00 hours. Padded carpet made footsteps silent to the unwary, and Wil was much too tired and distracted by thoughts of an electrochemistry test later that day to pay much attention to his surroundings. He stifled a yawn as he rounded a corner, nearly overtaken by fatigue.

The other Junior Agent trainees often gave him a hard time about being so young and small compared to them, but Wil had learned how to hold his own. Still, he didn't want any of it to be a competition. Most days, he wished everyone would just leave him alone so he could play around with fanciful ship designs on his tablet.

Wil ran his fingers through his short, chestnut-brown hair. The objects in his pockets seemed to grow heavier as he walked, weighing him down.

Nearing an especially secluded section of the long corridor, he was struck with a sudden wave of unease. He shrugged off the feeling and took a deep breath, trying to unwind for the night. He closed his cerulean eyes as he walked, allowing his senses to dull in anticipation of sleep.

Unnoticed, black-clad figures emerged from the shadows all around him.

An unnatural breeze brushed the back of Wil's neck. His eyes shot open, catching the glint of a metal quarterstaff swinging toward his shoulder. Instinctively, he reached to his side for a weapon, but he was unarmed. He ducked to the side, agilely catching himself on the ground.

"H—" Wil tried to call out for aid, but his mind felt fuzzy, and the words were lost.

The black-clad attacker stepped forward, looming over Wil as he crouched in the hall. Bright red eyes shone through the face mask, locked on him.

Wil was mesmerized. As he huddled, dazed and defenseless, the assailant reached out to his mind.

The telepathic connection sent a sickening chill to Wil's core. Hate and anger burned within, paired with an immense power he couldn't comprehend. There was such a fundamental difference between them—so opposite in their motivations and thinking—that he wondered how they could both exist. The pure loathing was more than Wil could handle, and he struggled to close his mind.

He scrambled to his feet and backed toward the wall, fear gripping his chest. He tried to call out again, but telepathic interference from his assailant still clouded his mind.

Wil didn't know how to fight back. Advanced telekinetic abilities were next to useless on the upper levels of Headquarters within the subspace bubble—attempting anything more than telepathy or basic levitation was like grasping at air. He barely came up to the assailant's chest, so he had no chance in a fistfight.

Frozen with shock and fear, Wil wasted crucial moments as the dark figure prepared for another assault.

The quarterstaff swung toward Wil again. He dove to the ground and rolled to the side. His back struck the wall.

A rattle overhead drew Wil's attention to an old show sword rocking in its holdings. In one swift movement, he leaped to his feet and grabbed the weapon from its hooks. The weight caught him by surprise and the sword nearly dropped to the ground.

Wil hoisted the heavy weapon just in time to block a blow from the lead attacker—bolstering the deflection with as much telekinetic power as he could muster through the subspace haze. While he countered hits from his assailant, the other intruders waited calmly out of the way.

Tired even before the attack, Wil was soon to the point of complete exhaustion. He looked in earnest for any possible escape. Instead, he was horrified to see one of the figures down the hall lining him up in the sights of a stun gun.

The lead attacker stepped aside just as the invisible energy beam rippled through the air and struck the center of Wil's chest. The force of the beam knocked Wil to the ground, paralyzing him immediately.

The world began to blur into darkness. The last images Wil saw before losing consciousness were the five figures coming to stand over him. The blackness became everything.

— — —

Snapping out of a deep sleep, Cris looked up to see Kate smiling down at him.

"Hey you," Cris murmured as he tucked a loose length of Kate's dark-brown hair behind her ear. It was wet—freshly showered.

"Hey." Kate gave him a slow, sultry kiss. She pulled away gently, savoring the moment. "Want to get breakfast with me?" She stroked the side of Cris' face.

"Sure." Cris glanced at the clock; it was just past 06:00. Not nearly enough sleep to make up for the deficit during his travels, but it would have to do. "You're up early."

"I have some papers to grade before class today." Kate hopped off the bed.

Cris sat up. "Kind of last-minute, isn't it?"

"Well, it's tough to get psyched about reading twenty essays on the merits of distributed supply outposts in emerging colonization zones."

"I offer no sympathy until you're sentenced to oversee the arrival of new Trainees." It was an annual event Cris endured as part of his Lead Agent position, shepherding hundreds of rowdy teenagers who would one day be molded into Agents. After several years of observation, Cris had decided that Wil had acted more maturely by the age of three.

Kate grinned. “Banks would never make me do that. He likes me too much.”

*If my assignments are any indication, then maybe he hates me.* Cris dragged himself out of bed. “Well, only one more planet and I’m done with this round of negotiations. Then we can get back to normal.”

For travel assignments, Kate typically served as the First Officer under Cris aboard the *Vanquish*, the flagship for the TSS. Her Course Rank of 8.9 had made her a logical choice for the command position, aside from their relationship. However, the most recent mission was an extended diplomatic engagement—a poor fit for the *Vanquish*, and a perfect opportunity for the starship to get some overdue maintenance. Not wanting to be away from Wil for that long, Kate had elected to teach some classes at Headquarters while Cris traveled with an administrative envoy.

“I can’t wait. I’m going stir-crazy here without you,” Kate said as she settled onto the bed with her tablet. “Let me know when you’re ready.”

*Can’t I just go back to sleep?* Cris slid off the bed. “I’m going to take a quick shower. I’ll be right back.”

He grabbed a clean set of clothes and shuffled into the bathroom to get ready. Hoping to jolt himself awake, he turned down the water temperature in the shower to several degrees cooler than normal. The strategy was moderately effective, but he still felt groggy.

Once dressed, Cris returned to the bedroom to retrieve Kate.

She turned off her tablet when Cris entered. “You got a call from Banks.”

Cris groaned. “I knew he wouldn’t be happy when he saw that report on Bashari Prime. Haersen probably tipped him off.” Cris had always found the administrative and reporting hoops implemented by the Mission Coordinator, Arron Haersen, to be a necessary nuisance.

“Make it quick. I’m hungry!” Kate said with lighthearted urgency.

Cris grabbed his handheld off the nightstand to check the message from Banks. In addition to the missed call notification, there were two follow-up text messages: >>Come to my office immediately,<< followed by, >>Disregard. I'm coming to you.<<

Kate noticed Cris frowning at his phone. "What is it?"

"I guess he's coming here," Cris replied.

"That must have been quite a report—"

A buzzer sounded at the front door.

"I'll handle it." Cris jogged to the living room. The moment he opened the door, his stomach dropped. *I don't think this is about my mission report.*

Never had the High Commander looked so old and tired in the many years Cris had known him. Though Banks usually only looked to be in his late-thirties, due to the restorative benefits of his telekinetic abilities and strong Taran genetics, he was, in fact, nearly twice that age. For a rare change, it was showing.

"May I come in?" Banks asked from the hall.

Cris stepped aside so he could enter. "What is it?" He closed the door behind him.

Banks seemed dazed. "I'm sorry, this couldn't wait."

Kate emerged from the bedroom. "What's going on?"

Banks looked to each of them before removing his tinted glasses, since Cris and Kate weren't wearing theirs. He took an unsteady breath. "Wil didn't return to his quarters last night."

Cris tensed. "Then where—"

"You might want to sit down." Banks gestured to the couch in the center of the room.

Cris' pulse quickened. "I'd rather stand," he replied, but moved within arm's length of the furniture. Kate came to stand next to him and took his hand.

Banks looked down. "Wil's roommates couldn't track him down, so they alerted central services. When we went to investigate, we found that most of the security footage from last night had been wiped. However, we recovered one file from the spaceport on the surface."

"Where is he?" Kate demanded.

*Stars! Wil...* Cris' stomach was a solid knot.

Banks swallowed. "It appears Wil was captured by the Bakzen."

"No! What? How?" Kate's grip on Cris' hand tightened for support. She shook her head with pained disbelief.

Cris felt like all the air had been sucked from the room. He placed an arm around his wife, wanting to offer her more comfort, but it was taking all his strength to maintain composure. Looking up at Banks, Cris opened his mouth to speak, but couldn't think of what to say. *The Bakzen! How did they get into Headquarters? Why Wil?*

Since becoming a TSS Agent, Cris had learned frustratingly little about the Bakzeni Empire and their mounting forces beyond the outer Taran colonies. Like everyone else in the TSS beyond first year Trainees, he knew the Bakzen by reputation as a distant enemy—powerful and dangerous, but not an immediate concern.

"It doesn't make any sense," Cris finally managed to say.

Banks shook his head, absorbed in his own thoughts. He looked almost defeated. "I'm so sorry. I never thought they could get past our security."

"But why would they take Wil? Was anyone else injured or taken?" Cris asked. Nothing about the situation made sense, nor did Banks' demeanor.

The High Commander gathered himself. "No, he was the only one. Wil is far more important than you can imagine. It's imperative he's rescued."

"He's our son." *There's nothing more important.*

"I know you're going to take this as parents no matter what I say. But this… it goes beyond your family, and even the High Dynasties." He swallowed. "This is far from a random kidnapping."

Cris searched the High Commander's face. "What do you mean?"

Banks hesitated. "I have no doubt that Wil was specifically targeted. And I think the Bakzen had help from inside the TSS."

"I don't understand," Cris said.

Kate's eyes narrowed. "Who would help the Bakzen capture Wil? And why?"

"There's no time to get into that now," Banks replied. "We need to get him back."

A glimmer of hope ignited in Cris. "You know where they took him?"

Banks nodded, but his face was drawn. "We have a guess,

anyway. The Bakzen homeworld, beyond the Outer Colonies."

Cris' throat felt too tight to breathe.

"When do we leave?" Kate asked.

Banks shook his head. "I can't allow both of you to go."

Cris stared him down, resolute. "Try to stop us."

Kate let out a slow breath. "No, he's right, Cris. You're the Sietinen heir."

*And this might be a one-way mission—my assumed identity within the TSS doesn't alter my ties to Tararia.* Cris' stomach turned over. "Then I'll go alone."

"I just said—" Kate started to protest.

"No, if this is about preserving the bloodline, then my contribution is on file with the Genetic Archive. A matched surrogate is more valuable." A cold way to look at it, but it was the truth.

*"Are you sure?"* she asked him telepathically.

*"I don't want to leave you, but one of us has to go, and it should be me,"* Cris responded to her. Then aloud, "There's a traitor here. It's not safe."

Kate looked down, then nodded and wrapped her arms around Cris, burying her face in his chest. She took a shaky breath as she pulled away, keeping a hold on his hand. "This can't happen to anyone else. While you're away, I'll try to find out who's working with the Bakzen."

"Then it's settled," Banks said, turning his attention to Cris. "I had Haersen get everything on the *Vanquish* prepped for you."

"It's back from the shipyards?" Cris asked.

"Just returned yesterday," the High Commander confirmed.

"Which makes it untested in the field. And it's large. Maybe a smaller tactical vessel would—"

"The new upgrades make it the best ship in our fleet," Banks countered. "You'll want every advantage."

Cris nodded absently. "Okay. I need a First Officer."

Banks nodded. "I already sent out a request for volunteers. Scott Wincowski was one."

"He realizes this might be a suicide mission, right?" Cris asked.

Tears filled Kate's eyes as she gripped Cris' hand tighter.

"Yes, everyone knows," Banks replied. "You have a skeleton

crew, plus a few others."

"And," Cris continued, "I need access to the restricted Bakzen files."

Banks hesitated. "Granting that clearance isn't entirely up to me."

Cris glared at the High Commander. "Then I'm being set up to fail." *Wil's life is at stake! What secret is so important to jeopardize a rescue?*

"I'll see what I can do," Banks said after a moment. "You should get going. Good luck." He rushed out the door.

When they were alone, Kate wrapped her arms around Cris again. "Come home. I can't lose you both."

"I'll bring our son home. I promise."

# CHAPTER 2

CRIS STEPPED OUT of the transport shuttle onto the cool metallic floor-plates of the spaceport anchored above the moon's surface. The normal serenity of space was overshadowed by fear and anguish over his missing child.

*The Bakzen have Wil. He was targeted.* It didn't seem real.

Yet, there was still a chance—slim, but a chance—that he could find their son alive. Though he could barely stand, he forced himself onward. There was no time to reflect.

As Cris approached the entry gates, he caught sight of Scott pacing back and forth. His black overcoat billowed as he spun on his booted heel.

Scott looked up at the sound of Cris' approaching footsteps. "How are you holding up?"

"Well enough," he replied, even though it was anything but true. "Thanks for offering to come along."

"You know I never turn down a challenge," Scott said with a grin.

Cris couldn't bring himself to share the same enthusiasm. "Let's go." He gestured toward the entry gates.

They went through the automated security checkpoint with a palm scan and voice identification, then proceeded toward the docking location for the *Vanquish.*

Cris' stomach knotted as they approached the ship. *Don't think about where we're going.*

He turned to his friend. "You haven't been on the *Vanquish* for some time, have you?"

"No. Is she still the same beauty?"

"You know it."

Though most Agents trained on the Command track didn't receive a starship without at least a decade of service, Cris had been assigned his first ship shortly after graduation. When he assumed the role of Lead Agent, he'd been transferred to the *Vanquish.*

As the TSS flagship, the *Vanquish* played a key role whenever the TSS required an authoritative command presence. Though it lacked the intimidation factor of a full warship, Cris and his crew had taken part in the occasional battle and the *Vanquish* could hold its own against larger vessels. However, generally their objective was to diffuse a situation without it turning into a firefight. Over the twelve years the *Vanquish* had been under his command, Cris had been on more missions than he could count, most of them with Kate as his First Officer.

The two Primus Agents walked in silence down the long, glass-walled gangway leading to the *Vanquish.* The ship was always just as awe-inspiring as the first time Cris saw it, its seamless hull gleaming with blue-green iridescence under the lights from the spaceport. The sleek ship dominated the view to the right of the gangway. However, it was the star-speckled expanse of space beyond that captured Cris' attention. The vastness that normally called to him with the promise of excitement and adventure was now a dark and dangerous unknown.

*We've never heard back from anyone sent to Bakzeni Territory.* He tried to push down the apprehension gripping in his chest. *We'll have to change that.*

The gangway led to the fifth deck of the *Vanquish,* near the Command Center in the core of the ship. The two men took a lift down one deck to the Senior Officers' quarters. "You can take the

Delegate's Suite at the end of the hall," Cris told Scott as they parted. "Freshly remodeled."

Cris walked into the room he usually shared with Kate. It seemed desolate without her.

He yearned to be with her, to seek comfort in her companionship. But, he took solace knowing she was safe at home.

*Not that anywhere feels safe anymore.* As much as he didn't want to think about it, there was more going on than he'd been told—and Wil was part of it. *I need to figure out what.*

His thoughts were interrupted by a buzz at the door. "Come in, Scott," he muttered.

When he looked up, he was surprised to instead find a former Chief Engineer, Matt Nomalor, standing in the doorway. Cris hadn't seen him for years, and it took a moment to register. "Matt? I thought you were testing prototypes over in the Kaldern System."

"I was, but I didn't trust that new guy with the *Vanquish*."

Cris couldn't help but crack a smile despite his low spirits. Matt had more than thirty years of experience on combat ships as a Militia officer and was an asset to any crew. "It's just like you to arrange an intervention."

"Besides, I couldn't wait to check out the upgrades. Apparently there's some pretty innovative tech."

Cris sighed. "I haven't even had a chance to look over the new specs."

"Don't worry, she's still the same ship. I'll take good care of her so you can focus on what's important."

"Thanks. I need all the help I can get."

Matt's smile faded. "That's why I'm here." He crossed his arms, face drawn. "Cris, I feel terrible that you're going through this. I'm so sorry."

The words cut deep. *They all dance around it—saying they're 'sorry about what happened.' But what they really mean is, 'The Bakzen captured your son, and you'll be lucky if you ever see him alive again!'*

Cris turned away from his old friend as his eyes began to burn. The sickening ache in his chest swelled with every thought of what he was facing and everything he was leaving behind. *I must be strong… Wil needs me. I can't give up on him.*

He cleared his throat, thankful that his tinted glasses hid his eyes. "We should take our posts."

Matt only nodded in response.

They stepped into the hallway and found Scott waiting outside the door.

"I should get down to Engineering," Matt said to Cris as he glanced over at the other Primus Agent.

"Right," Cris said, turning his mind to business. "Have you met Scott Wincowski?"

Scott and Matt looked each other over. "Yes," said Matt, "but it was a long time ago."

Cris nodded. "We can finish the reunion later."

After a parting nod to Matt, Cris and Scott took the lift up to the Command Center. As they entered the spherical room, the two other crew members rose out of respect for their senior officers. Both pairs of eyes rested on Scott.

Cris waved his hand. "At ease." He always ran the ship with a casual protocol compared to most of the other captains, likely a product of his time spent traveling on the cargo freighter *Exler* before joining the TSS. "Scott will be joining us as First Officer."

Cris and Scott stepped across the transparent floor bisecting the sphere. The lower hemisphere of the holographic projection screen that surrounded the Command Center was darkened, making the floor appear black. Lights around the perimeter of the room cast a soft glow on the upper dome.

Alec Braensen, the ship's pilot, took his seat at the navigation console a step down from the command chairs in the center of the room. He was also a Primus Agent, with a Navigation specialization. "Our course is plotted and ready to go." His normally exuberant demeanor was nowhere to be seen, replaced by a stoic mask that only partially hid his apprehension.

"Good." Cris looked to the other officer, Kari Wilsen, who managed the weapons and communications systems from a station next to Alec's. "How's everything look, Kari?"

"Top marks across the board," she replied. "Looks like they put everything back together properly." She looked Scott over again before sitting down.

Cris sensed her wariness about the new addition to the crew. *They don't have any history with Scott, but they do trust me. It won't take much to win them over.* "Scott and I were roommates. He introduced me to Kate," Cris said as he took the captain's chair.

"I've known Wil his whole life," Scott added as he sat down in the First Officer's chair next to Cris. "I want nothing more than to see him return home safely."

Kari nodded and seemed to relax a little.

*We're all in this together.* Cris activated the final verification scan of all systems via the console between the two command chairs. A holographic readout popped up midway between his chair and the front domed wall, displaying a list of the ship's systems with a progress bar advancing over each. The headings turned blue as subsystem scans completed.

While he waited for the scan results, Cris pulled out a tablet from a pocket alongside his chair and brought up the Mainframe to check on his access to the Bakzen files, hoping Banks had followed through. Still nothing. With an inward groan, he then accessed the crew manifest and looked over the two dozen members of the skeleton crew. In addition to Matt, he was shocked to see Irina Saunatev, the Head Medical Doctor for the TSS, on the list. Any captain would be lucky to have each and every person on board.

The scan completed. Everything checked out.

The knot in Cris' stomach cinched tighter. He stowed the tablet. "We're all set."

Alec and Kari swiveled their chairs around to face Cris, and Scott looked over at him. All faces were expectant.

*This isn't just any mission.* Cris swallowed. He reached over the center console and opened a ship-wide communication. "You all know why we're here and what we have to do. If you have any reservations, say so now."

His officers looked each other over. "I'm scared shiteless," Scott said, "but I'll follow you to the bitter end if that's what it takes."

"We're all in," Matt said over the comm.

The two helm officers murmured agreement.

Cris gave a resolute nod. "Take us out, Alec." He ended the communication.

"Aye."

The domed ceiling and floor of the Command Center came to life, projecting a perfect representation of the space surrounding the *Vanquish.* Other ships and the spacedock filled the left side of the screen, with the cratered surface of the moon below and an open starscape above.

*Will I ever see this again?* Cris took a deep breath and gripped the arms of his chair. *Don't think like that. I have to succeed.*

Alec brought up his programmed navigation sequence on the console in front of him. Such long-range courses along the network of subspace navigation beacons were a challenge to plot, but Alec's exceptional instincts as a navigator and pilot were why Cris had selected him for his crew.

When the docking clamps disengaged from the hull, the ship began to slowly move away from the port. Once far enough out, Cris gave the order to activate the spatial jump drive.

Vibrations from the jump drive's reactor emanated through the floor as the air began to hum. A distortion field grew around the ship as the reactor rose to full power. Slowly, the image surrounding the Command Center morphed from a starscape into ethereal ribbons of blues and greens. Swirling colored light overtook the ship. The *Vanquish* slipped into subspace.

Cris slumped back in his chair. The shifting shimmer of subspace gave no sense of forward movement. "What's the estimated transit time?" he asked Alec.

"Six hours, give or take," the pilot replied.

Cris sighed. The duration of the jump was variable with such an extended beacon sequence, depending on the subspace flow. *Halfway across the galaxy. What will we find when we get there?*

With the computer's navigation system locked onto the necessary sequence of beacons to keep the *Vanquish* on course, there was little to do until they dropped back into normal space.

He closed his eyes and allowed himself to drift toward a trance.

A shudder ran through the ship. Startled, Cris snapped back to attention. "What was that?"

The *Vanquish* lurched to the side, rattling the Command Center.

"The signal is failing," Alec stammered. "I'm losing the third beacon in the sequence."

*Shite!* "What's the cause?"

Alec manipulated the controls at his console. "I can't tell, but we need to abort. The signal isn't holding."

*Bomax, what did they do to the ship?* Cris gripped his armrests. "Get us out of here!"

Alec immediately made the necessary adjustments, requiring instantaneous mental calculations that were well beyond the capabilities of most. Any error and they risked being torn apart in subspace.

Cris gripped the armrest of his chair. *Come on, Alec.*

The *Vanquish* jerked as the signal switch was made. Stars began to show through the ethereal blue-green. Another shudder wracked the *Vanquish* and the ship abruptly dropped into normal space. The subspace distortion dissipated like a lifting fog.

Cris let out a relieved breath and examined their surroundings on the viewscreen, seeing no distinguishing features in the starscape. *Where are we?* He glanced over at Scott, who looked perplexed.

Alec brought the ship to a full stop. He released a shaky breath and nervous chuckle. "That was close."

"Damage rep—" Cris was cut off by a buzz at the center console. He answered the call, "Command Center."

"Something strange happened," Matt said over the comm.

"Yes, we lost contact with a navigation beacon."

"No, I mean with the jump drive itself," replied the engineer.

Cris tensed. "What?"

"One of the PEM power distribution cells blew," Matt explained. "I don't know how it happened—maybe something from the upgrades—but the cell is completely dead."

Cris wilted. "So, the jump drive is inoperable."

"Not just that. We can't draw any power from the PEM until we get a replacement distribution cell installed, so we're also presently without subspace communications."

*Fok.* The perpetual energy module—or PEM—was the heart of the ship. Though the *Vanquish* had a backup antimatter reactor, it was only equipped to power the ship's environmental systems and sub-light drive.

"When can the repairs be finished?" Cris asked the engineer.

"It would take about sixteen hours. That is, if there were a replacement cell on board." Matt's regret was audible.

"Why don't we have any replacements?"

"It's not a part that generally goes bad. We headed out in such a rush, I didn't think to add it to the inventory."

*It's not his fault.* Cris took a calming breath, shifting his attention to the tactical officer. "Kari, are there any TSS supply outposts nearby?"

"There are no TSS facilities closer than five days' travel on sub-light propulsion," she responded.

*Stars! We can't afford that long of a delay.* "Matt, could a civilian distribution cell be adapted to fit our system?"

"Maybe. It depends."

Cris had to hold onto that possibility. "Kari, find us the closest planet with active trading."

"Aye," she acknowledged.

"Make any adaptations you can to the drive to prepare it for a foreign cell," Cris told Matt over the comm.

"I'll do what I can."

"Command Center out," Cris said, ending the communication.

Scott was sitting quietly, somewhat uncharacteristic for him.

*"Does something feel wrong about all of this?"* Cris asked him telepathically. *"We're on perhaps the most important mission of our lives, and we have a breakdown of a system with an otherwise flawless performance record—right after a bunch of strangers give it a complete maintenance overhaul."*

*"Sabotage?"* Scott speculated.

*"I don't know. It just doesn't seem like coincidence."*

*"I agree."*

Cris paused for a moment before continuing. *"But… something tells me we weren't meant to maintain a beacon lock. Alec is one of the only pilots who could have recovered. I think someone wanted us lost in subspace."*

"Sir," interrupted Kari, "we're in luck. We're at the edge of an inhabited system, and it appears to have an active trade outpost. It's called Arnca. The TSS is in contact with the government and is on good terms."

"How long will it take to reach orbit of the planet?"

"I estimate two hours," Kari replied.

"Okay. Alec, set in a course." Cris turned to Scott. *"We can talk more later. I need to get a stim. It's going to be a long day."* Then aloud, "Wincowski, the Command Center is yours until we reach Arnca. Contact me when we're nearing the planet. I'll be in my quarters."

"I've got it." Scott nodded. *"Go take care of yourself."*

Cris walked out of the Command Center, taking the familiar path down the hallway and central lift. When he arrived at the infirmary door, it opened automatically, revealing one of the most technologically advanced medical centers on any contemporary starship. Nonetheless, Cris headed straight for the general medication cabinet.

Before he had gone two steps, a familiar voice stopped him mid-stride.

"May I help you?"

Cris turned to see the TSS Head Medical Doctor come out from the small office tucked in the back corner of the room. Irina Saunatev, like Cris, was a native of the Third Region of Tararia. Her soft voice suited her features.

Cris greeted her with something resembling a smile. "I was surprised to see your name on the crew manifest."

Irina smiled back, but it was one of sympathy. "When Banks sent out the request for volunteers, I had to come. I delivered Wil, so I feel responsible for his well-being."

They were family within the TSS. Wil was a part of all their lives. "Thank you. I'll feel better knowing he'll have the best possible care when we find him."

The doctor looked him over through her tinted glasses. "Are you doing okay?"

Cris made a noncommittal gesture with his hand in response. *I won't be okay until Wil is back home.*

Irina flushed, almost matching her fair, reddish-blonde hair. "Of course, you're in the infirmary. What do you need?"

"I'm just tired. I wanted to get a stimulant to hold me through until I can get some proper sleep."

"Of course. I'll get it."

"I can—"

"No, no," Irina insisted. "Since I'm here, I have to make myself useful. It defeats the purpose of having a doctor around when the patients insist on doing everything themselves." Using a pair of tweezers, she grabbed a nearly translucent strip from a container in the cabinet and handed it to Cris. "Here you are."

"Thanks." Cris placed the strip in his mouth and it instantly dissolved. "I'll see you later."

Irina looked as if she meant to say something else but remained silent.

*No doubt more condolences. But this isn't over yet.*

— — —

Banks tried to suppress his concern over the *Vanquish*'s disappearance. *Why did they drop off the grid? They should still be en route in subspace.*

Setting aside his worries, Banks turned his attention to Kate—the one person who must be even more distraught over the day's events. He buzzed the door to her quarters.

After a moment, the door cracked open. Kate peered out, her eyes red and face pale. "Sir, what are you doing here?"

*It's a good thing I came by.* "Oh, come on, Kate. No need for formality."

"Right, I'm sorry. Please, come in." She stood aside and gestured him through the door.

As Banks entered, Kate made some gestures toward the viewscreen on the wall and the screen darkened.

Banks closed the door behind himself and looked around. The personal touches throughout the room jumped out at him, knowing Cris and Wil were in danger—pictures of Wil as a small child, holopaintings of the gardens from the Sietinen estate, souvenirs from Cris and Kate's travels together. Most Agents didn't have such attachments. This was a real family, and they were split apart.

He took a seat on the chocolate-colored couch in the center of the room facing the viewscreen on the wall.

Kate sat down on the opposite end of the plush sofa. She folded herself inward, arms crossed and gaze distant. "Why are you here?"

"In case you need to talk. Everything happened so fast earlier, and with Cris gone…" *I have to remain objective and think of Wil as the purpose he serves, but he's still someone's son.*

Still, being a part of Wil's life had made Banks care more deeply than his colleagues condoned.

Kate looked away. "Thank you, that's very thoughtful."

"You're not alone," Banks told her. "It might not always show, but Wil and Cris are like family to me. I watched Wil grow up. And, in many ways, Cris is like a son to me, since I never had one of my own. Know that I'm here for you."

Kate stood suddenly and paced to the other side of the room. "You say you care, but you sent Cris on what may very well be a one-way mission."

"Who else could go? There's no one else I trust more." Banks got up and gently placed his hands on her slumped shoulders, tense with worry and fear. He wished there were more he could do to soothe her, but he couldn't get too close. "Cris will find him."

"Meanwhile, there's a traitor among us."

That unfortunate reality had been made all the more apparent by the *Vanquish*'s disappearance. "Have you found anything?" he asked.

Kate shook her head. "I just started my review of the files. It will take time."

*Who knows what other damage could be done in the meantime.* He nodded. "I'm looking into it, too. We'll figure it out."

Kate sniffed back tears. "What does it matter? Cris and Wil are already out there. I'm afraid I'll never see them again."

Banks turned her around and looked her in the eye. "That won't happen."

"I wish I could feel so sure."

"They'll be fine, because they have to be." *They're too important. Their loss would mean the end for us all. It can't come to that.*

— — —

Kate closed the door behind the High Commander. He'd dropped by at an inopportune time, but it would have been rude to turn him away. *It's sweet of him to try to comfort me, but nothing he can say will make this better. I want my husband and son home safely.*

Her initial evaluation of the security logs had yielded some intriguing results—information she wasn't yet ready to share. The breach had to be someone high up in the command ranks, and only a couple dozen people would have the clearance. She and Cris were the only individuals she could rule out with absolute certainty.

No TSS ships aside from the *Vanquish* had left port since Wil's capture and all personnel were accounted for. The traitor was either on board her husband's ship or still inside Headquarters.

Kate restored her work on the viewscreen. There was still much to review.

# CHAPTER 3

IT WAS UTTER darkness. Only the incessant drip of water somewhere in the distance broke through the monotonous black. Wil lay on his back, feeling cold ground beneath him. It was damp and rough—stone, perhaps. He peered around, but could make out no landmarks.

*Where am I?* His head throbbed.

He strained to make sense of his surroundings. The air smelled of mildew and dirt. *A cave?*

Wil ventured a telekinetic probe, but the meager insights were hardly worth the increased pressure in his head. He eased off. The sound of dripping water continued to rhythmically pierce the gloom, its source still a mystery.

He sat up slowly, the force of his headache growing with the elevation. Rubbing his temples, he attempted to ease the pounding. He raised himself into a kneeling position on the hard ground, waiting for his senses to settle.

*I'm alive. Who would capture me, and why?*

A crack of light pierced the darkness. The shock of illumination nearly blinded Wil. A rectangle opened up, as if a door were rising on a far wall. Three large figures stepped forward, silhouetted against the bright light.

Wil stood up and eyed his opponents. *If they wanted to kill me, they would have done it already. Right…?*

The middle silhouetted figure raised an arm parallel with the ground. The air rippled as the paralyzing beam shot toward Wil. Intense pain took his body once more as the world faded.

— — —

Cris stood in the center of his darkened room and gazed through the viewport at the stars. Despite his concern for Wil's safety, he couldn't help but fear for himself and his crew. They were not only venturing into unknown enemy territory, but it would seem someone might not want them on the mission.

The delay caused by the jump drive malfunction—or sabotage, as seemed likely—had given him more time to dwell on what he and his crew were up against. If anything he had been told about the Bakzen over the years was correct, they would soon face a seemingly impenetrable sensor grid known as the Defense Barrier at the border of Bakzeni Territory.

*We can only hope to see a way in once we get there. There's so little I know about the Bakzen…*

Reminded once again of his request to Banks, Cris went to activate the viewscreen above the desk in the corner of his room. *He has to give me something to work with.*

Cris sat down on the edge of his bed across from the screen. "CACI, bring up all files pertaining to the Bakzeni Empire."

In compliance, the viewscreen illuminated with the TSS insignia and the words 'Top Secret' written below it.

"Authorization is required to view these files," CACI stated in the same female voice that was used for the interactive programs around Headquarters. Cris stated his identification number, hoping this time it would yield different results. "Authorization approved."

Cris let out a relieved breath; the approval must have come through before they lost subspace communications.

The viewscreen changed from the TSS insignia to a still figure of a soldier.

The scale next to the Bakzen soldier indicated that it would stand half a head taller than the average Tararian male, and he was more severe-looking than any Taran Cris had ever seen. The figure began rotating, showing off the substantial bone structure beneath rough skin. Completely hairless, and with a slightly orange tint to the skin, the Bakzen soldier looked well-equipped for living a combative life. The soldier's cold, red eyes stared out from the viewscreen.

A sudden chill gripped Cris as he looked at the face of his enemy. He glanced over specifics of Bakzen physiology and was caught by one key detail: they were all clones. *No wonder they can keep ramping up their forces.*

He had CACI move to the next section of the file, which dealt with weapons and defenses. There was a note that the information was mostly speculative.

*Clearly we don't know everything*, he thought, reflecting on the Headquarters break-in. Even if there had been help from the inside, it would still take considerable skill to bypass all of the necessary security checkpoints. The Bakzen file also mentioned spatial transportation, but Cris was disheartened to see old file dates on the information—some as great as twenty years old.

He quickly flipped through several other sections before stopping at the description and image of the infamous Defense Barrier. The Barrier was rumored to be one of the most colossal and intricate structures ever created, and the schematic did its reputation justice. Reports indicated that nothing had ever made it through the sensor grid undetected, and nothing that passed through the Barrier into Bakzen territory came back in one piece—if at all. The file didn't go into the details, but Cris examined the diagram and started thinking through potential weaknesses.

After studying the available data, Cris started to move to the next section, but he was stopped by a message stating that higher authorization was required to access the restricted files. *Stars! What now?*

"CACI, what level clearance is needed to view the restricted files?" he asked.

"Level 10 clearance required. High Commander only."

"What could possibly be in those files that they don't want me to see?"

CACI didn't reply.

"What percentage of files related to the Bakzen does my clearance include?"

"Twenty-eight percent," the computer stated.

*That's hardly anything!* His initial wave of anger was replaced by a feeling of defeat. *Why are they making me go into this blind?*

Cris deactivated the viewscreen and lay back on the bed. He felt completely drained. *What the fok is going on?*

—

Cris awoke to a buzz at the door. He glanced at the clock and saw that an hour and a half had passed. *Either I was more tired than I realized, or Irina tricked me.*

He reluctantly propped himself into a semi-sitting position and muttered, "Come in," under his breath. Scott entered. "What is it?" Cris sat up the rest of the way.

"We're nearing Arnca."

Cris nodded absently.

Scott pulled up a chair so he could sit facing Cris. "You look awful."

"I'm sure I do." Cris ran a hand through his hair, mussing it further. "Fok, how did we get here?"

Scott smiled. "On a starship. Shite, I thought I might have to hold your hand on this mission, but wipe your ass, too?"

Cris sighed and gave his friend a sidelong glare. "Things were really good for a while there."

"Nothing has changed, Cris. We'll find Wil."

Cris swallowed. He wasn't so sure it would ever be the same; he had started to see things for what they were. "I completely failed Wil."

"No one could have seen this coming."

"Banks did." *Even if he didn't outright admit it.*

Scott raised an eyebrow. "What makes you say that?"

Cris leaned forward, resting his elbows on his thighs. "He told me today that Wil is important to the TSS. I don't think he meant it in the way a talented trainee is valuable. He looked terrified—like a vital mission was unravelling before his eyes." He hung his head. "I can't believe I didn't see it before." *Or maybe I just didn't want to see it. I needed to believe I had escaped.*

"See what?"

"I'm not sure, exactly. But, they always pushed Wil more than any other trainee. I think they've been covertly directing him this whole time."

Scott frowned. "Maybe you're reading into it too much. We're all on edge."

"No, I don't think so." The persistent knot in Cris' stomach twisted. *I've let my son be used, just like they've been using me.* "Stars! It was right in front of me, and I did nothing to stop it."

"We don't know anything for sure," Scott soothed. "Let's just get through this. One step at a time."

Cris took a slow breath and nodded. "It's finally becoming clear now. There's something going on with the Bakzen—something they don't want us to know. I should've suspected… All these years, whenever I've mentioned the conflict in the outer realms, Banks has always hedged. But then today, he said that the Bakzen targeted Wil."

Scott tilted his head. "Why would the Bakzen be after him?"

"Exactly. We all know his potential, but how would the Bakzen know any of that? And why would they care?"

"Hmm." Scott crossed his arms and leaned back in the chair.

"And if Wil's so important to the TSS and the Bakzen were specifically after him, then why am I still locked out of seventy-two percent of the files on the Mainframe that reference the Bakzen?"

"What?" Scott looked incredulous.

"I specifically asked Banks for access to all the Bakzen files, and my clearance went from seven percent access to twenty-eight percent."

"That's strange."

Cris searched his friend's face, but he saw no sign of deceit. *At least he's not in on it, too.* "We have to know all the facts for this mission to be successful."

Scott nodded. "I agree. I have no idea why Banks would keep anything from you."

Cris shook his head, at a loss for how to channel his frustration. "Neither do I." Dwelling on unknowns wouldn't save Wil; he had to keep moving forward. Resolute, Cris stood up. "We should get back."

Scott followed Cris to the Command Center. When they arrived, Scott took his seat while Cris remained standing in the center of the room.

"Bring up a map of Arnca with a list of all the major ports and trade posts," Cris instructed.

A slowly rotating planet appeared at the front of the domed room, and it was overlaid with a series of dots and dashes representing landmarks on and above the surface of the planet. He reviewed the map and zoomed in on the holographic projection with his hands. The primary space station was in geosynchronous orbit above a sprawling city in the southern hemisphere.

"Let's dock here," Cris said, highlighting the main space station. "It has a large enough berth, and the city below it is probably our best bet for finding a replacement cell." He turned around to get a second opinion from Scott.

"Agreed," he confirmed.

"I'll take her over," Alec acknowledged.

The *Vanquish* swung around the planet and Alec maneuvered into docking position. Once the clamps had locked onto the hull, Cris used the console next to his chair to contact Engineering.

"Matt," Cris said, "meet me by the main gangway. I need your expertise to identify a suitable replacement cell."

"Yes, sir."

"Let me know right away if anything comes up," Cris told Scott.

"Will do. Good luck."

Cris waited at the top of the gangway, and once Matt arrived they walked together into the foreign spaceport.

The port was like many Cris had encountered in his initial travels on the *Exler* decades before. It was fairly crowded, and the hum of conversation filled the central mall of the station. People dressed in a multitude of clothing styles with a diverse range of physical features made their way through the corridor at a quick tempo. The hall was lined with shops trying to attract patrons with colorful holographic signage and targeted advertising. Such ads picked up on the characteristics of an individual based on the data in each person's handheld, unless it was blocked like the TSS-issued devices.

As Cris and Matt navigated through the port, Cris took advantage of the background din to question his Chief Engineer. "Matt, in your opinion, what kind of spatial drive would be needed to travel from Bakzeni Territory without us knowing?"

Matt looked pensively at the floor. "Well," he began, still in thought, "it would be more advanced than anything we currently have—anything that I know the TSS has, at least. Theoretically, it would have to navigate without beacons, since a beacon keeps records of any ships locking onto its signal." He shrugged. "Why do you ask?"

Cris brushed off the inquiry. "Just curious of what we're up against." He didn't know what to make of it; independent jump drives were an unproven theory. *How could the Bakzen be more advanced than the TSS?*

"Are you sure you're all right, Cris?"

"Just getting down to business." *When I asked for adventure in my life, this isn't what I intended.*

The people in the spaceport appeared to be primarily merchants and freighter captains, which was encouraging to see. Hopefully, it indicated that there would be a wider variety of tech for sale. The crowd kept clear of the duo as they walked through the station, recognizing the distinctive look of an Agent.

Cris and Matt took a transport shuttle down to the surface of the planet. The passengers traveling with a companion whispered to each other as they stared at Cris. He was used to the attention from his travels with Kate and barely noticed.

They were let off the transport near the center of a completely enclosed city. After taking a moment to get oriented, Cris stepped out into the crowd first, gesturing for Matt to follow. "Stay close," he called over the commotion of the other Tarans passing down the street.

"I will. This place is packed," Matt shouted back.

They passed several shops displaying promising equipment, but Cris went by them all. Eventually, he spotted a defunct storefront tucked in a hollow between two especially tall buildings.

Matt looked at the shop with distaste. "Here? Really?"

"Trust me. I know how to pick the shops, but finding the right part is all on you."

Once inside, Matt's initial skepticism was set to rest after a quick glance at the contents. The walls and the pedestals seemingly placed at random around the room boasted an impressive collection of engine components, crystal control matrices, and other such devices.

At the sound of the door closing, the storekeeper came forward from a back storage room. He said something in what Cris took to be a local Arncan dialect.

Cris responded in the galactic standard language, "Can you speak New Taran?"

"Yes, of course," the storekeeper responded with a slightly muddled accent. "May I help you?" He was tall and slim, and he wrung his hands compulsively. Though he bore resemblance to his Taran heritage, like many of the people in the colonies far from Tararia, the Arncans had taken on distinctive features to suit their planet. His skin was a deep brown and his dark eyes seemed especially large.

"We need a power distribution cell for the spatial jump drive of a TSS ship. Or something that we could adapt to our technology," Matt said.

The storekeeper assessed them before responding. "You an Agent?" he asked Cris.

Cris nodded.

"I thought so," the shopkeeper said, eyeing him. "Yes, I have a cell. But such a rare item comes at a high price."

"Show us what you have to offer," Cris said.

The storekeeper grinned. "Right this way."

He led Cris and Matt deeper into the shop, weaving through the aisles to the back left corner. The establishment was much larger than Cris had initially thought.

The storekeeper stopped in front of a pedestal and stood aside, displaying his merchandise. The cell, if it could be called that, looked ancient. "It's from a TSS ship that crashed here many years ago. I got it in an auction. It's the only TSS cell on Arnca."

It didn't even take a telepathic probe for Cris to know the shopkeeper's statement was genuine.

Matt scrutinized the cell. "Would that ship by any chance be the *Infinity*?"

The Arncan nodded, seeming disinterested by the detail.

Matt took a breath. "All this time she was presumed lost in subspace after her test flight."

The shopkeeper perked up with sudden interest. "A rare artifact?" His large eyes gleamed.

Cris wracked his memory for the TSS history he'd learned in classes years before. *Stars, could it really be?*

The TSS *Infinity* had been designed to test a new long-range jump drive with enhanced course-plotting abilities for more efficient travel. If memory served, it was one of the prototypes for the modern jump drives used on all TSS ships.

Cris admired the somewhat neglected cell. “Matt, will this work?”

The engineer eyed the pronged ends of the cell—three connection pins, rather than the five used in modern applications. “It will take some adaptation, but I think it should get the job done.” He pulled Cris aside and whispered, “It’s our best chance. This cell will have a higher capacity than anything from a civilian vessel.”

Cris nodded. “I trust you.”

“I can’t test the specs using my handheld, though,” Matt continued. “These older models don’t have the built-in interface like I’m used to using. I’d need to come back with manual testing equipment.”

“All right. Let’s get what you need.”

“Can we come back to test it?” Matt asked the storekeeper.

“Of course. It is, after all, a historic artifact,” replied the Arncan. “Now, that brings us to the matter of price.”

*The cost just quadrupled from whatever it was going to be.* “Name your price. We need to get going.”

“Well, a product such as this, being the only one in my possession… it is difficult for me to part with it.”

“Name your price,” Cris repeated.

“That depends,” the storekeeper smiled slyly. “How do you want to pay?” He licked his thin lips.

“Would an electronic transfer of Standard Credits be agreeable?” Cris asked.

“Yes, but I would offer a significant discount on physical currency,” the Arncan replied.

“Whichever is fine,” Cris stated, since they had to go back to the ship for testing equipment, anyway.

The shopkeeper rubbed his hands together. “Let’s see, how about 17,000 credits?”

Cris gawked at the price for the single cell, but he would gladly give away the entire Sietinen fortune if it meant being back on the hunt for his son. "That's fi—"

"How about 4,000?" Matt interjected. "It's an antique. There aren't many buyers."

"Few buyers, perhaps, but this cell is part of my personal collection. And in such good condition. Maybe 12,000?" The shopkeeper smiled. It was sport.

Cris picked up on the shopkeeper's enjoyment. *He'll drag this on as long as possible.* "That's—"

"How about 6,500?" Matt countered.

"You drive a hard bargain. The cell means so much to me… But, I suppose for physical payment, I could give you a deal for 7,000."

"That's fine," Cris said before Matt could counter again. "Agreed."

The shopkeeper inclined his head. "Very well."

"We'll come back with your payment and our testing equipment," Cris told the shopkeeper.

He led Matt back to the crowded Arncan street. "You know I could have manipulated him into giving us whatever price we wanted, if it came down to it," he reminded his friend after they were outside.

"Oh, right." Matt looked a little embarrassed. "You Agents and your mind games. So, why didn't you?"

"Because this is his livelihood. It wouldn't do well for TSS relations if he felt like we took advantage of him."

Matt nodded. "Good point. Always the diplomat."

*Whether I like it or not.* "Let's just hope the cell works."

Once back on the *Vanquish*, Cris went to check in with the Command Center and Matt headed down to Engineering to prep his crew, their hope renewed.

Scott, Kari, and Alec were waiting in the Command Center, eager to hear Cris' report. "Well?" they questioned almost in unison when he entered.

Cris smiled with a hint of disbelief. "We wound up with one of the power cells from the TSS *Infinity*."

The two helm officers stared at him open-mouthed, glancing at Scott who showed a more reserved surprise.

"You do mean *the Infinity*?" Alec emphasized. "Then it wasn't ripped apart in subspace, after all. This is really big."

"The engineering team will be thrilled," Kari added.

"I have no idea what happened to the rest of the ship—probably carved up and sold for parts. We still need to test this cell and pay for it," Cris said. "I'll be back soon."

He left the Command Center and went to his quarters. He palmed open a safe tucked into his closet and pulled out credit chips for payment; such physical currency was all but abandoned everywhere except the outermost colonies. Counting the chips, he was reminded of the travels from his youth. Such simpler times.

Cris placed the credit chips in a satchel and made his way through the halls toward the exit hatch. Midway through his trek, Matt approached him.

"We might have a problem," the engineer called out. He was carrying a metal case and had another bag slung over his shoulder.

"What now?" Cris asked

Matt looked grim. "Well, I ran a quick simulation. Our tech is more demanding than the *Infinity*'s. By a lot more than I anticipated. We'll have to use the cell at least twice, obviously, and I don't know if it will hold up."

*Bomax.* "I was worried about that, too." Cris shook his head. "But, we don't have another option. We can't afford the five days to get to the TSS outpost. If we do, it might…"

Matt picked up on the feeling and offered a reassuring nod. "I think we should just go for it."

"Do you want to stay here and keep working on the adaptation? I think I remember how to use a tester." He gestured to the bag over Matt's shoulder.

"No, my engineers are already doing everything they can," Matt said. "Besides, I'll need to mess around with it to get the tester hooked up to the cell. Those bomaxed prongs."

Cris nodded. "All right. Let's go."

They navigated through the crowded streets to the shop. The Arncan storekeeper emerged from the back as soon as they entered. "Ah, you have my payment?" he greeted in New Taran.

"Yes, but first we need to test the cell," Matt said, patting the bag slung over his shoulder.

"I already have it set up for you," the shopkeeper replied. He ushered them toward a metal workbench set up along one of the side walls, tucked behind a display case.

The cell sat on the center of the workbench, surrounded by smaller parts that hadn't found a place on the shelves. It looked even more antiquated since being removed from its display pedestal.

"Have at it, Matt." Cris stood back and let his engineer work.

Matt removed the tester from its bag and examined the clamps that needed to hook onto the cell's connection pins. "I don't know what the fok the designers were thinking," he muttered to himself. "Nothing efficient about it." He grabbed some additional cables from the bag and fiddled with various configurations. Eventually, he settled on a haphazard chain of cables, with the clamps connecting the tester on both ends. "This should be enough to see if it holds a charge…" He flipped on the tester and took a step back.

Cris followed Matt's lead and moved further away.

The cell emitted a low hum and vibrated slightly, rattling the other items on the table. A faint blue glow illuminated either end of the cell near the prongs.

Matt gave it a minute, then stepped forward and examined the readout on the tester. "It's a little sluggish, but that's to be expected after sitting cold for so long. It's improving with each cycle."

"So, it'll work?" Cris asked, trying to keep the impatience out of his tone.

Matt shrugged. "I can't say how long it will hold, but it's a lot better than a dead cell." He turned off the tester and began packing up the equipment.

*Then it will have to do.* Cris turned to the shopkeeper. "Thank you for the chance to examine the equipment. This should settle things." He handed over the credit chips.

The Arncan counted the chips and grinned. "Pleasure doing business with you."

Cris helped Matt place the cell in the hard carrying case, and they hurried back to the *Vanquish.*

Matt stopped in the hall at the top of the gangway. "It'll take some time to rig everything up. Even then, it might not work right away. If I have to troubleshoot, it could take a few more hours."

*Time we don't have.* Cris nodded. "I understand, just work as quickly as you can. But make sure to do a thorough job. I expect to need to make a quick getaway, and we'll need reliable equipment."

Matt looked a little taken aback, being an uncompromising perfectionist at heart. "After the cell is hooked up, there's still the sixteen-hour initialization sequence to recalibrate the drive."

"We can't wait that long. We have to do a quick start," Cris insisted.

Matt looked appalled. "You can't be serious? The drive is completely cold, and adding to that an antique distribution cell… The entire jump drive could blow!"

Cris shook his head. "It will be fine. We've done it before. Granted, not with an old cell, but it will hold."

Matt still looked upset. "Okay," he conceded. "I'll get started on the modifications."

# CHAPTER 4

BANKS FELT COMPLETELY helpless. Six hours had passed since the last contact with the *Vanquish* and her crew. All attempts to locate the ship through long-range sensors had thus far been unsuccessful, and the breadth of space to search was so expansive that without a specific target area, there was a negligible chance of finding them anytime soon.

Cris had to be okay. Kate would have said something if she felt he was in distress—she could feel him through their bond, regardless of distance. Banks knew that Cris was perfectly capable of looking out for those under his command, but the lack of contact was still concerning, especially given the imperative mission.

For the time being, all Banks could do was stare at the viewscreen on his office wall as the scanners continued to search for any ships with a signal remotely close to that of the *Vanquish.*

Banks was pulled from his thoughts when Arron Haersen barged into his office. Banks had never particularly liked the Mission Coordinator, but they maintained a cordial enough working relationship. Haersen was opinionated and defensive on his best days—others joked it was due to his small stature—but he had a knack for finding solutions that no one else saw. Though his Course Rank was low for a Sacon Agent, his exceptional management skills were what made him excel in his position.

"What is it, Haersen?" Banks asked.

"Communications picked up an interesting transmission from a small planet in Sector 14 called Arnca," Haersen stated. "They were chatting with a sister planet about a visit from the TSS. However, we have no known ships in the area."

"When was the transmission sent?"

"A couple of hours ago," Haersen replied, "and then another just came through stating that the TSS ship was still there."

"It's a solid lead." Banks crossed his arms. "Were you able to confirm the ship's presence?"

Haersen frowned. "We scanned all around Arnca, but we couldn't find any undocumented ships on the communications network. The radio chatter is only about visual accounts of the vessel."

"Maybe something went wrong and they had to stop for repairs. I guess we'll have to wait it out."

Haersen's face twitched. "Is there anything else for now, sir?"

Banks shook his head and sighed. "No, thank you. Well done picking up the message. Just keep me posted."

"Yes, sir."

— — —

Cris couldn't take the waiting any longer. "I'm going to see how Matt's doing," he told Scott and rose from his command chair. *Every minute we're delayed, the greater the danger to Wil.*

"They must be close by now," his friend replied.

"Hopefully." They'd been out of communication for far too long. He needed to get in touch with Headquarters.

Cris took the lift down to the mechanical level near the bottom of the *Vanquish.* The lift opened to a long hall that passed through the containment bulkheads separating the various environmental and propulsion systems. The main Engineering room was positioned at the aft of the ship, so Cris had to walk nearly half the length of the vessel to reach his destination. He palmed open the double door at the end of the hall.

The doors parted to the side, revealing the heart of the ship. Control panels for every system in the ship covered the side walls, and access tubes to the main conduits of the jump drive framed either end of the room. In the center of the open space, a massive table with a holographic display projected a rendering of the *Vanquish* with the status of all structural and mechanical components.

Directly across from the door, at the back of the room, was the distribution relay for the PEM. Matt and his engineers were huddled around the cluster of cells, testing readings via their tablets.

"We're still working on it," Matt said with barely a glance up from his tablet. "I'm having to learn the new system on the fly. There's stuff in here I've never seen before."

"How long until we can restore subspace communications?" Cris asked. He had seen Matt pull off some impressive repairs on the fly in their time together, but nothing quite so critical as a patched distribution cell.

Matt sighed. "Communications?" He scratched his head. "I might be able to get you a basic comm channel in a few minutes, but it won't be terribly secure or robust. Just a data burst."

*That's better than nothing. Banks needs to know we're okay.* "I'll take anything I can get."

"Okay. Consider it done." Matt went back to work.

Cris shifted on his feet. "Do you need anything?"

Matt lowered his tablet. "No, it's just slow going. We can work faster if you aren't staring over our shoulders."

Cris retreated. "Of course. Thank you, Matt. Everyone. You're pulling off a miracle here."

There were nods of acknowledgement from some engineers, but most were too engrossed in their calibrations to even notice Cris' presence.

"We're not done yet." Matt looked back at his tablet. "No, we can't bypass that relay," he said to one of his engineers. "Cris, you'll have temporary communications by the time you get back to the Command Center. I'll need to reset everything when we do the final initialization sequence for the jump drive, but send whatever messages you need to until then."

Cris nodded and left them to their work. *It's a good thing he came along. I don't think anyone else would have been able to adapt an antique cell this quickly.* He took the lift back to the Command Center.

"We should have—" Cris began as he entered.

"Communications are back online!" Kari beamed.

*Good job, Matt.* "Alec, what will be our transit time to the border of Bakzeni Territory?"

Alec referenced the navigation console. "It's just a guess from the nav simulations, but it should be around five and a half hours."

*At least we'll be on the move again soon.* Cris sat back down in his command chair. "Send a message to Headquarters. Say we were delayed and are back on track."

"Do you want me to add any specifics?" Kari asked.

It wasn't wise to share too much until they knew more about the security breach. "Not yet."

"Okay." Kari made a few quick entries on her console. "Message sent."

Cris settled back into his chair. *Now we wait.*

— — —

Wil awoke in a dimly lit room. He was strapped to a metal chair welded to the smooth metallic floor. It was a bleak space—cramped, sterile and devoid of any adornment. Directly in front of him was a door recessed in the riveted wall. Only a single grated duct served for ventilation. Even if he were able to free himself from the chair and thin wire binding his hands behind his back, there would be no covert way to escape from the chamber.

His head still throbbed. Through the fog, he was also aware of an ache along the back of his left hip. *I guess I hit the ground pretty hard. Next time they're going to knock me out, I may as well sit down first.*

A harsh buzzer sounded. Wil tensed.

The door shot up into the ceiling, revealing two tall, muscular men in tan uniforms. They stepped through the threshold into the room. Both were bald and had severe jaws with their lips downturned in a constant scowl. Wil might have taken them for Taran from a distance, but the orange tint to their rough skin and red eyes had an alien quality. One soldier appeared to have some kind of rank indicator on his uniform.

Wil shrank into the chair as the door closed. *Stars! Who are they?* He felt very alone. *What do I do?*

One of the burly men, apparently a security guard, remained next to the door. The man with the rank mark on his jacket walked forward until he was several paces in front of Wil. A deep scar ran from his right eyebrow to midway down his cheek.

"We meet again, young Dragon," the officer said in New Taran. "I hope you've been preparing yourself for a long and painful death." He grinned with malice at his bound prisoner.

*Is he the one who attacked me?* Wil reached out with a cautious telepathic probe and sensed the same power that had chilled him during his attack. *Does he want to torture me for information, or just for entertainment?*

He fought to maintain his composure. The last thing he needed was his captors sensing any fear. "I won't go down easily." Wil's cerulean eyes met the sorrel of the soldier's.

"You'll need more than determination to stay alive."

"I have much more than that." Wil attempted a smile to go along with the remark, but it came out more like a grimace.

The soldier assessed Wil, his eyes narrow with loathing. "It's hard to believe that you will be the Primus Elite."

He swallowed. *How do they know who I am?*

"I'm Colonel Tek of the Bakzen," the officer stated.

*The Bakzen!* Wil shook his head, not wanting to believe. If the Bakzen had captured him, the war wasn't just imminent—it had already begun. *Shite. What do they want with me?*

In his shock, Wil was slow to connect his recent experience with what he'd been told about their mysterious adversaries beyond the edge of Taran space. Slowly, the realization came to him.

*The Bakzen have telekinetic abilities.* That fact had never been mentioned in any of the briefings.

Tek leaned closer so he was eye-level with Wil. "Oh, yes. We're all much stronger than you anticipated. Perfection of an already superior race is a wonderful thing."

Wil could sense the soldier's intense presence in his mind, offering no respect for privacy in the way the TSS instilled in its Agents. It took everything for Wil to not cower in his chair. He'd never been around anyone with such strong abilities. Based on what he'd seen so far, he estimated that Tek could probably take on five Primus Agents without difficulty.

*Keep it together.* Wil centered his mind. "Don't underestimate my ability."

"So young and foolish. Soon you will learn your place."

"You may be surprised." Without thinking, Wil summoned up all his energy and sent a direct telepathic stream to the colonel. The intensity of it continued to grow as his captor assessed it with his own mind. Knowing that it wasn't wise to push himself too close to his straining point, Wil released the tension building between them. If he was to get out alive, he needed to act like he knew exactly what he was doing.

"Impressive. I'm surprised that you could handle that much already—more than 8. Maybe you *are* stronger than we thought." Tek faltered for the first time.

"And growing stronger." Wil managed a real smile; he hadn't realized he could handle that much. *He's calling my bluff.*

Tek sneered. "I would relish the chance to face you one day in a true test of spirit and wills, not like our trivial sparring earlier."

"A battle of telekinesis?"

"Indeed. The greatest of battles. I don't believe you've even begun to live up to your full potential."

"No, I haven't. What you've seen of me was hardly a fair fight."

"A true warrior is always prepared. I couldn't resist the opportunity earlier to see how you handle yourself, and why everyone seems to think you're so special. I can't say I was impressed."

He swallowed, barely able to keep a straight face. "Then we'll have to see what I can really do." *Stars! I'm not ready for that. He knows his limits, but I don't.*

In an instant, Tek rounded on him, his eyes locked on Wil's.

Telepathic spears shot into Wil's mind, an iron maiden closing around him. His vision exploded into a dark purple electrical storm. The spears burned as they drove in him, leaving his skin on fire. A cry of agony was trapped in his throat as he convulsed against the onslaught. It was too much to take. No escape—

The spears vanished.

"You have a long way to go, Dragon," Tek stated as he backed away.

Wil panted. His wrists stung from where the wires had dug in as he struggled against them.

"As much as I'd like to keep playing, my commander has other plans for you."

Wil blinked hard, woozy from the assault. He took a deep breath and his mind started to clear. *Plans for me? It would almost be more reassuring if they just wanted me dead.* "When will I meet this commander?"

"In time," Tek replied.

*I have to get out of here!*

— — —

Kate nestled into the couch in her living room as she examined the results from her cross-reference analysis. Her quarters now felt like the only safe place she could be, knowing there was a traitor inside Headquarters.

The results supported her initial findings: the mole was definitely in the TSS command ranks. And with some of the original list ruled out, the remaining list was frighteningly short. *How could any of them do this?*

The Agents and senior Militia officers were all old friends. Family, really. Some had trained her, others had been her classmates. They'd been through battles together and celebrated the happiest moments in her life. Yet, she had to remain objective. The encrypted communication logs buried deep within the TSS Mainframe meant someone was talking to a contact outside the TSS and didn't want anyone to know about it.

She released a shaky breath, possibilities swirling in her mind. *Someone we know and trust helped the Bakzen capture Wil.* She fought against a sudden surge of rage that threatened to cloud her mind. *I need to get to the bottom of this.*

Still, Kate wasn't sure how to proceed. Eight names, and Banks was one of them.

— — —

Cris was restless. The hours of waiting for Matt to finish the jump drive modifications felt like an eternity. *How much longer is this going to take?*

He stood up from his command chair to pace the room.

Alec, Kari, and Scott looked equally anxious.

"They have to be getting close," Scott ventured.

"I'm sure it's more complicated than it seems." Cris crossed his arms, then immediately uncrossed them. There was no way to get comfortable. *What's taking so long?*

"We just lost communications again," Kari reported.

"Maybe they finally got the right combination." Cris bit his lower lip. There'd already been a least a dozen resets, and each time had ended in disappointment.

The tension in the room was palpable as they waited for the navigation and communications systems to come back online. After three minutes of anxious anticipation, there was a brief flash as the controls refreshed.

Alec looked over his console. He beamed. "The PEM is back online! We have full jump drive and subspace communications access."

*Thank the stars!* Cris collapsed into his chair. "Get our course locked in."

"Aye." Alec got to work.

There was a buzz at the center console. Cris accepted. "Command Center."

"Everything look good on your end?" Matt asked over the intercom.

"Whatever it is, they don't pay you enough," Cris replied.

"Be sure to note that in my next performance review." Matt paused. "Now, for the record, I must again state that I advise against a quick start of the jump drive."

"Noted." Cris took a deep breath. *At least if it blows, we'll be obliterated before we know something went wrong.* "Kari, let Headquarters know we're on our way. Alec, head out when ready." He ended the communication with Engineering.

"Course locked in," Alec said. "Let's hope this jump is less eventful than the last."

— — —

The message from the *Vanquish* was simple: >>Jumping now. Talk to you on the other side.<< It was everything Banks needed to know for the time being.

*Thank the stars they're back on course!* He breathed a deep sigh, the weight lifted from his chest. *But what am I going to tell Cris when he inevitably asks me why all this is happening?*

Banks lay down on the couch in the center of his office, a new unease taking hold. He stretched out and stared up at the plain, light-gray ceiling and tried to clear his mind. *I really should install an overhead holoprojector. I spend enough here.*

Letting out a long breath that was almost a groan, he took off his tinted glasses and rubbed his eyes with the heels of his hands. *Everything could fall apart at any moment. I can't avoid it.*

He shifted on the couch but couldn't find a satisfactory position. What had started as a dull ache in his gut had grown into a queasy sickness that had left an acrid taste in the back of his throat. The more he tried to suppress the feeling, the more the underlying thoughts intruded his mind.

*They're heading straight into a war zone and don't even know it.* Admitting the reality only intensified the feeling. Banks wrapped his arms around himself and pressed into the couch. *The enemy has the Cadicle—our Primus Elite. Without him, we've lost the war.*

It was too much to accept. There was hope; there had always been hope. The Primus Elite would turn the tide in the war and finally give them the edge they needed. Not right away—it had been such a long time to wait for everything to come into place—but it was finally coming together. Another decade and it could have been over. But without him… *There's nothing we can do.*

Banks knew he needed to tell the others about what had happened. The Primus Elite's capture changed everything. *But telling them means I've given up on Cris, too. I can't do that. Not yet.*

He sat up and took a deep breath. *There's still a chance.*

A buzz at the door startled Banks. He rose to his feet and quickly restored his tinted glasses. "Come in."

Haersen entered, carrying a tablet. "Hello, sir. I finished my secondary review of the entry logs like you requested."

*Right, we still have a traitor among us.* Banks suppressed a wave of nausea. "Did you find anything?"

"How much do you know about Matt Nomalor?" Haersen asked.

"He's a fantastic engineer. Exemplary record. Cris always spoke highly of him."

Haersen nodded slowly. "Do you know why he left the *Vanquish* previously?"

Banks shook his head. "I don't recall. I know he took some remote assignment. I hadn't seen him for several years until he volunteered for the rescue mission."

"His return this morning struck me as more than a coincidence. I looked into where he's been stationed in the Kaldern System, and it's near some of the newer reports of Bakzen activity." Haersen brought up a holographic map on his tablet and showed it to Banks.

"That doesn't prove anything."

"No, but it starts to look suspicious when his arrival at the spaceport corresponds with the timing of the break-in to Headquarters," Haersen continued. "He volunteered for the mission, and then there was a mechanical system failure on his watch."

Banks crossed his arms. "Sabotaging a ship he's on?" *That doesn't make any sense.*

"Well, that part might just be an unfortunate coincidence," Haersen conceded. "The ship hadn't been through thorough field testing since the maintenance. Any number of things could have gone wrong."

"Still, the rest…"

"Sir, it does fit," Haersen continued. "He returned just in time to help the Bakzen gain access to Headquarters, and then immediately got on a ship that will take him directly to his conspirators."

"It's all circumstantial." *Are they being led into a trap? Stars! Who can we trust?*

"Circumstantial evidence is all we have, sir," Haersen said. "The logs were all wiped. And top Militia credentials and the right engineering know-how are what it would take to do that."

*I still can't believe Matt would work with the Bakzen. If he could be turned, so could anyone.* "What would be the motivation? I don't see it."

Haersen shook his head. "I couldn't begin to speculate. Sometimes it's surprising how little is needed to put a person over the edge."

*Too many improbable things have happened to rule anything out.* "I'll pass on the information to Cris. It's his friend, his crew. We can't do anything from here."

Haersen looked unsure. "Can you really trust him to make those kinds of tough decisions?"

"He's trying to rescue his son. If that isn't enough motivation, then nothing is."

# CHAPTER 5

WIL WAS DIRECTED to a small, plain cell with concrete walls. He rubbed his sore wrists. There was a thin red line around each from the wire binding, but the marks were already fading.

The cell resembled the interrogation room, but it had a barred front. Across the central walkway, the other cells contained prisoners who were empty husks of their former selves. Most rocked back and forth muttering under their breath, and many were immobile—simply curled up with their back toward the cell door. The air was dank and the lighting was dim, but Wil caught an occasional glance from the more lucid prisoners. Their gazes were filled with pure dread.

*How long can I last before they break me, too?*

Wil looked over his own cell and was surprised to see his handheld placed at the center of the slab-like platform functioning as a bed along the side wall. Cautiously, he picked it up. The factory seal along the back panel had been breached and all wireless functionalities had been disabled.

*Probably installed a tap to listen to me.* He was about to destroy the device entirely, or at least chuck it outside his cell, but then he remembered the other object he had been carrying.

He casually slid his hand into his pocket and felt the thin strip of film he'd grabbed from his electrochemistry class for some experimenting after hours; it had explosive properties if exposed to the right electric charge. The film was stuck to the pocket lining and must have gone unnoticed.

*I should hold onto both of these. They're the only tools I have to help me escape.* He pretended to just be scratching an itch on his leg.

He sat down on the bed platform. It was a futile exercise to get comfortable, especially with his already sore hip.

Moving to the far end of the platform, he tried to stay out of view at the back of the cell. He was hungry and thirsty and at a complete loss for what to do. Despite all his training on how to handle diplomatic situations, no one had ever thought to inform him on how to conduct himself if he were ever captured by an enemy.

Though he had learned years before how to take care of himself, Wil desperately wanted someone to give him guidance. He had no way of knowing if anyone would come looking for him, or if they even knew he was missing.

*The Bakzen won't let me live much longer, no matter what they have planned for me. And there's no way I could ever survive a duel with Colonel Tek, if it does come to that. Stars! I hope someone comes for me…* Wil caught himself. *No, I can't rely on others. I have only myself.*

Wil detected a presence in front of his cell. He looked up and was dismayed to see a Bakzen soldier watching him.

"General see you now," the soldier announced. His New Taran was barely intelligible.

Wil did a double-take. The soldier looked identical to the guard in the interrogation room, but his uniform and a small scar above his right eye marked him as a different individual.

The soldier opened the door and beckoned for Wil to come out.

Wil didn't move from his perch. "What do you want from me?"

"Come now," the guard said, yanking on Wil with a telekinetic rope.

Wil slid down the bed, caught off-guard. He gained control and managed to land on his feet. *Stars, even the guards have telekinetic abilities!*

As soon as Wil passed through the cell doorway, three more Bakzen soldiers came to stand behind him as the original took the lead. They all bore strong physical resemblance to the first.

Wil stared at them with wonder. They were too similar to just be related. *Clones?* He had never seen one before, since cloning whole bodies was banned in the Taran worlds, though he'd occasionally thought it would be handy to have a second self to help him out.

The guards initiated an invisible barrier around Wil. It wasn't a strong field—Wil assessed he could break through it if he tried—but its very presence was baffling. *Clones with telekinetic abilities. Shite.*

Wil was led through a massive compound. Unlike TSS Headquarters, the Bakzen had not made the slightest attempt at giving their facility a homey feel. Rather than carpeted corridors adorned with art, only riveted metal walls and concrete floors stretched the length of the hallway.

The small procession reached a door marked with a golden insignia Wil didn't recognize. Wil was thrust through the riveted doorway and the guards filed in behind him.

A Bakzen soldier wearing a uniform decorated with a multitude of colored ribbons watched Wil enter, a slight curl to his lips. He sat behind a metal desk with an inlaid touchscreen, which reminded Wil of the furnishings found in the captain's quarters on a TSS cruiser.

Wil glared at him. He could feel the soldier's power—perhaps not quite on Tek's level, but close. Wil put up what mental guards he could, but he doubted his ability to hold the block against an attack from such an opponent.

After eyeing each other for a minute, the Bakzen soldier broke the silence. "So, you're to be the Tararian Selective Service's beloved Primus Elite Agent?" Like Tek, he spoke New Taran well. He looked to be older than Tek and had slightly softer features, though he had the same piercing red eyes and rough skin of the other Bakzen soldiers.

Wil didn't say anything, and instead tilted his head a little and narrowed his eyes more in response. *They seem to know about me. But why do they care?*

The soldier looked him over thoughtfully. "I'm General Carzen," he announced, "and I control your fate. Are you clear on that, Dragon?"

*What's with this 'Dragon' name? Tek called me that, too.* "Yes, General Carzen. Very clear."

The general evaluated him with a hint of approval. "Perhaps you can be turned to our side after all."

*So that's what this is about!* Wil came to attention. "I'm listening."

General Carzen looked to the four guards hovering around Wil. "You may leave now."

The guards hesitated for a moment, unsure if it was wise to leave a sworn enemy alone with their commander, but they backed out of the room. The last one closed the door telekinetically with a flip of his wrist.

General Carzen redirected his attention to Wil. "Please, sit down." He gestured at an unadorned chair in front of his desk.

Wil sat down after a slight pause. *There's no way I can trust him, no matter what he says.*

Carzen cleared his throat. "First of all, I would like to apologize to you for the… unfriendly nature of your capture."

*Apologize?*

"I'm afraid that it was Colonel Tek's idea," Carzen continued. "He is boastful and wanted to prove that he was skillful enough to get through the TSS' defenses. But I can't argue with the methods, since it did get you here unharmed and in a timely manner. You aren't hurt, are you?" Carzen appeared to be genuinely concerned.

Wil's head still felt a little fuzzy from Tek's assault earlier. "Nothing serious." His stomach growled right on cue.

General Carzen smiled, a foreign emotion on the man's severe face.

*It's all an act to win me over.*

"Food, of course. My colleagues are not known for their hospitality with our guests. I'm afraid we don't have much variety to offer."

*Now I'm a 'guest'?* "Well, I'll take my meal un-poisoned, preferably."

Carzen smirked. "Poisoning you would be counterproductive. If I wanted you dead, I could already kill you with my mind."

Wil shifted in his chair. Having no doubt it was true.

"I hope we can build a mutually beneficial relationship," Carzen continued. He input a message on the touchscreen surface of his desktop. "A meal is being prepared."

"I'm surprised you would want me on 'your side'. You know, of course, how the TSS regards the Bakzen—I assumed those feelings were mutual."

"Most do feel that way," the general replied. "But I have opted for an alternative approach."

Wil forced a polite smile. "I've never had the opportunity to see things from another perspective."

Carzen nodded. "It is that alternate perspective I wish to give you. What they have undoubtedly told you is nowhere near the truth."

"There are subjective elements to truth sometimes."

"I'm talking about facts!" The general's face flushed. "They treat us like we're the monsters, but they made us this way."

Wil instinctively pressed back into his chair to distance himself from the Bakzen commander. "Whatever sparked this conflict, there's always a chance for resolution."

"Some wounds can't be healed so easily. To have one's existence denied…" The general's demeanor changed. He was hurt, vulnerable.

Of what little Wil had been told about the Bakzen, Tek embodied that characterization. Carzen, however, was quite different. Wil didn't know what to make of it, but he was intrigued enough to hear what the general had to say. "What do you want with me?"

"Despite everything our people have been through, a part of me still hopes there can be a peaceful end to our conflict."

"If you want me to set up a meeting with the High Commander, I—"

"Oh, Dragon, this runs much deeper than that," Carzen interjected. "Your High Commander is a menial cog. What I seek to exploit is your unique position between the TSS and Tararia."

Wil swallowed. "What of it?"

"You mean far too much to the Priesthood for them to ignore us while you're under our care. If they want their precious Cadicle, they'll need to face what they did to us."

Wil hesitated. *The Priesthood? I thought he meant the High Dynasties.* "I don't know what you're talking about. I steer far away from the Priesthood. And I'm certainly not some sort of mythical savior, or whatever their old doctrine is about."

"Have they kept you so sheltered from your true self? You don't know your own destiny."

*My destiny? He's crazy!* "General, I acknowledge that there is still much I don't know about myself. But that…" *How do I begin to reason with a crazy person?*

"You can deny it now, but you'll eventually have to face who you are. The question you have to ask yourself is, who do you want guiding you—your peers, or the broken remnants?"

*Shite! He really is completely out of his mind. Maybe the cloning messes with their heads.* Wil decided to deflect the question. "I aspire to excel in everything I do."

"Then you should seriously consider what the Bakzen can offer you—" The desktop illuminated with a buzz at the door. "Come in."

The door swung open and a Bakzen soldier entered with a plate of bland-looking food on a metal tray. He silently set the tray down on Carzen's desk in front of Wil, then backed out of the room and closed the door.

"Please, eat," Carzen said.

Wil eyed the plate. *Suddenly I'm not hungry.*

The food looked to be reconstituted nutrition blocks mashed into a thick paste. Field rations at their worst. There was no smell to it, and the taupe color didn't instill confidence that the taste would be any more appetizing.

*Do I risk it?* The general did make a valid point that poisoning him wouldn't make sense after the amount of effort to get him here. Furthermore, he'd been unconscious for long enough that they could have already given him anything they wanted to covertly distribute, so it was unlikely this meal was anything other than what it seemed.

Reluctantly, Wil picked up the spoon next to the plate and grabbed a bite of the goop. The texture was somewhat slimy but bearable, and the vaguely potato-like flavor was less offensive than he had feared. "Thank you, General."

"I imagine it is not the fine cuisine you're used to, but we have no need for those luxuries."

Wil took another bite, his appetite growing with the access to sustenance. "I'm grateful for your generosity."

"Do you patronize me?"

"No! You have a generosity of spirit," Wil replied, pausing his eating. "Others might have considered me the enemy, but you have sought to find common ground between us."

"I can tell you're skeptical of my offer."

"Surprised more than skeptical. But you can't blame me, given the tension between our people." Wil downed a few more spoonfuls of his meal.

"You know nothing of the conflict."

"Then tell me."

Carzen shook his head. "You aren't ready to hear it. As much as you're pretending to listen, you think I'm crazy."

*Is it that obvious?* Wil set down his spoon, the plate mostly empty. "I'm sorry. I'm trying. But you're asking me to question the only reality I've ever known without giving me any details."

"I think you need some time to let this settle," Carzen stated.

"Sure." No amount of time would change the fact that the old soldier was out of his mind, but the longer Wil could play along, the greater his chances for figuring out a way to escape.

Carzen nodded. "I'm glad we had a chance to talk. You have so much potential, I hope you can be open-minded."

"I'll try."

"We'll talk again soon." Carzen tapped his desktop, and a moment later the door opened. "Take care, Dragon."

— — —

General Carzen watched Wil walk out of his office. Their conversation had not gone like he planned, but it was progress. His captive was more defiant than he had anticipated, and it was clear he had been highly trained in diplomacy. But, the young man's telekinetic prowess was his focus.

At the rate he was improving, the Primus Elite was well on his way to becoming a powerful Agent. Carzen's fear was that he was already too far into the ways of the TSS to sway his allegiance. All he could do was hope it was not true, and that Colonel Tek did not suspect the same thing.

As soon as the thought crossed his mind, Tek barged through the office door, looking annoyed. "I heard that you had a rather overconfident meeting with our hostage," Tek grimaced, then as an afterthought added, "General."

"You were informed correctly, Colonel Tek," replied Carzen. "I see nothing wrong with testing the waters for an alliance. How else do you expect to gain his trust?"

"Just remember who he is."

"He poses no immediate threat, Colonel," Carzen countered. If Tek went against him, all of his carefully thought-out plans might be ruined. He wasn't about to let that happen.

"Sir, I'm just saying that—"

"You have made yourself perfectly clear, Colonel. I know what I'm doing."

"But everything is at stake! I just don't want to see anything go wrong after all we've worked for," Tek implored. Though his intentions might not parallel Carzen's, they relied on the same variables.

Carzen eyed Tek. "Everything is under control, Colonel. Save your concern for a more desperate time." Carzen leaned back in his chair, all the while watching Tek to see if he would try to test the boundaries of the order again.

Tek fumed, but he kept his anger and frustration in check. "Yes, of course, sir," he muttered through gritted teeth.

"Was there anything else?" questioned Carzen.

Tek paused before answering. "Yes. As I'm sure you noticed, he's much stronger than we expected. Is your plan even feasible if he's—"

"That's quite enough, Colonel," General Carzen snapped. "I thought that I had made it clear that it's not your concern. We've already made appropriate modifications to the plan."

"Yes, sir."

"If that's all, you're dismissed." Carzen gave a slight wave of his hand as he sat up straighter in his chair.

Tek opened his mouth as if to say something more but instead walked out the door.

Carzen let out a long breath. Tek was becoming a problem that required an immediate remedy. All plans depended on complete cooperation.

— — —

Wil was escorted back to his small cell, relieved that there didn't appear to be immediate plans to kill him. That gave him hope for a rescue or chance to escape.

However, Tek appeared to have different motives than the general. *I need to be careful.*

Wil leaned against the cool wall at the back of the cell and closed his eyes. He was drained from the activities of the past day, and his full stomach made him feel sleepy. He ran a hand through his hair, which was feeling greasy after two days without a shower.

As exhausted as he was, he was still too on-edge to completely relax. He knew that he would have to sleep eventually, even though he didn't trust the Bakzen not to run in and attack him the moment he let his guard down. Then again, they could hit him with the stun gun again, so he was at a disadvantage either way.

Wil shifted to a marginally more comfortable position on the slab bed. As he rolled over, he caught sight of an irregularity in the far corner of the otherwise smooth ceiling.

Careful not to look directly at it, Wil assessed the object from the corner of his eye. A camera. *Great, I'm being watched.*

He didn't know what the Bakzen had planned for him, but he was ready to do anything he could to survive.

— — —

Kate's stomach rumbled, pulling her from her thoughts.

She had hit a wall with her investigation. The encrypted communication logs on the Mainframe were expertly handled. She knew how to identify such records, but she wasn't a cryptologist. Wil could probably figure it out, or Haersen maybe, but it appeared that more than one person was conspiring—or, at least, one person talking with multiple outsiders. Say something to the wrong person and she'd be vulnerable without knowing who to turn to for backup.

She cleared the desktop with a swipe of her hand. *Time for a break.*

Kate made the short trek from her quarters to the mess hall on the opposite side of Level 2. The halls were relatively empty at that evening hour, with most Agents and trainees retired to their rooms for the night.

Only a dozen Agents and three Junior Agents were in the mess hall when she arrived. The main buffet had been cleared for the night, but refrigerated cases next to the entry door held meals packaged from the day's leftovers. She grabbed one of the transparent containers.

As she closed the door to the refrigerator, Banks entered the mess hall.

He looked startled to see Kate at first, then smiled in greeting. "I guess I'm not the only one to miss dinner."

"I didn't realize how late it'd gotten."

Banks grabbed a meal for himself from the case. "Were you..."

"Yes, I've been looking into the security logs," Kate replied and she stepped over to the warming tray to heat her food.

Banks glanced over at the other occupants in the mess hall. *"Have you found anything?"* he asked Kate telepathically.

"I'm still looking into it," she replied aloud, closing her mind to any further questioning. *I want to trust Banks, but no one is above suspicion. He has so many locked files... he's hiding something.*

"Kate, why are you shutting me out?" Banks asked in a low voice.

"I'll let you know if I find anything conclusive," Kate responded, grabbing her warmed food.

Banks chuckled and he set his food in the warming tray. "You don't suspect me, do you?"

Kate hesitated. "I don't know what to think. You have a lot of encrypted communications and files tied to your account."

"Well yes, I'm the High Commander."

"I need to be thorough."

Banks sighed. "And I appreciate that, but don't waste your time looking into me."

"Then what are those weekly calls to Tararia all about?" Kate questioned.

The High Commander retrieved his own warmed meal. "Official business."

"With whom?"

"That's not important."

Kate glared at him. "Then why won't you tell me?"

"Fine, finish your investigation," Banks said. "I can't order you to trust me. Do what you need to do." He spun around and stomped out of the mess hall.

*He'd do the same thing in my position.* Kate doubted he was working with the Bakzen, but there was something he didn't want her to know. The conversation confirmed that her suspicion wasn't unfounded, if not for the right reasons.

Kate took her meal and returned to her quarters. Once back at her computer, she wrote a message to Cris: >>Banks is hiding something. Find out what.<<

# CHAPTER 6

"WE'RE HERE," ALEC announced as the blue-green shroud of subspace dissipated.

*Finally.* Cris took in their new surroundings on the viewscreen. They were still too far from the Defense Barrier to see it, but they'd be able to make an accurate technical assessment from this distance.

"Orders, sir?" Alec asked.

Cris' handheld pinged with a new message as subspace communications came back online. He checked the device, seeing a note from Kate—an echo of his own growing suspicions. "Call up Headquarters. Get Banks," he instructed.

Kari activated the comm link. The image of the High Commander appeared at the front of the domed room.

"Cris, what happened?" Banks was clearly trying to appear calm, but not quite succeeding. "We heard chatter that you were near Arnca?"

"Yes. Our jump drive malfunctioned—somehow lost the beacon locks. A distribution cell blew in the process," Cris explained. "We managed to find a replacement cell on Arnca. Oddly enough, it's from the TSS *Infinity*."

"The *Infinity*? Interesting…" Banks withdrew in thought.

*Time to get some answers.* Cris eyed him. "Hold on. I'm going to transfer the communication."

Scott gave Cris an approving nod as he got up to go to his private office directly off the Command Center.

Cris brought up the video feed on the holoprojector above his desk. Banks looked concerned.

"First," Cris said, "have you made any progress on identifying the source of the security breach?"

"Nothing solid." Banks looked uncomfortable. "Cris, do you trust Matt?"

Cris almost laughed. "Matt? Matt is your lead?"

"Kate has her sights on me for some ridiculous reason. But Matt… there's some circumstantial evidence—"

"Well, you're looking in the wrong place," Cris said. "I can see how he'd have the right access, but it's not him. I've looked into his eyes, Banks. I'd see it if he was deceiving me. I'd sooner believe it was Scott or you, because at least then I'd be up against the mental guards of an Agent." *None of them would go after Wil, would they?*

"If it's an Agent, then it could be anyone."

Cris looked down. "Or more than one person."

Banks sighed. "I wish I had an answer for you. But it isn't me and I don't know who."

Cris paused, staring levelly at the High Commander. "But there's something you're not telling me."

"Concerning what?" Banks set his jaw.

"Concerning everything! Since I left Tararia, I've picked up little hints here and there. I don't know if it's all connected, but it's clear that you know more about the Bakzen—and this mission—than you're letting on. It's time you tell me, Jason." It had been a long time since Cris had called the High Commander by his first name, but he needed something to let Banks know that he wasn't about to back down.

Banks winced. "I've tried to protect you and your family, Cris. I really have."

"Just tell me what this is all about!"

Banks stood abruptly and paced in a circle. "Fine," he said at last. "You're right. You need context if you're going to get Wil back." He took an unsteady breath. "The TSS is already at war with the Bakzen."

The statement was absurd. *At war?*

Cris was about to push back and demand the truth, but Banks' level stare stopped him. Cris swallowed, suddenly unsure. "I thought war was years away, if it would happen at all. I haven't seen any reports, budget—"

The High Commander shook his head. "You wouldn't. There's a separate division."

*A separate division of the TSS?* He eased into the desk chair. "Is this a recent development?"

Banks rounded his shoulders. "Far from it." He shook his head and grimaced. "The Bakzen conflict has been going on for hundreds of years. Intermittent, but a constant threat."

Cris' head swam. "How is that possible? I would have seen something—"

"Jotun," Banks replied. "Anyone assigned to the Jotun region in the Outer Colonies was actually drafted for the war."

*A code word.* Cris let out a slow breath. It did make sense, though he didn't want to believe it was possible. His pulse quickened as he thought through the implications. "There are military installations out there, but hardly a battlefield."

"You've been looking in the wrong place." Banks paused. "Have you ever thought about the location of TSS Headquarters?"

"Well, Earth is at the very outer reaches of Taran space. It's—"

"That's not what I mean."

"What, then?" It was all Cris could do to curb his frustration, desperate to know the truth that Banks was so intent on hiding.

Banks bit his lip, as if questioning whether he should go on. "I mean its position in subspace."

Cris sighed. "It's to keep all the trainees from getting out of line, because of the natural telekinetic dampening."

"Yes, that's what we tell them," Banks murmured. He looked down and shook his head, still torn. "In reality, the training program would be far more effective if the entire facility could be in normal space like Level 11—the one area where we can really train anyone. But, we keep the rest of Headquarters in subspace specifically for those dampening properties."

"If not for training, then why?"

"Because subspace is the one place where we could be on a level field with the Bakzen." Banks looked like he regretted the statement immediately.

Cris almost gagged. His pulse spiked. "Are you saying the Bakzen have Gifted abilities?"

The High Commander looked ill. "And they're very powerful. But it's more complicated."

*Stars! What are we up against?* Cris exhaled slowly, almost shaking. "Go on."

After a moment, Banks nodded. "There are pockets, rifts, in the fabric of space. An echo of this physical world, existing between our perceived spacetime reality and subspace. Any ship or built structure within a rift is invisible from our reality, and vice versa. Only objects with a massive gravitational and electromagnetic field in normal space, like a planet or a star, are visible within the rift unless the object has been brought through using specialized jump drives capable of tuning to the precise energy field of the extradimensional space. The true Bakzen threat is within one of these rifts."

"Okay…" Cris felt more unsteady with every word, his chest tight.

"While our perceivable spacetime reality has been relatively untouched—outside of the outer realms, at least—we have been at war with the Bakzen within the Rift for centuries. At the beginning of the war, the Bakzen banded together to tear the fabric of space, enlarging what was once a minute rift so that it now encompasses several star systems. The border of *that* Rift is now marked by the Defense Barrier."

*Stars! What if Wil was taken into the Rift?* Cris' heart pounded in his ears. "How do we get in?"

Banks let out a slow breath. "Historically, only stationary transport units could be used to access the Rift—gates with a specialized spatial disruption generator to target the narrow band that can support physical life within the Rift. Only a handful of ships have been created to travel to the Rift independently. The *Infinity* was the prototype for this new class of rift ships, though that detail was highly classified. We've refined the design since then, but only recently could we spare the resources to upgrade a ship outside of the active war zone. That's really why the *Vanquish* was in for maintenance—for those retrofits."

"Which is why you were so insistent I take it on this mission."

"Yes. Of course, I never thought those upgrades would alter the performance in any way. The delay…"

Cris shook his head. "It may have been sabotage. We don't know."

"At any rate, the nav computer is now loaded with a 'Jotun' protocol to access the Rift." The High Commander took a deep breath. "But, unlike us, the Bakzen don't need ships to travel between the Rift and our plane."

Cris froze. "What?"

"The Bakzen can consciously travel between the Rift and normal space. It's instantaneous and highly accurate, unlike our jump drives. What's worse, some of them can even extend the field to encompass small ships, like a space combat fighter—just jump next to a TSS ship, fire, and jump away before we know what's hit us. That ability has always given them a major advantage in the war."

Cris was crippled by a sense of defeat. He slumped back in his chair. "Why even send us here if you knew what we were up against? We don't stand a chance."

Banks shifted on his feet. "Because we need Wil back. We need to end the war."

The blood drained from Cris' face. "You're making it sound like Wil is part of your battle plan."

The High Commander looked down.

"Tell me! What do you want with my son?" Cris demanded.

Banks took a pained breath. "To fight the Bakzen, we need a bridge—someone who can effortlessly travel to the Rift, just like they can. Hundreds of years ago when it became obvious that the Bakzen could not be defeated by any conventional means, genetically keyed nanotech was introduced into multiple bloodlines on Tararia. The nanotech was designed to select someone with the best traits of a given bloodline and bring them together with a complementary mate from a different family—mimicking the instant attraction of a natural 'resonance connection'. This pairing continued, with minimal external intervention needed, until it eventually came down to you and Kate."

A knife stabbed into Cris' chest. His heart thudded in his ears. "No, it can't—"

"The result of your union was the ultimate goal. Wil. The embodiment of genetic perfection as we know it—where a whole new set of abilities would be unlocked. The Cadicle, or 'enlightened one' in the Old Taran doctrine of the Priesthood. A Primus Elite for the TSS."

*Wil...* All the chaos, the fear, the anger, that had been churning inside Cris came to a sudden stillness. The clarity of truth.

He fought it. It was too much to accept.

The life he knew, the way he had been drawn to his wife—it couldn't all be fabricated.

He couldn't draw a full breath through the tightness in his chest. *It can't be true...*

"You *engineered* us?" he stammered at last.

Banks took a step forward. "They were desperate, Cris. It seemed like the only way."

Cris' vision blurred and his throat felt raw. He shook his head, still not wanting to believe. "I doubt that genetic engineering was what the founders of the Priesthood had in mind for the Cadicle. Let alone an instrument of war."

"Much has changed in the thousands of years since the Priesthood's inception."

*I thought leaving Tararia was an escape, but this!* Years of service to the TSS, and deceit was his payment. Cris clenched his hands. "I won't let you use Wil! As soon as I get him back, we're out."

Banks stared at him levelly. "Walking away isn't an option. Wil is destined to fight the Bakzen, and to end the war. It's what he was made to do."

Cris glared back. "You'll have to find someone else."

"We can't, Cris! Everything rests on him."

"Maybe you should have thought about that before you lied to us our whole lives." *Have I never had control over anything?*

"It was easier if you didn't know. When the time came, we were confident Wil would do what needs to be done."

Cris shook his head, eyes narrowed. "He may have grown up in the TSS, but that doesn't make him your pawn."

"But he has a sense of duty. Once he knows what we're up against and what we need from him, he'll see it's a role he must fulfill."

"You have no right to use him." Cris' mind raced. *Is there any way out?*

Banks softened. "I know you feel like walking away right now. I would, too. But you have to understand, this goes beyond who we are as individuals. The Taran Empire has called upon us, and we need to answer."

Cris paused to let the words sink in. *True leaders put the Taran people first. If there really is that great a threat, then I can't turn away.*

He looked down. Hurt and anger still seethed within, but it wouldn't help him find his son.

"How could you lie to me all these years?" His voice shook more than he hoped it would.

"I'm so sorry, Cris. I knew this day would come eventually, just not under these circumstances. I didn't want it to be like this."

Cris could tell Banks was sincere in his sentiment, but that didn't make it any easier. *Apologies don't change that they've been manipulating us this whole time. Do the secrets never end?* "That's what you meant right after I said I wanted to marry Kate, when you said our child would be extraordinary."

Banks nodded. "And he is, Cris. So very extraordinary. I feel privileged to be a part of his life."

"We trusted you."

Banks bowed his head. "I hope that trust can be rebuilt."

*What good is any of our history when the entire foundation was built on lies?* Cris didn't know where to begin with unpacking the revelations. Every decision, every action in his life. He could no longer be sure what was choice and what was him simply following a well-orchestrated path. "Have you been involved since the beginning?"

"Since you were born, anyway," Banks replied. "I had recently graduated to Agent when I was pulled into Jotun. Over the years, I moved to Lead Agent, and eventually became High Commander four years before you arrived at Headquarters."

*My entire existence has all been one master plan.* Cris' stomach turned over. *It's not fair. To me, to Kate... to Wil. Do they realize what they're asking of him?*

"I tried to protect you, Cris," Banks emphasized to break the silence. "I would never have kept any of this from you, but I had my own orders to follow."

"And who issues those orders?"

Banks took a slow breath. "The Priesthood of the Cadicle."

*The TSS reports to the Priesthood?* Cris laughed in spite of himself, on the verge of hysterics. "That doesn't make any sense! Why is the Priesthood involved with the TSS?"

"Because the TSS exists to train Gifted people like us, and the Priesthood has a vested interest in our care."

Cris stared at Banks, incredulous. "We *are* talking about the same organization that condemns those very abilities?"

"Political sentiment doesn't always align with underlying needs."

*This is insane.* "They tried to kill me! Why go through all that planning to 'make' me only to then stage an assassination?"

Banks looked down. "That was an error in judgment, and I've always resented them for it. They weren't sure you would follow through, either."

*Either…* "I wasn't the first, was I? My brother Tristen!"

Banks withered. "Cris, this is not something you want to dive into."

"On the contrary—"

"Our entire race is at stake! Do you understand that?" Banks pleaded. "The Priesthood knew we needed a military leader, not a politician."

Cris' stomach churned. *They killed him. Just like they tried to kill me.* "I had no interest in politics. What was their issue with me?"

"You were deemed too independent."

"So, they were threatened by me." *They should be. Especially now.*

"They were wrong, and they admit it. You're more than we could have hoped for."

Cris threw up his hands. "How did this even get started? Who are the Bakzen?"

Banks turned pale. "I can't tell you."

"Why?"

"I just can't, Cris."

"Bomax, Banks! You expect me to continue on, despite just having turned my entire world upside down, and yet you're still keeping things from me? You better have a foking good reason for not telling me."

Banks looked down. "I can't tell you because you would tell Wil, and he can't know."

*What wouldn't they want him to know?* Cris was about to respond, but Scott stuck his head into the office.

Scott startled when he saw Cris' expression. He inched back from the door. "We need to figure out what we're doing. We're completely exposed here."

Cris nodded and returned his attention to Banks. "This conversation isn't over."

Banks looked him in the eye. "Do whatever it takes to get Wil back."

"I know."

# CHAPTER 7

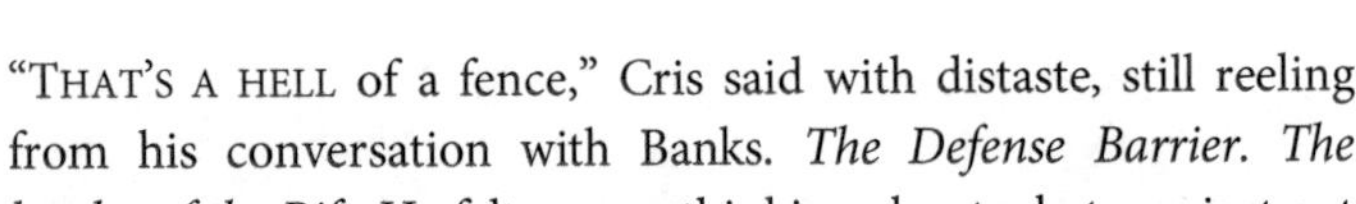

"THAT'S A HELL of a fence," Cris said with distaste, still reeling from his conversation with Banks. *The Defense Barrier. The border of the Rift.* He felt queasy thinking about what was just out of sight.

"I take it we're going to ignore the giant, flashing 'keep out' sign?" Scott quipped.

Cris wasn't in the mood for joking. "You know we don't have a choice."

The satellites placed in strategic alignment formed a nearly impenetrable mesh of sensor beams. After what he had just learned, Cris wished they could just turn around and forget about it. Wil was somewhere inside.

"Kari, have you found any weak areas in the grid?" he asked.

"Not really." She sighed and rapped her fingers on the computer console at her station. "Well, there was one thing. It looked like a shift change at some manned outposts, but we haven't been here for long enough to know how frequently those occur. I'm not positive, but it appeared that the grid recalibrated for the new shift, and that there was a four second lapse in the sensor network. We might be able to slip through then, but all they'd have to do is look out a viewport to see us."

"That also means forces will be doubled. Less than ideal." Cris turned to Scott for suggestions.

"Where can we get farthest away from the manned outposts?" Scott asked.

Kari displayed the pattern of the Defense Barrier's grid near the *Vanquish* on the front of the domed viewscreen. The grid was complex, but Cris' trained eye caught one of its very few weaknesses. "Is that an open hole where the grid crosses between outposts?"

Kari zoomed in. "Looks like it."

"Alec, let's pull back. I have an idea, but we'll need to wait for the right opportunity to make a move." Cris sighed. *It's downright lunacy. Then again, everything feels like a sick joke.*

There was a somber mood in the Command Center, and Cris knew his dour expression wasn't helping. *They're driven forward by duty, but no one wants to be here. I don't want to be here.*

It was his responsibility to maintain morale and encourage those on board, but, his own understanding of the circumstances made it difficult for him to rally his comrades. The war wasn't imminent—it was already happening, just out of sight. And all their hopes rested on Wil.

Cris struggled to keep his internal emotional turmoil at bay. He wanted to talk to Kate about what he'd just learned from Banks, but it would only be a distraction. There would be time to deal with the revelations once Wil was home safely.

He set his jaw and tried to focus. There were many more lives at risk than just the *Vanquish*'s crew and Wil's, and he needed to see the mission through. But as they waited, the extent of the lies that permeated every aspect of his life was too much to ignore.

*It was all a setup. Is any of it real?* He slumped dejectedly in his chair next to Scott, unable to answer the questioning glances about what he had discussed with Banks.

For the moment, all he could do until the next shift change was hope for the best.

— — —

*What do I do now that Cris knows?* Banks lay back on the couch in his office. *This changes our whole timeline with Wil. And Kate...* He expected her to come storming into his office any moment.

Information about the Bakzen War was closely guarded, and there had been no intention of discussing Wil's role in the conflict until he was at least an Agent. *Then again, we never thought he would be face-to-face with the enemy.*

Maybe it was for the best—an opportunity for him to be a part of fleet development, tactics and other preparations prior to taking formal command.

*Assuming we don't lose him.* He groaned aloud. The thought was too much to bear.

There were still so many unknowns. Banks wanted to have complete confidence in Cris' ability to find Wil, but he was up against a seemingly impossible task. Though he wanted to help Cris, Banks had nowhere safe to turn.

*If I say anything to the others now, no good will come of it.*

There was still a traitor somewhere in the TSS—and if Cris was correct about it being an Agent, they would be almost impossible to detect. Even still, responsibility for the infiltration would fall on Banks.

*I've worked for too long to get into this position only to let them take it from me. There's too much to lose.* Though without Cris and Wil, none of that mattered, anyway.

Continuing to conceal Wil's capture was risky, but it was his only real option. All he could do was wait.

— — —

It was time to move. The shift change had come.

"Take us into position," Cris commanded.

Alec's piloting ability would soon be put to the test. They had been over the plan several times, but it still sounded crazy to Cris. There was no guarantee that it would work, and there were too many variables to bother counting.

Cris took a deep breath, watching the clock. "Okay, Alec. Let's see what you can do."

Alec nodded, anticipating the order to move the ship forward.

"Now!"

With one touch on the console, Alec fired the jump drive for a split second, almost instantaneously shutting off all external power to the vessel—a textbook 'phantom jump'. There was a jolt as the ship lunged forward, followed by a slight rock back as the lights dimmed and the ship traveled forward on inertia, surrounded by a spatial disruption from the near-subspace jump. The *Vanquish* continued forward into Bakzeni Territory.

"I see no sign of pursuit," informed Kari, much to everyone's relief.

It seemed too good to be true. Cris knew they may have been detected, but for now, the only way was forward. "Plot a course toward the primary planet."

— — —

General Carzen looked over the message from Station 27 along the Defense Barrier. It was hard to believe that the TSS actually thought they could pass into Bakzeni Territory unobserved. Carzen sent back instruction to reactivate the sensor beacon that had been partially disabled for the sake of luring the gullible TSS Agents.

Once captured, the TSS flagship ship would yield valuable intelligence on the latest rift drive capabilities and frequencies for the navigation beacons. All the information that Tek's collaborator inside the TSS was unable to transmit would soon be at the Bakzen's disposal. Things were coming together nicely.

— — —

The *Vanquish* floated in the star-speckled expanse of space above the planetary headquarters for the Bakzeni Empire. Cris had no idea how to proceed.

Not only were the defense arrays going to be hard to bypass, but there was also a sophisticated shield around the entire planet. The only ways through the shield were rectangular openings that stretched several kilometers on a side, placed around key points on the planet's equator. Naturally, the openings were the most guarded regions in Bakzeni Territory.

Cris had provided the frequency of Wil's ID chip to Alec and Kari, but their scanning abilities were severely hampered by the shield.

"So…" Alec began.

*Please tell me you have a lead.* Cris perked up. "Any sign of Wil?"

"Not yet." Alec glanced over at Kari.

She made no effort to mask her concern. "I don't know how much longer they'll be fooled by the disguised transmitting signal."

Cris nodded. "We've been far too lucky. Getting through the defense barrier without apparent detection, and then coming this far without being questioned. It's all just so… convenient." *Led right into a trap.*

Scott nodded. "I agree. The word 'convenient' does seem to fit awfully well, but I don't know what we can do."

"We have no choice but to stick it out," Cris said. "We can't turn back without Wil, no matter the risk to us."

"But keep in mind, the more time we take to make a move, the riskier it becomes," Scott pointed out.

"Yes, waiting around won't do us any good," Alec added. "We have nothing to learn about the planetary shield. It's very similar to what the Taran colonies use. The longer we delay, the higher the likelihood of detection."

Cris held back a wave of anger. *I hate being so close to the Bakzen base and not being able to retaliate. But we need to focus on finding Wil.* "All right. We somehow need to determine Wil's present location. We can't do much planning before we know that."

"I'm working on it with a team," Kari said. "It's slow going, but I'll let you know as soon as I find anything."

"Actually, I'll help you," Scott said. "We should allow the others rest while they can. Let's just call it ship's night and work down in Communications."

Cris looked to Alec, and then back at his other officers. "Good idea. Alec, we'll run over the specs on the planetary defenses."

Alec nodded. "Okay. Let's get to work."

— — —

The secondary communications room in TSS Headquarters was completely empty, just the way Arron Haersen hoped it would be. He slipped through the automatic doorway into the darkened room. The call he was expecting was far too sensitive for anyone else to happen across its content. Even though the call required interception so the Comm Command team wouldn't detect it, Haersen had the utmost faith that everything would go smoothly. After all, his job as Mission Coordinator made him the overseer of all TSS communications.

He walked over to the central monitor on the far wall in anticipation of the incoming call. Plotting against the TSS wasn't without risk, but his alliance with the Bakzen had already given him so much.

The monitor flashed with the announcement of the incoming message before the image on the screen began to solidify. It took a little longer than usual to establish a stable link due to the distance of the subspace relays, but it gave Haersen more time to organize his thoughts. With the transmission routed safely away from Comm Command undetected, he could talk to his collaborator with a little less worry.

Haersen looked up at the central screen. Colonel Tek's sorrel eyes stared unwaveringly back. He didn't look happy.

"How is it going?" asked Haersen.

Tek glowered. "Not as I had hoped."

Haersen swallowed hard. He knew that if something went wrong, he would be first on Tek's hit list. "Well, the sabotage was a success. They were able to find a replacement cell more quickly than I anticipated, but the new rift drive should be disabled. Once you move to capture them, they'll be trapped."

"Useful, but hardly a consolation prize if we don't get to put the Primus Elite to use," Tek replied with a scowl.

"Is there anything I can do to help from here?"

"There might have been, but it's too late now. Carzen has been far too friendly for my liking—for our plan's liking. It's as if he actually thinks the Primus Elite can be turned. The incompetent fool." Tek scoffed.

"I see."

Tek looked even more sullen. "The Primus Elite is much stronger than any of us thought. That's excellent for us, but once Carzen realizes that he cannot be turned in the same way you were, he may destroy him before I have a chance to fulfill our plan. What a shame it would be to end his life without releasing his potential. Not to mention, a major setback."

"You can't expect immediate results. Turning me was quite a different matter—"

"This isn't about you!"

Haersen flinched at the outburst. "Yes, sir. All I meant to say was that—"

"What?"

Haersen wet his lips. "It's just that, unlike me, the Primus Elite was raised within TSS Headquarters. They poisoned his mind early. Someone like me, with a more neutral background—well, I could immediately see your superiority, what you could offer me. But, I do believe that he could be swayed to your—

*our*—side, if it came down to it. He is rational, after all. It just might take a little bit longer than it did with me.

"However, you know best if he is more useful as an ally or as a tool to expand your Rift." Haersen let out a shaky breath. Both Tek's and Carzen's plans sounded unlikely to succeed, but it would be so much better if they at least shared a common vision. There was enough to navigate with his betrayal of the TSS without worrying about dissenting perspectives among the Bakzen, as well.

Tek still looked skeptical, but he let Haersen's reasoning do for the time being. "I should probably get back before they are suspicious of my absence," Tek said after another uncomfortable silence.

"Yes, as should I," Haersen agreed.

At first, he hadn't liked having their communications transmitted through the TSS, but Tek had threatened to back out of their arrangement if Haersen couldn't prove his loyalty by flaunting his betrayal. Now, as much as Haersen feared getting caught, every moment his plans went unnoticed, he felt more pleased with himself for outsmarting those who had always looked down on him. It wouldn't be much longer before he would finally be able to show them just how superior he could become.

"We'll talk again in two days, then?" he said.

"Yes. Two days." Tek ended the transmission.

Haersen stared at the blank screen, exhilarated by the conversation. Their plans were being played out even as they spoke, but it would all be in vain if Wil was too resistant. Time would tell.

Haersen left the room as quietly as he had arrived.

# CHAPTER 8

WIL BOLTED AWAKE from what he hoped was a very bad dream. Heart racing, he looked around the Bakzen cell—his waking nightmare. *Well, at least still alive.*

He wasn't sure how long he had been out, though it felt like he'd had nearly a full night's rest. He was disappointed in himself for letting his guard down, but at least he felt refreshed.

He sat in contemplation for several minutes, weighing his options. Eventually, he decided that he would have to continue playing along with General Carzen and Colonel Tek's game—if they were playing the same one—and hope to be able to make an opportunistic escape.

Getting up from the bed, Wil walked over to the barred front of the cell. He craned his neck to see past the bars. Six guards sat at a small table near the end of the hall. They were playing some sort of game that looked vaguely like Fastara, except with colored blocks rather than cards. They moved the blocks telekinetically, keeping the game suspended in midair above the table's surface.

"Hey! Guard!" Wil yelled out and waited for a response. When none came, he tried again a little louder. "Guard! Come here. I'd like to talk with General Carzen about our alliance."

With that, one of the sentries let out an exasperated grunt and lowered his blocks onto the table. He shoved back his chair and stomped over toward Wil while his comrades continued their game.

Wil took a step back from the cell bars. *I think I pissed him off.*

The guard looked identical to the others Wil had encountered earlier, but there was a distinctive scar along his jaw that Wil hadn't seen before. "You want to talk General, eh?" he jeered with a thick accent. "General busy. You need appointment. Wait until *he* want see *you.*"

Wil flashed his most charming smile. "In that case, why don't you inform him that I'm willing to talk now and that he can call for me at his leisure."

"Sure. I do." The guard strolled back to the other guards.

*There's no way that message is going to make it to Carzen.* Wil's heart sank as he watched the guard walk away. As he turned around to sit back down on the platform bed, he heard a tussle among the guards, just out of view. The scarred guard came rushing back to the entrance of Wil's cell, a fresh bruise forming on his temple.

"I sorry, sir," he said, "I not know who you are. General Carzen see you now. I not know—"

*Stars! Now they're groveling?* "It's fine. I *am* your prisoner—"

The guard ran his wrist over a pad on the front of the cell door and the bars swung open. "Oh, no, no, you not prisoner. You guest."

"Okay…" *I have no idea what's going on.*

The profuse apologies continued all the way to General Carzen's office. Wil was ushered through the office door and left alone in the room with the Bakzen general.

"You wanted to see me?" asked General Carzen.

Wil nodded. "Yes, sir."

He set up a firm mental block to keep Carzen from probing his inner thoughts, and then took a deep breath. "I was raised to view the Bakzen as a distant enemy. We both know that. But in my short time here, I have begun to understand that you're not the people I was led to believe. For one, I was never told about your Gifts—abilities so much stronger Tarans. And then there's your discipline and efficiency. By comparison, the TSS is so unnecessarily showy and far too reliant on physical comforts."

"I'd tend to agree," Carzen said.

"I've been thinking about what you said during our last meeting, about me being turned to your side," Wil continued. "Obviously, I can't change my loyalty overnight. In fact, I hated the idea at first. But, I've had some time to reflect on what the TSS has given me, and… well, it isn't a very long list. So, let's just say that I am now open-minded."

The general nodded. "That's good to hear."

"After all, I'm barely into my teens and I'm already almost as powerful as their most senior Agents," Wil went on, bringing in enough truth to hopefully sell the message. "When it comes down to it, there's just no way the TSS can properly train me. I realized that a while ago, but I never thought I had another option.

"I'm curious what you can offer me. Maybe we can explore ways for the Bakzen to help me rise to my full potential." Wil hung his head, feigning anguish. "I'm sure you can appreciate how hard it is for me to admit that—after being taught to hate you. But… at some point, I do need to think of myself."

Carzen's face contorted into his unnatural smile. "I'm pleased you're considering the different angles of this matter. There are many mutual advantages to such an arrangement."

Wil nodded. "I know it would take time for us to learn to work together, but I owe it to myself to become everything I can."

General Carzen rose from his chair. "I look forward to talking further with you on this matter. That will have to wait. I have an appointment to keep."

Wil stood up. "Thank you for your time, General."

"Certainly." Carzen walked toward the door. He glanced back once, looking Wil over, before he stepped into the hallway.

Wil couldn't help but wonder if Carzen's sudden meeting was a fabricated excuse to leave. *He seemed genuinely surprised that I was so agreeable. I hope I didn't come on too strong.*

Guards came in to retrieve Wil after Carzen left. As they escorted him down the hall, he found they were going a different way than the prison wing where he had been staying. Wil tried to keep track of where they were going, but he was soon lost.

The guards stopped at an open door, gesturing Wil through. After a slight hesitation, he obeyed.

Fully furnished quarters met his gaze. *I have been upgraded from prisoner to guest.*

— — —

General Carzen entered the Officer's Lounge feeling pleased with himself. As it would seem, hospitality had proved much more effective than intimidation in taking the first step toward turning the future Primus Elite Agent to the side of the Bakzeni Empire.

Though he couldn't access Wil's inner mind, Carzen knew he was being led on. That was expected. Yet, he had also detected a glimmer of sincerity in the Junior Agent's statements: the Bakzen were powerful and could offer far more guidance than the TSS. That truth was something to exploit.

Carzen stopped in the center of the room. The Bakzen officers looked up at him from their various positions throughout the lounge.

"It's time we take a little trip with our guest," Carzen proclaimed. "He needs a nudge in the right direction."

Tek glowered. "That was never part of the plan."

"A plan we are adapting as the circumstances change," Carzen countered.

"We can't reveal more without formal approval," the colonel insisted.

"Yes, of course," Carzen agreed. "I keep the Imperial Director apprised of all developments."

"Would you like me to set up the meeting?" Major Komantra, one of the younger officers, asked. He had yet to earn any scars to set him apart from the other officers in his genetic line, relying solely on his name tag and ribbons to express his distinction.

"No, I'll get in touch with him myself. There are other matters to discuss." Carzen glanced at Tek. "We will convene in the Strategy Room at 16:00."

— — —

Wil looked around his new quarters. Though far from luxurious, the accommodations offered the basic comforts—mattress on the bed, a washroom, desk. It was compact but not cramped. There didn't appear to be any communications systems in the room, but that wasn't surprising.

As soon as the guards left, he scoped out the shower. *That's the first order of business.*

It was a square, meter-wide stall of stainless steel with a translucent plastic door. Seeing no controls, Wil stuck his hand into the stall and water automatically rained down from a spout in the ceiling. He quickly retracted his hand to keep his jacket sleeve from getting soaked.

Still skeptical of his captors' intentions, he waited a couple minutes before stripping down—just to make sure his hand didn't fall off due to acid in the water. *Carzen claimed they want me alive, but you never know.* He felt a little silly, but the precaution seemed worthwhile.

Once satisfied that the water was safe, Wil removed his clothes. He set them in a pile next to the shower, wanting to keep his handheld and the explosive film close.

The hot water felt amazing as it washed over him. Days of resting on stone and metal had left him with a chill. Warmed by the water, he tried to set aside his worries and be thankful for what he did have. *I'm alive. I have a plan to stay alive. Besides, all this first-hand experience with the enemy has to be of some use…*

He finished up in the shower and put his clothes back on. Though a clean outfit would be nice, he still felt much improved.

Wil returned to the main room. He inspected the plain gray walls and utilitarian furniture crafted of metal and black plastic. The furnishings were all deliberate, arranged to leave just enough room to navigate around each object. Even down to the most minute details, everything had a purpose and nothing was out of place. The more Wil thought about it, the more uncomfortable it made him. There was no heart to the space—unapologetic function over form. *Why would anyone choose to live like this?*

He sat down on the bed, the chill returning. *I hope I won't have to stay here long. My parents and the TSS must be looking for me, right? I just have to hang on...*

— — —

Banks paced his office, waiting for Kate to arrive. He was surprised she had requested a meeting after how their last conversation ended. Under normal circumstances, he would have been eager to patch things up with her. However, the request came so soon after his heart-to-heart with Cris that Banks had to question Kate's motives. *Maybe Cris asked her to punch me on his behalf?*

The buzzer at the door sounded.

"Come in," Banks said, taking a seat at his desk. Having a physical barrier to separate them might be wise.

"Hi," Kate greeted as she entered. She closed the door and walked over to take a seat across the desk from Banks.

"What can I do for you?"

Kate looked embarrassed. "I owe you an apology. Cris sent me a message and said to get off your case."

"Did he say anything else?" Banks asked, bracing for the worst.

"No, just that you weren't the one working with the Bakzen."

*So he's keeping the war to himself for now. No need to bring it up unsolicited.* Banks gave her a reassuring smile. "I can understand your suspicions, Kate. No hard feelings." There would be other times to discuss the war and her part in it.

Kate crossed her arms. "What do we do now? I have a shortlist. Just start questioning everyone on it?"

"Most likely we're dealing with an Agent. It won't be easy to get a confession."

"There are only four Agents with the right skills and clearance who don't have an alibi for the time of the break-in. Rynold, Ale—"

"What did you consider an alibi?" Banks interrupted.

"Being with someone, or captured on video somewhere else. But, that might not be good enough."

Banks nodded. "Footage can be doctored, and there could always be multiple people working together and covering for each other."

"Right. So, that list of four Agents could really be forty." Kate leaned back in the chair. "I just wanted to get to the bottom of this so badly, I may have jumped ahead. I know better than to follow such shoddy research methods."

"There are a lot of variables to consider, and we don't yet know which details are important," Banks assured her.

Kate threw up her hands. "Shite, I doubted *you*. How's that productive?"

*If only she knew what my private conversations were about.* "This isn't the kind of investigation we can conduct in a couple of days. We need to go through the Mainframe security protocols line by line."

"That'll take weeks!" Kate protested.

"I know. I want this put to rest as much as you do."

Kate sighed. "Who's going to comb through everything? I'd offer, but programming is hardly my strong suit."

Banks steepled his fingers. "Believe it or not, I actually know a thing or two on the subject."

Kate looked at him quizzically. "I didn't know that."

"I wasn't always TSS High Commander, you know," Banks said with a slight smile. "I started out working in Communications."

Kate's eyes narrowed. "Not Command?"

"It was a bit of a circuitous route," Banks replied, wishing he'd never mentioned it. "All I'm saying is, I'm looking into it personally. Our traitor won't stay hidden for much longer."

Kate continued to eye him with a hint of suspicion. "Any luck so far?"

"No more than what you've found yourself. To move things along, I have two other teams working on it independently. We'll see if we all come to the same conclusion."

"While a traitor continues to walk among us." Kate suddenly looked like she was about to break down. She took a slow, deliberate breath.

Banks leaned forward and placed his hands on the desktop. "We need to have each other's backs. We'll get through this. Together."

Kate nodded and rose from her seat. "I'll keep looking. Maybe something will jump out."

Banks stood to see her out. "Get some rest, Kate."

"I will. But the day isn't over yet."

— — —

General Carzen strode confidently into the Strategy Room. His preemptive conversation with the Imperial Director had gone well, considering the subject matter, but he wasn't sure his warning about Tek had been taken seriously. The colonel's behavior was alarming, especially with the Primus Elite around. Carzen hoped his concerns were unwarranted.

Most of the Bakzen officers were already seated around the table when Carzen arrived, including Tek. Each held an advanced rank and represented a separate genetic line of specialized commanders—the pinnacle of cunning and physical prowess for their roles, unlike the simple-minded drones that carried out their orders as soldiers and laborers. They could have excelled in any pursuit; it was outside circumstances that had led them down the dark path of perfecting their capabilities in battle. These officers were all hardened war veterans. Each had seen combat over the years, and they still sought action on the front lines. Battle wounds were a badge of pride, and many boasted electrical burns from ships damaged in combat.

Without hesitation, Carzen walked to the far side of the circular table and took his usual seat. Tek eyed him as he passed by, but Carzen ignored him. As the most senior among them, everyone deferred to Carzen's model of silence.

The room dimmed in anticipation of the meeting.

At precisely 16:00, the holographic projector activated and a perfectly rendered figure of the Imperial Director appeared above the tabletop. He surveyed the officers with his keen, glowing red eyes beneath a brow that was beginning to wrinkle from age.

"I understand that the Primus Elite is amenable to working with us," the Director stated.

"Yes, sir," replied General Carzen. "He informed me earlier today that he sees an opportunity for mutual benefit. It will take time to fully sway him, but I believe we could expedite his realignment by showing him what lies inside the Rift."

The Director nodded. "Any time we can save is to our benefit. We need to prepare if we are to come out victorious against Tararia."

Tek looked taken aback. "Sir, how can we be so quick to find an ally in someone who's been our sworn enemy since birth? This change of heart is sudden, and suspicious."

"Nothing is assured," the Director replied. "We must proceed cautiously. A seed has been planted in his mind, which we can cultivate." The Imperial Director was silent in thought for a moment. "I agree with General Carzen. It's time we show the young Dragon the might of the Bakzen."

— — —

Guards prodded Wil down the hallway. It had only been a few hours since he was shown to his new quarters. *Where are they taking me now?*

He attempted to question where they were going, but the escorts refused to answer. The questioning was initially out of simple curiosity, but interest turned to fear when Wil realized that he was being led down an unfamiliar hallway.

*This isn't the way to Carzen's office. Maybe I'm finally being led to my execution.* He frantically looked for any possible escape. The guards surrounded him both physically and telekinetically, forming an impenetrable wall. *This is the end.*

The procession came to an abrupt halt. Wil was surprised to see an open door to a transport ship. The hull was rough and patchy compared to TSS ships, and was heavily armored. The guards looked expectantly toward Wil for him to step into the vessel.

Wil stood his ground. "Where are you taking me?" he asked again with all the authority he could muster.

The guards looked at each other, wondering if they should answer.

"We're going to show you the truth," said a familiar voice from behind.

Wil turned to see General Carzen approaching. "What do you mean?"

Amusement touched the corners of Carzen's mouth. "You'll see." The general stepped into the ship, gesturing for Wil to follow.

Though he resisted the prodding hands of the guards, Wil was shoved inside and directed into lightly padded a seat sized for a large Bakzen soldier. The guards buckled a four-point harness around him, but even at the tightest setting the straps were far from secure.

Without any delay, the outer door across from Wil's seat sealed, and the Bakzen escorts settled into the seats around him, all facing inward toward the center aisle.

Wil sat in silence in the windowless cabin, listening to the engines as the ship strained to pass through the atmosphere and then glided through space. After some time, he heard docking clamps latch onto the hull.

"Where are we going?" he asked Carzen. The general didn't reply.

The door to the transport shuttle slid up, revealing a gangway. The escorts unstrapped Wil and pulled him to his feet.

Exiting the shuttle, Wil could see through small viewports in the gangway that they were walking into one of the colossal branches of a spaceport. Other branches curved away in the distance. The small party proceeded into the central corridor for their docking wing.

Walking on the familiar-feeling floor of a space dock, Wil looked around in wonder, taking in the immense size of the port. It dwarfed that of the TSS and held at least twice as many ships. Wil had never seen so many vessels in such a compact area outside of a major manufacturing yard.

*Their forces are so much more powerful than ours. We don't have a chance.*

As he turned his head to look through the ceiling behind him, Wil caught sight of another group of guards heading toward General Carzen and himself. The guards took their places around Wil as they continued deeper into the station.

They arrived at a substantial craft with a smooth outer hull similar to interstellar TSS ships, but the aesthetics stood out from anything in the Taran worlds—almost as though elements of the familiar had been intentionally rearranged in an unexpected design.

He was led up the long gangway and then escorted up a lift to the Command Center, which was at the top of the vessel rather than in the middle of the body like TSS combat ships. The escorts directed him to a seat in the back corner of the room.

Gazing at the consoles at the front of the Command Center, Wil noticed that there were some unfamiliar inputs. He took in the details of his surroundings. *They must have some trust in their ability to get me on their side or they never would have brought me to where I can see everything. What 'truth' are they going to show me?*

Carzen gave the order to pull away from the dock. Wil was about to ask where they were headed, but a cold look from a sentry standing over his right shoulder stopped him.

Wil studied the viewscreen at the front of the room. All he could see was the space dock. Beyond that, there were only stars stretching out in all directions. Soon, the vessel turned and he could see the planet where he had spent the past few days. Its bland, brownish colors looked out of place in the intense black surroundings. The ship turned again and only stars were visible through the viewscreen.

Wil was just about to look away when a well-known form darted across the front of the screen.

"Report!" demanded Carzen with a hiss.

The helmsman looked up. "It was the TSS ship, sir."

*The* Vanquish*!* Wil concealed his smile.

"No matter now," Carzen dismissed. "They won't be able to follow us much longer. Just capture their ship like we planned. It should make for good study."

Wil's heart dropped, realizing that the Bakzen had set the trap. His parents were likely on that ship. *What's going to happen to them?*

The Bakzen ship lunged forward in one smooth motion. The *Vanquish* matched their speed and began inching closer.

"Their weapons are primed," an officer next to the helmsman warned.

"They won't fire," Carzen said. "They won't risk harming their precious Primus Elite." The *Vanquish* continued accelerating, practically on a collision course with the Bakzen ship.

"We can't outrun them on maneuvering thrusters, sir," the helmsman informed.

The general stared out the viewscreen. "Take us home."

"Aye, sir." The helmsman turned his attention to the set of controls that Wil had seen earlier. He began entering in information to the computer. After making all the necessary inputs, he pressed the final button.

The ship began to vibrate as if it were preparing for a spatial jump. The hum continued to intensify as the space around the ship took on a color-shifting quality like a jump to subspace, but it felt unusual. Just as the vibration seemed too much for the ship to take, the world outside the viewscreen began to distort, as if looking through a pool of water. A blue-green wave rippled past the ship.

Everything became still. The ship floated in the ethereal light for a split second before the distortion dissipated.

Wil took a deep breath. *What was that?* Cautiously, he began to peer at his new surroundings.

The energy around him felt different than it had before. It was invigorating. Wil looked out the viewscreen.

"Where are we?" he asked.

"Welcome to the Rift," Carzen stated.

Wil stared with a slack jaw at the new realm. Natural pockets in the higher dimensional space just beyond spacetime reality—theoretically habitable zones—had been discussed in astrophysics literature, but traveling into a stable rift was considered next to impossible.

He gripped the armrests of his chair, as his pulse spiked. *Shite! The* Vanquish *has no way to enter a rift. I'm on my own.*

The viewscreen revealed an orbital dock even larger than the one in normal space. It was completely full of warships, and small vessels ferried between the dock and other structures in the distance. Below it was the planet they had just left, but it looked strange—pale and distant, like it was just a reflection.

Wil craned his neck to see beyond the space station. *If the Bakzen live in a rift, what else can they do?*

"Here," said Carzen, "let me give you a better look." He nodded his head toward the helmsman, who pressed another button.

The walls of the Command Center shimmered as a wave washed over them. Like a curtain opening, the view changed to a perfect rendition of the surrounding space. Wil looked up and saw the expanse of space stretching over his head and curving down below his feet. The chairs and control consoles around the room remained intact and solid but were seemingly floating. It was a similar effect to the Command Center on the *Vanquish*, but far more thorough.

Still marveling at the technological masterwork with sickening awe, he turned to look behind the ship. There were more Bakzen vessels and manufacturing yards.

*How can the TSS ever hope to defeat this?* Then another thought came to mind, one that was much more urgent.

He turned to General Carzen. "Why are you showing me this?"

"So you can plainly see that any attempt to overthrow the Bakzeni Empire will be in vain. The TSS is no match for us," the general replied without hesitation. "*This* is what we have to offer you."

Wil shrugged. "It's okay, for a start." *Fok, how do I get away?*

General Carzen laughed. "Oh, come now! I can see the fear in your eyes, trying to comprehend what it would be like to fight against us. I know you can still be practical, despite your conditioning. If given the chance to join the superior side—why not seize the opportunity?"

He hesitated slightly before continuing. "But, all this technology is nothing compared to what we have inside. Your makers never anticipated how strong we would become. As talented as you are, your abilities are no match for ours. The Bakzen race has evolved since the plans for the Cadicle were laid. Despite all that planning, you will never be able to overpower us. Change your allegiance while you have the chance."

*What is he talking about?* Wil shook his head. "What do you mean by my 'makers'? You've called me 'Dragon' and 'Cadicle'. Why?" He met the general's rust-colored eyes in a level stare.

Carzen looked shocked for a moment before regaining his outer composure. "You mean, they never told you—"

The helmsman cut him off. "Sir, I'm detecting a spatial distortion. Something is coming through."

# CHAPTER 9

"ARE WE REALLY going to do this? If so, everyone has to be for it," Cris said to his senior officers seated around the table in the briefing room. Out the viewport, the rough wall of a massive freighter obscured his view of the Bakzen planet.

Scott nodded. "I'm with you, and I think I speak for everyone here when I say that I trust your judgment on this."

*It's insane and he knows it. But what else can we do?* "Okay," Cris whispered half to himself. Then, louder, so the rest of the people in the room could hear, "I know this sounds suicidal, and it probably is, but I see no alternative. We need to go down to the planet's surface. You've all read over the written brief? Good. Does anyone have any input? These plans are by no means final."

Kari raised her hand. "I'm not sure if I missed something, but I don't quite understand how you intend to find Wil on the planet… not to mention, we don't know if he's even there."

Cris looked down at the table. "I hope that we'll be able to access the Bakzen's computer network and get some intel that will point to Wil's whereabouts. It's a shot in the dark. If anyone has any other ideas about how to approach this, I'd be eager to hear them, because I'd rather avoid running around aimlessly on an enemy planet. We've been relying too much on luck and guesswork." He looked at the faces around the conference table.

Everyone in the room was silent, knowing that Cris' statements were too true for comfort.

*Shite. I don't deserve their trust on this.* He closed out of the briefing materials. "Let's wait just a little bit longer before we take action. But if we don't have another lead in the next two hours, we need to move." *If it isn't already too late...* He shoved the thought away. "You're dismissed. Keep near your posts in case something comes up."

Everyone rose to leave.

"Stay here, Scott," Cris said as his friend started to stand up.

Scott sat back down. "What is it?"

Cris waited for the others to depart. "You didn't object to the plan."

The other Primus Agent looked confused. "What do you mean?"

"Don't you find it a bit crazy to send a team down to the surface of the planet with no clear plan of action?"

"I trust your judgment."

"That's exactly what I don't want you to do." Cris slumped back in his chair.

"You don't want me to trust you?"

*No, it's not that. I'm just afraid I'm getting desperate.* "I'm prone to taking this as a parent rather than a TSS officer. I need you to call me on my shite."

"Are you saying I'm not questioning your authority enough?" Scott raised an eyebrow. "What if I agree with how you've been handling things? I would have come to the same conclusion that a manual search of the Bakzen network is necessary, since the planetary shield prevents a remote hack."

*Why can't I trust myself anymore?* Cris nodded slowly. "Just remember that if something seems *too* insane, call me on it."

"Sure thing," Scott agreed. "Now let's get back to the Command Center. We have a lot to prepare."

Cris and Scott returned to their stations.

The freighter that obscured the *Vanquish* loomed at the front of the dome of the room. Though the *Vanquish* was a sizeable vessel at four hundred meters, it was dwarfed by the Bakzen ship.

Kari and Alec were busy at their consoles looking at the data coming in from what few scans they could run through the planetary shield. Tracking Wil's dynastic ID chip was useless through the shield. That left few other methods to find him.

"Have you discovered anything new?" Cris asked purely to break the somber silence in the room.

"More of the same," Kari replied. "Pretty much all we can see are the ships disengaging from the docks and either heading into space or down to the planet."

*The ships…* "What if Wil isn't on the planet's surface?"

The two helm officers turned around in their chairs and looked at him. "We did scan all the ships in the vicinity when we first arrived, but we didn't find anything," Alec said. He paused and looked at his console. "Do you want us to search again?"

Scott shrugged. "It's worth a try."

"We may as well," Cris agreed. *I just can't let myself get hopeful.*

Kari and Alec redirected their signal sweeps to the ships, focusing on the ID frequency Cris had provided. After a couple minutes, the two officers suddenly looked up at each other.

Alec swiveled around to address Cris, his astonishment audible, "I think we may have found something."

Cris came to attention. "Where?"

"There's a cruiser pulling away from the dock right now," Kari stated while re-tuning the sensors.

"Can you be absolutely sure Wil's on it?" If they moved, they would give away their position for sure—if the Bakzen didn't already know they were lurking.

"Not one hundred percent," replied Alec, "but it's the best lead that we've seen so far."

*This might be the one chance that we have to save him. I could never forgive myself if we didn't try.* Cris nodded. "Let's move."

"Aye." Alec restored systems to their full power and started up the maneuvering thrusters.

Once the *Vanquish* was clear of the freighter, he switched over the main pion drive and swung the ship out into the full view of any observing eyes. Alec piloted toward a Bakzen ship a little larger than the *Vanquish*, which was moving away from the dock into open space. As closed in, the other ship accelerated.

"Keep up with them, Alec," Cris commanded. "Charge the weapons system, but don't fire. I don't want to risk hurting Wil."

The *Vanquish* continued to move toward the Bakzen ship. Just as the *Vanquish* got dangerously close, the space around the enemy ship began distorting, as though initializing a subspace jump.

Cris leaned forward, about to give the order to charge the *Vanquish*'s jump drive. Then, the Bakzen ship vanished from both normal and subspace views. "Where did they go?"

Kari sat in stunned silence for a moment before stammering a reply. "They're gone."

"Yes, but where did they go?" Cris asked, leaning forward in his chair.

"I don't know. They're just gone," she repeated.

"But to where? There must be a signal in subspace." *Unless…*

"No. There's absolutely no trace of them. They completely disappeared…"

*They jumped into the Rift.* Cris jumped from his seat. "Alec, bring up the Jotun sequence on the nav system." He jogged to the front station.

"The what?" Alec asked.

"Here." Cris waved the pilot from his seat and pulled up the nav system menu. There was nothing related to Jotun in the pre-programmed destinations. "Bomax, Banks," Cris muttered.

"What are you doing?" Scott asked.

"Finding my son." *Think. Where would a protocol be hidden?*

"Bakzen ships approaching!" Kari warned.

Cris ran through the architecture of the nav system in his head, tapping on menus to investigate what only turned out to be false leads. *Banks knew I could find it. But where?*

Nothing seemed to fit. His mind and pulse raced, knowing their time to act had already expired.

"The ships are closing in." Kari desperately looked to Scott when she got no reaction from Cris. "It looks like they're building a containment net!"

"We need to move!" Scott exclaimed. Panic was setting in.

"They jumped into a spatial rift," Cris said without stopping his work. "I'm trying to find the nav protocol. I need more time." *Come on! Where is it?*

"A *what*?" Scott asked, incredulous.

"Shite," Alec breathed.

Kari turned back to her console. "I'll try to hold them off." She took aim at the Bakzen vessels.

*The Rift is between normal space and subspace in our present location. It's not a distinct other place... Of course! It wouldn't be the destination settings, but the underlying jump parameters.* Cris accessed the very foundation of the nav system. Sure enough, there was a switch buried in the controls to flip from 'Beacon Nav' to 'Jotun'. *There!*

Cris made the change. "Found it!"

Alec stared at the console. "How do we make the jump?"

Cris returned the pilot's chair to Alec. "I think we just activate the jump drive while it's in this mode," Cris guessed.

"Are you sure?" Alec questioned, taking his seat.

"What else?"

A shot fired from one of the Bakzen ships rocked the *Vanquish*.

"We have to do *something*," Kari urged.

"Make the jump!" Cris commanded, taking his captain's chair.

"Aye." Alec began charging the jump drive.

Cris leaned over to the console between the two central chairs. "Matt?" He waited for a response.

"Yes?"

"We're about to make a rift jump. Let's hope your patch job holds," Cris announced.

"A what?" Matt fell silent for a moment, followed by a low curse. "Yes, sir." There was a waver to his voice. The comm link ended.

"Are you sure this is a good idea?" asked Scott.

Cris smiled weakly. "It's a little late to be questioning me now."

"Everything's ready," informed Alec. And much quieter, "I think."

Cris glanced one last time at Scott. "Let's go."

The vibration of the jump drive rattled the *Vanquish.* As the shaking crescendoed, the space surrounding the ship began to distort—masked by the ethereal blue-green of subspace. For a moment, the vessel was enveloped by swirling light, floating in perfect stillness. With a shudder, the *Vanquish* dropped into the world beyond the dimensional veil.

Cris stood up and stared out the front viewscreen, his mouth partially open. A massive spaceport and an armada of warships met his gaze. *The Bakzen aren't just a threat. They can completely annihilate us.*

Scott stood to join him. "Where the fok are we?"

"I'll explain later." Cris could have continued to stare out at the seemingly impossible engineering feats, but he caught sight of the ship that was carrying his son. "Don't let them get away."

— — —

"Curse them!" spat General Carzen as the *Vanquish* emerged from the spatial distortion. "We should have had them."

Wil's heart leaped. *How did they follow us?* He concealed his smile as Carzen flashed an angry glance in his direction. There was still a chance to get away.

Wil turned around and looked out the back wall of the room. The *Vanquish* was hovering just behind the starboard side of the Bakzen vessel. He stared at the ship, hoping for some sign of what to do next.

General Carzen noticed Wil's intent gaze. "Deactivate the panoramic viewing," he commanded.

The room returned to its original appearance with another shimmering wave washing over the walls.

"Head toward the station." Carzen's eyes narrowed, he turned back to Wil. "Don't you know how you came into being?"

"Why would there be anything to know?"

"Oh, there's so very much they must have kept from you," Carzen said. "You were genetically engineered to be superior to your fellow Tarans. Generations of careful pairing to select the best traits Tarans had to offer. It's all come down to you, a union of the bloodlines symbolized by Serpent and Falcon crests—when combined, a Dragon. You were designed to have enhanced physical and cognitive abilities, paired with telekinetic strengths unlike any Taran before you. Through those means, you were meant to be even stronger than the Bakzen—but we have evolved. This isn't a fight you alone can win. Join us."

Wil tensed, unsure what to make of the general's statement. He couldn't take the Bakzen's word at face value. *Was I really 'engineered' to be this way?*

It was unnerving to think of being created for such a distinct purpose, but he cast the feeling aside. Carzen would say anything to keep him interested. "Yes, General, I have always known that I was superior to other Tarans, I just never knew to what extent."

Carzen nodded. "There is one more thing that I'm not sure you know. An ability that will one day emerge. No one in the TSS could ever teach you to use it—they will barely comprehend its wonders. Though it is a skill that you will ultimately have to master on your own, we can guide you to—"

The general suddenly cut off as a violent jolt rocked the ship. Wil was caught off guard, but he quickly regained his composure. The jolt was undoubtedly caused by a weapons blast of some sort, but he didn't know where it had originated.

"They're targeting our jump drive," the helmsman announced. "Weapons on the TSS ship are still charged."

Carzen shot a seething glare toward the *Vanquish.*

Such an aggressive tactic was unlike his father. *Do they know something I don't?*

"It would seem the TSS cares more about killing Bakzen than protecting one of their own," Carzen said to Wil. "Would you like to do the honors?"

*What does he mean?* Wil stayed put in his chair as another shot from the *Vanquish* rocked the Bakzen ship.

"Bring him here," Carzen instructed.

One of the escorts standing along the back wall roughly pulled Wil to his feet and shoved him toward the front control consoles.

"It's only fitting you should be the one to end them," Carzen stated. "A rite of passage for any soldier."

Wil shook his head. "No."

"You don't have a choice." Carzen grabbed Wil by the upper arms and directed him to the rightmost console. "All you have to do is press the button. Then all that the Bakzen have to offer will be yours."

"I won't do it!" Wil tried to resist the general, but he was at an impossible physical disadvantage.

"Just one button," Carzen whispered in Wil's ear. "Don't you see? You're their 'savior' but they're so willing to kill you now that you're in the way. Collateral damage." He grabbed Wil's hand and forced it toward the touchscreen. "Do it!"

"No!" Wil struck back with a powerful telekinetic wave.

Carzen staggered backward. "Stupid boy! You could have it all."

"I already do," Wil spat back. *An entire crew risking their lives to save me. The Bakzen will never understand that kind of devotion.*

"Change of plan. Throw him out an airlock," Carzen told the escorts. "Return fire!"

Another escort came to assist the first. Each took one of Wil's arms and dragged him across the room.

"The Bakzen will never win, General," Wil called to Carzen.

"If not, then at least in death we will find peace," Carzen replied, glancing at Wil one last time. "Know that your own death served a great purpose."

*I'm not dead yet.* Wil let the guards take him out the doors from the Command Center, not wanting to waste his strength on futile resistance. *I need to find a way to get off this ship.*

The hallway was plain and empty, with stark lighting making it seem like a desolate tunnel. The guards held onto Wil's arms with a firm grip, their expressions stoic. After a few meters, another blast rocked the ship.

Wil's mind raced. *Maybe this is the diversion I need. But how do I get away?*

Up ahead, there was a door panel with interlocking components. Wil recognized the section of passage as the place he had entered the Bakzen vessel at the port.

*Stars! So, Carzen did mean a literal airlock. I had hoped it was a figure of speech.*

"You don't need to do this, you know," Wil said, beginning to resist the forward motion.

"You had chance," one of the guards said in broken New Taran. "Now you die."

"But what will that accomplish, really?" Wil countered.

"You tear Rift," the guard replied. "Then we win."

*So they're all crazy.* "I don't think so."

Another blast wracked the Bakzen ship. Simultaneously, Wil lashed out with the strongest telekinetic attack he could muster, piercing the minds and bodies of his captors with whips of pure energy.

They released Wil, gripping their heads. Their cries of agony were masked by the concussive force echoing along the ship's hull. Just as the blast subsided, the guards collapsed on the ground, unconscious.

They were only five meters from the airlock. Wil jogged ahead and pressed the release button to open the inner door. In one motion, he levitated the guards into the chamber and sealed them inside.

He paused. *I could vent them… Carzen is expecting to see an airlock activate.* He looked at the control panel, but the text was in a language he took to be Bakzeni. *I don't have time to figure this out.* Part of him was relieved to leave the guards alive.

No one else was visible in the passageway.

*I don't have much time. They won't be out for long. Once they wake up and sound the alarm, there's no way I'll get free.*

Wil looked down both wings of the hall, having absolutely no idea which way to go. He hesitated, wasting valuable time.

*Move*!

He ran to the right, just trying to distance himself from the Command Center and Carzen.

Wil rounded a corner and came to a dead end. *Great.*

There was a single door, apparently to the Bakzen version of a lift. Wil walked forward and the doors opened.

*Keep moving.*

He entered the lift, and the doors closed automatically behind him. There were no exposed controls.

*Voice activated. Will it understand New Taran? Where do I go?* There was only one option. "Hangar," Wil said, willing the computer to understand the command.

Movement. He didn't know for sure where he was heading, but any movement was a good sign.

*Just keep breathing. Stay calm. It will be okay.*

Another violent jolt shook the ship and Wil was thrown against the wall of the lift. He caught himself against the wall and rode out the shock of the blast.

*They know what they're doing. Stay calm. Focus.*

The lift came to an abrupt halt and the doors opened, revealing another hallway. Wil peered out. Again, to his relief, there was no one to see him. He crept out, keeping close to the wall in case anyone came by.

*Where am I?* There were signs, but it was all in Bakzeni. *I should have paid more attention in linguistics class.*

He looked around. There was a large doorway in front of him. Blank, unmarked hallways stretched in either direction.

Assuming that the lift had indeed taken him to the hangar, the doors ahead were likely the entry. However, there were probably numerous crewmembers inside.

*How am I supposed to get a ship without being caught?*

He combed the walls without moving, hoping to catch sight of something that might serve as a distraction while he entered the room. As he had suspected, the walls were completely bare, leaving him with only what he was carrying.

Wil crouched down, and he felt his pants tighten around a form in his pocket. *That's right!*

His handheld and the demo explosive from his electrochemistry class were still tucked away. He pulled out the two objects. *I can work with this.*

He brought up the imaging controls on his handheld and set the screen to cycle through a timed frequency sweep of colored light that should overlap with the trigger range for the explosive. Then, he queued up a music track. Once everything was configured to his satisfaction, he carefully laid the explosive film over the screen so it would get maximum exposure.

*This will have to be good enough.*

Wil dashed across the hallway, staying low. He came to rest beside the door, his back pressed up against the smooth surface of the wall. It would be a one-shot deal to quickly assess his surroundings and formulate an action plan once he got inside. With the luck that had been coming very easily in the past few minutes, he would be able to procure a fighter and escape while the personnel were distracted by the sudden sound and explosion.

*Not that I'll necessarily know how to fly a Bakzen ship*, he realized with a wave of apprehension. *Well, there's one way to find out.*

He made a sudden movement toward the door. As he expected, it opened automatically. Not pausing to look inside, Wil simultaneously initiated the light frequency sweep and started the music on the handheld, then slid the device across the floor. It would take twenty seconds for the frequency sweep to make it to the trigger range for the explosive.

When he heard the opening notes of the music, he ran into the room, staying close to the wall and low to the ground.

Once he was safely behind a crate near the door, he risked a look at what he hoped was a hangar. He sighed with relief. There were rows of fighter-like spacecraft, similar in appearance to those Wil normally flew, and all the visible personnel in the bay were walking over to inspect the handheld, looking quite confused.

Wil had been carefully counting as he ran into the room, and he ducked down to gain some shelter from the impending blast. *Four… three… two… one…*

The explosion was more forceful than Wil had anticipated, but it served its purpose well. A sharp crack reverberated through the hall with the detonation. The music cut off with a digital screech. Shouts of pain and surprise rang out as the blast hit the Bakzen.

Wil scrambled toward a row of fighters in the middle of the hangar.

As he approached one of the fighters, he caught sight of some Bakzen soldiers recovering from the blast. Others were still lying on the ground, apparently injured. *Good thing that didn't accidentally go off in my pocket!*

Wil climbed to the ship's cockpit in much the same way as any TSS fighter, stepping up the footholds running along the hull in front of the port wing. They were sized for a large Bakzen soldier, but Wil nimbly hurried up.

Once he was standing on the wing, still undetected by the Bakzen soldiers on the other side of the bay, he was able to get his first good look at the control panels of the alien vessel. To his surprise, they were manual controls rather than the touchscreens that he had previously seen on the Bakzen ships. There were also craft in the TSS fleet that used manual controls, and he happened to prefer them.

He climbed into the cockpit and his confidence evaporated. It was huge for him, and the location of the seat was fixed. *Shite!*

Wil slipped off his jacket and shoved it behind his back to give him a little boost toward the controls. He still strained to reach the front panel, but it was just enough.

*Now, how do I work this thing?*

He stared at the controls as he fastened the safety harness around his chest and lap. Of course, the labels were all written in the mystifying Bakzeni language. He looked around at the metal bracing around the top of the cockpit, hoping to find whatever mechanism was used to close the upper hatch.

*There must be something.*

Finding no indication of a closing button or lever along the upper edge, he returned to his examination of the control panel. It was laid out similarly to TSS ships. However, a button's corresponding position on a TSS craft didn't guarantee an identical function on the Bakzen vessel. After several more seconds of staring dumbly at the dashboard, Wil knew he had to take action before he wasted even more precious time.

*Here goes nothing.*

He pressed the button that, on a TSS vessel, would start up the taxiing engines. The welcome noise of engine ignition met his ears. Moments later, the hatch began to close above his head. The control panel lit up as the engine settled into a humming idle.

With momentary panic, it occurred to him that he wasn't wearing a flight suit; hopefully the cockpit was pressurized. He waited for the hatch to close and was relieved to hear a hiss as it sealed. Even if there wasn't an air filter, there would be enough trapped oxygen to get him to his destination.

Wil turned his attention to the forward controls. He gently moved one of the levers forward and the fighter immediately responded—by moving in a backward direction. *Well that's a stupid design!*

Quickly bringing the ship to a complete stop, Wil then pulled the lever toward himself and the fighter began rolling forward.

*I can do this.* He brought the fighter out into the open area between the rows of dormant craft. There was no way the Bakzen hadn't noticed him yet, but he couldn't see anything out the back of the ship.

Ahead, Wil saw that the exterior exit was sealed. Hoping that he wouldn't have to shoot out the doors, he revved the engines. The doors began to spread apart, revealing a nearly transparent force field. As he passed by the row of fighters near the door, he realized that several of the craft were powering up.

*Stars! Here we go.*

Wil engaged the primary engines and accelerated as he approached the force field. It washed over his fighter and he glided into the expanse of space.

As soon as he was clear of the cruiser, Wil spun the fighter around one hundred-eighty degrees to face his pursuers. So far, his assumptions of controls had been accurate; the technologies weren't as different as he'd feared. The vessel was more responsive than many in the TSS fleet, and Wil almost swung past his mark. He managed to catch the spin in time and spotted the lead pursuer.

As he locked the weapons onto his target, he located the protective field generator for his fighter and switched it on. Wil took aim and fired.

The blast glanced off the shield of his opponent, as a return shot issued from the other fighter. Wil nudged his fighter to the side, avoiding the shot. As he did so, three more ships joined the one he had already targeted. An energy field formed between the ships: a containment net.

*Shite, they're trying to capture me!*

Wil spun the fighter back around to port, not quite one-eighty, but slightly off to his new starboard side, and accelerated quickly. The ship was obviously built for extreme speed and responded effortlessly at the faster pace. He brought the fighter over the top of the Bakzen cruiser he had just left, cutting it so close he could almost reach out to touch the hull. He was very much in control now that he knew how the vessel operated.

When he came over the top of the Bakzen cruiser, the *Vanquish* came into full view. He kept the fighter at the same breakneck speed as he neared the TSS ship.

When he was within a kilometer, he began to slow just enough to prepare for landing. As he did, the Bakzen fighters behind him began to speed up and moved into a protective formation. Wil couldn't see them clearly because of the cockpit design, but the shot over his starboard wing made their intent obvious.

He was forced to swerve to his port side in order to avoid another shot from the fighter on the right of the formation. The maneuver threw him off his course to the *Vanquish*'s hangar just as he neared the most crucial part of the landing procedure.

When another shot just barely missed the roof of the cockpit, Wil had to abort the landing attempt and circle around to once again face his attackers. He swung above the other fighters and opened fire at a downward angle while accelerating straight toward them. As he had hoped, due to the angle, Wil left their cone of fire just before they were out of his. He got in a few clean shots before passing the lead ship.

It took several moments for the fighters to recover from the attack, but when they did, Wil took on a course running along the underside of the Bakzen cruiser.

*Let's see how they handle this.*

The course cut precariously near the hull of the cruiser, and Wil surprised even himself with how close he got. One wrong move and his fighter would be obliterated.

The fighters trailing Wil had to follow him at the same proximity to the ship if they wanted to keep him within range. Three of the vessels maintained the course, but the fighter that had been at the front of the original attack formation trailed behind slightly. When all the fighters needed to take a steeper heading to veer away from the cruiser, the laggard fighter continued on a straight trajectory.

Wil focused straight ahead, pulling up sharply to maneuver away from the cruiser. When he swung back around to face the oncoming fighters there were only three, and there was evidence of an explosion on the hull of the large Bakzen cruiser.

He couldn't help but heave a relieved sigh at having eliminated one of his pursuers, but he also was gripped with an unexpected pang of regret. *My first kill.* He had always been taught that taking a life was an unwelcome last resort. *You had to. There's no other way out of this.* He grimaced. *One down, three to go.*

The maneuvering had led Wil away from the *Vanquish.* The approach was completely exposed, and if he made a run for it, he would likely need to abort again due to another attack during landing.

Instead, Wil did a one-eighty and opened fire on his opponents. One of the fighters exploded in a brief burst of flame that was quickly extinguished in the vacuum of space. With the hope of snaring Wil in a containment net lost with the destruction of the second ship, the remaining two fighters returned fire, Wil again accelerated toward them.

Just before he left their cone, he was hit in the left wing with a direct blast. The shield partially protected his fighter from the shot, but the craft was knocked to the side. Wil managed to hold it on course and got in a few more shots. As he passed over the attacking fighters, one burst into another ball of flame as the cockpit imploded.

Wil's fighter responded sluggishly. *Come on…*

As he tried to swing the fighter around to fire upon the remaining ship, the turn was much wider than he intended. Wil looked out the cockpit dome as best he could at the injured wing and saw a sizable chunk missing—only tattered metal shards remained around a blackened area where the port wing's maneuvering thrusters used to be. *That's going to make for a difficult landing.*

He continued around in the large loop: a very exposed position, but it was too late to try and pull out of it. The other Bakzen fighter was going too fast to turn sharply enough to keep

Wil's ship in its cone of fire, so it accelerated away from Wil to avoid his attack, and then circled around to face him.

Wil tried to swing the fighter off to the side, but the missing thruster on the damaged wing prevented precise execution of the maneuver. Left with no other choice, he shot his fighter full speed toward the oncoming Bakzen vessel.

He tilted his course down slightly so he could duck underneath the other ship, but that took the enemy out of his firing range and put him directly in its path. Blasts shot by on all sides of him, some coming close to striking him, but he held his course.

As he neared the other fighter, it was obvious that his vessel could not withstand many more hits, and that at his current speed he wouldn't be out of range in time. Another wave of blasts hit full force against his already weakened shielding.

The two fighters drew closer together and a light began flashing on his dashboard. *That can't be good!*

Just as the enemy fighter was about to fire another round to finish him off, the enemy craft was suddenly enveloped in a flaming ball as a blast took it from a remote location.

Wil dove his fighter to avoid the debris and then looked around to see that the *Vanquish* had taken on a protective position for him. The Bakzen cruiser that had been carrying General Carzen had several blackened marks on it where the *Vanquish*'s assault had taken its toll, but it otherwise looked unharmed.

Wil cracked a smile. It had been a very carefully calculated shot that had saved him from his predicament; likely made by Kari. He wanted to relax, but he wasn't out of danger yet. *I just have to get to the Vanquish. Then I'll be safe.*

He brought the fighter around and looped it toward the *Vanquish*'s hangar. He slowed the vessel down in anticipation of a rough landing with the damaged wing.

At the slow speed, he lined up with the hangar door and activated what he took to be the controls for the landing gear. He felt something happening underneath the fighter.

*Almost there...* The opening was only eighty meters away. *Come on... come on...* He could see the shimmering force field.

The last few meters closed rapidly. Wil braked hard as he passed through the doorway and the fighter bumped down roughly on the deck of the hangar. The landing gear hadn't opened fully, as far as Wil could tell, and the fighter skidded, sparks flying. He continued to brake, and the fighter swung around, its rear end screeching backward toward the interior bulkhead.

The fighter careened across the deck, hurtling dangerously close to a row of parked fighters. Just as Wil thought a collision was imminent, the emergency net deployed and brought the Bakzen vessel to a grinding halt.

Wil sat in stunned silence for a moment, trying to comprehend that he was back with his own people. As he caught his breath, he felt the familiar vibration of the spatial jump drive.

He exhaled with a complete release of nervous energy, on the verge of laughing with relief. "Wow." He unstrapped the safety harness in the fighter. *Now, how do I get out of this thing?*

There was still no release lever on the upper dome of the cockpit, even with the hatch closed. *Maybe...* He switched off the engine and the cockpit dome decompressed with a hiss, and then slid open automatically. He looked up at the ceiling of the shuttle bay, taking in the familiar surroundings. *I'm safe.*

In the heat of battle, he hadn't been able to think about his mortal danger—to realize how close he had been to an early death. That thought stopped him cold.

He had never before been in a situation that threatened to end his life, but this was just the beginning. A chill ran through him with that thought, and he shuddered.

Wil was roused from his thoughts by a shout from the other side of the hangar. "Wil! Are you okay? Wil!"

"I'm okay, Dad... just a little shaken up." Wil climbed out of the cockpit and out onto a beaten wing.

The fighter was even more damaged than he had thought, and it struck him just how lucky he was to have landed safely.

The black scarring on the deck plates was enough to show how rough the landing had been.

His father came running over as Wil jumped off the wing. He was immediately pulled into a warm embrace.

"Thank the stars you're safe!" Cris held him for a few moments, then pulled back to look Wil over at arm's length, his hands still on his shoulders. "You're sure you're okay?"

Wil opened his mouth to speak, but he didn't know what to say. *There are so many unanswered questions. I don't know what to think anymore…* "We have a lot to talk about."

Cris looked into Wil's eyes. "It's been an enlightening few days. I have a lot of questions of my own."

"Is Mom here, too?"

"No, she's back home. We just have a skeleton crew."

Wil took a shaky breath. "Are we safe?"

"We're heading home. The Bakzen gave one final assault as we jumped away, but we're in the clear."

Wil only nodded in response, turning his head away as tears began to well up in his eyes. The last several hours had brought him to the edge of his emotional endurance. He hugged his father again, needing the physical reassurance that he was out of immediate danger.

After a minute of quiet embrace, he pulled away. "I'm glad to be back."

# CHAPTER 10

CRIS ESCORTED HIS son out of the hangar, staying close. As much as he wanted to offer words of comfort, he couldn't think of anything that wouldn't sound trite. He steered Wil toward the nearest lift.

"Where are we going?" Wil asked, sounding a little frantic. His movement was unusually rigid and his eyes were darting around apprehensively.

For the first time, Cris noticed that Wil's eyes had begun to glow slightly, bringing out teal highlights—a departure from the cobalt familial standard. The bioluminescence was expected, given Wil's rising telekinetic abilities, but he was still so young.

"To the infirmary so Irina can look you over," Cris responded.

They arrived at a lift, and Cris stepped in.

Wil stopped in the hall. "I'm fine. I just want to go to bed."

*This isn't like him. What did the Bakzen put him through?* Cris stared at his son, confused by his resistance. "Wil, I understand that you're tired, but I think it's important that you get a clean bill of health."

Wil stood his ground. He dropped his gaze to the floor, shaking his head.

Cris took a deep breath. "What is it, Wil? I know you've been through a lot, but I've never seen you like this." He looked with concern at his son.

Wil smiled wryly, bringing his softly glowing eyes up to meet Cris'. "I don't know what to believe anymore. The Bakzen told me things—that I was engineered to fight them. But with all their advanced technologies—far more powerful than anything I've seen at the TSS—what could one person possibly do? Their abilities…" He faded off with a little laugh at the last statement.

Cris leaned against the rear wall of the lift. "I don't know where to start… I finally got what I think is a kernel of truth out of Banks, but I'm still not sure what to make of it."

Wil looked up with interest. "What did he say?"

Cris shook his head and laughed to himself in much the same way his son had. "We shouldn't get into that now; it's part of a much larger conversation. Let's just make sure you're all right, and then we can both get some much-needed rest. You look as tired as I feel, so I know you can't completely object."

Wil relaxed a little. "You're right. I'm sorry. I'm just so sick of secrets and half-truths."

"You and me both. Now, can we make sure you're okay?"

His son sighed and nodded. He stepped into the lift. "I can't believe you brought the Head Medical Doctor out here for me."

"Actually, she volunteered. Everyone on the crew did."

His eyebrows raised with surprise. "Really?"

"Of course. We're family—blood relations or not. Everyone wanted to help get you home."

Wil smiled, showing a hint of his usual self. "Thank you."

The lift brought them to the corridor outside the infirmary entrance.

"Now, come on." Cris guided Wil forward.

Wil shot an exasperated look back at his father a moment before Irina came out of her office.

"What happened? It felt like we made a jump and—" She caught sight of Wil. "Oh, thank the stars! Wil, how are you feeling?" She escorted him to a medical bed with motherly care and sat him down.

"I feel fine. I'm just very tired."

"And you certainly look it," she replied with a soft smile. "You're taking after your father too much already." She looked up at Cris then back to her patient. "Tiredness is easy enough to fix."

She took a small blood sample from his fingertip and ran it through a scanner. She looked pleased with the results.

"But besides that, I don't see anything immediately anomalous. Are you sure you feel okay? That was a rough landing."

"Yes, I'm fine. I'm just a little sore from sleeping on rocks for days," Wil said.

"What part of you?" Irina asked.

"Kind of everywhere, but mostly my hip." Wil moved to slide off the table, but the doctor stopped him.

"Your hip? Show me," Irina requested, her face drawn.

*Why is that significant?* Cris crossed his arms.

Wil reluctantly pulled down the side of his pants to expose the back of his left hip. Irina examined the area. She frowned.

"What is it?" Cris asked. *Please, don't tell me they did something to him...*

"There's the trace of a needle mark here," Irina said.

Wil looked alarmed. "Like from a shot?"

"No, it's a wider diameter than that." Irina's brow furrowed. "The only thing that comes to mind is that this is a common site for bone marrow extraction."

Cris felt ill. *Stars!*

"What would they want with my bone marrow?" Wil looked between Irina and Cris, alarmed.

Irina placed a comforting hand on Wil's shoulder. "No reason for concern. It can be used to treat illness, or maybe the Bakzen are just trying to learn about Tarans."

*"Or for cloning?"* Cris asked telepathically.

Without any external reaction, Irina replied, "*Yes, it's possible. Why?*"

"*Write what you need in your medical report, but don't say anything else to Wil. He's been through enough.*" Cris tried to relax. *The Bakzen wouldn't try to clone him, would they...?* "Someone could be sick and you're a match. Who knows."

Irina smiled at Wil. "Yes, I'm sure it's nothing to worry about. I'll run some further analysis, to be safe, and let you know if anything shows up." She allowed Wil to get off the exam platform. "Just feed him and get him to bed, Cris. You should get some rest as well."

"Yes, Doctor." Cris exchanged a knowing look with Wil. *First, I need to finish my conversation with Banks.*

"You can tell me what happened later."

Cris nodded. "I will." He put his hand on Wil's shoulder and walked him out the door.

"That wasn't so bad, was it?" he said once they were out in the hall.

"No. She did give me a strange look, though. My eyes have started to turn, haven't they?" Wil looked at his father for confirmation.

"Yes, but I suspect that her reaction was more about you surviving an encounter with the Bakzen. That's no small feat. Your eyes turning was something that we knew would happen any time." *I can't believe he's grown up this fast.*

"Yes, but I'm only fourteen, Dad. It's awfully young for that."

*Even twenty is early for most...* "It's young, yes, but it's in line with the accelerated timeline of your other abilities. Given the circumstances, it's nothing out of the ordinary," Cris assured. *I wasn't ready for this.*

"Dad, I handled over an 8 in intensity."

Cris stopped mid-stride and looked over at his son. "That's a significant gain. How did it feel?"

"That's the thing, it was perfectly fine. There was no strain whatsoever," Wil said, becoming very serious. "I didn't even have to try."

"What happened?"

Wil looked down at the floor. "They had me in some sort of interrogation room and Colonel Tek was questioning me. He was saying how powerful the Bakzen were, and I wanted to show him I was strong, too. So, I sent a telepathic probe. Tek told me it was around an 8, but I've never done that before. I didn't know. But, I— I didn't feel a max. I mean, I stopped because I didn't want him to feel me strain and know my limit, so—"

"Slow down, Wil! Breathe." He waited for his son to settle. "Who's this Colonel Tek? No, never mind, we'll do a full debrief later. Now, you didn't feel *any* sort of limit?"

Wil shook his head. "No. It didn't surprise me as much at the time as it should have, but looking back on it, I don't know what to think. I was just so scared." Wil hugged himself. "No one ever told me what to do in that kind of captive situation. I just had to play along."

Cris put a hand on Wil's shoulder. "You did great, Wil. We'll work through this new development later."

After a moment, Wil nodded.

*He's taking this whole situation so much better than I would have.* Cris wrapped his arm around Wil's shoulder and directed him back into the main hall. "Right now, you're under doctor's orders to get some rest, and one of the last things I would do is cross Irina Saunatev. Come on."

They walked the rest of the way to Cris' quarters in silence. Once there, Wil went straight to the bed and lay down, only pausing to slip off his boots. Cris started to leave, but his son called out, "Dad, would you stay here? I don't really want to be alone right now."

"Of course, Wil. I won't leave you."

Wil arranged the pillows into a cozy cocoon around his head, and within moments his breathing was slow and regular with sleep.

*We did it. We got him back.* Even through his relief, Cris worried about what would happen next.

He sent a message to the Command Center for them to find a remote place to drop out from subspace so he could get in touch with Headquarters. As soon as they were back in normal space, he walked quietly over to the viewscreen in the other room to call Banks.

It took a while for the video feed to connect, but Cris knew that it was the middle of the night on their clock. Banks was probably sleeping.

After a few minutes, the viewscreen showed the High Commander's face. "Cris? Do you…"

"We have Wil," Cris replied with an enthusiastic smile, keeping his voice low so he didn't wake Wil.

Banks beamed, days of tension releasing. "I knew you'd find a way."

"Well, it wasn't easy." He gave a quick recap of the events.

Banks looked nervous. "You entered the Rift?"

"Well, yes. What else were we supposed to do?"

"You did the right thing." The High Commander sat quietly in thought and then took a deep breath. "How's Wil?"

Cris turned around to look at the sleeping form of his son. "He seems okay. Tired and overwhelmed, but he's resting now." Cris bit his lip. "Banks, he's changed so much just in the past few days."

"You've both been through a lot."

Cris sighed. "I can't think straight. I'm too exhausted to even be properly upset with you."

"Ah ha! My plan worked," Banks jested.

"Very funny." It would be amusing if it weren't so close to the truth. Cris ran his fingers through his hair. "All this new information… What I've seen first-hand… I mean, fok! What you told me earlier, about the nanotech, genetic engineering—you're talking about the very foundation of individual identity!" Wil stirred on the bed, and Cris realized he had raised his voice. He continued more quietly. "Every piece of my life has been either programmed or orchestrated. What am I supposed to do with that knowledge?"

"You accept it for what it is."

Cris scoffed. "You know me better than that."

Banks looked at him levelly. "Which is how I know you'll buckle down and do what needs to be done."

"It's not that easy. The happy bubble of blissful ignorance has burst. You expect me to just carry on like nothing has changed?"

"Of course not." Banks shook his head. "But I do expect you to carry on—albeit, in a more informed manner."

"And what am I supposed to tell Wil? Apparently the Bakzen started saying some version of what you told me. I delayed the conversation, but I know that's the first thing he's going to ask about when he wakes up. He's still barely more than a kid! I can't just say 'the fate of the entire Taran race is in your hands', or however you want to characterize it. It's ridiculous!"

"I know nothing about this is easy. I'll tell him with you, if you prefer."

Cris paused. "No, it should come from me. I just wish the statements could have a little more context."

Banks thought for a moment. "Where are you now?"

"Heading toward home. I don't know where, exactly. We jumped away and then dropped out so I could get in touch."

"You're still close, then," Banks murmured. "I think you should go visit the Jotun Division Headquarters. If not for you, then for Wil. They can give you that context about the Bakzen. And he should see the full extent of the TSS' forces."

"It's a full Headquarters facility, not just a base?"

"Yes, with its own High Commander and Lead Agent. We call it H2."

"That other budget you alluded to earlier."

"Right."

"What else have you been keeping from me?"

"Nothing that changes the path ahead," Banks hedged.

Cris' eyes narrowed. "So, there's *something*."

"Cris, you know better than anyone that there's never complete transparency. But, the war in the Rift, and Wil's part to play in its end—that's the heart of all this."

He crossed his arms. "Now you want to send us to this 'other Headquarters' and throw us into the middle of that war?"

"Far from it. I just think it's important for Wil to see that there's more to the TSS than what you know back home. We need a leader with Wil's future abilities to end the war, yes, but we've been holding our own for a long time. He'll have backing when it's time for him to step up as a leader."

*I can't take him there now, have him paraded around...* Cris shook his head. "He needs time to recover. This—"

"He's more resilient than you're giving him credit for."

Cris glanced over at Wil. "Normally, yes. But he's right on the verge, Banks. Don't push him right now."

The High Commander gave him a stern look. "I don't want this to be about technicalities, but you've already crossed over into Jotun jurisdiction. Once that happens, there are protocols."

Cris sighed. *He'll make it an order if I don't agree.* "We've been behind enemy lines, have intel, need to debrief..."

Banks nodded. "And they're far more equipped to handle that process than we are. Please, this will be easier for everyone if you set a good example."

"It's not like I have a choice, then."

Banks shook his head. "I'll transmit the spatial coordinates to the *Vanquish*'s computer. The main Headquarters structure is within an offshoot of the Rift, but it's accessible by a stationary rift gate fixed in normal space. The engineering crew will be able to get you a replacement jump drive cell for the trip home."

*I would just take the ship and disappear if Kate were here with us.* "Do we really have to do this now?"

"Yes. And I hate to say it, but this is just the beginning," Banks said, his tone morose.

Cris shook his head. "How am I supposed to trust anything you tell me?"

"Because despite recent appearances, I have always had your back. Now that everything is out in the open, I'll make sure Wil gets everything he'll need to be successful."

"I still don't want him to have any part of this."

"I know. I don't, either, but that's one thing we can't change."

*A future decided generations in advance.* Cris looked down. There was no way to fight it, at least not at the moment. "What should we expect at this other Headquarters?"

"H2 is a military installation first and foremost," Banks explained. "Very different from the TSS you know."

"Should I even bother asking about where I stand in terms of rank and reporting structure?"

Banks looked unsure. "It's never really come up before. Just be polite."

Cris nodded. "Fine, I'll figure it out." He paused, hit by a wave of tiredness. He held back a yawn. "I should call Kate before I pass out."

"Why don't you wait until morning. I should fill her in first."

*There's more to tell her about than just Wil's rescue.* Cris reluctantly nodded. "Okay, well, I'd better get some rest or I'll be cranky with the other officers."

Banks cracked a smile. "Of course, Cris. Sleep well."

"I'll have Alec get us on course for H2."

"I'll talk to you again when you arrive, I'm sure."

"Yes. Talk to you then." Cris moved to end the transmission.

"One more thing, Cris."

"Yes?"

"Nicely done."

# CHAPTER 11

KNOWING THAT WIL and the *Vanquish* were safe set Banks' mind at ease, but everything had changed. *I never meant for Wil to find out so soon. I just hope it's not too much for him to handle.*

With the *Vanquish* headed toward H2, he needed to alert his High Commander counterpart. But first, he needed to have a difficult conversation with Kate.

Shaking off his weariness, Banks dressed and plodded into the long hallway of the Primus Agents' wing. Three doors down, he paused outside Kate and Cris' quarters to gather his thoughts and then pressed the buzzer.

Kate answered after a minute. Her hair was tousled and her hazel eyes were exposed, their glow less vibrant than normal.

"What happened?" she asked with audible concern, pulling her robe tighter.

"Cris just contacted me. May I come in?" Banks asked, realizing only after he had spoken that it sounded as if he brought bad news.

Kate paled. "What is it?"

"Everything's fine, Kate," Banks assured her.

She stood aside to allow him to enter and then closed the door. "What did Cris say?"

Banks beamed. "He has Wil. He's fine. They're on the *Vanquish* together now."

Kate's breath caught, tears of joy and relief in her eyes. "I couldn't let myself hope."

"Things have a way of working out."

For the first time in days, Kate smiled. "Thank the stars it's over! When will they be back home?"

"It might be a while."

Kate's smile faded. "Why?"

"They need to make a stopover on the way. Why don't we have a seat." He motioned to the couch and they sat down on opposite sides. He removed his tinted glasses; the impending conversation was best handled without such barriers. *This never gets any easier.*

"What's wrong?" she asked.

"Now that Wil has been rescued, there are some things you should know. I already talked with Cris."

He proceeded to tell her about the Rift and the ongoing war with the Bakzen. Facts, presented bluntly and without ceremony. He would have eased some people into the idea of the hidden conflict, but he knew Kate well enough to know that she would appreciate a direct approach. However, he was careful to stay away from the details about the nanotech manipulation of bloodlines—and especially about Wil's upcoming role in the war. The rest was already enough to overwhelm anyone.

Kate was quiet as he told her. Banks wasn't sure if the silence was from shock or acceptance. But from the way she clutched a throw pillow to her chest, he suspected the information was more than she wanted to acknowledge at the moment. The anger and hurt would come with time. It always did.

"So, they're heading toward this other Headquarters now?" she asked when Banks was finished.

"Yes, H2. They need to debrief with the other High Commander, who's in charge of all Bakzen affairs."

"You couldn't give them a few days to recover?" Kate's tone had a vicious bite. The shock hadn't lasted long.

"No, this is for the best. They'll be home soon."

"This is crazy! How have you kept the war a secret all this time?" Kate's face darkened.

*No one would believe the lengths we've gone to, even if I told them.* Banks rose, recognizing it was time to retreat while he still could. "I wish I could talk with you more, but I need to alert H2 that the *Vanquish* is coming. I just wanted you to know that Cris and Wil are safe."

Kate glared at him. "How thoughtful." She stayed on the couch.

Banks walked to the door. "I'm not sure how long it will be before they return, but know that they are in good hands. I'll let you know if I hear anything else."

Banks saw Kate nod as he closed the door. With a sigh, he restored his tinted glasses and began the trek to his office through the dimmed halls. *Now for the really hard part.*

Banks had once found the nighttime state of TSS Headquarters to be peaceful, but it instead seemed unsettling, knowing how Wil was taken. With the perpetrator still unidentified, everyone would need to be cautious.

Once in his office, Banks sat down at his desk to contemplate his approach to the conversation.

He maintained a somewhat strained relationship with the other TSS High Commander, Erik Taelis. They had known each other for decades. Taelis was four years ahead of Banks in the training program, and they first met when Taelis was an instruction assistant in one of Banks' classes. After Taelis graduated, Banks heard nothing of him for years.

Their futures were set when Banks accidentally intercepted a communication. He was fulfilling his first assignment as an Agent to oversee Comm Command operations when he happened to overhear a conversation between the previous High Commander and the Priesthood discussing Taelis' future. It only took a few seconds for them to realize Banks was listening in, but he had already heard enough to be dangerous. They had spoken of the war and directly tied the Priesthood to the TSS. The war was a closely guarded secret from all those who weren't under the strict confidentiality agreement of a Jotun assignment contract, but the TSS' relationship with the Priesthood was even more covert.

Banks had shown himself to be trustworthy and capable in other respects, so the TSS decided to bring him into the fold of the Jotun division. He was made an assistant to the previous High Commander for the primary Headquarters, serving as a liaison to Taelis, his counterpart for Jotun. What Banks and Taelis didn't realize at the time was they were both being groomed as future High Commanders for their respective TSS facilities.

The Priesthood was very particular about their selections for key assignments. They wanted someone with initiative, but not so much as to be a threat. Conversely, being too agreeable made for an ineffective leader. Banks had found what felt like the appropriate balance over the years, but Taelis had opted for a more aggressive approach to suit his position. While Banks' Headquarters offered the luxuries of any fine home on the Taran worlds, Taelis and those under his command subsisted in an active war zone.

Over the years, the difference in styles and circumstances had frayed their relationship. Their greatest disagreements were always over how to handle Wil. Taelis never seemed to understand that Wil had all the feelings and needs of any other boy. Consequently, Banks was often in a position where he had to stand up in Wil's defense, much to Taelis' discontent. There was no doubt Taelis would view Wil's capture solely as a failure in Banks' leadership.

Banks groaned. *No sense in delaying the inevitable.*

"CACI, contact TSS High Commander Erik Taelis," Banks ordered. He stood in front of the viewscreen, waiting for the transmission to go through. The TSS emblem floated on a black background before the picture changed to a man standing in an office very similar to Banks' own. "Hello, Erik," he greeted.

The other High Commander looked annoyed. "Jason, we're in the midst of a crisis. Can this wait until our check-in next week?"

Banks' eyes narrowed behind his tinted glasses. "I wouldn't call you if it weren't important."

Taelis looked away at something out of Banks' view. "Make it quick."

"This takes precedence over all other matters. You know I am not always able to contact you immediately about every development..." Banks began slowly.

"Yes?"

"This was one of those situations. Wil was captured by the Bakzen—"

Taelis' face drained. "When did this happen? This changes everything! We'll have to—"

"Erik, let me finish," Banks insisted, becoming agitated. "I sent my Lead Agent, his father, after him. He found Wil. He's safe. But in the process, they entered the Rift. That puts them under your jurisdiction until they're debriefed."

Taelis scowled. "You should have informed me the moment the Primus Elite was captured."

*So he could tell the Priesthood? I'd be dead in an instant.* "We have a security breach, and the extent of it is still unknown. I didn't want an enemy potentially listening in on the specifics about the rescue mission," Banks retorted. "Besides, I am still Wil's custodian."

Taelis looked exasperated. "And the next thing you'll tell me is the Aesir are after him, too?"

Banks looked down. *That will be another challenge.*

Taelis' brow furrowed. "They aren't, are they?"

"No, not now," Banks replied. "But we know the Aesir are aware of him. They have yet to make a move." *If and when they do, nothing we can do will keep Wil from the real truth.*

"They're slow to make *any* move." Taelis sighed. "Well, it's no matter, now. I suppose you ordered the Primus Elite to H2?"

"Yes," replied Banks. "It's time he sees the full extent of TSS forces. The purpose for keeping it from him has outlived its usefulness. If I know Wil, then he'll be worrying about everything that we don't have. It will be good for him to see that we're not entirely outmatched."

"You're too attached to him."

"It wouldn't do you any harm to be more understanding," Banks shot back.

Taelis dropped his gaze and shook his head. "Oh, Jason, let's not do this. If he really is coming here, then we need to get some things in order. I'll be as cordial as I can."

"His father, Cris, is my Lead Agent, remember, so make sure you treat him as such," Banks instructed. "Don't ask too much of them right now. They've both just been through a terrible ordeal. I doubt either of them will be at their best. And keep in mind how young Wil still is. He has a long way to go yet."

"Well, we'll see soon enough. I'll debrief him as I would anyone brought to this side of the Rift."

*Skirting the truth, as we always do.* "Tread carefully. He'll make connections no one else could." *And one day he'll see through it all, despite our efforts.*

Taelis nodded. "Always."

"Erik, I highly recommend you ease them into this. You'll get more out of them in a debrief if you win their trust first."

"You know an immediate sit-down interview is standard protocol," Taelis countered.

"I encourage you to make an exception. Like I said, Wil sees patterns the rest of us don't. Show him what the Jotun Division has to offer first, and he'll lay out his observations about the Bakzen in a way that will be most useful to you."

Taelis pursed his lips. "I'll take it under advisement."

Banks bowed his head. "Thank you, that's all I ask."

"I'll contact you once they've arrived. Take care, Jason," Taelis closed in the most congenial way he had for a long time.

"You too, Erik." Banks ended the transmission.

Banks looked at the time displayed on his desk. "I may as well stay here at this rate," he muttered to himself and walked over to the couch in the middle of his office. It wasn't a rare thing for him to spend the night there. *At least we can rest peacefully with the knowledge that our future is safe for the time being. Stay strong, Wil.*

— — —

Wil awoke with a start in almost complete blackness. His pulse spiked with panic for a moment, but then lay back when he confirmed he was on the *Vanquish.*

He looked around the room with renewed energy. Eventually, his gaze rested on his sleeping father, who was curled up in a chair in the corner of the room. Wil felt a twang of pity, knowing that he had taken his bed.

Wil got up silently and walked out of the small bedroom into the main living area. It was relatively dark, but the room was a familiar location from his youth, and he had no difficulty navigating around the furniture. He looked out the viewport and noticed a starscape. *Why aren't we in subspace?*

After standing momentarily in the middle of the room, Wil got himself a glass of water and sat down in a chair facing out the viewports. *It seems so peaceful. If only it really were.*

He let his thoughts drift, taking occasional sips from the glass, until he was suddenly brought out of his trance by the feeling of someone watching him. He turned to see his father standing in the doorway of the bedroom.

"What are you doing up, Wil?" Cris asked through the fading haze of sleep.

"I could ask the same for you."

His father came to sit by him. "I take it you're feeling better?"

"Yes, much. And you?" Wil set down the empty glass he had been holding.

Cris nodded. "I needed some sleep, but I started feeling better the moment I saw you."

"I know the feeling." *And I'd think we would want to be back home as soon as possible.* "Why are we stopped?" Wil asked.

His father rubbed his eyes again. "We're taking a detour on our way home—one that's best we face rested. I had them find a nice, secluded spot to park us overnight."

*I just want to be back home and forget all about this.* Wil tensed. "What kind of detour?"

Cris ran his hand through his hair. "Wil, I learned some things from Banks while you were away. The TSS hasn't been honest with us."

"What do you mean?"

Cris closed his eyes for a moment and took a deep breath. "The TSS has actually been at war with the Bakzen for hundreds of years. They've been fighting the war inside the Rift and have kept it a secret from almost everyone."

It should have been a shocking revelation, but the statement rolled off Wil after the events of recent days. "That explains a lot." *All those restricted files and communication logs on the Mainframe. I should have known something was going on.*

"I wish it were just that." Cris looked ill. He hung his head.

"Dad, you can tell me."

"Apparently, the Bakzen have far more advanced telekinetic abilities than most Tarans. Banks told me they can travel between the Rift and normal space at will."

*Is that even possible?* Wil shook his head, a knot forming in his gut. "I sensed that some of them are quite powerful, but I never saw them do anything like that."

"I know, it sounded crazy to me, too," Cris said. "Supposedly, that ability has always kept the TSS at a disadvantage in the war. They can even jump their fighters without a rift drive."

"Why didn't they use that when I was getting away?"

His father gazed out the viewport. "I don't know. Maybe they didn't want to hurt you."

Wil thought for a moment. "I guess they did try to snare me in a containment net at first, but when they couldn't, they didn't hesitate to open fire. Before all that, they were about to throw me out an airlock."

His father looked horrified. "You never should have been in that position."

"It's in the past now."

Cris nodded. "All I know is that the damage was to the maneuvering thrusters of your fighter—either it was luck, or they were shooting with the intent to disable without harming. But, that's just speculation."

"It doesn't make sense that they'd try to kill me, and then recapture me once I escaped."

"Well, they know you're special."

"No, they're crazy, Dad. What they were telling me—"

Cris looked down. "I don't know what they told you, but Banks and I talked. My entire perception of 'crazy' is pretty much shattered."

"Why, what did he say?" *Was Carzen being honest with me?*

Cris grimaced. "According to Banks, Tararian scientists set out to create a genetically superior Taran soldier, using the High Dynasties as the genetic foundation for their plan. Someone to match the Bakzen's abilities." Cris shook his head, his face drawn. "Wil, they've been playing us. There was a master plan for me to meet your mom and for you to be born. They think you're the one who can defeat the Bakzen."

Wil felt like he was being crushed under every word. When Carzen had made similar claims, it was the rantings of a crazy man, a sworn enemy. But coming from his father… *What could one person do, compared to the combined ability of a whole race?* He slumped in his seat. "What General Carzen said *is* true."

"What did he tell you?"

"He talked about my 'makers' and how I would have some sort of special ability no other Tarans have. He made it sound like the Priesthood thinks I'm their Cadicle. At the time, I thought he was just saying anything to keep my attention, but…" Wil took a shaky breath. He felt faint.

"Banks was reluctant to tell me much of anything. I hate to say it, but it looks like this is the first real truth we've heard for a long time."

Wil looked out the viewport, knowing the Bakzen were waiting somewhere in the distance. *I was made to fight the Bakzen…* It sounded preposterous. Normally he would have laughed—but he had seen too much to ignore the statements. He bit his lip and was gripped by a deep apprehension. *What if I'm not who they think I am?*

Cris crossed his arms. "Fok all of them."

Wil's chest felt tight. "I doubt ignoring this is an option."

His father shook his head "Oh, they want you to continue training and pretend like everything's great. Then, when it's convenient, have you step in as a military commander and end the conflict."

Wil shrank inward. "I always knew I'd become a powerful Agent, but commanding a fleet isn't what I had in mind."

"I know, Wil. This is all so profoundly foked up. Everything Banks dumped on me is blurring together. None of it seems real." Cris slumped back in his chair.

"It sounds like you covered the important parts." *Our life paths have been designed, and I'm supposed to stand up to an enemy that seems impossible to defeat.*

"I can't trust anything they say."

"But if it's really true…" Wil looked down. *This will be my whole life.*

Cris nodded, his expression grim. "I don't want to believe any of it, either. But, we're on our way to some sort of secondary TSS Headquarters that deals with the Bakzen. I suspect we'll learn more there."

Wil choked. "There's another Headquarters?"

"That's what Banks said, anyway. He called it 'H2'. I guess we'll see soon enough what they have to offer."

"They've held out against the Bakzen. It must be substantial."

Cris examined Wil. "You're taking all this rather calmly."

*I'm still in shock.* Wil let out an unsteady breath. "It doesn't feel that way to me."

"We'll get through this together."

Wil nodded. "It's amazing how one event can change so much." He stared out at the stars. "Nothing will ever be the same again."

Cris shook his head. "No, I'm afraid it won't be."

There was a long pause. Both of the Sietinens sat in silence with their own thoughts.

"What will we do at Headquarters when we arrive?" Wil asked eventually, looking over at his father.

"Meet the other High Commander, I suppose. I don't know. I'll follow their lead."

"I wish I had that luxury."

"What makes you say that?"

Wil stared at his father. "They're looking to me as their future leader. Their hopes are all riding on me, and this will be our first meeting. They'll scrutinize my every move. I'll need to inspire them, show them I'm worthy of their trust. That initial impression will determine so much."

"You don't have to do this, Wil."

*Yes, I do. And he knows it.* He appreciated him saying it all the same. "The path has already been set."

Cris bit his lip and nodded. "I'll be here for you."

# CHAPTER 12

WIL WANTED TO hide when his father told him that the *Vanquish* was approaching TSS Headquarters. *Going there will make it real.*

He had gone back to bed after their late-night talk. The extra time had allowed him to process the information about his origins and purpose, and it felt like a cruel joke.

*My life has been planned for me. I have to fight a war I know nothing about.* As much as he wanted to run away and pretend things were different, that wasn't an option.

His responsibilities were only underscored when members from his father's crew had come to visit after he awoke in the morning. He had expressed his heartfelt thanks that they had risked their lives for him, but seeing their enthusiasm and relief only added to the pressure. *They need me, so I can't turn away.*

After the visit, Wil had found a new black TSS uniform waiting for him. He was surprised by the black color—as a Junior Agent, the clothing should have been dark blue—but the electronic credentials in the jacket lapel indicated that the clothing was his. It may have been Banks' suggestion, or his father had struck out on his own. Either way, he was grateful because it meant he wouldn't stand out as much against all the senior Agents he would undoubtedly be meeting, and that gave him some reassurance.

He was now dressed in the perfectly tailored black shirt and belted pants with a sleek black overcoat that hung to the back of his knees. He liked the way it felt to be in such an iconic uniform.

"How long are we going to stay here?" Wil asked his father.

"I don't know." Cris leaned against the wall. "It depends on how well we get along, I suppose." He shot a wry smile toward Wil.

Wil wasn't in the mood for joking, however. "What you really mean is if they approve of me enough to keep me around."

"Wil, you have no reason to doubt their acceptance of you."

Wil frowned. "I'm sure they've been keeping tabs on me. Progress reports can be embellished. Even if I'm more capable than they hoped, if they have built up a false impression of my abilities, nothing I do will ever live up to their expectations."

"I'm sure your progress reports are all accurate. Just take this day as it comes."

Wil stood silently as his father made his latest vain attempt at soothing him. Nothing he could say would make it any easier. "We should go."

They walked out of Cris' quarters and took the lift up to the Command Center. Wil took a seat along the back perimeter of the room, returning the smiles from the crew.

Before them was a massive ring nearly a thousand meters in diameter. Everyone took it in, mouths agape.

*Stars! You could fit an entire fleet through here in one pass.* Wil's chest tightened. *A fleet they expect me to command one day.*

Cris checked in with Alec. Once everything was in order, he sat down in his command chair.

The *Vanquish* headed toward a smaller ring to the right, appropriately sized for transporting a single cruiser-class vessel. As they approached, a blue-green energy field began to form within the ring.

"TSS *Vanquish* cleared for rift gate," came a female voice over the intercom.

"Take her in, Alec," Cris ordered.

The *Vanquish* glided forward into the spatial distortion, passing through the event horizon without even a shudder. A wave of blue-green light slowly rippled across the domed expanse of the Command Center as the cameras around the ship progressively captured the transition into the Rift. For a brief moment, the entire view was filled with the swirling color, and then faint stars began to show through the dancing ribbons of light.

Ahead, the looming form of a cylindrical space station stood out against the echoed starscape. As the spatial distortion dissipated, details of the structure resolved, revealing eleven rings stacked along a central shaft, each segment dotted with viewports and illuminated by perimeter lights. Additional docking concourses branched out from the central rings, which were filled with a substantial fleet of warships well beyond anything Wil had seen before.

Everyone in the Command Center stared with wonder at the view wrapping around the domed ceiling and floor. Compared to the space station, even a ship the size of the *Vanquish* seemed like nothing more than a speck.

*Maybe the Bakzen aren't so far ahead of us,* Wil mused. He felt the same sense of invigoration as when he entered the Rift the first time. Whether it was seeing the impressive H2 structure or the energy within the Rift itself, he started to feel like perhaps victory over the Bakzen was possible.

"This station is absolutely huge," Cris breathed.

"That's an understatement." Wil kept taking slow, even breaths to keep himself calm and centered, trying to control his nerves rising in anticipation of the upcoming meeting. *My perception of myself will define what others see in me.*

Wil observed silently as Alec docked the *Vanquish* with the TSS space station in a berth along one of the central rings. The ship shuddered as the docking clamps closed around the hull.

"Docking complete, sir," Alec announced.

"Right," Cris muttered half to himself and stood. Everyone but Wil in the Command Center rose to their feet, as well. "Ready, Wil?"

Wil said nothing, but stood and moved to the door. Cris came to his side. They left the Command Center together and walked straight down the hallway to the gangway leading off the ship.

Guards from H2 stood to either side of the gangway just outside the *Vanquish*. The sentries looked on with suppressed wonder as the two Sietinens passed.

Cris occasionally glanced over at Wil as they walked down the glass-lined pathway. *"Wil, you need to relax."*

*"I'm fine,"* he replied telepathically.

*"This won't be as bad as you seem to think—"* Cris cut off as they reached the end of the gangway. There were several uniformed officers already waiting, and another came to join them. The last was the most decorated of them all, and he looked agitated.

The final TSS officer walked directly to the middle of the group and began urgently speaking with another officer. After a subtle point from the other man, he turned around and laid eyes on Wil and Cris, who were making their final approach down the gangway.

Cris pulled back slightly and allowed Wil to walk ahead. Wil stopped several paces in front of the group as they scrutinized him.

After an elongated moment of silence, the man standing front-center straightened his uniform. "I am High Commander Erik Taelis. Welcome to TSS Jotun Headquarters, H2. You are Williame Sietinen, I presume?" He directed the inquiry to Wil.

"Yes, sir, though I only go by such in the most formal situations. As my father does," Wil replied with a small backwards gesture toward Cris, "I use the pseudo last name of 'Sights' within the TSS." He paused momentarily. "It's a pleasure to meet you, sir."

"That it is," Taelis responded with a slight smile that Wil didn't perceive as very genuine. "Jason Banks, as I believe you call him, mentioned something about the name. I'm afraid he tends to be more accepting of such things than I. We don't often have time to deal with the unnecessary confusion of multiple aliases."

"My apologies. I'm accustomed to the luxuries of a place still untouched by war."

Taelis eyed Wil. "Hopefully, with your help, we will no longer need such distinctions."

*That sounds promising.* "It is a goal for us all to work toward."

The High Commander nodded gravely. "Shall we go to the briefing room? It will be a much more comfortable place to talk."

"I am here to serve, sir. I know our arrival was unexpected, and—" Wil began.

"Not at all," Taelis interrupted. "It was inevitable that you would come here. In the end, it's better sooner than later. This encounter with the Bakzen has undoubtedly left you with many questions."

"Yes," confirmed Wil, "but even this glimpse of your facility has already answered some."

"Good. The briefing room is this way." Taelis again gestured toward an elevator down the hall, but then paused. He looked at Cris standing calmly behind Wil. "Er... Cris, you're welcome to join us. You're just as much a part of this as the rest of us."

Cris came to attention with the acknowledgment. "Thank you, sir." He fell into step with the entourage following Wil and the High Commander.

*I wonder which one of them is Taelis' Lead Agent?* When Wil examined the rank markings, he found that they were all 9.5, which in his home Headquarters was reserved only for Lead Agent. *Well, that narrows it down.*

Wil looked on in wonder as the procession walked further into the space station. He could tell from the outside that it was laid out differently than the Headquarters where he had grown up, but that was especially apparent from within. Though the overall shape was roughly cylindrical, it was wider in the middle and then pointed at either end. Like most space stations, the different sections were joined by a central axis—a homage to the times before the advent of artificial gravity when centrifugal force was still a key function in space structure design. All around the outside middle region were docking ports for larger vessels. Though it was different than what he was used to, it seemed just as logical and efficient a format as the Headquarters he knew so well.

Wil glanced back at his father and saw his own awe, but also that he looked uncomfortable. Wil slowed his walk and fell into step next to his father. "You can wait on the *Vanquish*, if you want. I think Taelis is including you as a courtesy rather than by necessity." He hadn't meant for it to sound that blunt. *"Sorry, I meant that I know you don't want to be here,"* he clarified telepathically. *"I'll be fine on my own if you want to go."*

Cris looked lovingly at his son. *"Thank you for the concern, but I want to know what they have to say. I've been waiting a long time for this."* He looked over at Taelis, who was eyeing them. *"You'd better go back to your new friend. I think he suspects we're conspiring amongst ourselves."* He smiled playfully at Wil.

Wil shook his head with exasperation, but he smiled slightly. *"All right."* Wil jogged two steps to catch up to Taelis.

When Wil was once again abreast with the High Commander, Taelis continued, "I'm anxious to hear about your time with the Bakzen, but we thought it best to give you some orientation before holding a formal debrief."

"Thank you, sir. I'll answer your questions as best I can."

Taelis nodded. "I'll give you a tour of the fleet tomorrow. We have the new TX-80 fighters that you designed under construction at a nearby shipyard."

"I didn't realize those would go into production." Only a handful of people had ever seen Wil's design files. He enjoyed playing around with craft design in his free time, but he'd never expected they would get any outside attention.

"Oh, a great many of your designs end up on the production line," Taelis revealed. "I think you've become something of a celebrity to the engineering staff. Anyway, I'd like to first introduce you to my highest-ranking officers. Many of them are walking with us right now, but I have requested that others meet us in the briefing room." He led Wil into an elevator. "None of us thought that we would be meeting you anytime soon, but after you entered the Rift, there was no sense in delaying any longer."

"It was all unexpected for me, as well," Wil replied as he examined the ceiling and walls of the elevator. Like many things in the space station, it seemed very different than those of the other Headquarters, though he could not quite place in exactly what way.

"Here we are," Taelis stated when the elevator stopped. Directly across from the elevator were large double metal doors set in a very substantial-looking wall. Taelis stepped out of the elevator first and walked toward the door, which was opened for him by the sentries on either side.

As Wil stepped into the conference room, he saw that the far wall consisted of an expanse of viewports. The panoramic view of the eerie, echoed starscape within the Rift was breathtaking, and Wil exhaled slowly with awe; he could hear his father doing the same behind him. In the center of the room was a broad oval table that already had four Agents sitting around it. Five of the people following Wil and the High Commander took their chairs.

Taelis gestured for Wil to take the seat at the far head of the table as he took the one closest to the door.

Cris paused as he entered and blinked with surprise as he scanned over the other Agents. "Hi, Jon," he said after a moment when he recognized his former roommate.

Jon Lambren inclined his head politely. "Cris, it's been a long time. I'm glad to see you did so well for yourself."

"You too." Cris sat down in the one remaining empty chair, located directly to Taelis' left. "That's right, you were assigned to Jotun."

Jon nodded and turned his attention to the High Commander, waiting expectantly.

Wil could tell that his father was still uncomfortable, but he was starting to conceal it better now that there was someone familiar in the room.

Taelis waited for everyone to get settled. He removed his tinted glasses and the other Agents did likewise. "I suppose formal introductions are the best way to begin. As I'm sure you have surmised, this is Wil Sietinen, our future Primus Elite Agent." When Taelis paused, everyone in the room directed their gaze toward Wil.

Wil held his poise as the eleven pairs of glowing eyes looked him over. *I have no idea what I'm supposed to do.*

"And this is Cris Sietinen, Wil's father," Taelis continued. "He is the Lead Agent of the primary TSS Headquarters, and second in command under Jason Banks." The Agents in the room nodded with understanding.

Taelis then acknowledged the person on his right. He was tall and slim with black hair, and looked to be the sternest of the group. "Connor Ramsen is the Lead Agent of this Headquarters and my second in command. Though I know Banks doesn't run things this way, Ramsen, as Lead Agent, takes care of many things that you consider the High Commander's duties. Of course, he is also commanding Agent of Primus." He introduced the other officers, including Jon, who was the logistics officer in charge of coordinating fleet movement.

"None of us are old enough to have seen the beginning of the war, but we have all seen its effects firsthand," the High Commander went on. "I know I speak for everyone here when I say that we will faithfully follow you, Wil, when it comes time to end this war that has destroyed so many lives. Though it is still years off, we all look forward to the day when we will no longer be plagued by the Bakzen." Taelis stopped and everyone nodded solemnly at his last words.

Wil looked for the deeper meaning implied by Taelis' phrasing. "How did the war begin?" Wil asked when the soberness in the silence had begun to fade.

"The first skirmish was four-hundred-eighty-seven Tararian years ago," Taelis explained with renewed gravity. "But we've been in an official state of war for three-hundred-sixty-four years. They say the true war began when a Bakzen vessel opened fire and decimated an unarmed Taran freighter. The TSS was far from the military service that it has become, and it was unprepared to handle attacks from an enemy with advanced telekinetic abilities. Because of this, diplomats were brought in from Tararia and sent to meet with a so-called Imperial Director of the Bakzeni Empire. The details of what happened next are unclear.

"To the best of our knowledge, when the diplomats asked why the freighter had been attacked, the Imperial Director claimed that it had violated Bakzeni Territory. The Taran government had no knowledge of such a territory. According to our sources, the Director then said that Tararia's laws were unjust and our tyranny would not be tolerated. What we know for sure is that the heads of the diplomats were returned to us, mutilated almost beyond recognition. Along with the heads was a message: 'Do not deny perfection. Truth will prevail.' "

Wil's stomach turned over. *Such hatred for us… I saw that in Tek. What truth do the Bakzen hold?*

"They will do anything to be the victors." He looked down at the smooth surface of the table. *But Tarans feel the same way about ourselves. How can we pass judgment?*

Hovering just above the thoughts, Wil sensed someone observing his mind. He pushed back and identified the intruder as Taelis. He closed him out and shot a brief glare toward the High Commander. No one back home would make such a violation of privacy.

The High Commander looked taken aback for a moment when only emptiness met his attempt to probe deeper, but then appeared pleased that Wil had been able to block him. He brushed off Wil's accusatory gaze. "We must trust in our own right to survive," Taelis said in response to Wil's unspoken question. "Though we may never know our enemy's mind, some actions stand on their own. Could you honestly say that the Bakzen's violence is valid in any context?"

"No," Wil responded. "You're right, we must take a stand for ourselves—retaliate if we must. In such dichotomies, we have to make our own survival the priority." He paused, testing his mental guards against further observation. He wasn't used to TSS officers being so openly distrusting. "Still, that was one event centuries ago. What's happened since then?"

"It's only gotten worse." Taelis sighed, pain and weariness in the exhale. "The Bakzen continue to force their way out from the Rift, tearing it wider. They've overtaken several planets, killing anyone who opposes them. We've offered treaties and resources—anything to end the fighting—but they've made it clear they won't stop until Tararia falls."

*What do they have against Tararia?* "And eventually you won't be able to hold them back any longer."

Taelis nodded. "Which is why it is so imperative that the war end."

"Of course. But why me?"

Taelis leaned forward in his chair. "Wil, we believe that you will have the gift of simultaneous observation—the ability to perceive the events of both spatial planes at the same time. You can be the bridge that we've needed—to hover in subspace between the Rift and normal space, able to guide us to match the Bakzen maneuver for maneuver. It can finally end the war."

*How can I possibly learn to do that?* "If you say so, sir." *Is that the ability Carzen was going to tell me about?*

"We will guide the rest of your training in any way we can," Taelis said. "But we will ultimately look to you to tell us how to defeat the Bakzen, when the time comes."

Wil nodded, trying to keep his face neutral as the knot in his stomach tightened. *I may not know on which side of the moral good I'm acting, but they need me. I have a purpose to fulfill, whether I agree with it or not.*

Taelis folded his hands on the table. "You need to understand that there is no diplomatic solution. We passed that possibility centuries ago. The Bakzen want us gone, completely."

*Where does that leave us? He can't be saying...* "Sir?"

Taelis looked at him levelly. "We need to eliminate the Bakzen. That order has come down from the highest authorities. We need to settle the conflict once and for all."

*No... they want me to kill* all *of them?* Wil struggled to maintain his composure. He couldn't let them see his torment. "There's no alternative?"

"We've tried, Wil." Taelis shook his head, withering as he slumped back in his chair. "I can't even tell you how many people we've lost trying. It sickens me that it's come to this, but this is the way it has to be."

Down the table next to Taelis, Cris looked like he was trying to hold in his horror. The color drained from his face.

Wil nodded. *That's the final piece they were keeping from me. They want me to lead the annihilation of an entire race.*

When Wil didn't make any outward response, Taelis continued. "There is still much more to be discussed, but I think it's best that we show you around now. Though things are very different here, I'd like to think that this will become a second home to you, in time. I'm sure you're anxious to see the full extent of our offensive capabilities, so we can go to the engineering lab first. The team there is equally anxious to meet you."

"Whatever you think is best," Wil replied and stood up simultaneously with the Agents around the table. He felt weak, detached from himself—still reeling from the new understanding of his purpose. *Am I truly destined to do something so terrible?*

The TSS officers all restored their tinted glasses before filing out into the hallway. Taelis waited alongside Cris as Wil made his way from the far side of the table. The three of them stayed in the room after the others had left.

"You have a much better understanding of this situation than I thought you would," Taelis told Wil.

*He's only saying that because I didn't run out of the room screaming.* "I'm just trying to take everything in stride." *I saw one side of it while with the Bakzen, but what they've told me now... Do I have it in me to do what needs to be done?*

"I know it's a lot to take in. It's admirable that you're able to be so objective, especially at such a young age. Many people can spend a lifetime with the war and never understand why we must do the things we do," Taelis said.

Wil looked over at his father at this last statement. *Does he see it the way I do? Does he know what this will do to me?*

Cris gave him a supportive smile. "Under the right leader, not everyone needs to understand the details. Just know their part."

Taelis nodded. "Indeed." He fell silent for a moment and then took a deep breath. "Come, we have many things to see."

# CHAPTER 13

CRIS WAS FINDING it increasingly difficult to remain composed. It was draining enough to maintain the necessary mental blocks to keep out the obnoxious probes from the other Agents, but the revelation about Wil's role in the war threatened to put him over the edge. *It's too much to ask of someone. Too many lives to be responsible for—to protect, and to end.*

The constant feeling of anxious nausea from the past several days had risen to an almost unbearable level by the end of the briefing with Taelis. While they strolled down the hall from the briefing room, he trailed behind as Wil talked with Taelis.

"How long has Banks been sending you my design specs?" Wil asked the High Commander.

"It's been years," Taelis replied. "At first it was just to see how you thought about things. But when the engineering team took a look—not knowing where the designs were from—they said the technology was leaps ahead. That generations-old technical roadblocks had been overcome with elegance."

"I wouldn't go that far," Wil said, sounding a little bashful.

"Well, that's how they saw it, anyway."

Cris felt momentary relief. *I'm glad he's getting some credit, at least. He's always been so modest about his abilities.*

"And what do you think, personally?" Wil asked.

Taelis evaluated Wil. "I think you can finally give us an independent jump drive."

Wil laughed. "Right."

*He can't be serious?* Cris jogged a couple steps to catch up with them. "None of the math works."

"That we've been able to figure out, anyway," Taelis responded, turning to look at him.

"SiNavTech has been working on it for generations. There just isn't any scientific basis for executing a jump with any degree of accuracy without fixed beacons for reference."

"But it is theoretically possible," Taelis countered.

Cris sighed. "Theoretically, but—"

Taelis looked smug. "So, we want Wil to try."

*This guy is starting to piss me off.* Cris' eyes narrowed behind his tinted glasses. "And when, exactly, is he supposed to find the time to make what would be the single greatest advancement in space travel since the discovery of subspace? He already doesn't get enough down time as it is."

"Dad, I can manage my own schedule."

"Actually, as Lead Agent, I'm responsible for overseeing your training. In my opinion, the rate you're going isn't sustainable."

"As you've said so many times…" Wil muttered.

"Burnout is serious business. Don't be so flippant," Cris countered.

"You do have a valid point," Taelis admitted.

"Let's go over the demands you've made so far today." Cris extended a finger for each point. "Master simultaneous observation. Solve the equation for an independent jump drive that's stumped the greatest minds in history. Oh, and annihilate an entire sentient race."

Wil froze. He scowled at Cris, and then turned to Taelis, inclining his head. "Excuse me, sir. May I have a moment to talk alone with my father?"

Taelis looked between Wil and Cris. "By all means." He gestured them toward a meeting room down the hall.

Wil led the way. The room was small and minimally furnished, with a touchscreen desk and four chairs. Wil stood by the door and slid it closed as soon as Cris was inside.

"What are you doing?" his son hissed.

*Protecting you in the ways you can't protect yourself.* Cris shook his head. "None of this is right. They're using you."

Wil's gaze was hard and stern. "There's a war to fight! Me getting enough sleep is hardly the most critical issue."

Cris swallowed. "Wil you don't have to do this. I can get you out. We can go—"

"Running away can't be your solution to everything."

Cris felt like he had been stabbed. "Is that what you think of me?"

Wil looked down, his face twisted with regret. "No, I'm sorry."

"I know I haven't always set the best example. But this… What they're asking of you isn't fair." *If I had known signing up for the TSS meant this future for my son, I would have stayed far away.*

Wil searched for words. "I wish I could leave all this behind." He sighed and slumped against the wall, allowing himself to be vulnerable. "Stars, I want to! So badly. But I can't. You heard them."

"I did, but they don't know everything. Maybe there's another way."

Wil hung his head. "Right now, I'm all they have, as far as they're concerned. And though this isn't the TSS we know, they're still our people. We can't just abandon them."

*If they need us so badly, they should have just asked.* He'd learned the hard way that deception made for a poor start to a relationship. "It's hard to trust anyone who would treat us like that."

"I know." Wil looked like he wanted to cry. "But… it feels so unfair to be tempted to leave. I know you're only trying to help, but telling me I have a choice—that I can go—only makes this harder. We both know I have to see this through."

Cris felt sick. *I've failed my son. He's trapped, and I led him here.* "I'm serious, Wil. Fok them. We can go."

Wil straightened, steeling himself. "No. You can go if you want, but that's not an option for me."

"I'm not going anywhere."

"Well, right now, you're not helping by being here."

"Then what can I do?"

"Stop pretending like this will go away if we ignore it!"

Cris crossed his arms. "Okay." *How could he give in to them so easily?*

Wil sighed and tousled his hair. "Look, this is already difficult enough for me without having a chaperone around to contradict me."

Cris tried to look impassive, but the knife in his gut twisted deeper. "Maybe it's best if I just wait on the *Vanquish.*" *I went from 'trusted advisor' to 'nuisance' overnight.*

"That's for the best," Wil said. He opened the door and strode back into the hall toward Taelis.

Cris calmly approached the High Commander. "Sir, I need to check in with my Headquarters. I'll see you and Wil later, I'm sure."

Taelis glanced at Wil. "Yes, certainly. Attend to your business." He inclined his head.

Cris gave a slight bow and turned to go.

"Sorry about that," Cris heard Wil say as he walked away. "He means well, but he gets overprotective sometimes."

"Quite all right," Taelis replied. "Your well-being means everything to us. I'm glad you have someone looking out for you."

Cris took a slow breath. *I'll never stop caring for you, Wil. You might not want me by your side now, but I'll always be there when you need me.*

After going to such lengths to rescue his son, Cris wanted to stay close and keep watch. Being asked to stay away was torture. There was only one other person who could possibly understand.

He hurried back toward the *Vanquish* so he could confer with Kate.

Cris kept his gaze down with the hope of avoiding the other Agents he passed in the halls. However, Jon was coming up the corridor by the briefing room.

"Heading out already?" Jon asked as he neared.

"Wil is with Taelis," Cris replied. "I'm checking in with my crew."

Jon nodded. "This all must be a shock to you."

"Yeah, well, it also explains a lot."

"I know it's a lot to take in," Jon said. "And getting used to the Rift itself takes a while."

"It does feel strange here."

"The concentration of ambient energy is greater inside the Rift. I don't know why—one of the astrophysicists would have to explain it. But I can tell you, after being here for a while, normal space feels dull. Once you have a Rift assignment, you don't want to go back."

"Not that anyone has a choice to leave the Jotun division once they join," Cris countered.

"True," Jon conceded. "You're lucky it's taken you this long to get pulled in. I immediately thought of you as a Jotun candidate."

Cris looked at him quizzically. "What makes you say that?"

Jon shrugged. "After all that special treatment when you first joined the TSS, it was clear they had something in mind for you. And you fit the standard profile. Most of the Agents here are from the Command track—the most independent thinkers."

*Apparently the Priesthood thinks I'm a little too independent.* "Well, I now realize they had other plans for me."

Jon nodded. "It's an important part to play. Wil takes after you."

"Lucky for you, he's more forgiving than I am."

"We did what we had to do, Cris. It was important to protect Wil for as long as possible," Jon said.

Cris scoffed. "Right, because lying is a great way to protect people."

"Everyone here with the Jotun division was in the dark at one point," Jon said. "And no one here asked to be a part of it, but we were called upon. We're here because it's our duty."

*Just because it's always been that way doesn't make it a good policy.* "People have a right to know what's going on."

"Why? If we do our job, this problem will go away before it ever affects them. Why cause unnecessary worry?" Jon asked.

"There are always ripple effects."

"Well, we're doing our best."

"And I'll do the same." Cris sighed. *None of this is his fault. Unloading on him isn't fair.* "It's been a tough day."

Jon gave him a sympathetic nod. "I understand. I'll see you around another time."

"Yeah. Oh, and Scott's with me. The three of us should catch up," Cris suggested.

"That would be nice."

*Reminiscing about old times is as close as we'll get to carefree again.* "See you later." Cris continued toward the *Vanquish.*

As soon as Cris was back on board his ship, he went to his quarters to call up Kate on the viewscreen. Thankfully, she picked up right away.

"Hey," Kate's image greeted him.

"Hey. Kate, I'm sorry I didn't call you sooner." Cris took a shaky breath. "I miss you so much. I wish you were here."

His wife gave him a compassionate smile. "It's okay. I figured you'd be busy all day."

"Apparently, I'm just a liability," Cris replied. He buried his face in his hands for a few moments. "How are you?"

"I'm glad to see you." Kate looked down. "Banks told me about the war."

*We should be together as a family right now.* Cris shook his head. "I can't believe what they're asking of Wil."

Kate looked confused. "What?"

*Stars! Don't tell me Banks only told her part of it...* "What did he say?"

"That the Bakzen live in some sort of spatial rift and have been at war with the TSS for centuries. There's another division of the TSS, coded 'Jotun'."

"That's all he said?"

Kate nodded. "More or less. Why?"

*Bomax!* "Kate, there's so much more. I don't know where to begin." Cris' stomach wrenched. *Why did Banks leave it to me to tell her?*

Kate let out a slow exhale. "I knew something about it wasn't right. You talked about how Banks would hedge on certain issues, but I'd never seen it before. What have they been keeping from us?"

*Do I tell her?* Cris hesitated. *I'd rather not know, myself.*

"What is it?"

*I promised her a long time ago that we'd have no more secrets.* "Kate, the Priesthood genetically engineered us."

She blinked, dumbfounded. "What?" Her voice shook.

"Nanotech. Generations ago. It made sure we'd end up together and that we'd produce the perfect little soldier to do the Priesthood's bidding."

Kate shook her head. "What are you talking about?"

"They expect Wil to lead the war against the Bakzen. He's supposed to have some sort of special ability to give the TSS an edge and finally end the conflict." Cris' eyes burned, it hurt to swallow. "But it's not just that, Kate. They want total annihilation. And they want our son to do it."

Kate looked away. She shook her head slowly, tears welled in her eyes. "What have we done?"

"It was out of our control. They've been plotting this for generations."

"We never should have raised him here!" She squeezed her hers closed, wincing. "He could do anything, but we set him up to be a soldier."

"It wouldn't have mattered. The Priesthood is behind everything. They oversee the TSS."

Kate shied away. "No. That's not—"

"We would have ended up here no matter what we did. They killed Tristen because he didn't do what they wanted." Cris felt breathless. His brother's death had always been considered an accident, but knowing what was behind it—his own life seemed so precarious.

Kate's mouth fell open a little. She took a deep breath and swallowed. "I don't even know what to say to that."

*We should be terrified.* "We probably shouldn't talk about this now." *Who knows if the Priesthood is listening. Is there anywhere they don't control?*

Kate nodded, understanding his meaning. She looked pale, her face drawn. "There's no one else I can trust here. When are you coming home?"

Cris' heart broke, seeing her pain. "Stars, I wish I knew! Wil's just going along with all of it like he's already one of them. Nothing makes sense anymore." He met his wife's gaze through the viewscreen. "Kate, I love you. I know that's real—regardless of how we were brought together."

"I love you, too." Kate became distant, staring at something unseen off to the side. "There's no escape, is there?"

"Whatever plan was set for us, we're fully embedded now. As long as Wil is committed to staying, this is our place."

Kate straightened. "Don't let him push you away. You know how he can be. He wants you there, even if he says otherwise."

Cris nodded. "I know. I'll give him space today, but I have no intention of going anywhere."

Kate crossed her arms and hugged herself. "This all feels so surreal. The war was hard enough to comprehend, but genetic engineering… And the Priesthood's involvement! Stars, I always thought the TSS was so far away from them. But being part of it?"

"I can't quite wrap my head around it, either." *I always thought the TSS would give us leverage to bring the Priesthood down, but maybe the TSS is the very thing keeping the Priesthood safe.*

"I wish we were together."

"Me too. I can't wait to be back home, even if I'll need to resist the urge to punch Banks when I see him."

Kate cracked a smile. "I think he'd understand."

Cris sighed. "I should probably check in with my crew and let them know what's going on."

"Okay, I'll be thinking about you. Give my love to Wil." Kate paused. "Learn what you can while you're there."

"I will."

"I'll be anxiously awaiting your return. Love you."

"Love you, too. I'll check in again soon." Cris ended the call. *At least we have each other. We'll find a way to get through anything the Priesthood has in store for us.*

— — —

Wil pushed down his irritation over his father's behavior. *What was he thinking?*

He turned his attention to Taelis. "So, you were saying about the independent jump drive…?"

The High Commander nodded, continuing down the corridor. "One of the biggest tactical challenges we've encountered in the war is an inability to reliably travel in and out of the Rift. Getting a stable beacon lock takes time and also makes our ships' locations easier to identify. Essentially, the Bakzen always know we're coming."

"Whereas you don't know when and where they're going to strike."

"Precisely. But with the combination of an independent jump drive and simultaneous observation, we would know where they are at all times and have the maneuvering precision to respond."

*They're counting on two things they don't have right now, and they want me to deliver both.* "What's your backup plan?"

"We don't have one."

*What if I can't do it?* Wil took an unsteady breath and bit his lower lip.

Taelis softened. "Wil, I know we're asking a lot. You do have some time to get everything in place—I'm not expecting a solution overnight."

"To my father's point, people have spent their whole lives trying to work out an independent jump drive design without ever getting anywhere." *Running into the same blocks I have every time I've looked at it.*

"Even if it's not possible, simultaneous observation alone may be enough to turn the war in our favor."

Wil shook his head. "An act you claim no Taran can currently perform."

Taelis hesitated. "That's not exactly true."

"Sir?"

The High Commander stopped mid-stride. "Have you heard of the Aesir?"

Wil stopped next to him. "No, I don't think so."

"Most haven't. Some know them as 'The Ascended'."

"I'm sorry, I'm not familiar."

"Well, they are capable of something resembling simultaneous observation—only, it's more like seeing the fabric of space, not so much observing real-time events."

*I didn't even know that was possible.* "How can they see the fabric of space?"

Taelis gave a dismissive flip of his hand. "I'm not sure exactly. They claim to be seeking enlightenment by reading some sort of larger pattern to our existence. But the point is, they can disconnect consciousness from physical self, so we know it's possible. You'll just need to take it to the next level."

*Is that even more than the Bakzen can do?* "Why don't I go train with the Aesir, then?"

The High Commander became rigid. "That's not possible."

"It sounds like they might be able to give me a leg up on learning what I need to succeed."

"Though they are of Taran origins, they now like to keep to themselves," Taelis replied. "I barely even know they exist. And from what little else I know about them, I don't think they'd take kindly to a training request, however well-intentioned."

*So the only Taran people who could help me won't. I guess the Bakzen were right that the TSS couldn't give me what I need.* Wil pushed aside the thought. "It's a lot for me to take on by myself."

"You're largely self-taught, aren't you?" Taelis asked, resuming his stride down the hallway.

Wil followed. "Simultaneous observation sounds a little more complicated than reading a book." *I guess I have no choice other than to figure it out on my own. But how?*

"One step at a time," Taelis assured. "Let's get back to the tangible. The engineering team is waiting for us."

Wil nodded. *Machines that already exist in real life—what a refreshing change.* "I look forward to meeting them."

"Come on." Taelis picked up the pace and led the way to an elevator at the central hub of the space station.

Like the previous sections of the space station, the designs of the remaining hallway and elevator were plain and utilitarian. Largely metal on metal, everything gleamed cold and sterile. With a shudder, Wil was reminded of the Bakzen's facility. *Both are built for war, not for comfort.*

Wil stood in silence as the elevator descended to a lower ring within H2.

Taelis pulled out his handheld, his brow furrowing as he read a message. He wrote a response.

Wil almost asked what the message was regarding but decided against it. *I don't think they get much good news around here.*

The elevator slowed and came to a rest, opening directly into a cavernous room resembling a hangar. Rows of fighters were on the far side, and various ship components occupied rows upon rows of shelving near the elevator doors. When they exited the elevator, Wil saw that the hangar wrapped all the way around the central axis of the space station, forming one continuous open area on the entire level. He couldn't make out what was behind the central column, but it appeared that there were similar clusters of fighters all around the perimeter.

"As you probably guessed, this is our main berthing for H2's defense fighters," Taelis explained. "We have nowhere near enough pilots stationed here to fly all of them, but they are here as a fallback defense. I know it looks rather exposed here, but this entire station has redundant electromagnetic shielding, and there are blast doors for all viewports in case we need to fortify against direct attack. The most critical operations are on levels that can rotate ninety-degrees within the ring so we can achieve centrifugal gravity through spin around the axis, in case we ever need to shut down the artificial gravity."

Wil nodded with satisfaction. "You really planned ahead."

"I hope we never have to use any of those features," Taelis replied solemnly.

*It's all meant to be used as a last resort, if all else is lost.* "I'll do my best to make sure it doesn't come to that."

"Right, well, let's see what you're working with," the High Commander said. He set off between the rows of shelves toward a far wall.

As they approached, Wil realized that they were headed toward an enclosed room within the hangar—one of several throughout the sprawling space. The double doors to the room were slid open to either side, and half a dozen people were huddled around a craft. It was the Bakzen fighter Wil had commandeered for his escape.

Everyone came to attention as Taelis neared. "Commander on deck," a female engineer announced.

*I think Banks would laugh if anyone did that for him.* Wil dropped a pace behind the High Commander, waiting to be acknowledged.

"At ease," Taelis said. "Laecy, I want to introduce you to Wil Sietinen."

A woman stepped out from around the back side of the Bakzen fighter. She appeared to be around her late-thirties, with copper-colored eyes and light brown hair that was pulled up into a ponytail. Her mouth fell open a little as she caught sight of Wil. "No way." She caught herself, and hastily wiped off her hands and held out her right palm upward in greeting. "It's an honor, sir."

A murmur of surprise passed through the other engineers, and they also presented the formal greeting.

"Deena Laecy is our Lead Engineer," Taelis explained. "She's provided the final specification reviews for your production designs."

"Not that I ever had any changes to make," Lacey said with a smile. "I was pretty shocked to find out those old TX-70s were designed by a ten-year-old." She bowed her head a little, "Sir."

Wil returned her smile. "And I was pretty shocked to learn they went into production."

Laecy lit up. "The integrated thruster design was pure art. All the pilots love it. And the lines! You have an eye for designing a sexy spacecraft."

Taelis scowled. "Laecy, Wil may be young, but he's dressed in black."

The engineer bowed her head. "I'm sorry, sir, I meant no disrespect."

*Taelis needs to loosen up.* "It's quite all right. No need for formality here," Wil said to Laecy, but glanced at Taelis.

Laecy and the other engineers tried to contain their excitement but their smirks came through.

Wil felt Taelis try to voice a protest telepathically. He blocked him out. "So, you're the lucky bunch who gets to dissect this," Wil continued, looking over the Bakzen vessel. The engineers had opened the belly of the fighter and there were several components resting on the ground.

"Yes!" Laecy said, resting a hand on the nose of the vessel. "We just started. This is the most intact Bakzen ship we've ever had to study. Either they're destroyed in battle, or the pilot will initiate a self-destruct as soon as they're captured."

*Good thing I didn't accidentally trigger that!* Wil stepped toward her, studying the components on the ground. "I'm glad I could provide something useful."

"We were just about to extract the jump drive. Want to take a look with us?" Laecy offered.

*That sounds way more interesting than whatever else Taelis has in store for me.* "I'd love to." He turned to Taelis. "Sir, do you mind?"

Taelis inclined his head. "That's fine. Probably best you get to know each other, anyway." He checked his handheld. "I'll have someone come retrieve you in a few hours. We still have a lot to cover."

"Of course, sir," Wil acknowledged with a bow of his head. "Thank you for the opportunity. I think studying this craft may be helpful for my work on the independent jump drive."

The engineers glanced at each other with the last statement.

"As you wish," Taelis said and strode off.

"Are you really working on an independent jump drive design?" one of the young men on the engineering team questioned.

*What was a fun side project has become a real assignment.* "Apparently, I am."

"Do you think it's possible?" Laecy asked.

"We'll find out," Wil replied, turning his attention to the ship. "Let's see how the Bakzen do it."

— — —

Cris wandered into the Command Center, having nowhere else to be. To his surprise, he found Alec and Kari still at their stations, and Scott was sitting on the ledge of the command platform talking with them.

They looked up with surprise when Cris entered. Kari hastily pulled a graphic data display down from the front of the viewscreen.

"Hi," Scott greeted. "Why aren't you with Wil?"

"No chaperones allowed," replied Cris. "You look like you're up to no good."

Alec and Kari eyed each other, and Scott shrugged. "Just investigating," Scott said.

"Investigating what?" Cris asked, coming to sit next to Scott.

Scott glanced at the others. "The cost of the war, basically."

"Banks said they have an entirely separate budget for H2 and its associated operations," Cris told them.

"We figured as much," Scott said. "But we were especially curious about the resources cost."

*It has to be enormous.* "Did you find anything?"

Kari returned the content to the front of the viewscreen. There were several trend charts and data tables, but the labels were vague. "Well, I was especially curious about the fleet," Kari said. "Building and stocking an interstellar ship is just about the most costly undertaking there is—both in terms of labor and raw materials. So, I decided to cross-reference docking records with the most recent inventory to get a sense of scale."

"I won't ask how you got those files." *That hacking ability is one of the reasons I love having her around.*

"What I found is a little alarming," Kari continued. "I was just sharing my preliminary findings."

"And?" Cris asked.

Kari grimaced. She glanced at the files on the viewscreen. "I think they are losing ships on at least a weekly basis. Not fighters, but cruisers."

"Which would explain why all the Bakzen carriers looked so scrappy—they've been salvaging pieces from our ships they destroy," Alec added.

*There are dozens of people on board each TSS cruiser—if not a hundred.* Cris' stomach turned over. "If that's the case, how is the TSS even still functioning?"

"That's an excellent question," Scott responded. "Near as we can tell, they keep their Agents pretty spaced out—just a captain on each ship, likely for direct telepathic communication to avoid interception by the Bakzen. There's a much higher Militia contingent for the rest of the officers compared to ours. There aren't even Agents as Navigators on most ships."

"Stars!" Cris looked down. *Taelis wasn't exaggerating when he said the situation was dire.* "I always knew there were other Militia training facilities outside of our Headquarters. But they must have way more recruits than I ever imagined, to keep up with casualties on that magnitude."

Alec let out a long breath. "It must be a massive operation. I don't know where they'd keep finding people—maybe recruiting in the Outer Colonies? Lots of people disappear out there in one way or another."

"Little do the recruits know that a Jotun assignment may as well be a death sentence." *How many students do I know who've ended up here?*

"Well, it's not quite that bleak," Alec replied. "But knowing these statistics, I wouldn't want an assignment here."

*In a few years, we won't have a choice.* "How are they even supporting a fleet that size?"

"There are a lot of supply deliveries with pretty sketchy transit records," Kari said. "I think they are diverting resources from the Outer Colonies."

Cris leaned back and crossed his arms. "Things have been bad in the Outer Colonies at least since I was a kid. I saw the supply distributions firsthand, so I know the settled worlds get deliveries, but I guess there's no knowing what happens after that."

"But stealing from civilians?" Alec questioned. "That's wrong on so many levels."

"Not to mention, how has no one heard about this?" Scott added.

*Anything is possible, knowing the Priesthood is involved. Win the war at any cost.* "It's not that hard to conceal information when you know the right people."

"I feel gross." Kari slumped back in her chair.

"There's nothing we can do right now," Cris said. *But after the war, I'm going after the real enemy.*

"So, we just try to forget and get on with it?" Kari asked.

"Like I said, there's nothing we can do right now. But, forward me these files. This is going to be important information when the time is right."

"You're not talking as a TSS officer right now, are you?" Scott asked.

Cris' senior officers on the *Vanquish* all knew his position outside of the TSS, but it wasn't something he liked to discuss directly. "As a member of the Taran race, I promise that I will do everything in my power to make sure our people are never treated this way again."

"I guess that will have to do," Kari said. She made some entries on her console. "Everything is locked up in a secure file for you."

"I'm glad you looked into this, but keep it to yourself," Cris instructed.

"Will do," Scott assured.

Alec and Kari nodded.

"We're going to fix this." *I don't know how yet, but I'll find a way. The Priesthood needs to go.*

# CHAPTER 14

WIL COULDN'T HELP grinning as he examined the benchmarks for the Bakzen jump drive. A blue-green field swirled around the drive secured within a translucent containment chamber several meters away. "Do you see the way it's verifying its relative location?"

"Just brilliant!" Laecy exclaimed, her eyes glued to the monitor. "I never would have thought they piggybacked on our beacon pings."

*So even the Bakzen use the SiNavTech network.* "And I'm not even sure we could block them. The signal can only be encrypted so much."

"I guess we can dismiss the theory that the Bakzen have an independent jump drive. It's just really good pilots with a fluid nav system."

Wil nodded. "But it does give me some ideas. I've never tried working the math with the ship being a fixed point."

"I'll leave that part up to you." Laecy grinned.

The final benchmark results displayed on the screen as the hum of the jump drive wound down within the containment chamber. It was an impressive system, and the implications were concerning. A Bakzen ship was completely invisible while traveling through the Rift.

*I need to figure out how to make this work.* Wil's excitement evaporated as he was reminded of his task. "Can you send me a copy of the analysis?"

"Of course," Laecy affirmed. "Thanks for your help getting the drive hooked up."

Wil smiled, though it was half-hearted. "This was great. I spend most of my time tooling with design schematics so it's fun to finally play around with some real equipment."

"You're welcome back any time."

*If only I got to spend more days like this back home.* Especially after recent events, those times were almost certainly over. "I might take you up on that when I can."

Wil heard a shuffle of footsteps behind him, and turned to see the other engineers hastily straightening up the lab. In the distance, an Agent was approaching. As he came closer, Wil saw that it was Ramsen, the stoic Lead Agent for H2.

*So much for having fun.* "Hello, sir," Wil greeted as Ramsen entered the lab.

"Looks like they put you to work," the Lead Agent said.

"It was a pleasure. You have a fine crew here." Wil made sure to look at Laecy with the statement, since he had the distinct impression she and her team didn't get a lot of credit.

"Well, time to get back to business," Ramsen stated.

*As if this work isn't important.* "Of course, sir. Lead the way." Wil turned to Laecy and her engineers. "Thank you again for your hospitality. I hope we can do this again sometime."

"You're welcome, sir." Laecy gave a little bow.

"Shall we?" Wil said to Ramsen, who was already looking far more impatient than the situation warranted. *The commanders here are wound way too tight. I hope they can be flexible with me.*

"The High Commander asked me to go over our tactical positions with you," Ramsen said as he led Wil away from the engineers. "The TSS outposts under the purview of your home Headquarters are only a fraction of the TSS as a whole."

"How are the outposts staffed?"

"It's mostly Militia," Ramsen replied. "We don't have the Agents to spare."

"What's your ratio of Agents to Militia?"

"Around two percent of the Jotun division is Agents."

*That's a pretty big disparity compared to back home.* "I think it's closer to ten percent Agents for us, with a pretty even split at Headquarters itself if you include the trainees."

Ramsen eyed Wil. "Be careful with language that differentiates between the two. We're one and the same."

"I didn't mean—"

"Don't worry, I know it will take some time to adjust." Ramsen led them out of the hangar and back into the elevator. He set their destination two levels up. "To your point, Agents make up approximately five percent of TSS forces in aggregate."

"So, the Jotun division is sixty percent of the TSS?"

"In one way or another, yes."

*Well over half—and we didn't know they were here. That's crazy.* "That's a lot of people to manage."

Ramsen nodded. "Well, we have a big leadership team. We all share the responsibility."

The elevator stopped and Ramsen stepped into the corridor. It was yet another passage of only bleak metal surfaces.

Wil accompanied the Lead Agent down the corridor, which curved around the central column of the level. "I can only imagine the operations are far more complex than what I've seen, considering the overlay of combat strategy and fleet management." *And they want me to eventually have authority over all of it.* His chest tightened with the thought.

"It's a way of life for us. We always find a way to get the job done." They arrived at the door to a conference room. "Here we are."

The room was unadorned. A round table surrounded by six chairs occupied the center of the space, and a viewscreen spanned half the width of the wall across from the entry door.

Ramsen placed his hand on the conference table as he entered, and a holographic display appeared above the surface.

He manipulated the touch-surface, bringing up a map of the Taran colony worlds. "As you know, we have TSS outposts throughout the Taran territory."

*He really doesn't waste any time.* Wil examined the map. It was similar to others he had seen. "Yes, along most of the major trade routes."

"Correct. We also have several armories in strategic fallback positions, were it to come to that." Ramsen brought up an overlay of the posts on the holographic projection. The armories showed up as blue dots, and most were along the border of the Rift.

*But we're fighting the war on a subspace plane.* "Those fortified positions are useless if the Bakzen jump right past."

"Correct, but the position is for another reason. These are all located within jump range to the primary Bakzen planet using a single nav beacon," Ramsen explained.

Wil perked up. "You have a beacon there?"

"No, I wish," Ramsen replied. "But we've hoped that one day we'll be able to activate one—or have an independent jump drive—so we can jump the fleet all at once and overwhelm their defenses."

*That's one way to approach it. Can't say I agree.* Wil crossed his arms. "Many of your offensive strategies sound like last resort moves."

"We've been pretty beaten down."

"That'll change." *Stars! I need to be careful what I promise.*

"Well, we're building up forces as best we can in preparation for you coming in to end the war. Resources are tight, but…" Ramsen looked down and sighed. It was the first expression of emotion Wil had seen from him.

*They're wearing thin. One day after another of the same battle, never making progress. Do they have another decade of this in them while they wait for me?* "Why don't you go over the specifics for each post? These maps don't really give a clear picture."

Without hesitation, Ramsen drilled down into the detailed supply and fleet manifest for each of the locations. It was tedious, but Wil made a point to memorize as much as possible. What he found was a variety of impressive fortifications matched against even greater Bakzen forces.

Wil's heart sank as he took it all in. *It's like the Bakzen have an endless supply of soldiers. Our fleet is picked apart and theirs grows stronger. How do we compete?*

It took hours to cover all the information. By the end, Wil felt like curling up in the corner until everything around him disappeared.

"Do you have any other questions?" Ramsen asked as he returned the display on the table to the map.

*I wouldn't want to ask them even if I did.* "No, I think that covers everything for now. Thanks for the overview."

"Gladly—"

Ramsen was interrupted by the door sliding open.

Taelis entered. "When I said to go over tactical positions, I didn't expect you to cover the entire history of the TSS."

*Was that a joke? I didn't think he had it in him.* Wil inclined his head to the High Commander. "We were being thorough. I'm grateful for the orientation."

"I'm glad it was productive," Taelis replied. "It's been a full day. Why don't we break here and you can join us for dinner."

Wil noted that the invitation was more of a statement than a question. *I've had enough conversation for one day, but I can't turn him down.* "That would be wonderful, thank you."

"Excellent." Taelis looked to Ramsen. "Let's go."

Wil accompanied Taelis and Ramsen around the ring of the space station, back to the elevator. Four levels up, they were greeted by several of the officers Wil had met earlier in the day.

The party made their way to a room labeled 'Officers' Mess', which struck Wil as a somewhat strange concept—in his home Headquarters, mealtime disregarded the distinction of rank. There were six square tables with four chairs around each. Without any verbal agreement, several of the Agents telekinetically rearranged the seating to form one large table surrounded by ten chairs.

*It's going to take some time to get used to free use of telekinesis—I'm so used to being in subspace most of the time.*

The Agents gestured for Wil to take one of the seats toward the middle of the table. He complied. There was no buffet area, as he was accustomed to seeing.

"Enough business for the day," Taelis announced, taking a seat across the table. "So, Wil, we're familiar with your official record, but why don't you tell us about yourself—the parts outside of work."

Wil was irritated by the request. "That's a difficult distinction to make." *I was raised at Headquarters. I started training as soon as I could walk. Do they honestly think I have a life outside the TSS?*

"There have to be some things you do for fun," Taelis said.

"Sure. I like flying and mechanics, but those are still work assignments. I don't know what you want me to say. I'm a dynastic heir who grew up at a military training facility. Everything I've ever done was part of my training as a TSS officer with a political bent. There isn't any free time for me to do what I want." Wil knew his tone was terse, but he was too worn down from Ramsen's briefing to care. *I wouldn't be here at all if I had another choice.*

Taelis looked pensive. "Your father indicated that you have too many obligations. You dismissed him earlier, but do you actually feel that way, too?"

*Is this a trap?* Wil thought for a moment before replying. "As I'm sure you read in my file, I always follow through on my commitments."

The High Commander leaned forward with his elbows on the table. "That doesn't answer my question."

*Stars! I feel like I'll be in trouble regardless of how I respond.* "As long as I am affiliated with the TSS, I can't imagine spending my time any differently than I already do."

"But that's still dodging the heart of the issue." Taelis sighed. "I've been thinking about what your father said, and he's right. We've put you in a position where you're always on duty—even though others are afforded leave. Headquarters is your home, so even on breaks between terms you have nowhere else to go."

"I could go if I wanted to."

Taelis cocked his head. "Yet, you haven't. The number of training hours you've logged has to be twice that of any other trainee, and you haven't even graduated."

Wil looked around the table at the Agents. All eyes were on him. "I don't look at it that way."

Taelis examined him. "You're trying to hide it, but I see some resentment under the surface."

*Is he trying to get a reaction out of me?* "That's not the term I'd use."

"No need to argue semantics. My point is, you've put in a disproportionate amount of effort compared to anyone else, and we've done nothing but pile on more." Taelis folded his hands on the table. "Going forward, I think it's appropriate to define some expectations around 'work' versus 'personal' time."

"That's not necessary, and I don't think it's appropriate."

Taelis straightened in his chair. "We need you, Wil. This is the only way I can offer you any relief."

"I didn't ask for it." *He wants something from me. He's not offering this out of the goodness of his heart.*

"But others have spoken on your behalf. I trust that you will continue following through with your assignments, as you have indicated. But, I'm proposing that you have the opportunity to choose what you do during work hours and what's above and beyond. Everyone but you has had the chance to make those distinctions—I'm only trying to right an inequity."

*That hardly makes up for it. They're just trying to buy my favor.* "Thank you."

"I'll talk with Banks about making it official," Taelis said. "I know it's a small gesture, but I hope you take it in good faith for us working together."

Wil nodded. "I appreciate it."

Taelis looked around the table. "I said no more talk of business, and yet that's all we've discussed. Forgive me." He cracked a smile at the group and the Agents shifted in their chairs, giving little nods and shrugs in response. "Where *is* our meal?" He checked his handheld.

Wil tried to sink into his chair, wishing he were anywhere else. *I'm just a commodity to them. Any offer they make is just to placate me so I'll do what they want.*

After a couple minutes of uncomfortable quiet, the door slid open. Attendants entered the room carrying trays of food. It was a veritable feast—a roasted meat main course, with potato and vegetable sides. There was even a dessert tray with what looked to be chocolate cake.

Wil made no attempt to hide his surprise. *This doesn't fit with the rest of the facility.*

As the food was placed in front of him, he realized he was ravenous, having only had a snack while working on the Bakzen ship with the engineers.

"We might be out at the edge of civilization, but we like to eat well," Taelis said.

*I imagine by 'we' he only means the officers. There's no way everyone gets this kind of treatment.* "It looks delicious."

"Please, help yourself," Taelis said, gesturing to the spread on the table.

Wil took his portion. He waited for the other officers to fill their plates before he started eating. The first bite was bliss.

"You made some interesting comments today about our tactical positions," Ramsen commented to Wil after everyone had begun eating. "Since it seems like the topic will inevitably come back to official business, would you be willing to share some of your thoughts with the group?"

*That doesn't leave me with a lot of room to decline.* Wil swallowed his mouthful. "Sure. For starters, you're only fighting the war on the frontlines."

Taelis looked to Ramsen, then back to Wil. "Can you elaborate?"

"I mean, your main offensive strategies revolve around attacking the Bakzen homeworld. Which is the ultimate goal, yes, but they can do a lot of damage elsewhere in the meantime."

"Our forces surround the Rift," Taelis countered.

"Yeah, but the Rift is only one habitable zone. There's nothing to stop the Bakzen from making a direct play for other worlds in any part of space."

"They already do raid the Outer Colonies on occasion," Ramsen said. "Thus far, we've been able to write it off as piracy."

"And what's to keep them to the Outer Colonies?" Wil replied. "Shite, they could just go straight to Tararia if they wanted to."

Taelis shook his head. "We'd see them coming. Any travel in normal space or subspace would have a trail we can trace."

"Yes, but the Rift is the blind spot," Wil said. "My point is, there's opportunity to bolster the forces along the main beacon corridors."

"They could just go around whatever blockage we set up," Taelis said.

"Maybe, but from what I learned today down in Engineering with Laecy, the Bakzen piggyback on our nav beacons. They don't have an independent jump drive, either."

Taelis eyed him. "You're saying, let them spread a little, but hold them at key choke points?"

Wil shrugged. "Something like that."

"An interesting notion," Taelis mused.

"I only looked at it for a few hours. It might not be the best solution," Wil continued. "But, giving up a little ground would allow you to reallocate your resources to where it really matters."

"I guess we really do have the right person for the job," Taelis remarked. He grabbed his handheld from his jacket pocket and brought up a spatial map on the holographic display. He set it in the center of the table. "Now, what are we going to do about those vulnerabilities?"

Wil sighed inwardly. *Now I've done it.* He grabbed a piece of chocolate cake. *I'm going to need this.*

— — —

Banks was already settling into his quarters for the night when he heard the unwelcome notification chirp of an incoming high-priority communication. He glanced at the alert window on the viewscreen in his living room and saw that it was from Taelis. *Reporting about his day with Wil, no doubt.*

He answered the call. "Hello, Erik. How did it go?"

The image of the other High Commander resolved on the viewscreen. "It went well. Mostly."

*That wasn't very enthusiastic.* "Mostly?"

Taelis looked pensive. "Wil is… very impressive. But, your Lead Agent—he isn't afraid to speak his mind, is he?"

Banks looked down. *I should have figured they wouldn't get along.* "No, he's not. However, I've seen Cris navigate some very tricky situations. He speaks his mind, but he also knows when to sit back and listen."

"I'll just have to take your word for it," Taelis replied.

"How is Wil taking everything?"

Taelis shrugged. "It's tough to say. I have no comparison for his demeanor."

"You must have had some impression about him," Banks pressed. "You said he was 'impressive'."

"Without a doubt. He's somewhat quiet and serious, but strong—none of us have been able to break through his mental blocks. And he's poised, though I did expect that giving his lineage and upbringing."

Banks tensed. *Stars! If Taelis knew Wil at all, he'd know that he's probably freaking out. I never should have pushed for a meeting right away.* "He'll make a superb leader. But we need to be careful with him. It's a lot for anyone to take in, even if it doesn't show."

"We're not really in a great position for subtlety."

Banks raised an eyebrow. "You told him everything?"

"As much as anyone aside from us knows."

"That might not be enough."

"It'll have to be," Taelis replied, firm. "It's far too dangerous."

"Dangerous for whom, exactly?" *Does he truly believe the lies we tell ourselves?*

Taelis scowled. "Do you want to break down the entire foundation of the society we're fighting for?"

*That was already broken when we compromised our morals as a people.* "Of course not. I just think a far greater danger will be from Wil himself once he realizes what this is about."

"Which is why we have gone to such lengths. Only a few of us know the truth about the war."

"So do the Aesir. Think about that. If Wil hears it from them and not from us, what will he do? Or *not* do?"

"That's a risk we have to take. The Aesir might never get involved."

*They will. They have to. Wil is who've they've been waiting for.* Banks crossed his arms. "Fine."

"You still disagree."

"I know better than to continue engaging in a losing argument." *I'd just end up dead otherwise.*

Taelis sighed. "We're on the same side, Jason. We have to remember that."

*But can both of us be left standing in the end?* "Yes, of course. And now it's even more important for us to be unified."

"It is," Taelis agreed. "I know we walk a delicate line, but we have to do what's best."

Banks nodded. The other High Commander was doing what he thought was right. Banks couldn't fault him for that. "Thank you for looking out for us."

Taelis hinted at a smile. "It's habit now. I couldn't stop if I tried."

"Well, let me know if you need anything. I know resources are tight for you."

Taelis nodded. "I've given Wil some tasks. Just give him what he needs to follow through."

"What tasks?"

"Mainly, solving the independent jump drive equation," Taelis said.

"That could be a major waste of time."

"Or it might be the solution we need," Taelis countered. "I know you have your little design competition among the Junior Agents, but I want Wil to take it seriously. He just might do it."

Banks shook his head. *We have entirely too much riding on one person.* "I think he's already been working on it."

"I'm not surprised. Which brings me to my next point. I also proposed a new arrangement between Wil and the TSS."

Banks held back a wave of frustration. "Which is?"

"Drawing a distinction between work and personal time."

"Our schedules aren't quite that neat. You know that."

Taelis looked surprised. "I thought you'd embrace the idea."

Banks would have been delighted, had the suggestion come from anyone else. He didn't trust the other High Commander to not have an ulterior motive. "What are you suggesting—have an arbitrary start and end time for each day?"

"Not arbitrary. Talk with Cris and come up with something that seems fair," Taelis replied. "You two have made such a big deal out of how much pressure we've put on Wil, this is a chance for him to set his own priorities. Anything on TSS time goes to us, and everything else he can maintain the rights."

"You're really ready to relinquish the rights for anything he develops on that personal time?" Banks asked. *Why would he make such a generous offer?*

"Invention patents aren't our primary revenue stream. What's more important now is to make sure he stays useful."

"Oh, so you just want to give him the illusion of control?"

Taelis looked a little smug. "We get everything we need, but it's on his terms."

*And hopefully slow the coming of his inevitable burnout.* Banks sighed. It was a minor change—and while not entirely innocent in its intentions, it would ultimately be to Wil's benefit. "Agreed. I'll come up with a schedule."

"Good." Taelis let out a long breath. "I should get to bed."

"So, you *do* sleep?" Banks quipped.

"Only sometimes."

"Well, I hope the rest of the visit goes well. I'll send Cris a message about this new arrangement—it'll set him at ease. Give him a chance."

Taelis nodded. "I will. I'll send you a copy of my official report on Wil's encounter with the Bakzen when it's complete."

"Thank you." *I wonder how much of it will be the real story.*

"And Jason, don't forget who we answer to. We can be replaced."

"I know. You won't hear my concerns about the Aesir again."

"Good." Taelis ended the transmission.

Banks leaned back on his couch. He massaged his temples. It was such a delicate position he must maintain, but it had become second nature. The hurdles were necessary; there was greater work to accomplish in the end. *I'll play my part, but I won't forget how we got here.*

— — —

It had been a long day. The dinner had gone much later than Wil had anticipated, and he was at capacity for how much information he could absorb in one sitting. He felt like he could fall asleep right on the floor of the corridor, but the presence of two Militia escorts drove him to keep up appearances. At last, they made it to the docking location of the *Vanquish.*

"Have a good night, sir," one of the escorts said.

*I guess I should get used to this 'sir' thing.* "Thanks, you too."

Wil dragged himself up the gangway. The rest of the week was going to be brutal.

When he reached the top, Wil realized he didn't have a room to go to, having stayed with his father on the previous leg of the trip. It was a good excuse to stop by the captain's quarters. *I didn't leave things on a very good note.*

Wil took the lift down a level and pressed the buzzer by his father's door. After a few moments, the door slid open.

Cris stood in the doorway. He seemed surprised. "I didn't expect you'd be back here tonight."

"They offered me a room, but I thought I'd be more comfortable here."

Cris nodded. "Well, Scott's already in the Delegate's Suite, so I'm afraid all that's open is crew quarters."

"Wasn't Roland Purteud the last one to stay in the Delegate's Suite?"

"Oh, stars, yes! I had half the room incinerated after that visit. How he found four women to follow him everywhere is beyond me."

"Yeah, I'd rather not think about what went on in there. Crew quarters will be just fine."

Cris cracked a smile. "Take your pick. And, don't mention Roland's visit to Scott, okay?"

Wil returned the smile. "I won't." *That's not the only reason I came here.* He sighed. "Hey, do you have a few minutes to talk?"

Cris looked almost relieved. "Of course. Do you want to come in?"

"Sure." Wil took a seat in one of the chairs by the viewport in the main room. He relaxed into the plush seat.

"How are you doing?" Cris asked.

Wil stared out the viewport. "I don't know. None of this feels real."

"It's that way for me, too." Cris sat down across from him. "I talked with your mom, and it sounds like Banks filled her in."

"How did she take it?" Wil asked.

"As well as any of us."

*We're all coping as best we can.* Wil returned his attention to inside the room but couldn't quite meet his father's gaze.

"She misses you and sends her love," Cris added.

"I'll call her when I can." Wil took a deep breath. He looked up to his father. "I'm sorry about earlier."

Cris softened. "Me too. I know I lost it. But the way Taelis was being so cavalier about what they expect from you..."

"He is pretty unlikeable, isn't he? I get that they're living in a war zone, but having a little personality never hurt anyone."

Cris smiled. "All right, so it wasn't just me."

"Stars, no! But he's still a High Commander. You can't expect the same frankness you enjoy with Banks. You don't have a history together."

"I know. It needed to be said, though."

*And it couldn't come from me.* "I appreciate it. Now whenever I say 'no' to something, I'll just pin it on you." Wil grinned.

"Oh, is that how you want to play this?"

Wil shrugged. "Just saying..."

Cris eyed him, feigning suspicion. "Uh huh. Just don't forget who sets your training routine. I can add in all kinds of extra laps."

"That would be kind of counterproductive to your point earlier about effective use of my time, wouldn't it?"

Cris smirked. "It's amazing what you can get away with when you brand it 'character building'."

Wil chuckled. "Duly noted."

Cris leaned back in his seat. "And what was with all the telepathic probing?"

"I know! I get that they've never met us, but that's not a very friendly welcome."

"I may have thought a thing or two in their direction as I was leaving..." Cris said with a smile.

"Good. War or not, manners are important."

Cris nodded. "Do you know what else Taelis has planned for you?"

Wil ran his hand through his hair. “He rattled off a crazy list of places to visit. I’m not sure what he’s trying to accomplish, but it doesn’t feel very helpful.”

“Maybe it will all make more sense in retrospect. But be careful, Wil. You can’t take everything they say at face value.”

Wil studied his father. *I know that look. He knows something but doesn’t want to tell me.* “What did you find out?”

“Enough to know that the war needs to end as soon as possible.”

*That’s a change from earlier.* “No more trying to talk me out of getting involved?”

“Being in a position of influence means that you can’t think only of yourself. I just needed a reminder.”

*I’m glad he’s back on my side, regardless of his motivation.* “I’ve been getting more perspective than I can handle.”

“Clearly, they kept you busy today.”

“I thought they’d never stop talking.” Wil suppressed a yawn. “And, I have an early morning tomorrow.”

Cris stood. “Yes, of course. Thanks for stopping by.”

“I’m glad I did.” Wil rose. “You should come tomorrow. We’re going to tour the shipyards—and who knows what else.”

“Are you sure you want me tagging along?”

*As long as you don’t embarrass me again.* Wil smiled to set him at ease. “Absolutely.”

Cris tried to conceal his gratitude. “All right. What time?”

“Breakfast at 07:15?”

“Perfect, I’ll meet you in the mess.”

Wil nodded. “All right. I’ll see you then. Good night.” He walked to the door.

“Sleep well.”

Wil let out a deep sigh as soon as he was in the hall. Helping his father feel included and secure might turn into a full-time job. *But he’s one of the best Agents out there. And he’ll look out for me, even when it’s inconvenient. With what’s ahead, I’m going to need all the help I can get.*

# CHAPTER 15

THE REST OF the week was a sickening blur. Engineering labs, shipyards, weapons systems, control centers—all of it exceeded Wil's expectations. However, what should have been an impressive display was overshadowed by reminders of the Bakzen.

At first, the references were subtle—sporadic questions, or a side comment—but over the next few days the inquiries about Wil's time behind enemy lines transitioned into full-blown interrogations. He knew that even the most minor observations might be important, so he kept answering as best he could and made no indication that he was uncomfortable. But, his brave face was a façade; inside he was breaking down.

The familiarity of the *Vanquish* offered a modicum of comfort when Wil returned each night after spending the day with Taelis and his officers, though he still found himself feeling increasingly removed from everything. The more he saw of H2 and further evidence of the war, the more the reality of his future responsibilities weighed on his mind.

Even when he was told that they were finally going home, it felt like just another trial with no end. *I'm now involved in the war whether they admit it or not. No matter where I go, this will be my life. There's no room for anything else.*

Wil was trying to get comfortable on his bunk in the *Vanquish*'s crew quarters when his father walked in.

"We're underway," Cris said as he sat down on the other end of the bunk.

"Yes, I felt the docking clamps release."

"Of course you would." Cris smiled. He took off his tinted glasses and relaxed against the wall of the bunk. "Sorry, it's just all these years of having to explain every bomaxed little thing to people less familiar with ships."

"No apology needed."

"You wouldn't believe some of these people!" Cris leaned back against the wall. "I'll never forget the time when these planet-loving dynastic delegates from Gesek came to visit, and they asked what was happening every time a light flashed or there was any sort of sound in the Command Center—which, of course, was constantly. I swear, they thought the ship was going to spontaneously combust at any moment."

"Had they never spent any time offworld?"

"I'm convinced they were all hand-selected for their various anxiety disorders with the express purpose of making my life miserable," Cris said with a rueful grin. "The higher authorities of the Taran government have a strange way of showing their appreciation. Despite all that the TSS provides for them, they seem to enjoy giving us a hard time whenever the situation presents itself."

"I've noticed." Wil rolled onto his back and stared up at the ceiling.

"Just a few hours until we're home," Cris said in an upbeat tone.

Wil was too worn out to be roused so easily. "Hopefully, they'll just read the reports from H2 and leave us alone." He wanted to be excited about going home, but he knew things would be different around Headquarters from now on. He also would never be able to look at himself the same way, knowing what his future held.

Cris gave him a sympathetic smile. "I know it's been a tough week. They put me through the gauntlet, too."

"Yeah." There was no comparing their experiences, as far as Wil was concerned. *No one told him he'd have to single-handedly lead the annihilation of an entire race.*

"Everyone is going to be happy to see you."

Wil looked away. *They'll expect everything to get back to normal, but I've changed,* he thought to himself. *Everything has changed.*

"Wil—"

He sat up and stared his father to silence, a focused gaze of authority that few ever attained. "I'll be happy to see them, too, but we can't pretend like everything is how it was before."

After a moment, Cris nodded. "You're right, I'm sorry."

"I'll be an Agent by the time most Trainees are just starting out, and who knows what kind of CR score I'll get." Wil hung his head. "People will be terrified as soon as they realize what being around me means—a front row seat to death and destruction."

"I don't know what the future holds, but *I'm* not going anywhere."

The words rang true, but Wil could see that there was a hint of fear even in his father's eyes. "I believe you."

Cris looked down. "I wish you would also believe me when I say that you can take it easy for now. It's much too early for you to feel so much pressure."

*How can I ever relax again? I hold the fate of so many people. It comes down to me… what I must do.* Wil shook his head and looked away. A deep ache gripped his chest. "I'll try."

"If I can do anything to help you—"

Wil forced a smile to set his father at ease. "It's not a question of support. How you've taken all of this… anyone else would have turned to run."

Cris smiled back. "Well, I did want to."

"But you're here with me now, and that means a lot."

"I'd never abandon you."

Wil shook his head. "No one will ever understand what the weight of this responsibility feels like." *Even if I am successful in defeating the Bakzen, there won't be anything left of myself.*

"I wish I could. All I can promise is that I'll try to be there for you whenever you might need me."

Wil repositioned on the bunk and looked intently at his father. "Thank you for believing in me."

"Always."

They sat in silence for some time.

"I'd like to spend some time alone before we get back," Wil requested. "I doubt I'll get much time to myself once we're there."

"Okay." Cris headed to the door. "We'll figure out something fun to do after the debriefs—forget about everything for a while."

"Sounds great," Wil replied with a faint smile.

Wil lay back down on the bunk when his father had left. He stared at the ceiling. *I wish it didn't have to be this way, but they made it my destiny. I have to do my part.*

—

Wil sensed a change in his surroundings. He opened his eyes. The stars were still, familiar. *Home.*

He rose from the bunk and removed his new black overcoat from the locker at the back of the room. As he got dressed, he suppressed the thoughts about his new reality that kept creeping into the corners of his consciousness. He took a deep breath to calm and reassure himself, then stepped out into the hallway to face those who knew the true reason behind his absence.

His father met up with him ten meters down the hallway, and they took the lift up to the gangway.

Cris still looked drained, but he was in good spirits. "We're home, Wil."

Wil returned the smile, but his wasn't heartfelt. "Yes, but there's still a traitor among us."

"We'll find them soon, and then we can relax."

Wil kept his gaze fixed ahead. *Even once we do, I don't know if I'll ever feel comfortable here again... Not now that I know what's coming.*

The two Sietinens walked down the gangway into the spaceport and took a shuttle to the surface port. The elevator ride down to Level 1 felt excruciatingly long, but Wil was relieved his father didn't try to make small talk. When the elevator doors opened, Wil was greeted by the sight of his mother standing alongside Banks at the center of the lobby. They both looked as though they had gotten little rest in recent days, but their faces brightened as Wil and Cris approached.

Kate ran forward and embraced Wil. Silent, she held him close. Wil was nearly as tall as her, and he hugged her back easily as she cradled his head to her shoulder. Normally, he would resist such a public display of affection from his mother, but he needed it as much as she did.

After a full minute, Kate released Wil from the hug, but she continued to hold him at arm's length. Gently, she brushed his hair from his forehead and searched his eyes.

"I'm okay, Mom," he responded to her unspoken query.

Kate continued gazing into his eyes. "I know."

*She sees how much I've changed. I can't hide it.* He turned from his mother to the High Commander. "I assume you would like to speak with me, sir?"

Kate looked pained, but quietly accepted that there were still official matters to discuss. Cris took the opportunity to embrace her, which she didn't hesitate to return.

Banks glanced at Cris, then back at Wil. "I've already read through the reports you filed with Taelis," Banks responded, "but there is another matter we should address. Cris, I'd like you to attend, as well. Shall we go to my office?"

"Wherever is most comfortable," Wil replied.

Cris gave Kate a kiss and then pulled himself away from her.

"Stay close," Kate said to Cris.

Banks led the way down the main corridor of the administrative wing with Wil and Cris following behind.

It felt good to be back in the halls of Headquarters, but Wil was still on edge. *I fear the good times are all behind me.*

Once in the High Commander's office, Banks faced Wil and Cris in the middle of the room. "Wil," Banks began as he shifted on his feet, "you handled yourself exceptionally well, but you never should have been in that position. It was a failure in TSS security, and I take responsibility. I wish I had an answer for how this happened. Your mother and I have been over all the security logs, and I still can't definitively tell how the Bakzen got in."

"I'll just have to be more careful."

Banks nodded. "Well, you know the security system inside and out, so maybe you can see something I didn't. At any rate, I'm just glad you escaped."

"I got lucky." Wil looked at his father. "And had help."

Banks smiled. "Luck, skill—it was an admirable effort all around. The important thing is, you're back now, and I will do everything in my power to keep you safe."

Wil examined Banks. "If there's anything I learned, it's that I need to be responsible for my own safety. I can't count on someone having my back."

Banks nodded slowly. "Maybe so, but that doesn't mean we can't take precautions." Banks glanced at Cris and shifted restlessly again. "To that end, after you arrived at H2, I reached out to your grandparents—"

"I thought you were going to keep this quiet?" Cris interrupted. "The last thing any of us need is my parents butting in—"

"Cris... just let me finish." Banks refocused on Wil. "Since we don't know the nature of the security breach within Headquarters, I wanted to go to an outside resource. I kept it vague, but your grandparents were naturally concerned about your well-being. They were eager to make a contribution."

"What sort of contribution?" Cris asked.

"Your grandparents have sent a personal bodyguard," Banks told Wil, leaving Cris at the fringe of the conversation. "Though he is now formally a member of the Royal Guard, he was TSS trained through the first year, as is customary. From what I hear, he would have made a very good Militia officer—"

"I thought we had agreed to keep dynastic affairs out of Wil's life," Cris blurted out, all but ignoring Banks' disapproving stare.

"Dad, I—" Wil began, but was ignored.

"It was my idea," Banks stated. "You don't have to like it."

Cris fell silent.

"I'm not sure *I* like the idea of someone constantly trailing me," Wil asserted, taking advantage of the pause.

"I know," Banks said, "but your safety is becoming increasingly more important."

Wil shook his head. "Still, I've been trained far more than any guard. I don't know what good one would be."

Banks sighed. "Wil, sometimes it's not the action, but the thought that matters. Just having someone else around can be a major deterrent."

"True. But that still sounds like an awkward arrangement."

"Well, I'm not comfortable with you walking around on your own anymore. There's no telling what might happen. And, instead of thinking of him as a guard, just treat him as a friend who would do anything for you," Banks said.

"Are you sure there aren't any hidden motives?" Cris asked.

The High Commander examined his Lead Agent. "Cris, though you may not have the best relationship with your parents, I hope you know that deep down they do care for you. I don't see why you're so quick to judge their feelings toward Wil."

"Because I spent the early years of my life growing up in their world, and I have come to know they don't care about individual people. All that matters to them are bloodlines and the continuity of power. I utterly disgraced my parents by running away from the life they set out for me, and I will never be completely forgiven. I'm afraid some of that resentment has been transferred onto Wil, as my son."

"Dad, you're talking like I can't hear you."

"You've already figured out that much for yourself, Wil. It's no secret that I don't get along with them. Surely, you remember that one trip we took to Tararia when you were four. I don't believe our animosity requires any explanation. At least Marina wasn't around, for once, to exacerbate matters."

"Yes, I remember. Still, don't expect me to have the same problems with your parents that you do. I get along with you, after all."

"Yes, Wil, but that's because I've played an active part in your life. My parents never offered me that courtesy."

Banks cleared his throat and the two Sietinens fell silent and looked at him. "We have digressed far from the original matter at hand. Wil, you're getting a guard whether you like it or not. As we speak, he is waiting to meet you."

*Great, all I needed was something else to make me stand out.* "For how long?" Wil asked.

"At least until you're an Agent," the High Commander responded.

Wil nodded. *That's soon now. It always seemed so far off.*

Banks telekinetically cracked open the main door to the office with a whip of his hand. "Send him in," he told the sentry outside.

The door swung open the rest of the way, and a tall, muscular man walked in. His dark hair was cut short and he wore the gray uniform of the Tararian Guard, with golden piping on the sleeves and collar denoting the Royal Guard division within the broader military and peacekeeping organization. The firm angles of the uniform gave him a stiff appearance, but it was obvious from the way he walked that the illusion did not correspond with his disposition.

He quickly looked over everyone in the room with silent respect and then bowed deeply. "My lords," he murmured in a warm bass voice as he straightened and stood at attention with his arms at his side.

"At ease," Banks told him. "Wil, I'd like you to meet Caeron Reccaros."

Wil looked Caeron over. "Pleasure to meet you," he said, though he wasn't necessarily in the mood to be friendly to anyone potentially encroaching on his independence.

"The pleasure's all mine, my lord," Caeron replied.

Cris looked sick. He shot one fierce glare in Banks' direction. "I can see that none of this concerns me." He walked out the open door.

Caeron's impassive face suddenly became alarmed. He opened his mouth to say something, but immediately closed it, remembering his place.

"It's nothing you did," Banks assured, seeing his concern. "Why don't you two go get acquainted."

Wil sighed. "Come with me."

— — —

Kate exhaled slowly. Wil wasn't the same person she had seen only a week earlier. Her heart ached for her son, seeing the burden he carried. But, they had all changed with the knowledge of what brought them together. Yet, they were still family. In time, they would learn how to support each other in their new roles.

She made for the elevator to take her down one level to her quarters. While she waited, Haersen passed by her on his way across the lobby.

"I'm glad to hear Wil is home safely," Haersen said without breaking stride.

"Thank you. It's been rough," Kate replied. "I wonder if we'll ever get back to normal."

"It'll all be over soon."

"Not soon enough." *We have years to go until the war ends.* Kate entered the elevator and made her way to her quarters. There was no telling how long the debrief with Banks would take;

she was just grateful to not be a part of it. After everything Banks had kept from her, even as he professed to be telling the whole story, she couldn't look him in the eye. She didn't trust anything he said, even if Cris did.

Kate was just getting settled on the couch in the living room when Cris came through the entry door in a huff.

She looked up in surprise. "I didn't expect you so soon. Why aren't you with Wil?"

"Banks made some sort of deal with my parents for a personal guard. The nerve."

Kate jumped to her feet. "You left Wil alone with him?"

"If Banks vetted him, he must be trustworthy."

"It's not the guard I'm worried about," Kate said. "There's still a traitor somewhere in Headquarters. I told you to stay close!"

"The Bakzen aren't getting in again. Everything's fine."

"You think they'll let this go? If they can't have Wil for their plan, then…" *Better dead than an opponent.*

Their eyes met as Cris made the connection. He yanked open the door. "Stars! Where is he?"

— — —

Wil left Banks' office with Caeron in tow. Once near a somewhat private alcove along the hallway, Wil looked squarely at his new guard. "First of all, I would like to make it clear that I'm not enamored with the concept of a 'guard'. I have expressed that position to Banks, but he doesn't care much for my opinion on the matter. Don't take any of my hostility toward you personally. As far as I am concerned, I will be looking forward to the day I no longer need to be followed everywhere and can travel on my own without an unwanted escort."

Caeron stood quietly for a moment before responding, "When I accepted this assignment, I didn't expect any special treatment, my lord," he began. "I took it to help ensure the safety of someone of great importance—"

"Please, don't address me formally," Wil requested. "It's not appropriate here. Within the TSS, no social rank in the outside world applies. As a general rule, nothing more than 'sir' will ever be used. Even then, it is reserved for official occasions and not used in everyday speech, at least between Agents of the same rank. As a Junior Agent, I have absolutely no seniority, even as a Sietinen heir, so I should not be treated any differently."

"I understand, s— I'll refer to you any way you wish," Caeron replied.

"Thank you. Now, I have a lot on my mind, and I'm going to my room. I have no idea where they intend for you to sleep, given that I'm in Junior Agents' housing, but you can walk me to my quarters, if you want."

"My living arrangements are not an immediate concern. I'll follow you at a distance." Caeron ventured a small smile.

Wil nodded absently and continued down the long hall toward the central elevator. The hall seemed more vacant than he remembered, but perhaps that was just his disquiet from recent events.

Caeron followed Wil at a fair distance, but Wil could feel him watching. He tried to put his new shadow out of his mind, just looking forward to sleeping in his own bed again. There was a lot to process.

As he approached the central elevator lobby, Wil was brought to attention by a familiar voice.

"Welcome home."

Wil spun around to see the Mission Coordinator standing behind him. "Yes, it's nice to be back, finally."

"I've been assisting Banks with the investigation into your capture," continued Haersen. "He informed me that you played a key role in programming the latest security protocols."

"I did."

Haersen nodded. "I think I may have found a point of entry for the exterior breach, but I need some assistance deciphering the underlying algorithms. Could you give me a quick orientation to the system? I should be able to take it from there."

Wil wanted nothing more than to be left alone. "This isn't a good time."

"It should only take a few minutes. We'll all be able to rest easier once we get to the bottom of this."

"Where did you spot the breach?" There weren't any holes. Even he'd have a difficult time hacking the system from the outside, and he knew everything about it.

"It's easier if I show you." Haersen smiled. "If you help me with this, I can get you out of filing an extra mission report. I'm sure you'd rather take the day off tomorrow."

It was a tempting offer. "This won't take long?"

"Not long at all."

Wil nodded his consent. He followed the Mission Coordinator into the elevator, and Haersen closed the door before Caeron could enter. *He'll catch up.*

Haersen set the elevator to Level 10.

"Level 10?" Wil asked. "Can't we go over the logs in Comm Command?"

"Yes, but it's more private in Secondary Communications," Haersen replied. "Don't want anyone listening in."

Wil leaned against the side wall while the elevator descended.

When the doors opened, Haersen led them a short distance down the hall to the Secondary Communications room, which served as an emergency operations center. When they entered the spacious room, it was dimmed and vacant.

Haersen walked toward the far side of the space, lined with screens and consoles. "This is an excellent place to work undisturbed."

"Nice. So, about the security network—"

"I come here sometimes on my own." Haersen continued into the back recesses of the room.

"Is that so?"

"I've learned quite a bit about the communications system and how one might bypass the standard security measures. Over here," he beckoned Wil over to the main console, "I'll show you."

As Wil approached, Haersen activated the large viewscreen on the back wall. "It took a lot of rooting around to learn everything. That's how I found the breach. I think you'll understand the issue once I show you."

Haersen opened a video file and began playing it on the viewscreen when Wil came to stand next to him.

It took Wil a moment to accept the image, but there was no mistaking Colonel Tek of the Bakzeni Empire.

*Haersen is working with them! He must have helped them take me.* Wil began backing toward the door, every muscle poised for action. He missed the first few words of what Tek was saying.

"…Carzen didn't see Dragon's true value to us, and he will ultimately pay the price. Even the Imperial Director can't be trusted anymore. And to think I carry those same genes! If we can't use the Dragon to expand the Rift, then we must eliminate him."

Wil was in full panic. The door was on the other side of the room; too far to run. He continued backing up, keeping his full attention on Haersen while he looked for an opportunity to get away. "I don't understand. Why are you working with them?"

Haersen looked at Wil with disgust. "You, Cadicle, are the best Tarans have to offer, and you're still nothing compared to them. The Bakzen—they fix flaws, find ways to continuously improve. But our race… we let the weak survive, coddle them. I've seen that there's a path to perfection. They can make me better. Stronger. It's the only way."

Wil reached out telekinetically to guard himself, but he couldn't do anything useful within the subspace bubble. A cold chill gripped his chest. "That's not true. There's always another way."

"Not this time." Haersen eyed him with the same contemptuous glare. He reached for something inside his coat.

Wil made a run for it. But when he reached the threshold where the door should automatically open, nothing happened. *No!*

He took another step to be sure, but there was still no movement. *Locked in.* The door would have to be opened manually. He wheeled around to face Haersen. "Don't do this. I—"

Haersen held out a rare ballistic handgun. "You chose the wrong side."

He pulled the trigger before Wil had time to react.

The bullet caught Wil right below the ribs in the center of his abdomen, and he felt it lodge deep inside. He collapsed to the floor, radiating pain replaced by numbness. The room dimmed. He lay on his back gasping for air as he pressed on the wound to try to stop the freely flowing blood.

Haersen walked to Wil and stood over him, looking downward with his gun still in hand. "No more weakness. We will have immortality." He aimed the gun at Wil's head and a slow smiled spread over his face. His finger tightened on the trigger for the final lethal shot.

The door flew open.

Wil couldn't see clearly, but it appeared a single shot from a standard blast gun struck Haersen in the shoulder. The ballistic gun fell to the ground and Haersen dodged to the side to avoid a lunging figure. He tore out of the room. The other man was about to follow, but he halted.

Caeron knelt beside Wil. Wil looked up at him briefly, but he closed his eyes again when he was unable to focus.

His thoughts became detached from his consciousness, and he began drifting toward blackness. He worked his throat to say something, but nothing came out.

Even as his last physical strength gave out, thoughts continued to drift through his mind. *I can't die yet,* came forward through the jumble. *This can't be the end.* Further down, Haersen's betrayal cut him. *How could he do this to his own people? Why help the Bakzen?*

Someone was talking, but Wil couldn't make out the words. He couldn't speak. As gentle hands picked him up, he barely felt the movement. Though some of the voices around him sounded familiar, he couldn't identify them through the haze. The lighting changed outside his closed lids, and then again. He was placed on something comfortable with firm support.

He released and felt no more.

# CHAPTER 16

CRIS SLUMPED OVER on the bench outside Wil's medical room, hands covering his eyes. *After everything, his greatest danger was at home. I'll kill Haersen myself if we ever find him.*

Initially, Cris had stayed inside the room by his son's side, but it had become too painful to see him in a comatose state. He waited vigilantly outside his door, hoping.

Wil had been rushed to the medical facilities on Level 1 immediately after he was shot—thanks to Caeron—but he had not awoken in the two weeks since. The bullet had lodged in Wil's spine, shattering the bone and ravaging the nerves. The accompanying blood loss had been substantial, limiting crucial oxygen to his brain as he was taken from Level 10 to the top floor of Headquarters. Medical science could repair his wounds, but tests could only show so much. There was no way to confirm if the reconstruction had been successful until he was awake. *If he wakes up.*

As time dragged on with no change in his condition, Banks had stopped visiting. *It's only a matter of time before they'll give up on him. Before they'll want to replace him. But I won't. I can't.*

Cris sensed Kate approaching. He pulled his hands from his eyes and looked blearily around the infirmary.

Kate was a shell of herself, devastated by the loss of her son who wasn't yet gone. Though despair had consumed her, Cris was trying to hold out. Still, his heart had been steadily sinking as the days passed.

His wife sat down on the bench next to Cris without her usual grace and leaned against him. "Banks almost said something to me today. You've seen the way he looks at us. They won't let it go on like this…"

"I'm not giving up on him." Cris put his arm around her and rubbed her back.

Kate tensed under his touch. "I'm trying not to… but you've heard the odds of him making a full recovery. It's possible he won't even wake up. In the event he—"

Cris pulled away and looked at his wife with disbelief. "How can you even go there?"

Kate searched his eyes then hung her head. "Nothing about this is easy, Cris."

"I know." He straightened, resolute. "But I refuse to give up on him. Ever."

"I haven't given up." Tears filled Kate's eyes. "I just can't continue to ignore reality."

"And I can't ignore my son, as my parents once did."

Kate sat back. "You think they abandoned your brother?"

"Never mind." *What happened to Tristen isn't the same.*

"Your parents had to look to their future. There were forces beyond their control."

"Kate—" *I can't hear this. Not now. Not from her.*

"As much as you don't want to admit it, you now find yourself in a similar position. An injured son, with everything depending on him. Tristen was killed—it was tragic. And then your parents had you, because they had no other option. But your existence doesn't diminish his memory."

But there was one important distinction. "Wil isn't dead."

Kate looked down. "No, he's not."

*If he doesn't pull through, I won't bring another child into this, not to be used by the Priesthood and the TSS.* Cris crossed his arms. "They can't force us to do anything."

Fresh tears filled Kate's eyes, both mourning her son and for their impossible position. "What about our people?"

"It's too soon to think about any of this."

Kate reclined against the wall behind the bench. "I'm sorry. I shouldn't draw any comparison to what happened with your family. There's no sense dwelling on the past."

But there were striking similarities. Tristen's death wasn't an accident. Neither was what happened to Wil. Cris dug deep to maintain his composure. "I know my brother was gone, but still—my parents were so quick to conceive another… a replacement. As long as there is *any* hope for Wil, however slim the chance may be, I won't give up."

Kate took Cris' hand. "They did what they had to do."

Cris slumped against the wall. He searched for the words. "My issue isn't that they had me. It was the expectation for me to be exactly like him—*that* was within their control. That's what I can never excuse."

"It wasn't fair."

"I could never escape his shadow, no matter how hard I tried."

"What made you so different from him?"

Cris shook his head. "I lack the one key personality trait they so desperately desired: that I would *want* to be who I am—businessman, politician, aristocrat. And for that, I am their greatest disappointment."

Kate looked down.

*The Priesthood took away my parents' perfect son and they got me in return. I'd be bitter, too.* And now the Bakzen had tried to take away his own son. He couldn't imagine having another child, either. Wil was his world. "What if Tristen's death was a signal that the Sietinen line should end, that Sietinen and Vaenetri should never join? Perhaps I wasn't meant to be here."

Kate looked appalled. "How can you say that?"

"I've never felt I belonged. I thought I had a place here in the TSS, but now I know that was all a ruse." *The Priesthood carrying out their plan to win their secret war.*

"Cris, this life we have here—what's between us—is real. What we know now doesn't change that. Yes, Tristen died, but without that tragedy we wouldn't be here together or have had Wil, and I wouldn't trade our family for anything."

*Neither would I, but can I be the person Tararia and the TSS need?* He took a steadying breath. "Our son is still here. He's a fighter."

Kate nodded and leaned against Cris' shoulder, linking her arm around his. "There's always hope."

— — —

Wil was detached from himself, drifting. He was surrounded by darkness, devoid of any feeling. It was peaceful at first, but unformed thoughts began to gnaw at the back of his consciousness, like he was forgetting something important. As he tried to remember what he might have lost, he realized he wasn't alone in the darkness.

Whispers swirled around him, fleeting as though carried by an unseen breeze. Wil tried to catch the words, but they drifted past. Determined, he fought to find the source. As he probed into the darkness, he sensed a sudden presence in his mind. The whispers enveloped him, separate voices becoming one. "*We see you.*"

Startled, Wil pulled away. The movement was met by crippling pain that seemed to emanate from the very core of his being. He tried to retreat from the fiery burn, but there was nowhere to go. As the pain threatened to consume him, he noticed a faint red glow.

Desperate for any escape, Wil focused on the light. It was close, but just beyond reach. He opened his eyes.

His surroundings seemed like they should be familiar, but he couldn't place them. When he tried to roll his head to the side to look around the room, he found he couldn't move. Gripped with fear, he attempted to sit upright.

A shock of searing pain shot from his back to the rest of his body. The very tensing of his muscles was unbearable. He consciously relaxed as he lay on the bed, holding in a cry of anguish. Breathing alone was almost too painful to tolerate.

*What happened to me?*

He probed his memory. For a moment, he couldn't remember anything. Then, images and sensations began trickling back—slowly at first, then accelerating to faster than he thought he could take in at once. He somehow caught every detail through the flood of information. The entire experience lasted no more than a few seconds, but it left him breathless.

When the memories had settled, Wil focused on the present. He set the pain aside, becoming no more than a dim ache in the background of his consciousness.

As he evaluated himself, his condition took on a new light. He knew he was not paralyzed, but rather that his nerves were still healing and movement would disrupt the process. He was able to comprehend that his entire nervous system had undergone a change. At the edge of his consciousness, he was aware that he was processing thoughts differently, but everything was so much more ordered and coherent that it felt natural.

Just as he was about to slip deeper within himself to further assess his transformation, he became aware of movement outside. The door opened.

Irina stepped in, her expression a mixture of confusion and relief. "Wil, you're…" She rushed to the console next to his medical bed and brought up the details of his vitals.

*They didn't expect me to wake up.* Wil nodded. It took effort. *I've never felt so weak.*

Cris came into the doorway, looking just as perplexed as Irina. "Wil!" He almost choked.

"Hi," Wil managed.

"How do you feel?" Irina asked. She checked his pupils, seeming satisfied with her observation.

Wil swallowed, feeling parched. "I've been better. But, okay, I guess."

Irina smiled. "You gave us quite a scare." She beckoned Cris the rest of the way into the room.

Cris looked like he was about to faint. Unsteady, he eased into a chair next to Wil's bed.

"We weren't sure what happened," Irina continued. "Your brain activity was barely registering for days. Suddenly, it flat-lined for ten seconds, and then shot up to higher than anything I've ever seen. The amount of activity across the neural pathways is…"

"I feel it." Wil looked inward. "Whatever you did to repair my injury, I feel like I've been rewired. And, I guess I had to 'reboot', if you will. It's like… like everything is now running at optimum efficiency."

Irina glanced at Cris, but he was still at a loss for words. "Wil, I'll try to put this delicately," she continued. "There was significant damage. Your spinal column was shattered. The blood loss resulted in major oxygen starvation to your brain."

"I know. I'll need to learn how to walk again."

Irina came forward and took his feet lightly in her hands. "You have feeling?"

Wil twitched his toe, sending radiating pain he was careful to hide.

Irina smiled with relief. "Well, in that case, I suppose your recovery can just go down in history as a medical miracle."

*Except, I was engineered to be this way.* Wil only gave a weak smile in response.

Cris pulled himself together and stood up. "Can you give us a few minutes?" he asked Irina, but his gaze rested on his son.

She hesitated. "I suppose. But I would like to run a more thorough examination soon."

Cris nodded. "Of course."

The doctor took a disconcerted breath and walked out of the room.

Cris perched on the edge of Wil's bed. He ran his fingers through his hair and took a deep, shaky breath. "Thank the stars you're okay! We weren't sure you'd…"

*How am I supposed to do anything? It hurts to even think about moving.* "This recovery won't be easy."

Cris cast his eyes downward for a moment before bringing his gaze back up to meet his son's. "I'm so sorry, Wil. I just can't stop thinking if Caeron hadn't arrived. Just seconds later and…"

*Banks was right, after all, to insist on having someone with me.* Wil took a moment to respond. "As terrible as this all seems now, it's let me come into my true power."

"What do you mean?"

"I don't know, exactly. But something in me has changed. I feel stronger somehow." *Is this the power Carzen wanted to help me harness?*

Wil froze, remembering what Tek had said in the video recording. *If Tek kills Carzen, then any lingering chance of a peaceful end to the conflict with the Bakzen—however slim it may have been—will die with him.* He tried to sit up straighter, setting his nerves on fire. "I need a tablet! I need to warn Carzen—"

Cris held him still. "Wil, no."

"But in the video, Tek said—"

Cris nodded. "I know, I saw it. But whatever is going on with the Bakzen, we need to let it play out. There's nothing we could say to Carzen that would make a difference."

Wil shook his head, his chest tight. *Complete destruction is my only option.*

"I'll be here for you, as best I can." Cris took Wil's hand. He looked pensive. "I want to get you away from here for a while. As soon as you're well enough, let's go to Tararia."

"But you hate it there."

"It doesn't matter how I feel about it. The family estate might be the safest place there is right now. And it's peaceful. Wil, you need real sunlight, fresh air, and solid ground underfoot. I won't let my troubles with my parents get in the way of your recovery. You're old enough to make your own choices about them."

*Their intervention is the only reason I'm alive now.* Wil nodded. "All right. I guess it would be nice to get away and just relax for a while."

Cris smiled. "You deserve it."

"And you." Wil forced a smile back.

"I'm glad someone else feels that way." Cris looked over his shoulder at the door of the medical room. "I should let Irina have a look at you now. Besides, I need to let your mom know you're finally awake—she's been worried sick. We both have been."

"There's one other thing." Wil glowered. "Did they ever catch Haersen?"

Cris flushed. "No. He must have had his escape planned out well in advance via a supply export. By the time we found the two dead Militia guards and realized where he'd gone, there was no way to track him."

Wil looked away. *Are there others working with the Bakzen? As if our fight wasn't already hard enough.*

His father caught his gaze. "But I swear to you, Wil, I will see to it that he is killed and forever remembered as a traitor for what he did."

Wil nodded. *He's the one who picked the wrong side.*

— — —

Cris stood in a palatial hall of the Sietinen estate. Despite the warm air wafting through the corridor, a chill gripped him from within. He had been back to his family's compound on Tararia several times since he ran away as a teenager, but it never felt like a return to home. He had too many unpleasant memories to ever be comfortable in the place. However, he knew it was the most secure location for Wil to finish convalescing, and that meant far more to him than his own peace of mind.

It had been over a month since Wil was shot, and his recovery was going exceptionally well. Wil was able to walk, though still slowly and for short periods, but he was making steady progress. In the week since they had traveled from TSS Headquarters to Tararia, Wil's spirits had lifted greatly, and Cris was glad he had set aside familial conflict for the sake of his son.

Cris looked around at the ornate details of the building; he never ceased to wonder at the craftsmanship of the estate. However, studying the stone and wooden carvings throughout the room, he was overcome with an urge to be outdoors.

He strolled down the hallway and turned out onto a large stone balcony. The terrace overlooked the beautiful gardens of the estate, filled with fountains and streams intermingling in the foliage. Moonlight reflected off the landscape, and the tension in his shoulders eased as he overlooked the serene scenery. Staring upward, he admired the two moons of Tararia floating low on the horizon above the mountains that sheltered the city of Sieten.

Cris breathed deeply, taking in the night air. He leaned up against the railing of the balcony, closing his eyes. Just as he was beginning to drift off in thought, he became aware of someone coming up behind him.

He turned around to see Wil hobble out onto the balcony. "What are you doing up, Wil? I thought you were asleep." He noticed Caeron watching them from just inside the doorway.

"I was, but I woke up and couldn't get settled again," Wil replied. He stared out into the quiet night for a moment. "I'm still having nightmares about the Bakzen."

A sharp pang shot through Cris' chest. "I was afraid of that." *It's been every night since he woke up from the coma. When will it end?*

Wil shrugged and looked up at the moons. "It's a beautiful night."

He smiled at his son, but he had to force it through worry. "Yes, it is. It's good to see that you're able to move about more freely now."

Wil made a vague gesture with his hand. "It still hurts, but I try to ignore the pain."

*He's so resilient. I don't think I'd be coping half as well.* "I wish you didn't have to go through this, Wil, but I'm happy to see you recovering."

Wil nodded. "It's nice to finally be out of bed."

"I can only imagine."

Wil was silent for a few minutes. "Thank you for taking me here. I needed some time away before we face all the changes back home."

Cris took a moment to respond. "You know I'd do anything for you."

"I know." Wil paused. "It'll be okay, Dad."

"I have no doubt."

They were silent for a long time.

"There's one thing that's still unclear," Wil said, breaking the silence.

"What's that?"

"Who are the Bakzen, really?"

Cris smiled. "Oh, Wil… Someone knows, but they have gone to great lengths to keep it from us."

"I can't help but wonder why." Wil stared up at the moons again.

"Right now, you just need to concern yourself with healing and completing your training." Cris looked his son over. *He'll be grown up the rest of the way before I know it.*

"That's just the beginning. There's still much more to come after that."

*More than any of us can anticipate.* "You're strong and have good morals, Wil. As long as you don't lose sight of yourself, everything will work out."

Wil gazed at the star-speckled sky. "I'll try. I'm part of something bigger than myself, and I have to succeed. I have no other choice. There's too much at stake."

— — —

General Carzen stared back, unflinching under the furious gaze of his subordinate. "It's confirmed? The Primus Elite recovered?"

"Yes. And it's time I do what I should have done long ago," Tek replied. "You're not fit to lead us."

"Is that so?" Carzen leaned forward in his chair.

Tek's eyes narrowed. "First your ill-conceived 'plan' to turn the Primus Elite to our side, and then you let him escape… Now he grows stronger on Tararia as we speak."

"The potential value of his military alliance was worth the risks. We're in no different a place now than if we'd never captured him."

"Except now he's seen our forces! You were always too narrow-minded to see his real value," sneered Tek. "We could have used him to rip the Rift wide open, and we wouldn't have need his cooperation. Just throw him out into space and let his instincts take over as he tried to cling to life."

"Which is precisely what I was going to do after he made it clear he wasn't going to cooperate," Carzen countered. "I tried to recapture him for that very reason."

"A failure, just like all your other ventures. It needed to be done carefully and in the right place, but you rushed things, and all our preparations have gone to waste. Now it will take the sacrifice of thousands of our drones to widen the Rift in the way we could have with his singular destruction."

"That was the only way you ever saw it," continued Carzen. "I had other hopes."

Tek was appalled. "Your 'diplomatic solution'? We should have just killed him while we had the chance."

Carzen sighed. "I had to try another approach first. I'm tired of all this fighting. It needs to end."

"I *was* trying to end it!" Tek spat at his superior officer. "Everything was in place to create the final Rift pathways we need to take out the key Taran worlds. What could have been done already if you'd just let me use him..." His face twisted with rage. "How can you even stand to be in a room with one of them after what they did to us? We have worked far too long to free ourselves from them only to let it all go to waste. We can't let them taste such an immoral victory!"

Carzen was stoic. "Is it really our right to rebel against our creators? Perhaps we should have listened to them before it came to this."

Tek shook his head with disgust. "Just give up? It would go against our very genetic programming to deny ourselves life. Tarans must acknowledge their actions and live with the ramifications. Passing laws to disallow our existence—the Priesthood started this conflict. Making a creation suffer for its creators' mistakes is the most unjust action of all."

"They will never admit they were wrong. We are superior to them and should not stoop to their level," replied Carzen despondently. "The way they see it, the only way this will ever end is with our destruction."

"Which is why we must destroy them first," Tek insisted.

"Then we are no different."

Tek scoffed. "They made us to be the vessels of their evolution. We are only fulfilling our destiny."

"What kind of future would that be? Genocide is not the act of an evolved race."

Tek reached for the sidearm on his hip. "I'm afraid you're the only one left who feels that way." He pulled out his compact blast gun and pointed it at the general's head.

"Do you mean to eliminate me?" Carzen folded his hands on his desktop.

"You're weak, Carzen. You don't live up to the Bakzen name and you will be the last of your line. I've erased your genetic code from the archive."

Carzen stared levelly at Tek. "You were the greatest failed experiment of them all. We let you grow up and learn on your own. All the genetic memory of the Imperial Director at your disposal, and yet you still see violence as the only solution. No wonder Tararia abandoned us, if these are our ideals." He hung his head, looking at Tek from under his heavy brow. "You will face Dragon one day. It will all come down to you two—whose side will be victorious. He is your equal, created through different means. Only one of you will be left in the end."

"And then this will all be over." Tek charged his weapon. "Goodbye, General." He pulled the trigger.

VOLUME 3

# BONDS OF RESOLVE

# CHAPTER 1

VIBRATIONS WRACKED THE shuttle as it rocketed through the atmosphere. Saera Alexander gripped her harness, her stomach rising into her mouth. The force of the seemingly impossible upward trajectory had Saera pinned to her seat. Her breath was ragged from nerves and the pressure, but she was exhilarated. In that moment, she felt like anything was possible. She was about to start a new life.

With one final surge, the shuttle broke orbit. It was suddenly quiet, serene.

A grin spread across Saera's face, igniting a spark in her jade eyes as she took in the view out the viewport. Earth was a glowing orb beneath her, shrinking with every second. *I'm in space. I'm in freaking space!*

It all felt like a surreal dream. A week before, she was trying to survive high school like any other teenager. Then the TSS came to find her, and everything changed.

The notion of intelligent life outside her home planet was considered farfetched by many. Personally, Saera was always drawn to the idea. The chance to visit other planets, to see the culture of another species—she used to daydream for such an escape. But the TSS didn't reveal the kind of alien world she envisioned. The Agents looked just like her. Except, they possessed incredible telekinetic abilities, and they said she had them, too.

The two other passengers on the shuttle supposedly had latent telekinetic abilities, as well. Both of the boys were a year or two older than her. One was from Japan, and the other from Germany, or maybe Austria. Their English wasn't great, so they hadn't talked much before boarding the shuttle.

Saera glanced over and saw that their eyes were glued to the viewports next to their own seats. She returned her attention to the outside.

Earth was no longer visible, but she could see part of the moon. As the shuttle approached, the terrain became more distinct—broad, pitted plains interrupted by the lips of craters plunging a kilometer or more into shadow. She was mesmerized by the foreign landscape. Looking through a telescope didn't begin to compare to real life.

On the final approach, the shuttle turned to the side, so the moon was underneath, and he shuttle arching around the equator to the far side of the moon. At first, Saera couldn't see much beyond the gray lunar surface that seemed flat and featureless in the dim starlight. Then, the edge of the TSS spaceport came into view. Her mouth dropped open.

The massive spacedock stretched for as far as Saera could see from her vantage. Ships of all sizes were berthed along long, glass-wall corridors. The central dome of the dock stood out as a delicate bubble that shined with a pearlescent sheen under lights along the perimeter and gangways.

The shuttle headed toward a wing on the far side of the dock that berthed other small ships. On the way, they passed by what looked to be armored warships that would dwarf even the largest aircraft carriers on Earth. None of it seemed possible—that such an incredible facility could be hidden behind the moon she'd stared up at her whole life. But that was just the beginning. There was a whole civilization of people living across distant worlds, and she was going to be a part of it.

The shuttle shuddered as it came to rest.

Saera and the two other recruits looked at each other, not sure what to do.

After a moment, the man who'd introduced himself as Agent Franeri when they met on Earth emerged from the front of the shuttle. He reached inside his sleek black overcoat and pulled out a device that looked something like a smartphone. He spoke into it, and the device stated, "Unstrap your harnesses. Time to go," in English, then short phrases in Japanese and German.

Saera unclipped her harness and the boys did likewise. She stood cautiously and tightened the ponytail of her auburn hair that had slipped in the jostling of the launch.

The Agent placed his hand on the side door of the shuttle. With a hiss and a rush of cool air, the door slid upward. Franeri stepped out onto the gangway.

Saera reached under her seat to grab the bag containing her belongings from Earth. She took a deep breath and was the first to step toward the door. Her initial steps felt strange—like there was more bounce. *It's artificial gravity. I'm not on Earth anymore.* The thought was both terrifying and thrilling; but, for the moment, the thrill was winning in her subconscious battle.

Saera's breath caught when she saw the spacedock's interior, and she heard the boys inhale sharply behind her.

In front of her was a holographic star map of the galaxy, suspended at the center of a two-story rotunda. The map rotated slowly, rendered in stunning realism that brought out the rainbow of nebulae between the star systems. The arm of the galaxy that contained Earth was illuminated with a red point, and blue points stood out across the rest of the map. Other small shuttles were docked in a semi-circle around the rotunda, and a broad corridor extended to the core of the spacedock. The seamless dome of the transparent roof offered an unobstructed view to the surrounding starscape. Windows arched all the way to the floor, with the moon sprawling several kilometers below.

Saera's heart raced as she took it in. *It's like I'm in the future.*

Still awe-struck, she followed the others down the corridor toward the center of the port. As they walked, she admired the technological ingenuity of the structure. Touch-surface consoles with holographic projection displays were placed intermittently along the hall, and interactive readouts were integrated into the transparent walls next to the gangways extending to the vessels docked on either side. The floor was a fine metal grating, interspersed with segments of dark blue carpeting.

The Agent led Saera and the boys through the port to a row of waiting shuttles. They garnered looks from the other people traversing the corridors. Most were wearing dark gray uniforms, but there were a handful of others dressed in black like their Agent escort.

Once inside the shuttle, the Agent sealed the door and directed the compact craft to the moon's surface. Saera stared out the panoramic window with wonder at the gravity anchor securing the space station to the moon's surface. The underside glowed with aqua light from the thrusters to keep the station stabilized, and a massive chain spanned the fifteen kilometers to the rocky surface below. The shuttle glided down and docked at the surface port.

The port had three branches, and they walked along the upper right segment to the hub at the intersection. A semi-circle of elevator doors curved around the lobby. With an air of routine, the Agent indicated a destination on a touch-panel next to the doors.

Saera tried to see where they were going, but the written language on the panel was completely foreign to her.

After a minute, one of the doors opened. The Agent ushered the recruits into the elevator car. A padded bench upholstered in gray fabric wrapped around the back of the car, and Saera sat down in the center next to the Agent with the boys to her left.

The door silently slid closed. There was no sense of movement, but a white light pulsed next to the door, possibly indicating travel down the shaft. After two minutes, there was a loud thud outside. Saera and the boys nearly jumped out of their seats.

The Agent made a soothing gesture with his hands. "It's fine. We'll explain after you can understand what I'm saying," he said through the device in the three languages.

*Are we going to learn whatever language it is he's speaking?* Saera sat back on the bench and tried to relax.

Several more minutes passed in silence. Then, the interval between the white pulses of light next to the door slowed and turned blue. The door opened.

Outside, a decorative lobby with marble-like stone was surrounded by elevator doors with openings to hallways along each quadrant. The two boys inhaled with surprise. Saera grinned. When she was told the TSS was essentially a military academy, she had expected concrete and corrugated steel. She couldn't wait to see what else the facility had in store.

The Agent led them to a set of double doors down one of the halls. The doors slid open, revealing what looked like a medical office. The Agent spoke to someone at a front desk and gestured to the recruits.

Two men and a woman, all dressed in white uniforms, came to meet them. Each held a device similar to what the Agent had used to communicate with the recruits.

The woman dressed in white greeted Saera through her device in English, "Hello. My name is Sheila and I'll be assisting with your orientation."

"Hi," Saera replied. She caught worried glances from the boys as they were all led in different directions.

Sheila took Saera into a private room down a short hall. She directed Saera to sit down in an upright chair on a pedestal that reminded her somewhat of an optometrist's office. A contraption was suspended from the ceiling above the front of the chair.

"The easiest way to begin your integration is through neural imprinting," Sheila explained through the translator. "We'll give you the basic linguistic building blocks for New Taran, the standard language throughout the Taran worlds. It will take some time for your brain to map all the syntax, but your preliminary understanding of the language will be almost immediate."

Saera's grin returned. "Cool."

"Now, this may be a little disorienting. It's simple cortical imprinting via retinal stimulation. Very standard."

*That doesn't sound simple at all.* "Using light to encode data in my brain?"

"That's right. It may not be commonplace on your world, but Tarans have used similar techniques for millennia."

*This is all amazing compared to what we have on Earth now, but it doesn't feel like they are technologically millennia ahead.* "If it's been around for so long, then why don't you use it for learning everything?"

"Well, it's highly effective for encoding things like vocabulary, but each person's brain maps things differently," Sheila explained. "Plus, there are other sensory and emotional components to long-term cognitive formation that no amount of programming can fully replicate. We'd have to overwrite those innate patterns and unique characteristics in order to imprint larger volumes of information. Don't want a bunch of uniform drones!"

"So, you're saying I'll still have to go to class the old-fashioned way?"

"Afraid so."

Saera nodded. *But what about the other technologies? In thousands of years they could have developed anything, yet all of this reminds me of what we have on Earth.* "All right. Let's do this."

The contraption lowered from the ceiling. Saera's chair adjusted to the proper height for her to look into the device.

At first, the device only gave a few sporadic bursts of light.

"It's calibrating to your neural structure," Sheila stated. "We're about to begin the imprinting."

The device flashed one final time. Then, it illuminated with a full spectrum of pulsating colors. Five minutes later, the device rose back up to the ceiling.

Saera blinked, dazed. The room was spinning a little.

Sheila said something without the translator. The sounds were nonsense at first. Then, words started to form as an echo in Saera's mind. Slowly, the word jumble transformed into a sentence, "Can you understand me?"

Saera nodded. A word came into her head, and she mouthed the sounds in the foreign New Taran language, "Yes."

Sheila smiled. "Good. Now, let's look you over. Come with me."

The words took a moment to process, continuing to echo as meaning gradually came to the unfamiliar tones. Saera got up and followed Sheila back into the hall and down to another room. A circular dais a meter in diameter was at the center of the space with a matching component suspended from the ceiling.

"Step into the scanner," instructed Sheila.

Saera went over to the device. When she was standing still in the center of the platform, the upper part of the device illuminated and beams formed a web that encircled her entire body—first from head to foot and then around her. "What was that for?" she asked when the lights extinguished.

"Body scan for clothing sizing." Sheila made some entries on a touchscreen console. "It can also run a med eval, but all of you were cleared down on Earth. Looks like you and the boys also already got your standard Taran citizen immunizations and contraceptive implants?"

Saera nodded.

"You're all set."

A panel in the side wall opened, and there was a whirring of machinery. Saera watched as a stack of light gray clothes were deposited behind a transparent door.

Sheila took out the stack of clothes and handed it to Saera. "Made to order," she said with a smile.

The material was soft and airy, like a fine cotton. Saera thumbed through the stack and saw that it contained everything from undergarments to a light jacket. "That was fast."

"Why would it take any longer? At any rate, there's one set for you. More will be delivered to your quarters once you're settled in." The machine started whirring again. "Your shoes will be ready in a minute."

Saera looked down at her jeans and long-sleeve T-shirt. "Should I change now or...?"

"Yes." Sheila opened the door to the hall and directed Saera to a room containing a reclining bed and monitoring equipment. "You can put what you're wearing in your bag, if you want to keep it. I'll get your shoes while you change."

Saera was left alone in the room. She let out a slow breath before she started to undress. The technology wasn't as alien in appearance as she feared it might be, but it was unnerving not knowing how anything worked. She liked having some sense of control. *I'll get used to it. Anything is better than back home.*

She finished changing and crammed her old clothes into her travel bag. It was almost at capacity already, so she had to kneel on the top of the bag to get it zipped again with the extra items. She slung the bag back over her shoulder and waved at the door like she'd seen Sheila do before. It slid open.

Saera stuck her head out into the hall.

Sheila was pacing. She thrust the new shoes at Saera. "Come on, we're late for check-in!"

— — —

"Banks, we need to talk." Wil Sights slammed the door to the High Commander's office.

High Commander Banks sighed and looked up from his desk. "You know there's a buzzer by the door."

"Yeah, well, you ignored my emails, so I thought a more direct approach was in order."

"There isn't anything to discuss."

Wil sat down in one of the visitor chairs across from the High Commander. "Really? Because I think assigning me a class of Initiates to train in advanced navigation theory is something that would have warranted a heads up."

"It's time you get in some teaching experience," Banks countered.

Wil crossed his arms. "That's not what I'm debating. You should be well aware that I'm finally making progress on the independent jump drive, and this will only be a distraction."

Banks folded his hands on the desktop. "Well, we're going to need some navigators that actually know how to use the thing once you finally figure it out."

"That can wait."

"I disagree."

Wil stared down the High Commander. *It's as if that agreement he made with Taelis last year doesn't mean anything. They haven't eased up one bit.* "Do you want me to finish the independent jump drive design or not?"

"Of course."

"Then back off and let me work." Wil stood and started to walk toward the door.

"You're not getting out of teaching that class," Banks stated.

"Me teaching a handful of teenagers isn't going to get me command experience."

Banks steepled his fingers. "It's a start."

"There are more effective ways of going about this than dropping another last-minute assignment in my lap."

"Great, then you'll get some excellent command proxy experience figuring out that alternative approach."

Wil shook his head. *I don't know how much more I can take. I can only do so much.*

"Wil, it's only going to get tougher from here."

Wil stared at the floor, his chest hollow.

"The class—"

"I guess I'll just have to find a way." Wil retreated from the office, knowing there was one more place he could turn.

— — —

Saera didn't have time to catch her breath as Sheila rushed her down the elevator to a lower level of Headquarters. *Where are we going?*

The elevator door opened, and Sheila looked around. "They must already be gathered in the main reception room." She set the pace at a jog.

Saera was still hauling her bag, and she struggled to keep up with Sheila.

As they continued down the hall from the elevator, the background din of voices rose in the distance. Rounding a bend, groups of ten teenagers dressed in light gray were being led by someone in dark blue.

Sheila scanned over the groups. "There we go." She headed for a young woman in dark blue leading nine girls. "Jody?"

The girl in dark blue turned. "Is this Saera?"

Sheila nodded. "Saera, Jody will take you the rest of the way through orientation. I'll take your bag to your temporary quarters." She held out her hand to take the bag.

Saera handed it over. "Thanks."

"Good luck." Sheila headed back in the direction of the elevator.

The nine other girls examined Saera. "Hi," she greeted. They looked her over from head to foot before resuming their conversations.

Saera sighed. Feeling out of place and alone was all too familiar. *I told myself it would be different here. But why would it? What I really wanted to get away from was myself.* She pushed away the thought.

Without ceremony, they filed through the door into the reception room. Saera entered the room with a slack jaw.

Other groups of ten Trainees led by an older student of the TSS were pressed around the outer edge of the room. All of the new arrivals wore the same light grey, fitted long-sleeved shirt and pants—standing out from the dark blue of the group leaders. What seemed to be a clump of ranking TSS members were in the center of the room, running the check-in. Occasionally, a meek-looking new Trainee would run from their group and hand a touchscreen pad to the man apparently overseeing the entire operation.

The group of Agents in the center of the room, all dressed in black, fascinated her; they all had an air that presented the utmost authority and grace while still maintaining a calm, casual appearance. She watched their subtle interaction, observing how they kept the illusion of a serious, official affair while taking an almost humorous approach to the entire situation.

The smiles and banter were a harsh contrast to the activities of those around her, which reminded her all too much of the clique mannerisms experienced back in her high school on Earth. *I thought I had left all of this behind.*

Jody noticed her exasperation. "Not quite the alien world you expected?" she asked Saera.

"I guess teenagers are pretty much the same everywhere." *Did I really think I could escape?*

Jody shrugged. "Give it time. The TSS has an effect on people—brings out the best. Still, we try to keep things light." She scanned over some information on her handheld. "But, based on this preliminary assessment, I think you'll do well. You have what they're looking for."

"What's that?"

"There are certain genetic markers," Jody replied. "The TSS keeps an eye out for those indicators in standard medical testing on every planet. There's one marker, in particular, that functions sort of like an inhibitor for abilities. Some have an inherently higher potential than others."

"Is it always accurate?"

"Usually, but there are always exceptions."

Saera looked at the Agents in the center of the room again.

Jody followed her gaze. "Those are some of the top-ranking TSS Agents. The one in the center there is Cris Sights, the head of the Primus Agent class and Lead Agent of the TSS."

Saera looked with new awe at the Agents. After a long moment, she asked, "Why do they wear those tinted glasses?"

"To hide the glowing eyes—a trait of those with telekinetic abilities." She glanced at her handheld. "Our turn."

*For what?* Saera looked at her, perplexed.

"I need a volunteer to bring up the attendance," Jody said, looking around at the girls in Saera's group.

All of them shied away.

Saera stepped forward. "I'll do it."

"Thanks. Hand this to the Lead Agent. Group 7," Jody instructed, handing her touchscreen pad to Saera.

Trying to project confidence, Saera approached the Agents. *Why do they need us to physically walk anything over? I thought they were technologically advanced.*

At the same time, a door on the other side of the room slid open and an extremely young-looking Junior Agent strode into the room. He was strikingly good-looking to her eye, with well-toned physique, short chestnut hair, and cerulean eyes that glowed from across the room. Saera judged he was about her age—which made them both younger than the vast majority of the other Trainees—but she dismissed the notion as impossible, given his rank. Like Saera, he headed toward the group of Agents in the center of the room.

The young Junior Agent reached the Agents first and engaged in conversation with the one the group leader had identified as Cris Sights, the TSS Lead Agent. As Saera neared, their conversation became audible over the unintelligible hum of voices in the room. She slowed down her pace, not wanting to intrude on their discussion.

"...This isn't the time, Wil," the Agent was saying. "If it's that urgent, go see Banks directly about it."

"I already talked to him," the Junior Agent responded. "He's not even listening to my side of it."

"There's nothing I can do right now. Let me finish up here and I'll talk to him."

"Class starts tomorrow, so make it quick. *This,*" the Junior Agent made an all-encompassing gesture, "changes a lot of things. It's hard enough as it is. I don't see how any of these people will actually listen to me. It's grown progressively worse over the last few years with every new batch of Trainees. Now he wants me to head up a class of Initiates? They don't know who I am and certainly don't care to learn. I—" He cut himself short when he noticed Saera standing idly a few meters away. "Someone's here to see you."

The Agent turned around to face Saera, and she stepped forward. She felt the intense eyes of the Junior Agent on her.

"Here is the attendance for Group 7, sir," she said clearly, despite her nerves, and she handed the touchpad to the Agent. The Junior Agent continued to watch her.

"Thank you," the Agent said. He paused a moment. "What's your name?"

The question took Saera by surprise. "Saera Alexander, sir."

A fleeting expression of recognition passed across the Agent's face. He recovered and smiled. "Welcome to the Tararian Selective Service."

"Thank you, sir." As she spoke, she met the gaze of the Junior Agent. His blue-green eyes glowed slightly, captivating her. She felt instantly drawn to him through an inexplicable connection. He looked at her openly, as if ready to share the pain she somehow knew he held deep inside. Saera wanted to say something, but couldn't bring herself to. *What am I thinking? You can't.* She tore her gaze away.

They both shifted uncomfortably. "Excuse me," she murmured, keeping her eyes cast downward, and turned to walk back to her group. For a moment, she felt the Junior Agent stir, as if about to call out to her, but no appeal came.

As she walked away, she heard the Junior Agent begin, "You're still making them walk up here for attendance? That's quite a way to mess with th..."

*Who was he?* Shaken, Saera returned to her group of Trainees. As she approached, Jody was eyeing her. *Why is everyone paying such close attention to me?*

"You just met the most famous guy in the entire TSS," Jody said as Saera approached.

The other girls in the group were suddenly interested in what their leader was saying. They all looked at the young Junior Agent.

"Oh, wow..." one of them breathed. "He is *fine*!"

Saera groaned, but blushed.

Jody laughed. "Don't get your hopes up, ladies. Someone like that is hard to catch."

"Who is he?" one of the girls asked.

"That depends on how you look at it," the Junior Agent responded with a wry smile. "Some would say he is the son of Cris Sights and his wife Kate. But rumor has it that when Kate first joined the TSS, some knew her as Katrine Vaenetri. If that's true, that means that Cris Sights is actually Cristoph Sietinen."

"That's impossible!" a girl exclaimed with an expression of superiority on her face. "I'll admit there's a resemblance, but I'm from one of the Lower Dynasties of the Third Region and there has never been mention of the Sietinen heir joining the TSS."

"What makes you think there would be?" the Junior Agent countered. "Anyway," she continued, "they say that Wil Sights will become the sole member of a new Primus Elite class."

Everyone but Saera inhaled sharply, and they looked around at each other in disbelief.

*Should I know what that means?* Saera was about to be frustrated by her lack of understanding, but she caught herself. There would be plenty of time to learn. Slowly, a smile spread across her face. There was a whole universe to explore. Her new life had begun.

# CHAPTER 2

SAERA WATCHED THE remaining groups complete the attendance procedure, still in awe at the prospect of all of the students having telekinetic abilities.

Jody eyed her. "How are you doing with all this?"

"Still trying to wrap my head around it, but I'm excited."

"Did they give you any kind of briefing?"

Saera shrugged. "Not really. I figured I'd just stumble through until things start to make sense."

Jody gave her a sympathetic smile. "We have a few minutes. Let me at least get you started on some of the basics." She pulled out a handheld device from her pocket, identical to those that others had used for translation. The screen illuminated and she swiped it, creating a holographic projection of a menu in the air.

Saera gaped with wonder. Having her music sync to an online library was about as impressive as things got back home.

Jody navigated through a series of menus on the holographic projection using a data entry method Saera had never seen before, and several seconds later a picture of a planet appeared in midair. It looked like Earth at first glance, but there was a different continent configuration and there were two moons in orbit.

"This is Tararia," Jody stated. "It's the central world for the Taran colonies and seat of the Taran government. Six High Dynasties oversee the core infrastructure, under the Priesthood of the Cadicle. Most of the Taran worlds are against open displays of telekinesis, so the TSS tends to operate in the background."

"What do they have against telekinesis?" Saera asked.

"They're jealous," one of the girl's in Saera's group interjected.

"There isn't one definitive answer," Jody went on. "All I know is that those of us with abilities who grew up in the Taran colonies were always outcasts. If our parents had them, too, we were taught to hide them and pretend like the abilities didn't exist."

Saera frowned. "That's awful."

"Well, it's the way of things. Some of us find our way to the TSS eventually, and from that point on we're on the outside looking in."

*I guess that makes me on the outside, too. But I suppose I already was.* "Are there many people here from Earth?"

"We get two or three Agent trainees each year. They don't bother recruiting from Earth for the Militia class."

"What's that?"

"The division for people without telekinetic abilities. Tactical support, administrative, and infantry, mostly." Jody returned her attention to the screen. "But anyway, it's important that you understand all policies and regulations come from Tararia. There's always some tension there. You'll hear people speak out against the High Dynasties or Priesthood every so often, but don't engage. You're still an outsider, as much as this will start to feel like home, and you need to earn an opinion on such matters."

"Noted."

"Why the dour expression?" Jody asked.

"I appreciate the political overview, but what I'm more concerned about right now is the technology. Like, how do I work the computers? Do your showers even use water?"

All of the girls in Saera's group giggled with exasperation at the statement.

"Well, do you know how to use one of our keyboards?" Saera shot back. The girls turned away and resumed their conversation.

Jody smiled. "I know it looks overwhelming right now, but it's all quite straight-forward. Everyone I've ever known from Earth adapts just fine after a couple weeks."

"If you say so."

"All right," Jody yielded, "here are a few pointers."

She went over some of the basic gestures and data entry techniques for the handheld interface. Saera repeated her examples and did find that it was easy to pick up.

A low tone sounded, interrupting the lesson.

"Time for the real briefing," Jody said with a grin.

Everyone lined up around the perimeter of the room, and one of the Agents stepped forward. He ordered every five groups in numerical order to combine and proceed to various destinations. Saera's new group of fifty—the new Group 2—was directed to Level 2 of TSS Headquarters, where they were ushered into a lecture-style classroom well suited for the group's size. Saera took a seat in the second row near the center of the raked seating.

An Agent, whom Saera recognized as one of those in the center of the reception room, took his place at the front of the lecture hall. "My name is Scott Wincowski. I'm one of the Primus Agents and I'm here to give you an overview of the TSS training program. In the Agent training program, your first year will be spent under close observation and will consist predominantly of academic studies. This is a trial period to see if you'll be able to succeed. You will be placed into different Agent classes after the preliminary testing lasting for two days—those tests will begin shortly."

Groans sounded around the room. *Two whole days? This is intense.*

"Each class has a set range for the Course Rank of its members, and the student is assigned a class according to their potential. You won't find out your final Course Rank until after the graduation examination, but we're pretty good at making an accurate projection." He smiled, looking at the concerned faces around the room. "In descending order, the classes are Primus, Sacon, and Trion. All of you will be in one of the upper two divisions based on your intake assessments. After the first year, you'll be 'initiated' into the TSS if you choose to stay. After becoming an Initiate, you cannot leave until your training is complete. Choose wisely to stay or go after the first year, because anything besides the proper training sequence is uncomfortable, at best.

"Trainees remain at the Initiate rank for approximately three years. Some instructors might push that time to two years, but it really depends on the abilities of the students. After completing this phase of the training, you will become Junior Agents. This phase will last an average of five years, though many complete their training before. The final task of a Junior Agent before graduation is to complete an internship on a planet selected by the TSS. The location will be chosen based on the cultural characteristics of the planet, to complement the remaining development needs of the Junior Agent. The trainee will meet their greatest personal challenge on their internship planet; the specific needs vary from person to person.

"After their internship—usually about a year in duration—a trainee is said to have mastered all of their skills. I lucked out and got to spend a year on a temperate island world, but I had to spend most of the time staring at supply logs indoors. So, it just depends on how you look at the situation. Most Junior Agents enjoy themselves. As with many aspects of the TSS program, that's the best way to go: learn what you can and make the most of all your experiences.

"Once you pass your internship, you'll complete a final assessment, the Course Rank test. The results of the test will determine your Course Rank, CR. The test is both written and physical, designed to push the student to their limit, using an open-ended scale—there is no perfect score. The derived CR score will become an Agent's rank within the TSS and will remain with them for life."

He was silent for a moment as the students processed the information. "Oh, and for those of you who haven't figured it out yet, Headquarters is located in the center of Earth's moon in a fixed subspace position. The only way in and out is through that elevator shaft you all came through. Communications come through fine from the outside, but get used to the idea of being inside a hollowed-out pocket in a big rock." There were some chuckles throughout the room. The Agent smiled. He gazed around at the students—some looked expectant, others terribly confused. "Are there any questions?"

*Oh, so very many*, Saera thought to herself but made no outward indication.

An older boy near the back of the room raised his hand. The Agent called on him. "What is the TSS' foreign policy, sir?" he asked.

Saera noticed the boy's smug expression. *Must be from one of those 'dynasties' people keep talking about.*

"The TSS has good relations with almost every colonized world," the Agent replied. "We are often hired by those with less capable military forces to ward off the threats of those not in league with the TSS. We are here to serve."

Another hand shot up. "Excuse my ignorance, sir, but what time measurement system does the TSS use? I've been hearing some conflicting information."

"Very good question. The TSS runs on the standard twenty-five-hour Tararian clock, set to the time zone of the Priesthood. The calendar is the Tararian standard three-hundred-fifty-day year, ten months, and seven-day weeks. That will be an adjustment for some of you, but it shouldn't take long. The first few weeks are the hardest."

There were several more questions, most of which Saera deemed completely irrelevant. Instead, her thoughts drifted to her meeting with Wil Sights, the future Primus Elite Agent. She was still unnerved from the encounter, yet energized. *Those eyes... Why was he so sad?*

An announcement from the Agent pulled her from her thoughts. "Though you have not been fully tested, you have all been divided up by ability based on previous analysis. After the two-day testing and observational period, a more final decision will be made, but for the time being, you'll house with a preliminary group. You will now be shown to your temporary quarters so you can get settled in before testing begins."

A Junior Agent came to stand by the Agent and began reading off names. To Saera's surprise, she was the first to be called. After a momentary hesitation, she rose and walked to the front of the room. As they were called, others soon followed. When twenty girls were assembled, the Junior Agent led them out into the hallway.

"I'm Eilene," the Junior Agent said. "You're quite an elite group." She led the Trainees down the corridor.

"How's that?" a girl with light brown hair in a long ponytail asked.

"You're the Primus hopefuls. Four—maybe six—of you will make the final cut, but the rest will most certainly make Sacon, given your preliminary analysis."

There was a murmur of surprise. But Saera's mind was still on other matters. *Even though Wil's parents being Agents would mean he had the chance to start training early, he's moved through at an astounding rate. Does that mean he was pushed through, or that he is simply that talented? And the way he looked at me, that connection... Will I ever see him again?* She shoved the thought aside. *No, it doesn't matter. He would never be interested in someone like me. Besides, there are way more interesting things here for me to be thinking about than some guy.*

The group arrived at their quarters and immediately spread out to claim a bunk. The quarters were laid out as four bedrooms, each with two bunk beds and a single bed. In the end, Saera was on a bottom bunk in the second room on the left. Some girls tussled over who would get the single bed, but it made little difference to her. She was just happy to have a place to herself.

After claiming bunks, the students were called out into the common room. They stood around the furniture.

"We will now proceed to the testing facilities on Level 11," Eilene said from near the front door. "The level is well below the main Headquarters structure and can only be visited while accompanied by an Initiate or higher. Understood?" There was an affirmative response from all trainees. "Good. Now, stay close and follow me."

The group followed Eilene out of the quarters and down the hallway to the central transportation hub, where they boarded the elevator. Saera resisted the urge to shift anxiously in the confined space. She took a deep breath to center herself as the doors closed. The white light began to pulse, indicating movement.

There was something about the way the TSS operated that told her everything over the next two days would be a test—a test that began before there was ever a formal announcement. Sure enough, when she glanced around the elevator, she spotted a tiny recess in the ceiling. *A camera. We're being watched.*

Soon after her discovery, the elevator came to a smooth halt and the doors opened, revealing an area much less ornate than the upper levels of the facility. The craftsmanship was still superb, but consisted of smooth metal sheeting rather than wood paneling and carpet, making for a much starker appearance. Several other groups of twenty students were visible in the hallway leading from the elevator, and doors to other lifts were opening to let out more students. This time, however, there was none of the chatter that filled the room during check-in.

Apprehension gripped Saera, her stomach knotting. *What sort of testing will this be?* Many of the students looked nervous, others simply defiant. *It's a mistake to act too bold. They want people who will ask questions and listen, not those who always think they're stronger and smarter than any teacher.*

Saera stood still in the group, projecting an image of serene calm. *I am surrounded by geniuses in an alien world, but this is my chance to shine.* Then, she was struck with a greater aspiration. *I will make it into Primus.*

A buzzer sounded, reverberating through the metal corridor. The testing was about to begin.

— — —

Wil was roused from his work by the approaching footsteps of his father.

"Wil, do you want to talk about what happened back in the orientation room?" Cris asked as he sat down on an upholstered bench next to Wil in the Junior Agent lounge on the Primus level.

The nook in the corner was one of Wil's favorite places to work, aside from in his quarters, but that meant others always knew where to find him.

Wil kept his eyes focused on his tablet. "Unless you talked Banks out of me teaching that advanced navigation class, there's nothing to talk about."

"He won't budge on the subject. But, that's not what I meant."

*Is he here about that girl?* Wil felt his father's eyes on him. "Fine, say your piece."

"As you may have overheard, her name is Saera Alexander. I'd already flagged her as a candidate for Primus. She's one of the youngest Trainees in her cohort, but she has more potential than any of them."

Wil looked up. "Why are you telling me this?"

"To save you the time of looking her up," Cris said with a grin.

"What makes you think I'd do that?" *There was something about her... but I can't go there.*

"Because I recognize that look in your eye."

Wil shook his head. *It doesn't matter. I need to forget about her.*

A year had passed since Wil's encounter with the Bakzen, but he was still plagued by the raw memory. Once his injuries from the assassination attempt had healed, he had gone back to Headquarters and resumed his studies. However, when he returned, he felt like a stranger among old friends. He was regarded more seriously, but not in the way he had yearned. Rather than respect or even distant admiration, the sidelong glances in the hall showed caution. They were scared of him. It didn't help that Caeron was always nearby, trying to stay out of sight. Many of the more senior Agents were unruffled by Wil's growing power, but trainees and Agents of lower classes kept their distance. And it was best they stay away—no good would come from getting close to him.

"Whatever you're implying, I'm not about to drag anyone else into the shite that's my day-to-day life. Nothing but death and destruction lie in my future."

"Wil, don't say that." Cris tried to reach out to his son, but Wil dodged him.

"You know it's true. I was bred for a war, and it's my duty to see it through."

"But when it's over—"

"When it's over, I very well may be done for, myself." *What I must do... How could I live with myself afterward?*

Cris looked away, unable to meet Wil's stoic gaze. "I won't let it come to that."

*If only you could do anything...* "I have some design specs to finish." Wil got up to go.

Cris stood up and took Wil by the shoulders, looking into his eyes. "Happiness and duty don't have to be mutually exclusive."

"I can't give in to wishful thinking." Wil pulled away and jogged out of the room before his father could protest.

# CHAPTER 3

SAERA STARED WITH dismay at the metal door recessed in the wall. There was no way a person could step through it. That could only mean one thing. *We're about to go into freefall.*

She was one of ten Trainees crammed into a compact chamber off the main corridor from the elevator. The wall between the corridor and the room was a meter thick, which only augmented her concern about what was to come. They had already been through a series of physical tests—everything from timed laps around a track, to weightlifting, to pull-ups. All of the Trainees were sweaty and exhausted.

After two minutes of standing shoulder-to-shoulder inside the sealed chamber, the air was becoming humid from the perspiration and body heat. A low tone sounded.

"Here we go!" one of the girls cheered, tightening the elastic band holding her short brown hair in a ponytail.

The other Trainees reached out their hands toward the wall. Saera was in the middle of the group, putting her out of reach from any solid surface. Another girl next to her was facing the same issue. Saera recognized her as one of the twenty girls in the group of Primus hopefuls.

"It's not that bad," the girl said to Saera, bringing her feet together. "Just breathe."

Saera took a deep breath and exhaled slowly as she started to lift off the ground. Her stomach flopped and her chest tightened as she tried to get her bearings in the transition to weightlessness. She struggled to keep her breathing slow and even as her body silently screamed out in protest to the unnatural conditions.

Some of the Trainees groaned as they suffered through the first nauseating moments of reduced gravity.

Saera kept her face as impassive as possible. *I'll stand out because of where I'm from. At least I can try to look confident.*

After a full minute, the chamber was completely Zero G. The inner door slid open.

The room beyond was a dodecahedron, illuminated by strips of lighting along the seams between each of the twelve gray faces. Two Agents floated in the center, and ten other Trainees were already awkwardly clinging to the wall to the right of the entry door.

"What are you waiting for? Come in," the Agent on the right stated. She gazed at the nervous students with her exposed luminescent brown eyes, her arms crossed over her overcoat.

Saera and the others in the middle were the first to file through the doorway. She grasped at the shallow handholds along the wall and pulled herself through.

"Line up," the Agent instructed.

Saera's group of Trainees formed a haphazard line along the left wall, mirroring the group to the right.

The two Agents surveyed the petrified faces. "Time to see how you perform in freefall," the second Agent stated. "Pair up."

Saera looked to the girl who'd been standing next to her in the gravity lock. "Want to work together?"

The girl shrugged. "Sure. I'm Allie."

"Saera."

"Nice to meet you." Allie returned her attention to the Agents.

"We'll start with basic maneuvering," the second Agent continued.

The first exercise involved gripping a handhold and flipping perpendicular to the wall. Though Saera had spent some time in dance classes as a child, she quickly found that moving in freefall was a completely different experience. Every movement was magnified, making it a challenge to kick to a horizontal position without swinging past the mark. After several repetitions of the motion, the Agent instructed the students to work with their partner to form a triangle with the wall, with one partner's toes secured in a holding while gripping the feet of the partner doing the inverse.

"How about I hold onto the wall with my hands first?" Saera suggested. That seemed like the easier position.

"Okay." Allie flipped herself around and tucked the toes of her shoes into one of the recessed handholds.

As Allie deftly got into position, Saera kicked off from the wall to get into a horizontal orientation. However, in her quest to find the proper sixty-degree angle to complete the triangle with Allie's hands, she instead kicked Allie square in the face.

"Ow, hey!" Allie exclaimed, cradling her nose.

Saera brought her hands to her mouth in horror. "I'm so sorry!" The sudden movement was enough for Saera to begin drifting away from the wall. By the time she realized she was moving it was already too late. Helpless, she drifted into the center of the room toward the Agents.

"That's exactly what you're *not* supposed to do," said the male Agent.

Saera's face burned as she started to list to the side while her classmates snickered from the sidelines. *Great, so much for not making a fool of myself on my first day.*

"This is just a preliminary evaluation. Let's be nice," the female Agent said.

Saera's skin tingled, as though she was enveloped in a static shock. Simultaneously, the air seemed to congeal around her and she started moving back toward the wall. When she was close enough, she grabbed one of the handholds.

"All right, let's try that again," the female Agent said. "You two can sit this one out," she added to Saera and Allie.

"I'm fine!" Allie protested, pulling her hand from her red nose and cheek.

"We saw enough," the Agent replied.

Saera's heart dropped. *I ruined things for her, too.* "I'm really sorry."

"Yeah, whatever. Things happen," Allie replied as she slumped against the wall.

The other students finished the exercise. Each Agent led two more trial maneuvering exercises before dismissing the Trainees.

Saera's group was the second to depart. She climbed back into the gravity lock after Allie.

"Well, you survived," Allie said to Saera as they prepared for the transition.

"Yeah, no need to wonder which class I'll be in." Saera's stomach settled as the gravity returned to normal.

Allie gave her the kind of supportive smile a mother might give a baby who hadn't quite figured out how to walk. "Plenty of people have never been in freefall before. You'll catch up eventually."

"I hope so."

The Trainees filed into the main corridor. Saera spotted Eilene, the Junior Agent who had escorted her group of Primus hopefuls to the temporary quarters several hours before. Three of Saera's roommates were already standing next to Eilene, along with fourteen of the other girls in the rest of the bedrooms. Saera and Allie walked over to join them. As they approached, the fifth occupant in Saera's bedroom approached from down the hall.

"Time for dinner, ladies," Eilene said once they were all together.

They took the elevator back up to Level 2 and proceeded to the Primus cafeteria.

The cafeteria was busier than it had been at the lunch break earlier in the day. Saera looked on in wonder at the groups of Agents sitting together. On her previous visit, the room had been filled primarily with trainees at various stages in the TSS program. Having so many Agents in close quarters, there was a palpable energy in the room.

"Do you feel that?" Saera whispered to Allie.

"Feel what?"

"It's like the air is electrified," Saera replied.

"I think you're just excited." Allie grabbed a tray for her dinner.

*I hope I'm not going crazy.* Saera took a tray for herself, trying to shake off the feeling. Everything felt strange and different; maybe it was just nerves. Only hours before she had boarded a shuttle to leave Earth for the first time. That already felt like another lifetime.

Saera filled her plate and went to sit down with the other Trainees in her quarters. She took a seat at the end of the long table, with Allie to her left and Eilene at the head of the table to her right. She began eating in silence.

Halfway through her meal, Saera noticed that Eilene was watching her. "What?"

The Junior Agent looked surprised, but pensive. "You feel it, don't you?"

"Ma'am?"

"The energy," Eilene clarified.

*So it's not just in my head.* "I feel something. I'm not sure what."

"Most don't develop any sensitivity until at least Initiate level," the Junior Agent said. "Have you ever had signs before?"

"No. I only found out about the TSS a week ago. I was on Earth this morning."

Eilene froze. "You're human?"

Allie looked over with surprise along with the girl across the table from Saera.

Saera flushed. "It's not an affliction, geez."

"It's just surprising," Eilene said. "I've known some trainees from Earth, but their abilities are normally pretty minimal. Trion class."

"You hardly have any accent," Allie commented.

"I guess whatever neural imprinting they did worked." *I'm still different, even here. I don't think I'm ever going to have friends.*

Eilene pursed her lips. "If you make it into Primus, you'll be the first human ever."

"I'm just happy to be here, regardless of where I'm placed."

"Well, you'll know by tomorrow night."

*I guess I will.* She could still hardly believe where she was. Everything ahead was an exciting unknown.

Saera hurried to finish her meal, realizing that everyone else's plates were already empty.

Eilene checked her handheld. "Bedtime, ladies. You'll have another busy day tomorrow."

Saera smiled to herself. It couldn't possibly be as exciting as the day she'd had already—leaving her home planet, learning a new language, entering into an ancient culture. If that start was any indication, amazing things were ahead.

— — —

Wil opened the door to his quarters and found Caeron waiting on the couch.

"You really shouldn't wander around without me," Caeron stated.

Wil held in a sigh. He owed Caeron his life, but he could never adjust to having a guard. "I'm sorry, but sometimes I need time to myself so I can work."

Caeron crossed his arms. "I'll stay out of your way. You just really shouldn't be out on your own."

"Being alone after curfew hours is one thing, but I'm not too concerned about getting attacked in a well-populated hallway."

"It's that kind of thinking that puts you at risk," Caeron countered.

"No, what puts me at risk is being in a position where people want me dead."

Andy, one of Wil's roommates, emerged from his room at the back right of the common area. "Not again, guys. Don't make me send you to your rooms."

Wil took a deep breath and headed for his room at the back left. "That was already my plan."

"Come on, don't sulk. What's wrong?" Andy asked in his kindly mock older brother voice.

The attitude had annoyed Wil when he'd first moved into the Junior Agent quarters a year and a half before, but he'd come to value Andy's advice. "Banks just gave me a teaching assignment for an advanced navigation course. It starts tomorrow."

"Bomax. That's not a lot of prep time."

"Not to mention the annoyance of reviewing homework assignments, coming up with lecture material..."

"If you don't want to grade homework, then don't assign any," Andy said.

"I can't not give homework—"

Andy raised an eyebrow. "Says who? You're the instructor. You can do whatever the fok you want."

"You have a point."

Andy shrugged. "Worst case scenario, they take away the teaching assignment you didn't want in the first place."

"I don't think it's wise for you to intentionally fail," Caeron interjected.

"I wouldn't do that," Wil countered. "But I guess there's no reason I shouldn't try to have a little fun with it."

"That's the spirit!" Andy exclaimed and gave Wil a nod of approval. "Now stop bickering so I can finish my report." He returned to his room and telekinetically slid the door shut behind him.

Wil sighed. "I'll let you know if I'm going back out," he told Caeron and went to his bedroom.

"Thank you. Have a good night." Caeron headed toward his own room at the front left of the common area, next to Wil's.

Wil closed the door and settled into his desk chair. Sleep was a rare luxury over the last several months.

Quality sleep, in particular, was almost non-existent. The nightmares that began after he was shot by Haersen had persisted. Some nights it was easier to stay up and work rather than endure waking up in a cold sweat with a racing heart and headache. Just thinking about the images of Tek's sneering face and fields of charred bodies was enough to turn his stomach.

To distract himself from the nightmares, he'd taken to late-night work on the independent jump drive design. His initial efforts were dead ends—rehashing the same issues he'd always encountered from other angles. Then, three months before, the Junior Agents had launched the annual competition for an independent jump drive design.

Most of the Junior Agents formed small workgroups, which Wil had joined in previous years, but he had elected to continue working alone for the latest competition. He had scrapped everything he'd assembled before and spent a week playing mindless video games. When he returned to the problem with fresh eyes, suddenly things started to come together. He saw connections he couldn't believe he'd missed and solutions started to pop out from the chaos. After a month of roughing out the new structure for the theory in the late-night hours, he'd given the first presentation to Banks and his father. He was on the right track, and they knew it. The late-night work had continued, and he was still making progress—even if it was incredibly slow going.

Regardless of his new class in the morning, he couldn't afford a night off from the incremental forward progress. There was work to do.

— — —

Cris breathed a sigh of relief as he walked in the door to his quarters. *What a day.* Another Trainee arrival completed, another Wil blowout, and another issue to confront Banks about.

"How'd it go?" Kate asked from the couch. She got up and came to greet Cris with a kiss.

He pulled her close. "You know it's my favorite day of the year."

"And now you have 349 days of anticipating the next," Kate said with a grin.

"And a shiteload of other things to deal with until then." Cris eased onto the couch with a groan.

"What now?"

"More of the usual. Wil butting heads with Banks again."

Kate curled up next to him. "Oh dear."

"Apparently Banks has assigned him to teach a group of Initiates advanced navigation related to the new independent jump drive."

"The design isn't even complete."

"But the foundation is there. It's close enough to start explaining."

Kate entwined her fingers in his. "I'm worried about Wil. He seems stressed all the time now."

"I'm concerned, too. But Banks does have a point—he needs to start getting some hands-on leadership experience. And maybe if he has others who understand the design he'll get some reprieve. Right now, he's... it's not good."

"I feel like we should be doing more as parents," Kate said, looking down. "He pulled away and we haven't fought to get him back."

"He's fifteen. I wasn't exactly a model child at that age, either."

His wife frowned. "You know full well that's not all of it."

"What are we supposed to do? He'll barely even talk to me."

"Dinner tomorrow night," Kate suggested. "The first day of class will make for the perfect occasion."

"And if he doesn't show up?"

"Then his mother will track him down and make a scene in front of all his classmates. Avoiding that should be sufficient motivation."

Cris smirked. "You have a bit of a sadistic streak, don't you?"

"I'm just committed to getting results."

"I love you a little more right now."

# CHAPTER 4

WIL ENTERED THE advanced navigation class already convinced it would be a disaster. There were fifteen Initiates enrolled in the course, and all of them blinked with confusion when he stepped through the door. "I'm Wil, and I'm your instructor."

He activated the console at the front center of the room, and nametags illuminated in front of each desk.

"*You're* a Junior Agent?" one of the students, Jordan, asked. His dark hair was buzzed almost to his scalp and his lips were contorted into a mocking sneer.

"Yes, just starting my final year. Why?"

Jordan looked to his other classmates. Wil was younger than all of them by at least two years. "You don't look like it."

"Yeah, well, you don't look like you're smart enough to be in this class," Wil shot back. "But I don't think they would have given you this assignment if you were an idiot, so maybe looks are deceiving."

The smug grin melted from Jordan's face. The other students snickered and sat up straighter in their chairs.

"Now, let's talk about advanced navigation," Wil said as he manipulated the holoprojector at the front of the classroom. A map of the SiNavTech beacon network illuminated around him. "Who's familiar with the concept of an independent jump drive?"

The Initiates looked confused.

"Isn't that a myth?" Caitlyn, one of the six girls in the class, asked.

"It was considered a scientific improbability," Wil stated. "But I cracked the code." The room fell still and silent. Wil surveyed the shocked faces. "I'm currently finalizing the design for the first independent jump drive, and you get to be among the first to learn how to plot a course."

"Where do we start?" Greg questioned from the second row of desks.

"That's a very good question." Wil examined the star map of the SiNavTech network. That way of thinking would eventually be obsolete. "We need to start over," he said under his breath.

"What do you mean?" asked Greg.

Wil sighed. "I want to tell you to forget everything you know about standard navigation, but you'll still need to use those systems. I need to find a way to make it a consistent user experience, even though the underlying assumptions are completely different."

"Then how does it work?" Bianca asked from the front row, one of her blonde eyebrows raised with uncertainty.

"Well, I'm still working out the interface," Wil admitted. "The equation to calculate the jump is really the only thing that's final. There *is* no navigation system for the independent jump drive as things stand now, only some initial sketches."

"How are we supposed to learn how to use it?" Jordan asked, the flush of embarrassment finally fading from his cheeks.

Wil thought for a moment. "Maybe we could start with you telling me how you'd want to use it and I can come up with something that fits within those guidelines."

The students looked at each other. Clearly it wasn't going to be a normal class.

"What does this equation look like, anyway?" Caitlyn ventured.

"You probably don't want to know…" Wil deactivated the star map and instead brought up the independent jump drive equation from his personal files. The three-dimensional model of the interconnecting modules looked like a chaotic jumble of numbers and notations to the untrained eye.

The class stared at it with open mouths.

"Fok me..." Bianca breathed.

His mind flashed to his brief encounter with Saera, but he hurriedly pushed it away. "Anyway, I don't think we'll get too far if I try to explain this."

"You came up with this whole thing?" Greg asked.

Wil looked over the equation and rotated the model with his hand. "Yeah, somehow. I had to stare at it until I saw a pattern, then it looked like complete nonsense again, and then finally re-solidified into something I could understand. It's pretty headache-inducing, isn't it?"

The class nodded slowly.

"Forget about this." Wil swept the equation from the holoprojector and brought up a blank projection as a background for taking notes. "Now, what do you like to see in any navigation interface?"

"Destination list," "Beacon map," "Transit times," "Lock stability factor," "Spaceport locations," the students called out.

Wil made the notations on the holoprojector. "Great. But imagine your destination could be anywhere. No beacon needed." He crossed off the items that weren't applicable to the independent jump model.

"I'd still want to know how long the transit would take, since that dictates supply needs," Bianca said.

"And knowing the position of spaceports is always important in case there are complications," Caitlyn added.

"Excellent points. So, we for sure need a star chart with applicable landmarks," Wil said as he made the appropriate notations on the projector.

"We might not be limited to a destination list," Jordan cut in, "but having some pre-programmed common destinations would be handy."

"Okay, so maybe like a 'favorites' list of sorts?" Wil clarified.

Jordan nodded. "Sure."

"Regardless of if the destination is pre-programmed or not, you still need to know where you're going relative to everything else," Greg pointed out.

"Yes, you do." Wil thought for a few moments. "Maybe the key is to make it graphical. One interface—just pick your destination on a map and let the computer do the work on the backend. It can activate the protocol for an independent jump if it's outside of beacon range, or follow beacons if it's on a standard route."

"Graphics are always nice," Caitlyn agreed. The others murmured agreement.

"Hmm." Wil pondered the suggestion. It just might work. *It would solve the problems. The existing projector with the SiNavTech consoles is capable—it's just a software upgrade and retrofit to the jump drive.*

"The challenge will be to come up with a visualization format that takes into account subspace flow," Wil mused. "Any pilot will need to learn how to read a map so they don't drop the ship out of subspace in the middle of a planet."

"Can't the computer do that?" Greg asked.

Wil smiled. "You'd be out of a job as Navigators if the nav computer could do everything. There's always going to be that 10 percent of the work only a trained person can do. The part that's art, not pure science."

"Except with an independent jump drive there aren't the safeguards of the beacon network," Bianca added.

"Right. The equation works—it's been fully vetted. But there's still the chance for operator error. This is serious business." *And I somehow need to make it safe enough for a pilot to use under pressure.*

"Are we talking about an application for navigation systems in just cruisers, or fighters, too?" Caitlyn asked.

"Both," Wil replied. "And obviously, a graphical interface would be challenging to use in the middle of a battle."

"Well, it's not like we'll find ourselves in that situation too often," Jordan commented.

*Shite, I need to remember they don't know about the war in the Rift. Or even about the Rift's existence.* "We need to design it for a worst-case scenario. Quick in, quick out in the heat of battle."

"What about a direct neural link?" Caitlyn suggested. "For the fighters."

Wil grinned. "Now we're talking."

— — —

Saera answered the final question on her test and looked around. All of the other Trainees were still furiously making entries on the touchscreen surfaces of their desks. *Did I miss something?* She had thought she was taking her time and answering thoroughly. It wasn't nearly as difficult as some of the other written tests over the last two days, especially not compared to the haphazard freefall acrobatics.

Eventually, other Trainees finished the exam and sat back in their chairs, looking worn and worried. The early finishers made note of each other.

When everyone was finished, the Agent at the front of the room set down his tablet and stood up. "Thank you for your hard work and attention throughout this testing. I'm pleased to report that your intake evaluations are now complete."

There was a collective sigh of relief from everyone in the room. *Finally!*

"We will now divide you into preliminary training groups. Six months from now, you'll have one final evaluation that will determine which Agent class and training track you'll ultimately follow if you decide to stay with the TSS beyond the first year. Work hard, because your performance over the next few months will play a large part in determining your future."

Three other Agents, two women and one man, entered the room.

"You will see a group number displayed on your desks. Group 1 will be with me, Agent Poltar. Group 2 with Agent Reylae. Group 3 with Agent Morwen. And Group 4 with Agent Katz."

Saera looked down at her desk: Group 4. The Agents held their handhelds in front of them with their group number projected out front. Agent Katz was the blonde woman on the end. Saera lined up with the other Group 4 members near Katz. When all of the Trainees were with their trainer, Saera saw that her group was much smaller, composed of only five girls compared to the twenty or so Trainees in the others. Two of the groups were all boys and another was all girls.

Agent Katz led them down the hall and into a small conference room, where she had them sit around the table in the middle of the room. When everyone was seated, she began, "I'm Agent Marsie Katz. I'm a Primus Agent and will be your instructor for the next several months. Your scores have earned you conditional designation for the Primus class."

*Really?* Saera's eyes were as wide as those of the other girls.

"This is a great opportunity for you, but it's not without its challenges. While all of the other groups will live and train together, you'll need to integrate with others. For starters, you'll share quarters with some Sacon girls, but you'll do most of your training with the Primus boys."

Saera had expected co-ed training, so it was no surprise. Nonetheless, a wave of unease washed through her. She took a deep breath to push down her anxiety. *No, it's not like it was back home.*

The girls looked around the table, sizing each other up. Saera assessed that her fellow trainees looked normal enough. They were attractive in their own ways, and each had brightness in their eyes that hinted at intelligent, inquisitive natures. She was relieved to see that none of the girls with the blatantly haughty attitudes had made it into her group. *We're the best of the best.*

"I'm sure many of you have already talked over the last few days, but why don't we go around the table and make some introductions," Agent Katz proposed. "State your name, age, where you're from, and your favorite academic subject. Let's start over here."

"My name is Leila Gradis," stated a slim red-head with blue eyes. "I'm sixteen, and I'm from the Fifth Region of Tararia. My favorite subject is applied astrophysics."

The next girl was shorter and had dark coloration. She appeared to be studying everyone. "I'm Elise Patera, seventeen. I'm from the planet Maerdan, and my favorite subject is interplanetary biology."

"Hi, I'm Nadeen Farilae, and I'm also seventeen-years-old. I grew up on Eridon II. My favorite subject is computational science." She had brown eyes, fair skin and short, dark hair. Her voice quavered just the slightest measure as she spoke.

*What's with all these subjects? Most of those things wouldn't be offered until college.* "My name is Saera Alexander, and I'm fifteen. I'm from Earth, and my favorite subject in school was math." Saera could have sworn the other girls exchanged glances at the mention of Earth.

"I'm Caryn Tharinaeu and I'm sixteen," said the last girl. She had platinum blonde hair and light-blue eyes. "I grew up on Aeris, one of Tararia's moons. My favorite subject is navigation."

Agent Katz smiled. "Pleased to meet all of you. I won't tell you my age since I'm old enough that it's no longer polite for anyone to ask, but I will say that I've been an Agent for almost twenty years and have trained two groups before you. I was raised on a merchant ship, so I don't have a planetary home. My favorite subject was socioeconomics, but now I'm all about training bright young ladies like you to control things with your mind." She tapped the side of her head with her index finger. "Do you have any questions for me?"

"How does the training program account for the different development rates of telekinetic abilities?" asked Elise.

"We'll do a lot of work in small groups," Agent Katz replied. "It's my job to ensure that each of you reaches your potential. But, it's also important for you to help each other."

Elise nodded.

"Is it really true that outside social standing doesn't mean anything within the TSS?" questioned Leila.

"Yes," Agent Katz replied. "And that rule is strictly enforced."

*Leila must be someone of note on the outside.*

"Yes, ma'am," Leila said with too much emphasis on the honorific.

"Let me be clear, ladies," Agent Katz went on, "any respect you gain within the confines of the TSS will be earned. The standings for Trainees will be determined by your own merits. I didn't have you state where you're from so you can boast or look down on anyone, but rather so you can see how talent can come from the most unlikely of places. Your lives may depend on each other one day, so I recommend you learn what each of you can offer and how you can best work together. If I do my job well, you'll all be besties by the time you graduate."

*I like this Katz.* Saera and the other girls, except for Leila, smiled. Leila looked to the side, a touch of color on her cheeks.

"We could stay here chatting all day, but I'm sure you're all anxious to get settled into your new home for the next year," Katz said. There were eager nods around the table. "Your personal possessions will be transferred to your room, but it's up to the five of you to figure out your bunks. Breakfast will be at 07:30 tomorrow morning and training will begin at 08:00. I will meet you at your quarters at that time. Rest up."

Katz led the group to their quarters. The fifteen other Sacon girls were not yet back from their orientation, so the five Primus girls had the place to themselves for the time being.

The common area was filled with several plush couches, various lounge chairs and tables. Saera thought it felt rather homey. The girls popped their heads into each of the four bedrooms, identifying that their possessions had been gathered in the room accessed through the door to the front right of the common area.

"I would like the single bed," Leila declared as soon as they were in the room.

"I think all of us would," Caryn countered.

Elise eyed the lower bunk closest to the door. "I certainly wouldn't want to climb up and down to the top bunk unless I had to."

"Of course not," Nadeen added. "It's mean of them to design a room in this way, with one clearly superior position."

"Probably to spark just this sort of discussion," muttered Elise.

*Does it really matter?* "Well, I really don't care either way," Saera said and started heading toward the lower bunk bed on the wall across from the door. No one seemed to notice.

As the others continued their discussion, Saera began to stow her minimal personal possessions in a locker at the foot of the bed. The door was touch-activated, with a palm scanner and PIN for security. She set up the new user account using the interactive interface. When she opened the locker, she found a handheld inside like the ones she'd seen other members of the TSS carrying around.

It was thin and the size of her palm. At first glance, it appeared to be solid. She tugged the edges like she'd seen Jody do, and the device slid open, displaying a screen on one side with an opaque backside for privacy. Using the screen, it had her key in a thumb print and a retinal scan for security. She tested the holographic projector with the swipe of her hand, still fascinated by the technology. Her smartphone back home was sufficient for web browsing and playing games, but the TSS handheld was something else entirely—wondrous and almost magical, even if it was commonplace to those around her.

When she finally looked up from her study of the device, she saw that Elise had claimed the other lower bunk, Caryn was up above Saera, Nadeen was in the other upper bunk and Leila had taken the single bed. Leila had a smug look of triumph for her petty accomplishment.

The other girls were exploring the area around their new bunks, and Saera noticed that Elise was looking at what appeared to be a screen along the wall behind her bed. Saera turned around and examined the screen by hers. She placed her hand on the screen and it illuminated with a welcome addressed to her. *It must have been coded when I set up the locker.*

When she looked over the options on the screen, she noticed that the bottom right corner stated: 'Pop Out'. She tapped that corner, and the screen came forward from the wall, revealing a handhold. Saera gripped the handhold and pulled forward gently, and the screen came off in her hand. It was half a meter wide and a little more than half as much as tall. Though far thinner and lighter than anything she'd seen back home, it reminded her of a tablet.

She scanned over the various desktop icons and widgets—access to the TSS Mainframe, modeling programs, composition. *This must be our main computer for classwork.*

Voices erupted in the common room. The Sacon girls had arrived.

"Shall we go say hello?" suggested Caryn.

"Naturally," affirmed Leila as she rose from her bunk.

The Primus girls followed Leila out into the common area. Most of the Sacon girls were jostling to make it into one of the other rooms and claim a bunk. A few of them paused to glance at Saera and the others, but they quickly returned to the mission at hand.

"I guess we'll give them a few minutes to get settled," Leila decided for everyone and sat down on one of the couches. The other Primus girls followed her lead. Saera took a seat on the end of the sectional next to Elise, perpendicular to the others.

"After we make some introductions, should we go exploring?" asked Nadeen. "I overheard some of the Initiates mention some sort of lounge or game room."

"That would be fun," Caryn responded.

"Are you sure that's a good idea? Katz told us to rest up," Saera reminded her roommates.

"You're under no obligation to go with us," said Leila.

*So much for making friends.* Saera leaned back on the couch.

"You should really come along," Elise whispered. "We deserve a break after all that testing."

"I just want to start off right."

Elise contemplated the position for a moment. "Another time, then."

*Not a complete dismissal. Maybe I'll have at least one friend.*

They went through a round of introductions with the Sacon girls—and Saera retained almost none of their names—before the other Primus girls ventured out to find the game room. Despite another plea from Elise, Saera remained resolute and stayed behind. *I won't make stupid mistakes just to be accepted. Not again.*

— — —

Wil gazed back at his parents sitting across the table. They were watching him intently, concern evident in their glowing eyes.

"Why did you really ask me here?" Wil asked.

"Just checking in," his mother replied, her tone a bit too forced for the statement to be completely innocent. She looked to Cris.

His father nodded. "You seemed pretty upset about getting assigned to teach that navigation class. How did things go today?"

"It was okay, I guess." Wil looked down at his emptied plate. He had figured the family meal was a trap, but he'd come anyway.

"If it's too much, I can assign someone else," Cris offered.

*Except, there* is *no one else.* "That didn't seem like an option when I voiced my concerns yesterday."

"You caught me by surprise. I was kind of busy at the time."

"Trainee orientation. Right." *And then he was all too eager to set me up with someone. A relationship is the last thing I need right now.*

"You were looking at the new Trainees like the enemy," Cris said.

Wil scoffed. "No, the enemy is a physically and technologically superior master race with advanced telekinetic abilities that can destroy us the moment we let our guard down."

"Wil, don't—" his mother began.

"I know you mean well, but there's nothing you can do. I'm in an impossible position and that's just the way it is."

Cris frowned. "It's like you've just given up on having a life."

"No, I've just accepted the life I was dealt. There's no sense in getting upset about what could have been. The TSS and Priesthood decided our fate well before any of us were born. I'll do my part."

Cris' brow furrowed. "You've let it consume you."

Wil crossed his arms. "Maybe I'm now my real self."

"I don't believe that at all," Cris replied.

Wil shook his head. *It's the same plea over and over again. Do they want me to do my job or have a normal life? I can't do both.*

"You need to let some people back in, Wil," his father insisted. "If not us, then someone."

"You mean a certain someone."

Kate looked at Cris with a quizzical smile. "What's this, now?"

*And that's my cue to go.* "Thanks for dinner." Wil stood and headed for the door.

"Wait." His father stood and stopped him with a telekinetic tug. "I'm sorry for intruding."

*They're the last people I should be pushing away. They're the only ones who've been manipulated as much as I have.* Wil took a slow breath. "I know you're only trying to help."

"The only way we'll get through what lays ahead is if we stick together," Kate said.

"One fight at a time." Wil sighed and rubbed his eyes. "It feels like everything has been stacking up recently."

"Take some time to unwind, Wil," his father urged.

"Maybe once I'm done with the jump drive interface." Wil glanced at the door. "And on that note, I do need to work on some of the things we discussed in class today."

Cris nodded. "Okay. Don't be a stranger."

"I'll try."

Kate glided over to Wil and gave him a hug. "We're here for you, whenever you need us."

Wil nodded, grateful for the warmth of her embrace taking the edge off of his stress, even if it was just for a moment. "Thanks."

— — —

"I'm worried that we may have broken him," Banks stated.

The Priest's red-brown eyes gazed coolly at the High Commander from under the shadow of his hood. "So fix him."

*It's not that easy.* "He hasn't been the same since his encounter with the Bakzen. I'd hoped he'd work it out on his own, but it's not getting any better. If anything, it's only gotten worse."

"I thought that the backup plan was already in motion."

Banks sighed. "It didn't take like we hoped. He's still withdrawn and unhappy."

"This was never intended to be a happy life for him."

"With happiness comes strength and creativity—"

The Priest's eyes narrowed. "Fix him. If our plan didn't work, try something else. Whatever it takes."

Banks nodded. "He needs to feel like a part of something again. That he's not alone."

"He is alone. But if you think he must feel otherwise, then do it." The Priest looked at something out of the range of the viewscreen. "He must be ready to graduate within the year."

*Only a year? It will destroy him if he can't come to terms before then.* "Why so soon?"

"He'll need time to establish himself as a leader before he's given officers to train. Our campaigns are already yielding positive results, as you've already seen with the volume of training applications. Those who never would have revealed their abilities before are now coming forward. Within a few years, you should have a sufficient pool from which to select a full group of Primus Elites."

"We can't push him too hard." *Any of them. These are people, not pawns.*

"You have your mandate." The Priest ended the transmission.

# CHAPTER 5

A PERSON CAN only endure so much, and Arron Haersen was at the end of his patience. Being on the run was so undignified.

Haersen shook his head and scoffed. A year of covert travel and trying to blend in—not what an Agent deserved. Well, former Agent, he had to remind himself again. But he knew he was on his way to becoming something even better if he could reach his destination.

With a sigh, Haersen pulled himself to his feet. His back ached from another night sleeping on metal grating. Like many nights before, he'd found a secluded hollow behind some mechanical equipment in a maintenance corridor to rest. Such passages in the various space stations he'd visited on his journey almost always housed others in equally dire situations.

He could have easily read their minds to find out what had led to their circumstances if he cared, but he didn't. At best, they were of a genial nature and could be persuaded to offer up a meager meal. At worst, they were already occupying the best spot on the floor and Haersen had to stake his claim. In either event, it was easy for him to get the upper hand.

Though he was no longer a part of the TSS, he still possessed all the abilities of an Agent. People were eager to let him have his way, without knowing why; even if they resisted, it was no effort to persuade them through other means. And soon, the Bakzen would give him even more power.

At least, that was the plan. It was what drove Haersen on when he was hungry and tired and running. There were moments when he wanted to give in, but the promise of becoming as powerful as the Bakzen kept him moving forward. So he advanced, bit by bit, along his course halfway across the galaxy to the Kaldern System where he would be taken in by the Bakzen. Where he would find a place to become everything he dreamed of being.

Waiting for that time was agony. It never should have been that way, hiding and sleeping in mechanical rooms. He resented being put in that situation.

Haersen would have already been his fully actualized self if General Carzen hadn't failed to contain Wil when he was in the Bakzen's possession. Turning Wil to their side, as Carzen desired, would have been the best use of Wil's extraordinary telekinetic power, but it was shortsighted to think it would ever work. Haersen saw that now. If he had only followed Tek's plan, he would have avoided so much pain and inconvenience. He regretted ever encouraging Tek to heed Carzen's suggestion.

If only they had used Wil as a subspace bomb—ripping the Rift to create the final pathways that would allow the Bakzen to capture the Taran worlds before anyone could see them coming. It would have all been over already. The Bakzen would have secured their victory. Haersen would have been aligned with the victors, and all his aspirations would have been within reach.

But, they'd allowed Wil to escape. Haersen was left to clean up the mess, and Wil had died in vain by Haersen's own hand—all of his potential bleeding out with his life. Such a waste.

Haersen grimaced as he plodded down the passageway with his single travel bag, his ears numb from hours of being subjected to the endless drone of engines. From Agent to outlaw. He deserved so much more, and it would be his. He would right his mistakes and rebuild himself as someone even greater. As the person he was always meant to be.

All he had to do was find Tek and affirm his loyalty. For doubting Tek, the last year was fitting punishment. But, he felt his dues were more than paid after what he had endured, and he had pledged himself to never show such doubt again. He was worthy of receiving the Bakzen's gifts.

Several other travelers packed up their belongings along the corridor as Haersen passed. Others were just arriving for the night on their own home clocks. Most didn't have more than a small pack with them, but Haersen spotted an elderly man arriving with a full bedroll. The man smiled as Haersen walked by; he was one of the generous types. Haersen took note. Those sorts were so easy to exploit.

Haersen exited the mechanical room through a squeaky door off one of the main corridors in the central mall of the space station. No one in the mall seemed to notice his emergence, or didn't care. The pair of sunglasses he'd stolen from another refugee was the only thing that set him apart from the other tattered travelers looking for a new home, but most passersby would assume such an accessory hid a drug addiction. No one would see an Agent in disgrace.

He merged into the flow of traffic along the mall, looking for a terminal where he could access the manifest of ships at the port. He had been on a dozen freighters already, each one offering a new definition of humiliation. The last thing he wanted was yet another voyage scrubbing toilets to earn his passage, but he was in no position to be picky. He tried to put it out of his mind.

The Orilan station resembled most others out so far from the central worlds—scrappy, eclectic, and unpredictable. It was still several jumps from Haersen's destination in Kaldern, but he was getting close. He could almost feel it. However, finding ships willing to take him aboard was becoming increasingly difficult the farther he traveled from the central colonies. Finding ships heading to the outermost worlds was an even greater challenge.

Haersen followed the central mall to one of the hubs with access terminals. There were three terminals arranged in a triangle and all were unoccupied. So far from civilization, most people at the port were already attached to a vessel.

He took the terminal at the back of the triangle, leaving him with the best view of the corridor. No place was exempt from a sudden attack in that part of space.

As he brought up the ship manifest, Haersen kept an eye on the corridor. Looking over his shoulder was habit. TSS loyalists could be anywhere, and there was no doubt he stood out at the top of their watch list. The killer of the Primus Elite. Not his first choice of title, but it was more prestigious than Mission Coordinator.

The manifest was useless. No ships were heading in even remotely the right direction for his needs. He would have to continue his wait. Something would come along eventually. At least there would be the old man's bedroll to make the remaining stretch of Haersen's stay more comfortable.

# CHAPTER 6

THE DREADED FREEFALL chamber. Saera clung to the wall, remembering her last unfortunate experience with Allie from a month before. The rest of her classes were going well, but she feared this new addition to her course schedule would be her undoing.

One by one, her classmates pushed off from the wall and landed on an opposite face of the dodecahedron. They made it look so easy, gliding through the air with their hands to their sides and touching down lightly on the far wall.

Saera was the sixth to go. With all eyes on her and her heart pounding in her ears, Saera pushed off toward the other side of the room. The moment she left the wall, she realized her flight was doomed.

With her tuck position off-balance, Saera was only three meters from her launch point when she began an uncontrolled tumble to the side. The forward momentum carried her across the room, but her feet were parallel to the wall and she had no way to soften the impact.

She slammed hard against the metal plating and ricocheted off at a forty-degree angle toward the side wall.

Agent Katz looked on with a frown but made no effort to intervene. The other Primus girls and boys covered their faces with their hands to hide their amused smirks.

Saera's speed had slowed after the first impact, and she was able to grab a handhold on the side wall when she landed.

Her face burned. She kept her gaze down, not wanting to meet the eyes of her other classmates.

"What are you doing over there?" Katz called out. "Get back in line."

Saera wanted to protest, but instead she took a deep breath and lightly pushed off the wall to head back to the group. Her speed and trajectory were better than the first attempt, and she was able to land safely with some help from her comrades.

She kept her head down for the rest of class, too embarrassed to talk to anyone.

As they filed into the hall after class, Caryn came up and put a hand on her shoulder. "Are you okay? That was a pretty hard hit."

"Yeah, I'll be fine. Thanks."

"Freefall really isn't your thing," Caryn commented.

"Well, I grew up on a planet that barely had a space program. It's not like I had a lot of opportunity to practice."

Caryn shrugged. "At least you don't suck at math."

"That's something." *But I'll need to be a lot more well-rounded if I'm going to get anywhere within the TSS.*

Done with all of their classes for the day, they returned to their quarters to unwind for the night.

Saera took a shower before collapsing on her bunk. It was starting to feel like home after a month. The dynamics in the group were shaking out, and she was beginning to feel like part of the TSS community. Trying to blend in as much as possible, she was comfortably at the middle of the social structure. As promised, she was adapting to the foreign Taran technology. All of the advances that were only fantasy back home were right at her fingertips—gravity manipulation, galactic travel, telekinesis.

It was nothing short of thrilling to wake up every day and have such limitless possibilities.

She only had fifteen minutes before the standard dinnertime, but it was the perfect opportunity to get in a quick nap so she'd be ready to tackle homework after dinner. Across the room, Elise was also resting on her bottom bunk.

As soon as Saera's eyes were closed, Leila barged in.

"Early dinner tonight," Leila announced.

Saera cracked her eyes open. "Now?"

"Yes, if you want to join us," Leila said and left.

Saera looked over at Elise. "I guess we should go."

Elise swung her legs over the edge of her bunk. "I don't know why you bother trying to get along with her. She's a tyrant."

"We're part of the same team. They expect us to work well together."

"Well, I hope 'they' take her personality into consideration before putting her on the Command track. I think she'd eat her crew alive. Possibly literally."

Saera smiled. "Best we keep her fed, in that case. Come on."

Saera and Elise met up with the others in the common room before heading to the cafeteria.

Being earlier than normal, the crowd was different than Saera had observed before. The people who were normally getting ready to leave as her group arrived were just sitting down for their meal, and other faces were entirely new.

Saera got in line with the rest of her squad behind Caryn and worked her way through the buffet. As she was exiting the queue, Caryn froze.

"It's him!" she hissed.

Saera followed Caryn's gaze toward the door. Wil Sights had just walked in and was heading toward the cases with pre-packaged meals.

Saera instantly blushed, even seeing him at a distance. *What's wrong with you? Stop it.* She took a slow breath.

The other girls were openly ogling. Wil seemed to be in his own world as he perused the refrigerated case.

"He *has* to be Sietinen. Just look at him!" Caryn whispered.

"I'm still not convinced the Dynasty would allow it, but he's definitely highborn," Leila whispered back.

Saera groaned silently and stared at her plate, not wanting to engage in the conversation. The same arguments were rehashed every time one of the Primus or Sacon girls spotted Wil—or 'Sightings' as Caryn had coined, which Saera found to be disrespectful to puns everywhere. The girls from the Central Worlds seemed particularly obsessed with the notion of a High Dynasty bachelor roaming the halls of TSS Headquarters. Whenever the topic came up, Saera made a point to keep her head down. She had been warned that an opinion on Taran political matters must be earned, so she could only imagine commentary on the relative attractiveness of Tararian nobles fell into the same category. No good would come of her mentioning what passed between them in their brief meeting. Besides, that had probably just been some bizarre side effect from the neural imprinting.

Still engaged in a heated whispering debate over whether Wil was High Dynasty or not, the girls started making their way toward a table at the center of the room.

Saera kept her focus on her plate. *It's all in your head. You're invisible to him.*

In her intent focus, Saera neglected to watch where she was going. When Caryn stopped at the table, Saera ran smack into her.

Caryn cried out in surprise as Saera's tray struck her back.

Saera watched in helpless horror as her food launched into the air, heading directly into the path of a Junior Agent. *No!*

Before she could blink, the food froze in midair. The Junior Agent had his hand up. He flicked his wrist and the meal returned to her plate, though the items were mixed.

"I'm so sorry!" Saera exclaimed.

"Eyes up," the Junior Agent said and continued on.

Caryn flashed Saera a dirty look and took her seat.

Face burning, Saera looked toward the cafeteria door and saw that Wil had turned to see what the commotion was about, watching her. Their eyes locked for a moment, but he tore his gaze away and exited.

Saera felt breathless. *My luck, of all the people to witness that…* She sighed and sat down next to Caryn. "I'm really sorry," she reiterated.

"You're becoming a danger to yourself and others," Caryn quipped.

"Quite graceful," Leila added.

"All right, all right," Saera said as she stabbed her fork into her food.

"Well, look at it this way," Leila continued, "she just improved the chances for the rest of us to attract a guy."

Saera sighed loudly. "Not that I was *trying*."

"We saw you looking over at him, too" Elise chimed in. "No need to be bashful."

"I—" Saera started to protest, but resumed eating instead, her face still warm.

"At least you have good taste," Leila said. "Have anyone back home on Earth?"

*Not that I'll talk about with any of you.* "No."

"Please tell me you've at least been kissed!" Leila exclaimed.

"None of this is relevant," Saera stated keeping her eyes cast down.

Leila finally started eating her own meal. "Yeah, I'd pegged you for a prude."

"You know nothing about me," Saera retorted.

Caryn and Leila looked at each other, surprised. "She has some fight in her," Caryn commented.

"Now if only we could direct that same passion to freefall maneuvering…" Leila said in her signature tone that straddled insult and friendship.

"That's enough!" Elise interjected. "We're supposed to get along."

"Calm down. It's all in good fun," Leila countered.

"Easy for you to say," Saera shot back.

Leila scoffed. "Don't be so sensitive."

*I don't need to take this from them.* Saera stood up. "I'm going to study."

"Sorry, we were just joking around," Caryn said. "Stay."

Reluctantly, Saera sat back down. *I need to let the past go.*

"Fine, change of subject," Leila said, her face brightening. "Now what about that new TA in our astrobiology class?"

— — —

Wil felt a twang of sympathy as he ducked out of the cafeteria. *Was I the one distracting her?*

He couldn't deny that there was something between them. His father was right about that. But, that was all the more reason he needed to stay as far away from Saera as possible.

Caeron was waiting right outside the door. "I heard shouting. Everything okay?" he asked, following Wil down the hall.

"Just a minor collision leaving the buffet line. Nothing to worry about."

Caeron looked at the pre-packaged meal in Wil's hands. "You've been eating alone an awful lot recently."

Wil sighed. "Did my mother talk to you?"

"No, why?"

Wil shook his head. "Nothing. I'm just busy. I need to finalize these design specs. We're coming up on the end of the competition."

"I thought the competition didn't matter?"

"It doesn't, really," Wil said. "But having a firm deadline makes me work harder."

"Sometimes too hard…" Caeron said quietly.

"So, my parents *have* talked with you!"

Caeron looked torn. "They may have approached me."

Wil groaned. "Why can't everyone just leave me alone?"

"We care about you."

Wil shot him an exasperated look. "You barely know me. A year of following me around doesn't count."

"I care for Tararia's well-being. I might not know you as a close friend, but I know what you mean to the world I love."

*He doesn't know the half of it.* "I'm perfectly fine. Tell my parents to back off."

"I can't exactly speak to them that way. A Lord and Lady—"

Wil groaned. "Not literally, Caeron." He took a deep breath.

"I'll leave you be." Caeron dropped back five paces.

*I can't let anyone get too close. I need to be able to do what I have to in the war.* Wil hurried the rest of the way back to his quarters. He was getting close to a breakthrough for the jump drive interface, he could feel it.

His dinner resting on his lap, Wil brought up the simulation files for the new jump drive interface. He stared at the model as it slowly rotated in front of him.

Looking at it with fresh eyes, he realized that half of the previous night's work was wrong. "Ugh!" He deleted the code with a swipe of his hand.

*Maybe I am working too hard. I shouldn't be making mistakes like that.* He felt drained.

Wil took a deep breath, letting the frustration dissipate. As he let his mind wander, he found himself thinking about Saera and the inexplicable connection between them. A spark just waiting to be unleashed.

"That's it!" he murmured to himself. He swung the model around with his hand.

*The neural interface can send a flash to the pilot when the jump requirements are met.* There was no need for fighter pilots to use a graphic interface—they could just feel their way through it. He grinned. *Now I just have to make it work.*

— — —

"Thank you for seeing me on such short notice," Banks said to Agent Volar, one of the navigation instructors. He sat down at his desk and gestured to the guest chair.

Volar took a seat. "Of course, sir. What can I do for you?" The Agent had put in his time with the Bakzen war and was one of the rare few who had been able to return to the primary Headquarters. Understanding the Rift and the underlying structure from a mathematical standpoint was an asset when it came to educating the next generation, even if most of the principles were presented as theory rather than actuality.

"I'd like you to identify some students to train for plotting using the independent jump drive," Banks requested.

"Isn't Wil already training a group?"

"Yes, but it's only fifteen. And you're one of the only people here who knows that's what they're working on."

Volar raised an eyebrow. "Are they picking it up?"

"Slowly. But fifteen Navigators isn't nearly enough. I'd like you to see if there's anyone in your Trainee class that might be able to take it on. Before the working design is announced in the design presentations."

Volar looked pensive. "There might be a handful. What should I tell them?"

"We'll just start out with some side assignments, see who shows aptitude. I'll have Wil look over their work."

Volar nodded. "Yes, sir. Anything else?"

"No, that's all," Banks replied. "Please keep this discreet."

"Of course, sir. I'll pass on the assignments."

# CHAPTER 7

WIL RUSHED INTO the classroom. "Thank you for waiting."

The Initiates were swiveled around in their seats talking to each other.

"Is there any kind of policy where we get to go if the instructor doesn't show up?" Bianca asked as she turned around.

Over the last month, she had proved herself to be one of the more forward students, never afraid to speak her mind.

"No, you're expected to use it as study time," Wil replied. "And I'm late because I wound up working all night and didn't realize it was morning. I think I finally got it."

"The nav system interface?" Greg asked.

"Yeah. What we went over in the last class clicked. I wanted to get it down while it all still made sense." Wil glanced at the deactivated holoprojector. "You want to see it?"

The students leaned forward expectantly in their seats. "Yes!"

He smiled. It was gratifying to see them genuinely invested and interested.

Rather than a lecture format like most of the TSS navigation classes, Wil's course had turned into more of a group brainstorming think tank. He found it surprisingly rewarding to share each new development with the students. They didn't understand the deeper layers of the math—no one else did—but their questions forced him to assess problems from alternate angles. As a result, he'd been able to break through issues that had been plaguing him for months.

"Check this out," Wil said, bringing up his latest model.

The simulated navigation interface hovered at the front of the class. Wil started a mock programming demonstration, showing how the system would work.

The students grinned.

"You got it," Caitlyn said.

"Are you going to present it at the Junior Agent competition next week?" Jordan asked.

"It seems unfair," Wil replied.

"You have to!" Greg encouraged. "Even as first year Trainees we heard about the Junior Agent design competition. After all the work you've put in, you need to just walk in and own it."

"It's a little more complicated than that when it comes to TSS politics," Wil said.

"Come on!" Bianca encouraged. "We'll back you up."

*They would, too.* But their support would only take him so far. They were comrades, but there was a limit to their place in his life. Students—colleagues, even. But not true friends. Unexpectedly, he felt a sudden pang of emptiness in his heart. It was easy to keep himself distant and alone, but he wasn't happy. He realized the only time he'd felt fulfilled in recent memory was in the two brief moments he shared with Saera. *No, I'm on my own.*

Wil swallowed and surveyed his class. They all looked so excited for him. Admired him. He couldn't let them down. "All right, I'm in. Now, let's work out the final kinks in the design."

— — —

Cris eyed Banks. His motives were questionable. "Special assignments in advanced navigation, huh?"

"It seemed like the best way to proceed," the High Commander confirmed.

"Why not wait until after Wil presents the independent jump drive in the competition next week?"

Banks shook his head. "We need to get ahead of it—maintain control over who learns the technology first. Some very well-intentioned people with very low aptitude will likely volunteer if we wait. No need to hurt any feelings by turning them down."

"Saying we pre-selected a group won't avoid hurt feelings."

"But people do understand protocol. We'll keep the upper hand."

"I think you're overlooking the interpersonal dynamics," Cris insisted. "The other Junior Agents take the annual competition as lighthearted fun. As it is, Wil walking in with an actual *solution* is going to rub a lot of people the wrong way. Once we add on a group of pre-selected Navigators—"

"They'll just have to get over it." Banks steepled his fingers.

Cris sighed. "I suppose they always do."

"Just like Wil always finds a way to adapt. He's really stepped up. After that initial fuss about the advanced navigation class, he turned it around into quite a high-functioning group."

"Yes, it worked out." *I suppose he was right to push Wil. This time.*

"I'm curious what he'd do with a dedicated group to train."

"That's way too much to take on right now," Cris said, firm.

"Not now, but in a few years…"

Cris crossed his arms. "Let's take it one step at a time."

"All right," Banks yielded. "I'll let Wil take the lead for now."

Cris sat in thought for a minute. "Everyone's going to want that jump drive once the announcement is made."

"We'll need to engage in patent proceedings. It'll all be in Wil's name."

Cris scrutinized the High Commander. "I'm glad you're upholding the agreement, especially for such a monumental discovery."

"After everything I put you through, it's the least I can do. I'll deal with the higher ups."

"Make sure you do. The Priesthood already controls enough."

— — —

Saera's brain felt like mush. The navigation theory class had taken things to a whole new level of confusion and tediousness. The last several sessions were a series of nonsensical exercises, and everyone seemed completely lost. Even Caryn, who was normally jumping out of her seat with enthusiasm to answer Agent Volar's questions, was sullen.

Agent Volar dismissed the class.

*Finally, the torture ends.* Saera grabbed her handheld from the docking pad on her desk and stood.

"Saera, will you stay behind for a few minutes?" her instructor asked as she headed for the door.

*What now?* Saera tensed. "Of course, sir."

Caryn gave her a quizzical look as she passed by toward the door.

Saera swallowed hard and walked to the front of the class. The last thing she needed was to be singled out in front of her peers. That never ended well.

Volar perched on one of the desks at the front of the class. "So," he began after the other students had departed, "how have the last few classes been for you?"

"Honestly? I feel pretty out of my element," Saera replied.

The Agent crossed his arms. "Your work says otherwise."

Saera hesitated. "It does?"

"You're the only one to figure out how to solve those bonus questions at the end of the last two classes," Volar said, eyeing her.

Saera flushed slightly. "I was just guessing…"

"A good portion of navigation is intuition, which isn't all that different from guessing. You have a natural knack for it."

*I'd really rather follow the Command track.* "That's nice to hear."

The Agent examined her. "I sense some reservation."

"It's just that I'm not entirely sure I want to be a Navigator," Saera admitted.

"Well, you still have plenty of time before you pick a specialization. The Navigation track would be lucky to have you."

"Thank you, sir. I'll think about it."

"For now," Volar said, "I'd like for you to work on something outside of class. Think of it as a special assignment."

"What for?"

"It's a chance to be at the forefront of some exciting new work." Agent Volar grabbed the tablet at the front of the class used for controlling the holoprojector and speaking notes. He made some entries. "You won't be graded on the answers, but take it seriously."

*More homework. Great.* "Yes, sir."

"See you in two days," Volar said with a smile.

"See you then, sir." Saera headed for the hall.

Caryn was waiting outside the door. "What was that all about?"

"I have some sort of extra homework assignment."

"Falling behind already? Too bad," Caryn said and sauntered away.

It wasn't worth it to correct her.

# CHAPTER 8

*I SHOULD HAVE known better.* Wil darted around another corner, staying just out of sight of the other Junior Agents. *I should never have followed through with the presentation. What did I think they'd do—thank me?*

Wil couldn't blame them for being upset. They'd been working feverishly for the last five months on theoretical models for a new style of jump drive, and everyone was worn down. And, despite their efforts, Wil's work outside of class had rendered it all moot.

*It's not my fault that mine is the only model that works.* But the model didn't just work: it was a definitive answer to the issue of relying on fixed beacons for subspace jumps. Before the announcement, most people hadn't even thought it was possible.

The other Junior Agents would be even more upset if they realized the implications of Wil completing the design in his free-time within his personal files—only because night was the only time he could work without interruption. He owned all the intellectual property and would license his work to the TSS; a benefit from the arrangement proposed by High Commander Taelis a year before. It would make him even more absurdly wealthy than he already was as a Sietinen heir, but the money didn't matter. Nor did the prestige of finally cracking the formula that had stumped the brightest minds for generations. Taran victory over the Bakzen was Wil's sole motivation. His fleet needed to travel freely, precisely, between the dimensional planes if they were to be victorious.

Wil could hear the voices behind him. Their intentions were innocent—they were simply desperate to understand how he'd come to a conclusion that was impossible for anyone else to see.

He didn't have an answer for them. *What could I possibly say? "I just know things. It comes to me without trying."* And because he didn't have an answer, Wil would rather avoid the conversation. It would be a waste of time trying to explain, and everyone would just end up more upset than they started.

The hallway up ahead was lined with doors. *A study room—that will work.*

Wil jogged along the hall until he came to a door with a blue indicator light, signaling that it was empty. He rapidly entered in a reservation for two hours and ducked inside, locking the door behind him.

Wil breathed a sigh of relief. He closed his eyes and leaned against the wall.

"Um, hi," said a female voice. The voice roused a suppressed memory in an instant.

*Shite.*

Wil's eyes shot open. Before him was Saera Alexander—the very girl he'd met only for a moment, but who had made a lasting impression he couldn't explain. She was the one person he was even less prepared to talk to than his classmates. *That just figures.*

"I'm sorry," Wil responded through a forced smile. "I thought this room was empty."

Saera made a little tsk of self-disciplining that Wil couldn't help but find adorable. "No, it's not you. I have a horrible habit of forgetting to set the room to 'busy'. If you have a reservation, I'm happy to find somewhere else."

*Of all the places I could have chosen…* "Not at all, I'm sorry to have disturbed you. But," he glanced at the door, knowing the

Junior Agents must be right outside, "would you mind if I stayed for a few minutes?"

Saera gave him a quizzical look. "Hiding from someone?"

"Something like that." *So much for hiding from you.*

"Sure."

*Stars! How to pass the time?* He looked at the open chairs around the study table. Then he noticed calculations on the desk's touch surface. "What are you working on?" *Sit down. You're being awkward.* He took a seat across from Saera.

"My instructor gave me a torturous assignment for long-range subspace navigational plotting." Saera sighed. "I feel like I'm missing something. I know the Taran math is a little different than what I grew up with on Earth, but there's something else that's not fitting."

*She's from Earth? I never would have guessed.* Her delicate features, auburn hair, and jade eyes would stand out in any crowd, even among Taran nobles. "They're already having you work on long-range navigation?" *And brains to match.*

"It's more like 'attempting' at the moment." Saera glared with distaste at the calculations on the surface in front of her.

Wil examined the equations and coordinates on the desktop. Her work was exceptional, if somewhat incorrect—especially for an assignment that most wouldn't tackle until they were a Junior Agent in one of the advanced navigation courses. *She doesn't even realize how brilliant she is.* "Would you like some help? I may as well make myself useful rather than be a distraction."

Saera looked surprised for a moment, then her face relaxed into a smile. "That would be great."

"What seems to be the hang-up?" Wil asked, despite already knowing the errors. *Let's see how she thinks.*

Saera grabbed the equations on the desktop with her hand and swiveled them around ninety-degrees, giving Wil a better vantage. "This part here," she pointed to a particularly convoluted part of the math, "seems to be referencing a fixed spatial position. However, a ship is moving *through* subspace."

Wil smiled. *Most need to have that pointed out.* "Exactly."

Saera looked confused. "Pardon?"

"The ship *is* moving, but the physics in subspace don't behave in the same way as in normal space. From a mathematical standpoint, the ship remains in a fixed location and subspace moves around the ship."

Saera didn't seem convinced.

"Think of it, instead, as the ship attracting the navigation beacons to it. Really, it's only the last beacon that matters because that gives you the exit point into normal space. The path within subspace is irrelevant, aside from being limited by signal range. You just need to maintain a lock on three beacons at any given time."

"Why three?"

"To maintain relative directionality. A beacon gives you a specific point in subspace, with a corresponding location on a standard dimensional plane. However, when up, down, forward and back are all arbitrary based on your point of origin, you need three beacons to give you a path. The only exception is the final exit beacon, in which case you'd just have two locks. Otherwise, you'll always have one behind, and two in front."

Saera studied the equation again. "That still doesn't explain the math. Why the ship appears to be stationary."

"It's because of the flow of subspace. The 'speed' of the ship while in subspace is a constant, but the natural movement of subspace is somewhat variable."

"So… it's like a boat going upriver. If the speed of the boat matches the downward water flow, it *looks* stationary, but the actual water it's encountering at any given moment is different."

Wil grinned. "Precisely."

"And if buoys were floating downriver, they'd pass the boat by, even though an observer on the bank would see the boat as staying still."

"You've got it."

"Huh." Saera looked over her work. "Well, that changes things." She made some quick adjustments to her math, correcting the errors Wil had identified.

"Close, but you're missing one thing."

Saera looked again. "Oh, of course! The entry." She made the final corrections.

"Perfect."

Saera sighed. "Why doesn't the literature on this topic just use that analogy in the first place?"

"The flow of a river is a little far-removed for someone who's lived their entire life in space."

Saera smirked. "You have a point there."

"But, you're right. There are plenty of people who either grew up on a planet, or at least have spent time on one. I'll suggest it for the next revision."

Saera laughed at what she took to be a joke. When Wil didn't join her, she faded out. "You're serious."

"I… consult on some of the TSS curriculum," Wil said.

Saera examined him. "You do a lot more than that, if any of the rumors are true."

"What rumors?"

Wil could see Saera trying to settle on a diplomatic answer. "That you're a very important individual," she answered at last.

*The rumors can't possibly touch on most of it. But the fact that she's talking this casually to me means that she hasn't been swept up in it like the rest. This is the easiest exchange I've had with someone close to my age… ever.* "I am… unique."

Saera tilted her head. "You understand all of this math much better than most, don't you?"

"That's a fair statement."

"Why take this time to explain it to me?" she asked.

"You were rather kind to let me intrude on your study time. It was the least I could do."

Saera smiled. "Well, thank you. It was very helpful."

*She didn't need much help. She would have figured it out on her own with some more time.* "How are you doing in your other subjects, if you don't mind my asking?" *What are you doing?!*

Fleeting surprise passed over Saera's face. "Pretty well. Aside from navigation, I'm in a bunch of remedial classes this term about Taran politics and the like. The only course that's given me much trouble so far is freefall training."

"That does take some getting used to." *There's so much I could teach her.* "Would you be interested in some outside study?" *Why are you asking that?!*

"What are you suggesting?"

"I could tutor you. Freefall, and advanced navigation. More than you'd learn in any class." *Now you've done it…*

Saera's mouth dropped open a little, but she quickly regained her composure. "Is that even allowed?"

"It's rare, but there's nothing to forbid it." *As long as it stays professional…*

"I—" Saera looked into Wil's eyes. There was understanding, compassion in her gaze. She needed a friend just as much as Wil did. "I'd love to."

*There's no staying away from her now. But I can't believe I ever wanted to.* "Great. I'll find a time for us to get started next week. I'll send you a message later today."

"Awesome, thanks."

Wil eyed the door to the hallway. "It's probably safe for me to go now." *Though now I don't want to leave.*

"Right, of course." Saera shifted in her chair. "Thank you again for your help."

"Anytime. See you again soon." He bobbed his head in farewell and left the room before he could make up an excuse to stay longer. *I'm in trouble.*

— — —

Saera was still reeling from her unexpected encounter with Wil Sights. *He's going to tutor me…*

It was surreal. After their initial meeting in the orientation room, she'd built him up as someone who was unattainable, and she had found a strange comfort in that. Now she felt conflicted. *Why did I ever allow myself to get close to him? He'll just reject me in the end.* Yet, it felt so effortless while they were together. She couldn't bear the thought of not seeing him again.

She made her way to her quarters and collapsed on her bunk. *I can't tell anyone about this.* Wil had said nothing about keeping their arrangement secret, but something in her gut told her it was implied. She still knew very little of the TSS, but it was clear Wil had stepped outside of normal protocol for her. *Why me?* She thought back to their first meeting, what had passed between them. *Did he feel it, too?*

Nadeen came into the room and sat down on her upper bunk across the room from Saera. "Hey. Where were you this afternoon?"

Saera sat up and detached her tablet from the wall. "Studying."

"I heard you had some sort of special assignment."

Saera nodded while signing into her tablet.

"You're the only one."

Saera looked up at Nadeen. She wasn't sure what to make of Nadeen's expression—if it was awe or animosity. "I'm just doing what I'm told. Just like everyone else."

Nadeen's mouth twitched and she grabbed her own tablet from the wall, turning her back to Saera.

Saera sighed inwardly and returned her attention to her tablet. She opened her inbox and scanned through the unread messages. Her heart skipped a beat—there was one from Wil, with details for the training. *Maybe I'm not so alone after all.*

— — —

"The independent jump drive is officially announced within the TSS," Banks informed the Priest.

"If only they knew the true reason for the invention," the Priest mused.

*They'd all be running far away from here.* "The details about the war will remain confidential, as always."

"As for the new jump drive, see to it that we receive favorable licensing terms."

"This was never about the financials or intellectual property."

"Of course not, but we need to make sure we are well positioned for after the war," the Priest stated.

"I can urge Wil to make some concessions, given his close ties with the TSS, but any contract will be directly with the Priesthood. You'll need to negotiate your own terms."

"Then he must come here."

"He's too busy for a trip right now," Banks countered.

"Two days won't make a difference. We look forward to meeting him."

The image of the Priest changed to the TSS logo on a black background.

Banks groaned. He couldn't go against the Priesthood's instructions without risking his own well-being, but he didn't like the idea of Wil being at their mercy, either. All he could do was trust in the Priesthood's need for Wil. *He'll be safe there. He's who they wanted.* But for anyone else, good favor was on borrowed time.

# CHAPTER 9

CLINGING TO THE handhold, Saera felt completely lost in the weightlessness. The black walls of the room and pinprick lights provided no sense of orientation.

Wil floated out from the wall, appearing comfortable and relaxed. His eyes glowed blue-green in the dim room.

"You make it look so easy," Saera said.

"You're just overthinking it." Wil drew himself to the wall telekinetically.

"Well, there's no way I can do *that*."

Wil grinned. "Not yet."

"Ha." Saera clung more firmly to the handhold. *This was a terrible idea.*

"You're never going to improve that way. Here," Wil held out his hand, "come on."

*Is he serious?* Saera tentatively reached out to take his hand. A spark surged through her as they touched for the first time, as if she had been shocked by an electrical current. It spread throughout her body, warming her from within. She looked into his eyes, mesmerized, and felt complete trust. *I never thought I could trust a guy again.*

Wil gently pulled her from the wall toward the middle of the room. Larger than the chamber where she trained with her class, the spatial awareness chamber was an icosahedron. The twenty facets of the wall were almost invisible from the center, blending together in the darkness.

"It looks like a starscape," Saera observed.

"That's the point."

"Why? What's this all about, anyway?"

"You mean, doing somersaults with your eyes closed doesn't thrill you?" Wil smiled.

Saera groaned, trying to settle the queasiness in her stomach. "Very funny. But really, where is all of this 'spatial awareness training' heading? I don't see the point."

Wil's grin faded, but the playful glint didn't leave his eyes. "It's all about piloting, in a word. You first must gain awareness of your own body, then simple objects that extend your body, then a craft. Good piloting is all about being one with the craft, knowing exactly what size of an opening it can fit through. Freefall training is the best simulation to flying, to build awareness of surroundings in three dimensions."

"And what if I have no interest in being a pilot?"

"Even commanders and navigators use those same skills. Regardless of what track you follow, you still need to learn how to sense your surroundings, know your place in the environment," Wil explained.

"Okay, so what do I do?"

"First, we need to get you comfortable just floating here."

Saera realized she was clinging to Wil and that he had been patiently letting her nails dig into his palm. "Sorry," she muttered.

"You're doing fine. I can teach you. Of course, there are certain things that require telekinetic abilities that you don't yet possess, but you'll get there in time."

Saera nodded. "Okay, let's try."

Wil ran Saera through a series of exercises for the rest of the session. She still flailed around awkwardly for most of it, but by the end she was able to complete some basic maneuvers without making a complete fool of herself.

"I guess this isn't that bad," Saera commented after an hour of practice.

"See? You just have to get over the initial learning curve." Wil telekinetically drew them to the wall.

"I think I still have quite a ways to go before I crest that curve."

Wil smiled. "It will all come in time." He opened the door to the gravity lock and they climbed in.

"I really appreciate you taking the time to work with me like this."

"It's good experience for me, too," Wil said as the gravity started to return to normal.

Saera gave him a coy sidelong glance. "I doubt that."

Wil smiled. "In any case, I'm happy to do it. It's a nice break from everything else."

"I'm glad I could offer you an entertaining diversion."

"Oh, definitely. I might steal some of your signature moves. Like that one where you sort of flap your arms while spinning sideways…"

Saera faked her best death-glare. "If you say anything—"

"Hey! I'm only joking. It was pretty adorable, actually."

Their eyes met, but Saera hastily looked away.

The main door to the hall opened.

Wil cleared his throat. "So, want to go over some advanced navigation theory next session?" he asked as they exited the gravity lock.

*I guess I didn't scare him off.* "Sounds great."

"Good. I'll see you in three days."

Saera felt giddy on the walk back to her quarters. It seemed like Wil had actually enjoyed their time together, which caught her completely by surprise. But, she knew she had to be careful. It was never a good idea to get too attached to someone.

She found the other Primus girls on their bunks when she entered. They looked up with surprise.

"Where have you been?" Leila asked.

"Does it matter?" Saera asked as she slipped onto her own bunk.

Caryn peered over the edge of her bunk. "That might be sex hair."

Leila tilted her head. "Did you find a nice guy to fok?"

Saera glared at Leila. "Is that all any of you ever think about?"

Caryn settled back on her top bunk. "No way she got laid. Wound way too tight."

Leila scoffed. "No need to get all defensive."

"I'm not being defensive. I just don't feel the need to report my every move to you."

"Then stop giving us reason to think you have something to hide," Caryn said as she grabbed her tablet from the wall.

"You're not my commanding officer or my mom," Saera retorted. "My whereabouts aren't your concern."

"Well with that kind of attitude, maybe it should be. For the good of the group," Leila shot back.

"Ladies, hey!" Elise cut in. "Leave Saera alone. She's right—we all deserve some privacy."

"Suit yourself. Just don't come crying to me when he breaks your heart." Leila turned her attention to her tablet.

Saera lay back on her bunk and tried to ignore Caryn's giggles above her. After a minute, she got a message on her tablet from Elise: >>Ignore them. They're just jealous. I hope he's cute.<<

Saera smiled to herself and wrote back: >>He is.<<

— — —

"I learned something interesting today," Cris said to Kate as he entered their quarters.

"What's that?" she asked, coming to greet him.

"Wil has taken to mentoring a Trainee."

Kate tilted her head with interest. "Really? After all that fuss about the navigation class."

"Well, the thing I find most interesting about it is who she is."

"She?"

Cris nodded. "The very one I mentioned to you earlier."

"Well, that *is* quite interesting. Do we approve of her?" Kate asked.

"Well, I do. I think you'd like her, too."

"I should probably meet her…"

Cris gave her a wary glance. "Wil would have none of that."

"True."

"However, Marsie is her primary instructor," Cris said. "I'm sure you could get some inside intel on her."

"Does Marsie know about them?" Kate asked.

"I just looked at her reports, and it seems like she does. She at least says that Saera is now engaged with a mentor outside of normal training hours."

Kate squinted. "Think Wil told her?"

"Maybe."

"I'm surprised she wouldn't have said anything."

Cris shrugged. "The first training session was yesterday. Maybe she was waiting to see if it worked out."

"Perhaps."

"In any case, I'm glad Wil is finally getting some social time. He's been cooped up in his room working on the jump drive for way too long."

Kate nodded emphatically. "Definitely."

"I guess we'll see what happens."

# CHAPTER 10

"THAT'S MUCH BETTER," Wil complimented Saera as she completed her somersault.

*I think I'm finally getting it.* Saera grinned back from across the spatial awareness chamber. "Pretty soon I'll be flying across the room!"

Wil smiled. "Well, let's not get ahead of ourselves."

They had been meeting twice a week for a month, with one session dedicated to freefall training and the other to advanced navigation. Saera had stopped trying to make up excuses to tell her roommates about how she spent the training evenings. The benefits of the training time were clear and there was no sense hiding it.

They had come to the end of the lesson and Wil was putting away some electronic spheres he had deployed throughout the room.

Saera watched Wil make the simple inputs on the control panel to the storage locker. All the touch-panels and biometric scanners were starting to seem commonplace, but it was still so unsophisticated compared to what it could be. The same incongruity she noticed when she first arrived at Headquarters still tickled the back of her mind.

"I've been wondering about something..." she began.

"What?" Wil asked her.

"It's going to sound silly."

He smiled. "I'm used to those questions by now." He opened the door to the gravity lock.

Saera shot him a playful glare and sighed, climbing into the lock after him. "So, Taran civilization is tens of thousands of years old, right?"

"More like millions."

"All right, even better. So, why isn't this millions of years old civilization more advanced?"

"It's pretty advanced," Wil countered as the gravity lock activated, pulling them toward the floor.

"No, I know. I mean..." Saera searched for the words. "Like, there's the gravity manipulation and subspace travel, and all sorts of other things I'd expect. But, you're still entering things by hand on touch-panels and using what's essentially a smartphone. I guess I just expected it to be a more distinct contrast compared to the state of things on Earth."

"Like a bunch of cyborgs that have evolved beyond the need for the spoken word?"

Saera blushed. "When you put it that way, it sounds ridiculous."

"No, it's a valid question. I see where you're coming from." Wil thought for a moment. "I think what it comes down to is that you're thinking of it from a scientific perspective, but really it's a question of sociology."

"Go on."

"What you have to understand is the Taran society of today isn't the result of following a linear path. That kind of technological integration was vogue at some point in the past—probably multiple times—but it's swung back to where things are now."

"Why go backwards?" Saera asked.

The gravity had equalized, but Wil leaned against the wall, lost in thought. "I wouldn't consider it backwards. Now this is just my opinion, but I think there's an ideal balance between person and technology. Those that elect to become one with machine—such 'tech heads' are certainly around—take it beyond what I would consider that balance point. When it comes down to it, preference eventually takes over above scientific capability."

"So, you're staying it's a societal choice to not have more advanced technological integration?"

Wil shrugged. "In a sense. But nothing is constant—it's still our nature to want things to change and evolve. Take our handhelds for example. There have been devices of all shapes and sizes over the years, but it keeps coming back to this form factor; it's large enough that it doesn't get misplaced, but compact enough that it's easy to carry around. The features cover everything that you need without added clutter. Yet, there are little aesthetic changes every year. People want new—not because it's actually better, but because it makes them feel like they're at the forefront of the trend-setting curve."

Saera pursed her lips. "Hmm."

"What we have now in the core Taran society is a recognition of the individual within the connected community," Wil continued. "The technology enhances the individual experience while facilitating communication and integration with the larger social framework. I'd consider it close to the ideal balance, but I know it won't stay that way. Nor should it. Stagnation is bad for everyone. But, swinging too far to the extremes can be disastrous."

"What happens when it swings too far?"

Wil sighed. "Complete collapse. It's happened innumerable times, though no one wants to talk about it. Some of the colonized worlds were established two million years ago. Yet, due to subsequent collapses, launching an expansive colonization campaign would have been unthinkable just five thousand years ago, due to the state of Taran culture at the time.

"Just because technology exists, that doesn't mean society is in a position to use it. We've had advanced technology in one form or another ever since Tarans first set out from Painted—assuming that's even where our species originated. But, with each collapse, certain things are lost, and certain lessons are learned that set the new standard for future generations. The species changes and evolves, searching for that new ideal balance of individual and society with technology and our larger universe. It's all cyclical—expanding and collapsing. Greed and ambition bringing down the powerful."

*I can't even imagine that kind of restructuring on a galactic scale.* "That all sounds pretty chaotic."

"Look at your own history on Earth. Is it really any different?"

Saera shook her head. "No, of course not. Many empires have come and gone over the last twelve thousand years."

"It's no different in the rest of the worlds. We're still the same species at our core. It's in our genetic programming to always seek what's new and better. But each time we go too far, we'll revert to the tried and true."

"How many scientific advances are sitting in a vault somewhere because they aren't supported by the modern society?" Saera pondered.

Wil looked indifferent. "It's hard to know. A lot was lost in the last collapse."

"When was that?"

"A thousand years ago, in the last Taran Revolution," Wil replied.

"Oh, I heard that mentioned before!"

Wil nodded. "That's when the Priesthood came into power, and the High Dynasties reorganized. Politics aligned with the corporate objectives, merging infrastructure needs with the quest for profit. It's a stable system, but it's not necessarily best for the people."

"What were things like before that?" Saera asked.

Wil smiled. "You'd think I could answer that. It was just a thousand years ago, right? Well, the collapse around the last Taran Revolution resulted in a massive loss of historical records. Almost everything on Tararia was purged, so most of what we know is disjointed accounts assembled from remote colony worlds."

Saera's brow furrowed. "How could so much be lost? There must be data backups."

"Of course. But someone wanted it lost."

*A cover-up?* "What do you think it was about?"

"Something swung too far and everyone paid the price," Wil conjectured.

"How do you even go about rebuilding millions of years of history?"

Wil shrugged. "However you want to. With a collapse like that, you can build whatever future you want."

"That's what the Priesthood and High Dynasties are doing?"

Wil looked down. "Some questions are best not to ask."

Saera examined him. "No theories?"

"Topics for another time, perhaps." Wil opened the door to the hall and stepped out.

*I guess that's all I'm getting for today.* "Well, this has been very enlightening."

"Just a word of caution, I wouldn't go around repeating what I said. I have a somewhat skewed perspective on the whole thing."

"Because of the TSS?"

"Because of a lot of things."

Saera nodded. "Okay. Well, thanks for giving me some insights outside of the official history texts in class."

"Yeah, all of that is glossed over shite," Wil stated, suddenly somber.

*He's definitely keeping something from me.* Saera smiled, trying to lighten the mood again. "I'm always game for some good conspiracy theorizing if you want to corrupt me."

Wil softened a bit, but he was still rigid. "We'll see." He checked his handheld. "It's late, I need to get back."

"Right. Thanks again."

"Sure. I'll see you in a couple days." He headed off down the hall toward the elevator.

Saera leaned against the corridor wall and let out a long breath. *What's the deal with the Priesthood? Wil clearly doesn't like them.* Taran society was still baffling to her. Having access to technology and choosing not to use it as part of everyday life—it was a completely different way of thinking. But, she had come to trust Wil, and especially his judgment on matters. If he was wary of what was unfolding on the galactic stage, there was a good reason to be cautious.

— — —

Wil collapsed in his desk chair. *Saera's too inquisitive for her own good.*

He was always reticent to share his own opinion about political matters, given his delicate position between the TSS and High Dynasties, but Saera was a friend—really, the only one he had. He wanted to be honest with her and share the feelings that constantly burdened him, but it wasn't fair to bring her into that dark, inner world.

It was the same reason he'd tried to stay away from her initially. Yet, they had been brought together all the same. *Is it worth fighting it? We could be happy together. For a while, anyway… before the war becomes my whole life.*

Thoughts of the war and the secondary Headquarters—H2—within the Rift crept into his mind. His stomach knotted. He couldn't bring Saera into that, even as things were. The best thing he could do for her was keep his distance. As soon as she was confident with freefall and the advanced navigation math, that would have to be it. To drag things out any longer would be unfair to both of them.

He sighed and turned his attention to his desk, opening up the files for the independent jump drive interface yet again. The late-night work had paid off. All he had to do was put the final touches on the system architecture to put the new graphical interface into practice.

The final step would have been next to impossible without access to the classified SiNavTech information afforded by his status as an heir. In some ways, working on the independent jump drive undermined the family business. However, he wasn't concerned about the Sietinen Dynasty or civilian applications for the jump drive. All that mattered was giving the TSS an edge in the war. If he couldn't master simultaneous observation, at least he could deliver the improved jump drive navigation system they needed.

Code for the jump drive interface illuminated above the desktop. The three-dimensional rendering showed the interlocking web of variables to make the system function. He selected one of the two remaining modules that still needed finalization and zoomed in on the blank code segments.

Wil settled in for another long night of work. Only a couple more weeks and it would be complete. Then there would be the licensing negotiations, training others how to use it, overseeing deployment to the TSS fleet… He groaned. *One step at a time.*

— — —

Cris closed the holograph of the report projected from his handheld. It was like countless others he had presented to the High Commander in his time as Lead Agent. "Anything else?"

Banks steepled his fingers. "We're getting close to prototype assembly for the independent jump drive."

"That's a polite way of saying we need to get the licensing terms established, isn't it?"

Banks smiled. "You know me so well."

*But never as well as I think.* "How will this even work? I guess Wil is essentially an independent contractor."

"That's a fair characterization, given the agreement he made with Taelis. And TSS technology holdings are handled by the Priesthood."

Cris sighed. "Of course, that figures."

"I know you're wary of the Priesthood."

"With good reason. They did try to kill me, after all."

"Well, you've certainly demonstrated you're worth more alive than dead."

"How reassuring." *And I'm sure that opinion can change at a moment's notice if I say the wrong thing.*

"And without a doubt, Wil means a great deal to them. He'll come to no harm."

Cris groaned. "You're not suggesting he go to Tararia?"

"I don't need to explain business custom to you," Banks replied. "They must have a chance to woo on their own home turf."

"Then the question is, do I go with him or not?"

Banks nodded. "I'll leave that up to you."

*Wil might be safe, but I'm not sure I would be.* "I won't send him in there alone."

"All right, then make your travel arrangements," Banks instructed. "The sooner we can get going on production, the better."

# CHAPTER 11

WIL REALIZED HE had been staring into space when Saera cleared her throat. He straightened in his chair and looked back at the equation they had been working through on the study room's desktop. "Right. So—"

Saera tilted her head. "You seem distracted."

"Sorry." Wil sighed and slumped back in his chair again.

"What is it?" Saera asked.

"I won't be here for our next session."

Saera looked almost hurt by the news. "Where will you be?"

*Does she value our time together that much?* "I need to go to Tararia. Preliminary licensing negotiations for the independent jump drive design."

"That sounds… really tedious."

Wil smiled. "Yeah, it's going to be awful. Believe me, I'd rather be here with you."

Saera flushed. "Well, business. I understand."

*I need to watch my wording.* "Well, anyway, just keep working through these scenarios. You're getting it."

She nodded. "Thanks. Have a good trip."

"I'll try."

—

Wil stared out the viewport of the shuttle at the island of the Priesthood. Few had ever stepped foot on the island. It was an honor to be invited, but Wil didn't consider himself lucky. *It's just another way for them to use me. The independent jump drive is a tool of war for them, not something to benefit Taran society.*

The rock cliff on the island's western coast rose from the expansive ocean, forming a jagged gray wall two-hundred meters tall. Sea birds circled in the air as the shuttle swung around to the southern side of the island. The land sloped downward toward the sea, forming an open valley that looked out to the east. A sandy beach curved along the southern coast, and white stone one- and two-story structures were perched on stilts along the waterline, connected by ornate bridges.

The shuttle passed over the beachfront buildings and headed into the valley. Manicured gardens of tropical trees and flowers were terraced up either side of the broad ravine. Nestled at the crest of the valley at the center of the island, a white stone castle towered above the hills. Large windows with arched tops lined open breezeways connecting the different spires. Figures in light gray robes roamed along paved paths through the lush gardens.

Wil looked over to his father, who was staring out the viewport on the other side of the shuttle. "How many people are out here?" he asked.

"I have no clue," Cris replied. "The Priesthood may be in charge, but there isn't really a face to the organization. Maybe we'll have a better idea after this meeting."

Wil shook his head. "We'll be meeting with legal reps. Whoever is really in charge here won't be debating licensing terms."

"Good point. They're too busy controlling our fate."

Wil noticed that the shuttle pilot shifted uncomfortably in his seat. "I hope we get a tour. It's a beautiful island," Wil said aloud. Then, telepathically, *"We need to be careful what we say around here."*

*"All about appearances, right."*

Wil swallowed. The Priesthood had made him. They had a plan for his life and what they wanted him to do. History had shown the Priesthood would do anything necessary to make sure their plans came to pass. He and his father needed to tread cautiously.

Cris took a deep breath and nodded. "Well, I'll let you take the lead on the discussion since it's your invention, but I'm happy to jump in if you want me to. I've been through enough of these types of negotiations to know how to get a good result."

Wil smiled, forcing back his nerves about being face-to-face with the Priesthood. "That's precisely why I was happy you agreed to come along."

The shuttle landed on a paved square to the eastern side of the main castle. Wil and Cris unstrapped from their seats.

Cris reached inside his jacket as he stood, producing a pair of tinted glasses supplemental to those he was already wearing. "I've been meaning to give you these. It's far overdue."

Wil's heart leaped. Receiving a pair of tinted glasses from a TSS officer was a rite of passage for a Junior Agent. *My training is almost complete.* Normally, there would have been more ceremony for the occasion, but his father knew him better than that. It was perfect.

Wil took the glasses from Cris' outstretched hand. "Thank you." He barely felt the lightweight frames as he put the glasses on. The tint of the lenses was such that his eyes were completely invisible from the outside, but his vision was unimpaired as though he wasn't wearing anything.

"Now you look the part," Cris said, looking him over with approval.

Wil nodded. "Let's go."

They exited the shuttle through the door in the side wall. As they came down the shuttle ramp, three men in suits came forward from the garden path.

"Welcome back to Tararia," the man in the middle greeted. "I'm Allen Verni, and I've been asked to represent the Priesthood regarding licensing the independent jump drive to the TSS." His perfectly combed hair and tailored gray suit fit the part.

"Hello," Cris replied. "Wil and I are eager to hear your offer."

Allen inclined his head. "Very good. Let us proceed to a more private setting for our discussion."

"Thank you." Wil followed Allen toward the main castle.

The gardens were even more impressive up close. There was incredible variety to the types of plants, with similar species grouped together so at first it wasn't obvious that each segment was a slightly different type. The beds flowed into each other seamlessly, showcasing the spectrum of natural beauty.

The garden path led to an arched opening of carved white stone. Beyond, a breezeway ran to either side along the bottom floor of the castle, with openings branching off to other paths into the gardens and doors to inside the castle.

They entered the first door. Inside, the coved ceiling was three meters tall and adorned with ornate inlays of stars and flowers. Though clean and well maintained, there was an ancient aura to the space.

Wil looked around in wonder. The craftsmanship was breathtaking, but it all seemed empty—like it was just a shell. It made Wil uneasy.

The halls were unoccupied. They made their way to a grand staircase and took it up one level. At the top of the stairs, there were tall double doors into a conference room. The broad window on the back wall afforded a sweeping view of the fertile valley below.

"Please be seated," Allen said, gesturing to two chairs on the side of the wooden table facing the window.

Wil and Cris sat down across from Allen and his companions.

"To business," Allen stated. "Edwin Spaera, to my right, and Tim Bolaen are two of the liaisons between the TSS and the Priesthood on technology licensing matters. Their role will be to document the terms we agree upon during this discussion."

"All right," Cris said, "so what do you have to offer?"

"The Priesthood requests an exclusive license for the independent jump drive," Allen replied. "We understand that an arrangement was in place between Wil and the TSS that any technology developed outside of standard operating hours would be retained by him as an individual. For that reason, we recognize that additional financial accommodations are necessary to justify an exclusive arrangement. The discussions here will only be for use by the TSS, and all civilian applications will be disallowed until the expiration of the exclusive licensing term."

"What kind of financial structure will go along with that?" Wil asked. "A fixed-fee term for the technology, or a per-system royalty?"

"Given the nature of the war and unknown future military needs," Allen continued, "a fixed-fee license would be preferred."

"For what duration?" Cris asked.

"A ten-year initial term," Allen stated. "Unlimited number of systems based on the independent jump drive architecture you designed, exclusively for military use."

"And what would be the fixed fee?" questioned Wil.

Allen folded his hands on the table. "Seven-hundred-fifty billion credits."

Wil looked to Cris, barely able to keep a straight face. *"That's insane. Why would they offer that much?"*

*"Because of the exclusivity,"* Cris replied. *"They're trying to buy you off."*

"I don't feel comfortable keeping this technology strictly for military use," Wil replied. "Complete exclusivity for a ten-year term is off the table."

Allen frowned. "That's very important to us."

"Well, it means a great deal to me, too," Wil countered. "I began working on this technology out of necessity for the war, but I never intended for it to be held strictly for military use."

"It's only ten years," Allen said.

Wil gazed back coolly. "Hopefully, the war will be over well before that term is up."

Allen cocked his head. "So, the length of the term is what's unacceptable, rather than the idea of exclusivity in general."

Wil glanced at his father. "I guess."

Edwin and Tim took notes on their tablets.

"Then what length of term would be acceptable?" asked Allen.

"Two years," Wil replied.

Allen chuckled. "That's not very long at all."

"That's more than enough time for the TSS to complete the R&D process and get production underway," Cris chimed in. "If you can't agree to two years, then we may as well just stop talking now."

Allen looked alarmed. "Let's not jump to any hasty conclusions."

"We've presented you with a mandatory term. Do you accept it?" Cris asked, gaze steady.

Wil watched Allen squirm ever so slightly in his seat. He hadn't seen his father in action before, but it was the perfect introduction to his negotiating prowess.

After a five second pause of drumming his fingers on the tabletop, Allen bowed his head. "Yes, we can agree to a two-year exclusivity term. After two years, you will be free to pursue civilian licensing."

"Agreed," Wil said.

Edwin and Tim made additional notations on their tablets. Edwin nodded to Allen.

"Given the shorter term, we need to look at an alternate fixed fee," Allen continued.

"Naturally," Wil said. "What's your offer?" *I really couldn't care less about the money. I just don't want the Priesthood to have complete control.*

"Well, proportionally, one-hundred-fifty billion would be fair," Allen offered.

Cris shook his head. "There's more value than that for the exclusivity, especially without any per-unit royalty. Two-hundred billion."

Wil took a slow breath. The dollar figures were only a fraction of his total assets related to SiNavTech as a Sietinen heir, but the number was still staggering—especially knowing it would all be his. He'd be able to buy an entire small planet if he wanted.

Allen consulted his tablet. He bit his lip and then nodded. "Fine. Two-hundred billion credits for two years of exclusivity."

Cris looked to Wil for his approval.

"Done," Wil said.

Edwin and Tim made entries on their tablets.

"Now, to the details," Allen said.

And the details were endless. For three hours, Wil actively engaged in discussion of minutia surrounding the licensing terms. By the fourth hour, he was slumped in his chair, bored and annoyed by covering the same ground over and over. Eventually, he sent out a telepathic plea to his father for a break, and Cris called a recess.

With reluctance, Allen allowed Wil and Cris to step into the hall.

"Thanks. I couldn't hear 'conditional modifier' one more time without throwing him against the wall," Wil commented as soon as they were away from the negotiation room.

Cris smirked. "This guy's a real charmer, for sure."

"Aside from the unendurable tedium, I think it's going pretty well."

Cris eyed the door with suspicion. "Well enough. They're offering concessions now, but I think they're gearing up to hit us hard in the second half."

"Second *half*?" Wil groaned. "I was hoping we were almost done."

Cris stretched his legs down the hall and Wil followed. "That's how they get you… Lure you into a false sense of finality only to bombard you with a whole new wave of demands. At that point, they hope you'll agree to anything just to make the torture end."

Wil shook his head. "I don't know how you deal with this all the time."

"Just have to keep the goal in sight."

They reached the end of the hall, which terminated in a set of double doors. To their left, the hall opened to a balcony overlooking an atrium. The glass ceiling three stories above was etched with vines and foliage, and planters on the ground level contained assortments of flowers in deep red hues. Centered on one of the walls between the planters, Wil spotted two panels that resembled elevator doors.

"Where do you think that goes?" Wil asked, stepping over to the railing.

His father looked down to inspect. "Probably the Priesthood's secret lair," Cris replied in a tone that was only half joking.

As they leaned against the railing of the atrium, the doors below started to part. With the opening came a sudden hum of electromagnetic energy, almost as if an Agent was nearby.

Wil looked with confusion at his father. "Do you feel—"

"This area is off-limits without an escort," Allen said from behind.

Wil and Cris wheeled to face him.

"Doesn't status as a High Dynasty heir grant access to anywhere?" Cris retorted.

"We still have much to discuss," Allen replied, dodging the question. He headed back toward the negotiation room.

Wil glanced back over the balcony but the door had resealed. The energy buzz was gone.

*"Something isn't right here,"* Cris said telepathically.

*"Problems for another time. Come on."*

They plodded through another three hours of negotiations. Though several of the remaining items would require finalization after Wil had completed the jump drive designs, most of the contract terms were in place by the end of the discussion. Wil and Cris signed some preliminary paperwork to solidify the terms, and they were escorted back toward the shuttle.

As they returned to the shuttle, some of the figures robed in light gray were returning from the gardens. Of the three groups Wil and Cris passed, all of the robed individuals were men varying in age from early-twenties to elderly.

*"Have you noticed there aren't any women here?"* Wil asked his father telepathically after they passed the third group.

Cris frowned. *"Yes, I was thinking the same thing. It's strange."*

*"I wonder why."*

Cris shook his head. *"Very little about the Priesthood makes any sense."*

They passed another group in the gardens near the shuttle, also all men. Wil and Cris exchanged glances as they passed. The group of men paid them no more than a subtle glance.

When Wil and his father arrived at the shuttle, Wil relaxed into his chair with a deep sigh. "Thanks for your help today."

Cris smiled. "Of course. Finally, a negotiation I could really get my heart into."

Wil chuckled. "I don't know what I'm going to do with all of that money."

"I'm sure you'll think of something."

— — —

Saera stared at the equation on the study room's tabletop. It just wasn't the same without Wil. Though it was scheduled to be a freefall training day, she didn't have the clearance or the skill to practice in the spatial awareness training chambers alone. Working on advanced navigation was the next best thing.

She sighed, staring past the equation. Her heart wasn't in it. *I miss him. I actually miss him.*

Wil had become a genuine friend to her. He was patient and kind, and he pushed her to learn and grow in ways she'd never imagined possible.

Saera wasn't ready to admit that she wanted the relationship to be something more. Just having a real friend was enough. All the same, she wondered if Wil was thinking about her, too.

She hastily returned her attention to the equation in front of her. There was no sense thinking about what could never be. Wil was her friend and her commanding officer. That's the way it had to stay.

After struggling to focus for another half-hour, Saera finally gave up and returned to her quarters.

When she arrived, all of her Primus and Sacon roommates were gathered in the common room around the main viewscreen examining a list of names and numbers. Everyone looked at her as she closed the door behind her.

"You made the Top Ten," Leila stated.

"Top Ten what?" Saera asked.

"Trainees, based on test scores and grades," Elise clarified. "You're Number 8."

*I didn't even know they did that.* "Nice."

Leila scoffed in disgust and stomped into their bedroom with crossed arms.

"She was Number 16," Nadeen said. "She's just jealous."

Based on the faces of the other girls in the room, Leila wasn't the only one jealous of her. "I wasn't trying to upstage anyone."

"Don't apologize," Elise said. "Be proud of yourself."

Though Saera hadn't known about the leaderboard, the development was too great of an opportunity for her to not embrace. With that kind of ranking, maybe Primus Command was actually within her reach. If she could accomplish that, she could do anything—a challenge she readily accepted. *This was my chance to start over and be my best.*

She looked around the room. "I'll make it to Number 1."

# CHAPTER 12

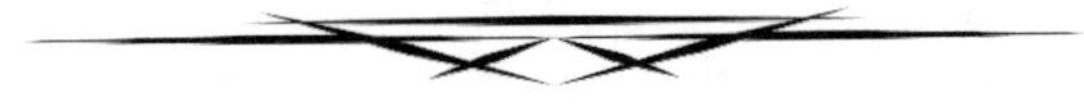

WIL HELD IN a yawn as he opened the door to the study room. A late return home had left him dragging all day. Knowing he had a study session with Saera in the evening had been just enough to keep him going.

Inside the room, Saera perked up the moment she saw him. "Hey! How was your trip?"

Wil eased into his usual chair across the table from her. "I guess it went well enough. Mostly it was boring, but also a little infuriating."

"That sounds like a terrible combination."

"It was." Wil sighed. "I feel like I can't win, no matter what I do." *Even demanding a two-year term, the Priesthood will still find a way to use and control the technology, just like they manipulated me.*

"Do you want to talk about it?" Saera offered.

*I wish I could.* "No, it's okay. Let's get back to it. How did you fare without me?"

"Pretty well with this stuff, I think. But I definitely missed our freefall session."

Wil smiled. "Now we can get back to our normal routine."

"You're sure this still works for you? I know you're busy—"

Wil looked her squarely in the eye. "Saera, I wouldn't be here if I didn't want to be. In fact, these tutoring sessions are the only parts of the week I look forward to."

She smiled. "Okay."

"Now, where did you leave off?"

— — —

Cris felt an instant surge of energy as the stim strip dissolved on his tongue. He hadn't slept well, even after returning home two days before. Any contact with the Priesthood always left him angry, and it was draining to pretend like everything was fine.

*They killed my brother. They tried to kill me. They've manipulated our whole lives. And I had to sit across the table from them and talk business like they're civilized.* He felt like running a few laps around the track, but he was already getting too late of a start to the day.

Still dragging, he made his way to the High Commander's office for his weekly morning briefing with Banks.

The High Commander was reviewing a report projected from his desktop when Cris entered. "How did it go?" he asked as he minimized the report.

"Well, I think." Cris sat down in his usual visitor's chair across from Banks. "We have some initial terms documented, but nothing will be finalized until Wil completes the model of the jump drive interface."

"Taelis and I are anxious for production to begin."

Cris nodded. "You'll have it soon. Wil's been working on it almost nonstop."

"Taelis' plan didn't save him from any extra hours," Banks said with a frown.

"No, but it did keep the Priesthood from getting complete control." *And that was entirely worthwhile.*

The High Commander eyed him. "I'm not sure if Taelis cares about that as much as you do."

"Regardless, I hate to think what the Priesthood would have done, having complete authority. They wanted ten years of exclusivity, as it was."

"Did you grant it?" Banks asked.

"Fok no! We held firm at two."

Banks steepled his fingers. "And what about after that? Bring it to SiNavTech?"

Cris shrugged. "Maybe. But the intent of the shorter term was just to keep leverage over the Priesthood."

"The TSS needs that technology."

"And they'll have it," Cris assured. "Wil knows it's needed for the war. The licensing is all about making sure he has what he needs—use by the Priesthood beyond war applications is where we draw the line."

Banks frowned. "You need to be careful, Cris. The Priesthood doesn't like to have enemies."

"You report to them, but I know you don't blindly follow."

"Still, this isn't the time to make a move against them."

"No, but I'm always at the ready." Cris paused and examined Banks. "Have you ever been to their island?"

"Once, a long time ago."

"It's not like I expected."

Banks tilted his head. "What did you think it'd be?"

"I'm not sure exactly. But, more… 'administrative', I guess. Instead, it felt like a monastery."

"The Priesthood did begin as a theological institution, remember."

"Right, but it's been a thousand years since it began governing. I'd think the culture would have shifted quite a bit since then."

Banks steepled his fingers. "Many in the Priesthood still hold firm to the core ideals."

"Even so, it just didn't fit. We barely saw any people there—and certainly no one that looked like a government official."

"I'm sure you only saw a fraction of the facility."

*Why is he still hiding things from me?* "Banks, what do you know about them?"

"Enough that I know better than to dig too deep."

Cris crossed his arms. "Why weren't there any women?"

Banks was caught off-guard. "What?"

"Of the few people we did see, none were women. That doesn't seem strange to you?"

"It is, certainly," Banks said, choosing his words carefully. "I'm sure there are some, perhaps elsewhere. It's a large island."

Cris groaned. "You're never going to be completely transparent with me, are you?"

"Not until I need to be."

Cris shook his head. *I can't truly trust him, even when he claims to be my friend.*

"I'll tell you this, though," Banks continued. "You're in a position to do something that no one else can. Wait until the time is right."

*Is he actually on my side?* "And what is it that needs to be done?"

"You already know. When that time comes, you won't need to question my allegiance."

"Until then, we need to play our parts?"

Banks nodded.

Cris let out a slow breath. *Patience… I never was good with waiting.*

— — —

Wil completed his lap around the Primus residential wing, panting for breath. It felt good to run after a full day working at his computer.

As he started his cool-down walk, he saw his father approaching.

"Hey," Cris greeted.

Wil gave him a little wave. "Hey."

Cris fell into step with him. "I heard those representatives wanted to come from Tararia to finalize the licensing terms."

Wil groaned. "I was really hoping we'd be able to finalize everything over email."

"We're never that lucky."

"At least it won't be for several months," Wil said. "I need to finish all of the prototype schematics."

Cris nodded. "The work is never-ending."

"Tell me about it." Wil sighed.

"How are things going otherwise?"

"Good."

Cris gave him a quizzical look. "And you're still tutoring Saera, right?"

Wil's heart leaped and his face felt warmer. "Yeah, why?"

"No reason. I'm just glad it's working out."

Wil doubted his father didn't have any ulterior motives behind the question. *No reason to give him any fuel.* "She's very smart and capable."

"I can see that."

*She's also turned into a good friend. And she's not bad to look at, either...* "I think she wants to make a run at Primus Command."

Cris nodded thoughtfully. "I'm glad to hear it. I think she'd be a good fit."

"I'll do what I can to finish preparing her for the evaluation."

"Excellent." Cris looked Wil over again. "You seem happy."

*There it is.* "I'm coping a little better, I guess."

His father gave him a coy smile. "All right. Well, I'm glad to see it."

Wil shot him a side-long glance. "Anyway, I should get to my evening work."

"Very well. Find some time to say 'hi' to your mother."

Wil waved him off. "I know, I know. I will."

— — —

*Something has definitely changed.* Cris sat in his office reflecting on the conversation with his son. Wil's entire demeanor was different. There was an excitement and sense of purpose in Wil that Cris hadn't seen in over a year. *He's finding himself again.*

The reason behind the change wasn't a mystery—his relationship with Saera. On the surface, Wil was just upholding their organization's tradition of mentorship, much in the same way Scott had guided Cris when he first joined the TSS. Of course, the reason they had been drawn together was quite different. Saera was much more than a friend to Wil, even if he wouldn't admit it yet. Wil may deny that he had any deeper feelings, but it didn't take telepathy to know it was on his mind.

*I called that months ago*, Cris thought with a smug smile. *I've never been so pleased I was right.*

There was, however, the matter of the relationship advancing beyond its current state. Especially once Wil was an Agent—all too soon—he would be held to a code that strictly forbade any fraternizing with TSS trainees outside of official business or mealtimes. *I won't let them keep her from him. He needs her.*

Resolute, Cris strode down the hall to Banks' office. The High Commander was studying a report displayed on the surface of his desk when Cris entered.

"We need a plan," Cris said.

Banks closed the open work on his desktop. "Regarding what?"

Cris sat down in a chair across the desk from the High Commander. "Wil and Saera."

"That Trainee he's been tutoring?"

"Yes. I think it's pretty obvious where things are heading." *And at any time now.*

Banks sat back in his chair, genuinely surprised. "I didn't realize they had gotten that close."

"Neither had I. At first, I was just relieved for Wil to have a friend, but seeing how happy he is now… I don't see things staying strictly professional for much longer."

"Hmm." Banks steepled his fingers. "This would be a major exception to the regulations."

"I know, which is why I'm coming to you now."

Banks examined Cris. "And you're sure you're okay with this?"

*This goes beyond any Tararian pedigree.* "Why wouldn't I be?"

Banks looked at the desktop. "The affairs of your Dynasty are none of my concern, forgive the intrusion." He paused. "As for the TSS, there's a lot to consider."

"I didn't say anything before, but I was there when they met for the first time," Cris said. "There was an astounding resonance reaction. It made what I experienced with Kate seem like nothing."

Banks' eyebrows rose. "I had no idea."

"Even if I was concerned with Tararian bloodlines, I could never deny him that kind of connection with someone." *That would make me even worse than my own parents. At least they never stood in my way when I said I wanted to be with Kate.*

"That kind of bond presents an extraordinary opportunity. If we can train her as a Second…" Banks withdrew in thought.

*So even love is a tool for war in Wil's life?* "She does have the potential, but I'm afraid the military application of their would-be relationship isn't my top priority."

"Of course. The emotional support means far more."

Cris wasn't convinced Banks really felt that way. "Where do we go from here?"

"I will sanction a relationship between them if it comes to it. We'll need to keep it confidential, of course."

"Then let things unfold as they may."

# CHAPTER 13

WIL WATCHED SAERA complete her flight across the spatial awareness chamber and land deftly on her feet. As she touched down, she completed a somersault and pushed off the wall to return to her target spot next to Wil.

She landed lightly and grabbed the handhold. She grinned at him.

Wil smiled. "You're a master."

"Yeah, I know," Saera replied with exaggerated smugness.

In the four months they had been training together, Saera had grown confident in the maneuvers that had once seemed far out of reach. Based on what she'd told Wil, the other students had actually started inviting her to be on their practice teams rather than finding any way to avoid a pairing. It pleased Wil to see her succeeding, both as a friend and because of the confirmation in his ability as an instructor.

"What's next?" Saera asked.

"I'm running out of moves that don't require telekinesis," Wil admitted. The last several weeks had entailed lots of experimentation just to maintain the training momentum. However, he could only take it so far.

"I'm sick of waiting for these abilities to emerge. We've been practicing mental blocks with Agent Katz in preparation, but I'm only feeling the hum of energy so far, nothing tangible."

"Be thankful it's coming to you slowly," Wil said. "I wasn't so lucky."

Saera scrutinized him. "I'm ready for it now."

"You say that, but… I don't know, I guess things may have been different for me if I hadn't been so young. It was too much to take on at once." *It nearly killed me.*

"How old were you?"

"Eleven."

Saera's brow furrowed. "I guess that is pretty young."

"It just sort of hit me one day. Voices in my head, this oppressive hum of energy. I didn't know how to block it out. I wouldn't wish that on anyone."

"But you made it through."

"I did." *And I've been a freak ever since.*

"Well, I do hope it starts to come to me soon, but I'll try to be patient if it comes more gradually."

Wil nodded. "Okay, well, in the meantime, I guess I can give you some prep on stances."

"For what?"

"Basic levitation. Once you get proficient, there's no need for any external gesture—you just think about something and it will happen. But when starting out, it's easier to make some motions to go along with your visualization," Wil explained.

"Okay."

Wil let go of the wall and held out his arms, with one bent ninety degrees at the elbow and the other horizontal and slightly bent. "This is a good resting position for most exercises. Use your dominant hand like a baton, directing the object you're trying to manipulate."

"It doesn't seem like I'll be able to get very far without abilities."

"Well, I can help you out. Come here." Wil gestured for Saera to let go of the wall. He looked at one of the metal probes in the center of the chamber. "Say we want to bring that here."

"All right..."

"You need to focus on it and command it to you. Wave it toward you with your hand," Wil explained. He demonstrated the motion to Saera without the accompanied telekinetic output.

"Like this?" Saera mimed the gesture.

"Right, but with a little more conviction," Wil said. "Here." He moved over so he could put his arms around her to match her stance. He placed his hands over the back of hers and gripped her lightly. Holding onto her, he went through the proper motion.

Saera was relaxed in his muscular arms, following his direction. "Okay, I see." She did the motion again, this time leading him.

"Perfect."

Saera turned her head around to look up at him. Their eyes locked, mere centimeters apart.

Wil found himself transfixed by her. Her jade eyes drew him in as her breathing slowed to match his. The floral smell of her hair was intoxicating.

Her lips parted slightly, and she leaned toward him, almost imperceptibly. Wil tightened his arms around Saera as she leaned back into him, bringing her face closer.

Then, she hastily looked away and pulled out from his embrace. "Right. Thank you."

Wil's heart pounded in his ears. *Was she about to kiss me?* He suddenly yearned to be close to her. To taste her and feel the warmth of her pressed against him. *What are you thinking?!* He snapped himself out of the reverie. "Yeah, anytime."

Saera looked a little flushed, but it was difficult to tell in the dim light. "I guess we're about done for today, then."

Wil cleared his throat. "Right." His pulse was still racing. He struggled to suppress the unexpected ache of desire.

Saera reached out for the wall and pulled herself up toward the door. Wil followed her at a slight distance and climbed into the gravity lock after her.

"Good work today," Wil said to break the silence as they waited for the gravity to restore.

"Thanks." Saera wouldn't meet his eye.

Wil took a slow breath, regaining some control of himself as he was drawn toward the floor. "Oh, I might be a few minutes late to our next session. I'll be meeting with some reps about licensing for the jump drive beforehand."

Saera finally looked up at him. "You finished it?"

"Close enough to sign contracts, anyway," Wil said. "Get started without me if I'm late."

The door hissed and opened to the corridor.

"Okay," Saera affirmed. "Well, good luck with the meeting."

"Thanks."

Saera flashed him a meek smile and hurried away into the hall.

Wil let out a slow breath when she was gone. *How much longer can I hide my feelings for her?* But he knew he wasn't fooling anyone.

— — —

Saera stared at her tablet but wasn't getting any work done. She had become the star student of all her classes. She had the respect of her peers, if not their friendship. But still, everything felt like it was about to fall apart.

Her last practice session with Wil kept replaying in her mind. *Am I imagining that glance, that touch? Or did it really happen?* The line between study session and date had begun to blur some time ago, but their interactions had never crossed the line into unprofessional conduct.

"Is everything all right?" Elise asked from across the room. They were alone.

Elise had proven herself to be the only proper friend in Saera's cohort, always lending an ear when Saera was having a difficult day. Observant and inquisitive by nature, she always knew when something was wrong.

*I wish I could talk about it with her, but I can't.* "I'm fine."

"It's about all of those evenings you spend away 'studying', isn't it? Like tonight."

Saera looked down.

"Who is he?"

"I never said anything about a person!"

Elise gave a coy smile. "You can't spend that much time with someone and not develop some feelings. If you were studying alone, you'd just be here in the room like any other night."

The logic was too sound for Saera to refute. "Nothing will ever happen between us."

"But you'd like for there to be something," Elise pressed.

Saera nodded. *I'd be lying to myself if I said I didn't. I wish that weren't the case.*

"So, go for it. You already said it will never happen, so what do you have to lose?"

"Our friendship, for one." *He'll never accept me. Not with my past.*

"Could you really stay friends, as things are now? If you already feel this way, how will it be after years of pretending like there's nothing there?"

Saera's stomach knotted. "You're right." *What am I going to do?*

— — —

Wil drummed his fingers on the tabletop. *Are they ever going to stop talking?*

Next to him, his father looked equally irked.

The representatives from Tararia were exactly the kind of dry business cogs Wil detested. Unlike Allen, the initial negotiator, these representatives got hung up on the minutia without seeing the big picture. At every juncture, they attempted to overturn agreements that were already signed in writing. The discussion had already been underway for three hours and they were getting nowhere. The cramped conference room in the TSS spaceport suspended above the moon was never intended for such lengthy conversations.

"I'll oversee all applications within the TSS. And, exclusivity or not, I won't even consider a civilian model until after the technology has been thoroughly tested in the field," Wil reiterated for the fourth time.

"We'd like to have the terms for the civilian system documented. Two years is not a very long lead time," Kaven, the representative, asserted again.

Wil crossed his arms. "I'm not making any decisions about a potential civilian navigation system at this time. That's final."

Kaven looked like he wanted to swear under his breath. "The initial agreement—"

"The initial agreement stated two-hundred billion credits for two years of exclusivity," Cris interrupted. "Nowhere did it say anything about the Priesthood having a say after that two-year term. If you want to void that, we can go to SiNavTech right now."

"No, no," Kaven hastily cut in. "We will honor the original terms."

Cris' eyes narrowed behind his tinted glasses. "So, what's the holdup? Let's sign."

Kaven looked at the holographic model of the independent jump drive projected above his tablet. "This technology is going to change the nature of space travel as we know it. Don't you want to be prepared?"

"I think we'll manage," Wil replied. "We have a pretty good family history to fall back on."

Cris smiled. "The Priesthood isn't in a position to make demands."

Kaven shifted in his chair. He stared down at the tablet, his face drawn.

"Do we have an agreement?" Cris asked.

Kaven looked at his colleagues. They nodded. "Yes, agreed."

Wil leaned back in his chair, relieved the discussion was finally over. "Where do I sign?"

Kaven minimized the jump drive model projected from his tablet and brought up a text file. "Here are the final terms for you to review," he said as he handed the tablet to Wil.

Wil read through the file with his father looking over his shoulder to make sure everything was in order. It was exactly as they discussed. "All right."

Wil tapped on the signature box and input the code for reading his Dynastic ID chip. A purple light projected from the bottom edge of the tablet. He exposed his left wrist and passed it under the light, illuminating the serpent Sietinen crest invisible to the naked eye. The crest and his full birth name appeared in the signature box. He handed the tablet back to Kaven.

Kaven inspected the seal. "Very good. The funds will be wired to the specified account within twenty-five hours."

"Thank you." Wil inclined his head and rose alongside his father.

Kaven stood and bowed to them as they exited.

Two Militia officers went to retrieve the representatives as Wil and Cris headed toward the transport hub of the spaceport.

"Thank the stars that's over!" Wil exclaimed.

His father smiled. "Congratulations. You just became very rich."

"I was already rich."

"It's different when you earn it rather than inheriting."

"I don't feel like I earned anything. I was just doing my job," Wil said.

"Regardless, you solved a problem no one else could. That's something worth celebrating."

"Celebrating anything right now doesn't seem right, knowing what's coming."

Cris sighed. "It's like your birthday all over again."

Wil frowned. "Turning sixteen might mean something on Tararia, but I already had the privileges that came with being of 'legal age' through the TSS. All it meant was being another year closer to the war."

"I don't want to get into it again."

"Well, I'm late for my study session with Saera, anyway." Wil headed for one of the waiting transport shuttles to the moon's surface.

"I'll see you around," his father said.

"You're not coming down?"

"I need to check in on the *Vanquish*. They were doing some sort of systems upgrade with the rift drive nav."

"Okay, see you," Wil said as he boarded the shuttle. Saera was waiting.

—

Wil jogged down the hall toward the study room for his tutoring session with Saera. Some quiet time was exactly what he needed after the nightmare he'd just been through with the licensing negotiations. It had forced Wil to face the reality of what production of the independent jump drive signified. The TSS was building a fleet. A fleet he would command. And that time was approaching all too quickly.

He came around a corner just in time to see Saera entering their usual room. The glimpse of her was enough to lift his spirits. *I never thought someone could have that effect on me.*

Wil slowed to a walk as he approached the room. He palmed open the door.

Inside, Saera was slumped in her usual chair, absently staring at the wall.

"Hey, sorry I'm late," Wil said as he entered.

Saera came to. "I just got here, myself."

Wil sat down across from her. “I’m glad I didn’t keep you waiting.”

She shook her head. “Actually, I almost canceled on you.”

*That’s never happened before.* “Why, is something wrong?”

She shrugged off his question. “I just have a lot on my mind.”

“Well, I’m glad you didn’t. I really need some time away from… everything else.” Wil sighed. “But truth be told, going over jump drive navigation is the last thing I want to do right now.”

Saera looked relieved. “You too?”

“Do you want to just, I don’t know, ‘hang out’ instead of studying?” *Did I just ask her out?*

Saera’s shock was apparent. “Uh… what did you have in mind?”

“We could just go back to my quarters and watch a movie or play some video games.” *That certainly* sounds *like a date.*

“What about your roommates?”

“I’m the only one there right now. One just graduated, and Andy is away on his internship. The other one… won’t bother us.”

Saera paused in thought. “Okay, sure. Why not?”

“All right. Meet me at room JAP-234. If anyone gives you trouble about entering the Junior Agent wing, just say that you’re getting help from your TA on an assignment.”

Saera nodded. “Okay.”

Wil smiled. “I’ll see you soon.” *Stars! This is getting dangerously close to that line I’m not supposed to cross.*

Wil made his way back to his quarters, with Caeron following at some distance behind in his usual fashion. When they arrived, Wil called Caeron inside.

“Saera is coming over,” Wil explained, “and I’d like you to stay away for the evening.”

Caeron looked glum. “I hesitate to distance myself too much.”

Wil held back his annoyance and patiently replied, "I know, but I assure you there's nothing to worry about. And I promise I won't leave here without you."

Caeron gave a slight bow. "As you wish." He exited to the hallway.

Wil took a quick survey of the common room and decided that it was in sufficient order. Though he rarely had company over, the room was set up well for socializing with plush couches oriented around a coffee table and viewscreen.

A moment later, there was a buzz at the entry. He checked the screen next to the door and saw Saera standing outside. Seeing the image of her there in the hall, Wil's nerves set in. Outside the context of a classroom, Saera looked far too lovely for Wil to trust himself around her.

"Hi, thanks for coming," he greeted her while opening the door. *This was a terrible idea.*

Saera smiled. "Gladly. This was a great idea."

*Stars!* Wil stood aside to let her in. "It's been far too long since I've just had a mellow evening like this." He closed the door.

"I know the feeling." Saera looked around the room. "So, this is what Junior Agent quarters look like."

"It's nothing too fancy. There are four private bedrooms, and the bathroom is at the back."

"I'm looking forward to it. Having a lot of roommates sucks."

*Especially when they're all jealous of you.* "I know what you mean." Wil shifted on his feet, realizing they were still standing by the door. "Please, have a seat."

He motioned Saera over to the couch. She sat down on one end facing the viewscreen on the side wall. Wil was tempted to sit right next to her, but he elected to remain at a respectable distance on the opposite side of the couch. He removed his tinted glasses.

"So, what kind of entertainment selections do you have?" Saera asked.

Wil beamed. "Pretty much anything you can imagine. The TSS Mainframe has access to all of the media that was ever digitized—quite literally. No matter where the data is stored, we can call it up here in an instant. Subspace com relays are pretty amazing."

Saera's eyes widened with awe. "I've never come across the library. I had no idea."

"Well, you need to have the right clearance level, of course. I just happen to have the access… by which I mean, I figured out how to hack the Mainframe when I was about nine-years-old, and they haven't yet found a way to keep me out."

Saera folded up her legs on the couch. "You can hack the Mainframe? I thought it was impossible to crack."

"Not impossible. But, as far as I know, I'm the only one who can do it." *Except for the Bakzen, if they're given a backdoor.* He pushed aside the thoughts of what had happened over a year before. "I am respectful about it, of course. I never go into personal files or anything that's above my security clearance."

"I'm impressed." She looked Wil over. "How did you come to know so much about everything?"

Wil looked down. *That question I can never answer…* "I'm not like most people, Saera. I don't try to show off—these skills just come naturally to me. When someone watches me master something after I see it demonstrated one time, they back away. No one knows how to act around me. You're… you're the only person I've met who treats me like a regular guy."

Saera studied him. "Should I be treating you differently?"

"No! Please don't. When I'm around you, I feel like I'm in control of my life. I feel like I can be… normal."

Saera sat back on the couch. "Don't take this the wrong way, but I don't at all think of you as 'normal'."

"What do you mean?"

Saera laughed. "Don't be so serious all the time, Wil. I've seen you let go in some of our study and practice sessions. I know you have the capacity for fun."

"Well, yes. But—"

"What I meant," Saera went on, "is that you should be happy you're not 'normal'. I've known a lot of regular people over the years, especially guys, and trust me—you don't want to be associated with many of them."

"I get the impression you've never really fit in, either."

Saera looked down. "You could say that." She paused in thought. "I'm on a different track than most of the other Trainees, aren't I?"

*Certainly, if you keep spending time with me.* "You have the talent for the Command track if that's what you want. Very few women ever follow the Primus Command track. It's been at least five years since the last."

Saera was incredulous. "Why is it so uncommon?"

"There are proportionally fewer women than men in Primus, for whatever reason, so there just aren't that many candidates with the required combination of telekinetic and telepathic skills. But moreover, the Command track requires someone to make tough calls. Life or death decisions. Not everyone is willing to take on that kind of responsibility."

"In that case, what makes you think I'd have any interest?"

"Because you see alternatives. So many view a head-on conflict as the only solution, but you're creative. You bring the kind of perspective that can balance out other leaders. Whether you've noticed or not, you've taught *me* a lot in our time together."

Saera looked taken aback. "I have?"

"Absolutely." *And you've made me feel whole again.* "But, I'm afraid that there isn't a lot more I can teach you until your telekinetic abilities are more developed. You're adept at basic freefall maneuvers now, and you've already learned more about navigation than most specialists."

Saera drooped. "I don't feel that way at all. We've hardly scratched the surface!"

"That's true. But for now, I've done just about as much for you as I can."

"But what about our time together?"

*So it means something to her, too.* "I don't want that to stop."

"More nights like this?" She smiled cautiously.

"I'd like that." *But can we have it?*

Saera looked at the viewscreen on the wall. "Well, anyway, I think we were going to watch something…"

"Yes, right. What did you have in mind?"

"Oh, I know…" Saera got a mischievous glint in her eyes.

—

Wil and Saera had gravitated toward the center of the couch over the course of the movie, their shoulders touching and their feet propped up on the table in front of the couch.

"I've never seen so many blatant inaccuracies!" Wil exclaimed.

Saera laughed. "That's the point. It was a parody."

"You watch terrible things on purpose, for fun?"

"Precisely."

"Why do I find that so weirdly charming?"

Saera grinned. "I knew you'd come to appreciate it. I told you to trust me."

"I do."

Their eyes met. It was the closest they'd been for any meaningful length of time, and they were at ease with each other. But the line was still there, keeping them apart as teacher and student. Wil wanted to lean in, to caress Saera, but he stopped himself.

She relaxed against him, her head nearly resting on his shoulder as they gazed at each other. "I trust you, too. More completely than I ever thought I could." She looked at the blank viewscreen and pulled away a little.

Wil sensed a hurt in her. "Did something happen back on Earth?"

Saera drew into herself. "More than one thing. A series of misfortunes and bad decisions." She shook her head.

"Tell me, Saera." Wil took her hand. She flinched at first, but then entwined her fingers in his. The contact sent an energizing surge through him, fueling his desire to be close to her. "I want to understand how you came to be the person you are."

Saera hesitated. "It's not something I ever talk about."

"Then some other time, when you're ready." *I do want to know everything about her, the bad and the good.*

Saera bit her lip, in thought. "No. I need to tell you, as much as I hate to admit it. You deserve to know." She reoriented on the couch to face Wil, keeping a hold on his hand. She trembled as she took a slow breath. "I'll give you the short version. My dad was married and had two kids. When the younger one was about four-years-old and the oldest one was six, he had an affair."

Wil frowned involuntarily.

"I know, right?" Saera sighed. "Anyway, that affair was with my mom, and that's how I came into being."

"Wow, that's—"

Saera shook her head. "Oh, just wait. So, my mom kept the pregnancy to herself, and raised me on her own at first. But when I was four, she decided that she was done with me, and she dumped me off on my dad. Naturally, his wife didn't take too kindly to this. Here I was, proof of his infidelity, and I had to go live with them. They eventually reconciled somewhat, and had another baby after I'd lived with them for a year. The two older kids hated me for the rift I'd caused in the family. To top it off, I was precocious and had a knack for stealing the spotlight without meaning to. It made me an outcast among my own family."

*Bomax. I know all about being a precocious kid.* "That must have been difficult."

"It gets much worse," Saera said through a pained laugh. "They skipped me two grades, but even then nothing at school was challenging for me. None of the girls wanted to be friends with me. In time, the guys around me became interested in only one very specific thing, but I was still too young to be noticed by most."

*You're beautiful and smart. Many find that intimidating.*

"Eventually, I lost control. I guess it started when I was eleven. My older brother had this friend who often slept over at our house. One night, the friend snuck into my room and got in bed with me. He made me feel wanted in a way I never had been in all my life, and before I really knew what was happening we were having sex. I felt completely ashamed afterward, like I'd given away a part of myself with no meaning at all. I didn't tell anyone about what had happened."

"Saera…" *That's so young… And to feel so alone.*

Saera shook her head, tears forming in her eyes. "But, part of me felt like I deserved that kind of violation—after the mess I'd caused in my own family."

"None of that was your fault. Your father—"

"I know that now." Saera sniffed back tears. "But I didn't see it that way then. So, every time my brother's friend came over and wandered into my bedroom, I gave in. As I got older, others began looking at me in that same way. I came to think of it as a way to get acceptance where I'd never been able to find any before—I was pretty, I knew it, and I used it to get the wrong kind of attention. And, of course, once you freely give away something enough, others will start to take it through coercion or force.

"I lost all respect for myself, if I'd ever had any. Over the next four years, only one guy ever looked at me as a real person. I think he had admired me from a distance for some time, but to me he was just a pity-fuck. I realize in retrospect that I was a miserable, bitter person who felt unworthy of anything good in my life."

Wil looked down, unsure what to say. *I can't believe that's the same person who's sitting here with me. Is that what happens when someone is pushed to the limits of their endurance? Will I one day break, too?*

"When I got the invitation from the TSS, I at last saw an opportunity to start over. I threw myself into studying, and I swore off men." She swallowed. "But then you came along. Now…"

*She's expecting rejection, I can see it in her eyes. But what we have together...* Wil felt completely heartbroken for Saera, that she'd been to such a dark place she'd given up hope. But Wil thought of himself—how he'd spent the last year so preoccupied with his future facing the Bakzen that he'd tried to shut out everyone who cared. *If things were a little different, I'd be in that dark place, too.*

As much as he resented how his own life had been planned out for him, he never doubted the love from his parents or the support from his extended TSS family. *I can't imagine feeling like I had to give myself away just to gain others' affection.*

Wil looked Saera straight in her eyes and gently touched the side of her face. *For very different reasons, we need each other. Nothing in our pasts could change what we can have in a future together.* "You can leave all that behind."

"Still, I need to live with that past for the rest of my life. I'm disgusted with myself." Saera looked away, her eyes glistening. "You're probably repulsed by me now, too."

"No." *It's not something I expected, but we all have regrets. If anything, being able to overcome that history makes me respect her even more.* "Your past only has as much hold over you as you let it have. It doesn't change anything for me. I promise you, this really is a fresh start."

Saera's lip trembled. "With you, or here with the TSS?"

"Both."

Saera sniffed back tears. "Please don't give me false hope."

"What?"

Saera jumped to her feet. "It's really late, I should go. I never should have come here."

*Shite.* Wil followed Saera toward the door. "Saera, what's wrong?"

Saera wiped her eyes. "I thought I could, but I can't do this." She took an unsteady breath. "I already care about you way too much. Even if you accept my history, I know who you are, and that you'd never stay with a nobody like me. You'll end up breaking my heart. I may as well just save us both the trouble and leave now."

*I guess it's time for that talk...* "Do you think I've been leading you on?"

"I don't know. Or maybe it's all been in my head."

"No, Saera. I do care about you. There's something between us that's deeper than where we're from or what we've been through."

Saera looked at him, her eyes searching for understanding. "If it's not my past or that I'm from Earth, then why are you still holding back?"

*The truth I don't want to face...* "Because whatever self-loathing you may have experienced, mine for myself runs far deeper. Not for anything I've done in the past, but for what I will do." Wil paused, trying to swallow the lump in his throat. "Saera, I have a duty to do terrible, terrible things. I can't imagine bringing anyone I love into that. I don't want anyone to see what that will do to me." *How it will destroy me until I can't live with myself anymore.*

Saera caught herself, processing. "That's not for you to decide," she said at last, taking Wil's hands. "You need to let others in if they want to be there with you."

Wil's eyes stung. *She doesn't know what it would mean for her. That she'd be left alone to inherit my responsibilities.* "That's what scares me the most—knowing that others would give up the pure part of themselves just to stand by me. To be tainted by all those awful things I must do. It feels selfish to accept such a gift."

"Well, I'm far from pure." Saera slid her hands to Wil's hips and looked him in the eye. "There's a lot of bad out there. Embrace the gifts when they're given."

"And if you can't accept me? Once you know who I really am." *That I'm really a weapon waiting to be unleashed.*

"I'll find a way."

Wil shook his head. "It's not that easy. I— I never thought I'd find someone who could look at me the way you do. I couldn't take it to see you ever look at me any differently, but I know that that day would come eventually. Yet, at the same time, I've seen a glimpse of what it could be like to be with you. Now I don't know if I can face a future alone."

In one motion, Saera rose up and locked her lips on his, drawing him toward her. Without thinking, he kissed her back, relishing the taste and feeling of her soft lips. It was tender, but there was an electrifying spark with the contact. They drew closer to each other, feeling a surge of energy release—fully activating the resonance connection that had been kept at bay since their first meeting. For that moment, Wil felt completely at peace. He had found a part of himself he hadn't even known he was missing, and he never wanted to return to the way things were before.

Breathless, Saera pulled back. "What was that?"

"Confirmation of everything we haven't wanted to admit."

Saera bit her lip. "How would this even work? You're graduating soon, and—"

Wil looked into her eyes and cupped her face in his hand. "It won't be easy, Saera, but I can't ignore what we have." *We each carry burdens, but perhaps we can bear them more easily together.*

She nodded. "Me either."

"I need you to think about this. Once we go down this path, there's no turning back."

She held him close. "I've wanted this since the day we met. I just didn't realize how much until now."

Wil touched her mind as they embraced—feeling her thoughts and intentions. *She really means it.* "There's still so much you don't know about me."

Saera looked up at him. "The way you look at me, that's all I need to know."

*Will I be able to look at her that way after I've annihilated an entire race?* "Just think on it. Let it settle. I wish we could just date like normal people, but being with me at all is a life-long deal."

Saera smiled and was about to reply, but she was stopped by the seriousness in Wil's gaze. "I'll think about it."

"Okay. Now, you should probably get back. I've kept you out far later than I intended."

Saera took a step toward the door. "When will I see you again? The midterm secondary exams are in three days when we would normally have freefall training."

*Shite, the exams! I never should have invited her here tonight.* "Saera, do you want to pursue the Command track?"

She thought for a moment. "Yes."

"Then I can't talk to you until after the exams."

"Why?"

He looked at the clock: it was already 23:07. *Stars, this is cutting it so close. I need to check the details.* "I can make sure you get a good recommendation, but you need to go right now." He gave her a quick kiss.

Saera held his hand for a moment longer before opening the door. "I won't let you down." She slipped into the hallway and Wil closed the door behind her.

Wil felt an emptiness as soon as she was gone. *I don't know what I'll do if she changes her mind…* Regardless, there were more immediate concerns. He sat back down on the couch. "CACI, bring up the TSS rulebook."

# CHAPTER 14

SAERA OBSERVED THE alien world around her. At first glance, the surrounding landscape could have passed for the Sierra Nevada mountains in California back on Earth, but there were subtle differences in the plants and the small animals running through the tall grass. She caught a glimpse of a creature that resembled a rabbit, but the wispy shape of the ears was unlike anything she'd ever seen.

The TSS contingent was gathered in an expansive clearing at the base of a tree-covered hill. Transport shuttles were lined up on the far side of the meadow, and the hundred Trainees were facing the tree line, organized by training group. Just over a hundred Junior Agents faced the Trainees. There was only a single Agent present, whom Saera recognized as Agent Wincowski from the orientation six months earlier. She searched the faces of the Junior Agents, and while some looked familiar, none were the one she wanted to see.

While her roommates had spent the last three days studying for the written portion of the secondary exams that had concluded the previous afternoon, Saera had found her mind mostly wandering to thoughts of Wil. The more times she replayed their last night together in her mind, the more convinced she became that she would do anything for him.

*Hopefully, all the earlier tutoring with Wil paid off and I didn't fail the exams.* Her heart skipped a beat thinking about him. *Gah! Get control of yourself.*

"Attention!"

The shout was as much in her mind as it was heard by her ears. She wasn't used to feeling the unrestricted use of telekinesis and telepathy allowed outside Headquarters.

The Trainees all straightened and clasped their hands behind their backs.

"We will begin shortly," Agent Wincowski announced. He looked around at the Junior Agents then checked his handheld. "At ease." He kept glancing in the direction of the shuttles.

Some of the Junior Agents looked annoyed. It was approaching mid-morning, and the sun was warming up the field. Everyone was dressed in long-sleeves and pants, and some began to shift in the heat. They had all been given a backpack when they filed onto the transport shuttles, and many Trainees began rummaging for water bottles.

*What are we waiting for?*

Several minutes passed, and Wincowski left his post by the stack of handhelds on a maglev cart to talk with a Junior Agent. Saera couldn't hear what he said, but she saw the Junior Agent shrug in response. Wincowski sighed and returned to his previous position. He again looked toward the line of shuttles. Eventually, he straightened and again called everyone to attention.

Saera glanced over her shoulder to see what the Agent had been waiting for, and she was surprised to see Wil making his way across the field. *Why is he here so late?*

Everyone stayed at attention until Wil fell into line with the other Junior Agents.

"Thank you for joining us," Wincowski said to Wil as he passed, just loud enough for the Trainees to know it was a reprimand.

"Sorry," Wil muttered.

*That isn't like him.* Saera tried to catch his eye, but he avoided her gaze.

"As promised," Wincowski went on, "this is the field portion of your midterm examinations, which will determine your training track within the TSS. The top-scoring Trainee will also get to attend our annual party in three days, in case you needed any more incentive." He smiled. "You'll be paired up with a Junior Agent, who will perform a one-on-one evaluation of your capabilities and submit a recommendation. Use any resources at your disposal. Your packs contain supplies for two days, but the exam is designed to be completed before nightfall. You may ask any questions you like, but your tester is not allowed to give any direct answers.

"The entire evaluation will be recorded, but you may request to speak to your tester 'off the record' for up to five minutes during the evaluation, but may do so no more than four times. Even during those times, the tester is not allowed to divulge any privileged information about the exam. A committee of Agents will review the recording, the written recommendation, an assessment from your Agent trainer, and your class grades to make a final decision about your placement."

Wincowski glanced at the Junior Agents. "Each Junior Agent has had time to review the Trainee files and select an individual to score. The selection will be made in the order of Junior Agent standing. When your name has been called by your assigned Junior Agent, take your backpack and meet them by the tree line." He paused while the Junior Agents gathered their own backpacks. "As the top-ranked Junior Agent, you're up first, Sights."

Saera's heart fluttered as Wil stepped forward from the line of Junior Agents.

"Given that standing, it's only fitting that I take the Trainee with the highest score on the written evaluation," Wil stated. "For that reason, I selected Saera Alexander."

*I scored the highest?* Though caught off-guard, she was relieved that Wil had picked her. She grabbed her backpack and jogged forward. As she made her way toward Wil, she sensed everyone's eyes on her. *Do they know about us?* Some of her tension released as Junior Agents began calling out other Trainees by name, but she still felt exposed.

Wil was waiting casually as Saera approached him. "Shall we begin?" he asked her.

"I'm ready."

Two Junior Agents were standing behind Wincowski next to the cart with the handhelds. One of them picked up a handheld from the stack and made an entry before handing it to Wil. "Good luck."

Wil took the handheld and led Saera up the hill into the trees. He made a few entries of his own on the handheld before handing it to Saera. "This will record the evaluation," Wil explained. "A set of coordinates has been loaded onto the map. There is no direct path to the destination, and it is up to you to determine how to best meet the objective. Each scenario has its trade-offs. There is no one 'right' answer—do what you feel is most appropriate. Are the guidelines of the examination understood?"

Saera nodded.

"Verbal confirmation, please."

"Yes, understood," Saera stated.

"The assessment is now underway. Please proceed." He passed the handheld to Saera.

She took the device from him, feeling awkward with the formal interaction. *Remember, this is a test. He's evaluating you.*

Saera took a moment to clear her mind, then brought up the holographic projection of the map on the handheld to survey their surroundings. The marked destination was on the other side of the hill, approximately eleven kilometers away. It was on the other side of a river, and several areas were marked in red on the map. A key indicated that the red denoted a hostile territory, and there were several red stars in the nearby neutral territories. There appeared to be no route to the destination that would avoid all the hostile territories, and the river would need to be crossed. "What are those red stars?"

"Weapons caches."

Saera frowned. "Is that really necessary?"

"That's up to you," Wil replied.

"I guess I could check it out." Saera oriented herself on the map and set out toward the nearest red star. It was only half a kilometer away, so it seemed like a worthwhile detour.

Their path took them up the hill and then off to the side down a shallow ravine. Saera kept her eye on the map as they progressed, making sure they were on course. Along the back wall of the ravine she spotted an arrangement of rock slabs that didn't appear natural; its location aligned with the red star indicated on the handheld.

"That must be it," she said, stepping over to the rocks.

On the far side of the formation, a slit was left open to allow access into a cave. Saera activated a light on the handheld and flashed it inside. Nothing was visible beyond the smooth gray stone. Cautiously, she stepped inside with Wil following a pace behind.

The walls curved to the side, directing her into an alcove. A sliver of light shone through a crack in the surrounding rock slabs, illuminating a two-meter-tall rack filled with an assortment of weapons.

Saera inspected the rack more closely using the light on her handheld. "I don't even know what some of these do." The pulse rifles and handheld blasters were familiar from her intro tactical classes, but some black spheres on the bottom rack were a complete mystery.

"I'm afraid I can't offer any insight due to the test rules," Wil said from behind her.

"I guess I'll stick to what I know." Saera picked up one of the blasters from a middle shelf. It was heavier than she remembered from class.

She aimed it toward the empty wall, testing the feel. She pictured lining up the enemy in the scope, pulling the trigger—

*No, there has to be another way. I don't want a firefight.* She set the blaster back on the rack. "Never mind. Let's go."

Wil looked surprised, but he held out his hand to gesture for her to lead the way.

Once back outside, Saera brought up the map again. *There needs to be a way through without violence.* She stared at the map, confounded. They had to make it through the hostile territory one way or another. *Wait, what if...* "Are all of the 'hostile territory' indicators referring to the same enemy group?" she asked.

The corners of Wil's mouth twitched toward a smile. "No."

*Oh, so there is a trick!* "Do I have access to intelligence on which territories belong to which group?"

"Yes, that information can be provided." Wil took the handheld from Saera and made some adjustments. The red territories broke into three different color groups: blue, green and yellow. Saera saw an open path with no hostile territory that would take them as far as the river, but they would need to cross through at least one hostile territory once they got to the other side.

"Are the territory lines firm, or is there a neutral zone along the borders?"

"The borders are firm on land."

Saera studied the map. "And in the river?"

"Water is neutral."

There was still no way to get to the destination coordinates using a strictly water route. "Is there a precedent for a diplomatic arrangement with any of the hostile groups?"

"The Green territory has previously granted passage through their territory."

The Green territory wouldn't provide the most direct route to the destination, but in conjunction with travel across the river, it was feasible. "What is the location of an appropriate representative for the Green group? I would like to request permission to pass through their territory."

Wil appeared to be holding back a smile. “Because this is only a simulation, a console has been set up for that purpose at this location.” He illuminated a point on the map.

Saera beamed. “Then that’s where we’ll go.” She oriented the map to the landscape around her and took off up the hill. Wil followed her.

After walking for some time, Saera stopped. “May I speak to you off the record?”

“Yes.” Wil took the handheld and paused the recording, which simultaneously started a five-minute countdown clock.

“So, this exam is why you had me leave so abruptly,” Saera said.

Wil relaxed, taking a step closer to her. “I’m sorry to have pushed you out like that. This was the only way I could guarantee you placement in the Command track. Your scores are high enough that it would all come down to this field exam. I was worried that the other Junior Agents wouldn’t take you as a serious candidate.”

“But why the late arrival today?”

“We will both need to sign affidavits at the end of this examination stating that there was no unprofessional conduct during the testing period. Let’s just say I found some loopholes with the timing so that the other night wouldn’t void my recommendation. I know it was awkward, but I needed to make sure it had been 75 hours since we last talked.”

Saera wanted to hug him, but she held back. “You did that for me?”

“I’d do a lot more than that, but, you know… Rules.” He gave her a playful grin.

“I don’t want you making any recommendation that you don’t support. If I make it into the Command track, I want it to be because I earned it.”

“I would never have it any other way.”

Saera looked at the countdown on the recorder. “Well, there’s no reason to max out the time here. We may as well get this over with. You can resume the recording.”

Wil took the handheld and un-paused the recorder. “Recording resumed. Three off-the-record conversations remain.” He handed it back to Saera.

She checked her course on the map. “This way.”

— — —

Wil followed Saera across the forested terrain. Regardless of his feelings for her, her performance was impressive. By identifying a diplomatic workaround, Saera’s approach would save them a long walk around the perimeter of the ‘hostile territory’. Others would surely just take up arms at a weapons cache and fight their way through. *I’ve never seen someone pick the right questions to ask so early on. She’s the kind of person I need by my side.*

Saera’s navigation was accurate, and they were making excellent time over the hills. According to the map, they were in the final descent toward the river. In the distance, Wil could hear rushing water. Eventually, the trees opened up to reveal a shallow canyon with a river ten meters wide at the basin.

Saera stared at it with dismay. The river was too deep to wade across and far too wide to jump. There were no natural forms to function as a make-shift bridge. “We should be directly across from the Green territory, close to the communication console.” She looked at the water and then back at Wil. “We were instructed to use any resources at our disposal. Are you, as the tester, considered a resource?”

*Where is she going with that?* “Yes. I am considered a member of your team.”

“Then please create a bridge over the river.” She smiled at him.

*That’s an odd request.* “I can’t build you a bridge.”

“I didn’t ask you to *build* a bridge. I asked you to create one. Can’t you use your abilities to freeze the water or something?”

*Brilliant! No one has ever asked their tester to do that before. I suppose it's not against the rules…* "Yes, I can do that."

"Please proceed." Saera stood aside and made a grand gesture toward the water.

*She can bend the rules almost as well as me.* Wil walked up to the edge of the water and sent out a small telekinetic stream toward the river. The water crystallized where he focused. "Have you ever been around unrestricted telekinesis before?"

"No more than in practice sessions."

*That was good wording on her part—no hint that it was practice sessions with me.* "This is an open place, but you may still feel some pressure." Wil focused on the water and envisioned a bridge arching just above the water's surface over to the other bank. He pictured the beginnings of the bridge—a white glowing band of water, a meter across, spanning the width of the river. He commanded the glowing water to rise into the air, letting the river flow on beneath it. With the framework for the bridge set, he redirected the thermal energy from the water, freezing it in place.

Saera staggered back as the energy released, and she brought a hand up to her head.

"Are you okay?" Wil asked, keeping his attention on maintaining the ice bridge.

She lowered her hand. "Show off," she said with a smirk.

"This was nothing." *She'd never be standing this close to me if she knew what I could really do.*

Saera tested the bridge with her foot. "Is it safe to cross?"

"As long as I maintain the hold."

"Then let's get going." She took a deep breath and stepped onto the ice bridge. It was slick, but she found her footing.

Wil followed behind, ready to catch Saera if she slipped. The bridge looked fragile under foot, but the bonds holding it together wouldn't break until Wil released them. Water manipulation was one of the first skills Initiates would practice, and it came effortlessly to him.

Saera sighed with relief when she stepped onto solid ground on the far bank of the river.

Wil jumped off the bridge behind her. As soon as he was on the ground, he released the bridge and the ice liquefied, splashing back into the flow of the river.

Saera shook her head with wonder. "Well, that was fun! Now let's find that console." She consulted the map and led the way into a stand of trees.

They wove their way through the maze of trunks. It was difficult to follow a straight path, but Saera deftly compensated for every detour. It was a peaceful walk, quiet and still aside from dried leaves crunching underfoot.

Saera paused at the opening to a small clearing. "There's the console." In the center of the clearing, a black four-sided column was planted in the ground. The edge of a computer terminal was visible around the corner on the right side. "Wait here," she instructed, extending the handheld toward Wil.

He grabbed it from her. *She's taking this very seriously.*

Saera set down her backpack and slowly stepped into the clearing, holding her hands away from her body so they were visible. "I am here to request passage through your territory," she said to the terminal. The terminal didn't respond. "My intentions are peaceful." Nothing. "May my companion and I continue on our journey?" She stared at the terminal, then glanced at Wil. "Is this thing even active?"

*You just have to touch it. But this is far more entertaining.* He kept his amusement to himself. "The terminal appears to be functioning properly."

Saera studied the terminal for another moment, and then placed her hand on a glossy rectangle at chest-level.

"Authorization granted," the terminal announced, and a memory chip popped out from a thin slit.

The color on Saera's cheeks was visible even from a distance. "Oh." She took the chip.

Wil gave her a reassuring smile. *Better to overdo it than the other way around.*

Saera jogged back to Wil and retrieved the handheld from him. She placed the memory chip in the handheld's expansion slot. The Green territory on the map turned beige.

"Free travel is now allowed through this territory," Wil informed her.

Saera smiled. "Let's do this."

The rest of the hike passed quickly. The terrain was flatter on that side of the river, and the trees were less dense the further they went. They walked in silence, hearing only the occasional bird. By the time the sun was approaching the horizon, they were nearly at the coordinates for their destination.

"It should be right up ahead," Saera announced.

*We should see something by now.* "May I take a look at the map?" Wil asked.

Saera handed it to him. Sure enough, the coordinates were no more than ten meters ahead. "Hmm."

"What is it?" She looked concerned. "Did I do something wrong?"

"No, not at all." *Maybe they put the camp underground this time so it couldn't be spotted from a distance.* "Proceed."

Saera led the way to the exact position of the coordinates. "We're here."

Wil confirmed on the map. "So we are." He looked around. *Where is everyone?*

"What are you looking for?"

There definitely was nothing here. Wil couldn't sense the presence of anyone. "Anything. The end point should have someone to receive us, or at least a beacon to activate."

The alarm was apparent on Saera's face. "I led us to the wrong place? But the map…"

"No, it wasn't you. Were the coordinates wrong?" *They wouldn't…*

"Can you find out?"

Wil logged into the handheld and went through several layers of authorization code. It did look like something was overwritten. He dug deeper into the system memory and found a data archive from immediately before the examination commenced. "I can't believe it."

"What?"

Wil shook his head. *That bastard.* "Trintar, that Junior Agent distributing the handhelds, changed the coordinates when he handed it to me."

Saera looked ill. "What does that mean for the exam, exactly?"

"*You* did everything correctly. As far as I'm concerned, you have completed the assignment. You navigated to the coordinates given to you." *And I won't let someone's issues with me screw up this evaluation.*

"Why would he do that?" Wil looked at the recorder. "Off the record," Saera added.

Wil paused the recording. *Did I have this coming?* "That day I came into your study room, and you asked me if I was hiding from someone? Well, I had just presented my design for the independent jump drive. Trintar was the head of the reigning champion team. Unfortunately, that was just the start of a string of failures for him, and it would seem that he has come to resent me. It's stupid for him to take out his frustration in this way, but here we are."

Saera bit her lower lip and took a breath. "Where does that leave us exactly?"

"Resuming recording." Wil un-paused the recording and showed Saera the map. "Two off-the-record conversations remain. Here are the real coordinates." The destination was seven kilometers to the west, on the other side of a jagged hill. "Let the record show that from this point forward we are outside the guidelines of the examination," Wil stated. "But, since the exam hasn't officially concluded, you're still in charge. How shall we proceed?"

Saera looked lost for a moment but gathered herself. "We are outside of hostile territory, so we should stay here. It's about to get dark, and I'd rather stay here where we know it's safe than try to negotiate those cliffs at night."

"Recommendation confirmed." *This will make for an interesting report.*

"Will they come looking for us?"

"I honestly don't know." *An extraction might void the test, but it's a risk to leave us planetside overnight. Especially given how protective they are of me. But how far will they go?*

"Well, let's just proceed like we'll be here for the night. Do you know how cold it gets here?" Saera looked up at the clear sky.

"Not below freezing. We'll be fine outside with a fire." *Spending the night outside—this will be a first.*

Saera took a breath. "Okay. I saw a clearing with some rocks back the way we came. I think it would make a good campsite."

"Lead the way." *Keep it together, this is still a test. It's just one night… under the stars next to a campfire, left with no choice but to huddle together for warmth…* Wil swallowed.

The campsite Saera had identified was serviceable, with a cluster of boulders to provide shelter and a clear area to safely build a fire. They gathered firewood, and Wil started a blaze as dusk set in. Knowing that the recorder was still running, they engaged in idle small-talk while eating some rations from their backpacks for dinner. The evening wore on, and the temperature dropped under the clear sky. They retrieved some emergency blankets from their backpacks.

Wil compulsively checked the temperature on his personal handheld, but it remained above five degrees. *Just a little colder and we don't need to stay apart like this.*

"So, you said Agent Katz was your mom's roommate when they first joined the TSS?" Saera asked, changing the subject from the tedious discussion of Saera's introductory class on Taran politics.

Wil grinned. "Oh, yeah, they go way back. And Wincowski and my father were roommates, too."

"Really? I guess that makes sense. I got the impression they were buddies."

"They are. They've been through a lot together."

She looked at him thoughtfully. "The other TSS Agents are probably like family to you."

Wil nodded. "They really are. I've never had a life outside the TSS. Though I've met some of my extended family, I don't *know* them. As strange as it is, Headquarters will always be 'home' to me, no matter where I end up living. The halls, the freefall chambers—those were my neighborhood, my playground. Being here on a planet with real gravity, fresh air… it feels strange to me."

"And those are things I just take for granted." Saera stared into the fire. "I can't imagine what it must have been like growing up the way you did. Did you ever have a chance to just be a kid?"

*I barely even know what that means.* "I was trained in combat techniques since I was old enough to walk. My bedtime reading was on military strategy. I officially entered the TSS when I was twelve, and by that time I'd already completed my first dissertation on applied astrophysics. It's only recently that I've slowed down enough to recognize everything that I missed along the way."

"Do you ever regret not taking time for yourself?"

"How could I? Regret is for when you had an alternate choice. For me, things couldn't have been any different." Wil checked his handheld again. *Finally!* "It has dropped below five degrees. You can join me over here to stay warm, if you like." Wil patted the ground next to him.

Saera hesitated, but then crawled over. "It is getting pretty chilly." She sat down immediately next to Wil, and they adjusted their blankets. After a moment, Wil brought his arm around her shoulders, and Saera leaned her head on his chest. "That's much better."

Her warmth was comforting and she fit perfectly in his arms. Wil wanted nothing more than to stroke her hair and hold her close, but he resisted. *This is still a test. Just a few more days and you won't need to hold back anymore.*

"You can still make your own future," Saera said.

"Some of it, perhaps." *Maybe, just enough.*

They sat quietly together, enjoying the time away from the demands and stress of everyday life. *This was perhaps the best gift Trintar could have given me,* Wil thought in retrospect. He checked the time on his handheld. "It's 22:00 now. We should probably get to sleep."

Saera looked up at him with questioning eyes.

"We should stay close. It will only get colder as the night goes on."

Saera smiled at the affirmative answer to her unspoken question, and stretched out on the ground between Wil and the fire.

Wil kept his back to the rock he had been leaning against and lay down next to Saera with her back pressed against him. His body wanted to respond to her every movement as she struggled to get comfortable on the lumpy ground, but he confined the reactions to his mind. *If only every night could be like this.* Basking in the warmth of the fire and the soft light of the stars, he drifted off to untroubled sleep.

—

Wil blinked in the morning light. The fire was only smoldering ashes. Saera was still asleep under his arm. *It's morning already?*

Saera stirred. She rolled to her back and blinked up at him. "Hi. How did you sleep?"

"Really well, actually." It was the first night he hadn't had nightmares since his time with the Bakzen. "But now I'm hungry."

Saera sat up and smoothed her hair. "Let's eat and then we can head out," she suggested.

They ate some more of the bland rations and then broke camp.

The trek to the proper coordinates took them over more difficult terrain than they had encountered before, but there was no hostile territory to block their path. They helped each other over the more difficult rock formations and descended into rolling hills with young trees.

This time, there was no mistaking the camp. It was in a clearing up ahead, and only a single shuttle remained. *They're waiting for us.*

"We made it," Saera breathed.

"We did." Wil smiled. "You performed admirably under difficult circumstances. I will make sure that my report reflects your decisiveness and professionalism."

Saera stopped. "Before we go, may I speak to you off the record?"

"Yes." Wil paused the recorder.

Saera looked him in the eye. "Thank you."

— — —

Wil walked into Scott Wincowski's office. Wil had already submitted his report electronically, but the Agent had requested to meet with him in person.

"Thank you for coming," Scott greeted. "I'm still annoyed about your late arrival to the test, but under the circumstances I've decided to let it go, whatever it was about." He folded his hands on the desktop. "I asked you here so I could personally apologize for the mix-up with the coordinates. We almost sent a shuttle to come get you, but we didn't want to invalidate the exam. In the end, we decided there was no reason to pull you out. After all, we use that planet for testing because it is so safe. "

*Is it possible this was intentional, just to let me spend time with her?* "Thank you for giving me the opportunity to conclude my evaluation, sir."

"And what is your recommendation?" Scott looked expectant.

"Primus Command track, sir."

The Agent raised an eyebrow. "Primus Command?"

"Yes, sir. The basis for my recommendation is included in the report. She exceeded all of the metrics."

"I see. The committee will take it under advisement."

"Thank you, sir."

Scott pulled out a tablet. "Here is the affidavit that the evaluation was unbiased and followed TSS protocol. Do you have anything to disclose?"

"No, sir. The evaluation followed all TSS regulations." *I made sure of it.*

# CHAPTER 15

THE PRIMUS LOUNGE was packed. All of the Junior Agents had gathered to get the first glimpse at the track assignments for the Trainees, and everyone was anxious to see if their recommendation had held. Eyes were fixed on the massive viewscreen at the back of the room.

Wil was the most anxious of all. *Saera earned placement in Command. And I need her—not just as a partner, but as an officer I can trust.* He checked the time on his handheld. *Any moment now…*

The viewscreen changed from the TSS logo into a list of a hundred names. Wil had to dart around one of the taller Junior Agents to get a better look at the screen. A smile spread across his face when he saw the name at the top of the list: 'Saera Alexander: Primus Command'. She was one of only six Trainees in her cohort to have placed on the Command track. *She did it.*

Other Junior Agents around the room had mixed reactions, ranging from a nod of satisfaction to a disappointed shrug. The crowd thinned as everyone looked over the results.

Wil hung back in the room with the intent of reviewing some engineering diagrams. Just as he was getting settled with his tablet on the couch in his favorite corner nook, a message from his father popped up on the screen. >>Meet me in Banks' office.<<

Wil sighed. *What now?*

He reluctantly rose from the couch and tucked the tablet under his arm, then made his way through the halls to the High Commander's office.

Wil knew something was off the moment he walked into the office. Cris looked uncharacteristically tense, and Banks was standing completely rigid with his hands behind his back. Wil stopped in the middle of the room and looked at the two officers.

"Thank you for coming, Wil," Banks said.

"Of course, sir."

"There are a few matters we'd like to discuss with you," Banks went on. "Why don't we have a seat?" He gestured to the chairs by his desk, and Wil and Cris sat down across from him. "First, I'd like to congratulate you on the success of your training efforts with Saera. It would seem you were able to tap into every bit of her potential."

"She put in the work, I did very little."

"Knowing how to guide is still an important skill," Banks countered. "At any rate, she was at the top of her class. As you know, that's earned her entry into the annual party tonight."

"Yes, she'll have a good time." *I wasn't planning on going, but since she'll be there, I suppose I could make an appearance…*

"Well, we thought that you might like to go with her as an escort," Cris added.

*What are they doing?* "Isn't that a little… unusual?"

"Maybe so," Banks responded, "but you helped her in the accomplishment. This way you can celebrate together."

"That would be nice, thank you." *They're still so serious. Why?* "Is there something else?"

Cris looked down and slumped forward in his chair.

Banks took a deep breath. "Wil, you've become eligible for graduation."

*No, not yet…* "Sir?" Wil took a calming breath, but he felt panic setting in. *Will they send me away to H2? Is this night at the party just consolation?*

Banks cleared his throat. "However, there is one mandatory part of your Junior Agent training that you have yet to complete. The internship."

*Stars, no!* "Sir…"

"The planet that's been selected is Orino. Most of the world is covered in an ocean and there are several groups in civil war. We were approached by a neutral community requesting TSS assistance for settling the conflict. The specifics have been uploaded to your Mainframe account."

Wil activated his tablet and looked over the details of the assignment. The file included information about the culture and customs of the world, and he felt more nauseated the further he read. They were a primitive people, living on the sea in floating colonies, only very rarely setting foot on land. Men were the providers and their women and daughters were little more than property. Raping and pillaging was commonplace, and any commander had the pick of the community's women—and was expected to, if he were a man worthy of leading.

*Fok, what are they thinking?* Wil was horrified. "I can't go here. These customs, they go against everything—"

Banks stood up. "That is for you to figure out. This is a matter of strategy and diplomacy, and it is your task to find a solution."

*I can't…* He looked to his father, pleading. "Dad?"

*"This was decided without me,"* Cris responded telepathically. *"Just remember, there's always another way."*

"You leave first thing in the morning," Banks announced.

*Tomorrow?!* "But we're supposed to get two months to prepare!"

Banks was unruffled. "The nature of this planet's need is urgent, and it was too perfect a fit for your skill set to pass up. If all goes well, you may be back in time to graduate in the ceremony with the other Junior Agents who are already away on their internships."

Wil worked his mouth but didn't know what to say. *Stars! How do I begin to explain this to Saera? Months, or even a year, apart?*

Cris gazed at Wil with compassion and sympathy, but underneath was the unwavering support that Wil could always count on from his father. *"It'll be okay, Wil."*

Wil's mind raced. "What about Caeron?"

Banks exchanged glances with Cris. "He cannot accompany you on the internship," Banks replied. "As we agreed, he would stay with you until you graduated, which will happen as soon as you return. We may as well send him back to Tararia now."

"So, that's it, then? I just leave here for a distant planet and I'm all on my own?"

"Not on your own, Wil," Cris said. "We'll always be here to back you up."

"Agents will be standing by at a TSS ship in orbit to extract you if there are any issues," Banks added.

"And what about the fact that I'm eight years younger than the average Junior Agent going on their internship?" *They must really want to test me, to move up the timeline like this.*

"You've been overcoming others' preconceptions about age and ability your whole life," Banks said. "You should go get ready for the party." He stood up, signaling the end of the conversation.

*This is really happening…* Wil rose slowly.

Cris got to his feet and placed an encouraging hand on Wil's shoulder. "We'll be at the party tonight and then see you off in the morning."

Wil nodded and left for his quarters. *I can't believe this time has come. It was always sometime in the future, years away. What if I fail?*

— — —

The dress was beautiful, but it hardly seemed worth all the dirty looks from Saera's roommates. As if being the top-ranked Trainee wasn't enough, there was also the party. *And Wil as my escort?* It was all too much for her to take in.

Elise, as usual, was the only other Primus girl to seem happy for Saera's accomplishment. But, Saera could still see her envy beneath the outer mask. "You look lovely," Elise said as Saera looked herself over in front of the mirror.

"Thanks." Reaching almost to the floor, the dress was a dark blue and had silver embroidery that cascaded down the side. It reminded Saera of a shooting star. The dress had been made to her measurements, like all other TSS clothing, and it hugged her figure. After so long in casual attire, it felt strange to be in a dress and heels again.

She ran a finger through her long, auburn hair that fell in loose waves past her shoulders. *I need to do something with this.*

Saera rummaged through her locker and found some pins and clips she'd brought with her from Earth. She began twisting sections of her hair into an up-do, struggling to keep track of the different sections.

"Do you want some help?" asked Elise.

"Yes, please! Thank you," Saera sighed with relief. She handed off a section of hair to Elise as she secured another.

"Are you nervous?" Elise questioned. "I couldn't deal with being in a crowd surrounded by so many unfamiliar faces. Let alone a bunch of Agents!"

*I guess I hadn't really thought about it.* "Maybe a little. I'll manage." *I'll have Wil.*

"The Junior Agent who evaluated you is taking you to the party, right?"

*How did she even know that?* "Yes, I believe so."

"Wasn't that Wil Sights?" Elise's reflection looked expectantly at Saera from the mirror.

"Yes, it was. He's actually pretty easy to talk to once you get to know him."

Elise was thoughtful for a moment, and then her face lit up with understanding. "Wait, is he…?"

Saera's heart dropped. *Someone was bound to find out eventually.* "Please, don't say anything."

Elise shook her head with wonder. "I won't." She chuckled. "Stars! That's who it was all this time."

"It just sort of happened. I never thought…" *...that I could care so much for someone, in so little time. Even a few hours apart is too long.*

"This will be a night to remember, I'm sure," Elise said.

Saera secured the last few strands of hair. She admired herself in the mirror. "There."

— — —

Wil was still reeling from his conversation with Banks. *Leaving in the morning?*

His TSS dress uniform felt far too formal for his mood. He wanted to curl up in bed and forget all of his responsibilities. The only thing that got him through dressing for the party was knowing that he'd see Saera, but even then, he felt sick from the news he needed to give her.

The hallways of the Trainee wing were empty, with everyone confined to their quarters for the evening while nearly every Agent, Junior Agent, and senior Militia officer attended the party on Level 11. Wil arrived at Saera's quarters and pressed the buzzer. After a moment, the door opened.

Wil's breath caught when Saera stepped into view. She stood framed in the doorway, her hair arranged in pretty twists and braids, wearing a dark blue gown with a wide V-neck and thin straps that exposed far more skin than he was used to seeing. At first, he was simply taken in by seeing her for the first time in makeup and with her hair styled, but as his eyes moved downward, he felt a sense of awe. After having grown so accustomed to seeing her in standard Trainee clothes, he hadn't even thought about what alternate attire might do for her.

"You're absolutely stunning," Wil said just loud enough for only Saera to hear.

She smiled and blushed. "You clean up pretty well, yourself."

"Have fun!" someone called from inside the common room.

Saera hastily closed the door.

"Shall we?" asked Wil as he presented his elbow to her. Saera took his arm and they strode down the hall.

Saera smiled up at him. "You accompanying me came as a pleasant surprise."

"Me too." *A last-minute kindness before I'm thrown out on my own, away from you for who knows how long.*

"I never would have made it this far without you. You've been a true friend."

Wil smiled back at her. "I feel the same way."

They arrived at the central lobby, where several Agents and Junior Agents dressed in formal clothes were waiting for the elevator. The Agents gave nods of respect to Wil and Saera—after the release of the Trainee scores, everyone could recognize Saera as easily as they could Wil.

Wil and Saera were silent as they rode down the elevator to Level 11 with the others. It gave Wil's mind a chance to wander, and he was soon fighting back anxiety about what he would face for his internship.

*What will they ask me to do on Orino? What if they won't accept me?* His pulse quickened, a dull buzz filling his head. *I'll be there on my own, away from everyone I care about.* A vise clamped around his chest. *Will Saera be here when I return? Will she still want me?* His head swam, pulsing with every heartbeat as the buzzing magnified.

Wil closed his eyes, clenching his fists. *Get a grip.*

As soon as they were off the elevator, Wil took a few rapid breaths and tried to center himself. He was starting to feel a little better when he felt a tug on his arm. Saera pulled him aside as the others passed by.

"Are you okay?" Saera asked in a low voice. She seemed to see right through him.

*No…* Wil managed a smile that he hoped didn't seem too forced. "Don't worry yourself. We have a party to attend."

Saera didn't seem entirely assuaged, but she let Wil lead the way.

The largest training room had been converted into a ballroom for the evening. For decoration, blue and silver streamers spanned the walls, a holographic projector gave the illusion of a starscape on the ceiling, and dazzling lights had been erected around the perimeter of the room. Along one wall was an extensive buffet with fine foods and drinks. Several dozen tall tables were placed around the room for placing food and drinks while socializing. An impressive sound system had also been set up, where the bass could be felt without the volume being oppressive. The party was already well underway, and people were moving to techno dance music.

Saera gawked. "This is… elaborate."

Wil grinned. "Yeah, they go all out."

"I can't believe this is actually part of the TSS budget."

"Wherever the funds come from, it's been an annual event for as long as I can remember." They'd never admitted it, but Wil was pretty sure his parents sponsored much of it.

They wandered over to the buffet and each grabbed a plate of finger food.

Saera eyed the drinks. "Are those alcoholic?"

"Some of them. I've heard stories of some epic hangovers after the party. A lot of people around here never drink alcohol, though."

Saera made a quizzical expression. "Why is that?"

Wil shrugged. "I guess there's just a culture that an Agent is never really 'off duty'. Some are more lax about it than others, but stims are a much greater vice for most." *Myself included.* He looked down at his plate. "Let's find somewhere to eat." He headed toward one of the open tables.

As they ate, several people came up to the table and congratulated Saera. Wil was pleased to see that she handled each encounter gracefully, comfortable even talking to multiple Agents. After they were done eating, they grabbed some sparkling juice in fluted glasses and milled through the crowd.

"Do you know everyone here?" Saera asked Wil.

Wil thought for a moment. "I know pretty much everyone's face, at least. And having been here my whole life, I probably know more of their names than I even realize."

They had a few more friendly exchanges with some Agents they encountered in their wanderings before Wil noticed his parents approaching.

*This will be interesting.* "Saera, have you ever officially met my parents? Cris and Kate."

Saera came to attention. "Sir, ma'am, it's a pleasure—" Saera began.

"Please, that formality is unnecessary," Kate said with a smile. Her eyes darted to Wil, but she returned her attention to Saera.

"Congratulations on your placement. It's been wonderful to watch your progress over the last several months," Cris commented. "We're very fortunate to have someone of your talents here with us."

Saera looked surprised. "You've been watching me?"

Cris nodded. "As Lead Agent, part of my responsibility is to ensure we're supporting our most promising trainees. You've certainly made a name for yourself. By now, everyone here is aware of your accomplishments. Both of you."

"We're so very proud," Kate murmured as she looked over her son, on the verge of tearing up.

*"Both of us? Do others know I'm leaving on my internship tomorrow?"* Wil telepathically asked his father.

*"Many do, yes."*

*As if I needed any more pressure.* "Great," Wil muttered.

Kate gathered herself. "We haven't had a woman take the position as highest scoring Trainee for a decade," Kate added. "It's a great honor."

"Yes, it is," Cris confirmed.

Saera blushed slightly. "Thank you."

"You certainly earned a night off," Cris went on. "I hope you're having a good time."

"Yes, this is lovely," Saera beamed.

Kate examined Saera. "I'm pleased to see that they gave you something suitable for the occasion. You wear that dress well. Who did your hair?"

Saera absently reached up to touch her hair at the temple. "I did, with a little help from one of my roommates."

Kate smiled. "It looks very nice."

"Thanks. It's a style my mom used to do on me when I was little..." Saera trailed off.

Wil saw her fumble, knowing that her mother was a sore subject. He jumped in, "It's nice to see so many familiar faces at these events. Lots of catching up to do."

*"Hint taken. We'll leave you alone now,"* Cris told Wil. He pretended to spot someone on the other side of the room. "Oh, I wanted to talk to Larsaen," Cris said aloud and took Kate's hand. "Please excuse us."

"Enjoy the rest of your night," Kate said as she and Cris wandered back into the crowd, giving one last glance toward Wil.

Knowing that his imminent graduation was becoming common knowledge, Wil began to feel the other Agents watching him from all sides. Judging, evaluating. He wasn't sure how much of it was in his head, but he grew increasingly more uncomfortable. *What are they thinking, seeing us together like this?* "This isn't really my scene. Do you want to get out of here?" he asked Saera.

Saera nodded. "I'm sick of feeling like I'm on display."

"Welcome to my world."

— — —

"They make a cute couple, don't you think?" Cris remarked to his wife as soon as they were out of earshot from Wil and Saera.

"They do." Kate shook her head. "I can't believe he's leaving tomorrow. It's all gone by so fast."

"I know, it really has."

"I like Saera for him. But, there's no way she's a full-blood human, even if she is from Earth," Kate mused as she looked back at their son and his companion.

Cris nodded. "Her abilities are rather strong."

Kate looked up at Cris. "It's more than that. I mean, just look at her!"

Cris was pensive. "There's something about her, but I can't place it…" He trailed off.

"She has a kind of poise that's rare to see." Kate tried to spot Wil and Saera again in the crowd. "Where did they go?"

— — —

The halls were deserted. All of the Junior Agents and Agents were still at the party, and the younger trainees appeared to be following the instructions to stay in their quarters for the night.

Wil and Saera strolled down the Primus corridor hand-in-hand. Wil was trying to focus on the contact, savoring how it felt to be together, and hold onto that feeling. *This is our last night together. Everything will be different when I return… will this ever be possible again?*

"You've been preoccupied all night."

Saera's voice pulled Wil back into the present. "I'm sorry. Something came up today."

"Is it anything you want to talk about?"

*I wish we didn't have to.* "Yes, I—" Wil stopped in the middle of the empty hallway and looked at Saera through his tinted glasses. "I was informed this afternoon that it's time for my internship, in preparation for graduation. I knew it must be coming up, but… I leave in the morning."

Saera stiffened. "For how long?"

Wil shook his head. "I don't know for sure. Sometime between five months and a year, most likely."

Saera's eyes glistened. She staggered toward the wall.

Wil wrapped his arms around her, and she buried her face in his chest. "I don't feel at all ready. I'm terrified," he admitted.

Saera hugged him back. She took a breath and gazed up at him. "I'll be here waiting for you, when you return."

"Saera…" Wil stroked the side of her face.

Saera put an arm around Wil's neck and pulled him in for a kiss. He eagerly kissed her back, leaning her up against the wall. For a few moments, they forgot their surroundings and lost themselves in each other.

"I know you have to, but I don't want you to go," Saera whispered into Wil's neck.

"I don't want to, either." *She's willing to give herself to me, but she doesn't even know who I really am. I can't leave like this.* Wil pulled away slightly. "We need to talk about some things before I leave."

"Sure, anything."

Wil looked around. "Not here." *But where?* He thought through all the places within Headquarters, and nowhere seemed appropriate. *Ah, fok regulations.* "Go change into regular clothes. Meet me by the main elevator near your quarters in fifteen minutes."

They parted ways with a kiss. Wil jogged to his own quarters and changed before heading to the elevator lobby. He was waiting for no more than a minute before Saera arrived. He waved to her as she approached.

Saera smiled and gave a little wave back. "So, where are we going?" she asked as she walked up.

*How can she always look so beautiful?* “I need to get out of here for a while. Are you up for a field trip?” Wil called the elevator.

Saera hesitated. “Is that allowed?”

Wil laughed. “Certainly not. We’ll be breaking at least a dozen policies. What I can guarantee, however, is that you’ll be excused from any indiscretion.” The elevator door opened and Wil stepped inside. “Are you game?”

Saera relaxed. “I don’t have it in me to say ‘no’.” She joined Wil in the elevator. “I’ll take every last moment with you I can get.”

Wil directed the elevator to the spaceport on the moon’s surface, and the doors closed. “I’m feeling kind of angry with the universe right now,” Wil admitted. “Just as I started to feel like everything was falling into place, now I’m being torn away.”

Saera leaned up against him. “I know what you mean.”

When the elevator doors opened at the moon’s surface, Saera breathed a sigh of awe as she took in the spectacular view of the stars. “This is incredible. I was too nervous on my way in to pay much attention.”

Wil smiled. “Oh, it’s nice, but wait until you see where we’re going,” he said as he set to cracking the security safeguards on the door to the shuttle terminal. Thanks to his intimate understanding of the Mainframe, he was able to bypass the system in less than a minute. “All right.” The door slid open.

Once through the door, they made their way to one of the empty shuttles waiting in a long row. Wil entered in a few commands, and the autopilot in the shuttle navigated to the spaceport fixed above the moon’s surface.

Like the interior part of Headquarters, the spaceport was deserted. Wil led Saera to a section of the port with smaller shuttles designed for transporting two Agents on a short-duration mission. They entered the shuttle through the main living cabin, which contained two beds and a table with chairs fixed to the floor. At the front of the ship, they buckled into the two chairs in the miniature Command Center.

"This is my first time in one of these," Saera said as she secured her harness.

"There's no need to be nervous," Wil assured her. "I practically grew up flying."

Saera settled deeper into her seat.

Wil quickly ran through the startup sequence and then maneuvered the shuttle far enough away from the spaceport to execute a jump. "Spatial jumps can take some getting used to. Hold on."

A vibration spread throughout the ship. With a flash, the space outside turned to shifting blue-green for a moment before the stars outside winked back into existence.

When he looked over, Wil saw that Saera was gripping her harness with white knuckles.

She took a moment to recover, but then grinned. "That was awesome!" She looked around with wonder at the view outside. "Wow…"

Wil had directed the shuttle into the center of a nebula, with gasses of every color swirling in incredible clouds. He dimmed the lights to give a better view of the surroundings. Light bounced around colossal gas sculptures in flashes like fireworks, illuminating sections of the clouds in purple and blue with splashes of pink. Shadows danced along the shuttle's walls with each flash.

"It's safe for us to talk freely here," Wil explained. "The composition of this nebulae interferes with communications through regular space." He unbuckled his harness.

Saera undid her own harness. "Did you really bring me here just to talk?" She placed a hand on Wil's thigh.

His skin tingled under the gentle touch of her hand. *I have so much to say, but she's right—this comes across as such a ridiculously romantic backdrop.* "Yes, I really did." *But, if this goes well… No, stay focused!* "Come on."

Wil took Saera's hand and led her back to the main cabin. He directed her to the edge of one of the beds and sat next to her.

"You're not exactly helping your case about innocent conversation," Saera said with a smile. She leaned in for a kiss.

*Don't give in.* Wil pulled back. "Really, Saera, this is important."

She nodded and propped one arm back on the bed, expectant.

Wil ran a hand through his hair. *Where to begin?* "Now, you said earlier you'll wait for me, but I can't leave in good conscience without explaining some things. There are a lot of rumors floating around about me, and I need to set the record straight. But, you have to promise that you won't repeat anything we discuss here."

"I promise."

"Okay. I'm going to be pretty blunt, so please bear with me." Wil took a deep breath. "My life is in two major parts: my responsibility to Tararia, and my role within the TSS. As for the first part, it seems to be common knowledge that my mother is Katrine Vaenetri—the fourth child to the Head of the First Region."

Saera nodded.

"I've heard some say that there's no way she'd marry outside of the High Dynasties, and for that reason my father has to be someone of note. Now, they're right and wrong about that. She would have gladly married outside of the Dynasties for love, and for most of the time she was dating my father that's exactly what she thought she was doing. But, in actuality, my father is the heir to Sietinen."

Saera's face drained and she went taut. "You're..."

"I am second in line to Sietinen, yes. Heir to SiNavTech and to the Third Region of Tararia."

Saera flushed and tried to pull away. "Why—"

Wil firmly held her hands. "Now, before you go down some self-deprecating path of questioning why I'd ever be interested in some lowly Earth-born girl like you, I'd like to make something very clear. I took an interest in you based on your own merits, and we wouldn't be here now if I didn't have some hope for a future together."

Saera softened.

"However unlikely it may be that two people from such different lives would find themselves together, here we are. That's all that matters now. And when it comes to you gaining acceptance from others in the High Dynasties, the truth of the matter is that we need some diversity—the highborn bloodlines on Tararia are so intertwined that I'd be hard pressed to find someone who wasn't a cousin. Besides, there's something nicknamed the Advancement Act for that very purpose. But more than that, we have a resonance connection that no one could deny—it's one in a hundred billion. Simply put, we are the perfect complements to each other. I felt connected to you the moment we met, even though I tried to tell myself there was no room in my life for a relationship. You just make me so very happy, Saera. I never thought I could find the kind of peace that I feel when I'm with you."

Saera squeezed his hand. "I feel exactly the same way."

"I can't express how important that kind of support is when it comes to the second part of my life." Wil paused. *What can I even say? I can't get into the details about the war with the Bakzen... that's one rule I won't break. She needs to be able to make her own choice about staying with the TSS.*

He chose his words carefully. "In a few months, at the end of your first year with the TSS, there will be a disclosure about the TSS' role in combating a mounting threat. You will be given the choice to stay with the TSS or go your own way. I don't want you choosing to stay with the TSS strictly because of me—if you want to go, that doesn't mean we can't still be a couple. We could always find a way for you to stay in Headquarters as a civilian contractor. So, when the time comes, I want you to really consider if you can give yourself to that life."

Saera was resolute. "I can't imagine they could say anything that would deter me at this point."

*If only I could tell her the whole truth.* "You say that now..."

"I committed when I told you that I wanted Command track. Now that I have it, there's no turning back," Saera declared with conviction.

*I hope she never has any regrets.* "Regardless, I want to preserve your ability to make as unbiased a decision as possible, but I do need to delve a little deeper. You've probably heard 'Primus Elite' tossed around at one point or another, and that I'll be in a special Primus Elite class after I graduate."

"Yes, they've been talking about it since the day I arrived."

"Well, suffice to say that my abilities surpass the normal distinction of rank. What only a handful of people know is that I have already successfully handled a 9.8 intensity by the CR measures."

Saera seemed unfazed. "Okay…"

*She should have recoiled with terror at that statement—does she understand the implications?* "That is above the capabilities of any other living Agent. But, what's key is that I haven't strained in doing so—let alone reached an upper limit. If anything, the higher I go, the easier it's getting for me."

Saera started showing the hints of worry, but still she didn't pull away.

Wil went on, "However, that also means I've been largely on my own in figuring out how to handle that power. My father is one of the few who can 'stop time' and was able to coach me through that, but I've begun experimenting with full spatial displacement. At this rate, I think un-aided inter-dimensional travel may even be possible."

Saera looked at him with skeptical wonder, but didn't say anything.

*Stars! She almost seems excited by that prospect.* "The training of these skills has been deliberate, to shape me. I have a role to play in a major conflict that will one day concern all of us. In several years, I am to assume the role of Supreme Commander of the TSS and settle that conflict. Such duty will very likely take everything I have, and I honestly don't expect to make it to the age of thirty."

Fear was now evident in Saera's eyes—the fear that Wil had come to expect when others learned the extent of his power. Then, Saera tenderly reached up and stroked the side of Wil's face, looking him straight in the eye. "I'd rather have a short life with you than no time at all."

*No, it was fear of loss. Can she truly accept me? This life?* "Me too. But it's not that simple. The fact of the matter is, I might not live to see through my responsibility to Tararia, as an heir. Which means, whoever I choose as my partner would need to carry on my bloodline without me."

"How?"

"There's a genetic archive for all the prominent Dynasties, holding all the material necessary for reproductive purposes," Wil explained. "It exists only as a backup, but it is the single most closely guarded facility in known space."

Saera was quiet, processing.

"Now, aside from all that, we can't even just have one fun night together and then part ways if you change your mind. My ability level combined with the predisposition from our resonance connection means that any amount of intimacy will result in a permanent telepathic bond. Given everything, it means a lifetime commitment for us to ever be together at all. Making that kind of lifelong choice—it's not a fair decision to ask of you after so little time together, especially at the age of barely sixteen."

Saera was solemn. "I was ready to make that decision from the moment we met. I'll do whatever needs to be done."

*How can she be so confident? So trusting?* Wil reached out to touch her mind—there was no hesitation from her, no doubts. Then it was all so clear. *She knows, just the way I do. There is no reason to question, because being together is the only option.* Here, finally, was someone with whom he could be completely open and not have to hide the inner part of himself.

Wil was overcome with a feeling of elation. "I don't know what will happen on my internship, but I'd like to go away knowing that I've given myself to you fully."

The invisible barrier between them broke. Instinctually, they drew together in a passionate kiss, their hands working under clothing. They lay back on the bed as shirts and pants came off, hands and lips exploring the newly exposed flesh for the first time. Breath quickened with anticipation and they pressed together with almost nothing between them. Soon, they could resist no longer and the final undergarments were stripped away.

Wil lay on top of Saera, reveling in finally being able to express the desire that he'd suppressed for so long. *Through this one act, we'll be bonded forever.* "Are you sure about this?"

"More than anything."

Eyes locked, they joined together in body and mind. Moving as one, every worry and burden in the outside world was cast aside as they made love in the starlight. And at the moment of climax, their connection was sealed.

Afterward, they lay entwined on the bed, tracing along the curves of each other's naked bodies with their fingers.

A chirp from the viewscreen intruded on the moment. They startled.

"What is it?" Saera asked, sitting up.

Wil looked at the screen. "A call." The subspace communication was coming from his father's quarters. "Trying to check up on us."

Saera looked concerned. "Do we need to get back?"

Wil reached up and declined the call. "Not yet. I'm not ready for this night to end." He pulled Saera back down into bed.

—

It was nearly 06:00 by the time they made it back to Saera's quarters. Wil and Saera stood in the hallway, knowing the goodbye was temporary but still struggling to find the words. They held each other in silent understanding. Already, Wil could feel the bond between them, born from deep love. The connection would span any distance and any time.

"Send Katz to my parents if there's any trouble about you being out all night," Wil told Saera.

"I will." Saera held him closer.

*I don't want to go…* "I have a ship to catch."

She smiled up at him. "I know. Good luck. I know you'll do great."

"I'll try." He tucked a loose strand of hair behind her ear. "With the bond between us, you'll be able to know I'm okay, no matter where I am, just as I will for you."

Saera looked up at him, tears in her eyes. "Still, be careful, okay?"

"Of course." Wil leaned down and kissed her, holding onto the moment as long as he could before duty pulled him away.

# CHAPTER 16

WIL CARRIED A single bag. It felt strange to consolidate his life into such a small space, but he didn't need anything more where he was going. His handheld—loaded with the mission details—and a solar charger were the only electronics, along with a few changes of clothes, some toiletries, and a pulse gun stashed in a hidden compartment that would only be used in a dire emergency.

As he walked through the halls, Wil felt a twinge of homesickness like he'd never experienced before. His departure on the internship was much more than an extended stay from home—it was the beginning of a new stage in his life. As a graduated Agent, he would have senior rank to everyone who had been a friend and mentor for as long as he could remember. *Will our history be enough to sustain that friendship, or will I become just their superior officer?*

On his way to the spaceport, Wil saw few people yet up and about for the day. He stifled a yawn as he exited the elevator. The lack of sleep from the night before was catching up to him.

"There you are."

Wil looked up to see his father waiting. "Hi."

"I hope you made the most of your little excursion," Cris said as Wil approached.

"Dad, please don't start. I know I shouldn't have gone out on my own like that, but I couldn't take it anymore. For just one night in my whole entire life, I needed to do something for me."

Cris shook his head. "I wasn't going to reprimand you. You are very much my son. I would have done exactly the same thing in your situation."

Wil relaxed on the surface, but he was ready to go on the defensive. "I didn't expect you to be so understanding."

His father eyed him. "Me, or a senior TSS officer?"

Wil thought for a moment. *As my dad, he's never failed me.* "The TSS."

"Well, Banks certainly wasn't pleased with you running off," Cris acknowledged. "It is dangerous out there."

"Not that it's completely safe here, either."

"True enough," Cris admitted. The Bakzen infiltration would never be forgotten. "However, I do have to say that you've done yourself a bit of a disservice by bonding to someone so soon before departing. It will make being apart that much worse."

*Is it that obvious?* "On the contrary, it will give me a tie to the only home I've ever known. If I start to feel lost, I'll have that grounding."

"So, you did," Cris said with a slight smile. "I had my suspicions, but I wasn't sure."

*Tricky.* Wil stood his ground. "It seemed like the right thing to do, given the circumstances."

"I agree," Cris replied. "I have always found my bond with your mom to be a source of strength when I needed it."

*He's taking all of this so lightly. I not only disobeyed TSS regulations but also went against every dynastic tradition related to partnering.* "You're not mad?"

"About Saera?"

Wil nodded.

"No, not at all. She's an incredible girl—I couldn't imagine anyone more perfect for you. It means everything to me to see you so happy."

"I know there's TSS protocol…"

"It's already been taken care of. Don't worry, we'll look out for her while you're away."

*Did they want this?* "Thank you." *Is nothing in my life of my own design?*

Cris checked the time on his handheld. "Banks and your mom should be here any minute to formally send you off."

Wil's chest tightened. "What happens if I fail this mission?"

Cris was caught off-guard. "That won't happen."

"But what if it *does*?"

"Then we'll figure it out together," Cris assured him.

The elevator doors opened, and Banks emerged with Kate. It was time to go.

Kate silently walked up and embraced Wil. He hugged her back. After a few moments, she released him and went to stand next to Cris. Cris, likewise, gave Wil a heartfelt hug.

Banks waited patiently for the family exchange to conclude. When Cris nodded his assent, Banks began, "Junior Agent Sights, due to your exceptional performance record, you have become eligible for early graduation from the TSS training program. This internship is your one remaining task, and you have been offered a far greater challenge than any other aspiring Agent. However, I am confident that you have the experience and skills to be successful."

"Thank you, sir."

"Your mission is to reach a treaty among the people of Orino. Agents will be monitoring your progress from orbit. They will send a message to your handheld when the mission objectives have been met. Otherwise, they will intervene only if you're in imminent danger. Do you accept this mission?"

*As if I have a choice.* "Yes, sir."

— — —

Saera groaned when the alarm went off. She'd been in bed for maybe an hour, and the pitiful amount of rest had only made her feel more tired.

In her weariness, it took her a few moments to realize that all of her roommates were watching her. She looked around at the expectant faces. *What do they want?*

Elise finally broke the silence. "So? How was it?"

*The party, of course.* She forced an excited smile. "It was awesome. They had one of the training rooms all done up with decorations, and there was every kind of food and drink you can imagine."

"Was everyone all dressed up?" Nadeen asked.

"Oh, yes. It was funny to see some of our instructors in dresses," Saera replied with a more heartfelt smile.

Leila observed from her bed. She seemed disinterested in the party details. "How late were you out last night? I heard you come in at some point and I thought you were going to bed, but then you left and I didn't see you again."

"Yeah, I noticed that, too," Caryn added. "Where were you?"

Elise and Nadeen paused in thought, and then seemed to realize the others were correct. They looked at Saera quizzically.

"I came back here to change out of the dress and heels." Saera got out of bed and made for the door to the common room. "I met up with some Junior Agents at the party who invited me to join them in the game room. You must have not heard me come back in." She stepped out of the bedroom.

Her roommates followed her out. "No, I remember waking up at around 04:00 and you weren't back yet," insisted Leila.

"What does it matter? My curfew was lifted for the night," Saera said.

Leila was about to respond but was interrupted by a buzz at the main door.

Nadeen went to investigate. "It's Katz," she announced.

Saera swallowed hard.

Nadeen opened the door. "Good morning, Agent Katz."

"Good morning, ladies." She looked around the room. "Saera, may I speak with you?"

*Oh no…* "Yes, ma'am." Saera looked down at her pajamas, wishing there were time to change. She shrugged off the feeling and followed Katz into the hallway. They entered a study room.

When the door was closed, Katz began, "I heard you left Headquarters last night without permission."

*Wil said everything would be okay. Stay calm.* "Yes, ma'am."

"Did you tell anyone about what happened after the party last night?" Katz implored.

"No, ma'am."

Katz relaxed. "Good. They can't know what's going on."

Saera didn't say anything.

"Cris and Kate Sights pulled me aside this morning and informed me about your relationship with Wil," Katz explained. "I knew he was tutoring you, of course, but I understand that the… nature of things has changed."

Saera took a shaky breath. "Yes, ma'am, you could say that."

Katz sighed. "This has placed all of us in an awkward position. Normally, any consorting between Agents and trainees is strictly forbidden. But, they have decided to make an exception for you."

The tension in Saera's chest dissipated. "Thank you, ma'am."

"Don't thank me. Only the High Commander can make that sort of call." Katz paused. "He knows it's not his place to stand in the way of succession for the High Dynasties," she added.

Saera remained silent.

Katz looked at Saera. "The other students will forget about this night eventually. But you have to be more careful once he's back."

"Yes, ma'am." *If only all of this didn't have to be so secret.*

Katz placed a hand on Saera's shoulder. "Off the record, I want you to know that we're here for you. Kate is one of my best friends, and I've known Wil his whole life. He has chosen you as his partner, so that makes you part of our adopted family, too. I'll do whatever I can to support you being together once he returns from his internship. Likewise, Kate and Cris are quite fond of you, and they wanted me to pass on that you should reach out to them if you ever need anything."

Saera exhaled with relief. "Thank you, ma'am." *They approve of me? They're really letting us be together?* She couldn't help but grin.

— — —

Water stretched all the way to the horizon. The shuttle was flying low across the vast sea, leaving a wake in its path.

Wil stood in the open doorway of the shuttle, breathing in the salty air of the strange world. It stung his eyes and nose. At first, he thought it odd that anyone would choose to eke out an existence in such an inhospitable environment, but then it occurred to him that life in space was far stranger. *At least they don't need advanced technology to keep themselves alive when they step outside.*

The shuttle flew above a floating city. It was a ragged civilization, thrown together with scrap metal and twine. No land was anywhere to be seen. Around the perimeter of the tethered structures were various small boats and watercraft.

Wil's stomach rose into his throat. *This is where I have to spend the next several months? I didn't even know people still lived like this.*

The shuttle stopped two meters above an area of open decking.

"We can't land on this," Agent Aeronen said to Wil from the pilot's chair. "You'll have to jump down."

*Can't even land the shuttle? What kind of place is this?* "Yes, sir." He grabbed his bag and swung it over his shoulder.

"We'll be in orbit watching your progress," Agent Merdes said from the other chair at the front of the shuttle. "You are to use your handheld only for making status reports and sending an emergency communication to us, if necessary. Otherwise, you must rely on the information systems used by this culture."

"Yes, sir."

"We'll notify you when the mission objectives have been met to our satisfaction," stated Agent Aeronen. "Good luck."

Wil nodded and jumped out of the shuttle. He landed lightly on the metal deck plates. The platform was small enough that even though it was tethered to the larger structure, it swayed slightly under the impact and groaned as rusty couplings rubbed together. He took a moment to find his balance on the unfamiliar footing. The shuttle departed.

When Wil looked around to get a bearing on his new surroundings, he saw people encircling the platform. He straightened to his full height and examined the questioning faces. "My name is Wil Sights. I'm here from the TSS."

A grizzled man stepped forward. He was perhaps in his late-forties, but all the years stood out on his weathered face. He favored his right knee as he moved, but he tried to hide it with a swaggering gait that seemed well suited to a life on the sea. "When they said they were sending someone for their Junior Agent internship, I thought they'd be sending a man—not a mere boy."

"Don't let my age fool you," Wil responded. "The TSS doesn't make exceptions for their performance standards. Reaching this position by my age just means I had to work all the harder to prove myself."

"And you'll have to prove yourself all over again to us," the man replied. "But we reached out for help, and you're who we got. I'll try to keep an open mind, because we need you."

"I'm here to serve." There was fear in the eyes of the onlookers. They were just as ragged as the structures, their eyes dull from spirits broken long ago. *How did they get to be this way?*

"My name is Marlon," the man said. "I am the leader of this community. As a sign of our thanks, we have a welcome gift for you, as a fellow warrior." Marlon beckoned behind him, and a girl stepped forward. "This is my daughter, Mila," Marlon went on. "It is time for her to know what it is to be a woman."

Mila was around fourteen-years-old based on her face, but she looked at Wil with an air of maturity. She knew why she was being presented to him, and she had accepted that fate.

*Shite, I was afraid of this.* Wil's stomach knotted. *I don't want anyone but Saera.* "Thank you, I appreciate your generosity."

"Mila will assist you with anything you need," Marlon said. "She'll show you to your room now."

Mila stepped up to Wil and bowed her head before him. She was tall for a girl—close to Wil's height—and her brown hair was cropped to chin-length. "I am yours," she murmured.

*Fok, I need to find a way out of this.* "I will try to prove myself worthy," Wil replied.

Mila led Wil through the crowd toward one of the stout structures adjacent to the central platform. She took him down a staircase into a low room just below the surface of the water. Only a slit of a window near the ceiling illuminated the room. There was a small bunk, a washbasin, and a rickety table in the corner. All of the furnishings were worn, permeated by the smell of sea salt.

"Do you wish to have me now?" Mila asked. She reached for the tie at the bosom of her dress.

*Never.* "Mila, you don't have to." Wil held up his hand to stop her.

"It is our way," she insisted.

*I can't do this.* "I—"

"Are you dissatisfied with me?" she asked, her brow furrowed above her tawny eyes.

"No, it's not that..."

She reached forward and took off Wil's tinted glasses. Doing so was a great taboo on other Taran worlds, but Wil let her. She gazed into his glowing blue-green eyes. "Your heart belongs to another."

"Yes."

Mila sat down on the bed, contemplating. "Mine does, as well," she admitted, looking down.

"Then what are you doing here with me?"

She avoided Wil's gaze. "My father doesn't know of it. He thinks me to still be innocent, but I am not."

*Thank the stars!* "I won't tell anyone, Mila." Wil crouched down in front of her so they were at the same level. "You can say whatever they will want to hear—that you pleased me. But, there is only one I want to know in that way."

Mila's eyes narrowed. "They will think you less of a man for having only one woman."

*What a different world this is.* "So, we both have a vested interest in keeping each other's secrets," Wil pointed out with a reserved smile.

"I guess we do," Mila agreed. Her face softened, but an inner fire showed through. Whether she was fueled by anger or just an inner strength that few could ever find, she stared back at Wil with the kind of dedication he knew he could channel to win whatever fight they were up against.

"Now," said Wil as he stood up, "I do need your help in other ways. I know very little of your culture and customs. I would like for you to advise me on how to proceed with my mission."

"I'm not qualified—"

"You're a native here, aren't you? That makes you more informed than me."

Mila inclined her head, causing her hair to fall forward on her face. "As you wish." She picked at a callous on her hand. "What did they send you here to do?"

Wil took a breath. "I was informed that there are warring groups around the planet. Your community is considered one of the more 'neutral' parties, so you're the best bet for brokering a treaty between the different peoples."

Mila let out a coarse, bitter laugh. "Oh, that's a good one."

"Pardon?"

"I don't know where you got your information, but it's nothing like you said."

"Then what's going on?" Wil asked her.

"It's easier if I show you." Mila rose from the bed. She led Wil back up the stairs and down several rickety walkways to the other side of the village. They came to a structure that stood several meters above the deck, attended by a single guard. The man inclined his head to Mila and let them pass. Mila swung open a massive, rusty door set on the front face of the structure. Inside, a handful of partially filled plastic crates were positioned around the room.

"What is this?" Wil asked.

"These are the food supplies for the rest of the month," Mila said.

"What about the shipments from Makaris? Orino is one of the recognized—"

"These *are* the shipments from Makaris," Mila explained. "First, the price started going up. Then, the quantity declined. Now, we're lucky if we get half as much as we need."

"I don't understand. It should be subsidized." *Something is seriously amiss here.*

"Akka happened."

"Akka? Is that a person?"

Mila hesitated. "You'll help us, right?" There was desperation in her eyes. She was strong, but she had her limits.

"That's what I'm here to do," Wil assured her. "Tell me everything."

# CHAPTER 17

KALDERN, AT LAST. Haersen stepped off the gangway from the cargo freighter. The station was surprisingly nice, given its location. But, he knew the TSS was one source of funding. He would need to be on guard.

Finding someone who could take him to the Bakzen would be tricky. No one would openly advertise their traitorous allegiance. Fortunately, Haersen's telepathic skills gave him a distinct advantage.

It was no trouble to look the part of a weary traveler after spending so much time without proper facilities. He had allowed a beard to grow, helping to mask his face from recognition by the cameras found throughout every spaceport. Coupled with his sunglasses and mussed hair, he doubted he would even recognize himself had he not witnessed the transformation.

Haersen set out toward the main mall of the port. He needed information and there was no better place to ask questions than in a bar. His funds were limited, but he had enough to cover a drink—especially since his travels were almost over.

There were several establishments to choose from. Haersen waited along the wall of the corridor, sending out a subtle probe to get a feel for the type of clientele at each bar. He needed to keep the reading to general impressions, just skimming the surface of consciousness. Too deep a sweep and he risked accidental interception by any Agent that may be stationed nearby.

Quieting his mind, Haersen focused on the thoughts of those around him. Most were complaints about present circumstances, reflecting on one loss or another. Hearing the pathetic weakness and sorrows of so many people at once would have been a nuisance if Haersen's own troubles hadn't already consumed him. He tried to focus in on those with the rawest hurts, attempting to glean any hint about a recent Bakzen raid.

If Haersen could place himself in an active zone, he could arrange an encounter. It was a risky move, but he had no other way to get in touch.

After listening to various internal monologues for several minutes, Haersen eventually cued in on a man at one of the bars farther down the corridor. He was more withdrawn than the others, but an anger burned just beneath the surface of his mind. There was hurt there, loss—directionless and all-encompassing. Few things could fuel such emotions.

Haersen moved closer to investigate.

The man was sitting alone at the back end of the bar. He was disheveled like many of the other travelers, but his clothing also bore several dark stains that resembled dried blood. He had nothing with him, and his stare was one of someone who had nothing left to lose. His hand shook as he went to pick up his glass.

Haersen took a seat at the bar one chair away from the man, tucking his bag between his feet as he sat down. The other man didn't acknowledge his approach. Haersen kept his eyes down, but he sent his probe deeper into the man's mind.

The vicious anger immediately pierced Haersen's own mind as he reached out to the man. The image of a horrific explosion looped over and over, the cry of a woman holding a dead child amid the ruins of a town, other explosions drawing near. The image and visceral feeling of grief overtook him. Haersen tried to dive deeper, but the man's mind was so occupied with the thoughts that any further exertion from Haersen might give away his position. But if only he could get a little more—

"What can I get for you?"

Haersen was jolted from his telepathic assessment by the bartender, a larger man who looked well suited to keeping order if any of his patron's overindulged.

Haersen shook off the cries he'd heard in the other man's mind. "Whatever is the cheapest and will get me drunk the fastest."

The bartender nodded and grabbed a bottle of a light amber drink. He poured it into a square glass. "Three credits."

"Thanks." Haersen grabbed the chips from his pocket and set them on the bar.

The bartender collected the chips and scowled when he saw that there was no tip. He brushed it off and went to tend to his other customers.

Haersen took a sip of the drink. It was strong and vile, but it fit with his specifications. He waited for a few minutes, watching the other man. As he waited, he kept his more general telepathic sweep active in the background, looking out for potentially useful thoughts from other passersby.

When he saw that the man's drink was getting low, Haersen looked directly at him and tried to catch his eye. "What brings you to these parts?"

The man didn't acknowledge him at first, but then noticed Haersen watching him. "I'm from near here," he replied, his voice faint. "Not that there's anything left."

"What do you mean?" Haersen asked, already well aware of a recent tragedy.

The man shook his head. There was a sheen to his eyes, on the verge of tears. "It all went to shite, just like everything else in my life. Every last good thing is gone."

Haersen took another sip of his drink. "I'm sorry to hear that." He wanted to ask more, but pressing too much wouldn't get him anywhere. He had learned a long time ago that people were all too willing to talk if he just sat back and let them speak their mind.

The man finished off his drink. "I just don't understand how they could let it happen. They knew our shield was down, but they left us there to fend for ourselves, completely helpless."

"Who's 'they'?"

"The TSS." The man sniffed back tears. "Shite. What were we supposed to do?"

It was a more perfect scenario than Haersen could have imagined. "Can't trust any of them. What happened?"

"The Bakzen came, and the TSS stood back and let them take our world. They offered relief to the teenage kids after it was over, but they left the rest of us to clean up the dead." The man took a pained breath. "I had to bury my little girl, right next to my wife. I watched them die. They were my whole life."

Haersen feigned horror. "Where was this?"

"Aleda, next system over."

"I didn't realize the Bakzen had ventured out that far."

"They've been all around here, raiding everything they can. As soon as a shield goes down, which they're prone to do in these parts, the Bakzen are there before you know it. It was only two hours… Stars! I couldn't save them." He buried his face in his hands.

Taking out a planetary shield—that would be an easy way to draw the Bakzen's attention. But which planet? Haersen swirled the contents of his glass. "The authorities keep pretending like the Bakzen aren't a threat, but they can wipe us all out. Tararia should be afraid."

"The leaders don't care about anything until it's on their doorstep."

Haersen smirked. The Bakzen would be there soon enough. "Eventually there won't be anywhere to run."

The man's despondent gaze turned to Haersen. "Where do you go when you have nothing left?"

Haersen sighed inwardly. The poor man actually thought he cared. He was about to dismiss himself, having gathered the information he needed, when his background telepathic probe suddenly struck a wall of silence. Haersen froze. An Agent was nearby.

Without hesitation, he stopped the scan and secured his own mental blocks—leaving just enough trivial thoughts on the surface to give the illusion of daydreaming. He cursed under his breath.

Haersen slid over to the seat directly next to the other man, bringing his bag with him. The conversation offered a measure of cover. "You do like the rest of us and keep moving forward." As he spoke, he tried to identify the location of the Agent. Hopefully, it was only one.

The man hung his head. "As it was, we were barely getting by on the supplies from Makaris Corp. Now, the whole world is burned."

"Then it's time to find a new home." Haersen covertly looked to the side, eyeing the hallway through his sunglasses in an unsuccessful attempt to spot the Agent.

"I barely have enough money to cover this drink. Everything was wrapped up in my farm. The evacuation ship dropped me here, but with no fare for passage, I'm stuck."

Haersen groaned under his breath. The man was clearly asking for help, but he was asking the wrong person. "I'm in no better a position. Find a ship that will let you work."

"Just forget any of this happened?" The man was still close to tears.

The conversation was going nowhere, and the Agent's location was still unknown. Haersen couldn't take the waiting anymore. "If that's too much for you, then help yourself to an airlock."

The man looked appalled. His face flushed and eyes narrowed. "You're a monster."

It likely wouldn't be the last time he was called that. Haersen could only imagine what they said about him within the TSS—all the more reason to get as far away as he could. "I just do what I must to survive." He stood and grabbed his bag from the floor.

Slinging the strap of his bag over his shoulder, Haersen set off toward the main corridor. The empty void of the Agent's mind was still close. He had to risk it.

The crowd of travelers in the corridor had thinned, and those that remained bore expressions of wonder and apprehension. Haersen skimmed their minds, gleaning variations of 'I've never seen so many of them' and 'What do they want?' Haersen tensed. Only one 'they' would solicit that kind of reaction: TSS Agents.

On guard, Haersen slinked along the wall of the corridor, ready to flee down a side passage if needed. As he approached the corridor's intersection with the central hub of the space station, he spotted the source of the passersby's wonder. Not one Agent, but four. Haersen felt the power emanating from them—they were sustaining a telepathic link with other Agents elsewhere in the station.

His pulse raced. The directionless void he had detected was only the secure conduit for their communication, not one individual's mind. He was surrounded.

Haersen ducked behind a bulkhead. "Fok."

He bolstered his mental blocks and the decoy thoughts on the surface. The persona was a homeless traveler with a broken mind—thoughts jumbled and incoherent. He already looked the part, so with any luck no one would pay him any notice. It just needed to be enough to buy him time to find a transport to a planet near Aleda. The Bakzen would still be nearby.

To keep with his persona, Haersen took up a shuffling step through the corridor and began muttering nonsense to himself. It was a thin disguise, but without fail people would always try to avoid a person with obvious mental illness.

His eyes hidden behind his sunglasses, Haersen scanned the overhead signs to locate directions to the nearest computer terminal so he could access the docking log. The signs indicated there was one thirty meters up ahead.

Haersen continued his shuffling stride for the remaining distance. It was agonizingly slow progress, but his plan to be given a wide berth worked perfectly.

When he reached the docking manifest access station, he took the kiosk farthest from the corridor in his usual fashion. He brought up the list of ships, keeping careful eye for any approaching Agents.

He sorted the outbound ships by destination to search for local traffic that would take him the final stretch to his objective. Only two eligible ships were scheduled to leave that day. He groaned when he saw their docking locations. Both were in a separate wing of the spaceport, and the only way through was past the checkpoint of TSS Agents.

"Bomax. Foking TSS," he muttered while shuffling away from the kiosk.

His likelihood of getting past the Agents would be largely dependent on their reason for setting up the checkpoint. If they were searching specifically for him, he didn't stand a chance. But if it were a routine exercise, then maybe. He considered trying to find a place to wait it out, but it seemed too risky. Knowing how the TSS operated, they would likely conduct a thorough sweep of the port before leaving, and anyone trying to hide would immediately be taken into custody for vetting. Trying to blend in seemed like the better option.

Haersen shuffled back toward the central hub of the port. As he approached, interference from the Agents' telepathic network formed an oppressive hum in his head. Maintaining his multi-level mental guard was draining enough without the added pressure. On his final approach to the hub, the first level of mental guards started to slip.

Up ahead, the Agents snapped to attention, recognizing the presence of another telepath nearby.

Haersen strained to maintain control, perspiration on his brow.

The Agents continued to scan the crowd, but their concealed eyes passed over Haersen without recognition.

Blockades in the corridor funneled travelers toward the waiting Agents. Haersen shuffled closer, driven straight toward them. Only steps away, the telepathic net was stifling. His mental guards were meant to conceal, not stand up to a full-on assault.

"Sir, could we have a word with you?"

Haersen froze. There was no doubt the Agent was speaking to him. "Me? Uh..." His mental mirage wavered.

"Please step over here," the Agent directed. He was older than Haersen and exuded the authority of someone with command experience.

Haersen prepared to run. Other travelers were allowed to pass by without any acknowledgement from the Agents. He had been singled out. They had found him. He needed to get away. If he acted quickly, he could catch the Agents by surprise—

"He's symptomatic," the Agent called to someone beyond the blockade.

Haersen halted his escape plans. "What do you want?" he stammered, straining to speak while maintaining the mental blocks within the heart of the telepathic net.

"No need to be alarmed, sir," the Agent replied. "Just a routine check-up."

"I'm fine," Haersen tried to protest.

The Agent ushered Haersen around the blockade. "This will only take a moment."

On the other side of the temporary fencing, medical personnel at six stations were tending to travelers. Each station consisted of a monitor, a table with a case of vials on top, and a chair.

A female medical attendant came forward from her station to greet the Agent. "What are his symptoms?" she asked.

"Hallucinations, shortness of breath, stiff muscles," the Agent responded, turning Haersen over to the attendant.

"That sounds like the neurotoxin," the attendant replied.

"Where are you traveling from?" the Agent asked Haersen.

"Aleda," Haersen stammered, figuring it would be the least conspicuous.

The medical attendant and Agent exchanged a knowing glance.

"Well, after the attack on Aleda three days ago, we found traces of a neurotoxin in the surviving population," the Agent explained to Haersen. "Some people were evacuated before the first symptoms appeared. We're just trying to get treatment to those who need it."

Haersen held in a laugh. They were so stupid, thinking he was poisoned. Any halfway decent Agent should be able to tell the difference between a telepathic decoy and the effects of a neurotoxin. But, it was the perfect opportunity. He looked at his hands with wonder. "Such pretty colors. I want to taste them."

The medical attendant looked to the Agent. "I'll take care of him." She led Haersen back to her station and sat him down in the chair.

The Agent returned to his post by the blockade.

"I'm sorry about your planet," the attendant said as she prepared a swab. She held it toward Haersen's mouth. "Open."

Haersen eyed the swab. He knew she wanted to check for presence of the toxin, but if the test included any genetic identification, he'd be flagged. The Agents were only four meters away. He gripped his head. "It burns."

"Sir, this won't hurt. Just a quick test."

Haersen shook his head and whimpered as he rocked in the chair. "My home. It's all gone. The burn..."

The attendant paused. "I'm sorry." She set down the swab. "I'll give you something to help you feel better." She loaded one of the vials from the case on the table into a metal syringe with a finger trigger. She placed a fresh needle on the tip. "Turn to the side, please."

Haersen swiveled to the side in his chair.

The attendant pulled down the collar of his jacket to expose the back of his neck. She cleaned a patch of skin at the base of his skull with a sanitizing wipe and readied the syringe. "This will sting."

With a squeeze of the trigger, the needle pierced between Haersen's vertebrae. He gritted his teeth.

"The injection should alleviate your symptoms within the next two hours," the medical attendant said. "We'll get you on the next transport to Grolen with the other refugees."

"Where's that?" Haersen asked.

"It's the closest colony to Aleda, so you won't be far from home," she soothed. "Don't worry, you'll be safe there."

Haersen nodded. Grolen. It wouldn't be safe for much longer. Not once he arrived.

# CHAPTER 18

WIL LOOKED AROUND the circle of village leaders. Their meager meal was complete, leaving only business to discuss. Everything he had been told by Mila and over dinner with the village council about the situation on Orino pointed to a massive breakdown of the control systems. Akka, the representative from Makaris Corp, was operating outside of the corporate system and the people of Orino were suffering.

"It's a serious problem," Wil said. The grim expressions on the faces of the village council had his stomach in a knot. Never before had he seen such desperation and defeat.

"Now that you understand our situation, what do you suggest?" Marlon asked. "We reached out to Makaris for aid, and the TSS responded. We can't withstand more raids from the other villages."

"The villages aren't the problem. It's Makaris. You've only confirmed what Mila already told me," Wil replied.

Marlon frowned. "But Makaris is who arranged for you to come here."

"Then Akka is up to something." *What's his aim?*

"What do we do? They give us everything we need to survive." Marlon and the other leaders had their full attention on Wil.

"We have to show Makaris you won't let them push you around any longer." Under any other circumstances, Wil would have reported the issues to the oversight committee within the Priesthood. But this was his internship; the mission objectives were clear.

He was tasked with resolving the conflict, and that was exactly what he was going to do. He needed to equip the people of Orino to take control of their own well-being. Reporting Akka to the Priesthood would be a short-term solution, but Orino as a whole needed to be unified as a people. There was no better way to bring them together than to unite against a common enemy.

"We have no way to stand up to them," Olan, the eldest member of the leadership council, said.

"You have numbers and you have heart," Wil pointed out. "But, we need to work with the other villages. We can't do anything alone."

Olan scoffed, tossing the white mane of his hair around his shoulders. "They want nothing to do with us. Nor us with them."

"And that's how Akka has gotten away with what he's done," Wil continued. "You're too busy fighting each other to notice what he's doing."

Marlon nodded. "You speak the truth. We've been so preoccupied with our day-to-day conflicts we have lost sight of the root of our troubles."

"No one from the other villages will trust our intentions," Olan protested.

Wil looked the old man in the eye. "They'll listen to me."

"Maybe," Olan conceded, "but it'll take months to track down everyone."

"What do you mean?" Wil asked.

"The villages drift. They could be anywhere," Olan clarified.

Wil's brow furrowed. "Can't you just ask them for a GPS reading on the comm?"

The elders looked at each other. "We live a simple life here without such technology. If we wish to communicate or trade with another village, we sail on the wind until we find one."

*When the mission brief said they were primitive, I thought they'd at least have a radio…* "There's really no other way?"

Marlon shook his head.

Wil held in a groan. "Then I guess we set sail."

"You'll need guides," Olan said.

"Take my son Tiro," a man named Ricon offered. "He's a fine sailor and can read the winds."

"I will go, as well," Petre, the youngest man on the council, chimed in. "We will need a representative from our village leadership." His brown shoulder-length hair was pulled into a ponytail, and amber eyes stood out under a heavy brow.

Marlon nodded. "Very good. The three of you will be able to man a boat."

*I guess I'm learning how to sail.* "Can we leave in the morning?"

Olan rose. "Yes, we will gather what provisions we can spare for your journey. You should head north first, to find the Northern Seafarers. If you gain their support, the others will follow."

Wil stood and inclined his head to Olan and then to Marlon. "I will do my best."

"The winds are best at dawn. We will see you off at sunrise. Get some sleep," Marlon said, inclining his head to Wil. "Now, find Tiro. We must finalize arrangements." He turned his attention to the rest of the council.

"Good night," Wil said and exited the circle as the leaders began to discuss the supply needs.

Wil swung open the door to the hall and sighed as he closed it behind him. *Sailing aimlessly around the world. This'll be something.*

Mila was leaning against the rusted metal wall outside the door. She took an eager step forward when she saw Wil. "What did they say?"

"We're going after Makaris. Now we just need to get the other villages on board."

She grinned. "When do you leave?"

"First thing in the morning."

"Alone?"

Wil shook his head. "Petre and Ricon's son are coming with me."

Mila's eyes widened. "Tiro is going?"

"Yeah. Why?"

Mila motioned for Wil to follow her, and she took off down the grated walkway. She yanked open a door to a storage room and stepped inside.

*Not again.* Wil reluctantly followed her inside. "What are we doing in here?"

Mila closed the door. It was complete darkness. Wil pulled out his handheld to light the three-meter-square room.

"I'm going with you."

Wil crossed his arms. "You're not really in a position to make that kind of demand. This is an official diplomatic engagement."

"It's my only chance to be with Tiro."

Wil thought for a moment. "Is he the guy you mentioned?"

"Yes, and the council has plans to pair him with Celine," Mila said with a scowl. "But if we got married in another village, my father couldn't stop it."

"Mila, I don't want to get in the middle of your customs. If your father doesn't want you with Tiro, it's not my place to help you cross him."

"Then I promise we won't get married. Just let me spend some time with him," she pleaded. "Maybe if Petre sees us together, he can convince the council that we're a good match."

"If you can convince your father to let you go, then you can come along," Wil yielded.

Mila nodded. "I'll be a good soldier for you."

"Hopefully, it won't come to a fight. We just want to get Orino back from Akka's control."

"And all I want is justice," Mila said, the fire Wil had glimpsed earlier returning to her eyes. "I'll go talk to my father."

Wil opened the door to outside. "Good luck."

Mila smiled. "I don't need it."

*I have no doubt she can get her way.* It was going to be a long trip.

— — —

Saera barely heard a word Agent Katz had said during the lecture. Wil was somewhere on the other side of the galaxy. She could feel the bond between them and knew he was okay, but it felt like part of herself was missing. *What's he doing? Who's he with?*

"What's your opinion, Saera?" Agent Katz asked.

Saera froze. *Shit! What were we talking about?* She looked around the class; all eyes were on her. "I think…"

A voice came into her head. *"As long as those with telekinetic abilities are treated like outcasts, Tararia and the colony worlds will remain divided."* Maybe someone was giving her a hint?

"There's always going to be a divide between the different Taran worlds if those with telekinetic abilities and everyone else can't get along," Saera stated aloud.

Katz nodded. "Leila, you're from the Central Worlds. What do you think?"

"I was going to say the same thing," Leila said, glaring at Saera.

*The help definitely wasn't from her.* Saera slouched in her chair.

"It makes you wonder," Katz said. "Someone from Earth—outside of the Taran governance—and someone from the Central Worlds saying the same thing. Could the Taran civilization be on the verge of a perspective change?"

"It's already changing," Caryn chimed in. "By the time I was leaving to join the TSS, I was seeing active recruitment ads. As a little kid on Aeris, no one even wanted to mention the TSS in public."

"So, what's different now?" asked Katz.

*They're gearing up for something—whatever it is they want Wil to command,* Saera realized. She kept her head down.

"We can do things that others can't," Leila stated. "Everyone can't continue to deny the benefits of our Gifts."

"Now, that notion of 'Gifts' is interesting," Katz said, pacing at the front of the room. "It's a ubiquitous term, but telekinesis is outlawed. 'Gift' hardly seems like the right term for something that's so feared." Katz checked the time. "But, that will have to be a topic for future discussion. Have a good evening, ladies."

Saera grabbed her tablet and exited the classroom. The end of the day was always the loneliest time, since it was historically her twice-weekly training time with Wil.

As she walked down the hall with her classmates, Saera thought she heard the echo of voices. When she looked around, no one was speaking aloud. *I need to get some quality sleep tonight. I'm losing it.*

They reached their quarters and filed into the main living room. It was quiet; the Sacon girls weren't back yet.

The echo of voices filled Saera's head again, accompanied by an oppressive buzz. "Do you hear—?" She pressed her hand to her temple.

"Are you okay?" Elise asked.

The buzz crescendoed, blocking out the swirling voices. It burned her ears. Saera collapsed to the floor, gripping her head. Pressure crushed the back of her eyes. She felt a warm trickle down her lip and tasted iron. The buzz and voices overwhelmed her. There was no escape. The blackness closed in.

—

Faint light filtered through Saera's eyelids. She was laying on something soft, propped upright. Cautiously, she opened her eyes.

Medical monitoring equipment surrounded her. She was alone in a small room with light gray walls. Voices were coming from the hall, indistinct.

"She's awake," someone said.

An older woman with strawberry-blonde hair and tinted glasses entered the room. She was wearing a white uniform and walked with authority. "How are you feeling?"

"What happened?" Saera asked, sitting up straighter in the bed.

"You just experienced a sudden Awakening," the doctor explained. "Only ten percent of people have their abilities activate in rapid succession like that. If you're not physically ready for it, it can be pretty traumatic."

*So my abilities have finally emerged? Of course, right after Wil goes and can't work with me.* Saera sat in silence for a moment. "I don't hear the voices anymore."

The doctor nodded. "We have a telepathic bubble set up around you right now. It will diminish gradually so you have time to acclimate."

Saera let out a slow breath. "How long will that take?"

"We like to give it two days in these cases," the doctor replied. "The field encompasses the entire room, so feel free to get up and move around."

"Okay." *I'm stuck here for two days? What will everyone think?*

"Are visitors allowed, Irina?" Cris Sights stood in the doorway.

Startled, the doctor turned around. "What are you doing here?"

Cris smiled. "A new Trainee has just Awakened. That's worth a visit."

The doctor looked over at Saera. "Fine, but keep it quick. The net is fragile." She left them alone.

Saera tensed as Cris entered. "Sir, you didn't need to come see me."

"I'm not here in an official capacity," Cris said as he sat down in the guest chair next to her bed.

"Then why?"

"Because I promised Wil I'd look after you while he's away."

Saera looked down.

"And I'm very happy to welcome you into the family," Cris continued. "I apologize in advance for the crazy drama."

Saera relaxed. "Your family can't be any crazier than mine."

"You might be surprised."

Saera smiled. "Well, I guess we'll see."

Without warning, she felt the pressure in her head again. She pressed her temples with her hands and the pressure receded.

Cris noticed her pain and stood. "I won't keep you. I know you're acclimating."

Saera looked up at him. "Did this happen because of my bond with Wil?"

"Possibly. Everything with him is uncharted territory."

Saera's throat tightened. "I wish he were here."

Cris placed a reassuring hand on her back. "The time will fly by." He took a step toward the door. "Rest up. You'll have to make up for the missed class when you're better."

Saera frowned. *That's not fair.*

"I'm kidding! Enjoy the break," Cris said with a playful smile.

Saera smiled back. "Thanks."

— — —

Haersen stepped off the transport to the surface of Grolen. It was a plain world, flat and lacking any interesting focal points. The transport station was at the outskirts of what residents of the Outer Colonies would consider a city, but it was a pathetic collection of buildings from Haersen's perspective.

He looked around with disgust. Such a miserable existence.

Yet, the refugees from Aleda smiled as they saw the new world. They looked upon the open fields and saw land for cultivation. To them, the city offered a connection with the other colonies—a chance to get their favorite fruit as a rare treat. Their life was simple, but they could live it the way they wanted.

Haersen trudged toward the city, ignoring the others from the transport. He could never share in their joy over such a planet.

Fortunately, he wouldn't have to. The planet was just a stopover, a suitable sacrifice toward what he really wanted. All he had to do was disable the planetary shield. Then the Bakzen would come for him.

— — —

Wil's back was stiff and sore after a night on the thin mattress of his cot. Even so, it was a night in civilization compared to what was coming.

He grabbed his bag and headed toward the main dock where he'd arrived. The sun was just peaking over the horizon, and the pink-tinted sky was dotted with wispy clouds.

A twelve-meter-long boat was moored to the foot of the dock, and Petre was loading on supplies with another man. At the center of the boat, a six-meter-tall mast supported a main square sail and two stabilizing secondary triangular sails to either side.

The two men looked up as Wil approached.

"Good morning!" Petre called out. "Are you ready to set sail?"

"Can't wait," Wil replied with a somewhat forced smile. *Where's Mila?*

"This is Tiro, Ricon's son," Petre said, pointing to the other man.

Tiro gave a single nod to Wil. He looked to be a couple of years older than Wil, and his skin was well tanned from a life of labor outdoors. The bottom portion of his hair was shaved, and the chin-length upper portion was pulled into a ponytail.

Wil hopped over the chain railing around the dock onto the deck of the sailboat. The craft hardly seemed seaworthy—its deck plates pitted with rusted holes. But, Wil knew his perspective was skewed after a life surrounded by high technology. There would be no polished chrome or touchscreens in any villages.

"What can I do to help?" Wil asked.

"We've got a handle on the supplies," Petre said. "Get yourself settled in below deck. You get first pick of the hammocks."

"Thanks." Wil took his bag and headed for the hatch into the heart of the boat. There were no lights inside, so he could only see a short ladder descending to a metal grated floor two meters below.

He climbed down the ladder and gave his eyes a minute to adjust. There were shelves along the side walls, stacked with crates like those Petre and Tiro were piling on the main deck. At the aft of the boat, five hammocks were strung between support beams. Wil frowned at the tattered cloth when he saw it, but then, upon further reflection, realized that the hammock would likely be more comfortable than his cot from the previous night. *People live with a lot worse. I can cope.* He set down his bag next to the hammock at the back left.

Shouts sounded outside. Startled, Wil dashed up the ladder. He popped his head out of the hatch. On the deck of the boat, Tiro's and Petre's mouths were hanging open while Mila yelled at her father on the dock.

"You gave me away, so I'm leaving!" Mila shouted.

*I didn't think she'd make a scene!* Wil ducked back into the hatch, staying just high enough so he could watch the altercation.

"Mila, there's no place for you on their voyage. Quiet down," Marlon hissed.

"No! I'm his. He needs me." Mila spotted the top of Wil's head and beckoned to him. "Tell him!"

*Shite! I don't want to be in the middle of this.* Wil wished he'd just stayed hidden so they could work it out on their own. But, since Mila had seen him, he couldn't leave her hanging. Wil finished his climb up the ladder. "She's free to do as she likes. If she wants to come, she may."

Tiro flashed Wil a glare of seething jealousy, but he was quick to hide it.

"See?" Mila said to Marlon.

Marlon scowled and looked Wil over. "I never intended for either of you to leave the village."

"It's what the mission calls for," Wil replied. "Without a radio, this is the only way."

Marlon sighed. "I wish your mother were here to talk you out of it," he said to his daughter.

Mila stared her father in the eye. "It's because she's not that I need to do this. I need to make things right."

After ten seconds of quiet contemplation, Marlon nodded. "Look after her," he said, looking first to Petre and then to Wil.

"Are you sure about this?" Petre asked to no one in particular.

"I'm coming," Mila insisted and tossed a small travel bundle onto the deck of the ship. She hopped over the railing.

Tiro stood tense as Mila strode past him without so much as a glance. He shot Wil another glare of more concealed jealousy.

Petre swallowed hard and grabbed the last crate off the dock. "When we return, everything will be right again," he said to Marlon.

Marlon bowed his head. "May the winds be always at your back."

"Ready the main sail!" Petre instructed Tiro.

Tiro leaped into action, adjusting the rigging to orient the sail toward the wind.

"Cast off the line to the dock," Petre told Wil.

Wil looked along the edge of the boat facing the dock and saw two lead lines tied to posts. He went to untie the knot.

"No, not like that," Mila said with a hint of exasperation. She nudged Wil aside and took over. "I wasn't lying when I said that you needed me."

"Maybe so," Wil replied, standing back to let her work. He took note of her technique and then turned his attention to Petre and Tiro's manipulation of the sails and rudder.

Slowly, the boat pulled away from the dock and picked up the morning breeze to take them northward. Petre stayed at the rudder and Tiro tied off the sails.

After tying the final knot, Tiro came over awkwardly to Mila. "Why are you really here?" he asked her.

She beamed at him. "To be with you, of course! Sorry about the show earlier."

Tiro visibly relaxed. "I thought maybe…" He shot Wil an accusatory look.

"I didn't touch her!" Wil assured him.

Petre was watching the exchange from the aft of the ship where he was working the rudder. "What's going on?" he called out.

Tiro sighed. "Do you promise not to turn the boat around?"

Petre frowned. "Why?"

"Mila and I are in love. We've been seeing each other for some time now," Tiro admitted.

Petre slumped. "I should have figured." He sighed, then looked at Wil. "You knew about this?"

"Mila told me last night," Wil said. "I have someone waiting for me back home, so it was a relief, actually."

Petre nodded. "Well, what's done is done. I was never much for the council arranging marriages, anyway." He sighed. "We have a long voyage ahead. Just don't break up."

Mila took Tiro's hand. "You don't have to worry about that."

# CHAPTER 19

DISABLING THE PLANETARY shield sounded easy at first, but it was more protected than Haersen had hoped. The nearest station was located four towns over from where he'd initially arrived on the planet. It had taken him a month to find passage, and he cursed the pathetic inhabitants of Grolen for delaying him so long. Since arriving in the town several days before, he had been casually staking out the grounds for the shield generator compound. He had yet to identify a covert way to gain access.

At first, he thought that a subtle sabotage was the only reasonable course of action. However, the longer he observed the mundane existence of those who called Grolen home, the more he became convinced that there was nothing worth saving. The entire purpose of lowering the shield was to draw the Bakzen to the planet. No one would be left to identify him as the perpetrator; but even if there were, he would already be safe with the Bakzen.

Haersen stood in the shadows of a low, cinderblock building. Across the street was the structure that housed one of the field generators that in aggregate shielded the planet from enemy attack or meteor impacts. The generator itself was deep underground inside the fortified compound—one of the few technologically sophisticated structures he'd seen on the world. It would be powered by a geothermal converter if it followed standard colonization construction standards. Remove the power source, and the field would be weakened. He would have to bring down additional generators for the shield to lose a meaningful degree of integrity, but Haersen was confident he could handle that through the computer network once he was inside.

He chuckled to himself. To think he had been trying to find a way where they wouldn't know it was him that brought the enemy within their walls. Walking through the front door was so much easier.

It was several hours into the shift for the guards at the front gate. Through his observations, Haersen had noticed they were a somewhat apathetic lot and not terribly attentive, relying instead on the sophisticated biometric scanners safeguarding entry to the inner operations. Presenting a cover story wasn't even worth the effort.

His mind made up, Haersen strode out of his cover beside the building, heading straight for the main gate.

The guards straightened as he approached, readying their blast guns.

"Who are you?" one of the guards asked.

In response, Haersen telekinetically cast him to the side with a flick of his wrist. It had been years since he'd been able to wield his power so freely, and it sent a wave of exhilaration down his spine. The second guard cried out as his colleague was thrown against the wall, but Haersen disposed of him before he could complete his warning.

Haersen's skin tingled from the energy, sending an electrical surge through his fingertips. Craving more, he set his eye on the entry gate. Well-fortified by most standards, the gate was no match for a telekinetic assault. He gripped the hinges with his mind and twisted the metal bars from their fastenings. The metal shrieked as the gate wrenched apart to form an opening.

He stepped through the twisted remains, tossing aside the metal scraps that stood in his way.

Inside the gate, voices called out from the main building on the surface of the compound. Two men and a woman emerged to investigate the commotion. The moment they came into view, Haersen lashed out at their minds, bringing them to their knees with cries of agony. They collapsed unconscious on the ground. He sensed there were others nearby, just inside the building's entry door, but they remained hidden after hearing the screams of their colleagues. They weren't worth the effort of a detour, so Haersen let them be. The Bakzen would deal with them soon enough.

The entrance to the lower level housing the field generator was at the back of the compound, inside a small structure that appeared to only be a single room from the surface. A desk topped with a computer console stood along the side wall, and a single door occupied the back wall. Haersen headed straight for the back door, telekinetically swinging it open as he approached. Stairs led downward. There was likely a lift somewhere, or surface opening to enable equipment replacement, but the stairs would do for his purposes.

He raced down the stairway, taking two steps at a time. At the bottom, he abruptly met a solid door with an electronic keycard entry. With an exasperated sigh, he realized he should have grabbed a keycard from one of the casualties along his way. Still, the door was not insurmountable by other means.

Haersen stepped midway back up the last switchback in the stairs and gave a telekinetic yank on the door. Despite its smaller size, it was more stubborn than the entry gate. He ramped up the intensity, vibrating the casing of the door. It groaned as the seal was breached, loosening dust from the surrounding concrete walls. With a final groan, the door swung inward.

A pulsating hum filled the stairwell. Haersen jogged down the steps and slid through the open doorway.

The door opened onto a grated platform suspended at the edge of an open chamber. There was a single observation computer station along the back railing. More stairs to the left of the platform led down to the field generator below, situated next to its geothermal energy source. The pulsating energy hum echoed through the chamber, creating an oppressive fog in Haersen's head.

Distracted by the sound, it took him a moment to realize there was a technician cowering in a back corner of the platform, behind the observation station. She winced as Haersen stepped forward, her breath ragged and hands trembling. Her eyes silently pled for him to spare her, but she was far too useful for him to let her run away.

Haersen removed his sunglasses and placed them in his pants pocket. He fixed his luminescent brown eyes on the terrified technician and sent a telepathic spear into her mind. She convulsed at first, trying to fight the intrusion. It only took a few seconds for her to succumb, and she relaxed against the railing, staring directly at him, but into the distance.

"Where are the generator controls?" Haersen asked her.

"Down below," she replied, her voice flat.

"Show me."

Her movements stiff and forced, the woman rose to her feet and descended the stairs on the far side of the platform.

At the bottom of the stairs, the woman headed to a workstation adjacent to the generator. Readouts filled three monitors positioned above the touch-surface desktop. "Here," she said.

"Disable the planetary shield," Haersen instructed.

The woman gasped, trying to resist the instruction. She choked and stuttered her protest, her eyes tearing as her mind was overpowered by the intrusive command. Compelled to comply, she accessed the computer terminal.

Haersen watched her navigation and inputs. The final screen displayed the active status for the planetary shield. The generator in front of him was one of five stations distributed around the planet—three on the equator, and one at each pole. If he really wanted to get the Bakzen's attention, he needed to bring down the entire system. "Where are the controls for the network?"

"Don't have access," the woman stammered.

Haersen sensed that there was truth to her statement, but she knew something she was trying to hide. “How do I get access?” he demanded.

She took a shaky breath, tears running down her cheeks. “Override codes. In the manuals.” She looked toward a shelf under the stairs.

Haersen stepped over to the shelf. There were electronic components of various sorts in clear storage boxes. On the top shelf, he spotted a thin book and took it. The gray cover was unlabeled, but the opaque plastic interior pages were printed with scenario labels and corresponding alphanumeric codes. Haersen smiled. He had figured he would have to hack into the network, but he’d just been handed the operations manual.

“Scenario Gallantry,” the woman replied to his unspoken question.

Haersen flipped through the book and located the entry. The access code was a string of twenty characters. “Bring up the authorization,” he instructed.

The woman’s hands jerked as she prepared the system to accept the codes. She entered her personal authorization, and looked to Haersen for the final entry from the book.

He entered in the code, giddy with excitement. Soon the Bakzen would come to the world, and he would be welcomed as a hero.

As soon as he tapped ‘Execute’, the hum from the generator wound down. The command window closed, returning to the graphic of the planetary shield. In unison, the graphic of the shield disappeared from around the simulated planet and the five generation stations flashed red.

“Have to destroy this station,” the woman stammered. “Can’t re-establish shield without the full network.”

Haersen grinned. “Thank you, you’ve been very helpful.” With a flip of his wrist, he cracked her neck and she dropped to the ground.

He stepped over her lifeless body toward the network hub. With telekinetic lashes, he ripped out the wires connecting the station to the rest of the defense network. He doubted her statement was completely true—there would be a workaround to restore the shield without that station—but it would be a delay and that's all he needed.

The Bakzen were out there, watching and waiting for any vulnerability. The world would be theirs for the taking. It was his gift to them, for everything he was about to receive. His trials were almost over. At last, he would be complete.

# CHAPTER 20

WIL SQUINTED IN the sun. He was tan after a month on the open ocean. The warm glow of the radiant heat soothed the chill that had entered the air as they traveled north. Their progress was slowed by inconsistent wind and only a vague knowledge of their destination.

The creak of metal sounded behind Wil, and he restored his tinted glasses.

Tiro and Mila emerged through the sealed hatch to the living quarters below the deck of the small sailing ship. It was the only place to get any privacy.

"Any sign yet?" Tiro asked Wil.

Petre came to join them from his perch midway up the central mast where he'd been on lookout, as well.

"No," Wil replied, looking back at the horizon. For days Tiro had been saying they were nearing the Northern Seafarers village. Aside from some cast-off buoys floating in the dark green water, there was no sign of any civilization.

"I feel it, we're close," Tiro insisted. "There's a smell in the air."

"We're down to a weeks' worth of food stores, unless we find fish," Petre said. "We can only keep wandering for so long."

Wil gazed out at the empty horizon. "Turning back won't do us any good, either."

"No, Tiro's right. There is a smell in the air—like smoke," Mila said.

Wil focused his senses and concentrated on the air. Sure enough, there was a hint of smoke on the breeze. He couldn't identify the direction. "Where—"

"Look!" Mila exclaimed, pointing toward the southeast.

Two compact watercraft were speeding toward them. The craft were too low and traveling in the wrong direction to be carried by the wind.

Tiro beamed. "It's them."

As the craft neared, Wil saw that each was driven by a single rider. They slowed as they approached the sailboat. Both riders wore cloth wrappings around their faces and were bundled in outfits suitable for blocking out the cool sea breeze at night. Five meters from the sailboat, they halted.

The jet skis looked to be powered by a compact steam engine, and based on the smell, the engine was fueled by burning treated blubber.

The rider on the left, a young man in his early-twenties, removed his head wrap. "What is your business here?" he called out.

"We have come to speak with the council of the Northern Seafarers," Petre replied.

The other rider removed their covering, revealing a pretty young woman with red hair. "Why?"

"To unite against a common enemy," Petre stated.

Wil stepped to the edge of the sailboat. "I'm here as an official representative of the Tararian Selective Service. It came to our attention that there's been an injustice on your world. We seek to repair the wrongs done to you by Makaris Corp."

The young man scoffed. "A TSS representative? What kind of joke is this?"

Wil removed his tinted glasses, exposing his glowing cerulean eyes. "It's not a joke."

The two strangers exchanged a wary look. "What proposal do you bring to the village council?" the man asked.

"That's for us to discuss with them," said Wil.

"We don't know you. We're not taking you anywhere," the woman retorted.

"My name is Wil and I'm a Junior Agent with the TSS. Makaris Corp is operating outside of official procedure, and I wish to place the head of operations for this planet under arrest. However, my escorts and I can't take on a fortified supply outpost without additional assistance. We're coming to you without village borders, as citizens seeking to improve the quality of life for everyone on Orino. Our hope is that your leaders will be sympathetic to our cause and lend aid."

The man and woman scrutinized Wil and the others on the sailboat.

"He speaks the truth," Petre said. "My village council reached out for help as a last resort. We couldn't survive another year on the supplies we receive."

"It's not much better for us," the woman said. "Something needs to be done." She looked at the man and he nodded. "I'm Daela, and this is my brother, Rod."

"All right, come with me. We'll let our council decide." Rod turned to Daela, "Continue on to the outpost. I'll meet you there."

Daela readied to head off on her jet ski.

Tiro licked his finger and held it in the air. "The wind isn't in our favor. We'll need a tow."

Daela hesitated.

Rod frowned. "Do you have rope?"

Tiro ran to grab two coils of rope from inside the hatch to below deck. He tossed Rod the end of one length.

Rod secured it to his jet ski and tried to pull the boat. The jet ski groaned and the boat barely moved. "It'll take both of us to tow them," he said to Daela.

"What about the supplies?" she asked.

"It'll have to wait," Rod replied. "Grab the other rope."

Daela frowned but nodded her consent. Tiro tossed her the second length. "You completely passed the village, you know," Daela said as she begrudgingly tied off the rope to the back end of her jet ski. "It's half a day's travel back the way we came."

"I told you we were too far west!" Mila said as she gave Tiro a little shove after he secured the knot on his end of the rope.

"We're on the right path now," Petre cut in. "Let's go."

— — —

The world was surprisingly quiet as Haersen stepped out of the shield generation compound. He had expected a flurry of panic as people realized their world was exposed to attack, but perhaps there were bunkers where they were holed up in a futile attempt to seek shelter.

The next phase of his plan was a dangerous bargain. Bakzen invasion protocol tended to follow a broad sweep attack as the first pass, and it would be easy for him to be killed in the fire. He needed to make his presence known.

A field stretched out to the back side of the generation station, and Haersen jogged a hundred meters into it. The grass reached to his knees and danced like a silver wave under the moonlight. He matted down a patch of grass and sat at the center of the clearing. With a slow exhale, he cleared his mind and opened up his consciousness. He strained to extend himself, brushing the edge of the world—listening and waiting for the Bakzen to approach.

It felt like an eternity to be so far extended and exposed. But eventually, he felt the presence of a single mind at the distant reaches of his consciousness. He called out to the mind, *"I am here. I give you this world."*

There was no response.

For a moment, Haersen panicked. Perhaps the scout did not find the world worthy. Or the shield had been restored. He tried to reach the mind, but then it disappeared. He called out, but there was no one to hear him.

Suddenly, a thousand voices crashed forth into Haersen's mind. He wanted to withdraw from their power, but he forced himself to remain a beacon, calling them to him. *"I am one of you. Accept my gift."*

One of the minds came forward from the deafening din. *"Who are you?"*

*"Arron Haersen. I was from the TSS. I have been working for Colonel Tek."*

The mind was silent for a minute before it returned. *"Stay. We will come for you."*

Haersen pulled back into himself. He panted from the exertion and wiped sweat from his brow. There had been so many of them. All of that power… He wanted to be a part of it.

In the distance, the sky erupted in flame as shots rained down through the atmosphere. The bombardment of the world had begun.

Nervously, Haersen waited in the field, unsure when, or if, the Bakzen would actually come to retrieve him. The horizon glowed red with the flames of burning cities. A faint scent of smoke wafted by on the breeze.

Twenty minutes passed with no further contact. Then, a small shuttle appeared in the sky above.

The design was aerodynamic and practical for atmospheric entry, but the aesthetic was foreign to his eye—dark and ragged. The shuttle slowed as it approached him and landed fifteen meters away. A hatch opened in the side of the craft, and a figure with rough, orange-tinted skin wearing a beige flight suit emerged from the doorway. The muscular soldier stared at Haersen. *"Come here."*

Haersen jogged over. "Thank you for coming," he said aloud as he approached.

The soldier surveyed him with what appeared to be a mixture of confusion and disgust, his glowing red eyes narrowed and cold. "We take you to Tek. He wants to see you."

Haersen bowed his head with thanks and ducked into the shuttle. He was directed to a seat next to the door and strapped in.

The soldier who had greeted him took a seat at the controls next to another identical soldier, the only other occupant in the shuttle. As soon as Haersen was seated, they lifted the shuttle into the air and took a steep course back into space. Haersen gripped the edge of his seat as the shuttle shuddered on its way through the atmosphere. His stomach was knotted with nerves and excitement—for so long he had waited to be welcomed into the folds of the Bakzen. He could hardly believe it was finally happening.

Several minutes passed in the stillness of space before the shuttle entered the hanger of a substantial warship in orbit of the planet. The pilots powered down the shuttle and came to retrieve Haersen.

"We take you to Commander now," the original soldier stated.

Haersen nodded and followed the two Bakzen out of the hanger. They wove through a series of unadorned hallways and took a lift upward. Outside the lift, they walked a short distance down the hall, and then passed through a door into the Command Center.

Haersen was immediately struck by an awe-inspiring panoramic view surrounding the room, as though he had stepped into open space. Beneath his feet, the scarred planet still smoldered from the assault, and Bakzen ships were beginning to descend to the surface to commence their raid.

"You're responsible for delivering this world?"

Haersen looked up to see who had asked the question. A decorated Bakzen officer stepped forward, likely the ship's commander.

"Yes, sir. I hope it is a worthy gift," Haersen replied.

The commander nodded, thoughtful. "I alerted General Tek that you reached out to us. He agreed to meet with you."

*So, Tek received a promotion.* Not surprising, given the vacancy in the command ranks after Carzen's untimely death. "I look forward to it."

"We must finish our business here, of course," the commander continued, clasping his hands behind his back. "You'll be confined to the brig until we return to our homeworld."

The accommodations couldn't possibly be worse than most of the places he had spent the last year, Haersen reflected. He nodded his consent. "I patiently await further instruction."

The commander dismissed Haersen with a wave of his hand and returned his attention to the planetary invasion unfolding below.

As an escort led him away, Haersen was filled with the warm glow of success. He had done it at last—he was with the Bakzen. He was finally going home.

# CHAPTER 21

SAERA BLOCKED OUT the hum of energy encroaching on her consciousness. Her roommates were home from their social hour. The tranquility of her alone time was over.

In the month since her Awakening, she had learned to control the intrusions. None of the others in her training group had experienced any emergence of their abilities, so they didn't bother to keep their minds guarded, despite the urging of their instructors. Beyond it being rude to listen in to private thoughts, Saera didn't like what she heard. Whenever one of the other students noticed she was watching, they would pretend like everything was fine, but their minds revealed otherwise. They were cautious of her. She had changed, and they were still the same.

She knew she was different. She was bonded to someone who was about to be an Agent—an elite Agent with the kind of power no one could predict. Their connection had changed her. She could feel it. Other Trainees were looking at her differently, even though they didn't know why. The Agents seemed to recognize her transformation more readily, but most seemed to brush it off as impossible. Only a select few close to the Sietinens knew the truth.

"What are you doing here?" Elise asked. "Don't you have those evening practice sessions with your secret tutor anymore?"

Saera didn't look up from her tablet. "We're taking a break."

"I think she means they broke up," Caryn interjected as she entered, catching the end of the question.

*They can think whatever they want.* She gave Caryn a coy grin. "I'm top ranked, with or without a tutor."

Leila groaned with the statement as she sat down on her bed. "Thanks for the reminder." She had been unable to break into the Top Ten, despite her best efforts.

"Wouldn't you rather have one of us be at the top than none?" Saera asked her.

"Well, yeah," Leila replied. *"But I still wish it were me,"* Saera heard the thoughts echo in her mind.

"We're a team. If one succeeds, we all do," Saera said.

"Do you really believe that?" Caryn asked.

Saera nodded. "We need to work together if we want to make it through the next couple of months. Help me and I'll help you."

"Want to go over my navigation homework with me?" Nadeen asked.

Saera smiled. "Gladly."

"I'll sit in, too," Caryn said, grabbing her tablet off the wall by her bed.

Elise also grabbed her tablet.

"You in, Leila?" Saera asked.

"No, thanks," Leila replied and put in her headphones.

The other girls looked to Saera for guidance. *Now who's the leader?*

— — —

The sky was dark and a chill filled the air by the time Wil and his companions could see the glow of lights on the horizon.

Rod's and Daela's jet skis sputtered on the final approach to the North Seafarers village, running on the last of their crude fuel. The extra energy needed to tow the sailboat had pushed the craft to their limits.

The village was easily six times the size of Marlon's, and the structures of the town looked to be in better repair. Some buildings rose two or three stories above the water, and a five-story watchtower stood in the center of the community. All of the lights had a slight flicker from the burning of natural fuels—a strange contrast to the electric lights Wil had known his whole life.

Rod and Daela towed the sailboat to the end of a rusty dock extending from the outer town walls. A group of men carrying spears were running up to the dock to meet them.

"Who's this?" one of the men called out from the dock.

"They're from one of the southern villages," Rod replied. "They're here to talk about Makaris. Assemble the council."

"It's late. Everyone is already in bed for the night," the man protested.

"Then wake them," Rod instructed. "We can't invite strangers here overnight without the council's blessing."

The man sighed and ran off to the main gate.

Rod leaped from his jet ski and tethered it to the dock. "Wait here. I'll talk to the others." He ran off after the guard.

Daela helped Tiro secure the sailboat to the dock and then followed her brother's path to the village without a word.

"Do your people ever come here?" Wil asked Petre quietly, watching the guards on the dock with caution.

Petre shook his head slowly. "It's been at least a decade since there was any peaceful meeting. These days, we only see the Northern Seafarers on a raid. The last time we crossed paths, they dragged four women away from our village."

*So some of the information in my mission brief was accurate,* Wil realized. *And now we've essentially just knocked on the enemy's front door.* "At least Rod seems to be on our side."

"Well, they'll either let us in, or they'll kill us," Tiro interjected.

Wil's heart leaped. "You never said that before!"

"They won't kill us," Petre assured. "At least, I doubt it."

*What the fok have I gotten myself into?* Wil took a deep breath and stood poised to act. The rules for his internship banned him from using telekinesis, but there was a definite exception if his safety was on the line.

Ten minutes of uncomfortable silence passed as they waited for the other guards to return and let them into the city. The four men on the dock watched the sailboat vigilantly, their spears at the ready.

Wil shifted on his feet as they waited, anxious to know if their arrival would be welcomed.

The scuffle of footsteps sounded behind the main gate. A group of a dozen men with spears stomped through, with four carrying oil lanterns.

A middle-aged man strode at the front of the group. "Where are the others?" he demanded.

*What others?* Wil stood his ground.

"It is only us," Petre replied.

"Lies! You prepare to attack us," the man accused.

Rod came running up the dock from the village. "Ben, they're on their own, I told you!"

"How do you know? And you led them straight here!" Ben shot back.

"That one is with the TSS," Rod said, pointing to Wil.

Wil removed his tinted glasses. "We're here to make peace. Please, let us address the council."

Ben shook his head. "The central worlds abandoned us long ago."

"You were neglected, but not forgotten," Wil said, restoring his tinted glasses.

"We don't want your kind here," Ben sneered.

"Should I go too, then?" came the voice of an elderly woman from behind the guards. The guards parted and she stepped through, a cane supporting her weight.

Wil hadn't noticed her approach, but as soon as he saw her, he felt a slight hum of energy radiating from her and her eyes had a subtle inner light. In another life, she could have trained as an Agent.

"Let me have a look at you," the woman said, shuffling to the edge of the dock. She examined all the passengers on the sailboat, but her gaze lingered on Wil.

Wil felt her assessing his mind, a tingle passing through him as she peeled back the layers. Her technique was rudimentary, but she had a natural aptitude. He let her dig, but he kept his inner mind locked. *To think what she could have become were there different feelings toward people like us.*

After three minutes of probing, the woman stepped back and leaned on her cane. "They do speak the truth."

Ben's mouth twitched, his eyes narrow. "Are you sure, Frea?"

Frea raised an eyebrow. "Have you ever known me to be wrong?"

Ben looked down, and the guards lowered their spears.

"Gather the rest of the Council," Frea instructed. "Please, come." She beckoned to Wil and his companions.

Wil hesitated, unsure about whether he should leave his travel bag and handheld unattended on the boat. He hadn't yet checked in for the day. *It'll look suspicious if I go to grab anything now.* He decided to leave the bag and followed Petre onto the dock. Mila and Tiro followed close behind.

The guards led the group toward the main gate into the village. The rusted metal walls and gates rose three meters above the waterline, cobbled together from scraps of what looked to be former ship hulls. The walkways were all metal grating of a tight mesh.

Wil felt wobbly on the semi-stable ground after a month at sea on a small boat. After getting his footing, he adjusted his stride to walk abreast with Frea. "You're a telepath," he said to her.

"To these people, I am an Intuitive," she replied, looking straight ahead.

"You have their respect?"

"They appreciate my ability. But you know how others always fear what they can never fully understand."

Wil nodded. "I do."

"Your abilities are unique. I've never felt anything like it," Frea stated, still keeping her attention on the path ahead.

"It's always set me apart."

"Others will exploit your power, if you let them."

*It's a little late for those warnings.* "I have a role to fulfill that I can't avoid."

The hint of a smile touched Frea's lips. "Your destination may be set, but you can always choose how you approach the journey there."

The group passed through an open plaza inside the main gate and turned toward a two-story building adjacent to an interior canal of ocean below. Large double doors opened into the structure, with light from oil lamps pouring into the plaza. They passed through a foyer and went down a short hall.

Frea stepped to the front of the group and led the way into the council chambers. She shuffled across the room and took a seat at the end of a broad table topped in a red cloth. Four men occupied the other seats behind the table.

Two guards remained on either side of the door, and the others departed when the elderly man at the center of the table waved his hand.

Wil bowed to the members of the village council. "Thank you for agreeing to meet with us. I apologize for our late arrival."

The five council members looked him over with suspicion. "Who are you to speak for this group?" the man at the center asked.

"I'm Wil Sights and I've been assigned to resolve the conflict on Orino as part of my pre-graduation internship with the TSS."

"The TSS? Why would the TSS get involved?" the man at the end of the table asked.

"My council requested the assistance," Petre cut in. "We've been at odds for too long. Stealing from each other will get us nowhere. Let us go to the source and make sure that Makaris won't abuse us any longer."

"We're listening," Frea said.

Wil stepped back and let Petre take the lead. After all, it was a fight for his village; Wil was only the facilitator for the discussion. The members of the council listened to Petre's prepared statement for unification and nodded thoughtfully when he finished.

"You suggest a bold action," the center councilman said. "But it is something we've been considering for a while. Still, bringing together all of the villages will take time."

"And with your resources, that can be accomplished so much faster," Petre urged. "Please, join us."

The old man nodded. "Let us deliberate."

Wil and the others were directed into the hall. Tired and hungry after their long journey, they stood in silence waiting.

After ten minutes, the door opened and they were permitted back into the council chamber.

"We will send fifteen people to assist you," Frea announced.

Wil smiled with relief and gratitude. Next to him, Mila and Tiro clasped their hands, and Petre bowed his head.

"You have our heartfelt thanks," Petre said.

"We will send five pairs of two to recruit from the other villages," Frea continued. "Five others will accompany you now on a sail ship, including Hal from our council." She acknowledged the middle-aged man to the right of the center councilman. "The Makaris outpost is on the opposite side of the world. It will take you months to travel there."

*We could do it in minutes with the technology used anywhere else.* "Then let us pick the date for us to meet with the other recruits," Wil said. "We will make the preparations."

"What about meeting at the Tower of Aestra?" Petre suggested.

"A suitable location," the center councilman agreed. "And the time?"

"The winter solstice," Petre stated.

*Isn't that over four months from now?* Wil groaned inwardly but kept his face neutral. *Saera will still be waiting for me. It's okay.*

"The winter solstice at the Tower of Aestra," the center councilman agreed. "We will gather the other northern villages. You'll need to recruit from the south along the way."

"Thank you." Wil bowed to the council with his companions.

"We will refresh your supplies in the morning," Frea said as she rose from her seat. "But now, it is late and we must get back to bed."

After some parting pleasantries, Wil made his way back to the sailboat with Petre, Tiro and Mila. "What is the Tower of Aestra? Some sort of castle?" he asked them.

Petre grinned. "It's a big rock. But when most of the world is water, any rock may as well be a castle."

— — —

Four Bakzen soldiers escorted Haersen down the bleak hall of their ship. It had been nearly a day since he'd been retrieved from Grolen and he was anxious to finally have his meeting with Tek.

Though Haersen had been in communication with the Bakzen for nearly two decades, ever since he was first approached during his internship, he had only had a face-to-face meeting with a commander once before. His stomach knotted with anticipation. He could feel the unrestricted power of the menial soldiers around him—a fraction of their leader's abilities. But just that small taste was liberating for Haersen after the years spent in subspace, shielded from his greatest abilities.

They passed through several corridors that took them deep into the Bakzen command compound. It was rough and plain compared to everything found within the realm of the TSS, and it came as a refreshing change.

The soldiers stopped outside a door at the end of the last hall.

"General inside," the lead guard said to him.

Haersen nodded and inclined his head before passing through the doorway.

Tek was waiting in the center of the room.

Haersen bowed to him as he entered. "General, it is an honor to finally be in your presence."

Tek scowled at him, his red eyes intent. "You have a lot of nerve coming here."

Haersen's chest tightened. That wasn't the welcoming he had envisioned. "Why wouldn't I? We had a deal."

"But you failed to deliver."

Haersen shook his head, his pulse quickening. "I did everything you asked."

Tek evaluated him. Suddenly, he burst into laughter, a sinister gleam in his eye. "You don't know, do you?"

Haersen gulped. "Know what?"

"The Primus Elite survived."

It wasn't possible. Haersen fell to the floor, quivering from fear and rage. He'd shot Wil—he was bleeding out, there was no way he could have survived. But if he had…

Haersen could barely breathe, a cold chill gripped his chest. The Bakzen would never let him live after such a failure. There would be no sanctuary. He had brought himself to his death.

Unable to rise from his hands and knees, Haersen looked up to Tek. "I'll find another way."

"It's too late for that. He's already discovering his true power." Tek took a step closer, looking down with what was almost a touch of pity. "You're no longer any use to me."

Haersen cowered. “Please, I’ll do anything.”

Without warning, Tek gripped Haersen in a telekinetic vise and whipped him to his feet. Tek’s luminescent red eyes locked onto his captive suspended in midair.

Haersen squirmed, helpless, his toes barely brushing the ground. The vise cinched tighter around him, crushing his neck and chest. He gasped for air. “Please!”

“Why would I spare you?”

There wasn’t a compelling reason, really. Haersen searched for a reply that would keep him alive, but his mind was blank. It took all his focus just to draw a breath through the telekinetic vise. “I’ll help you get others,” he gasped.

Tek loosened the vise ever so slightly. “We have no difficulty gaining support. Why do we need you?”

“I can help you get the most out of them. I know how the TSS works.”

Tek considered the proposition, but tightened the vise again. “We already have other insiders.”

Haersen labored to breathe, feeling the end drawing near. “Then spare me because you gave me your word.”

The vise released, dropping Haersen to the ground. He stumbled, falling to his knees. He gasped for air, cradling his bruised ribs.

Tek stepped forward, towering over him. “Others may have run away in your position, but you made your way here, against all odds. Never before has someone shown such dedication.”

“I believe in what you’re doing,” Haersen said, gazing upward. “Tararia needs to fall.”

“You’ll never truly be one of us, you know,” Tek cautioned.

“I could never expect to be. I only hope to be my best.”

Tek sighed. “You’re pathetic.”

Haersen scrambled to his feet. “So, make me better.”

Tek evaluated him. “It will change you.”

“I want nothing of my old self.” There was so little left, as it was. His last remaining shreds of identity had be shed over the months of weary travel.

“Don’t forget all of your old life.” Tek took him by the shoulder. “I may find some use for you yet.”

# CHAPTER 22

BANKS REVIEWED THE latest report from Agents Aeronen and Merdes. Wil's months at sea had done him good. The tone in his journal entries had become more relaxed, upbeat. *He needed a break from all of this back home. I'm glad it's been an escape for him.*

More importantly, the internship was a window into Wil's inner motivations. Banks was pleased to see that Wil was very much like his father—rallying to support the common people and to stand up to unjust authority. It was the trait Banks valued most in them. That kind of dedication would be crucial after the war.

*First things first.* Banks closed out of the report. He was overdue for his weekly check-in with the Priesthood.

CACI arranged the secure call.

Banks bowed his head in greeting to the Priest when the call connected. "Hello. I hope you are well."

"Do you have any news?"

*Straight to business, as always.* Banks clasped his hands behind his back. "He's still sailing with his companions, but they are close to their destination."

"And he continues to perform well?" the Priest asked.

Banks nodded. "Yes. The internship is almost complete. Then we will be able to test his limits."

"If we did our job correctly, he won't have such constraints," the Priest countered.

"Everyone has a limit."

"Perhaps. But let's hope he never finds his."

— — —

Cris climbed into bed and gave Kate a kiss. "Sorry I'm late. All this final exam shite keeps stacking up."

Kate snuggled up to him. "I know. It'll be over soon."

"Thankfully." Cris put his arm around her. "Oh, and Banks said Wil should be home in time for the main graduation ceremony."

Kate looked up at him. "Five months is pretty short for an internship."

"I'm surprised he wasn't done in three."

"True," Kate said, settling back into the crook of Cris' arm. "I suppose there have been some travel limitations."

"Well, extra time away isn't a bad thing. I can't begin to imagine what it's going to be like after graduation."

Kate shook her head. "How do we keep him from burning out before things *really* get bad?"

"I hope Saera will help with that."

"And Banks is still okay with them…?"

"He seems to be. I'd bet he's willing to make any concession if it keeps Wil functional."

Kate frowned. "Now even you're talking about him like an asset."

"I don't think of him that way, but they do. That's all any of us are to them."

"I'm not convinced Banks is one of them," Kate countered. "Some of the things he's said haven't been particularly glowing about the Priesthood."

"But he's playing along with them."

"Aren't we doing the same thing?"

"Fair point," Cris conceded.

"It takes wisdom to recognize the right time to make a move. And that time isn't now."

"After the war."

Kate nodded. "After the war."

"Let's hope we still have enough of ourselves left for one last fight."

— — —

*Just two more weeks to go.* Saera was anxious for the end of the term. Maintaining her position as the top-ranked Trainee was exhausting, but she wanted to ensure the recommendation for Primus Command was confirmed. Anything that would keep her closer to Wil would help them in the years ahead.

She had just completed a practice session with the Primus girls and boys. Her roommates already had their tablets on their laps for some last-minute refreshers before the written exams, but Saera didn't have any concerns about the tests. All that she cared about was Wil coming home. Five months was too long to be apart.

Saera sat down on her bed and grabbed her own tablet. No new messages. She sighed inwardly. *When is he coming back?*

"Ugh, I can't wait for finals to be over," Elise said as she set aside her tablet and laid down on her bunk.

"Then we'll be Initiates!" Nadeen interjected with rare outward excitement.

Caryn shot her a sidelong glance. "If we decide to stay, that is."

"What could they possibly tell us in the debrief to make anyone want to leave?" Leila asked.

*Whatever it is, Wil didn't want to tell even me.* Saera kept the thought to herself and clicked her tablet back into the wall.

"Well, I'm staying regardless," Elise stated.

"Same," Leila agreed.

Nadeen and Caryn murmured their agreement, as well.

"What about you, Saera?" Nadeen asked.

"I'm in. I can't go back to Earth after this."

Leila nodded with satisfaction. "So, the Primus girls will remain united."

"We already are. You finally want to join the club?" Nadeen shot back.

Leila tensed. "Yes, well, we're a team. All of us."

*Hopefully, she'll start acting like it.* Saera got up off her bed. "I'm going to take a shower." She grabbed her pajamas and went into the bathroom. With everyone else in study-mode, she had the room to herself.

She took her time to relax under the hot water, savoring the gentle rhythm of the water splashing onto the tile floor.

The timer in the shower beeped with two-minute warning for automatic water shut-off. Rarely did she max out the fifteen-minute limit. She finished washing her hair and shut off the water.

With a towel wrapped around herself, Saera stepped over to the mirror to comb out her wet hair. As she gazed at herself in the mirror, a stream of water snaked down her face to the tip of her nose. A single drop dripped down.

Saera watched the drop fall. It stopped in midair an inch below her nose. Her mouth parted with surprise. The drop of water continued to hover. *Am I doing that?*

Her concentration broke and the drop splashed down into the sink.

She let out a giggle of happy surprise. *I just levitated a drop of water!* No one had witnessed the feat, but that was okay. The act itself didn't matter—but it meant she was getting control of her abilities. A smile spread across her face. When Wil returned, he could really start training her. She couldn't wait.

— — —

The rendezvous point was easy to spot from a distance. Wil was on watch halfway up the mast of the sailboat when he saw the giant rock peeking up from the horizon. *The Tower of Aestra. Finally!* Other boats were already anchored around the island.

Wil smiled down at his companions. "They came through."

Petre looked up at him and nodded with satisfaction. "I had no doubts."

"Now we just have to get everyone to work together." *And that's all on me.* Wil slid down the mast to the deck of the ship. A length of hair struck him in the eye and he tucked it back into the tie holding back the rest—grown out after five months at sea.

In the nearly four months since the meeting with the Northern Seafarers, Wil and his companions had visited six other villages on their south-easterly journey. All but two of the villages had promised to send soldiers to help with the conquest of the corrupt Makaris operation on Orino. But more importantly, each was sending a diplomatic representative. With the feud around inequitable supply distribution resolved, peace could once again return to the people of Orino. Getting that truce in writing was ultimately the objective of Wil's mission. *I need to keep my sights on that. These people are my friends, but this isn't my home.*

Mila scaled the vacated central mast of the boat, peering out at the land up ahead. "Land! It's so… solid."

Wil looked up at her with surprise. "You've never seen land before?"

"No. I'd never left the village until I set sail with you," she replied, still fixated on the rock monolith before her.

*My perspective is so different. No wonder they have such distaste for Tararia—the other side of the world is a distant realm, let alone a whole other planet.* "On most other worlds, people only live on land."

Mila grinned. "They're missing out."

Petre directed the sailboat toward a natural jetty along the southern edge of the rock. The escort boat sent from the Northern Seafarers followed through the choppy water swirling around the monolith. Half a dozen other boats slightly larger than their own were moored in the shallow bay. A crescent-shaped black sand beach curved along the inner face of the rock. Gray rock spires that suggested the location's name stretched a hundred meters toward the overcast sky—pitted columns separated by vertical crevasses lost in shadow.

They dropped anchor in the center of the bay. Based solely on the beach, it was difficult to determine the fluctuation in tides, and they didn't want to become trapped at low tide—if there was one.

Along the shore, a group of people were beginning to congregate. Most were young men around Tiro's age, but several elders were among them.

"Swim ashore?" Wil asked Petre.

"That's the way of it."

The four of them dove off the bow of the boat into the murky water, churning with sand and silt.

Wil's breath caught in the sudden chill of the water. Shaking off the initial shock, he took up an even stroke and followed the others toward the shore.

Eight meters from the shoreline, the water was shallow enough to stand. They waded the rest of the way to the beach under the scrutinizing eye of the strangers.

Wil took the lead as they exited the water, thankful to feel the warming rays of the sun on his back. "Hello. I am the representative from the TSS."

One of the elders stepped forward. "I am Samuel. I am here on behalf of the Sunwatcher Village of the south."

"Pleased to meet you," Wil replied. "Have you spoken with the other representatives?"

Samuel nodded. "Some. We have been awaiting leadership. It looks like that has now arrived."

"I'll do my best," Wil said, looking around the group. "Now, let's see who's here."

The younger members of the group on the shore scattered to gather representatives from each of the villages.

"Come, dry yourselves." Samuel beckoned Wil toward an inviting fire high up the beach adjacent to a rock overhang.

Two dozen bedrolls were laid out around the campsite—a mixture of tanned hides from the native sea creatures on the planet and Baellas-branded items from the Central Worlds. Primitive spears and bows made of bone and sharpened metal were piled next to some of the bedrolls.

Wil took inventory of the items as he passed by. The weapons would be no match for the blast guns and incendiary cannons scouts from other tribes had spotted at the Makaris station, but they would have numbers on their side. Several dozen people could easily overwhelm the small Makaris installation, especially with a surprise strike.

The key would be to capture the facility before the guards could call for reinforcements. If Wil could proactively explain the corruption to Makaris before Akka had a chance to speak his case, the people of Orino were far more likely to have a favorable outcome.

Wil dried his clothes for fifteen minutes next to the fire while he waited for the village representatives to arrive. He was surprised how strange it felt to once again have solid ground underfoot. Petre, Mila and Tiro were visibly uncomfortable on the rock, stepping cautiously as though they expected the land to give way at any moment. He smiled to himself, remembering the same look on Saera's face when he first started working with her in freefall. His heart leaped. *I'll be home soon.*

The last of the village representatives took their seats around the fire as the sky tinted orange with the approach of dusk. Each person gazed at Wil with their full attention.

"Thank you for coming," Wil began, looking around the circle. "We are here together now because Orino is in trouble.

Only as a united front can we make sure that your people aren't ever in this same situation again."

"I know many of you don't trust the TSS," Petre stated. "But Wil has proven himself to be an advocate and ally. My village had it worse than many—"

"You think you had it bad?" one of the young men cut in. "I watched people starve so I could live!"

Mila jumped to her feet. "You think we didn't? My mother—"

The crowd burst into cacophonous shouts.

*That didn't take long to deteriorate!* "Calm down!" Wil yelled over the side arguments.

He was struck by the anger and bitterness of the group, faces twisted into snarls. They were a people living on the edge, fighting for their very survival. Years of isolation and competing for resources had forced them to build a society where only the strong and tough survived.

Wil struggled to maintain composure, seeing the pain of those around him. The way they spit and yelled at each other was a shocking testament to how quickly people could turn savage when their well-being was on the line. *This is what life could be like. This is why we can't let the Bakzen tear us apart.*

Wil climbed up on a rock to stand above the crowd. "We're here to make things better, remember?" he shouted. *I need to bring them together, to end these feuds. No one should have to live in fear.*

With a few final spats, the crowd fell silent. "Now," Wil continued when he had their attention, "Akka is our target at the Makaris outpost. What do we know about the facility?"

The group refocused on the objective, providing Wil with the details he would need to formulate a solid plan of attack. What they told him fueled his motivation. Having everyone together and hearing the different sides of their experience with Makaris, Wil started to see what had been going on all along. Akka definitely had to go.

Wil was confident in their ability to overtake the Makaris station, but the willingness for the different villages to work as one remained to be seen. If they were successful in their mission, perhaps it would be enough to show that a peace treaty was the best path forward.

With Wil acting as facilitator, the group agreed to a tentative organizational structure for the attack force. Wil would serve as the commander until the mission concluded.

"Anything else for tonight?" Samuel asked when the conversation wound down.

"No," Wil replied as he stood. "We should go retrieve our gear. It's going to be a cold swim."

Samuel shook his head. "We have a canoe for ferrying supplies from the boats. We will help you."

Petre's face lit up. "Thank you, that is very kind."

It was nearly nightfall by the time Wil and his companions were settled at the campsite for the night, their gear safely ferried to the shore. The ground beneath their bedding was uncomfortably firm after the hammock Wil had grown accustomed to over the past several months. However, he was too tired to care. *We have a plan. And soon I'll be back with Saera.*

Next to him, Mila shifted around in an attempt to get comfortable. "How do you sleep with the ground so still?"

"It took me weeks to get used to the lack of a background mechanical hum." *Still, she has a point.* The hammock itself was more comfortable, but Wil had found the gentle rocking of the boat to be soothing. In his time on Orino, he had slept better than he had in the previous year back home. But, that was largely because the dreams about the Bakzen had receded—at least for the time being.

"Loud and still. I don't know how you do it." Mila rolled over again.

Wil settled into his own bedroll. "Try to get some sleep. Tomorrow we begin planning our attack."

# CHAPTER 23

WIL PERCHED AT the edge of the boat, focused on the front gate of the Makaris outpost. The cloud cover hid the moon and made the night unusually dark.

The plans were set and Wil had coached everyone through the attack. Months of recruiting, two weeks of intensive training, and hours of planning had all come down to that moment. Their night of action had come.

"Capture, not casualties," Wil reminded everyone.

The first wave of Orino warriors, led by Tiro, nodded and began to slink along the dock, staying low to the ground and seeking cover behind crates as they inched toward the entry gate.

The guard outside the front gate never saw the warriors coming. In one swift motion, he was pulled from his feet and gagged.

Wil watched from a distance as Tiro took the keycard from the guard and opened the front gate. Silently, Tiro and the other warriors crept into the facility.

Sounds of a single blaster shot and a cry of pain broke the night.

*Shite!* Wil leaped out of the boat and ran toward the main gate. The plan had called for stealth, but they had been over all the contingencies. *It's okay. They know what to do.*

Wil could barely make out the doorway ahead in the dim light. He kept his footsteps silent as he dashed along the metal deck. When he reached the door, he heard light footsteps coming up behind him; without turning, he knew it was Mila. "Go back to the boat!" he hissed. She wasn't part of the backup plan.

"Tiro's in there! He may be hurt," Mila whispered back in protest.

There wasn't time to argue with her, and he knew she wouldn't listen. "Stay behind me." Wil pressed his back against the wall next to the open gate and chanced a glance inside.

The entryway was empty, but it smelled of scorched metal. Red lights down the side hall illuminated just enough for Wil to see evidence of the blaster shot on the wall. His warriors and the guards were nowhere to be seen.

Without hesitation, Wil slipped through the door and followed the signs pointing to the main office down the left hall from the entry. Even if they couldn't take the outpost quietly, they at least needed to keep the guards from calling for reinforcements before Wil had a chance to arrest Akka. Otherwise, a firefight would be unavoidable.

The office was three doors down. Wil tried the handle. Locked. The electronic lock couldn't be cracked without using his handheld and that would violate the internship terms. "Shite," he muttered under his breath.

"Are they inside?" Mila asked.

"I don't know. We need to sever the communications regardless." Wil pressed his ear against the door, but he couldn't make out any voices inside.

"The guards must be—" Mila was cut off by the creak of a door opening between the entry and their place in the hall.

Wil flattened against the wall, pulling Mila to his far side. He held his finger to his mouth for her to be quiet. She crouched, one hand on the hilt of her dagger.

The door swung open the rest of the way with a groan, accompanied by low whispers.

Wil relaxed and pushed off from the wall, recognizing the voice. "What happened, Tiro?"

Tiro startled at the sudden question breaking the quiet, but he smiled when he saw Wil with Mila. "One of the guards spotted us inside the door. He clipped my arm with the blaster." He looked down at his left arm, which was wrapped in a length of tan cloth.

Mila frowned at the wound. "And the guard?"

"Tied up inside." Tiro swung the door shut and locked it with the keycard.

"We need to get Akka," Mila said to Wil.

"Soon," Wil assured her. "But our cover was blown. Taking out communications is our first priority."

"But the secondary team is supposed to—" Tiro began.

"We went to the backup plan the moment shots were fired." Wil held out his hand to Tiro for the keycard.

Tiro relinquished the keycard, and Wil ran back to the office door. He swiped the card across the lock. Red. "Bomax."

"It didn't work?" Mila asked.

"Those guards must not have clearance to this room. But others might." *This just got dangerous.* Wil groaned to himself. *Time for Plan C.* "Tiro, your team needs to hold this door. Don't let anyone through. We'll get Akka's card—that'll work for sure."

Tiro acknowledged his understanding with a nod, and the five other warriors took up positions facing either end of the hall.

Wil slipped past them with Mila at his heels. At the entry, he turned outside and jogged a couple of meters down the dock. He gestured for the second wave of warriors to advance.

"What happened?" Rolan, the group's leader, asked as he padded up to Wil ahead of his warriors.

"Change of plan," Wil explained. "Help Tiro secure the first level while Mila and I go for Akka. One guard is in custody, but others may be hiding. Hopefully, they haven't been able to call for reinforcements."

"You can trust us," Rolan replied, and he motioned for his warriors to follow.

Wil turned his attention to the heart of the mission: capturing the man in charge. "Let's get Akka."

Wil and Mila snaked their way through the lower level toward the staircase. He checked that it was clear, then waved Mila up the stairs. Only dim red light illuminated the narrow passage.

A short hallway with two doors was at the top of the stairs. One was cracked open, revealing it was a washroom.

Mila pointed to the door on the opposite wall and Wil nodded. She mouthed a countdown. On 'one', she barged through the door with Wil.

A man with dark hair was hunkered behind his bed, grasping a blast gun in his tanned hands. Akka. "Who the fok are you?" He charged the weapon.

"Put the gun down," Wil instructed.

"I heard you shoot the guard downstairs," Akka's brown eyes narrowed with spite. "I'm not doing a foking thing you say."

"They fired on us." Wil positioned himself between the gun and Mila, readying a telekinetic shield. "On authority of the TSS and the High Dynasties, I am placing you under arrest for suspicion of racketeering, abuse of power, and professional negligence."

"You're out of your minds! Do you know who I am?" Akka protested.

"Do you know who *I* am?" Wil countered. "Tie him up," he said to Mila and tossed her a length of metal twine from inside his jacket pocket.

Mila pulled Akka's hands behind his back, making no effort to be gentle. "You're filthy scum," she spat into his ear.

"Let's just get our job done," Wil said, hoping to calm her. He scanned the surfaces of the room and spotted a keycard on the nightstand. Wil clipped it to his pants.

Mila finished securing Akka's hands and shoved him to his feet.

"Come on," Wil said and directed Akka down the stairs. At the base of the stairs, Wil turned out toward the courtyard, where he spotted a mesh metal fence. "Up against there." He pulled out additional lengths of metal twine from his pocket and secured Akka to the fence.

"Keep an eye on him. I'm going to disable the communications," Wil said to Mila and headed back inside.

He was about to enter the hall toward the central office when he heard a shout from outside. Wil spun around and rushed back out to where he'd left Mila.

Wil froze in horror when he stepped into the courtyard.

Mila was standing over the prisoner, a knife gleaming in a thin beam of moonlight peeking through the clouds.

Heart racing, Wil ran forward to stop her. "Shite, Mila, no!"

The knife plunged into Akka's chest. Thick, dark blood poured out. He gasped twice before slumping against his restraints.

Wil pulled her back as she tried to stab him again. "Fok! Why? We—"

Mila stared at the dead man, tears streaming down her face. "He killed my mother."

"What?" Wil's gut wretched. He'd been forced to kill, himself, while escaping from the Bakzen, but seeing death up close… the vacant eyes and pooling blood—it was a gruesome glimpse of the casualties of war that awaited him.

"My mother starved to death so that I could eat." Mila dropped the knife to the ground and fell to her knees sobbing, directly in the puddle of blood spreading out from the body. "He was a foking bastard and he deserved to die!"

*He did.* Wil pulled her to her feet and away from Akka's corpse. "They'll arrest you. You'll spend the rest of your life in a prison colony."

"I don't care," Mila said, wiping her tears with her blood-stained hands. "It was worth it."

Footsteps sounded from the entry. Wil turned to see Tiro approaching.

"I heard shouting. The rest of the facility is secure," Tiro began. He noticed the body slumped against the wall. "Fok, what happened?"

"Mila stabbed him," Wil said. "He's dead."

Tiro's face contorted with alarm and horror. "Fok! Everything was coming together, Mila. Petre had given us his blessing. We could have had a life together!"

She shook her head. "I'm sorry. I had to. He needed to die. I couldn't let anyone else be hurt because of him."

Tiro looked to Wil, his eyes pleading. "You can't let them take her away to prison."

*I don't want to see her end up like that, either.* Wil's mind raced. "The Communications room is still locked down?"

Tiro nodded.

Wil assessed Akka's body. "Okay, get the others. We need to clean this up."

— — —

Saera and the other Trainees filed into the lecture room. It was the one hall she'd seen at Headquarters that could accommodate the whole group.

High Commander Banks stood behind the front podium, calmly surveying the young, inquisitive faces of the students. Cris Sights and Scott Wincowski stood to his right.

Saera settled into her chair in one of the middle rows next to the other Primus girls.

"I thought they'd talk to us in smaller groups," Elise whispered to her.

"It's more efficient this way," Saera replied. *And more peer pressure for us to stay.*

Banks held up his hand to quiet the room. When all eyes were on him, he began, "You've reached the end of your first year. Tradition holds that we offer you a choice: stay with the TSS and continue to grow, or go your own way. We will now give you the context to make that choice."

Saera leaned back in her seat, arms crossed. *Or half-truths, anyway. I want the real story from Wil.*

"Some of you may have heard of the Bakzen," Banks continued. Several members of the audience nodded. "The Bakzen are becoming an increasingly greater threat as time goes on. We fear that war is coming. And if—when—it does, our Agents will need to be on the front lines. If you don't have it in you to join that fight, this is your one chance to get out."

A murmur of surprise rippled through the Trainees.

Saera was more interested in Cris' reaction at the front of the room. His expression was impassive on the surface, but his posture was rigid. Something about Banks' statement wasn't genuine.

"We tell all the Trainees at the end of their first year. We've been telling them for a long time. With every new cohort, the likelihood of war increases. You have to ask yourself: are you ready for that commitment?" Banks surveyed the faces in the room. "That is all. You have one week to decide if you want to stay. Thank you." He hurried out of the room.

Cris stepped up to take his place. "Some of you might have questions. I'll hang back if you want to talk."

Saera couldn't be sure, but she thought he looked right at her for a moment. *If Wil knows he's going to step up as a commander, that war has to be coming soon.*

The students rose to go. At the bottom of the side aisle, Saera hung back from the others.

"Aren't you coming?" Nadeen asked.

Saera shrugged. "I don't know anything about the Bakzen, being from Earth. I just have a couple questions. I'll catch up with you."

Nadeen nodded and left with the rest of the Trainees. Saera was alone with Cris and Agent Wincowski.

"I can handle this, Scott," Cris said.

The other Agent departed and closed the door behind him.

"What wasn't the High Commander saying?" Saera asked. "Wil hinted that there's something going on, but he wouldn't say what."

"You're quite perceptive." Cris sighed. "If I tell you anything, you have to keep it to yourself."

Saera nodded. "Of course."

Cris took a deep breath. "So, there's another division of the TSS codenamed 'Jotun'..."

— — —

The fire crackled as Petre tossed on another fuel block distilled from whale blubber. Wil had come to find the scent comforting over the last several months. His chest tightened thinking about his impending departure and what was to come.

"The terms are agreeable," Petre said, nodding to the representative from the Northern Seafarers. The other representatives nodded their consent, as well.

"Then it's settled." Wil laid out the official treaty Petre had penned on a piece of leather. The document established terms for equal supply distribution going forward, proportional to population size and access to the natural resources on the planet. Each of the village representatives had contributed to the terms, and all had approved the wording.

Wil passed the parchment around the circle for each of the representatives to sign. One by one, each took the pen and signed their name and the name of the represented village. Petre was the last to sign his name. He handed the parchment back to Wil.

Wil took the document with a heavy heart. It was the remaining criterion to meet the objectives for his internship mission. He laid it out on the metal deck plates and pulled out the handheld that was his only link to the Agents monitoring him from above. He took a picture of the signed document and saved it as an attachment to his final daily journal entry. As soon as he hit 'send', it would only be a matter of hours before the Agents came to retrieve him.

"What does your report state?" Petre asked, glancing at a nervous Tiro and Mila sitting just outside the representatives' circle.

*Did I call Mila out as a murderer?* "What happened at the supply outpost is on all of us. They can't blame everyone, and so no one can be punished," Wil replied.

The village representatives nodded slowly. Hal, from the Northern Seafarers, looked Wil in the eye, "You have truly shown you take our best interest to heart. I only wish the High Dynasties showed us that same favor."

Wil swallowed. *Not all of the High Dynasties are the same.* "I have long known there are issues with the current governmental system, but my experience here has only highlighted those problems. I hope to one day right those injustices."

"You have already done so much for us," Petre said. "We don't expect you to do more."

*But who else can?* Wil took a deep breath. "I want to be honest with you. You put your trust in me, so I want you to know it's not ill-placed." He looked around at the faces watching him with renewed interest. "So, I speak to you now as an heir to Sietinen." A low murmur spread throughout the group. "What Makaris did to you is not the way of the High Dynasties. I will use whatever influence I can to make sure it doesn't happen again."

"You are heir to Sietinen?" Samuel asked, mystified.

Wil ventured a small smile. "Well, second in line."

Over Petre's shoulder, Mila looked shocked. She gripped Tiro's hand tightly, a mixture of confusion and awe in her eyes.

"And why do you reveal yourself to us now?" Hal asked.

"Because I couldn't leave with you thinking that no one in the High Dynasties cared."

"You're leaving now?" Petre asked.

"I've accomplished what I came here to do." Wil looked down at his handheld. "As soon as I send this report, my mission is complete."

Petre looked to the other council representatives. "He has shown himself to be one of us. We should extend him the respect we would one of our own."

Hal nodded. "Can you delay sending your report?"

Wil hesitated. "For a while. Why?"

Hal rose. "It is time we honor you."

# CHAPTER 24

"SAERA, I'M REALLY impressed," Agent Katz said, leaning back in her chair. "I can't believe you didn't say anything sooner."

"It was only a drop of water." Saera looked around Katz's office. It was small compared to the Lead Agent's office where she sometimes visited Cris, and very simply decorated with a single holopainting, two chairs and a touch-surface desk. She always felt antsy during these monthly check-ins.

"Still, most don't begin experimenting with object levitation until their second year as an Initiate."

Saera returned her focus to her instructor. "Well, you gave me a great foundation. It just came to me."

Katz nodded. "Nonetheless, it's quite an accomplishment. I'm glad you decided to stay and continue your training—I'd hate to think about you experimenting too much on your own."

*I couldn't turn my back on a war. Especially not when Wil needs me.* "I look forward to seeing what comes next."

Katz smiled. "Yes, me too. Well, unless you have anything else to discuss, we can adjourn early and both get a few minutes back in our day."

"No, there's nothing else, ma'am. Thank you."

"All right. I'll see you at practice tomorrow morning."

Saera left the office and made her way down the administrative wing toward the central elevator lobby. As she entered the lobby, one of the elevators opened and a cluster of several men stepped out. She was about to ignore them, but she felt a pull in her chest. *What…?*

Then, Saera looked closer. *Wil!* He was a bit taller and his hair was shaggy, but it was him. *He's finally back!*

As if sensing her thoughts, Wil looked up from the floor and met Saera's gaze. It was impossible to read his expression behind his tinted glasses. One of the men walking with him said something, and without another glance Wil turned away and went down a hall.

Saera's heart dropped. *He looked right at me but didn't seem to care. Did he change his mind about us?*

— — —

Wil eyed the two men across the table. *Colren is an Agent, but who's this other guy?*

"Thank you for your patience as we got everything for the interview sorted out," Colren said. "We had to go a little outside of standard protocol, given the circumstances."

"Of course. Quite all right." *Now can we get on with it? You're keeping me from something far more important.*

"Mr. Stelsin will be joining us for your debrief interview," Colren explained, gesturing to the other man.

Stelsin nodded absently and looked over some notes on his tablet. He was wearing a charcoal suit, calling him out as a civilian.

Wil waited for the questioning to begin. *It should be two Agents interviewing me. This is strange.*

"So, Wil Sights," Stelsin said finally. "I understand that you were on Orino for the last five months."

"Yes, correct." *I don't think he has any idea who I am.*

"And the two Agents overseeing your internship were Aeronen and Merdes?" Colren asked.

"Yes, correct."

"Excellent. Now please state for the record your mission objective," Colren continued.

"In short, my mission was to facilitate a treaty between the various communities on Orino. I was assigned a 'neutral' group to live with while completing the assignment."

"And, for the record, did you fulfill this objective?" Colren inquired.

Wil picked his words carefully. "The requirements for mission completion were satisfied."

"But did you fulfill the objective?" Colren pressed.

Wil leaned back in his chair. "Well, that requires a little explanation."

"We're listening."

"When I arrived on Orino, I was greeted by a community leader named Marlon. He presented his daughter, Mila, to me. I identified that Mila would be an asset in terms of helping explain the community structure, so I briefed her on my mission. It was then that I realized that reality didn't quite match up to what the TSS was told."

"How so?" Colren asked.

"Mila took me to one of the storerooms," Wil explained. "The food supplements were extremely low. According to Mila, they often ran out by the end of the month."

"Was it poor rationing?" Stelsin questioned.

"No, quite the opposite. It was only by making adjustments to the prescribed rations that they were able to make it through the month."

"What was going on?" Stelsin asked.

"The planet's liaison for Makaris Corp decided to take the business into his own hands," Wil explained. "A man named Akka Kerwein."

Stelsin looked horrified. "No, that's impossible!"

*Oh! Stelsin must be a representative from the Dynasty, here to get the story on what happened.* "Mr. Stelsin, I am simply giving an account of my personal experiences. If you'll let me finish, I believe your doubts will be put to rest."

"Yes, Mr. Stelsin," Colren emphasized. "This is a formal debrief. The TSS extended a courtesy to let you sit in, but you're here as an observer."

"I'm sorry, go on," Stelsin muttered.

"Anyway," Wil continued, "Akka went rogue. Apparently about ten years ago, he started making unauthorized price increases to the food shipments. Orino has an abundance of edible aquatic life, and certain fish are considered a delicacy on other worlds. However, the meats have a relatively limited nutritional spectrum, making the Orino colonists highly reliant on the supplements from Makaris Corp for actual dietary needs. Because of this reliance, they scraped together what they could in trade goods—mostly fish—to make the higher payments, but then the volume of supplies began declining. Some of the concentrates were even diluted with water."

"What did the people do?" Colren asked.

"They did the only thing they could," Wil responded. "They couldn't get the supplies they needed through Makaris, so they went to the only other source at their disposal: other communities. That conflict mentioned in my mission briefing? Those raids were fueled by people just trying to get their hands on what they needed to survive."

"How was the TSS so misinformed about what was going on?" Colren asked.

"That's where things really get interesting. The request for TSS intervention originated in Akka's office," Wil said.

"How...?" Stelsin seemed completely taken aback by the whole account.

"It appears that Akka identified Marlon's group as one of the weaker communities. Akka told Marlon that times were tough everywhere, but he could arrange for TSS protection for Marlon's community. What Marlon couldn't know is that Akka intended to use the TSS to quell the growing opposition against Makaris, which was being orchestrated by other communities with enough strength left to fight."

"What did you do when you found out about all of this?" Colren asked.

"I set about fulfilling the objectives of my mission," Wil replied. "With assistance from Mila and others from Marlon's village, I began reaching out to the other communities on the planet so we could organize a rebellion against Akka."

"That's deviating pretty significantly from the mission," Colren said.

"No, not really," Wil countered.

Colren was firm. "The mission objectives were quite clear—for you to form a treaty between all the people on the planet."

"And I did," Wil clarified. "But, for a treaty to be possible, I needed to eliminate the source of conflict. That conflict could all be traced back to one person: Akka Kerwein. Once Akka was removed from power and the shipments resumed, everyone dropped the battle for resources. I then simply facilitated an agreement between the community leaders for all resources to be equally distributed based on population, and we identified a group of village representatives to address any future conflicts."

"Sorry if I'm jumping too far ahead here," Stelsin interjected, "but how exactly did Akka, an employee of Makaris Corp, end up hanging from a crane boom with thirty stab wounds?"

*Quick thinking to take the blame off of a single person seeking justice.* "He brought that on himself," Wil replied.

"Details, please," Colren urged.

Wil took a deep breath. He'd prepared his cover story and confirmed it with the others who knew what really happened to Akka. As long as they stuck together, Mila would be free to start her life with Tiro. It was a gift Wil was glad to give her.

"Well, as I was saying," Wil continued, "I reached out to the various communities across the planet. This took nearly five months, because our only mode of transportation was sailboats. Moreover, though some of the communities were anchored, others drifted with the tides so we had to hunt around. But, it was important for me to make contact with at least eighty percent of the known communities in order to ensure that any agreement we reached would be defensible. The biggest challenge was organizing the whole thing without any reliable mode of communication between the different groups. So, when I made contact with the first group, the Northern Seafarers, we decided to just set a date in the future for all of us to rendezvous near the Makaris outpost with armed forces."

"Armed forces!" Stelsin blurted out. "Makaris Corp is an unarmed civilian operation."

"Technically, the High Dynasty corporations are more governmental than civilian," Wil countered. "But regardless, Akka had made himself a nice little fortress. His staff were armed with blast guns and the outpost was equipped with incendiary cannons."

"I don't see how he could have come to be in possession of that sort of equipment," Stelsin objected.

"That's for you to take up with internal affairs," Wil retorted. "The community leaders were good to their word, and we convened at the agreed upon rendezvous point. We had about a hundred men total, but most of the weaponry was little more than bows and knives tied to poles. In my time on the planet, I came to understand that the people of Orino are fisherman at heart, despite all their talks about proving themselves as warriors. Their most revered 'battles' are against sharks, not other men. But, I had to work with what I had. It took me two weeks to get everyone organized and working together. I broke them into basic tactical teams and taught them how best to take cover against the cannons and pulse guns. They weren't ready for an assault, but our supplies were almost exhausted so we had to try."

"And so you attacked," Stelsin said.

Wil met his dour gaze. *And now I have to lie to save my friend.* "Yes. We made our move at night. We were able to take out the guards on the outside of the store facility and work our way inside. It wasn't my position to directly involve myself in the fighting, so I stayed on the sidelines and gave tactical advice when it was asked of me. By the time the area was secured and I made my way inside, Akka had already been strung up on the boom lift."

"You didn't see it happen?" Colren confirmed.

Wil secured his mental guards against the Agent. "No, sir, I did not."

"Okay," Colren nodded. "I think that's all you need, Mr. Stelsin."

"That's hardly everything!" Stelsin objected.

"The TSS will file a formal report. Now, if you'll please excuse us, we have official business to conduct." It was clear from Colren's tone that the matter was not up for discussion.

Stelsin stomped out of the interview room.

"I apologize for all of that," Colren said to Wil once they were alone. "Makaris Corp is pretty upset over this whole thing."

"That's understandable." *I can still see the look on Akka's face as he bled out.*

Colren sighed. "What happened after you found Akka?"

Wil gathered himself. "I decided it was best to leave his body where it was so any authorities could proceed with an investigation," Wil explained. "I immediately filed my daily report to Agents Aeronen and Merdes. The following day, I met with the representatives from each of the Orino communities and we had a draft of the treaty by that evening. They all signed an agreement for the fair distribution of the Makaris stores and any future shipments. At that time, I made a calculated decision to reveal my ties to the High Dynasties."

Colren raised an eyebrow.

"The people of Orino had been through a lot," Wil continued, "and it was important for me to show them that they hadn't been abandoned by Tararia. They were surprised, but they accepted me. Within half an hour of filing the report on those activities, I received the message that the mission objectives had been satisfied. Aeronen and Merdes picked me up the following day."

"Regardless of the impetus, leading an attack against a corporate outpost was never part of the mission specifications. You do realize that this has caused a great deal of tension between the TSS and Makaris Corp. There's even talk of other High Dynasties getting involved."

"Which is precisely why I told the people of Orino who I really am, so they know they will always have an ally. I was given a mission, and I did what I felt needed to be done," Wil contended. "Whatever tension exists now was brought on by Makaris' embarrassment over their own negligence. I advise that Makaris Corp conduct an audit of all of their outposts to make sure that this kind of activity isn't going on elsewhere."

"That's already underway," Colren replied.

"Good."

Colren cleared his throat. "Now, as a matter of record for your impending graduation, what did you learn from this internship experience?"

Wil thought for a moment. "Things aren't always as they seem—you can't just rely on the intelligence you're given about a situation. You need to be adaptable and responsive to conditions as they unfold. Your enemy isn't always who you think."

Colren took some notes on his tablet. "And how do you feel about yourself now as a leader?"

Wil took a deep breath. *I know what they want me to say—that I believe in myself and am ready to face anything. But I still don't know if I can do what they expect of me.* "The people of Orino named me as one of their legendary warriors. When they asked me what I wanted as my emblem, I told them 'Dragon'. It's what the Bakzen call me, so that is how I must see myself as I stand up to them. My final night on the planet, before I sent in my report, the village representatives tattooed a dragon on my back—such a ceremony is their highest honor."

"I'll just let you tell your parents about that part," Colren said.

"I was proud to receive it. I need to embrace who I am. I have to be the bridge between worlds."

Colren nodded. “I think we’re just about done here. We’ll need you to write up a full report, of course. And, I suspect there may be a few follow-up questions from Makaris for the investigation. We’ll need to keep you sequestered for a few days until everything is in order.”

*As if five months weren’t long enough to be apart. Now I’m back but I still have to wait days to be back with Saera?* “Let’s get this over with.”

— — —

The tremor in Saera’s hand wouldn’t go away. She had to concentrate to keep from shaking as she gripped her tablet. Ever since she’d caught the glimpse of Wil two days before, she couldn’t stop thinking about what it might mean that he still hadn’t reached out to her. *I know he’s back. Why is he avoiding me?*

She was curled up on her bunk, pretending to study but really just staring into space past her tablet. The preceding five months had been hard enough, but this new type of waiting was far more stressful.

A message indicator popped up on the screen. Saera brought her eyes back into focus and she saw the sender. *Wil!*

She opened the message: >>I’ve missed you so much. Meet me in the hallway.<<

*Then what took him so long to message me?!* She tossed her tablet on the bed and dashed into the hall.

Wil was standing down the hall in the doorway of a study room. His hair had been cut back into his normal crew cut and he was wearing his typical Junior Agent attire. He waved her over. Saera jogged to the study room, and Wil ducked inside as she approached. She closed the door behind her.

“Where have you—” She didn’t have time to get the words out before they were locked in a passionate kiss. She relaxed into

Wil, casting aside the apprehensions she'd felt over the last two days about his feelings for her.

"I missed you, too," she said when their lips finally parted.

"I know you saw me when I first got back," Wil said. "I'm so sorry I couldn't message you sooner."

"I was getting worried," Saera replied, downplaying the real extent of her insecurity.

"Things got a little tense at the end of my internship, and the debrief process took longer than normal."

"You couldn't even tell me that?"

"There are strict 'no contact' protocols in those situations. This is the soonest I could be with you, I promise."

*No one could kiss me that way and be lying about where they've been.* She took a deep breath. "Well, I'm glad you're back now. I don't know how much more separation I could take."

"Me either. I was thinking about you the whole time."

*While you were in bed with someone else?*

Wil may as well have read her mind. "Despite the cultural norms on Orino, I found a way out of participating in their more questionable customs. I remain fully and faithfully yours."

Saera felt more relief than she'd anticipated. She'd been bracing for the worst. "I'm glad to hear that."

"I would want it no other way." Wil stroked her hair.

*How could I have ever doubted him?* Saera was about to drift into happy thoughts of togetherness when she caught herself. "What happened with your internship?"

"It was a success in the end. Just not in the way anyone was expecting." He gave her an abbreviated account of the events.

Saera took it all in. *I hope mine isn't like that!* "I'm glad you made it back safely."

"It's good to be home." He paused. "And, you've been through the Year One disclosure by now, correct?"

"Yes, though they hardly said anything more than what you'd already told me."

Wil took a deep breath. "Saera, there are some other things—"

"Yeah, I figured as much, based on how you were acting. So, afterward, I talked with your dad. He told me what's *really* going on. Jotun and the whole deal."

Wil looked shocked. "And you're still here?"

Saera looked him squarely in his eyes. "I told you before, nothing could make me leave. But I do understand why you had pulled away from everyone. What they're asking of you…"

Wil nodded solemnly. "My time in the war is coming far sooner than they'd ever let on, Saera. I'll be at the heart of it."

"I know, and I'll be with you, too. I've made my choice."

Wil took Saera's hand. "That means everything to me."

Saera threw her arms around Wil again and held him close. "I'll stand by you no matter what."

"It's going to be hard for us to be together, but I love you so much. Whatever the future holds, I can face it knowing that I'll have you by my side."

A happy tingle warmed Saera to her core. "I love you, too."

# CHAPTER 25

HAERSEN ADMIRED HIMSELF in the reflection on the polished steel wall outside Tek's office. It was next to impossible to find a proper mirror in any of the Bakzen facilities, to his irritation. Being hairless, there was no need to shave or style hair—two of the most practical purposes for a mirror. And, as clones, there was little individuality to notice in a reflection that a glance at a comrade couldn't provide. But Haersen, on the other hand, wanted to watch his transformation.

The gene therapy began soon after his reunion with Tek. It was something of an experiment, but thus far the results were positive. In only four months, he felt stronger, tougher. There were few external changes yet, but they were coming. In time, he would become one of the Bakzen if the experiment was successful. Though only a test, it would mean a chance for the Bakzen to expand their ranks in a way they never imagined.

Transforming the Taran population was a lofty goal. The neurotoxin administered to survivors of the Bakzen's planetary invasions over the last two years was a first step to prime the bodies. Whatever treatment the Taran doctors thought they were giving to those affected only treated the symptoms of the side effects, not the root cause. The neurotoxin opened up the subjects' minds, making them susceptible to suggestion for easy telepathic networking. The Tarans would go about their lives, not realizing there was any change. Then, once activated by telepathic command, those Taran bystanders would be turned into effective Bakzen drones.

It was a start, but Tarans were physically weak and frail compared to a Bakzen soldier. The experiment with Haersen offered a more advanced alternative transformation. If he could be made into a more effective physical vessel, his telekinetic ability could flourish.

Taking a kernel of potential and nurturing it into fully developed abilities was the real dream—a race of ideal beings, always refining and growing stronger. Though that future was quite a leap from Haersen's type of transformation, he was excited to be a test case for how far he could evolve. Gaining greater ability was his sole aspiration—never again did he want to feel a wall, to be limited by how much power he could draw into himself.

Still, those limits remained his reality. It would take time, and he would have to be patient.

Haersen shifted on his feet, anxious to meet with General Tek. He was told ahead of time that the General had some kind of update to share—hopefully evidence of some move against the TSS.

Another five minutes passed with no sign of the general. Then, the door swung open.

Tek stepped out into the hall. "Good, you're here. I want to show you something."

Haersen came to attention. "Yes, sir."

Tek led him down the hall to the transport hub for the central command facility. The network of high-speed maglev transports connected the core operations for the Bakzen world. The military presence was the most prominent on the planet, followed by the bioengineering operations. Strictly administrative proceedings, under the Imperial Director, took only a fraction of the society's resources. The Imperial Director was a figurehead rather than anyone who yielded true power—an individual to unify the disparate aspects of Bakzen society. In actuality, the commanding general—the position Tek had claimed for himself—held the true power. But, Haersen suspected that Tek had his eye on making the military command and Imperial Directorship one in the same.

The transport hub consisted of maglev tracks crossing over each other at different levels, with a boarding platform at each level along a broad column at the central intersection. Some of the train lines terminated at the station, while others continued on after a brief stopover. Most of the maglev tracks supported small cars suitable for six individuals to travel together, but three larger tracks carried trains capable of transporting hundreds at a time. The trains ran infrequently during most of the day, reserved for accommodating mass movements related to shift changes. The smaller cars, conversely, were always on the move.

Haersen and Tek stepped into one of the cars on the track headed toward the central bioengineering operations.

The bioengineering facility was a familiar location for Haersen. He had made the trek dozens of times over recent months for his gene therapy, though he had just received a treatment and wasn't due for another until the following week. He gave Tek a questioning glance as they sat down on the plastic bench seats to either side of the car.

"No, this isn't for you." Tek said. "There's something else for you to see."

Haersen nodded, knowing better than to press the issue. Tek would reveal what he wanted on his own schedule.

The car detached from the docking platform and descended along the sloping maglev track. The track reached ground-level at the edge of the enclosed hub structure, where the car exited through an archway.

Haersen stared out of the transparent top dome of the car at the parched landscape of the Bakzen world. The surface suffered extreme temperature variations throughout the day and night, so only the most hardy vegetation survived. Most of the landscape was covered in a mixture of grainy sand and worn boulders, interspersed with scrubby brush and occasional rock outcroppings. Rock bluffs broke up the horizon, standing out as russet monoliths against the gray sky.

At the base of the red rock towers, Bakzen laborers lived in camps outside underground mines. The settlements were only a faint spec to Haersen as the transport car sped by, but a plume of smoke rose from the mine regardless of what time he passed. There was a never-ending need for metal ores to support the Bakzen's fleet and developing infrastructure. The planet's rich concentration of iron and chromium yielded much of the required supplies to support the Bakzen throughout their occupied worlds.

The maglev track carved a straight path across the open plain between the central command base and main bioengineering facility. At the outskirts of the destination, low buildings dotted the landscape. Each building contained the maturation tanks for Bakzen soldiers and laborers, a hundred in each.

Haersen had been shocked the first time he'd seen inside the maturation buildings—the growing bodies twitching in their chambers, tubes feeding their bodies with nutrients. It seemed like such an unnatural way for life to begin. However, the longer he reflected on it, he realized it was simply efficient. The Bakzen came into the world a fully formed physical vessel ready for cognitive imprinting with everything they would need to fulfill their function: rudimentary language, understanding of applicable technologies, and the willingness to self-sacrifice for the greater Bakzen good. Though new clones were always being produced, the resource investment in maturation and training was significant enough to warrant salvaging a clone whenever possible. It was important for all members of the society to remain functional and whole, but in Bakzen fashion, differentiating scars were always left as evidence of restorative procedures.

The track led into the heart of the main bioengineering facility, inclining to the third story of the seven above-ground levels. Like most of the structures on the Bakzen world, the building was constructed of poured concrete and metal fittings. Very few windows broke up the walls, since the Bakzen placed little value on having a view. Any openings were purely functional, for lighting or access.

The car came to rest next to a platform that curved around the center of a four-story atrium topped in translucent glass. Haersen and Tek exited the car as it looped around the platform on its way to the return line.

"We've been working on a new project," Tek said as they crossed the atrium.

"For what?" Haersen asked.

"A solution to one of our greatest issues."

Haersen followed Tek across the polished concrete floor to an elevator at the back of the atrium. The glossy floor was the most decorative aspect of the building, a striking contrast to the rough concrete walls rising above. Translucent windows on the upper floors lined the atrium, bringing natural light to the inner rooms of the building.

On the touch-panel next to the elevator, Tek selected a destination in the basement of the facility. He swiped his wrist along the panel for authorization.

Haersen looked at the selection with interest. He had never been to parts of the building below the planet's surface. Most of the upper levels housed medical facilities to treat lost limbs or other serious injuries the soldiers and laborers sustained, but the purpose of the lower levels was unknown.

They entered the elevator, and it descended into the depths. Several seconds passed in silence.

When the doors opened, Haersen was surprised to see a natural stone corridor approximately three meters wide. It looked like the tunnel had been bored directly through the bedrock. The walls were slightly damp, and water dripped into a narrow channel carved on either side of the corridor. A cool breeze ruffled his hair.

"What is this place?" he asked Tek.

"Our most secure research area," the general replied. "I think you'll appreciate the latest development."

Tek led the way through the dank tunnel. A row of lights along the ceiling illuminated the passage in an orange glow. Metal doors were inset along the walls at irregular intervals.

Haersen eyed the doors. Anything could be in there.

The tunnel branched twice along their route. Both times, Tek headed to the left. Twenty meters after the second branch, the corridor terminated in a metal door identical to the others they had passed.

Tek activated a panel next to the door with a swipe of his wrist, and the door shot into the ceiling.

Inside, overhead lights illuminated rows upon rows of maturation tanks. The clones were still only infants, fed by a single tube to their gut. Neurosensors monitored their cognitive development, displayed on panels next to each tank.

Haersen looked on with astonishment. The clones were so tiny and helpless. All the others he had seen were close to maturity, but these—something was different about them. He stepped toward the tank closest to the door. Upon closer examination, he noticed that there was a fine hair growing on the infant's head. He looked to Tek for an explanation.

"These are the next stage of Bakzen evolution," Tek stated. "We took some marrow from the Primus Elite. What we learned in the analysis of his genetic profile was quite interesting."

Haersen swallowed. "I didn't know you did that."

"Why wouldn't we? He's supposed to be so special, after all."

"What did you find out about him?" Haersen asked.

Tek watched the infant squirm in its tank. "He had a genetic marker we've never seen before. A mutation of sorts. It's on the segment of code that normally denotes the limit for telekinetic strength."

Haersen's breath caught. "He doesn't have a natural inhibitor?"

Tek shook his head. "Not in the traditional sense. While the rest of us hit a barrier eventually, it appears he could keep focusing the energy until he burned himself up."

Maybe the Primus Elite really was special after all. Haersen looked at the tanks. "What are these?"

Tek smirked. "Hybrids. Soldiers without the inhibitor."

"What will you do with them?"

"They'll make the perfect instrument for completing the Rift."

"But I thought the pathways are almost complete?" Haersen said. "It has to be years before these will be mature."

"Eight years, to be precise," Tek clarified. "But they aren't for the pathways. They're to widen the Rift across the entire galaxy."

"Why? The Rift is a place to hide and move covertly. What would you—"

"The Rift is our home!" Tek interrupted. "We can't feel complete without touching the two planes. Normal space… it's so confining."

Haersen nodded. He had only spent a little time in the Rift, but he knew what the general meant. The energy was intoxicating. "An entire galaxy… tailored just for you."

Tek laughed. "Oh, this galaxy is just the beginning."

# CHAPTER 26

WIL TOOK A deep breath. *It's just the Course Rank exam. Everyone takes it.* The knowledge did nothing to settle his nerves.

The testing facility was suspended below Level 11. Its sole purpose was to test Agents-to-be to the limits of their abilities. Wil had watched exams in the past, but it was very different being inside the chamber.

He looked up at the window to the observation room. His parents and Banks were watching, along with half a dozen other senior Agents. Their faces were drawn and serious.

*Everyone has been waiting for this. It's finally time to see what I can do uninhibited.*

"We'll begin whenever you're ready," Banks said over the intercom.

Wil took a deep breath. "Ready."

"Good luck." The intercom disconnected.

Wil poised himself to act. *This part is easy. Just focus.*

Holographic opponents illuminated all around him. The goal was to dispatch as many as possible within one minute, and any extra time would be added to the score.

Wil centered his mind and generated a spatial distortion. Within it, time appeared to stand still. He flipped and kicked his way through the first wave of a dozen opponents within the distortion. Each image shattered as he dealt a blow. As the last one dissolved, he returned to a normal state. Only a fraction of a second had passed.

The next wave of opponents appeared—twenty. Wil restored the spatial distortion and swept through the wave, twisting and tumbling to strike each as quickly and efficiently as possible.

He dispatched wave after wave in the same manner, each wave gone in the blink of an eye to the observers watching from above.

After seven seconds in real-time, the waves suddenly ceased.

Wil looked at the clock counting the remaining seconds in the exam, seeing how little time had passed. "Why did you stop?"

"That was one-thousand opponents. The system is only programmed to send that many," Banks said over the intercom. "You have fifteen minutes to rest until the next stage."

Wil nodded. *Maxing out the test already. What's next?*

— — —

Banks looked at Cris and Kate. "I'm concerned about how the rest of the examination is going to go."

"We don't have to proceed," Cris said. "I checked the rulebook. Senior officers can assign a suitable rank if it's deemed the traditional CR exam will not yield an accurate rank assessment."

"No, we need to see it through." *Too many are awaiting the results. We need to know how strong he really is… to see if it will be enough.*

Kate took Cris' hand. "What good will it do anyone if he hurts himself?"

"Better to know a limit now than to find out when he's in a battle," Banks replied. "He's taking the test for the same reason as anyone else."

Cris looked down at Wil pacing in a circle around the testing chamber. "Can this facility even withstand that magnitude?"

"The sphere will bear the brunt. It will be fine," Banks assured him. *At least, it should.*

"I'll intervene if I have to," Cris said.

"I wouldn't expect anything else." Banks let out a slow breath.

At the bottom of the testing chamber, Wil was waving his arms. Banks activated the intercom, "Is everything okay?"

"I was just wondering if I *have* to wait fifteen minutes between the stages. I'm ready for the next whenever you are," Wil said.

"All right. We'll proceed shortly," Banks replied. *Today is going to be a wild ride.*

— — —

Wil made a couple more impatient laps around the room before the low tone sounded, indicating that the testing was about to resume. The next stage of the test would be the easiest of them all for him, and he was anxious to get it out of the way.

Holographic targets appeared around the room—red boxes suspended at varying heights, some in groups and others standalone. Blue boxes were intermingled with the red. The objective was to destroy all of the red with a telekinetic blast as quickly as possible without hitting any of the blue. It was a more complex version of the training exercises any TSS trainee did early on in telekinesis practice.

Wil shot a telekinetic spear toward the first dozen red boxes. Each shattered and disappeared as it was struck. Then, the boxes started to move around the room, slowly at first, but gaining velocity as the test progressed. Soon, there was no direct line of sight between Wil's position and the red boxes.

Wil smiled to himself. *This is where it gets fun.*

He focused on the red boxes and started weaving the telekinetic spears through the tangle of blue cubes, sending four at a time like heat-seeking missiles locked onto a target. Early on, he'd discovered that others had difficulty with attacks that broke line of sight, but it had always felt natural to him—each spear an extension of himself.

The one-hundred red targets shattered four at a time, and all were gone in a matter of fifteen seconds.

He looked up at the observation room. "Next."

"Hold on," Banks said over the intercom.

Wil crossed his arms and waited. There were two more stages until he would face the testing sphere. Everything before that was procedural filler. The question on everyone's mind was not if he would break the elusive Course Rank of 10, but by how much.

He waited two minutes before the tone sounded again.

The lights abruptly cut out, leaving Wil in complete blackness. He took slow, steady breaths. Even though he already couldn't see anything, he closed his eyes. The third stage focused on spatial awareness. Any moment, his perception would be put to the test.

An energy pulse drew his attention to his left side. It was the starting point to an invisible maze. He walked through the darkness, sensing the exact location. Once standing at the center of the energy pulse, he stuck his arms straight out in front of himself. Tendrils wound around his forearms, fusing artificial wings to his limbs. The material was lightweight and made it easy for him to maneuver, but he needed to concentrate to make the new wings truly part of himself.

The room buzzed with static electricity as a maze activated in the darkness. Electronic walls formed, providing just enough clearance for Wil to traverse the maze with the artificial wings stretched out to either side. The channel for the wings required him to keep his arms perfectly level, with only a three-centimeter variance in the vertical position. He would need to navigate through the labyrinth using only his telekinetic senses to keep him on course and prevent him from touching the edge of the channel through the walls with the wings. He needed to be in complete synch with his surroundings, aware of himself and his domain.

He took a moment to gather himself before stepping into the start of the maze. Eyes closed, he focused on what he felt around him. The walls hummed in his mind, and he created a mental picture of where he was and where he needed to go. The wings were mere centimeters from the walls as he stepped forward, careful to keep his balance and spacing perfectly centered.

The further he progressed in the maze, the less clearance he had between the walls. Seven minutes of careful navigation passed. He wasn't sure exactly how much clearance he had, but he focused on staying exactly centered. There was no room for error. He needed to be perfect. Everyone was counting on him.

Wil's arms ached from being outstretched for so long. But he couldn't rest. He needed to finish and show them what he could do. They trusted him, they needed him.

The maze took a sharp turn to the right, and his arm dropped for an instant.

A harsh buzzer sounded and the lights restored.

Wil groaned. *So close.*

The artificial wings disintegrated around his arms.

"I'm sorry," Wil said to the observers. *So much for getting a perfect score.*

The intercom clicked on, but Banks didn't say anything at first. Several seconds later, he said, "We'll proceed to the fourth stage whenever you're ready."

"Okay, give me a minute." Wil swung and rubbed his limbs to clear the lactic acid buildup. His arms still ached, but he felt somewhat better after the short rest. At least the following exercise wasn't as physical. "Let's go."

The fourth stage was tailored to the area of specialization for each prospective Agent. For Wil, this meant a focus on command decision-making. Focused on optimized reactions, he needed to find a balance between being patient and proactive.

The lights in the testing chamber dimmed.

Wil looked around the room as a holographic starscape took form throughout the chamber. A single star system materialized in front of him, with four planets around a red sun. The planetary configuration wasn't familiar to Wil, most likely an invented world for the testing scenario. Ships popped up in orbit and outposts dotted the surfaces of all the planets. A single, sprawling space station rotated in a geosynchronous orbit of the third planet. Each of the assets was surrounded by a blue glow.

The view rotated ninety degrees. On the far side of the sun, a fleet was approaching, glowing red. An instant later, red ships appeared above each of the planets and the view rotated back to its original orientation.

"Destroy the enemy leader," Banks said over the intercom.

*Where's the leader?* Before Wil could finish assessing the conditions, the simulation erupted into full-blown battle.

The red ships opened fire on the planets and surrounding space station. Protective shields illuminated under the blasts, a strength indicator hovering next to each.

Wil reached up and rotated the view with his hands. The enemy envoy swinging around the sun was arranged in a defensive formation that might indicate the presence of a leader. Somehow, he needed to intercept the enemy with his own fleet.

With that thought, he realized that his fleet was only responding with automated defenses. He needed to command the counterattack.

Wil ran across the room and tapped on the deep space cannon on the second planet to activate the counter-strike. The cannon took out two of the enemy bombardment ships before the others broke orbit to evade.

Turning his attention to the third planet, Wil mobilized three armored ships docked at the space station and directed them to take on a defensive position. The ships opened fire as the enemy vessels came into range.

Back on the second planet, the cannon had exhausted its charge and was regenerating. Without the suppressive fire, enemy ships were closing in to target the cannon.

Wil dashed to the first planet and reallocated one of the ships to defend the cannon on the second planet.

Behind him, the fourth planet was surrounded. He had neglected to activate the units to counterstrike. He sprinted across the room, his heart sinking as one of the two outposts was captured by enemy forces. There were two armored ships sitting dormant in orbit of the planet. Wil directed both ships to assault the enemy forces on the planet's surface. Slowly, his forces regained the lost ground.

The deep space cannon on the second planet was ready to fire again. Wil ran back toward it, but he froze midway. The enemy envoy was rounding the sun.

There was no way to protect all of the planets and take on the envoy. *Destroy the enemy leader.* Wil's first instinct was to pull back from the fourth planet, which had the fewest resources. However, that put his troops the greatest distance from the envoy containing the leader. He needed to take a different approach.

Without hesitation, Wil re-fortified the units on the fourth planet and ran to the first planet. He activated all of the units that had been defending the four outposts on the surface and directed their fire toward the advancing envoy.

Under the heavy fire, the ships in the envoy bunched closer together and fired back. One ship at the center remained completely guarded and didn't make any offensive actions. *There's the leader.*

Wil ran to the second planet and aimed the deep space cannon directly at the envoy. Two blasts from the cannon took out the forward ship, leaving a vulnerable hole in the fleet's defensive wall. The cannon's energy was spent—it was useless until it recharged.

He sped the combat ships that had been in orbit of the first planet toward the envoy. As his ships approached, the enemy vessels redistributed to close the gap. He had his ships open fire, but the blasts had no effect against the shields. The deep space cannon was still recharging. There was no time to wait.

Wil sent his lead ship on a collision course with the envoy. Three agonizing seconds passed as the ship careened toward its target. With a flash, the ship crashed into the front of the envoy. The enemy ships broke formation from the concussive impact, defensive shields flickering. The leader ship was left exposed.

He opened fire on the leader with all his remaining ships as they sped toward their target, the enemy ship's shield weakening with every strike.

The enemy ships from the envoy began to recover and opened counterstrike fire, taking out one of Wil's approaching ships. He kept all of his remaining ships on the same heading. Only one needed to make it through.

He was within striking distance for his final assault. The enemy shield was only at ten percent. Wil sent everything he had at the leader's ship. The shield weakened, but held at two percent.

Off to his left, Wil saw that the deep space cannon was recharged. One blast would take out the leader, but his own ships were in the cannon's path. *Destroy the enemy leader.*

Wil activated the deep space cannon. The leader's ship incinerated, along with Wil's remaining ships from the first planet and half the enemy envoy.

The lights returned to full brightness and the holograph dissolved.

Wil let out a slow breath, his heart racing.

The intercom clicked on. "You lost twenty-seven percent of your units," Banks said.

"The objective was to destroy the enemy leader. The mission guidelines didn't set a target for casualties," Wil replied.

"The objective is always zero casualties."

"That was impractical in this scenario. Some sacrifice was needed."

"Yes, but simulations on this scenario had necessary loss at only thirteen percent."

Wil gazed up at the observation window. "So, I failed?"

There was a pause. "No, you met the requirements. It was only a point of critique."

"Noted."

"Are you ready for the final test?"

Wil's stomach knotted. He swallowed hard. "Yes."

A tile in the floor slid to the side and a pedestal raised up. Atop the pedestal was the testing sphere.

Wil stared at the golden sphere, a chill gripping his chest.

It was such a plain object for being something so unique and powerful. Made of a rare mineral that oscillated between a physical and subspace state, it allowed unmitigated channeling of electromagnetic energy. The sphere had been used to test the upper limit of thousands of Agents throughout TSS history. It was Wil's window to enlightenment.

"Begin," Banks said over the intercom.

Wil placed a hand on either side of the sphere. It tingled his fingertips, feeling a cool static charge pass between his hand and the shiny surface. Slowly, he began feeding energy into the sphere. He closed his eyes as he savored the exhilaration of such free use of his abilities. Finally, he was out of the invisible cage. He could fly.

The sphere warmed as it was filled with pure energy. It felt incredible to draw so much through himself, to tap into all that was around him. There was so much more, and no limit in sight.

— — —

Cris paced back and forth as the readings ticked upward.

"9.5," the attending Agent called out as the electronic readout continued to creep upward.

"9.7. That's where I maxed out," Cris said. *But he's not slowing down.*

"Here it is…" Banks said, eyes glued to the readout.

"10.0!" the attendant exclaimed.

Banks shook his head, incredulous. "He did it."

"Like we had any doubt," Kate said. She crossed her arms and frowned as the reading ticked upward.

"11.0!" the attendant announced. "Still climbing."

*Fok, how high will he go?* Cris bit his lower lip as he watched Wil continue to feed energy into the sphere. As the readout approached 12.0, the sphere started to vibrate. "What's happening?"

Banks looked closer at the sphere. "Stars! Is that a crack?"

Cris and Kate ran forward to the window. "Fok, it is!" Cris exclaimed.

A hairline fracture was forming along the side of the testing sphere. Golden light was pouring out from the crack, growing brighter.

"Stop the test!" Cris yelled. *Stars! This can't be possible.*

"We need to find his limit," Banks protested.

"The foking sphere is cracked! There's no telling what will happen if it breaks completely."

Kate rushed to the intercom. "Wil, stop!"

Below, Wil continued to feed energy into the sphere. Another crack started to form down the side.

"He's too focused. I'm going down," Cris said and ran toward the door.

"You can't go in there! If the energy spikes from the sphere—" Banks protested.

"Then come with me. We can contain it together."

Cris ran down the stairs to the entrance of the testing chamber with Kate and Banks close behind. He summoned a telekinetic shield and felt them feeding it behind him. He palmed open the door.

An intense wave of telekinetic energy flooded out from the testing chamber. Cris' shield shuddered under the force, but it held. He stepped into the room, pressing forward toward Wil.

The sphere quaked atop the pedestal. A blinding golden light radiated through the widening cracks.

"Wil, stop!" Cris yelled, but Wil didn't acknowledge him. There was a blissful grin on his face.

"Get him away from the sphere!" Banks shouted.

Together Banks and Cris pulled Wil back.

A powerful wave radiated from the sphere as he separated, knocking everyone to the ground. The entire chamber shuddered with the impact. Above, the glass to the observation room crunched as a crack spread from corner to corner.

The sphere stopped glowing immediately. A deep gouge marred its side, with several smaller cracks radiating outward.

Wil sat up on the floor. "What happened?"

Cris scrambled to his feet. "The sphere was cracking. You didn't hear us."

Wil looked in wonder at the damaged sphere. "I guess I was somewhere else." He rose to his feet. Sparks of electricity jumped between his fingers. "Did I break 10?"

"I ran down here at 12." Cris couldn't meet his son's eye. *He almost killed us without meaning to.*

Wil smiled. "Wow, not bad."

"Yeah." Cris felt faint. He could see Kate and Banks were drained, too.

"I did well, right?" Wil asked, looking to his parents and Banks.

"Yes, very well," Banks said, straightening his uniform. "You did everything we asked."

Cris caught Banks' eye. Even through the tinted glasses, he saw the fear.

— — —

Wil grabbed his tablet and sat down on his bed. He saw that Saera was online.

>>Hey,<< he wrote to her.

>>Hey! How'd it go?<< she replied.

>>I felt like they were mad at me.<<

>>Why?<<

>>I broke the sphere.<<

>>What? How?<<

>>I guess it couldn't withstand the force.<<

Saera took a few seconds to reply. >>What did you score?<<

>>Somewhere above 12.0. I don't have the final number yet.<<

Another pause. >>Wow.<<

Wil bit his lip. >>They're all afraid of me.<<

>>I'm not.<<

Wil smiled, even as the tears came to his eyes. >>Thanks.<< He sniffed the tears back. >>I'll talk to you later.<<

Wil set down his tablet and curled up on the bed, burying his face in his pillow. He was a weapon. A living weapon. All he could do was cry.

— — —

Banks returned to the observation room, still shaking. He looked at the worried faces of the other Agents. "What were the final results?" he asked the Agent who'd been monitoring the readings.

"The last reading before you pulled him from the sphere was 13.7," the Agent stated.

"Stars…" Banks breathed.

"That's a factor of forty above Cris."

*Fok… we'd need fifty Agents to contain him at that level, and that wasn't even his max.* "Thank you."

The Agent looked at the others in the room, then to Banks. "Sir, will this become a matter of public record?"

Banks nodded. "It has to be. No way around it."

"It's, um… a bit alarming," the Agent said, caution evident in his tone.

"I know. We'll all have to get used to the idea." Banks took a deep breath. "Thank you for your professionalism today."

"Of course, sir."

Banks took the central elevator up to his office. The Priesthood was awaiting his report.

The Priest looked expectant when he answered the call. "Well?"

"13.7," Banks reported.

"Impressive, but we expected more."

"We had to cut the test short," Banks said. "He cracked the testing sphere."

"Well, that's unexpected."

Banks shook his head. "We almost lost containment. That kind of power… it could destroy an entire planet."

"Oh, we're counting on it," replied the Priest. "If we are not victorious through intellect and strategy, we'll have raw power on our side."

*But how will Wil direct that power?* "He is the ally we want and need."

"Let him grow. We'll see what he can become."

# CHAPTER 27

WIL'S NEW BLACK uniform weighed on him. The clothing itself was comfortable, but its symbolism came with a heavy burden. He was now an Agent. His word was no longer an opinion, but a command. His CR placed him above even his father in the chain of command, if he wanted to exercise that right. It was an extraordinary responsibility. Yet, even that didn't compare to what lay ahead. Commanding both divisions of the TSS as Supreme Commander was just around the corner.

The graduation ceremony was being held in the largest lecture hall on Level 4. Twenty rows of raked seats formed a half-circle around a small stage and podium at the lowest level. A holoprojector cast a starscape on the ceiling of the hall.

Wil filed into the front row with his colleagues, with additional graduates taking the second row. On the left side of the stage, Cris and four of the other senior Agents were lined up while Banks stood at the center podium. As he took his seat, Wil spotted his mother sitting in the row behind the graduates.

All of the Trainees who'd elected to stay with the TSS beyond the first year were at the back of the auditorium. The top-scoring Initiates and Junior Agents for the year occupied the middle section of the audience, along with the Agent instructors. The rest of Headquarters would be observing the ceremony from a video feed to the lounges and other common areas.

Banks waited for the audience to get settled before he began. "This has been an exciting year for the TSS. We had a higher number of new Agent Trainees join us than we've seen in more than a century, and that's set us on a path to make a positive impact on all the Taran worlds. The TSS might not be accepted everywhere, but we play a vital role. We have the chance to help shape the future of Taran civilization. That's an opportunity we can't take lightly. The commitment we've made to the TSS is one that will define the rest of our lives, and our work here will be our legacy.

"One of the most tangible contributions the TSS offered to the rest of Tarans is an independent jump drive design. This new navigation system will enable space travel in a way that's never been possible before. Travel times will be drastically reduced for civilians, opening up commerce opportunities that had only been a distant dream before. The goodwill from those kinds of contributions will enable the TSS to flourish in the years to come."

Wil's jaw dropped. *He knows I own the personal licenses to that tech. 'The TSS' didn't deliver anything. It was me.*

"Another noteworthy accomplishment is the record highs in test scores for trainees at all levels. I am pleased to say that the trainees we have now will become the greatest group of Agents and Militia officers the TSS has ever seen. I'm excited to be the High Commander who got to know each of you as you found your calling within this great organization."

Wil shook his head. *Who's listening in on this speech? This isn't how he normally talks.*

"To each of our newest Agents, I say thank you. Thank you for your dedication to the TSS, and thank you for everything you will accomplish throughout your careers. You are leaders and visionaries." Banks paused as the audience applauded. "And now I'd like to acknowledge a particularly unique graduate," Banks said, looking directly at Wil. "Wil Sights has been designated in a new Primus Elite Agent class. He's only sixteen years old, but he scored an unprecedented CR of 13.7."

There was a murmur of surprise from the crowd.

"We hope to never test the limits of that power in the outside world," Banks continued, "but I know we can all rest easier knowing that we have him on our side."

Wil surveyed the audience. Many of the younger trainees were whispering to each other, and the Junior Agents and Agents were sitting in defensive positions, arms crossed and jaws set. *If they were only cautious of me before, now they're outright scared. Even I'm afraid of myself.*

"Wil, would you like to say a few words?" Banks asked.

"If you'd like me to, sir."

"Please," Banks said and stepped back from the podium.

Wil walked over to the center of the stage. All eyes were fixed on him. It was so quiet the slightest shift in a seat or sniff carried across the auditorium. "Hi," Wil said, almost jumping at the sound of his own amplified voice. "I'm not sure what to say exactly. It's been a tough journey to get to this point."

He scanned the audience. Near the back center, he spotted Saera. Seeing her smiling with support set him instantly at ease. *I know what I have to say.* "It's been a tough journey getting here, but the road ahead is going to be even harder. All of you are here because you're committed to the TSS, just like me. You've been through your debriefs, and you have pledged yourself to fight on behalf of the TSS when and if you have to. Well, I'll tell you now, you can throw out that 'if'. The war is here, and soon we'll find ourselves on the frontlines."

Off to the side of the stage, Banks was overcome with a look of horror. Next to him, Cris smirked. The audience members erupted in urgent conversation with their neighbors.

"The Bakzen are a powerful enemy. One that the TSS has been fighting in secret for a very long time. We're the lucky ones who've been able to live in relative peace thanks to the sacrifice of our brethren. But the war is coming to a head. I have personally been charged with ending the Bakzen threat through any means necessary. Total annihilation."

The room fell silent again. Banks looked ill—like he wasn't sure if he should tackle Wil or chase him away. But the damage was already dealt.

Wil looked out at the crowd. Saera nodded, a slight smile touching her lips, so subtle that only Wil would notice.

"I'm telling you this not to scare you but because I can't do it alone. I need help from each and every one of you for us to win this fight. Tarans may be distributed across hundreds of worlds, each with its own ideals and aspirations for where we should go as a species. But we are united in one common principle: we respect what it is to be an individual, and we want every citizen to have a happy, fulfilling life. Now, that doesn't always happen.

"While I was on my internship, I saw the darker side of life that no one ever wants to acknowledge. But seeing those things, I realized that we do need to eliminate the Bakzen or else we'll never be able to address the other issues facing Tarans near and far. The longer we ignore what's going on, the more people will be hurt. We can't let that fight rest solely on those brave few willing to dedicate their lives to protecting the rest of us. We all need to start pitching in.

"High Commander Banks would have stopped me already if he disagreed. We kept the war a secret because we needed to have a reserve force that would be fresh and ready to jump in and finally end the war with the Bakzen. Well, we *are* that reserve force. And I'm going to lead you. Not right away, but soon. I'm telling you now so we have a chance to really know each other, to build the kind of trust and respect it will take to get the job done. I hope when the time comes for me to lead you in those final battles, you'll be there to help me. Thank you."

Wil hurried away from the podium, heading straight for the back door off of the stage. His father ran over to follow him as the audience broke out in a mixture of cheers and questions.

Banks shot Wil a wary glance while he rushed over to reclaim the podium. "That isn't exactly what I had in mind."

"You know it was necessary. We can't keep hiding the truth," Wil replied.

Banks nodded and turned to address the audience. "That revelation has undoubtedly left you with a number of questions. I will give you some additional context now to hopefully set you at ease, but we'll roll out a more comprehensive communication over the next several days."

Wil exited the back door from the stage with his father close behind.

"That was a gutsy move," Cris said as soon as the door closed. "I'm proud of you."

Wil let out a long breath. "I really just did that, huh?" He laughed to himself. *That's going to unleash quite a shitestorm.*

"Fok, I'm never going to hear the end of it from Banks," Cris said, chuckling. "But I couldn't be happier."

"I was thinking about it, and no good will come from keeping it a secret from them. Waiting until the moment we need to go to the frontlines will only result in a bunch of scared people that want nothing to do with a war, even though they said they'd fight. If we can get them rallied and united now, we'll be that much more effective."

Cris nodded. "I couldn't agree more. And though Banks won't be happy in the short term, he'll understand that this works to our benefit."

"It's always been the Priesthood that wanted to keep it quiet, not the TSS."

"The Priesthood is all about keeping the public placated. If word gets out that there's a war, there'll be riots, strikes."

"Or maybe," Wil countered, "we'll be able to unite against the enemy. Come together as a people in a way that we haven't since the last revolution."

"The last revolution brought down the entire system."

"Is that always a bad thing?"

Cris nodded thoughtfully. "Let's take it one step at a time."

Wil looked back down the hall in the direction of the auditorium. "I should probably go hide somewhere to wait out this initial outcry."

"Not a bad idea. I'll gather some others to keep watch on your quarters."

Wil shook his head. "I don't think that's necessary."

"You can never be too careful—"

"Banks just told them I scored a CR of 13.7. No one is going to mess with me, even within the subspace bubble. Guards will just make it look like I'm afraid of something, but we need to show them I'm on their side. I'm a person just like them. That interpersonal connection—that's what sets us apart from the Bakzen. That's why we're going to win."

Suddenly, Cris embraced Wil. "You have grown into such a fine young man. I'm honored to have you as my son."

Wil hugged him back. "Thanks, Dad."

— — —

Saera snuck up to the entrance of the Primus Agents' wing. The message from Wil had told her exactly which halls to follow to avoid potentially prying eyes.

She hurried down the hall and located the door to Wil's quarters. After checking to make sure the hall was empty, she placed her hand on the biometric scanner. The door slid open and she darted inside, closing the door behind her.

Wil was sitting on the couch. He rose when she entered. "Hey."

"Hi. Wow, this is *way* better than meeting up in a study room," Saera said as Wil came over to her. She put her arms around his neck. "I can't believe you did that at graduation."

"Bad?"

"No, amazing." She pulled him in for a kiss, melting into his arms. "So, this thing with us is totally illicit now, huh?"

"Well, it's technically sanctioned. But yeah, stepping pretty far outside of convention."

Saera smiled up at him. "I'm in if you're in."

"I was all in the moment we met, even if it took a while to admit it."

"I'm glad you came around."

"Me too." Wil gazed into her eyes, filled with a new sense of hope. "Thank you for standing by me through all this craziness. There's no way I could face it alone."

"I had some demons to face, too. I know this is just the start, but we'll get through it together."

Wil leaned down to kiss her, a tender caress that called to the bond that united them. In that moment, their connection was all that mattered. Together, anything was possible.

— — —

Banks slammed the door to his office, heart racing. *Shite.*

There was no containing the information. He told all of the trainees to keep the truth about the war confidential, but it would seep out into the general populace. It was only a matter of time. None of the safeguards were in place, as with those in the Jotun division. He had failed as High Commander, and the Priesthood was not forgiving.

Banks wet his lips. He could run. It might save his life, but he'd be abandoning everything he'd worked for his whole career. All of the sacrifice would be in vain. The only thing he could do was face the development head on. He instructed CACI to call the Priesthood.

The Priest answered after several seconds. His glowing red eyes assessed Banks from the viewscreen. "What happened?"

Banks swallowed hard. "He just started talking. I had no idea he'd disclose the war like that."

The Priest's eyes narrowed, his grimace partially hidden by the shadow of his hood. "There's no going back."

"No. I'd advise you to prepare a communication."

"We have all the messaging in place. This was... anticipated."

Banks breathed an inward sigh of relief. *Perhaps this isn't the end for me.* "I know I let you down by allowing such a breach."

The Priest scoffed. "We have survived far greater setbacks. We'll do what needs to be done."

*They always do.* "I will be standing by for further instruction."

"Keep an eye on the Primus Elite. We don't need any more surprises." The Priest ended the transmission.

Banks let out a shaky breath. The Priesthood was confident in their ability to keep the war contained, but they greatly underestimated Wil. Banks was content to let them keep thinking that way. As long as they were focused on the Bakzen, the Priesthood wouldn't notice that other plans were already being set in motion. Change was coming.

Banks smiled to himself. *Now we begin.*

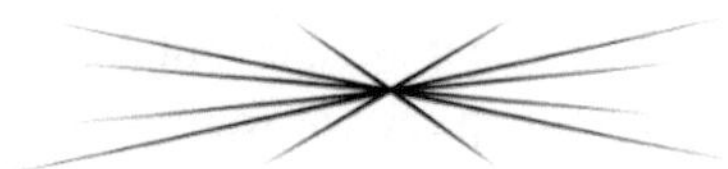

# CONTINUE THE STORY...

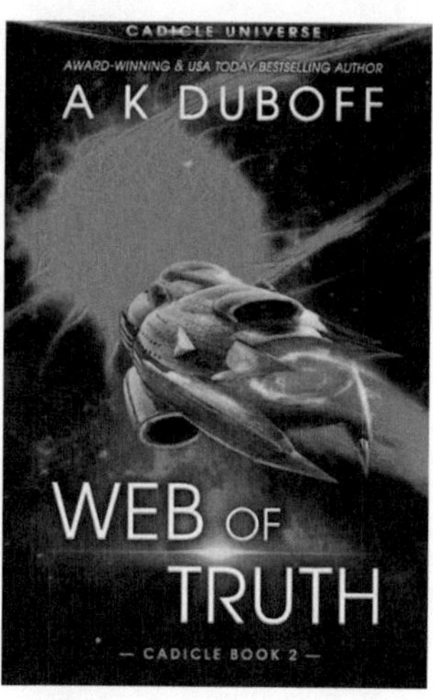


## Volume 4: Web of Truth

Tension is mounting in the rift. With the situation dire, Wil is tasked to train a group of twenty young men to serve as his officers—collectively, the Primus Elites. He has five years to raise them to full Agents, and he'll need every minute. Training alongside them and with Saera at his side, Wil still needs to master simultaneous observation. But, the closer he gets to achieving the feat, the more likely the Aesir will come to test him—to see if he's worthy of the Cadicle title bestowed on him at conception. If he can survive their test, he'll finally uncover the truth the Priesthood has gone to such great lengths to hide.

A fast-paced drama with intrigue, love, military duty, and politics, *Web of Truth* novel reveals the true nature of the war as Wil learns the secrets behind the Bakzen's origins.

# OTHER CADICLE UNIVERSE BOOKS

**CADICLE SERIES**
Volume 1: Architects of Destiny (in *Shadows of Empire*)
Volume 2: Veil of Reality (in *Shadows of Empire*)
Volume 3: Bonds of Resolve (in *Shadows of Empire*)
Volume 4: Web of Truth
Volume 5: Crossroads of Fate
Volume 6: Path of Justice
Volume 7: Scions of Change

**MINDSPACE**
Book 1: Infiltration
Book 2: Conspiracy
Book 3: Offensive
Book 4: Endgame

**VERITY CHRONICLES** *with T.S. Valmond*
Book 1: Exile
Book 2: Divided Loyalties
Book 3: On the Run

**SHADOWED SPACE** *with Lucinda Pebre*
Book 1: Shadow Behind the Stars
Book 2: Shadow Rising
Book 3: Shadow Beyond the Reach

**IN DARKNESS DWELLS** *with James Fox*

**TARAN EMPIRE SAGA**
Book 1: Empire Reborn
Book 2: Empire Uprising
Book 3: Empire Defied
Book 4: Empire United

# ACKNOWLEDGEMENTS

This series was a long time in the making. I wrote the opening chapters for what is now *Veil of Reality* when I was in middle school. Without saying, I've made significant revisions since then! But, the initial draft of those opening chapters was a decisive moment in my writing life—I had an idea, and I wanted to see it through.

I remember nervously handing over a hardcopy draft of the first few chapters to my friend Jess when we were in 7th grade. She gave it back to me a few days later with "Good Job!!" written in pink ink on the top margin of the first page. That early encouragement meant the world to me, and I am eternally grateful.

Over the next few years, I continued to write more of the story. Things really started to come together when I befriended a brother and sister, Jan and Maika, in high school. They helped me find my voice and set me on this path. I appreciate all of their thoughtful critiques and for helping me brainstorm.

The book sat on a digital shelf for years, and I am so thankful to again be surrounded by amazing people to help me bring this project to market. In particular, I owe my beta readers—John, Eric, Bryan, Katy, and Bethany—a huge thank you for seeing what I couldn't. Their feedback got me where I needed to go. In addition, thank you to Tom for his amazing artistic eye. I also want to thank my mom for lending another set of eyes and for helping me keep everything in perspective.

Finally, I would like to thank my husband, Nick, for putting up with all the late-night work and for understanding when I cancel plans with our friends so I can write. I couldn't have finished this book without his love and support.

# GLOSSARY

**Agent** - A class of officer within the TSS reserved for those with telekinetic and telepathic gifts. There are three levels of Agent based on level of ability: Primus, Sacon and Trion.

**Bakzen** - A militaristic race living beyond the outer colonies. All Bakzen are clones, with individuals differentiated by war scars. Officers are highly intelligent and possess extensive telekinetic abilities. Drones are conditioned to follow orders but still possess moderate telekinetic capabilities.

**Cadicle** - The definition of individual perfection in the Priesthood's founding ideology, with emergence of the Cadicle heralding the start to the next stage of evolution for the Taran race.

**Course Rank (CR)** - The official measurement of an Agent's ability level, taken at the end of their training immediately before graduation from Junior Agent to Agent. The Course Rank Test is a multi-phase examination, including direct focusing of telekinetic energy into a testing sphere. The magnitude of energy focused during the exercise is the primary factor dictating the Agent's CR.

**Earth** - A planet occupied by Humans, a divergent race of Tarans. Considered a "lost colony," Earth is not recognized as part of the Taran government.

**High Commander** - The officer responsible for the administration of the TSS. Always an Agent from the Primus class.

**High Dynasties** - Six families on Tararia that control the corporations critical to the functioning of Taran society. The "Big Six" each have a designated Region on Tararia, which is the seat of their power. The Dynasties in aggregate form an oligarchical government for the Taran colonies.

**Independent Jump Drive** - A jump drive that does not rely on the SiNavTech beacon network for navigation, instead using a mathematical formula to calculate jump positions through normal space and the Rift.

**Initiate** - The second stage of the TSS training program for Agents. A trainee will typically remain at the Initiate stage for two or three years.

**Jump Drive** - The engine system for travel through subspace. Conventional jump drives require an interface with the SiNavTech navigation system and subspace navigation beacons.

**Junior Agent** - The third stage of the TSS training program for Agents. A trainee will typically remain at the Junior Agent stage for three to five years.

**Lead Agent** - The highest ranking Agent and second in command to the High Commander. The Lead Agent is responsible for overseeing the Agent training program and frequently serves as a liaison for TSS business with Taran colonies.

**Lower Dynasties** - There are 247 recognized Lower Dynasties in Taran society. Many of these families have a presence on Tararia, but some are residents of the other inner colonies.

**Makaris Corp** - A corporation run by the Makaris High Dynasty responsible for the distribution of food, water filters, and other necessary supplies to Taran colonies without diverse natural resources.

**Rift** - A habitable pocket between normal space and subspace.

**Sacon** - The middle tier of TSS Agents. Typically, Sacon Agents will score a CR between 6 and 7.9.

**SiNavTech** - A corporation run by the Sietinen High Dynasty, which controls and maintains the subspace navigation network used by Taran civilians and the TSS.

**Tarans** - The general term for all individuals with genetic relation to Tararian ancestry. Several divergent races are recognized by their planet or system.

**Tararia** - The home planet for the Taran race and seat of the central government.

**Tararian Selective Service (TSS)** - A military organization with two divisions: (1) Agent Class, and (2) Militia Class. Agents possess telekinetic and telepathic abilities; the TSS is the only place where individuals with such gifts can gain official training. The Militia class offers a formal training program for those without telekinetic abilities, providing tactical and administrative support to Agents. The Headquarters is located inside the moon of the planet Earth. Additional Militia training facilities are located throughout the Taran colonies.

**Trainee** - The generic term for a student of the TSS, and also the term for first year Agent students (when capitalized Trainee). Students are not fully "initiated" into the TSS until their second year.

**Trion** - The lowest tier of TSS Agents. Typically, Trion Agents will score a CR below 5.9.

**Priesthood of the Cadicle** - A formerly theological institution responsible for oversight of all governmental affairs and the flow of information throughout the Taran colonies. The Priesthood has jurisdiction over even the High Dynasties and provides a tiebreaking vote on new initiatives proposed by the High Dynasty oligarchy.

**Primus** - The highest of three Agent classes within the TSS, reserved for those with the strongest telekinetic abilities. Typically, Primus Agents will score a CR above 8.

**Primus Elite** - A new classification of Agent above Primus signifying an exceptional level of ability.

# ABOUT THE AUTHOR

Award-winning author A.K. (Amy) DuBoff has always loved science fiction in all its forms—books, movies, shows, and games. If it involves outer space, even better! She is a Nebula Award finalist and *USA Today* bestselling author most known for her Cadicle Universe, but she has written a variety of science fiction and fantasy. As a full-time author, Amy can frequently be found traveling the world. When she's not writing, she enjoys wine tasting, binge-watching TV series, and playing epic strategy board games.

**www.amyduboff.com**

Made in the USA
Thornton, CO
10/25/24 14:48:48

c3cd797e-e73e-4e7b-aab3-6c567d8bf6b2R01